EXTRACURRICULAR

BOOK 1 - BOOK 2 - BOOK 3

JOSIE BROWN

A BOOK BY

SIGNAL PRESS

* * * * *

To write Josie, go to:
mailfromjosie@gmail.com

To find out more about Josie, or to get on her eLetter list for book launch announcements, go to her website:
www.JosieBrown.com

twitter.com/JosieBrownCA
facebook.com/josiebrownauthor
pinterest.com/josiebrownca
instagram.com/josiebrownnovels

CONTENTS

BOOK ONE

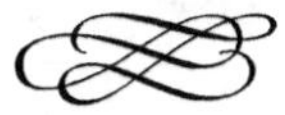

SOMETIME IN THE NEAR FUTURE

Book 2, in fact...

CHAPTER 1

The San Francisco restaurant chosen for the FBI's first sting in the college admissions investigation that went by the name "Operation Sis-Boom-Bah" was renowned for its exceptional wines (including a 2001 Pomerol Bordeaux), and the fact that it had just netted *Food & Wine*'s highest honor, its Grand Award.

None of this would be notated, however, in Transcript No. 1-00351 of the video recording made of that initial meeting between Cooperating Witness Number One and her targets, Suspects Numbers One and Two.

Nor would there be any reference to the fact that Cooperating Witness Number One insisted that the Bureau honor the restaurant reservation, which she had secured for the FBI's sting operation. Case in point: her clandestine client meetings only took place in the best restaurants. Those anxious for her services frequented the same renowned boîtes and expected nothing less of her. It was the unwritten rule that she would pay for these meals—or, in this instance, be reimbursed by the Bureau.

One of the two agents in charge of the case, SallyAnne Jagger, winced at this thought. Austerity was embedded in the rulebook of the country's domestic intelligence service. Still, proper consent from their very reluctant division director was given when the operatives in charge—SallyAnne, along with her partner, Lionel Porter Polk VII—made a believable case that the restaurant's mirrored walls would afford them close-range surveillance of the meeting from several angles, especially if they happened to wangle a couple of stools at the bar immediately across from their witness' dining booth.

"If we get there early enough, it's easily doable on a Thursday night," their witness had assured them as they made their way to the restaurant in an FBI-issue unmarked van, tricked out with state-of-the-art surveillance equipment that was to be monitored by a third Bureau operative, Riley Kemp.

Unbeknownst to their witness, this was just one of her numerous random acts of entitlement that had earned her the code name "Maleficent." SallyAnne had come up with it after listening to court-sanctioned surveillance audio in which their witness had coerced one desperate mother to participate in her scheme with a cruel lie: "Besides losing out on better jobs and being ostracized by her more successful friends, your daughter is much too pretty to end up in junior college—where surely, she'll be mauled by the gangs who roam the halls there."

SallyAnne, a product of a junior college that fed into the state university that eventually earned her a jurisprudence graduate degree, let loose with a litany of obscenities that would have impressed a prison yard bully.

From then on, the codename stuck.

The restaurant in which the sting was to take place was located in Presidio Heights, a well-heeled neighborhood of stately Edwardian mansions with the occasional Victorian townhouse thrown in for whimsy and a little color. As they made their way down Washington Street, Lionel pulled out something from one of the van's custom shelves: a tiny, soft flesh-toned disk.

"Put it in your left ear," he instructed. "It allows us to talk to you in case we need you to say something specific."

Maleficent shuddered. "How vulgar! It'll look as if I'm wearing a hearing aid."

"You can cover it with your hair," he suggested. To make his point, he loosened the lock she'd just pushed behind her ear. "See? Like that."

For a second, their eyes met. When she smirked, he turned toward the shelf again, but he was smiling.

SallyAnne wasn't. She knew Lionel hadn't meant it as a flirtation, but it was disconcerting that Maleficent took it that way.

Lionel next pulled a small alligator-skin clutch from the shelf and handed it to Maleficent.

She gawked, repulsed, then tossed it back at him. "What's this? Have you been slumming at Ross Dress for Less?"

"No! It's from, um, Macy's." Lionel pointed to the label, which read GIANI BERNINI. "It's a designer bag. We've embedded a camera. Since it matches your dress, I thought you'd—"

"Well, you thought wrong!" Maleficent rolled her eyes. "'Bernini' is a house brand—ergo, a cheap knock off. One look at the logo and I'll be the laughingstock of all my clients!"

"Oh…kay. Well…" Lionel looked over at SallyAnne and winked.

Maybe he was amused, but she wasn't.

Lionel shrugged off SallyAnne's scowl. As another idea struck him, he reached into a different shelf. This time he pulled out a bejeweled spider brooch. "Okay, then, you'll wear this. It's embedded with a state-of-the-art microphone and is somewhat less conspicuous."

He attempted to fasten it on Maleficent's little black dress, but in the moving van, the task was virtually impossible. Although Washington Street was mostly empty of traffic, Lionel was stymied by the periodic Uber pick-ups and drop-offs, not to mention the van's sudden stops at each corner crosswalk.

Suddenly, Riley took a sharp turn. To SallyAnne's horror, to brace himself Lionel's hands went to Maleficent's chest. To SallyAnne's relief, at the very last second, he dropped his arms to avoid a possible claim of battery.

They fell to the floor. Lionel landed on top.

Maleficent's response was to slap him, but she was smiling.

He leaped up first. Always the gentleman, he held out his hand to help her to her feet, but she smacked it away. Instead, Maleficent steadied herself on the van's built-in shelves. Then, with the regal bearing of a Victorian side-saddle equestrian (apropos, since Maleficent was quite adept at this revived sport), she rose upright—not an easy feat, considering her short, tight dress and four-inch heels.

Snatching the brooch out of Lionel's hand, she snapped, "Must you ruin my dress? My God, man! *It's an Oscar de la Renta!*"

SallyAnne rolled her eyes. Maleficent's disdain disgusted her, but not as much as Lionel's deference to the woman.

As if talking to a four-year-old on the verge of a tantrum, Lionel gently but firmly replied, "Sorry, but it's our best bet for getting clear audio."

"I've topped the *Nob Hill Gazette*'s 'Best Dressed' list three years straight. Just one glance at that cheap piece of tin and the marks won't believe a word I'm saying anyway," Maleficent retorted.

"Can't you just tell them one of your students made it for you?" Lionel replied.

His suggestion was met with a French curse.

Her response startled him. But by the blush creeping up his neck, Sally-Anne realized he was aroused too.

Figures, she thought.

They'd been partners for three years and through a baker's dozen cases —all high-profile white-collar crimes. At first glance, one couldn't imagine why their division director had seen fit to pair them. Standing side by side, they made an odd couple. Everything about SallyAnne was short: her height (she was just five-feet-two-inches tall), her hair (jet black and bluntly bobbed), and most definitely her temper. The daughter of a postman and a librarian, she had worked her way out of the Bureau's assistant pool after acquiring a night school degree in Criminology from the University of Virginia.

In contrast, Lionel was tall, fair, and had the stoic bearing that naturally comes from being the most recent of seven consecutive generations of Lionel Porter Polks, all alumni of Harvard Law School.

He wore the mantle of old money well. This invariably gave their more privileged suspects the mistaken impression that he would sympathize with their plight in getting caught. It also encouraged their hopes that, perhaps, he'd bend a rule or two for this wayward Cantab (Harvard), or that complicit Yalie (Yale), or the other imprudent Quaker (University of Pennsylvania).

Lionel encouraged this misnomer by talking their language: of private club memberships, friends they might have in common, and of the need these days to put up with those lucky enough to have gotten a leg up in their world via Affirmative Action (women, people of color, gay, trans, whatever). At this last, their gaze would shift toward SallyAnne, as if to imply, see what I mean?

After warming them up, Lionel questioned them gently on the specifics of their crimes. Viewing him a soft touch, they lied through their teeth, even after being warned that they were under oath.

Lionel's encouraging demeanor never changed. It was up to SallyAnne to bring down the curtain on their devious act. She played the heavy, countering with fact in response to their fiction. Then, in her blunt, unvarnished way, she'd bark away at them, an unrelenting bulldog digging up the bones of their crimes.

When they finally cracked, they'd eye Lionel as if he were a traitor to their class.

Lionel always answered their silent glares with a shrug and the appropriate Latin phrase: *Lux et Veritas* ("Light and Truth") to the Yalie. For the Quaker, it was *Leges Sine Moribus Vanae* ("Laws without Morals are Useless"). Only one word embodied a Harvard man's shame: *Veritas* ("Truth").

When presented with the evidence against her, Maleficent's face never twitched a muscle. And her response when Lionel reminded her of her alma mater's motto—Radcliffe's *Indsyria Didat* ("Industry Enriches")—was to snicker, "It does indeed."

Instead of being angry with her, Lionel chuckled at her audacity.

SallyAnne's knowledge of Latin was limited. Still, intuitively, it struck her that something had gotten lost in Lionel's translation. When Maleficent joined him with a coy giggle of her own, SallyAnne realized they were speaking the same language after all: attraction.

As with any suspect, Bureau operatives were just as adept at reading even the most trifling inflection in their partners. In Lionel's case, willowy blond ice queens with steely blue eyes and lips that never rose beyond a smirk were his Kryptonite. In SallyAnne's opinion, the fact that a well-heeled crook fleecing some investment firm had a closet filled with Brioni suits—or in Maleficent's case, was helping the parents of spoiled brats steal college admissions slots from hardworking, better deserving students while decked out in Oscar de la Renta—didn't make her any less culpable.

Up until now, she'd never doubted that Lionel felt the same way. She had to shut down his infatuation with Maleficent, and quickly.

"Listen, lady," she growled, "your dinner dates may be 'marks' to you, but to the Bureau, right now they're designated only as 'suspects'—which is a long way off from 'defendants.' *Ergo*"—SallyAnne loved that Maleficent winced upon hearing that word—"if they can't be incriminated, you are royally screwed."

SallyAnne tore the purse out of Lionel's hand and shoved it against Maleficent's taut, possibly Spanx-trussed abdomen. "Now, if you want to shave a few years off what could be a long sentence, I suggest you take your designer phone and your designer makeup and any other designer crap you have in that overpriced designer handbag and stuff it in here. That includes the credit card already approved by the Bureau. Now, when you get to your booth, you're going to place this flat on the table, like this"—by twisting Maleficent's wrist in a painful position, SallyAnne also flipped the small purse horizontally—"so that the clasp is pointed at the suspects. That way, the video camera will pick up your interactions with them."

Maleficent's eyes narrowed to the point where only her long, feathered lashes were visible.

For a while, it seemed as though time stood still.

SallyAnne had had enough. Grabbing the brooch from Maleficent's hand, she added, "If it ruins this overpriced *schmatta*, well too bad. You are wearing this bug, even if we have to stick it up your—"

"What Operative Jagger is trying to say is that any possible reduction in your sentence will be largely predicated on the success of this operation. It's strictly up to you, Ms.—"

"Really? '*Ms.*?' Come now, Lionel! A moment ago we were snuggled together on the filthy floor of this mobile monstrosity. Plainly, that puts us on a more intimate basis—"

"One block out!" Riley shouted.

To make the point that the time for coy innuendos was over, SallyAnne pointedly pinched the bodice of the de la Renta and then pierced it with the brooch.

Maleficent's painful squeal might have been in protest that the lines of her frock were now forever ruined, but more than likely it resulted from the brooch's pin prick. Riley had stopped quickly to avoid running over a nanny wrangling a double baby carriage and a leashed Doberman as she crossed the street.

Maleficent's screech was loud enough to wake the poor woman's charges. But by the time she calmed them down, the van was already a block away.

The sting couldn't start until Maleficent's curses, threats, and tears had subsided. Lionel watched her worriedly as she touched up the make-up smudges. "Why did you have to be so hard on her?" he hissed to SallyAnne.

"Don't you understand what she's doing?" SallyAnne retorted. "If she's lucky enough to shove these suspects and a few other narcissistic parents into the defendant column, sure, maybe some judge will be kind enough to carve a few years off her sentence. But as far as I'm concerned, for what she's already done to all the kids who should have gotten into those colleges but didn't because some over-indulged cheats took up their slots instead—well, hell, Lionel! I hope he throws the book at her. Don't you?"

"Of course I do," he declared.

SallyAnne exhaled, relieved. *Thank God he's not totally smitten.*

"You know, I can hear everything you're saying," Maleficent muttered.

"Good," SallyAnne snapped back. "And I'll bet you don't feel an iota of guilt."

"Of course I do," Maleficent retorted.

She was lying. SallyAnne knew this because her eyes stayed firmly on the mirror.

In fact, through the mirror, she could see Maleficent's sly grin.

"Ladies—please!" Lionel sighed.

SallyAnne couldn't wait to take her down.

THEY DROPPED MALEFICENT ON THE BLOCK BEFORE THE RESTAURANT.

Riley then turned the next corner. At that point, Lionel and SallyAnne got out of the van and walked back toward the restaurant. In the meantime, Riley had backed the van into a parking space right across the street, informing them and Maleficent via their earbuds of his great luck in finding a spot so close.

As they entered the restaurant, Lionel asked SallyAnne, "Do you think she'll behave herself?"

He got his answer: a snort.

THE HOSTESS WAS ALREADY SEATING MALEFICENT. THROUGH THEIR EARBUDS, the agents listened as she demanded a booth directly across from the bar, as per Lionel's instructions.

A moment later the hostess was back at the entrance. SallyAnne informed her, "We'd like to sit at the bar."

The young woman smiled. "Sure, follow me."

As Maleficent had predicted, the bar was practically empty. While passing by, they ignored her, but their eyes swept over the booth.

Watching them, Maleficent held up the Bureau-issued clutch purse. Then, with theatrical aplomb, she slapped it onto the table.

"Ouch!" Riley groaned into their earbuds.

Lionel frowned. Like SallyAnne, he was quite aware that surveillance equipment was sensitive.

"Cooperating Witness One, please angle the purse a bit to the right so that I have a fuller view of both you and the empty side of the booth where Suspects One and Two will be seated," Riley commanded.

Maleficent shifted the purse ever so slightly. "You mean, like this?"

"Yeah, something like that," Riley declared. "But without your middle finger blocking the center of the screen."

Lionel and SallyAnne took a closer look at the booth. Yes, Maleficent was indeed shooting Riley a bird, albeit upside down. Feeling their eyes upon her, she ignored their stares but flipped her wrist so that now her middle-finger salute was aimed in their direction.

Lionel groaned. Like her, he finally recognized Maleficent as a hostile asset.

About damn time.

By grabbing the two stools at the closest end of the bar, Lionel and SallyAnne were now directly across from the banquette where Maleficent waited for her clients: a couple named Gretchen and Seamus McCoppin.

The bartender frowned when Lionel ordered a glass of seltzer water with a lime. The goatee'd hipster's scowl deepened when SallyAnne echoed the order. Then, feeling guilty about it, she added, "Oh…and your house red."

She felt redeemed by the bartender's grudging nod.

Maleficent was also ordering. Through their earbuds, her command to her waiter—"Martini. Dirty, with two olives. And bring it fast!"—came in loud, clear, and obnoxiously snide enough to make Lionel wince.

The bartender placed their drinks in front of him. So that Lionel understood that in no way did she expect the Bureau to pick up the cost of her wine, SallyAnne pulled a credit card out of her purse.

"Don't be silly." Lionel patted her wrist, then handed the bartender the card he used for Bureau expenses.

"Oh!… Well, thank you," she murmured. For just a moment his hand lingered over hers. She wished time could stand still.

Sadly, it couldn't. They were on a mission. To get the optimum sight line, the agents twisted their barstools so that they were knee to knee—something SallyAnne didn't mind in the least. That way, they'd each have a partial view of Maleficent's booth while pretending to be a couple in love. One of them was pretending, anyway.

In seemingly no time at all, the restaurant filled up. Even the bar was getting crowded. Many standing there stared longingly at the lucky diners already seated at tables. A few of the bar's patrons were obviously regulars. When they walked in, all they had to do was nod at the bartender, and a minute or two later he'd place their drink in front of them.

The McCoppins came in on the next wave of diners. SallyAnne recognized them from her numerous stakeouts of the couple's grand mansion, which filled a half block on nearby Jackson Street. To exchange air kisses with Gretchen, Maleficent raised up from the banquette. She then offered Seamus a handshake. By the look on his face, she must have squeezed it firmly.

"Was she signaling him?" SallyAnne wondered out loud.

Lionel watched Seamus for a long moment before shaking his head. "Nah. It was a power play on her part. She claims this pair is low-hanging fruit, but the emails Seamus exchanged with her are still too nebulous for our case. If she doesn't nail them on this, she's got to come up with someone else."

He had a point.

Instead of worrying about whether Maleficent could pull it off, Sally-Anne would do what she knew he'd expect of her: play the role of the infatuated date.

This wasn't much of a stretch.

Not that she'd ever let Lionel in on that secret. Should he ever suspect as much, unlike some of the other agents, he would follow the rulebook to the letter and would request another partner.

No, she'd prefer to keep her mouth shut, even if it meant a broken heart.

***

"SHALL I ORDER A FEW HORS D'OEUVRES?" MALEFICENT FORCED HER LIPS INTO a smile that she hoped looked natural enough. To hide her jitters, she raised her hand and snapped for their waiter. "The amuse-bouche here is to die for! And having seen your wine cellar, Seamus, I know you'll appreciate the Bordeaux I ordered." She pointed to the bottle that the sommelier had already opened.

Seamus glanced around warily. "Well, maybe a glass—but no food. We want to make this short. I'll be damned why we have to do this in public! What if someone overhears us?"

Maleficent's heart skipped a beat when she noticed his eyes lingering on SallyAnne—until she realized he was gazing at her crossed legs.

Men are such pigs, Maleficent thought. And he's sitting with his wife, for God's sake!

Not that it would have mattered to Gretchen. They were two peas in a pod—both vain and covetous for attention from the opposite sex.

For that matter, if one hadn't known they were husband and wife, one might easily assume that they were twins. Together, they had sandblasted the ravages of middle age from their bodies, minds, and souls. Their faces, devoid of all laugh lines, had been stretched into caricatures of their more youthful selves. Not that they could smile naturally anymore. Their lips, plumped with fillers, drove their smiles into unnatural lines that ran beyond the corners of their mouths and into their cheeks, giving them the appearance of crazed clowns. Their bodies were tautly sculpted. Looking at Gretchen's chest, Maleficent wondered how many ribs she'd had surgically removed to get a waist thinner than Fawn, her seventeen-year-old daughter. As for Seamus, his arrogance was a given, but she assumed his flashpoint temper had something to do with the steroid injections that resulted in forearms that would make Popeye envious. No gray strands could be found in the unnatural chestnut hue on either of the McCoppins' lush heads of hair.

Maleficent stifled the urge to slap his face—not for Gretchen's sake, but for her own. She didn't have time to dawdle, what with the Feds breathing down her neck. If she wanted to lighten her rap, she'd have to make the McCoppins ante up—and fast.

"Hey, you called me, remember?" she huffed. "So if you have something on your mind, speak up."

"Yeah, okay, I do!" Seamus' fantasy of being entangled in SallyAnne's legs dissipated in the heat of his anger. "I want to know why I had to hear about your super-secret college admissions program from one of the other dads—some VC yutz who claims to have been behind Uber's third round of financing—and at a school basketball game, of all places!" He scowled. "Hell, if anyone deserves your personal attention, it's our Fawn! Jesus, when I think of the boatload of money we've given to Ashbury Academy—"

"And time!" Gretchen chimed in. "I've been the chair of every school auction since Fawn's sophomore year—"

"Don't interrupt me," Seamus boomed. Turning back to Maleficent, he added, "I sit on *the goddamned board, for Chrissakes!*"

His shout pierced right through Maleficent's ear. She wondered if it may have blown out the hearing device hidden there.

"Please, Seamus! Keep your voice down!" Glancing around, Gretchen nodded in Lionel and SallyAnne's direction. "You're attracting attention."

Maleficent's eyes shifted toward the FBI agents just in time to see them look away, mollified at being noticed.

Just my luck to have these Keystone Kops assigned to me, she fumed.

She forced an encouraging smile onto her lips. "Not to worry, Seamus. I'm expanding the program to include a couple more students—but fair warning, they will be accepted on a first-come basis only."

"Fawn is a perfect candidate for the program," Gretchen insisted. "If anyone deserves special attention, it's our daughter. Poor thing is always so distracted! Her cell buzzes constantly. Did you know she was diagnosed with ADD when she turned eleven?"

"Bullshit. She's boy crazy," Seamus grunted. "I'm beginning to think we should have signed her up for an all-girls Catholic school. Not that we remember our own experiences with those hard-assed nuns so fondly."

Gretchen blushed at her husband's indiscretion. "Truth be told, I'm at my wits' end! I'm doing everything I can to make Fawn understand how important the right college will be to her future. I've threatened to take away her phone if she doesn't study. And every year since second grade I've made sure she signed up for at least three extracurricular activities. My God, she's taken lessons on every kind of musical instrument known to man!"

"Only to quit them within a week," Seamus barked. "We could outfit a full symphony orchestra with all that noise-making crap in our basement."

"At least she's still cheerleading," Gretchen pointed out.

"Yeah, wow, great. So she shakes her pompoms in a damn uniform that leaves almost nothing to the imagination," Seamus groused.

Only because Fawn ordered her uniforms two sizes too small—on purpose, Maleficent thought. She knew better than to say that out loud.

"It still counts as an extracurricular," Gretchen argued. "It's all that testing that's holding her back! She hates them and refuses to study for them. Not that I blame her. She's taken Pre-SATs since sixth grade!"

"And we all know how well that's gone over." Seamus rolled his eyes. "Every time she takes one, the grade is worse than the last one!" He shook his head. "It's been a damn waste of money."

"The only thing left is—well, prayer." To prove she meant it, Gretchen crossed herself. "Seriously, what else is there?"

Maleficent looked down at her wristwatch. It was a Vacheron Constantin and had set her back about seventeen thousand dollars. She sighed deeply—not because she felt sorry for Fawn or for that matter her parents, but because she'd probably have to put it on eBay if she were to cover her defense attorney's already humongous bill. "Not to worry," she cooed soothingly. "Fawn is a perfect candidate for this college admissions program. You see, it's for students who are—well, to put it delicately, 'at risk.'"

Gretchen blanched. "'At risk?' Fawn is not mentally deficient! Granted, she's not the best test-taker, but that's because—"

"She's lazy," Seamus insisted. "Well, that, and she has the attention span of a gnat—"

"Let me be blunt," Maleficent interrupted. "Fawn is at risk *of not getting into an Ivy league college.* And, frankly, considering her GPA and her study habits, it's unlikely she'll get into any state school either."

Gretchen's face lost all of its color. "Are you telling me that our only option is junior college?"

"Not necessarily." Maleficent leaned in. "As Seamus has already told you, I've initiated an exclusive concierge college counseling program that guarantees acceptance to at least one of three Ivys."

Gretchen nodded. "Yes, he mentioned something about it. But he didn't explain how it works."

Maleficent shifted her gaze to Seamus.

He shrugged.

Why that son of a bitch. He hasn't leveled with her that they're here to sign off on the bottom line! What, was he too afraid to explain it to her, or was she just too stupid to get it?

Not that it mattered. It was parents like the McCoppins that irked Maleficent most. Getting them both on record agreeing to the scheme would be a delight.

Unless Gretchen said no.

Damn it, Maleficent thought. If she balks and talks him out of it, I'm screwed. They have to take the bait…

Maleficent smiled as if she'd just won an Oscar. "Quite simply, I've built a network of decisionmakers within certain colleges who act as— well, let's just call them 'pre-admission advocates' for those students who aren't readily identified as an exact fit."

"Oh…" Mystified, Gretchen murmured, "I didn't know the universities provided such services."

"Frankly, Gretchen, they don't. But rest assured these strategically placed staff members will point us in the direction of least resistance. Just as importantly, they are ready, willing, and able to sign off on students with unique qualifications for, say, certain little-known sports, or specialized academic programs, or clubs where fewer students are competing for the available spots."

Gretchen frowned. "For example?"

"Here's one: I have a contact at Fawn's first-choice school who runs a university-sanctioned club. He calls it 'Best Face Forward.' It actively recruits admissions candidates who are an inspiration to others and have proven this by volunteering for non-profit causes."

The guy she referred to was a teaching assistant who directed several quasi-legitimate clubs that met enough of the university's minimal requirements to be run on campus. Maleficent paid him handsomely to write enthusiastic recommendations on her clients' behalf.

Gretchen shrugged. "What with cheerleading practice and AA's sports events, Fawn won't have time for any volunteer work between now and the end of basketball season. And besides, it's like pulling teeth to get her to do anything that takes her away from her clique of besties."

Maleficent chuckled. "Not to worry! No one is asking her to actually *show up* at these volunteer events. She can get by with a few photo ops. We'll put Fawn in tee-shirts bearing the names of a few little-known non-profits and—*voila!*—we've got all the proof we need. Oh, and she'll write a few paragraphs imagining her experiences at such events. She'll then post them to her social media accounts. You know, Instagram, Snapchat—"

Gretchen shook her head. "We don't allow Fawn onto social media. Every parent knows that colleges troll those entities to find out all the ways our children are getting in trouble!"

"Valid point," Maleficent purred.

Especially in Fawn's case, despite her mother's assumption otherwise. After Seamus contacted her, Maleficent did a deep dive into Fawn's social media presence. The result was eye-opening. Too much so. Unbeknownst to her parents, Fawn was prominently featured on several sugar daddy websites. She'd also created a YouTube video in which she demonstrated a seductive way to eat a banana.

When Maleficent informed Seamus of his daughter's indiscretions, she'd quoted a fee of one hundred thousand dollars "to make Fawn catnip to college admissions directors." She now realized she'd sold herself short.

To offset Gretchen's concern, Maleficent added, "In this case, the photos won't be posted on Fawn's social media accounts but those of the benefiting nonprofits."

Creating websites for fake charities would be no small task, and the black-hat hackers up for the job weren't cheap. The McCoppins' rate just went up exponentially.

Gretchen nodded slowly, but by her pursed lips Maleficent realized she was still unconvinced. "When Fawn gets on campus, what if she's too busy to join this club?"

"Once your daughter is attending the university, going to club meetings are optional."

Gretchen frowned. "Wouldn't that be lying?"

Seamus guffawed. "That's the whole point, Gretch! It'll have to be faked because she's too lazy and too selfish to have done this do-gooder crap in the first place!"

"Oh!..." As if weighted down by this reality, Gretchen dropped her head. When she found the strength to raise it again, it was to fret, "Even so, what about Fawn's grade point average?"

"As part of the program, I will personally coach her on those subjects that seem to be the most challenging," Maleficent vowed.

"That would be all of them," Seamus muttered.

Ignoring him, Maleficent continued, "And I'll also nudge her teachers to do all they can to increase her comprehension of their test material so that we can inch up that meddlesome GPA."

Gretchen's lower lip trembled. "There's still the issue of her Scholastic Aptitude Test. And, from what I've heard, there's only one more scheduled before transcripts are due to the colleges."

"Yes, well that does present a major hurdle." Maleficent shrugged. "However, as part of the program, Fawn's test will be given a leg up at the discretion of the proctor."

"What does that mean?" Gretchen prodded.

"Woman," Seamus huffed, "what she's trying to say is that someone else will be taking Fawn's test for her."

Turning to Maleficent, Gretchen asked, "Is that… is that true?"

"Yes."

Gretchen's eyes grew large. "Then… this cannot be sanctioned by Ashbury Academy!"

So that there would be no mistaking her meaning, Maleficent looked her straight in the eyes. "It isn't."

"And it's got to stay that way," Seamus warned Gretchen. "Do you understand?"

Gretchen's mouth tensed into an anxious moue.

Maleficent froze as Gretchen processed this new reality.

Finally, Gretchen nodded meekly.

First crisis averted.

Maleficent found herself breathing again. She continued: "As I explained to your husband, I am not an employee of the school but an independent contractor whose job is to assess and assist Ashbury Academy's junior and senior students on their college admissions process. As for this specific program, it is of my own creation. But because the methods needed to guarantee success are somewhat unorthodox, the program is run independently of the school." She sighed. "And thanks to Seamus and a few other board members, it was approved so that, at my discretion, I could solicit specific parents whose children I deem are most at-risk."

Gretchen's blank stare seemed to go on interminably.

In Maleficent's ear, Riley murmured, "Did the mic go dead?"

That was Maleficent's cue to bring it home. Steeling herself, she added, "At this point, if you're not interested, no need to continue. Shall I?"

The McCoppins exchanged glances. Finally, Gretchen whispered, "Yes."

Maleficent stifled the urge to leap up for a victory dance.

Now, time to close this deal...
She smiled grandly. "Which brings us to a very delicate topic..."

SALLYANNE WAS SO ENGROSSED IN MALEFICENT'S DECEIT THAT, AT FIRST, SHE didn't feel the tap on her shoulder. When it dawned on her that someone was trying to get her attention, she looked up and found herself gazing into the eyes of a man who seemed vaguely familiar.

Her mind raced through the possibilities. An old acquaintance? Maybe a former colleague? Perhaps a prior conviction now out on parole?

It couldn't be the latter. Otherwise, his playful smile would not be lifting her spirits, making her heart race, and sending a thrill through her.

"Is this seat taken?" The man was pointing to the now empty stool on the other side of her.

That voice...

SallyAnne had an uncanny ability to hear a voice just once and remember it forever. In this case, she'd listened to his years ago: when he'd been interviewed on the radio.

By the way he now slurred his words, she was surprised she'd recognized it at all.

She had explicitly listened to the show because he was her favorite author. He'd earned that honor with his debut effort, a coming-of-age novel entitled *Extracurricular*.

The face on the back of that oft-read book's well-worn jacket cover now stared down at her.

When his author photo was taken, he'd been two decades younger. His hair had been thicker and longer, his physique thinner, and his life hadn't yet suffered the gravitational pull between great success and some catastrophic fall from grace noted so nonchalantly in the press.

She was so stunned that she murmured, "No, not at all—*Mr. Gable!*"

Her apparent interest in the stranger earned her a scowl from Lionel, who expected her undivided attention for the task at hand.

Intrigued by her recognition, Egan Gable plopped down hard on the stool. "Do we know each other?" He leaned in closer.

Too close. He exhaled enough Scotch to make her eyes water. Taken aback, she stammered, "I read your book—*Extracurricular*. In fact"—the words came out of her mouth before she could stop them—"it's my favorite."

Egan's eyes softened. "Thank you for that. In fact, *THANK GOD* for that! I thought you were another infernal AA parent!" Without pretense, he scanned her head to toe. "But of course, you're much too young to have children of your own."

When their eyes met again, she blushed.

Suddenly, SallyAnne noticed that Lionel was staring at her too. But unlike Egan, he wasn't smiling. "Um…AA?" she stammered. "You… you mean Alcoholics Anonymous?"

"In this case, no," he chuckled. "Albeit, many of AA's—that is, Ashbury Academy's—teaching staff are chip-carrying members." Egan's last word was accompanied by a burp. Noting her dismay, he quickly added, "Not me, mind you."

Her anxiety had nothing to do with his sobriety and everything to do with the mention of Maleficent's school. Was he here to meet with their cooperating witness?

Egan Gable waved at the bartender. "Speaking of which, may I buy you another"—he looked down at her barely touched glass—"wine? Or, perhaps something a bit more adventurous? I can vouch for the fact that the barkeep makes a mean Sneaky Pete: whiskey, coffee liqueur, and just a splash of milk—"

Lionel leaned over SallyAnne and proclaimed, "Sir, do you mind? The lady is on a date!"

SallyAnne gasped. She never thought she'd hear those words come out of Lionel's mouth, let alone so—*so fervently*. She turned to face him, only to realize he was staring back—

As if he were seeing her for the very first time.

It was the same look he'd shared with Maleficent when she'd teased him about her alma mater.

SallyAnne's cheeks felt as if they were on fire.

A deep blush was creeping up Lionel's neck as well.

Egan, obviously too drunk to notice, chortled, "Well, you've got an odd way of showing it, sir! Not only are you ignoring this, this"—a second burp came out loud enough to turn a few heads—"this beautiful young woman, the whole time I've been chatting her up you've been staring over there, at that over-inflated Barbie doll!"

Swaying precariously, he swung his arm toward Maleficent—

At which point he took a closer look at her.

Suddenly, his eyes opened wide, as if they were no longer hazed. "Well, well! It seems I know Barbie—and for that matter, her plasticine friends too—Ken and Midge." As if attempting some semblance of sobriety, he straightened his tie, and then patted it flat against his shirt. "If you kind gentlefolk will excuse me, I think I'll mosey on over and pay my respects."

He walked off quickly but seemed to be listing to port.

Like Lionel, SallyAnne's fear that Egan Gable might ruin their sting operation had them ready to grab him and yank him back. It didn't help that Riley was yelling something at them through their earbuds. From what they could make out he seemed to be saying: "Let him go! She just said she's expecting him!"

Maleficent knows Egan Gable? SallyAnne's jaw dropped at the thought.

For some reason, she found this new bit of information disconcerting.

In truth, it was downright depressing:

My favorite author of all time is not only a lush but he also has awful taste in women.

A Few Minutes Earlier...

"...Which brings us to a very delicate topic"—Maleficent was saying—"the cost of Fawn's participation in the program. As you can imagine, such guarantees aren't cheap." She faced Seamus. "In fact, after hearing some of the hurdles Gretchen just pointed out, to do Fawn justice I must reassess my previously stated fee."

Seamus's glare left Gretchen cowering. When he turned back to Maleficent, he snarled, "How much now?"

She thought for a moment, then declared with a shrug: "Two hundred and fifty thousand."

"You've got to be out of your mind!" Seamus sputtered.

"On the contrary," Maleficent assured him. "It took a lot of work to set up a network that assures your daughter will end up in a college worthy of your investment in her." She glanced at her watch. "Time for you to decide if she's worth it. If not, no harm no foul. However, in an hour I'm meeting another set of parents who were disappointed you'd beat them to this appointment slot."

The color went out of Seamus's face. "You didn't mention our names to them, did you?"

Maleficent frowned. "Of course not! When it comes to this program, I'm the soul of discretion—for obvious reasons."

Seamus muttered something indistinguishable.

Hell, if I can't understand him, Lord knows the Feds can't, either!

Irritably, she asked, "Can I take that as a yes?"

"Yeah, okay," he grumbled.

"Alright then." She handed him a business card. "When you return home, wire a donation in the correct amount to this charitable organization. In fact, it's the recipient of Fawn's new extracurricular activities. In return—*huzzah!* Automatically, you'll receive a tax-deductible receipt."

"Well, that's something anyway..." Her husband, who silenced her with a scowl, did not share Gretchen's relief.

"Tomorrow I'll begin Fawn's transformation into the student we all know she should be," Maleficent promised.

Unsaid was obvious: should be—*but isn't.*

Not that the McCoppins needed their noses rubbed into this unflattering reality.

Gretchen leaned in so close that Maleficent thought she was going to kiss her.

Why? For being some sort of lifeline for Fawn? Ha! If only she knew!

Maleficent's instinct was to recoil. Instead, she steeled herself, only to realize Gretchen was whispering in her ear: "Please… Fawn mustn't know anything about this!"

Maleficent shrugged. "Mum's the word."

The vow was barely out of her mouth when she heard her name followed by the exclamation, "Well, I'll be damned! Small world, isn't it?"

The McCoppins blanched at the man approaching them.

Maleficent stifled a curse—one that she might have shouted out loud, and in English, no less.

Egan Gable…?

What the hell was he doing here?

She forced her lips into a smile before declaring, "Ah, well, look who's here too—AA's illustrious literature professor, Egan Gable!"

Noting how Gretchen's eyes lit up, she then lowered her voice so that only the McCoppins could hear her say, "By the way, Mr. Gable is my top candidate for SAT proctor. I know how much Fawn dotes on him."

"Oh? Well, …that's great, I guess." For some reason, Gretchen seemed both elated and upset by this bit of news.

Has he… and she…

Ha! She is such a harlot!

Maleficent wasn't surprised in the least. Like daughter, like mother.

Egan's appearance gave the McCoppins the perfect excuse to skedaddle. No one was more pleased about this than Maleficent. She had nothing but disdain for her marks.

<hr>

OPERATION SIS-BOOM-BAH

[Transcript #1-00351(A) between Cooperating Witness Number One (CW-1) and Person of Interest Number One (POI-1)]

CW-1
Fancy seeing you here.
(Stares back at Agents Polk and Jagger)
Slumming?

POI-1
What, with that pretty little damsel at the bar? Are you jealous? Surprise, surprise! Not that I blame you. She struck me as smart and beautiful—and kind.

CW-1
She is also a…
(Pauses)
Jesus! Never mind! Enough of this bullshit—and enough of your little
head games, Egan Gable! Oh, and as far as I'm concerned, our little deal
is off.

POI-1
No… *NO!* You can't renege on what you promised!

CW-1
Says who?

POI-1
But—but… Please… don't!

CW-1
Well… Since you're begging. Perhaps we can work something out.

POI-1
(Sighs)
I told you twice already. I'm just not that into you—

CW-1
Don't be a fool! I don't mean sex, you imbecile! I'm giving you back what
you so desperately want—
(Pauses. Then:)
If you'll agree to be the proctor for Ashbury Academy's SAT test.

POI-1:
(Suspiciously)
Are you joking?

CW-1:
Not at all… But you must do everything the job entails—to the letter.

POI-1:
(Shrugging)
How hard can it be?

CW-1:
Just the usual. Of course, the most challenging task concerns the seven
special needs students. Their math portions must be substituted. Will you
have a problem with that?

POI-1:
Why should I? Like you say, they're special needs, and all that implies.

CW-1:
I thought not.
(Sighs:)
There's something I hadn't mentioned before. It is a necessary evil. It involves the essay portion.
(Pauses:)
You're also to provide substitute essays for those students.

POI-1:
(Frowning:)
How is that even possible?

CW-1:
It probably means pulling an all-nighter, but, unfortunately, it goes with the job.

POI-1:
Wait... I'll be staying up all night with the kids?

CW-1:
Don't play stupid, Egan. It doesn't suit you.

POI-1:
(Frowning:)
You've got to be kidding me!

CW-1:
Suddenly, you have a conscience?
(Clicks her tongue:)
I assure you, the pay will make it worth your while.

POI-1:
(Pauses. Then:)
Oh yeah? How much?

CW-1:
Fifteen thousand.

POI-1:
(Snorting:)
Knowing you, you're pocketing at least a hundred thou.

CW-1
You arrogant bastard!
(After a long pause:)
Alright then! Thirty-five thousand. Take it or leave it.

POI-1:
(Pauses. Finally:)
So, how does this little scheme of yours work?

CW-1:
A week from Friday I'm to get the SAT answer keys for both math and reading, as well as the essay questions. That night, I'll drop them by your place along with the names of the students involved. After they take their tests, you're to substitute the math and reading portions with ones that you've already filled in correctly—especially the math portion, although, so that the tests look valid, you're to miss one or two answers in the reading questions. And Egan, just make sure they are different mistakes on each student's test, okay?

POI-1:
Yeah, yeah, okay, whatever. And what about the essays?

CW-1
The way the SAT board weights things, a well-written essay is merely icing on the cake. I know you well enough to appreciate your bullshitting skillset. I'm sure elevating the students into the literary stratosphere should be child's play for you. And since you already teach these students, matching the essay topics to their voices shouldn't be that difficult for you.

POI-1:
If you say so.
(Sighs)
One caveat, babe: I'll want my money a week before the test, or it's no go.

CW-1:
(Seductively)
That's the easy part. In fact, tonight. Say, nine? I'll even give you the cash with a receipt for—let's call it "services rendered."

POI-1:
(After a pause, then a resigned shrug:)
Sure, why not?

REALIZING THAT EGAN AND MALEFICENT WOULD BE PARTING WAYS ANY moment now, Lionel directed SallyAnne to make her way to the van first. "That way, Romeo doesn't have a reason to stick around."

She nodded but said nothing. Still, she was flattered that Lionel would assume as much. She was out the door in a flash.

A moment later, Egan left the table too. By then, SallyAnne had joined Riley in the back of the van, where he was watching Maleficent on the monitor. Pointing to her, he muttered, "She's one cool bitch."

SallyAnne hoped he didn't mean that as a compliment.

AS DIRECTED, MALEFICENT PAID HER BILL WITH THE CREDIT CARD IN THE purse. When she rose to leave, she noticed that Lionel was now sitting alone at the bar. She'd been given strict instructions to ignore the agents, but she could not resist the urge to saunter over. She even dared to take SallyAnne's stool.

She waited until the bartender went off to make her signature martini when she murmured to Lionel, "I'm scared. I hope you know that. And I'm doing my best to help you—"

"Cut the bullshit," he muttered. His lips barely moved as he stared straight ahead, but his words came out clearly and firmly. "We're the ones helping you—*to save yourself.* And lady, from what I can tell you actually enjoy taking the others down with you. So if you want sympathy, look elsewhere. In the meantime, head for the van so that you can turn in your gear."

Maleficent stared at him but knew better than to say anything. Instead, she tossed a twenty on the bar, then did as she was told.

BETWEEN THE TIME LIONEL PUT MALEFICENT IN HER PLACE AND SHE ARRIVED at the van, Riley had finally stopped laughing at Lionel's putdown.

Although SallyAnne was also impressed, to hide it from Riley she merely shrugged.

Maleficent entered the van. Without a word, she pulled out the ear mic and tossed it along with the clutch purse to SallyAnne. As for the brooch, she practically ripped it off her dress. When SallyAnne offered to help, she snarled, "Don't you dare touch me."

A few minutes later, Lionel showed up. He sat up front with Riley.

When they dropped Maleficent in front of her home—a high-rise building on Russian Hill with a straight-on bay view—it was up to Sally-Anne to tell her: "You did a great job in covering your tracks. Too good, in fact. Unless you figure out a way to get evidence on the other six families, we'll have a difficult time convincing the judge that you're doing your best to cooperate. In these few weeks before the SAT test, I suggest you call to set up meetings with the other suspects to go over the process again with them. That way we can record their corroborations."

Maleficent purred, "My, my! Aren't you the little taskmistress! Silly me —I thought naming names would be sufficient." She stuck out her hand in a Nazi salute. "I'm on it, *mein Führer*." She slammed the van door on her way out.

RATHER THAN HEADING BACK DOWNTOWN TO THE OFFICE TO TRANSCRIBE THE video, Lionel suggested they tackle it at SallyAnne's place, which was just a few blocks away in San Francisco's Cow Hollow neighborhood. The idea seemed reasonable enough. Despite the look of longing he'd let slip in the restaurant, SallyAnne had no illusions that he'd breach protocol over it.

After she typed it up, they read it over. When Lionel got to the part where Maleficent was left alone with Egan, Lionel suddenly declared, "You need to change something." He pointed to the first time in the transcript that SallyAnne labeled Egan Person of Interest Number One.

"But...why?" she asked "He isn't yet a suspect or a defendant—"

"You're right, he wasn't—that is, up until the moment he agreed to participate in Maleficent's scheme. Ergo"—Lionel smirked as he said the word—"in keeping with Bureau policy since we'll soon be arresting him for conspiracy to commit fraud, we can go ahead and use 'Defendant Number Three' as his descriptive."

"Granted, he conspired. But how do we know if he committed the overt act of actually accepting the money?"

"Maleficent doesn't know it, but we're still recording her through her cell. Remember? In fact, Riley is still on surveillance. He followed her over to Gable's apartment and texted a confirmation ten minutes ago—along with a few jealous comments about your crush's staying power."

"Oh." The impact of this revelation was heard in her soft delivery.

Lionel clicked his tongue in mock dismay. "Agent Jagger, I'm beginning to think you're sweet on Defendant Number Three."

To deflect the heat she felt in her cheeks, she retorted, "Don't worry. I'm not. For that matter, if it were true, would the thought of it make you jealous?"

"Heck, yeah, it would." He shrugged. "But... Just... Never mind." To avoid her gaze, he looked at his watch. "I should take off."

She nodded.

SallyAnne followed him to the door. When he opened it, he stood there just long enough for her to give in to her impulse to do the unthinkable: she raised up on tiptoes to kiss him.

She'd aimed for his cheek but he turned his head, and their lips met instead.

He didn't pull away. In fact, he took her in his arms.

When they finally parted, neither said a word. But there was longing and shame in his eyes. She had no doubt hers reflected the same spectrum of emotions.

After locking the door behind him, she leaned against it and cried.

***

As SallyAnne's head hit her pillow, her feelings were still thrumming from Lionel's kiss. She didn't dare guess what would become of their friendship. But if their professional association were to survive, she'd have to keep her feelings for him at bay.

To put him out of her mind, she thought of Egan Gable.

From his writing, she'd always imagined he had a great strength of character. Frankly, now knowing what depths he was willing to sink to—and for so little money at that—made her want to cry.

How does that happen, she wondered. How could someone who writes so eloquently—and with such passion—be so callous, so unfeeling?

But then she remembered that she was judging him on a book he'd written two decades ago; and a work of fiction at that.

She teared up at her own naïveté.

People change over time, she realized. Really, it's tiny twists of fate that change us.

The proof was Lionel.

She smiled at the thought of him.

Suddenly, she pitied Egan. He's like Icarus, she reasoned. He flew too close to the sun, only to fall into a sea of despair.

And now he's drowning…

TWENTY-TWO YEARS AGO

Here's where the story really begins...

CHAPTER 2

*I*f Audrey Thorpe hadn't caught Jeremy Blake, her boyfriend of two years, nailing some cheerleader who, rumor had it, could tie a knot in a cherry stem with her tongue, it's just possible that she might not have been so susceptible to Egan Gable's charms.

The break-up happened during an SAT testing session hosted by a rival school, Saint Ignatius Prep. Both Audrey and Jeremy had taken the test once already, in the spring. And although they'd both scored over 1500, each was competitive enough to want another go at it. For Audrey, it was the math segment that tripped her up the first time, whereas Jeremy had gotten a perfect score there. He was, after all, San Francisco's Mathlete champ.

They'd gone over to St. Ignatius together, in Jeremy's father's car. But because their last names were at the opposite ends of the alphabet, they were put in separate auditoriums. Unlike their school, Ashbury Academy —which was relatively new and crammed all of its 120 students into a timeworn Victorian mansion on the outskirts of San Francisco's Haight-Ashbury neighborhood—S.I.'s campus was humongous, boasting two ball fields and two theaters, as well as the two auditoriums. In fact, the private school's coffers were so full that it was in the process of building a second gymnasium.

During the first hour of testing, Audrey and Jeremy tackled different sections of the test. For Audrey, it was Evidence-Based Reading and Writing. For Jeremy, it was Math, so it was no surprise that he whipped through it with at least twenty-three minutes to spare, giving Audrey a thumbs-up through the auditorium's exterior window, indicating that he'd wait for her outside until the break period.

Although creative writing was Audrey's strength, the essay question was stumping her:

According to Winston Churchill, "In wartime, truth is so precious that she should always be attended by a bodyguard of lies." Is there any personal situation in which a lie would be validated? Explain why or why not.

Hmmm, thought Audrey. Is there only one right answer to this question? And if so, what if I choose the wrong one?

Or, is this one of those times in which there is no one right answer, and therefore I'll be judged on not what I write, but how I make my case?

Audrey's dilemma was, in a nutshell, the Achilles' heel on her high school's academic philosophy. Although Ashbury Academy was known for its focus on its students' critical thinking skills, in some cases (at least, in Audrey's case) too much of it went on.

And on. And on.

Inevitably, emotional paralysis set in.

Twenty minutes later, Audrey was still in a panic. *This essay counts for a quarter of my total score! I can't afford to screw it up!*

The reason for her hesitation was personal: the notion of deceit was foreign to Audrey.

Unlike the majority of her peers, she had never lied to her mother, Lavinia. Granted there had been numerous opportunities, but Audrey just didn't see the point in it. During the few times they'd disagreed on something, Lavinia had never pulled rank. None of that "It's my way or the highway" crap, and certainly no guilt trips.

Instead, they'd talk things through and usually came to a compromise.

They even agreed on how Audrey should handle her relationship with Jeremy.

"Are you having sex?" Lavinia had asked her one day very nonchalantly.

Audrey shook her head slowly. "No… Not *yet*. But he'd like to."

"Would you like that, too?"

"I've thought about it, yes."

She would have felt guilty admitting this if it weren't for Lavinia's wistful smile. "Your first time making love is a special moment. But even more important than the desire or passion you feel now is the issue of trust. When the person you love has earned your trust, then the time will be right."

Audrey let that sink in. Did she trust Jeremy? For the most part, yes. At least she wanted to believe that, but it wasn't always easy to do. For one thing, he liked to flirt with other girls. For another, she'd heard him make several bald-faced lies to his parents. In fact, the whole reason they had driven over in his father's car—a brand spanking new Ferrari F355

Spider—was because he'd told his dad that his own car had a faulty brake line.

"Why don't you just tell him the truth," she teased him, "that what you really want is to make the other guys jealous when they see you drive up in it?"

Jeremy graced her with a smug grin. "Because that would piss him off. Besides, what he doesn't know won't hurt him."

"I hope you don't say that about me, behind my back."

He said nothing but gave her the same tightlipped smile he'd just given his father as they'd waved off.

That, and then he kissed her hard as if that would relieve her of any doubts.

Love means never having to tell a lie, thought Audrey.

Oh my God! That's it!

From that point on, the essay flowed out of her:

It's easy to tell a lie. You can validate doing so by telling yourself that those you lie to can't handle the truth, or that what they don't know won't hurt them, or that in fact, you're saving them a lot of pain.

But the reality is that, yes, your loved ones can handle it. You have to trust them to do so, just like they trust you not to lie to them. Wouldn't it hurt them much more should they discover that you didn't give them the benefit of your doubt?

If you're really worried about their pain, first think about the devastated looks on their faces when they realize that you didn't trust them to understand the truth.

Trust needs truth.

So does love.

Audrey fairly tossed her paper at the test monitor. She couldn't wait to tell Jeremy how well she'd done.

JEREMY WASN'T IN THE AUDITORIUM'S LOBBY WAITING FOR HER, OR EVEN OUT IN front of it. Finally, she found him: in his father's Ferrari—or, more accurately, rocking the car with some big-breasted harlot.

Audrey recognized the girl because she'd sighed throughout the essay test when she wasn't sucking on her Number 2 pencil. She had also cut out early from the English test. The frown on the girl's face indicated she'd be retaking it at a later date.

It suddenly dawned on Audrey that she'd seen the girl a week before, on SI's cheering squad during a home game with AA. The girl was easy to remember because, invariably, the timing on her jumps was off.

In hindsight, Audrey reasoned, that might have been deliberate. It got the crowd to notice her.

The players saw her, too. The very first thing they noticed was that she wasn't wearing a bra.

Like now.

Or for that matter, panties.

As Audrey watched Jeremy's ass cheeks rise and fall in unison with his paramour's squeaky yelps of orgasmic pleasure, she stumbled through all five stages of heartbreak:

- Denial, (Maybe that wasn't Jeremy, but some other guy who'd stolen his keys… But no, she'd recognize his Ashbury Academy letter jacket over that bare ass anywhere!)
- Anger. (How DARE he do it—and with a pea-brained tart, no less!)
- Bargaining. (Obviously, it was a hormonal lapse of judgment! And, besides, Audrey had already allowed him to get only as far as third base. Granted, whenever he'd attempted to go for a home run she'd slapped his hand away, or worse yet murmured some seemingly offhanded teen pregnancy statistic—but still!)
- Depression: Had her prudishness pushed him away? If only he'd give her a second chance, she'd... she'd what? Give in to his begging? Why do so when her love obviously meant so little to him? Was this how it was to be with her future relationships with men?
- Finally, there was acceptance: Jeremy wasn't hers anymore. He now belonged to some double-jointed cheerleader who would use him to tutor her for her next shot at the SATs.

And he'd enjoy every minute of it.

Audrey wondered how long Jeremy had known the girl. Not that he'd tell her the truth if she were to ask him. Even if he did, what would it matter? The bottom line was that her relationship with him was a joke; a total sham.

No, worse: it was a lie.

I guess the testers will laugh when they read my essay, thought Audrey. They'll think I'm just a stupid, naïve little girl.

Well, I guess I am.

She felt like running all the way home, but she knew that if she left now, she'd be forfeiting the second and third portions of the test, and that would ruin her score.

Nothing was more important than that. *Certainly not some horny boy.*

At least none of this had happened in front of Lavinia. Her mother would have insisted that addressing her heartache was more important than anything, including the test.

Considering her role as founder and Head of School at Ashbury Academy, it was an odd stance, but that was Lavinia for you. Feelings mattered most.

WHEN AUDREY TOLD HER FRIEND, TALLULAH WISHART, ABOUT JEREMY'S desertion—more to the point, with whom Jeremy had two-timed her—her friend had laughed so hard that she spewed her latte.

"Ha," said Tallulah, "I guess that proves the adage, 'Abstinence makes the heart grow fonder—*of someone willing to give it up.*'"

Audrey shifted uncomfortably on her stool. "The saying is 'absence makes the heart grow fonder,' and it has nothing to do with sex."

Tallulah snorted. "Trust me, little virgin, abstinence has everything to do with sex."

"No, what I mean is… Just never mind." It was useless to argue semantics with Tallulah, or anything else, for that matter.

Lavinia called Tallulah "an old soul," which, to Audrey's way of thinking, was just a polite way of saying that she spoke her mind on anything and everything, whether she knew what she was talking about or not.

Jeremy had always called Tallulah a blowhard. Audrey was too loyal to her dear girlfriend to let him know she agreed with him.

Thinking about Jeremy, Audrey teared up again.

Seeing this, Tallulah growled, "He's lucky I wasn't there. I would have tossed a brick through that Ferrari's windshield."

Audrey had no doubt about that. Tallulah had a horrible temper. She'd gotten away with a lot of crap because of her mother's fame. Maggie Wishart was the sultry lead singer for Chameleon, one of the legendary rock bands that had gotten its start during San Francisco's infamous Summer of Love.

At that very moment, Audrey vowed to stay a virgin forever.

Or to at least date grown rational men, as opposed to horny pubescent boys who wore their pants belted below their hips as if showing the top half of their boxer briefs was sexy or something.

By, say, twenty-five, she reasoned, any hormone-induced frenzy would have subsided, along with the urge to drop trou in public, let alone to lie to the woman he loved.

AS FATE WOULD HAVE IT, THE VERY NEXT DAY EGAN GABLE, WITH HIS CRISPLY creased khaki pants belted at his waist, came into her life.

The opening day of Ashbury Academy's fall term was still two weeks away, but Audrey, who was to be a senior that year, had made up her mind that she wasn't going to stay home and mope. Better to keep busy by helping out around the school. Since Lavinia was AA's headmistress, Audrey was well aware that there was always some task in need of someone's immediate attention. And because Clare, Lavinia's assistant, had extended her Mexico vacation through tomorrow, she knew Lavinia would welcome her help.

Egan had arrived early for his interview with Lavinia. He was applying for a position as the instructor of AA's Advanced Placement course called *Shakespeare's Influence on World Literature*. Unbeknownst to him, he was the one and only candidate for the position, and that made him a shoo-in—if he lived up to the *curricula vitae* he'd faxed over just the day before.

Audrey, who had just finished conducting a tour of the school with a prospective student and his parents, saw by the lit button on Clare's phone console that Lavinia was still fielding calls from parents preparing for the new school year. She smiled apologetically to Egan and then pointed toward the chairs backed against the administration office's large bay window.

Egan took the hint: prospective students and their parents came first.

Noting that the coffeemaker on the sideboard was still on, he poured himself a cup. But before settling into one of the reception room's folding chairs, he grabbed an old and well-thumbed copy of *Utne Reader* from the large coffee table, which was, in fact, the stump of a Redwood tree.

"'Magic circles are mandatory.' What the hell does that mean?" The applicant's father, Mr. Siler, who had been reading the admissions brochure, hadn't even realized he'd muttered his question out loud until his wife nonchalantly took his hand in hers and proceeded to pierce his palm with a French-tipped nail. Audrey knew this by the man's pained wince.

Nevertheless, he took the hint: *Shut your yap! Don't blow this for Seth. And keep it that way. At least until he is officially accepted into the school.*

To Audrey's mind, that was certainly still up in the air, considering that Seth—tatted up high above the collar of his Mötley Crüe tee shirt and sporting a nose ring to boot—had been a total pain in the ass throughout the tour. For his parents's sake, Audrey had pretended not to notice.

"A magic circle is how students here at the academy resolve conflicts," she explained. "You see, a river stone is passed around. Whoever has it is allowed to express their concerns or feelings. We find it quite effective in inspiring open debate amongst the students." Audrey's tone was gentle enough to use on a five-year-old, let alone a master of the universe such as Mr. Siler.

By his suspicious grimace, she knew he wasn't the type to appreciate the historical relevance of the custom. Understandable. Truth be told, it had more to do with Lavinia's misspent youth on a commune in Mendocino County and the potency of the psychedelic mushrooms that grew under the mammoth Sequoias. But had this been divulged, Mrs. Siler might not have been so pushy about Seth's acceptance.

"They told us on the phone that AA does have an opening for another senior in this year's class. Is that right?" Mrs. Siler asked anxiously. Noting Audrey's nonchalant nod, her quivering smile finally steadied itself. "That's good to know."

"Not to look a gift horse in the mouth, but what gives?" asked Mr. Siler. "I mean, it seems as if every other school has a wait list. And the tuition at the others runs a third higher than Ashbury's."

He had every right to be suspicious. According to their application, the Silers were recent transplants from Seattle, where he'd been one of The Chosen Ones: a Microsoft senior tech executive. From Seth's snarky comments about his previous school, Audrey gleaned that his teachers hadn't appreciated his study habits. Surely the corporate largess that came with his father's connections more than compensated for that.

But the Silers were in Apple country now. In fact, the city was rife with deep-pocketed corporate donors: not just Apple, but also Gap, Pacific Telesis, Hewlett-Packard, Bank of America, and Wells Fargo. The rosters of other schools were already filled with the progeny of their management staffs. This hot list included Charles Schwab, where Mr. Siler had just been hired to head up its fast-growing tech support division. If by some quirk of fate a student slot suddenly opened up, the first call would go to a corporate wonk whose company was underrepresented at that school. Why not bring one more industrial titan into the fold and help spread the wealth?

So yes, Ashbury Academy might just be the Silers's last hope, even if they didn't yet realize this.

What they couldn't know was that the school needed Seth just as badly as he needed it.

Ashbury Academy was only three years old. Despite this, Lavinia had worked hard to keep the school more affordable than the city's other private schools. Her vision was that the school would appeal to parents much like herself: those who, for whatever reason, were disappointed with the public schools but felt that the privates were too structured or unduly influenced by the whims of the parents as opposed to the needs of the students.

In fact, half the students at Ashbury were on either full or partial scholarships.

AA's great weakness was that it had yet to build its reputation among those whose corporate connections or old family money might fund its mission. Knowing this, Audrey's sales pitch played to the school's strengths: its school's class sizes and academic philosophy.

"Ashbury Academy has a few select openings because Lavinia and her staff have devised a curriculum model that is grounded in the essentials while remaining fluid," Audrey explained. "For example, we have several students who excel in the performing arts or have a unique facility for science and math. As such, they are often presented with learning opportunities outside the realm of the typical classroom environment. So, should a particularly promising student cross the school's threshold, AA's fluid student body model allows for him to be accommodated."

Her choice of pronoun was deliberate.

Audrey immediately segued into a usually well-received selling point: the respect she had for the school's instructors. "Lavinia only hires those who've had actual hands-on applied experience in their subjects," she explained. "That way, students are taught by someone with innate knowledge and a genuine passion for it."

"You mean, the sex-ed teacher was once a porn star?" Seth smirked. "Awesome! Does she tutor on the side?"

Hearing this, Egan choked on his coffee.

Audrey's smile suddenly set into a grimace. She hated the boy for making her sound silly.

No way will Lavinia let him into our school—

Oh, who am I kidding, Audrey thought. Schwab just hired this Neanderthal's daddy, and he's offering to pay full tuition. Provided the jerk isn't an arsonist, she'll let him in, if only to cover the new teacher's salary.

Seth's jibe was rude enough to make Mr. Siler look up from the school brochure and give his son a warning glance.

Little good that did. Seth smirked and rolled his eyes.

If Audrey had to guess, she was willing to bet that the sealed envelope holding his transcripts would reflect eleven years of mediocre grades. So why should the boy give a damn if he were accepted or not?

Seth may have given up, but obviously, his parents hadn't. It was natural to assume they'd already heard the horror stories about the San Francisco public schools from Mr. Siler's new co-workers. The scuttlebutt: if you couldn't get your child into the public school's crown jewel, Lowell (and no one could; not with a waiting list that was, perpetually, four years long) you had no choice but to cough up the bucks for private school.

San Francisco's more prestigious non-sectarian private high schools– University, Lick-Wilderming, the Lycée Francais, not to mention Urban just a few blocks away—had numerous students waitlisted for each class. Even without the tattoos, nose stud, and bad attitude, Seth Siler would have a hard time finding a slot.

That is, unless it turned out that Seth was a legacy or a sibling.

And the Silers were willing to donate a new wing.

No, the Silers were just as desperate to get into Ashbury as Lavinia should be to have them.

Resigned to this reality, Audrey glided toward the large double door marked HEAD OF SCHOOL. "Lavinia is off the phone now. Why don't I knock and see if she's available?"

Because it was his first time at Ashbury Academy, Egan wasn't aware that the pretty young brunette with the big gray eyes and dimples on both sides of her mouth wasn't named Clare, despite the placard that sat front and center on the school's reception desk.

Nor had it occurred to him that she was only seventeen years old.

And why should it? AA's receptionist was emboldened with a solemn maturity that belied her years.

Her sad luminous eyes didn't dart away with the giddiness found in most teenaged girls. No Madonna-esque corset peeked out from under a sheer blouse or denim jacket, no short flouncy skirt over fishnet stockings, no Doc Martens. Instead, she wore a long fitted black cashmere sweater over black slacks and ballet slippers: sensible for a traditionally chilly August day in San Francisco. Her hair wasn't big and frowsy, but straight and angled with the sides cut bluntly even below her chin line, and bangs that stopped just above her naturally arched brows.

"Zelda," Egan murmured, just loud enough for her to hear him.

She looked up to find him gazing at her.

"I'm sorry. I was admiring your, er, hair," he explained.

Obviously, she knew the reference to F. Scott Fitzgerald's wife because her dimples deepened again.

He had accomplished his goal.

He could see that she was struggling with a comeback, but before she could get it out the phone rang, giving her the perfect excuse to ignore him again.

What she didn't know was that he enjoyed eavesdropping on her because it gave him an inkling of what he was getting himself into. By the lecture she delivered, he assumed it was a parent new to the school's procedures: "No, students do not wear uniforms here, because Lavinia feels that how we choose to dress on any given day is part of a student's creative process." After a pause, she rolled her eyes in disgust, adding, "No, upper class-persons will not be allowed to go off campus for lunch. The food choices are less than desirable here in the Haight—"

Albeit the drug choices on every street corner of the 'hood are second to none, Egan thought to himself. This bit of public knowledge brought a slight smile to his lips.

Seeing it, Audrey smiled too and then held the phone away from her ear so that he also could hear the concern in the parent's petulant voice. When it finally broke off, she responded, "No, you've been misinformed. The traditional senior trip is not Lake Como, but *Mono* Lake... Yes, well again, the whole point isn't 'culture,' but self-discovery. The students separate and live on their own for three days... Accommodations? They take sleeping bags and camp under the stars! No, sorry, Lavinia would never consider Rome, Paris, or Madrid instead... Why? Because if you can't find yourself in the middle of nowhere, what are the chances of finding yourself anywhere else?" She moved to slam down the phone, but at the very last moment, she resisted the impulse. She murmured good-bye and gently placed the receiver in its cradle.

Egan waited until their eyes met, then smiled. "I for one found myself in Paris. If you'd allow me, I'd show you where."

My God... He's flirting with me!

Egan Gable's offer left Audrey speechless. Perhaps this was for the best because just then Lavinia opened her door to usher the Silers back into the reception area.

Noting the frowns on all their faces, Audrey closed her eyes, relieved.

Good, she thought. *Ashbury may be poor, but it's pure, too. That's what makes us so different. So special. That, and the fact that the school only exists because Lavinia created it for me.*

As if reading her mind, Lavinia met her gaze with a wide smile.

In that singular moment, Audrey vowed to live her life just as her mother had.

No lies. No secrets.

And I'll always put my children first.

Egan's polite cough broke the trance between them.

Lavinia looked over. "Oh, there you are," she exclaimed. "Egan Gable, am I right?"

Her smile now embraced him like a warm ray of sunshine. He'd already recognized her from the photo collages that adorned the students' lockers flanking the wide hallway leading to her office. She'd been front and center in many of the pictures. That same grin, shared with the students who embraced her in the photos, was also reflected on their faces.

Noting Lavinia's obvious delight in his presence, Egan relaxed a bit. "And you must be Ms. Thorpe!" He stood and shook her extended hand. "A pleasure to meet you."

"Call me Lavinia. Everyone does, even the students. Even my daughter. In fact, Audrey is one of our seniors this year." Lavinia glanced over at the woman behind the desk.

No—the girl.

Egan couldn't help but stare. He was embarrassed for having missed the resemblance between the two. In his defense, there were enough variations–in their physical looks, their mannerisms—to throw him off. For example, the daughter was more slender, the mother taller. There were also the slight nuances that came with an age difference of thirty years or more. Although not yet fifty, already the skin had pillowed out around Lavinia's chin line, and a delicate web of wrinkles had formed at the corners of her eyes. But what had thrown him off even more than Lavinia's long prematurely graying curls or her colorful mode of dress was her ecstatically cheerful demeanor.

It was the antithesis of her daughter's quiet reserve.

She's Mary Poppins for the Brat Pack, he marveled. Okay, yeah, I can dig it.

Noting his surprise, Lavinia said to Audrey, "Dear, do you think you'll finish inputting those new class schedules into the computer before Clare returns tomorrow?"

Audrey glanced at the clock on the wall. "Oh, I'd say I'll be done by the end of the day, no problem." She shuffled the pink phone messages into a neat stack and handed them to Lavinia. "By the way, thus far five parents have called begging that we reconsider the senior trip to Mono Lake." She was looking at her mother, but her sly smile was meant for Egan. "The overwhelming consensus is Paris."

Egan could feel the blood draining from his face. Great, he thought. I almost got caught coming on to Lavinia Thorpe's underage daughter! Talk about blowing a pretty decent meal ticket…

But she is adorable.

Lavinia sighed. "For many of the seniors, that would be their second or third trip to the City of Light. They'd be bored! The parents never seem to understand that the sole purpose of the senior trip is to—"

"Find yourself," Audrey and Egan said it in unison.

"Yes—exactly!" Lavinia looked from one to the other before scrutinizing Egan carefully.

He stared back innocently. He hoped she took it to mean that, instinctively, he understood their mission; that he got what they were all about, there at the academy.

At least, what she was all about. After all, Lavinia Thorpe was AA.

As he followed her into the office, she shut the door behind him.

CHAPTER 3

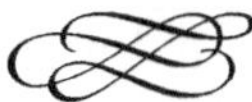

August 2

Phone tree message left for all parents via Ashbury Academy Parent Auxiliary:

"Hi, Regina, sorry I missed you! I hope your summer has been fab! Hey, are you guys still in Tahoe?... Oh, darn it, hope you're checking your messages! Listen, I'm calling because Lavinia asked the Auxiliary to call and remind all parents that Ashbury is breaking tradition this year. We are not—repeat, NOT starting the fall session on the day of this month's full moon, as in the past. Instead, we're starting on the day of the Lunar eclipse, which is August 17th. Isn't that cool? I think the significance of that will stay with our kids for a lifetime—"

"Tell me about yourself." Lavinia eased herself into one of her office's five comfortable armchairs that circled the perfectly round redwood stump sawed knee-high. She then motioned for Egan to do the same.

"Well..." he took a deep breath. "I got my undergrad at Berkeley—Lit major. I speak French and German. And I'm working on my thesis—"

"No, no...what I mean is—well, tell me about you. Where did you grow up? What was the most fun thing you did as a kid? What are the most important lessons your parents taught you? Why did you become a literature major? Is there anything you'd change about your academic journey?" Lavinia leaned back, as if in anticipation of some mystical revelations. "And lastly, why did you answer the ad for this job?"

Egan's mouth opened, but no words came out. He didn't dare tell her the truth: the whole truth, and nothing but. Instead, he massaged his life's sore realities into soft, pliable fibs.

For example, he was honest when he told her he'd grown up just north of the Golden Gate Bridge: in the lily-white suburban neighborhood of Greenbrae, where some seven hundred mid-century ranch homes were grubstaked on several hills. From Greenbrae's rocky peaks, San Francisco twinkled through the bay's pearlescent mist, like Emerald City before being swathed in Technicolor.

When Egan remembered his childhood, the word "fun" never came to mind. Boring was more like it. And yet, he told Lavinia that he'd spent "many joyous hours" making up adventurous tales that transported him to faraway places.

It was partially true. His real goal was to get away from his dull, disillusioned parents. Even going no farther than one of the larger cities across the bay—San Francisco, Berkeley, wherever—was far enough. His parents never crossed any of the bay's bridges. Why should they? Marin County was safe. The rest of the world was not.

As for any lessons he may have learned from his parents, one had indeed left an indelible mark. He saw firsthand how inertia killed everything in its wake—motivation, careers, dreams, and most importantly, love.

Egan doubted his parents still loved each other. At the very least their unity was a habit. Worse yet, it was an obligation.

He likened his father, a life insurance salesman, to a modern-day Willy Loman: stuck in a deep rut of boredom, but not imaginative enough to catapult himself beyond a mundane but comfortable life financed by automatically-renewing commissions and sweetened by the occasional bonus of a free company trip.

As for his mother, to Egan's mind she was her generation's Madame Bovary: dismayed at how her life had turned out, yet in denial of her role in its outcome. But unlike Flaubert's heroine, lust wasn't what she craved. The next Nordstrom Half-Off Sale would do just fine, along with a noontime shaker's worth of Negronis.

Regarding Lavinia's question as to why he chose literature as his calling, he answered, "Quite simply, because those I admire most were novelists."

He explained that he appreciated Hemingway's spare words and wanderlust; how he admired Fitzgerald's way to heighten his characters' emotions, but sympathized with his desperate yearnings for recognition and financial success. He marveled at Greene's aptitude for weaving intricate plots from his character's misguided motives.

At the same time, he prayed he'd never experience the depth of pain and depression that gave this celebrated British author the ability to create such complex characters. Not that he could admit that to Lavinia.

As for her next question—"Is there anything he'd change about his academic journey?"—he assumed she was asking about high school. In that regard, his answer would have been one word: EVERYTHING. His public high school was the largest in Marin County. Sports ruled, and the academic faculty was on rote. He'd felt invisible in the school's continually milling throng of a thousand students.

So instead, Egan answered as if Lavinia had asked about his years at Berkeley: "I had teachers who inspired me, and opportunities that challenged me. Everyone should be so lucky."

Wasn't a half-truth better than no truth?

In this case, yes. Otherwise, he'd have to admit that, as far as Berkeley was concerned, he was a failure.

Egan had just turned twenty-six. He hadn't exactly rushed to get out of college, tacking on the university's six-year Ph.D. track behind his major, Comparative Literature. It was understood that as long as he stayed enrolled, his father would pick up his school tuition and living expenses, which included a studio apartment in the basement of a small cottage elbowed between two old Victorians just north of the campus.

He'd worked tirelessly at his craft, inspired by his creative writing instructors, many of whom were renowned novelists. At the same time, he'd analyzed the English, French, German, Russian, and Scandinavian classics.

To his credit, he'd done his best to keep the requisite allotment of sex, drugs, and political activism in moderation. He didn't want it getting in the way of his creativity. And yet, at times it did—

At least, regarding sex.

Was it his fault he was a good-looking guy? Women responded eagerly to the lazy scratch in his voice and to the all too obvious invitation offered through the unflinching gaze of his deep-set pale green eyes.

It was to be expected, particularly on a campus that was known for its hot-blooded activists and frustrated intellectuals. Merely letting it slip that he was working on a novel was catnip to the girls he met in the many coffee shops that dotted Shattuck Avenue.

So yeah, sex got in the way.

After Egan's first year in the program, his faculty chair—the much-revered Pulitzer Prize-winning novelist, Clive Munt-Luckinbill—had encouraged him to submit his novel as his senior project.

By the program's third year, Gable Senior's pleas that Egan get a job —*any job*—to help out with his expenses were coupled with a threat: "Or else it's time you drop out."

Although worried that any sort of job would distract him from his writing, as a compromise Egan charmed the head of the Lit department into awarding him one of the coveted teaching assistant positions. It consisted of slogging through the lifeless term papers of undergrads.

But Egan's hard work was for naught. He turned in his novel halfway through his fifth year in the program. It earned a passing grade, but as a literary endeavor, it garnered only spare encouragement from the dissertation committee.

Even his faculty chair had gone so far as to declare that it "Lacks a soul. The voice is tentative, the narrative half-hearted, and the plot pedestrian. The author falters in developing an honest tone. Perhaps a different POV would have given it the needed gravitas…"

Fuck you and your gravitas, Egan thought at the time. I'll give you a different point of view, alright.

To get back at the man, he had seduced Clive's wife, Clementine, then added a scene in his novel that memorialized the pathetic experience, including the woman's inclination for naughty talk.

It gave Egan great pleasure to think that, were the book to be published ("No," he chided himself, "*when* it's published") his nemesis would read it and her oft-shouted command—"Show me that big, thick joystick, lover boy!"—would ring a bell with the old fool.

A recent sideways urinal glance had him doubting it.

In the meantime, Egan queried twenty-two literary agents. Unfortunately, the final rejection came the day before his lover's tearful confession to her husband.

Egan's teaching assistant position was immediately terminated.

That evening, Egan invited his father to Marin Joe's, one of the old man's favorite haunts. Three bites into their medium-rare prime ribs, Egan begged for an extension on his financial support.

"That way I can focus strictly on my writing for a year—in New York," Egan explained.

Gable Senior almost choked on a forkful of creamed spinach. His insurance commissions were hard won. Egan's undergraduate tuition payments had been a stretch, even with Egan taking out a student loan—which, having co-signed for it, turned out to be the nightmare about debt that kept Gable Senior up nights.

Gable Senior frowned. "Why New York, of all places?"

"It's the center of the book publishing industry. If I'm there, I can meet with literary agents and editors about my novel—"

"So, you've finished it?"

"Sort of." Egan shrugged.

"In other words, no." Gable Senior swiped his napkin over his mouth. Aggravated, he declared, "Seriously, Egan, why the rush to move away— and to one of the most expensive places on Earth—when you've still got your position at the college? That should impress them, right? When you're ready to show the damn thing around, you can set up a few appointments from here and then fly to the Big Apple, drop off the book, and fly out again–"

"About my job"—Egan winced—"I've…I've been let go."

Egan Senior deflated in front of his eyes.

"Look, if it puts your mind at rest, I won't even live in Manhattan," Egan promised. "To offset costs, I'll find a place in, say, Brooklyn. It's cheaper there, but still a great place for writers—"

Egan babbled on, but Gable Senior heard none of it.

Finally, the steam ran out of Egan's dream. The whole time his father hadn't said a word. Instead, he pushed back his plate, stood up, and walked out.

Gable Senior hated the thought of telling the boy's mother of their son's request. Should she then have the audacity to suggest that he cash in his 401(k), he'd give her an earful. He'd been saving that little pot of gold to build a cabin on the Tahoe lakeside plot he'd purchased years ago— which, thankfully, was more than a hundred miles from the nearest Nordstrom.

Egan came home to find his mother's shaking voice on his answering machine, imploring him to forgive her for standing firm with his father on the rejection of his request.

"I think we may have made life too easy for you, Egie." She sighed fretfully. "I'm not saying that your writing isn't good. Maybe it has potential… Oh, *I don't know*! All I'm trying to say is that real life isn't like baseball camp, where you're allowed to play all day, and everyone gets a trophy at the end of the summer. We can't all be Barry Bonds, sweetie—"

Egan threw the machine up against the wall.

He'd hated baseball camp.

The lid cracked off and one of the audiocassette tapes—he couldn't tell whether it was the one with his outgoing message or the other—popped out onto the floor. His black lab, Casanova, couldn't resist what he took to be an unexpected treat. The dog was gagging on it before Egan could wade through all the clothes and books on the floor to get to it. But he knew better than to wrestle it from Casanova's slobbery jowls. He'd just wait until the damn dog spat it out.

Maybe it was for the best. He had no desire to talk to anyone anyway, least of all his parents.

I'm doing this for all of us, Egan reasoned. When my novel is a bestseller, I'll insist that Dad retire. Maybe then he'll take Mom on a real vacation, not another Winnebago road trip to Tahoe.

It was their loss, he reasoned.

But Egan was a realist. His dream of being a bestselling author would have to wait—for now, anyway.

That afternoon, he pocketed a discarded copy of the *San Francisco Chronicle*'s help wanted section he'd found on a chair in the Peet's across from the Claremont Hotel, where he'd just applied for a job as a waiter. Lavinia's ad sounded like a good match for him. "Seeking an instructor for three courses: *Beginning English (two classes), Creative Writing,* and *Shakespeare's Influence on World Literature.* For the latter, you must be versed as well in Shakespeare as you are in classic Western literature, and adept at articulating your love of both to inquisitive high school students in a creative setting…"

It would do.

At least, for the time being.

———

AND SO, IN ANSWER TO LAVINIA'S FINAL QUESTION—WHY HE'D ANSWERED Ashbury Academy's ad for the position—Egan explained, "I feel it's a good fit. Shakespeare's plots and characters have inspired generations of writers. I look forward to giving your students a different perspective of the Bard through their works. Who knows? Perhaps the next great author will come from AA."

"Anything is possible," Lavinia replied. Leaning over, she held out her hand and declared, "Welcome to the Ashbury Academy family."

Egan was elated.

More importantly, he felt redeemed.

And then, because it bugged the shit out of him that the cuckolded Clive might just be right about his book, he tried to impress Lavinia by mentioning that he was working on a novel.

"An admirable and challenging endeavor, but certainly within reach for one with your passion for literature." She then added, albeit hesitantly: "By the way, the potential benefactor I met with—he's the senior partner in a law firm—he was curious as to whether or not Ashbury had a debate team. Seems he excelled in debate in college, and was hoping to inspire high schoolers to pick it up." Her lips bowed into a wicked smile. "So I told a little white lie: that we'd just established our own debate club. Of course, he offered to sponsor it." She put her hand on Egan's sleeve. "Would it be too much of an imposition on your time to mentor our newly established debate team, too? Of course, I'd raise your compensation to include this additional responsibility."

"Sounds great." What else could he say? To keep writing, he needed the money, so yes.

Even with that, Egan's new position didn't pay much. But it would undoubtedly sound better to say, "I teach at a private prep school" than "I currently work in the foodservice industry."

To hold onto the job, he knew he'd have to live up to Lavinia's expectations as well as his own.

In other words, Audrey was off limits.

Audrey waited until Lavinia ushered Egan into her office and closed the door behind them before rummaging through Clare's desk. Finally, she found the folder she sought in Clare's inbox:

The curricula vitae of one Egan Gable.

It told Audrey what she needed to know: that he was twenty-six and a Ph.D. candidate in Comparative Literature from UC Berkeley.

The university was Lavinia's alma mater. It was also Audrey's first choice.

So yes, Mr. Egan Gable was a shoo-in, in more ways than one.

For the first time since Jeremy's defection, Audrey didn't feel bereft.

She felt euphoric.

Audrey clicked onto Clare's computer and scrolled through its files until she found the Fall Term curriculum database. The new teacher's position was slotted for three courses.

Introduction to English Literature was a required course for ninth graders. Creative Writing was part of the tenth grade's curriculum. Thankfully, the third course, *Shakespeare's Influence on World Literature*, was something she hadn't yet taken. And because it was an AP course, she could drop an elective for it.

It only took a few seconds for Audrey to find her class schedule. By eliminating Glee, she could accommodate her Physics class in fourth period, freeing up her seventh period for Egan's class—

Except that the course was already filled: mostly with seniors, who would cry foul if they were bumped. It was one of the few APs offered, and their transcripts needed as many 5-plus GPAs as they could cram onto it…

But wait—there were four juniors on the class roster too. As AP candidates, they'd had the choice of Egan's seventh period class or one entitled *The Influence of 19th Century Female Authors on Current Fiction*. It was the only course still taught by Lavinia, who, until Egan's hire, had been AA's sole English Studies instructor.

Audrey wrote each junior's name on a slip of paper. After folding and placing the strips in Clare's empty coffee cup, she closed her eyes and plucked one of the names:

Mandy Blackwell

Audrey couldn't picture the girl. She must be new to the school, she realized.

Mandy's sixth period class was PE. When the change went through, she'd be taking it as her last class of the day. To Audrey's mind she'd be doing the girl a favor. At least now she wouldn't have to shower before her final class, right?

With a flick of a button, the change was made.

A thrill raced through Audrey. For some unknown reason, she just knew it was going to be a memorable year.

CHAPTER 4

About Your Interaction with Your Students:

Rule #1: No one is asking you to love every student. However, you should do your best to like them: if not as friends, then for the simple reason that they too are human beings.

Rule #2: Treat each student with the same respect you'd hope to receive in return.

Rule #3: When it comes to your students' feelings toward you, use the judgment of a parent. You are the adult, and he or she is the child. Never forget that.

—Excerpted from *The Ashbury Academy Teachers' Handbook*

"Well, well, well! Indiana Jones is back." Cornell, the prissy Chemistry and Biology teacher, patted a napkin to his thin lips but not in time to hide his smirk.

He shifted his glance from Egan to Berney, the tall, tanned man on the other side of the teacher's lounge. Berney taught Geography, World History, and Workshop, a required course where AA's students, both male and female, learned to use all sorts of tools. "Scrumptious, isn't he? All summer long he digs up dinosaur fossils somewhere in Wyoming. I wonder what he does to keep warm on those cold starry nights?"

Egan noticed that Cornell's vest was an original Harris Tweed. He'd seen a similar one in the latest issue of Esquire, so he imagined it had cost his co-worker a pretty penny. It bugged him the way Cornell held his coffee cup, with his pinky finger arched. The cup and its saucer were almost precisely the same shade of powder blue as the cashmere sweater draped casually over Cornell's shoulders.

Egan wondered if he accessorized this way every day. Did he have a rainbow hue of cups stashed in his desk?

If Egan were to guess, he'd say yes. And as the newest member of AA's illustrious staff, he'd soon find out.

Odette Pettigrew, who taught French and Spanish, giggled, "*Merde!* Berney is happily married, you little harlot—so back off! However, if he were to ever leave that sweet wife of his, remember the golden rule: share and share alike." She'd been hovering near Egan's elbow and touched it gently.

It's unfortunate that Odette looks like one of Notre Dame's gargoyles in drag, Egan thought. Still, he found her sense of humor somewhat attractive. Besides, she'd brought chocolate croissants for everyone, which she'd made herself. Paired with the freshly ground Peet's brewing in the faculty lounge's coffeemaker, Egan felt his new job was off to a great start.

Shrugging off Odette's admonishment, Cornell turned to Egan. "How about you, New Kid on the Block? Got any interesting hobbies?"

Both gave him such hungry looks that Egan almost burst out laughing.

Before he could answer, Lavinia, who seemed to hear every conversation at once even while standing halfway across the room, proclaimed, "I anticipate we will all be impressed with what Egan offers this school, its students, and the world of literature."

Egan blushed slightly at her declaration.

It was seven-thirty on the morning of the first day of the fall term. The school's main building took up one square block at the base of Ashbury Street, just across the street from the park greenbelt known as the Panhandle. Having endured 1967's Summer of Love, its most recent reincarnation as a progressive prep school for almost two-hundred precocious teenagers with overly indulgent parents should be a cakewalk for the grand old dame.

Or so you'd think.

Listening to his new colleagues' chatter, Egan realized Audrey had been right to boast about them. How had she put it? Oh yes—they had hands-on applied experience in their subjects.

Larry Tabke, a nuclear physicist who had retired from Lawrence Livermore Labs, taught Physics. Hardy, who had once been a researcher on the staff of the California Academy of Sciences, taught Earth Sciences and Astronomy. The head of the Math department, Robert Brownstein, had resigned ("on principle," he declared to Egan) from the IRS, where he'd worked as an accountant. ("I also count cards," he offered in a fervent whisper. "But don't leak that to the Feds.")

Paulo, a union activist who had worked the lettuce fields and marched in Sacramento and Washington with Cesar Chavez, helmed government and Political Science classes.

History—United States and World—was Nicholas Lavinsky's domain. Tweedy and softened with age, "History Nick" had written books on both subjects now used in the curricula of several state universities.

Even the part-time staff members were the real things. Nick McGregor, or "PE Nick," was also a personal trainer. The demure Art instructor, Osprey Talbot, had metal sculpture installations all over the world; and the honey-toned Music teacher, Andrée Conley, spent her weekends fronting a jazz band made up of A-list studio musicians.

I'm the imposter here, thought Egan. I've done nothing.

At least not yet.

Until he'd demonstrated he was the real thing, he'd do his best to make this his new home.

To prove it, when Lavinia asked the staff to consider ways in which they could use that day's anticipated lunar eclipse as an overriding theme across all academic disciplines, he quickly answered, "I'll walk the students through the relevance of the lunar calendar on the plot of King Lear."

"Ah, perfect!" Lavinia's approval swept over him like a warm, welcoming breeze. "Hardy, yours is somewhat obvious: perhaps a student field trip to California Academy of Science's planetarium? The eclipse isn't until eight o'clock tonight. Maybe the students can take in the show at, say, around five or so? We can order pizza for them afterward. What are your thoughts about that?"

Hardy's frown caused his bushy brows to arch downward. "Doable, for sure. I'll call over there and leave a message for a group showing tonight." He paused, embarrassed, he added, "But I'll need volunteers for this field trip."

Berney blinked. "Why? It is, quite literally, just a walk through Golden Gate Park. It's not like there's any carpooling involved."

Two pink spots appeared on Hardy's cheeks, the only part of his face that wasn't covered by hair. "Yeah, well, the last time I took a group over there I was the only one of a few looking up at the stars. Half of the kids were counting each other's molars with their tongues."

This drew resigned shrugs from many of the staff.

"Biology in its most primitive human form. Should be a piece of cake for you and your volunteers, Hardy," murmured Lavinia with a grin. "Any takers? I'd join you, but tonight I'm hosting the school's trustee dinner right before the eclipse."

There was a collective groan. Other than that, no one moved a muscle.

All Egan could think of was the long ride back to Berkeley via the Transbay Tube. Stuffed with commuters on the way into San Francisco earlier that morning, the ride in had been claustrophobic enough. Granted, it would be emptier by the time he came home from the field trip. Still, the thought of shooting through a tube 135 feet below San Francisco Bay with a bunch of hungry potheads heading to Gordo for burritos kept his hands at his side.

But then, glancing at Lavinia, he found himself mesmerized by the one feature she shared with her daughter: those luminous gray eyes.

Slowly his hand went up.

As if shamed by him, some of the others followed suit. Odette waved hers gaily and gave him a sly wink. Seeing Berney's hand go up, Cornell sighed loudly but lifted a hand as well.

Egan knew instinctively that they didn't resent him. Why should they? It was apparent to him that they all revered Lavinia; that she would have gotten what she wanted anyway.

In fact, she now had more volunteers than she needed.

"Super! Thank you all! We'll cap it at eight. The rest of you get the next go-round, right?" She laughed along with the others.

What followed was a lively, albeit friendly, debate among the teaching staff as to the mating traits of bonobos compared to that of human teenagers.

"At least with bonobos, there is less drama and more action," Cornell muttered.

As he looked around, it struck Egan that Lavinia's staff was a lot like the furniture that crowded the room: overstuffed and worn down, but comfortable and welcoming.

It's not like Berkeley at all: no infighting, none of the smugness or the petty politics, he thought. She's chosen well. They like her, and buy into her cockeyed mission. She'll never find herself amid a mutiny with this group.

As if reading Egan's mind, Lavinia murmured just loud enough for him to hear, "Welcome to my ship of fools."

AUDREY WAS NOT AT ALL SURPRISED THAT, BY THE END OF ASHBURY'S OPENING day assembly, Egan had been declared the school's top hunk.

After all, he was the youngest and the cutest of the teachers. This was all too obvious when Lavinia introduced him along with the school's other instructors.

The immediate shuffling of schedule cards could be heard throughout the assembly hall (not to mention a few delighted squeals and disappointed moans) as the female students in the school checked to see if, in fact, they'd somehow won the scheduling lottery that put them in one of Egan's four classes. Audrey could only imagine that the angry cry of "WHAT THE HELL—" she heard emanating from one of the back rows was the overachieving junior by the name of Mandy Blackwell, who realized she'd somehow been bumped from Egan's *Shakespeare's Influence on World Literature* class.

Validation of Egan's newfound status could be heard in the gossip being murmured all day through the hallways. But where it really hit home to Audrey was in the Senior Girls' restroom, where she'd gone to check her makeup before seventh-period.

"—And that Gable dude! My God, he is *bitchin'*! But I thought he'd never call on me! And when he finally did, I stuttered like some stupid airhead! What do you think, was it that noticeable? Did I make a total fool of myself?"

Audrey had been touching up in front of the mirror by the far window. Hearing this declaration, her lipstick stopped mid-stroke over her upper lip.

She couldn't see the restroom's two other occupants because they were in the toilet stalls.

"Honestly?... Okay, yeah. In Creative Writing, you sounded like an absolute dweeb," her friend said in all seriousness. The girl seemed to take joy in telling her so. "But don't worry. I don't think he was paying attention. That was the exact moment Lanie Henderson did that thing—you know when she yawns and arches her back so that her boobs practically fall out of her blouse? Like, how obvious is that?"

Audrey shuddered. She had seen Lanie do that exact move countless times. But Egan was too mature to fall for that, she reasoned. He'd graduated from Berkeley, where they burned bras, not stuffed them. That alone proved he was a serious guy who would never fall for petty flirtatiousness—

"And I love that whole 'intellectual vibe' he's got going. I mean, he quotes Voltaire as if he's the fifth Beatle! Isn't that totally righteous?" The girl in the first stall was on a roll. "I am, like, *so* ready to be teacher's pet!"

In the mirror, Audrey noticed her cheeks had turned the same candy apple red as the shade of her lipstick. As much as she wanted to believe that she was embarrassed for the girl who had admitted her lust so candidly, in truth she was ashamed that they were so similar to her own feelings for Egan.

What makes me so different from her? Audrey wondered.

The answer was all too obvious: Nothing.

No, that's not true. My feelings for him are more profound than just sex...

Hearing the toilets flush, Audrey tossed her lipstick in her purse and scrambled out the door. She was late for class anyway.

Egan's class.

CHAPTER 5

*A*ny presumptions Audrey had left about her connection with Egan were stomped into the ground (along with her heart) as she saw, first hand, the pull he had over her classmates.

All a student had to do was look into those deep-set green eyes, and immediately she—or he, for that matter—was drawn to the young instructor.

Davis Wong, Audrey's closest guy pal, slipped her a note that summed it up succinctly:

> *It's like watching a Klingon tractor beam lock onto a clusterfuck of Federation starships!*

He's right, Audrey thought. You can't help but feel completely sucked in. You feel as if you're the only two people in the world—

But then he lets you go, only to aim his charm at someone else.

When that happened to Cherry Conover, the girl seemed to deflate physically. In her case, that was not easy to do considering, as Audrey's friend, Bliss Thackeray, had pointed out on numerous occasions: "Those breasts of hers are natural floatation devices!"

But by the end of class it seemed as if Audrey was the only one who didn't get to mind meld with Egan. Instead, he called on everyone around her, tossing out backhanded compliments that had the chosen ones blushing or giggling at their own expense.

Worse yet, whenever his eyes swept over Audrey at all, he seemed to look right through her.

Hurt and confused, she wondered, Why not me? Am I not pretty enough?

Or is it because I look too desperate?

Even her friends were fighting for Egan's attention. When he casually mentioned to Davis that he thought his vintage bomber jacket was cool, Davis puffed up with pride.

Audrey had been with Davis when he'd bought it off of some old queen who claimed he flew with Jimmy Stewart during World War II. Hearing that, Davis didn't argue. The damn thing cost him all of ten bucks anyway: a great find at that price, for sure, so why quell the deal? But as they walked away from the man, Davis muttered, "Yeah, sister, we're all waiting for some flyboy to sweep us off our feet. Mine is Tom Cruise in *Top Gun.*"

Now Davis was acting as if it had come off a runway in Milan.

Tallulah let it drop to Egan that her mother was Maggie Wishart. When Egan mentioned that Chameleon's debut album, *Make Lust Not Love,* had been his favorite album as a teen, and that he'd played it so many times that he'd worn out the grooves, she offered to bring him another copy—autographed of course, by her mother.

Watching Egan's eyes open wide in gratitude, Audrey felt as if her heart had just broken into a million tiny shards.

Traitor, she thought.

Not of Egan, but of Tallulah.

Well, yes, of Egan, too.

Finally, the chimes in AA's bell tower rang out, heralding the end of the school day. Like the other students, Audrey gathered up her books and bags, only to find Egan standing next to her, scrutinizing her intently.

He was looking into her soul. Or so it felt.

But she was mistaken. She realized this when he gently tapped his bottom lip with his finger. "Um...Did you forget something?"

"I'm sorry... what?" Her mind raced to the obvious. Was he asking for a kiss?

He leaned in and murmured, "Your lipstick. I think you'd better look in a mirror."

Suddenly Audrey remembered she'd completely forgotten to apply it to her bottom lip before leaving the restroom.

Well, isn't that just perfect! All this time I've looked like a clown. No wonder he ignored me!

She only saw pity in his grin.

"Have a nice day," he said, as he sauntered back toward his desk. "Oh, and do tell Lavinia I had fun today in class. Better yet, tell her you did too."

Fun. Yeah, right.

That's when it hit her: He ignored me because I'm the Head of School's daughter.

The realization that she'd never connect with Egan on any other level—not even as a student—brought angry tears to her eyes.

Thank goodness he didn't see them. But that was only because he was too busy chatting up Tallulah.

Davis saw them. He pulled a folded kerchief from the breast pocket of his jacket. "Aw, hell, baby cakes! You look like a *raccoon.*"

She stared down at the crisp white square of linen. It was mono-grammed with his three initials: DXW. No doubt he had special-ordered it from Wilkes Bashford.

Only Davis had the style to match up an old bomber jacket with an expensive snot rag, she thought.

His life was certainly a study in contrast. A first-generation Chinese American, his parents had kicked him out onto the street for admitting to them that he was gay. Lavinia, who had seen him soliciting in the Panhan-dle, had offered him a full scholarship to the school.

Because he always seemed so sleepy in the morning, Audrey wondered if he was still hooking on the side for quick cash. He had promised Lavinia that he wouldn't do that anymore. It was the one and only prerequisite for him staying at the school.

Davis winced as Audrey blew her nose into his kerchief. A few of the other students turned to stare and snicker.

Well, too bad, Audrey thought. I'm still Lavinia Thorpe's daughter. I can get away with a lot of things, but walking out of class with snot hanging out of my nose is not one of them.

Neither is flirting with my teachers.

"L ET ME SEE YOUR BINOCULARS." A UDREY POKED B LISS, WHO SEEMED FIXATED on something on the other side of the starlit planetarium's auditorium.

To avoid the other students, Audrey, Bliss, Davis, and Tallulah had set up camp in the balcony of the planetarium so that they could observe everyone else while pretending to listen to Hardy's lecture.

"Keep your mitts off," Bliss muttered as she slapped Audrey's hand away. "I'm watching Kyle Moody go at it with some little junior. Man, his technique is so *whacked!*" She shook her head sadly. "You'd think he was milking a cow or something! I guess some girls are just so desperate that they'll put up with anything."

Obviously disgusted, she sighed and handed the binoculars to Audrey, who immediately lifted them to her eyes. "Wow," Audrey exclaimed. "You didn't tell me these were night vision binoculars."

"Let me see," begged Davis, but Audrey held on tight to them and leaned forward over the balcony's banister so that he couldn't reach them. He had a fear of heights, so she knew he wouldn't try again.

He gave her the finger then turned back to Bliss. "Where the hell did you get these, anyway?"

"They're my dad's. Cool, huh? Really, they belong to our store. He's put them on all the shop window mannequins. This week's theme is *The Matrix*."

Bliss's parents, Maude and Reggie, owned the hottest boutique on Union Street, which meant that she was the school's unofficial fashion diva. Like many of the parents who sent their children to Ashbury, they'd known Lavinia forever—or at least since the '60s, when, like she, they'd come to the Haight to turn on, tune in and drop out, only to eventually come to the conclusion that life was a participatory event.

Parenting, especially, had a way of doing that to you.

Creating Utopia was still the goal, only this time creating it for the whole family became the new mission. Maude and Reggie were a perfect example of this. From the pictures Audrey had seen in Lavinia's photo album, the store the Thackerays had opened in the Haight before Bliss was born, called Over the Rainbow, was no more than a hole in the wall where they sold long gauzy skirts, tie-dyed halter tops, jeans with the widest bell-bottoms imaginable, granny gowns, and velvet Sergeant Pepper jackets, along with incense, scented candles, and bongs.

After Bliss's birth, the store mirrored the personal changes in the Thackerays' lives. The sweet musky smells stayed, but the drug paraphernalia went out, as did the second-hand clothes. Instead, they displayed cutting-edge fashions created by many of San Francisco's up-and-coming designers, all made from fibers that were organically grown. One section of the store was even devoted to children's clothing.

By the time Bliss was six, ecstatic write-ups of the store were regularly appearing in the *San Francisco Chronicle* and the alternative weekly, the *Bay Guardian*. But a rave review from the tony *Nob Hill Gazette* put them on the radar of the town's socialites.

This gave the Thackerays the incentive to open a second store in the posh Union Street shopping district, right down the hill from San Francisco's most exclusive neighborhood, Pacific Heights. When the new store tripled the Thackerays' income, they realized that they had at last outgrown the Haight.

The year Bliss started high school, the Thackerays took their company public. In the three years since, they'd opened Over the Rainbow retail outlets in six other cities, and moved into their own Pacific Heights mansion, near their wealthiest San Francisco patrons.

But they weren't Lavinia's only friends who, with whatever fame and fortune they'd made for themselves, had moved from the Haight to one of San Francisco's more prestigious neighborhoods—Sea Cliff, Presidio

Heights, St. Francis Wood, Pacific Heights, Russian Hill—or even out to Marin County; or to one of booming Silicon Valley's exclusive communities like Atherton, Burlingame, or Portola Valley.

Tallulah's mom, Maggie, was another example. After her second album went platinum, she'd moved over the Golden Gate Bridge to Mill Valley, the rustic little village that sat at the base of Mount Tamalpais. With baby Tallulah and her latest boyfriend in tow, she held court to a myriad of musicians, singers, songwriters, and hangers-on in a rambling six-acre estate with picture-book views of the whole bay, accessed only by a tiny road that zigzagged halfway up the mountain.

It was a long way from the old Victorian that now housed Ashbury Academy, which had been a communal crash pad for Maggie, Lavinia, and the Thackerays among others.

It seemed to Audrey that sending their kids to the academy gave them a perfect excuse to reconnect with the youthful ideals that had brought them to San Francisco in the first place. She could just imagine the many crazy hazy memories sparking and flaring once more in full psychedelic color as they walked the hallways of the academy during the school's monthly family potluck nights.

The only light coming into the planetarium was from the simulation of a lunar eclipse. Audrey could barely make out her friends' faces. That was okay, because Audrey knew them by heart: blond wan Bliss would be smiling widely, despite her braces. And except for her perpetually naughty smirk, redheaded Tallulah had the face of a Botticellian angel. Davis's cheekbones were angled high, although pocked deeply with acne. He never smiled or frowned. In the three years she had known him, she had learned to read his thoughts in his almond-shaped eyes, not his mouth.

I wonder if the school will mean half as much to us as it does to Lavinia and the other parents, she thought. Probably not. High school is just— well, it's high school. Everyone wants to forget about it. It's too painful to hang onto.

Her feelings for Egan were proof of that.

"Oh my God, just think: In another twenty years, we'll all need night vision goggles because the sun will have been blocked out by pollution and all that other crap! Won't that be, like, so sad?" Bliss proclaimed this loud enough that Hardy's pontificating stopped cold.

Audrey and her friends ducked as he searched the room for his heckler. As Tallulah's head bobbed out of sight, the colorful Lobro Swatch, which she'd used to tie back her wildly coiling hair, glowed ominously, giving away their location.

Hardy sighed. "Once the balcony trolls will cease their declarations, I shall continue."

Silence.

Audrey lifted her head in time to see him shake his head in resignation.

Finally, his monotone drone picked up where he'd left off. "As I was saying, people: what makes this eclipse unique is that the moon is passing through the center of the earth's shadow—"

Tallulah went back to what she'd been doing before Bliss's outburst: flicking M&Ms off the balcony railing onto the students below. "Audrey, seriously, if you're looking for Jeremy, he's sulking in the far-right corner, under Orion." Then, with a knowing smirk, she added: "You know he's dying to make up with you."

Audrey frowned. "That's too bad. He's made his bed—his Ferrari, anyway—and now he can lie in it with his stupid new girlfriend."

"He was never your type in the first place," declared Bliss.

Audrey shrugged. True, her relationship with Jeremy was dead and buried, but her pride was alive and well. At least her friends had held off a few days before doing the postmortem on what they assumed was a broken heart.

"I don't have 'a type,'" Audrey insisted.

Davis lowered his sunglasses so that he could look her in the eye. "Sure you do. We all do."

"Speaking of heartbreakers, who's got the skinny on Egan?" Tallulah tossed an M&M at Audrey. "Your mama done good, picking *that* boy."

Audrey shrugged. "Don't look at me. I know nothing about him. Fair Master Gable is an enigma wrapped in a conundrum."

"I beg to differ." Bliss arched a brow. "That young man is an open book."

Audrey shifted uncomfortably in her seat. "I don't know what you mean."

"Well, I do." Tallulah declared. "He loves being big man on campus. Did you see the group of students on his heels as he walked here through the park? It looked like that old fable—what's it called again?"

"The Pied Piper." Davis shivered. "Frankly, I think that says more about us than it does about him. If he's really all that great, why is he teaching at AA? No offense to Lavinia or anything, but Ashbury isn't exactly Stanford or Harvard. And it's certainly not University High."

The others took that in silently. Audrey bristled at the inference: that Ashbury wasn't good enough for Egan.

She wondered if he thought that too.

The realization that he might made her hand shake slightly, but she kept her eyes focused through the binoculars, scanning each row slowly, left to right. She'd never tell her friends who she was really looking for:

Egan Gable.

But he was nowhere in sight.

59

To find him, Audrey had only to look up. Egan was watching her and her friends from the security catwalk that circled the top of the planetarium.

He couldn't hear them, but even their slightest moves were animated, their murmurs rising and falling in the currents of their capricious emotions.

He was jealous of them. If only he were as connected to his life as they were to theirs.

If only he could somehow be connected to Audrey.

So, this is what it's like to be in love, he thought.

Since puberty, lust had been his constant companion. A beautiful face never failed to put a smile on his lips. And somehow he always seemed to find the right words to entice its owner.

But Egan's attraction didn't come from his looks. He was more self-assured than handsome. His confidence intrigued women. His penetrating gaze dared them to ignore him.

Most didn't.

Should a potential conquest proffer a blush instead of an instant acquiescence, even better. Granted, he'd have to work harder to get her into his bed, but he'd relish the conquest all the more.

Egan loved a challenge. But Audrey was more than that. In every way, she was forbidden fruit: the daughter of his boss, and underage at that.

More to the point, Egan would hate himself if he broke her heart.

He had never felt that way about another girl.

Woman.

Person.

He held no illusions: in the mere twenty-six years since his birth, he'd disappointed more people than he could count on both hands. Hell, he'd upset his dad more times than he'd even admit to himself. He had friends whose girlfriends he'd bedded without a second thought. One guy's iron fist left Egan with a souvenir of the misadventure: a fake front tooth.

Egan could tell that Audrey was attracted to him, but so what? All kids her age were fickle. He'd been at AA for only a day and already he'd witnessed six romantic summer-love break-ups and three crying jags induced by unrequited love.

Life won't always be this way, he reasoned. This is just a singular moment in time. The obstacles standing between us won't always be here.

She'll grow up—

And so will I.

All the more reason to play it cool; to just wait it out.

If, somewhere in the future, the stars aligned, then so be it. Some things were just meant to be.

Perhaps this was one of those times.

CHAPTER 6

Debate Terminology

Ad hominem fallacy: Attacking a person rather than the argument.

Ad populum fallacy: Claiming that something is true because of popular belief.

Burden of Proof: The affirmative's responsibility to prove that the resolution is true. If the affirmative fails to prove the resolution, he/she/they ought to lose the debate.

—*National Forensics League Coaching Guide*

"*L*isten up, mam'selles and gents!" Egan's declaration cut through the classroom chatter like a buzz saw. At the same time, all heads turned in his direction. The sort of fidgeting that was usually found in a room filled with twenty high-achieving and highly hormonal teenagers stopped suddenly as if they were merely images caught in a camera's flash photo.

Satisfied, Egan honored them with his thousand-watt smile.

It was a month into the school year. Thus far, from what Audrey could tell, Egan was retaining his crown as Teacher with the Most Pets. It sickened her how anxiously her classmates vied for his attention. He rewarded them by doling out praise like fairy dust.

At least, it was better than the students who were quite literally throwing themselves at him.

Every day for the past four weeks she sat in his classroom while he conversed, cajoled, inspired—and yes, flirted—with her classmates. Sure,

61

every now and then he called on her, too. But on these rare occasions, his tone was always serious, completely deferential.

She hated that.

He treats me with kid gloves, like I'm—oh, I don't know, Princess Di or something.

No, worse… Oh my God, it's like I'm *the First Lady!*

Just the thought of that made her shudder.

From then on, she left her pearls at home.

Instead, she tried to break him.

She thought having the best grades in class would do it. Apparently, he expected that, so other than writing EXCELLENT on her papers, she got no other response.

For a whole week, she tried answering every question he broached to the students. But if he called on her at all, it was at the very end of the hour, just in time for the class chimes to cut her off.

The following week she asked countless questions in class, sometimes about the most obvious things. She could tell he was annoyed with her, but he answered patiently. But he never gave her the response she sought and would have been the most obvious: "Why don't you see me after class and I'll answer your questions at that time?"

Because he'd rather not see me after school.

He'd rather not see me at all.

Well, too bad.

Today, in desperation, Audrey decided it was time she lower herself to the ploy generations of women had used before her. Right before entering Egan's class, she freed the first two buttons on her blouse so that he couldn't miss the obvious: her generous cleavage, the result of a recently purchased purple push-up bra.

Her scheme backfired. Egan's sole glance in her direction was to chide her for being late, which brought her to the attention of every other male in the room.

Jeremy was practically panting. But when Egan intercepted the note Jeremy had scribbled to reaffirm his love for her, Audrey was mortified.

Holding it up to the class, Egan declared, "Seriously, Mr. Blake, if one is to profess one's love, one should skip the use of the term 'blue balls.'"

Everyone laughed uproariously—except for the writer, his subject, and their torturer.

Audrey didn't know if she was angrier with Jeremy for caring so much for her that he made a fool of himself, or at Egan for caring so little that he made her the butt of his joke.

I should give up, she thought.

But no, I can't. Because if I'm right and he likes me but is afraid to show it, he'll never know I love him too.

And eventually, he'll give up on me.

He'll forget about me.

If he really cares for me, he's doing the right thing: he'll let me know, even if there's nothing we can do about it.

At least not now.

From then on, she'd have to accept that he talked to the other girls in the class. She'd have to pretend not to care when he teased them. She'd ignore it when he flattered them with off-handed compliments.

And when he was the subject of the other students' personal musings or coy remarks, she'd act bored, feign nonchalance, or completely ignore them.

Anything to keep from crying.

Like now. She watched as Egan opened his bottom desk drawer, pulled out a stack of small pamphlets, and moved to the front of his desk. As he leaned against it, he scanned the students. Periodically, he paused while making eye contact: honoring one recipient with a wink, another with a nod, and yet another with the shadow of a smile.

When, finally, his glance shifted in Audrey's direction, her heart skipped a beat—

Until she realized he was actually grinning at Tallulah.

Audrey turned in time to see Tallulah's response: she stuck out her tongue at him.

Impressed at her audacity, Egan guffawed.

Tallulah winked at Audrey.

Thank you, my friend.

Egan smirked as he shrugged off the slight. "Great news, people! Lavinia has given me the honor of coaching Ashbury Academy's newest team: *Debate*."

The announcement drew an awed murmur.

"Tryouts will be held this Thursday. It'll be heralded in tomorrow's student bulletin. But because you're my favorite students, I'm giving you a head start."

"I bet you say that to all your classes," Davis declared.

Everyone laughed.

Even Egan, proving the jibe had hit its mark. "Despite my propensity toward universal favoritism, if you're serious about making the team I suggest you prepare accordingly. It will be small: only eight students, and made up of seniors and juniors." He held up one of the pamphlets. "This handy little booklet outlines the National Debate Society's rules and regs. You'll also find four debate questions on page sixteen. Be prepared to debate two of them—and, in debate parlance, both for and against. You must also be ready to debate a third question. Please write it down now: 'Should Ashbury Academy students be drug tested?'"

Snickers accompanied the scratch of pencils on paper. Egan waited a moment until all scribbling ceased.

"Got it?... Good," he said. "I'll be judging you along with Nick and Cornell."

"History Nick, or PE Nick?" Jeremy shouted out.

"You're in luck," Egan replied. "It's PE Nick. History Nick has a dental appointment that afternoon."

Everyone chuckled at Jeremy's expense. They knew that because Jeremy was a jock PE Nick might be more generous in his scoring.

"You'll be judged on four criteria." Egan counted them off with his fingers: "First, we'll grade you on your argument's organization and clarity. Then, we'll consider the reasons that support your argument. Next, we'll assess your cross-examination and rebuttal. A perfect score is sixteen. Times the three judges, that means you can earn as many as forty-eight points. Got it?"

The students nodded.

"The judges will be using a four-point rubric for each criterion," Egan added. "A full four points is granted for complete clarity and an orderly presentation, three points for being less than perfect of that, two points if you are not up to speed overall, and one point if you screw up miserably."

This time, the laughter was half-hearted: sour and unpleasant, like a fart which left both the culprit and the victims ill at ease.

Egan added, "Remember, making the team gives you what you desire most—another leg up on your college applications. May the best debaters win." Egan sighed. "Which brings me to another significant announcement. I've graded last week's essays, and I have to tell you"—he paused, as if seeing how high he could ratchet up the suspense—"I'm duly impressed. Almost everyone did their very best to draw an analogy between the Bard and the contemporary author of their choice." Egan's eyes rested on Bliss. "In particular, I want to give a shout-out to Ms. Thackeray's creative comparison of *Much Ado about Nothing* to Ms. Bushnell's sure-to-be-a-classic"—he rolled his eyes—"*Sex and the City.*"

"Wow! I'm glad you thought so!" Bliss preened at what she deemed was a compliment. "Frankly, I felt it was a stretch!"

"Ditto. And just so we're clear, 'creativity' doesn't necessarily translate to an A grade."

She frowned at this reality.

Bliss's most exceptional charm was her naïveté —or, so it was assumed by everyone *but* her three closest friends. Ashbury's clock tower chimes weren't going to stop her from making some cockamamie argument as to why Egan should reconsider her paper's grade.

And Audrey knew he'd enjoy every minute of it.

Until he's free to be with me.

Eight months from now, I'll have graduated from high school, she reasoned. The fact that I'm Lavinia's daughter will no longer stand in our way.

By that time, he'll finally realize I'm worth waiting for.

In the meantime, Audrey would make her way to the school library. She was determined to spend more time with Egan. If it meant making Debate Team, so be it.

She grabbed one of the pamphlets on her way out.

As the other students took off, Bliss went into her pitch for a higher grade.

Egan sat silently. Every now and then he'd nod slightly, but his mind was elsewhere.

He was thinking of Audrey.

Since the first day of school, it had hurt him to glance in her direction. It was too tempting to let his eyes linger on her.

He knew she was frustrated with him too. Still, he'd hoped ignoring her would discourage the apparent attraction they shared.

Boy, was he wrong. If anything, she'd come on even stronger.

He'd almost lost it today when he noticed her blouse was partially unbuttoned. He'd only succeeded in making things worse when he called attention to her tardiness. Every other guy in the room turned to gawk at her—especially that Neanderthal, Jeremy Blake. Egan had heard the rumors of their recent breakup, but watching Jeremy's note on its journey to Audrey had him thinking the worst:

That they'd gotten back together again.

That Audrey's plunging neckline hadn't been a wardrobe malfunction at all but a seductive ploy—

Not for Egan's benefit, but for Jeremy's.

Out of jealousy, Egan had taken the note and read its silliest part out loud to embarrass the boy. But in doing so, Egan had embarrassed Audrey too.

She hates me because I shamed her, he reasoned. *I can't say I blame her. It was a childish and despicable thing to do.*

It dawned on him that she might ask to be transferred out of his class. And after his callousness, she certainly wouldn't dare try out for Debate Team.

The thought saddened him. Having read her essays and listened to the ease with which she made her points in class discussions, he knew she'd be a natural debater.

Maybe it's for the best, Egan thought.

It would certainly make it easier for him to hold to his mantra:

Don't lead her on. Hold onto my job... Don't lead her on. Hold onto my job...

"So, what do you think, Egan?" Bliss's voice roused him from his worst nightmare: losing Audrey.

"Huh?... I think... I..." He tried to remember a single word she may have said, but nothing came to mind. The hope in Bliss's eyes only made him feel worse; not about tuning her out, but about hurting her dearest friend.

It's why he muttered, "Yeah, okay. Whatever."

Delighted, Bliss squealed. "Alright! Wow! If I can get a C minus changed to an A, maybe I should try out for Debate Team after all!"

Egan held his groan until she was too far down the hall to hear it.

———

FOR AUDREY'S DEBATE TEAM TRYOUT, SHE CHOSE THE TWO TOPICS LEAST likely to appeal to her competitors because of the amount of research involved: allowing the Internet to stay free, and eliminating the position of the vice president.

Because the former topic's merits were continually being debated, a myriad of information could be found online. As for the latter, Audrey knew the perfect reference source. One of the more arcane tomes in AA's library was a book on the lives of United States vice presidents. The book, no longer in print, chronicled every vice presidency up until Richard M. Nixon.

That alone is a perfect rationale for why the vice presidency should be eliminated, Audrey reasoned.

As the librarian, Eloise, stamped Audrey's selection with the return date, she exclaimed, "Well what do you know? This book has never been checked out! Ah, well, the VP is always the bridesmaid and never the bride, isn't he?"

Audrey thought for a moment. "Wouldn't that make him the best man?"

Eloise laughed. "Right you are."

Audrey took the book to her favorite corner: a small alcove tucked into the bookcase right behind Eloise's desk.

———

"EXCUSE ME, I'M LOOKING FOR THE BOOK CALLED *THEY WERE OUR VICE Presidents*. Do you know where I might find it?"

Audrey's ears perked up. For the past hour, she'd been making notes from that very book.

The student's voice, a girl's, wasn't one she recognized.

"I'm sorry," Eloise's clucked sympathetically. "It was just checked out."

"May I ask by whom?"

"Well..." Eloise's hesitation turned her one-syllable response into three.

"I just want to see if… Well, maybe this other student would consider sharing it with me."

Indignation stiffened Audrey's spine. *The audacity of this person!*

Eloise sighed. "It was one of the seniors—Audrey Thorpe."

"Oh." The student's reply was more like the plaintive wail of a wounded animal.

"I guess you'd have to ask her yourself—"

"Oh! You mean she's still here?" The girl's whine was replaced by a menacing wheedle—one that might have easily been growled by a Gestapo commissar.

"I…I don't know! I don't think so." The doubt in Eloise's tone was too tepid to hide the truth. Audrey wondered if, at the same time, the librarian's eyes had shifted to the alcove behind her, and thus betraying her.

"Oh. I see. Well, I'll just have a look around."

I'm trapped, Audrey thought.

Her ears followed the girl's slow, deliberate footsteps.

Audrey imagined her making her way through each row of bookshelves, peeking into every nook and cranny on the hunt for her prey.

As the footfalls receded, Audrey relaxed—

But not for long. Suddenly it seemed the footsteps were right next to her.

The alcove's desk was solid wood on three sides. Audrey ducked under it and pulled her chair in as far as it would go in the hope that the girl would walk right on by.

She did—

But then retraced her steps. She must have turned down Audrey's aisle because now the *clump-clump-clump* was slow but steady.

Audrey froze.

Finally, it stopped right in front of Audrey's desk.

Audrey held her breath. Only her eyes moved: downward, taking in the girl's shoes—Dr. Martens, an AirWairs style she'd never seen before. They were pale pink and illustrated with double-decker buses, telephone booths, the Queen's horsemen with their big furry hats…

Finally, the girl moved away—and fast. She was running. Clumping, really, what with those boots—

Audrey crawled out from under the desk. A quick glance at her workspace and she realized why the girl had taken off so quickly:

She'd stolen the book.

Damn it! Damn it! How could I have been so stupid?

As quickly as she could, Audrey stuffed the rest of her things in her backpack and ran from the library—

But it was too late. The hall was empty.

"Where have you been?" Tallulah asked. She, Bliss, and Davis were sitting on AA's front stoop.

"Isn't it obvious?" Audrey retorted. She stared down at her arms, which were loaded down with library books on politics and constitutional law.

The missing book was the one she'd needed most.

She'd asked Eloise about the girl. Eloise claimed she'd never seen her before—doubly troubling since the librarian knew every student in the school.

"If for any reason she doesn't return it, I won't charge you for it," Eloise vowed.

"I should hope not," Audrey grumbled under her breath. She'd have to make do with biographies of the presidents and pray that the vice presidents were mentioned too.

Bliss, who had been perusing a recent issue of *Vogue*, was mimicking the come-hither pout on Cindy Crawford's face. "Whoa, wait! Those books are about the government. Aren't you debating about killers?"

Both Audrey and Davis gave her a blank stare.

Annoyed, Bliss added, "It's about *forensics*, silly gooses! You know, murder and stuff like that!"

Tallulah rolled her eyes. "All by your lonesome you're perpetuating the 'dumb blonde' myth for the rest of your kind." She thumped Audrey's books so hard that they almost dropped. "By the way, in this case, 'forensics' means extensive research."

"Oh." Bliss's eyes glazed over as she stared at Audrey's haul. "Well, that leaves me out. I'd rather be shopping."

"Same here," Davis replied. "And besides, the kind of guy who tries out for Debate Team isn't exactly man candy."

Tallulah shrugged. "You're right. You'd be better off as the football team's towel boy."

Davis sighed. "If only!"

Audrey nudged Tallulah with her foot. "What about you?"

Tallulah snorted. "Who needs Debate Team? Hell, if I want an argument, all I have to do is go home. Every day, Maggie and I fight over some bullshit." Her tightly coiled curls bounced as she shook her head angrily. "And I win because I'm not the one who's always drunk and living with some gross creep."

Maggie's latest boyfriend had been coming on to Tallulah. For just that reason, the girl had taken to staying over in the spare twin beds in either Audrey's or Bliss's bedrooms. "We've got enough homework as it is. Aren't you going a tad too far to get Egan to notice you?"

"Oh, he noticed her today, alright." Davis slipped his finger around the top button on Audrey's blouse, releasing it from its hole.

Audrey's face turned bright red. "You've got it all wrong. It's a great extracurricular for college applications—"

Bliss giggled. "The lady doth protest too much, methinks."

"Jesus! Egan even has her talking in tongues!" Davis slapped his forehead. "Other than Tallulah and me, is there anyone who hasn't joined the Nefarious Cult of Egan?"

Audrey shivered. "Nefarious is right! And some of its members are willing to steal to be in it."

"What?" Suddenly Audrey's friends were all ears.

"I'd checked out a book to use as research for my debate study. I overheard some girl ask about the same book. Next thing I know, she stole it off my library desk."

Tallulah's eyes opened wide. "Who was she?"

Audrey shrugged. "I wish I knew. She was gone in a flash. The only thing I can remember is her boots. They were Doc Martens, but a style I'd never seen before. Pinkish with what looked like a cartoon map of London—"

Bliss squealed. "Oh my God! I'll bet they're these boots!" Furiously, she flipped through her magazine until she found the page: a Dr. Martens ad displaying the exact same boots.

Davis frowned. "I've never seen those before."

Bliss rolled her eyes. "You wouldn't have because this is British *Vogue*." She flipped back to the cover so that he could read the magazine's issue title. "Maude leaves them around the shop—along with the French and Italian issues so that customers can see that what they're buying is sometimes straight off the fashion runways."

"Or great knockoffs," Davis retorted.

Bliss stuck out her tongue at him. "So what? Someday we'll carry the real thing—"

"Well, now that we know something about Audrey's thief, we can find her"—Tallulah cracked her knuckles menacingly—"Even if we have to look under every girl's bathroom stall. Considering what she did, she shouldn't be able to just waltz into the tryouts and run rings around our champ here!" She stuck a thumb in Audrey's direction.

"She won't, I promise you that," Audrey vowed. "Even if I have to memorize the rest of this stuff just to play catch-up." She heaved the books. "Listen, Nancy Drew, if I'm to make up for lost time, I've got to get cracking. But don't let that stop you, Bess, and Ned Nickerson here from finding the culprit."

"Why can't I be George Fayne?" Davis asked.

Bliss snickered. "Despite her name, she's really a *tomgirl*, silly!"

Davis sighed. "That's my point, genius."

Tallulah swept her arm over Bliss's head.

Bliss cringed. "What's wrong? Did you see a bee?"

Apparently, the point was made to everyone but Bliss.

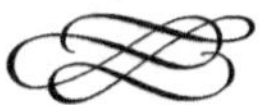

The hunt for the book thief went on all week. Although Audrey and her friends scrutinized the feet of every junior and senior in Ashbury Academy, by Thursday afternoon they had yet to identify the girl.

Audrey was just about to enter Ashbury's assembly hall for Debate Team tryouts when her friends fell into lockstep beside her.

Surprised, Audrey murmured, "What are you doing here? I thought you'd decided to sit this one out."

"We are—sort of." Tallulah nodded toward Davis and Bliss. "We're here to find the thief. That bitch has no right to make the team"—she lowered her voice to a snarl—"and to make sure she doesn't, we *will* expose her."

Audrey was startled by her friend's ominous tone. "How? And to whom?"

Tallulah threw up her hands, perplexed that Audrey couldn't grasp the obvious. "To Egan, of course! She's given us all the clues we need to trap her at the scene of the crime. So, if she's chosen for the team, we'll storm the stage and let her know she gave herself away by her choice in stylishly unique footwear, and demand to see the stolen book!" She put one arm around Bliss's shoulder and the other on Davis. "Am I right?"

Davis pumped a fist in the air. "Right on!"

"Power to the people!" Bliss shouted.

Audrey understood their frustration. Hell, she was madder than anyone. Still, the thought of a revolt made her cringe. If her friends stood up and made a fuss because somehow the mystery girl had gotten on the team and Audrey hadn't, it might look as if Audrey was jealous and had put them up to it.

And Egan would side with her against the girl—not because she'd won her way onto the team fair and square but because she was his boss's daughter.

He'd then think she was petty. And Egan Gable could never love someone who would sink so low.

Worse yet, Lavinia would suggest they resolve the issue with a Magic Circle.

Audrey shook her head. "No, Tal! You can't do it! I mean...So she absconded with the book. So what? I'm smart. I didn't really need it to make a few debate points."

Frustration darkened Tallulah's face. "But—it's the principle of the thing!"

Audrey took Tallulah's face in her hands. When she had her dear friend's eyes focused only on her, she whispered, "That's my point exactly."

Time seemed to stand still.

Finally, Tallulah shrugged. "Okay, have it your way. We won't make a scene." She nodded toward the others. "But we're still going in."

Audrey frowned. "Promise me."

Tallulah smirked. "What, now you want to pinky swear?"

"Yep. Exactly. The last thing I want is for you to wrestle the culprit to the floor while I'm making my closing argument." Audrey held up her hand, pinky extended.

Tallulah rolled her eyes but held up her hand anyway.

When the girls' fingers entwined, Audrey nodded her thanks but turned her head before the others could notice her eyes were glistening with tears.

Twenty-one other students were there to debate.

Audrey knew all but three girls and two boys. From what she knew about the sixteen students she recognized, at least nine of them would make worthy teammates. Like her, they studied hard, excelled at their classes, and readily took part in class discussions.

Jeremy was there too. Seeing him, Audrey almost groaned out loud.

Based on her assessment of the competition, there was no way Jeremy would make the cut. Not that he knew the rules of debate anyway. His way of winning any argument was to toss out a few snarky jibes or parry with a couple of stupid jokes. If neither method got him what he wanted, he'd close with some ominous sulking.

She doubted he'd get beyond the first competitive round.

If I'm going to make the cut, I can't let his silly attempt to woo me back get in my way, Audrey reasoned. I need to focus!

She'd created a mantra and repeated it now in her head:

CONTENT: know what you're going to say, backward and forwards...MAKE YOUR CASE: Summarize it succinctly; then break it down using logic, statistics, examples, and quotes...REBUTTAL: undermine the other side's contentions; then summarize the flaws of their case.

And do it all with a blend of persuasion and conviction.

Above all else, she'd make eye contact with those who count most:

The judges.

Cornell, Nick, and of course, Egan.

Smiling brightly with her head held high, she walked in and sat down.

SHE HAS THE GRACE OF A QUEEN, EGAN MARVELED.

He had fully expected her to disappear from his course; to transfer out without saying anything. Instead, she came to class each day, turned in her work, but did not participate or vie for his attention in any way.

Although it was contrary to what Egan knew was right, he greatly missed her attempts to garner his attention.

He was annoyed that Jeremy felt the need to use the debate team's tryouts as a chance to woo Audrey back. If the gossip Egan heard was true, Audrey wouldn't fall for Jeremy's malarkey.

At least, Egan didn't think she would...

Unless she's trying to get back at me for snubbing her, he suddenly realized.

In that case, she might consider making up with him just to make me jealous.

Cornell waved his hand in front of Egan's face. "Why the long face, buttercup?"

Egan shrugged. "No reason."

"Well, then, time to turn that frown upside down and get this show started," Cornell cooed.

"Sorry," Egan grumbled. He grabbed a stack of blank index cards. As he rose, he chided himself for having created the scenario in which Audrey was once again vulnerable to Jeremy's attentions.

It suddenly dawned on him how he could nip that disaster in the bud.

Forcing his lips into a smile, he faced the contestants and exclaimed, "I'm happy to see so many of you here for Ashbury Academy's debate team tryouts. As you already know, to make the team, you'll be playing by National Speech & Debate Tournament rules. PE Nick and Cornell have graciously agreed to act as my co-judges. So let's get started." He held up the index cards. "First and foremost, put your name on these index cards and turn them back in to me."

He passed the cards to the first person on each row, who in turn passed it to the next person, and so on.

Within minutes the students had turned in their cards—except for Davis, Bliss, and Tallulah, who ducked out of sight.

Egan collected them. As he walked back to the judges' table, he seemed to shuffle the cards.

As a child, he'd had an interest in magic tricks. This served him well now. With sleight of hand, he palmed the cards with two names—those of Audrey and Jeremy—and moved them to the bottom of the pile.

"To choose who debates whom, I'll pull two cards at a time from the stack," Egan continued. "Those two students will debate the question chosen for everyone: 'Should students be drug tested?' The first name called will be 'for' first, and then 'against.' The debates will take place in front of judges only. We'll be in the anteroom, there." He pointed to a set of double doors that belonged to a smaller room. "The eight students who win their matches with the highest scores will make up our team."

Egan watched as the students silently calculated their odds. They'd have to beat fourteen others.

For a moment, his eyes shifted toward Audrey. Her face looked as if it were carved from stone.

Unfathomable.

"Good," Egan declared. "Now, continuing: On Monday, those who have made the team will then get the chance to compete for team captain. Competitors will be sorted and matched by the two alternate questions they've chosen to debate." He scanned the competitors. "Any questions?"

No hands went up.

"Great," he finally declared. "Then the first two debaters are"—he turned over the first two cards—"Adrienne and Monica. Good luck to you, ladies."

THERE WERE TO BE ELEVEN MATCHES.

The first debate took all of ten minutes. Waiting for it to end was agony for Audrey. She just wanted to get hers over with. From the silence in the auditorium, the others must have felt the same way.

When the door to the judges' chambers finally opened, Adrienne came out. She smiled broadly and gave a thumbs-up to the others.

Monica was stoically silent.

Two more names were called. None were Audrey's.

Then two more. And another two. And yet two more names. Too antsy to sit alone, Audrey moved next to her friends. Two debates later, she was regretting it. Bliss was holding tight to her arm. Every time the doors opened, her friend's nails dug into her wrists.

"It's worse than waiting for the electric chair," someone muttered loudly.

Another student guffawed. "If that were our debate question, I'd gladly take the 'for' position."

That elicited a few nervous giggles.

But everyone went silent again as the door opened. The victor moon-walked out. His defeated opponent shot him a bird.

Egan could be heard calling out: "'Audrey Thorpe...'"

She sighed, relieved. When she stood up, she smoothed her skirt before picking up her debate notes—

"...and Jeremy Blake."

"Shit!" Tallulah squeaked. She slapped her hand over her mouth.

Audrey glanced over at Jeremy. She'd been so caught up in reviewing her debate points that she hadn't noticed he hadn't been called yet either.

Jeremy stared back at her. His tan from his many afternoons on the football field seemed to fade by several shades.

For a second, she felt sorry for him.

Just not sorry enough.

She smiled sweetly but made it a point to stroll into the judge's room before him.

Jeremy and Audrey each took a podium and then waited for Egan's signal to start.

Audrey noticed Jeremy wince when she began her opening argument in support of student drug testing. She wasn't surprised he was ruffled.

She was on fire; hitting all the bases.

She was annihilating him.

Audrey began by stating the school's mission: to enhance the health and wellbeing of its students and to create an environment in which critical thinking skills were learned, developed, and allowed to flourish.

She then pointed out that the school's mandatory rules forbidding the use of street drugs was the outgrowth of this stated mission. She followed with hard statistics about the effects of drug use on teens, their subsequent health issues, school dropout rates, and the financial and emotional cost to those who were early drug users.

Finally, despite fears it may cost her a few points, she ended with an emotional appeal: "The choices we make in our teens affect us for the rest of our lives. During these years, we are at our maximum potential—physically and mentally. We can't let social pressure dictate our actions. We have to think for ourselves. As Albert Camus said, 'Life is the sum of all our choices.'"

As she spoke, she stared straight at Egan. She hoped he'd deduce her message: *WAIT FOR ME.*

Egan gazed back. Then he winked at her.

Yes, he'd heard her.

———

JEREMY ISN'T YET OUT OF THE BARN AND ALREADY SHE'S SLAUGHTERED HIM, Egan thought.

Damn, she'd make a good lawyer.

He noticed the tremble in Jeremy's hands as the boy positioned his note cards on the podium. If the quiver in his voice wasn't bad enough, he stumbled over his opening argument: that if thirteen is old enough to be a man in the eyes of a religious faith five thousand years old, it should be the age in which students can make decisions for themselves—including what drugs to use, when, and where.

From there, his presentation went downhill.

Egan just sat back and let nature take its course.

He almost snickered when Jeremy quoted from the Torah. He then moved on to other societies in which a male's rite of passage began as a teen or younger: the Mardudjara Aborigines of Australia, the Satere-Mawe tribe in Brazil, the Maasai of Kenya, "...and even the Pacific Islander tribe, the Vanuatus, are considered men as young as age five."

In her rebuttal, Audrey countered that if every society used the cutting of a male's foreskin as a sign of manhood, toddlers could then be recruited into the U.S. Army. "And I suppose, by that standard, a girl is a woman on the day of her first menstruation."

Jeremy blanched at her statement. The men winced, but by their nods, they were duly impressed with this rebuttal.

The highest rating allowed was sixteen. Thus far, he'd only given that score to four students. Audrey's argument had been much better than theirs, but he'd figured he should shave it—but only by a point, so that it wouldn't look as if he were playing favorites.

He gave Jeremy a score of 10. Despite his personal animosity, in his opinion even that was generous.

———

"OKAY, GENTLEMAN," EGAN SAID. "LET'S HAVE YOUR VERDICTS."

Cornell and PE Nick handed him their scoring cards.

Audrey: 14 +15 + 10 = 39

Jeremy: 10 + 16 + 13 = 39

What the hell? THEY TIED?

Cornell had given Audrey the score of fourteen, which meant Nick had graded her a lowly ten.

"Students, will you wait in the hallway?" Egan hoped the anger didn't come through in his request.

Startled, Audrey and Jeremy rose. From their pace, you'd think they were being sent to the gallows.

Still, Egan waited until the door was firmly shut before growling, "Did we see different debates?"

Nick shrugged. "Frankly, I thought Audrey overplayed her hand."

"Oh yeah? Does that mean you preferred the way Jeremy underplayed his?"

Nick snickered. "Let's just say I rewarded him for giving it the old college try."

"If that's the case, he won't do better than junior college."

Nick guffawed. "Jeremy will end up in an Ivy. Hell, if he doesn't get there on a football scholarship, he'll make it based on his math scores."

"If he's such a shoo-in, why is he even trying out for Debate? And for that matter, why are you helping him?"

"Because the kid wants it badly," Nick insisted.

"No—he wants *her* badly," Cornell sighed. "Anyone can see that. Ah, *l'amour, l'amour!*"

Egan shook his head. "That's not what Debate Team is about."

"I'm sticking to my score," Nick insisted. "When Jeremy is happy, he carries the team with him."

Egan turned to Cornell. "How about you? Didn't you feel Audrey's argument merited more than a score of fourteen?"

"Well, yes, I did—up until she brought up that thing about lady bits." Cornell shuddered. "TMI, to say the least!"

"And yet Jeremy's mention of foreskin was okay in your book?" Egan smirked.

"Everything Jeremy says and does is okay by me," Cornell purred. "Hey, cut me some slack! I took off three points—legitimately. And I did it even though he ditches my class whenever he can."

"You're both very generous," Egan muttered. "To a fault, which could negatively affect everything I'm trying to do here."

Nick sighed. "Give it a break Egan! So what if Audrey and Jeremy are tied? They now both have a shot at making the team. Why is that a bad thing?"

If only you knew, Egan thought.

Not that he'd say that out loud. He shrugged. "Okay, I'll let them know they tied."

As Egan announced the tie, Audrey was able to keep the shock off her face that somehow Jeremy's score had matched hers.

How could that be, she fumed. My God, his presentation was all over the place! And his opening statement was so lame! I mean, seriously: *the Vanuatus*?

A realization hit her: Egan would have preferred having Jeremy on the team. He didn't want to show her any favoritism, so he scored her low on purpose—but not low enough to offset the other judges' scores.

The thought angered her.

He's decided he can't be himself around me. Well, that's too bad! Because at the same time he's stifling any attempt I make to live my life; to be myself.

Well, she wasn't going to let him.

There were still three sets of competitors left to debate. She prayed the winners' scores wouldn't beat hers. She deserved to be on the team.

Egan knew it too. She wasn't going to let him steal her chance to make it.

At least if my score is too low to make the team, Jeremy can't be on it either.

The thought gave her enough relief that she could smile again. In fact, she felt generous enough to thank Jeremy for holding the door for her on their way out.

He must have been shocked that she wasn't angry with him because he blushed. And then, feeling emboldened, he placed his hand on the small of her back.

She turned in time to see Egan flinch and took some solace that his misguided plan hadn't worked.

CHAPTER 8

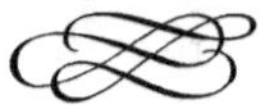

"That's the girl!" Bliss's frantic whisper was followed by a nod toward the row behind them on the right.

Tallulah flipped around to see their suspect. The girl, sitting by herself, was plump and wore square small-framed glasses. The frizzy shorthairs near the nape of her neck had escaped the tight topknot that held the rest of her dishwater blond mane.

It looked as if she were talking to herself too.

Probably memorizing her opening argument, Tallulah figured. "Bliss, are you sure it's her?"

Her friend nodded. "Heck yeah! She's wearing the Docs!" Now that the scouting expedition was over, Bliss stood up and waved Davis over. When she got his attention, he trotted their way.

Tallulah snickered. "If she wore them today then I guess she thinks those boots are lucky for her."

"Or comfortable," Bliss countered, "which they are. Our shop sells a ton of Martens." She nodded toward the girl. "So, what do you want to do about her?"

"She's yet to be called into the judges' chambers," Tallulah reminded her. "By then I'll have figured something out."

They didn't have to wait long. Just as Audrey and Jeremy were walking out, Egan shouted, "Mandy Blackwell and Franklin Zorn!"

Startled, Top Knot leaped up, spilling the note cards that she must have placed in her lap. Furiously, she gathered them, took a couple of deep breaths, and then made her way to the judges' room on the heels of her competitor.

"I've got a great idea!" Tallulah nudged Davis. "She left her backpack by her seat. Find her locker keys. Make duplicates. The workshop room should be open." Berney left it that way so that the students could work on their projects at all hours.

"On it." Davis sauntered up the aisle. When he got to Top Knot's row, he lifted her bag and walked off with it without anyone noticing.

* * *

"I'M SORRY, AUDREY. YOU SHOULD HAVE WON, FAIR AND SQUARE." JEREMY'S apology was too guileless to be anything but sincere.

"Thanks for that," she murmured. "It means a lot to me."

"And I want you to know…I mean, about us." He pursed his lips. "I know I screwed up—big time. If we could…I mean, if there were any way you could find it in your heart to—"

Jeremy—*groveling?* Audrey was so embarrassed for him that she shifted her eyes away—

To the students passing them on the way into the judges' room.

The boots…

That girl is wearing THE BOOTS!

Audrey's eyes moved up toward the girl's face: round, pitted with zits, pocked with anxiety.

And she had the misfortune to debate Franklin, a senior with one of the highest GPAs in the school. Everyone liked Franklin. He was quick with a quip. A real charmer.

At that moment, Audrey felt sorry for the girl—

Until their eyes met.

Until Audrey saw the girl's lips curdle into a smirk.

She then dared to wink at Audrey.

Audrey was too upset to do anything but watch as the girl walked around her.

By the time the fog of her anger had subsided, she had realized Jeremy was saying something: "So, you're okay with that?"

"Huh?… Yeah, sure." She shrugged helplessly. At that moment she noticed Bliss waving her over. "Look, Jeremy, I've got to go." Her legs seemed to turn to jelly as she stumbled down the aisle.

* * *

"THE BOOTS—"

Before Audrey could finish her sentence, Tallulah replied, "We know. On the girl who just went inside." She opened the girl's bag and held up an Ashbury Academy student ID card. "She's Mandy Blackwell. A junior. Lives in Pacific Heights."

Blackwell—Mandy…

For some reason, the name sounded familiar to Audrey, but she couldn't place it.

She reached for the girl's bag and opened it. As she'd hoped, the book was inside. "Bingo!"

Tallulah nudged the bag with her foot so that it was beyond Audrey's reach. "And it's got to stay in there—for now, anyway." She nodded to the students milling around them. "Think about it! She can always claim she found the book somewhere, and that you—we— had no right to open her bag, let alone rummage through it."

Audrey sighed. "Okay, alright! But what if she loses it?"

"You immediately reported it stolen to Eloise. Now that we have the name of the girl, Eloise can confirm she asked about the book right after you signed for it. In the meantime…" She shifted her glance to Davis, who was making his way toward them.

He landed in the seat beside Audrey. He was palming something, which he handed to her:

A set of keys.

"What's this for?" she asked.

Bliss hissed, "They open the Blackwell girl's lockers."

Audrey frowned. "What am I supposed to do with them?"

Tallulah arched a brow. "It's your chance to take back what's yours—when the time is right."

Davis opened Mandy's notebook. He rifled through the papers on the inside pocket until he found what he was looking for. "According to little Ms. Blackwell's class schedule, she has PE during seventh period."

PE?…

Audrey groaned.

Oh my God! Mandy Blackwell was the junior I bumped to get into Egan's class. Talk about bad karma…

"What's wrong with you? Tallulah asked.

"It's …nothing." Audrey shivered at this turn of events. "Debate Team's first practice is on Monday. We'll be debating to see who makes captain. If she makes the team, she'll hang onto it through the weekend."

"Tomorrow is Friday," Davis pointed out. "She'll probably stash her bag in the girl's PE locker room while they're playing on Kezar Field." This historic ball field was located just a few blocks from the school.

Tallulah grinned wickedly. "She'll freak out when she realizes it's disappeared."

"Hey, how are we getting out of Egan's class?" Bliss asked.

"We'll figure something out." Tallulah shrugged. "But if we all disappear, he'll suspect something. It's not like there's an outbreak of measles or something."

"Fine with me. I wouldn't be caught dead in the girl's locker room anyway," Davis assured her. "Tell you what—while you're B and E'ing, I'll create a diversion.

"Can I help too?" Bliss asked hopefully.

"No," the others declared.

She pouted for a moment. Finally, she groused, "What's 'B and E'ing'?"

"In police lingo, it stands for 'breaking and entering,'" Davis explained.

Bliss's eyes opened wide. "How would you know that?"

Davis shrugged. "Don't ask, because you don't really want to know."

"It's part of his dark, deadly past," Tallulah scoffed.

"Bottom line—if you get caught, it's not fun," Davis retorted.

Tallulah chucked his cheek. "Then be sure we don't." She pointed to the bag. "Speaking of which, maybe you should put this back by Mandy's chair before she returns."

Davis nodded. Holding the bag low, he walked away as if he hadn't a care in the world.

Noting Audrey's frown, Tallulah asked, "You're up for this, right?"

Audrey shrugged. "I'd feel bad if I embarrassed Lavinia."

Tallulah put her arm around her friend. "I'd feel bad about that too. But Audrey, be honest: what's worse, scaring that lunatic by stealing back the book she stole from you, or informing Lavinia about Light-Fingered Mandy's odious theft, whom she'd then have to suspend? The girl is new at AA. She'd take a public shaming pretty hard."

She's got a point, Audrey reasoned. If this Mandy person felt disgraced, she'd leave the school for good, Audrey reasoned. And AA would lose her tuition money.

No, Tallulah's way is much better. And besides, maybe Mandy won't make the team. If not, she'll return the book on her own, and we won't have to go through with the theft.

The thought was barely out of Audrey's mind when the doors to the judges' room opened. Mandy waltzed out as if she'd just danced with Prince Charming.

She beat Franklin? But... how?

Egan stood at the door behind them. He was smiling too.

Why? What has this Mandy person done? What has she said to make him so happy?

Audrey turned to Tallulah. "How long do we make her sweat before we tell her we returned the book to the library, safe and sound?"

Tallulah laughed. "If it were up to me, at least a month. But you're a much nicer person."

Not this time, Audrey vowed.

THE REST OF THE TRYOUTS TOOK UP THE NEXT HOUR.

When the last competitors emerged from the judges' room, they told the rest of the students: "If you won your match, you're to stick around while the judges pull the eight highest scorers."

While those who lost their matches shuffled out, the winners stayed seated, but barely. Skittishness came through in nervous giggles, ponderous pacing, and hands that wouldn't stay still. Anxiety seemed to suck all the air from the room.

Audrey spent that time staring at her feet and wondering if the quest to get Egan to admit his love for her was futile.

What if I imagined what happened? Worse yet, what if he was just flirting like he does with everyone else?

What if he doesn't love me at all?

She had to find out.

FINALLY, THE DOORS OPENED AGAIN. EGAN CAME OUT. CORNELL AND PE NICK were at his side. "Okay, gang. I want to just say that all of you gave spectacular debates. You left me in awe. I'm proud of each and every one of you." He sighed. "If I could, I'd put all of you on the team. But, unfortunately, I can't." He lowered his head as if their apprehension weighed heavily on him as well. "Okay, so, here we go."

Egan read each name deliberately.

He read Audrey's somewhere in the middle so that it wouldn't seem so obvious.

He hoped he'd kept the pride out of his voice—

And the guilt that he'd had to bump two students with higher scores to slip Audrey and Jeremy onto the team instead.

That Jeremy kid has no place on the team, he fumed. *And not just because he loves Audrey...*

No, he doesn't love her. He just wants to fuck her. To be her first.

As he watched Audrey's joy in hearing her name, he was ashamed to admit it to himself:

And so do I.

IT WAS JUST A FEW SECONDS AFTER THE FINAL BELL ANNOUNCING THE START OF seventh period that Egan noticed Audrey's absence.

Jeremy's chair was empty too.

Egan felt his heart drop into the pit of his gut.

Damn it! They skipped my class—together?

If Audrey and Jeremy wanted to be alone, Audrey would know where to go to make that happen. She knew every nook and cranny of the school.

Egan was overcome with the desire to find them—now.

I've got to stop her from doing…something stupid.

In the meantime, he had to take care of his students. He stood up. "Okay, class, it's time for a pop essay based on your homework assignment last night on *Macbeth*. Today's assignment: compare that power couple to another found in either nineteenth or twentieth-century literature." He looked down at his watch. "I'll give you a half hour. Afterward, you can regale me with your thoughts."

He waited until the groans gave way to the scratching of pencils on paper before making his way down the aisle in front of Bliss's desk. Reaching it, he murmured, "Bliss, may I see you for a moment?"

The girl raised her head. Her eyes widened in surprise. Instinctively, her eyes went to Audrey's empty seat.

She knows something.

"Would you mind following me out into the hall?" he asked.

By the time she stood up, her lip was trembling, but she did as she was told.

———

"Where is Audrey?" Egan didn't see the need in beating around the bush.

"She isn't feeling well." The words came out thick as if they were sticking in Bliss' throat.

"I see." Egan hoped his nod came off as sympathetic. "So, if I were to go to the reception office, I'd find her there with Clare?"

"No!" As soon as the word was out of her mouth, Bliss pursed her lips. "I mean, I'm sure she'll be back before class ends."

"Oh? What makes you so sure?"

"Because… she wasn't feeling *that* sick." Bliss had a nervous habit: twirling the ends of her hair. Egan watched as she did so now.

Egan nodded. "I see. So, where is she right now?"

Bliss gulped but stayed silent.

"Whatever she's doing, it's wrong, and you know it. Please, Bliss, tell me where she is so that I can stop her from making the biggest mistake of her life."

Bliss dropped her head. "The PE locker room…"

He nodded. It makes sense, he thought. This period's PE class would be out on the field. No one could bother them there.

"Go back to class," he commanded. "Don't mention what we've discussed to anyone."

Nodding, she scurried back into the room.

As Egan made his way through AA's halls, he tried to keep his thoughts from what he might witness as he entered the locker room:

Audrey and Jeremy's clothes piled haphazardly on the tile floor;

The two teens, naked and damp with the sweat of their desires; grunting from the high of their ecstatic union; groaning in the throes of climax…

He pushed these heartbreaking thoughts from his mind.

He wondered how Audrey might feel when she finally realized he was there. Surprised? Shamed?

Maybe triumphant.

What better way to thumb her nose at him, to make him realize what he could have had if only he'd asked?

But I care too much to ask it of her. Not now, anyway.

And after today, maybe not ever.

Audrey watched from Ashbury Academy's clock tower as the seventh period PE class made its way down Haight Street toward Kezar Field. When they were out of sight, she murmured, "We can go in now."

Tallulah's emphatic nod sent her tightly coiled curls into a frenzied dance. "Okay, let's do this thing!" She beckoned for Audrey to follow as she made her way down the tower's staircase, to the school's basement level.

As they'd hoped, the basement hallway was empty.

The changing rooms were never locked. They entered the one designated GIRLS and scanned the rows of lockers, which were stacked in columns of two.

"There it is!" Tallulah pointed to a bottom locker numbered 415.

Audrey followed her over. Her hands shook as she inserted one of the two tiny locker keys. The first one didn't work, so it must have belonged to Mandy's book locker, somewhere outside the Junior Class' homerooms.

The second key opened the shiny new lock.

"Eureka!" Tallulah squealed.

"Shhhh!" Audrey looked around. Satisfied no one had heard her friend, she pulled the lock from the door.

Mandy's bag was there, as were her clothes.

So were the boots.

As Audrey unzipped the bag and took out the book, Tallulah pulled the boots from the bottom of the locker too.

Audrey frowned. "What are you doing?"

"To the victor go the spoils." Tallulah shoved the boots into Audrey's arms. "Oh, and you're in luck! They're exactly your size."

"I can't wear these! She'll know we stole them," Audrey argued. "Or that *I* stole them."

"So? What of it? She wouldn't be able to prove it. You heard Bliss. Her parents' store sells all kinds of Doc Martens. Maybe they sold you this pair."

"Tallulah, I told you: we can't get caught!"

Ignoring Audrey, Tallulah shut the locker door, snapped the lock into place, and pocketed the key. As she slipped the boots and the book into her backpack, she argued, "And we won't—because Mandy won't dare tell anyone. Otherwise, she'd have to admit she stole your book."

Audrey shook her head. "I don't know…"

The sound of footsteps shut her up.

Tallulah must have heard them too because she shoved Audrey toward the locker room's back door. It was designated as the basement's fire exit and it led out onto Haight Street.

To avoid being seen by anyone who might be looking out the school's windows, the girls hugged the building's brick wall as they made their way back to the school's main doors. When Clare looked up from the receptionist desk, they ducked behind a wall. Then, when her back was turned, they flew up the grand staircase to the second floor and Egan's classroom.

***

They were surprised to see that Egan wasn't there. Except for a few whispering cliques, their classmates were in the midst of a writing assignment.

Bliss waved frantically to her friends. When they took their seats, she leaned over and hissed, "Egan went looking for you. Did he catch you?"

Perplexed Audrey shook her head adamantly. "You told him where we went?"

Bliss didn't have to say anything. Her answer was given by twirling a lock of her hair furiously with her index finger.

Tallulah slapped her forehead. "Damn it, Bliss!"

Audrey was about to scold her when she felt a tap on her shoulder: Jeremy.

"Where were you?" he hissed.

"What's it to you?" she muttered.

"Everything—since you promised to go with me to PE Nick and ask about our scores."

"Wait…*what*? I don't remember…"

Jeremy glared back. "Yesterday, when we walked out of the judges' room, I told you I was sorry we'd tied. Audrey, I'm no fool. You wiped the floor with me! If PE Nick scored you low on purpose, I wanted him to admit it—and make good on it."

Audrey couldn't believe her ears. "You were willing to do that for me?"

He nodded. "Audrey, I'd do anything for you."

"Jeremy, please... What we had—*that's over.*"

"That's what PE Nick said too." Jeremy's face hardened at the memory. "He said the fact that you stood me up was proof I'm wasting my time trying to get you to forgive me."

"Gee, he's a regular relationship counselor," Audrey retorted. "So, tell me: did he also admit he graded me lower on purpose?"

"Of course not. But... I know in my gut he did."

Don't be so sure, Audrey thought wryly. Her bet was still on Egan.

Jeremy continued: "He's worried I'm losing my edge on the field because I'm still hung up on you. He thinks I'm killing my chances for a sports scholarship. And he's right." He put his hand over hers. "But that's no reason to take away something you badly wanted and deserved. Audrey, if you ask me, I'll leave Debate Team."

For the first time since the day of the SATs, Audrey felt grief-stricken: not for her loss but Jeremy's pain. "Jeremy, I would never—"

"Ms. Thorpe and Mr. Blake, I'm so glad you finally found your way to class!" Egan's voice came from the front of the room.

Startled, they looked up in unison.

Egan tapped the blackboard. "Since you missed the class assignment, I'll expect you to stay after the bell and make it up."

Jeremy gawked. "But, I've got football practice—"

"I'm sure PE Nick will understand." Egan's tone sent a shiver through Audrey.

Jeremy nodded meekly.

They stayed silent as Egan called on some of the others to read their essays.

When the last bell of the day chimed, they stayed put while the others rose to leave. As Tallulah followed Davis and Bliss out the door, she nudged Audrey with her backpack. The outline of the book and the boots were easy to make out.

Egan waited until the last students trickled out before closing the door. When he turned around, he pointed to Jeremy. "You go first. What was so important that you had to skip my class for it?"

SAY IT. SAY YOU WANTED ANOTHER CONQUEST—THE ONE WHO GOT AWAY: Audrey.

Boast about it to me, just like you'll do to your jock buddies.

Give me a reason to knock that smirk off your face.

Despite Egan's silent wishes, Jeremy merely shrugged. Still, he kept some semblance of a casual grin on his face as he replied, "I stayed after sixth period PE to talk with Nick."

Egan rolled his eyes. "I see." No doubt Nick would vouch for Jeremy. Hell, he'd do anything for his star quarterback. To prove it, he'd almost ruined Audrey's chance to make Debate Team.

In fact, Egan wouldn't have been surprised to learn that Nick suggested that the couple use the locker room for their tryst.

He gave Audrey a sidelong gaze. "And where were you?"

Audrey opened her mouth, but nothing came out.

Hell, she's traumatized, Egan thought. That son of a bitch sullied her— and now she's in shock! I'll kill that little asshole—

"Audrey was…with me."

Egan seethed at Jeremy's admission. Not that he could show it. He cocked a brow. "With you, talking to PE Nick?"

Jeremy nodded.

"Why did you both feel the need to talk to him during my class?" Egan asked.

Jeremy sighed. "Because it was about Debate Team tryouts. I felt I didn't deserve my score. I wanted his assurance—in front of Audrey—that he hadn't been too generous on my behalf at the expense of her place on the team."

"How chivalrous," Egan snapped. He turned to Audrey. "Is what he says true?"

All the color left her face. Still, she nodded. "Yes. I was with him."

Egan flinched. *So she admits it. They were together.*

But where?

Egan knew he'd scared Bliss into telling him the truth. And yet, when he'd checked both the boys' and girls' locker rooms, Jeremy and Audrey were nowhere to be found—

Unless…

Unless Jeremy blew his wad too quickly.

Or, worse yet, he couldn't get it up.

Ha! Egan swallowed his urge to scoff at the irony of that. Maybe Audrey's long face had something to do with her disappointment in missing the big moment…

With the wrong guy.

Or maybe she just couldn't go through with it.

Hope surged through him. He looked at Audrey, praying he'd read this theory in her face.

She was staring back at him. There was no triumph in her eyes:

Just longing.

Egan hated himself for having thought the worst of her.

He felt ashamed for wanting her as badly as he did.

I care too much for her.

"I'll expect your assignments on Monday," he muttered. "And by the way, Jeremy, don't blame your coach for doing his best to save you from yourself. Every great teacher has the same instinct."

By Audrey's blush, he knew she realized the message was for her.

CHAPTER 9

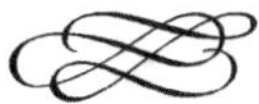

$\mathcal{L}$avinia knocked on Audrey's bedroom door. "Darling, you've been in there all weekend! Why don't you come out and spend some time with me in the garden?"

Audrey sighed. Her mother was right. Since leaving school on Friday, Audrey had holed up in her room, preparing for the first Debate Team meeting. In that regard, the library book on the vice presidents was providing a font of information for Audrey's for-and-against arguments.

She was determined to be the team captain. It was the best way to force Egan to see her as a competent person.

And maybe more.

Hopefully, much more.

Audrey knew why her mother was concerned. Lavinia's rule about homework was simple: there should never be too much of it—and none on the weekends.

AA's teachers were comfortable with that philosophy and managed their class time for new information and the open discussion of it. Any homework assignment was, at best, an item to read for discussion the next day, or an essay to write. Tests were short, and usually required an essay answer. The process was geared toward nurturing critical thinking as opposed to rote test taking.

Few nights or weekends went uninterrupted by some school event. Realizing this, Audrey cherished time alone with her mother. She knew Lavinia felt the same way.

This would have been such a time of joint solitude.

Audrey usually studied in their cottage's sunroom, so she felt doubly guilty for hiding out in her bedroom. Or, if it were a warm day, she'd sit on the chaise out in the yard, so that she and her mother could talk and laugh and gossip as Lavinia nurtured the flowerbeds. It was a futile attempt, but Lavinia never gave up hope that they'd flourish despite San Francisco's foggy nights, chilly summers, and a peek-a-boo sun that ducked and dodged the city's tall buildings and even taller hills.

Lavinia was right. This was *their* time.

"I'll be down in a second," Audrey exclaimed.

She was about to tuck the library book under her pillow when something fell out from between its pages. It was a contact sheet containing miniature black-and-white photos of—

Egan?

She could tell immediately that it had been taken by the professional photographer hired by the school for the formally posed headshots of teachers and students displayed in AA's yearbook.

One of the photos had a heart drawn around it in red ink.

Admittedly, it was the best one of Egan. He was gazing directly into the camera. His brow was arched as if he were about to say something intriguing.

His grin was an open invitation to come closer and listen.

So, Mandy has a crush on him.

And because of Audrey, Mandy had been bumped from the one opportunity she had to get close to him.

Until she made Debate Team.

Such irony.

But how did Mandy get ahold of these photos? Only the students who worked on the yearbook staff would have access to the school's photo archives.

Lavinia would know if Mandy was on it.

For that matter, maybe she just walked into the yearbook production room and stole it. Heaven knows she isn't above taking what isn't hers.

Audrey wondered what she should do with the contact sheet. There was no way she'd return it to the school, what with the red heart drawn around Egan.

I should burn it, she thought. But she knew she couldn't do it.

Instead, she put it in her keepsake box—antique, carved out of burlwood, and lacquered. She'd found it at a garage sale a couple of years ago.

After Monday's meeting, Audrey planned on placing the book in the library's overnight box. She could then ask Eloise if it ever showed up. Once Eloise confirmed it had, she'd be off the hook for it.

And Mandy would too.

"I can't believe Egan assigned homework for the weekend." Lavinia's swipe at the bead of sweat hanging at the end of her nose only replaced it with a smudge of mud. "The teachers know how I feel about that."

"Officially, it's not homework," Audrey assured her. "Monday's debate practice will determine who will be the team's captain. I want to take a shot at it."

"Ah! Well, then. I can't be angry with him, can I?" Lavinia was all smiles again. "And I certainly can't stifle your admirable desire to lead your team." Lavinia shoved her hand spade into the flowerbed's rich, dark soil, enlarging the hole by several more inches. "What with Debate Team and four classes, I hope I didn't burden Egan with too much responsibility."

"He seems to be enjoying himself—in my class, anyway." Audrey kept her eyes on her notes.

Lavinia stopped digging in order to look up at her daughter. "Is he a good teacher?"

"Everyone loves his class." *No lie there.*

Lavinia laughed. "Something tells me his popularity isn't just based on his teaching skills."

"You're right," Audrey admitted. "But he has a passion for teaching, and it shows. My class is also a lot of fun. He encourages us to think about what influenced the writers who came after Shakespeare, and why. And he makes everyone feel…well, I guess the right word is *special*." She turned her head so that her mother couldn't see her cheeks pinking up.

"That's good to know." Gently, Lavinia tapped the base of a plastic pot holding a small lavender plant. When she determined it had loosened the soil around the plant's roots, she lifted it out and placed it in the hole in front of her. "I was surprised to see your name on his Comparative Lit roster. I thought you'd decided on Glee instead."

Audrey shrugged. "I figured it wouldn't hurt to have one more AP course on my transcript."

"It was a full class," Lavinia reminded her. "Another student was bumped: Mandy Blackwell. She was very upset. Her mother called me about it."

What a cry baby!

It was on the tip of Audrey's tongue to divulge the lengths Mandy had gone to get close to Egan. But then she thought better of it. Her own actions toward him would seem questionable to a stranger.

For that matter, Lavinia would question them too.

But I'm not some lovesick schoolgirl. My God, I'm a year away from college!

"No class schedule is set in stone until the first day of school," Audrey argued. "And besides, seniors have always had first dibs on courses."

"All I'm saying is that you should have discussed it with me before going into the computer and making the change yourself," Lavinia continued.

Audrey muttered. "Isn't she on the yearbook staff?"

Lavinia nodded absently.

So, I was right. She stole Egan's photos from there!

"Mandy's mother didn't threaten to pull her out of the school, did she?" Audrey wondered if she'd sounded too hopeful. She and the girl had yet to exchange a single word and already she found her incredibly irritating.

"No," Lavinia replied. "Slowly but surely, Mandy is finding her sea legs at the school. It helped that she made Debate Team."

"Well, then, that should keep her busy," Audrey muttered. "And yearbook looks great on college transcripts. Frankly, I don't know why she's making such a big deal over getting bumped, and in her junior year, no less!"

Lavinia sighed. "I wish it weren't a big deal either. But when parents are paying for school tuition, they look at educators through a different lens. Everything is magnified—especially perceived slights. They feel their children deserve special treatment in all matters."

The memory of Egan laughing with Mandy as he walked her out of the judges' room came to mind.

I know what kind of "special treatment" Mandy is hoping for...

Audrey had a horrible thought. "Had you mentioned her disappointment in missing out on Comparative Lit to Egan?"

"No..." Lavinia paused from planting to think for a moment. "At least, I don't think so. Why do you ask?"

Audrey shrugged. "A lot of students tried out for debate. I'd hate for anyone to think he was playing favorites."

Lavinia frowned. "I wouldn't stand for it."

"I know that, and so does everyone on the staff. But you're Egan's boss. He's new and he wants to please you." *It's why he won't look twice at me.*

The thought of his disregard for her feelings made her even angrier about Mandy's crush.

"The Blackwell girl is a junior," Audrey huffed. "She can take Egan's class next year."

Lavinia patted the loose dirt around the plant's stem. "If he's still around."

That got Audrey's attention. "What do you mean? Where do you think he'll go? To another school?"

Lavinia smacked the dirt from her hands. "Doubtful. In his mind, teaching anywhere is just a temporary situation. He's young, and he has goals. He wants to be a novelist."

"He's not all *that* young," Audrey protested. "He's twenty-six."

"Twenty-six may seem old to someone in their teens, but in the scope of a lifetime, he's still young. Think about it: he's only eight years older than you. When he's forty, you'll be thirty-two."

Audrey enjoyed the thought that, in just a few years, no one would question their attraction, let alone their dating.

And certainly not their marriage.

She rewarded her mother's wisdom with a laugh. "You've got an excellent point."

At that moment, she decided to give Mandy Blackwell a very clear message:

Stay away from me.

And stay away from Egan.

She'd start by winning Monday's debate.

And so that Mandy understood just who she was messing with, she'd wear Mandy's boots.

CHAPTER 10

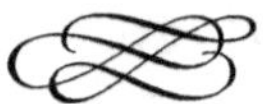

Only four students from Egan's seventh period class made it onto Debate Team. Jeremy and Audrey were two of them. The others were Gemma Sisley, whose father had been one of Berkeley's renowned Black Panther activists; and Johnny Ruiz, whose mother ran a free clinic in San Francisco's Mission district. They stayed behind when their classmates filed out as AA's clock tower rang Monday's end-of-day chimes.

Within minutes, the rest of the team filtered in. Two were the auburn-haired Kennedy twins—Caleb and Jeb, each whip-smart in some arcane form of trivia. Another was a junior girl: Portia Rosenberg, a pixie in stature who spoke rarely, but always eloquently.

Mandy Blackwell was the last to enter. She held her head high, but by her frown, it was obvious she wasn't happy.

Audrey could guess why.

TALLULAH WAS STILL LINGERING IN THE DOORWAY WHEN THE JUNIOR MADE HER entrance. As Mandy walked past her, Tallulah declared, "Wow, nice sneakers! They make quite a fashion statement."

Mandy's face darkened with anger. She was wearing shoes her stepfather, Simon, had insisted on buying her: Women's Air Jordans.

The sneakers were a name-brand cliché. Trimmed in black and sporting the red logo of a player palming a ball while leaping high in the air, the shoes were white and puffy, like marshmallows inflated by the heat of a campfire flame.

Mandy didn't play basketball. In fact, she despised sports in general. It showed in her doughy figure. Still, her mother had insisted she wear them, if only for PE class.

Mother will do anything to please that jerk, Mandy thought furiously.

She knew this from the disgusting sounds that emanated from the master bedroom on the far end of the third-floor hallway on any given night.

Mandy had no choice but to wear the sneakers home on Friday, after the discovery that the coveted library book and her Doc Martens had been stolen from her PE locker. The theft of the book upset her only because she'd hoped to spend the weekend making notes from it, whereas the boots were her pride and joy.

She cringed when her stepfather saw the sneakers on her. He puffed up with pride, under the assumption that he'd finally won her over.

As if!

Unlike her mother, his money didn't impress her. She refused to fawn over him, let alone coo and grovel like she'd seen her mother do for him.

And for what, a couple of hundred dollars in tip money?

Mandy wondered if Simon stuffed the bills in her mother's panties and then made her strip down. She wouldn't doubt it in the least. Her mother was just the most recent of Simon's three wives and she was hell-bent on being his last.

Maybe that's the reason Mom spends several hours a day working out, she reasoned.

Mandy's goal was much bigger: to make sure she'd never have to rely on a Simon of her own.

Besides, she preferred stealing from the wad of cash he left in his bureau drawer; not any of the numerous Benjamins crammed between the old fart's tighty-whities but a twenty or two, every couple of days.

Simon never even noticed.

The best thing about Simon was that he was willing to fork over the money for AA's tuition. Getting into a decent school with a reputation for strong academics was her ticket into an Ivy League school–preferably far away from the Simons of the world.

She knew AP courses were a great shortcut. It was why Mandy had made her mother scream bloody murder when she'd been cut from Egan's class.

Although Mandy had somehow gotten bounced from Comparative Lit, she'd accomplished the next best thing: making it onto Debate Team.

That's where Egan came in. Her goal: to be teacher's pet, one way or another.

Doing so would make her school of choice, Berkeley, very probable. She'd heard he was well connected with the Lit Department. It was an easy major, so why not make that her next academic perch?

Mandy wasn't a virgin and Egan was a hottie. If getting a recommendation to Berkeley meant sleeping with him, she'd do it, and willingly. If she sucked up properly, no doubt he'd write a recommendation for her.

She rolled her eyes at the thought that, in this case, "sucking up" would prove to be more than a double entendre. Granted, had he looked like a troll—like, say, Hardy or History Nick—the task would be harder to swallow—literally.

Mandy knew all too well that close personal connections were also key to her future success. Her goal: to get as close as possible to those who could do her the most favors.

Since the first day of school Mandy had made note of the kids, both the girls and the guys, who were deemed popular by their peers. Audrey Thorpe topped the list—not just because she was the Head of School's daughter or because she'd proven to be one of AA's smartest students. She had a reputation for kindness. She never had a bad word to say about anyone. She inspired others and was respected for doing so.

In other words, she was her mother's daughter.

At that moment, Mandy realized she was *her* mother's daughter too.

It's why she had given into the compulsion to take Audrey's library book. As for the fact that some nut felt the urge to steal it along with her Docs—well, that was now Audrey's problem. Since she was the last person to have checked it out, she'd have to cough up the money for its disappearance.

All the more reason to ignore Tallulah's smug observation. Making Debate Team gave Mandy a great opportunity to get close to Audrey. No one was going to stand in her way—certainly not the daughter of a drugged-out rock-and-roll whore! Once she had Audrey's ear, she'd work on nudging a wedge between her and that bitch, Tallulah.

Which is why Mandy met Tallulah's jibe with a withering glower.

Tallulah dared to stare back. When she finally looked away, it was to wink and nod at Audrey.

Mandy followed Tallulah's gaze. That's when she noticed:

Why, THAT BITCH IS WEARING MY BOOTS!

To top it off, Audrey held the missing library book in her hands. When the girls' eyes met, there was no triumph in Audrey's.

Just pity.

Then Mandy remembered the photos of Egan tucked away in the book.

Damn it! Why did I have to draw a heart on it? She'll tell her little posse about it and I'll be the laughingstock of the whole school—

Unless I make a fool of her first.

"Okay everyone, we've got a lot on our plate, so go ahead and take a seat," Egan commanded.

Although Jeremy was in the middle of saying something to Audrey, she shushed him and quickly turned away. Miffed at her snub, he shrank into his seat.

So there's still trouble in Paradise, Mandy thought.

She'd kept her ear to the ground and knew the scuttlebutt. Knowing that Jeremy was still pining after Audrey could work in Mandy's favor.

Especially if she made Debate Team captain.

She knew just how to make that happen.

EGAN OPENED WITH: "I HEREBY DUB YOU THE DEBATE EIGHT. AND, AS I mentioned on Friday, the first order of business is choosing our fearless leader."

Johnny raised his hand. "Why do we have to debate for it? Why don't we just vote on it?"

Egan shook his head. "This isn't a popularity contest. You're going to want someone who is a tent pole player. Someone who can strategize and play to each teammate's strengths. And besides, debaters are judged at the podium. That's where we'll find our team captain. So, any takers?"

Mandy and Audrey's hands rose simultaneously.

Johnny Ruiz's arm went up, as did Gemma's.

Egan nodded approvingly. "The winner of each match will face off for the prize of leading this motley crew." He held out a mug. "Who chose the first of the four possible debate questions, 'Allowing the Internet to Stay Free?'"

The hands of all four competitors went up. "Ah, well that makes life easy. We now have our first-round debate question." He walked to the blackboard. Picking up a piece of chalk, he asked, "Now, how about the question about whether statues of Confederate heroes should be taken down?"

Gemma and Johnny's hands went up.

He wrote their names on the board beside the word STATUES.

Egan eyed Audrey, then Mandy. "Make my day and tell me you two chose the topic of vice presidents."

They nodded.

"Okay, great. Now, if it turns out that either Mandy or Audrey must debate Gemma or Johnny, the topic will be the same question used Friday: about school drug policies." He nodded toward the students who'd chosen not to compete. "They will serve as your judges and use the same criteria as Friday's debates."

"You mean, you won't be judging us?" Mandy asked.

Egan nodded. "I'll fill out a score card but it'll only be used if there's a tie."

Egan had no intention of playing favorites. He'd watch as nature took its course. But he crossed his fingers that Audrey's debate skills, coupled with her popularity, would win over her voting teammates.

They drew from a cup holding four rubber bands: two that were blue, and two that were beige. "If your bands match, you'll debate each other. Beige bands go first."

Audrey's band was blue, as was Johnny's.

Egan put two of the bands back in the cup, one of each color. "Gemma and Mandy, you're up. Blue band argues for the Internet staying free, beige against it."

Mandy drew the beige band again. She was glad because if life experience had taught her anything, it was that nothing in life was free.

Audrey and Johnny went to opposite sides of the hall to read over their notes on their arguments.

That is to say, Audrey knew she should be studying them, but she was distracted at the thought of debating Mandy next.

She'd known Gemma to be a fierce competitor in all things. Then again, so was Mandy. Audrey flinched at the memory of Mandy's seething glare at the sight of her boots on Audrey's feet.

Perhaps I went too far, she thought.

But couldn't the same be said about bumping Mandy from Egan's class? Even Lavinia had chided her for doing it.

Then again, Mandy seemed bound and determined to get close to Egan, even if it meant stealing. If that weren't bad enough, the heart drawn on his photo proved she was obsessed with him.

It made Audrey sick to her stomach to think of Mandy becoming captain.

I can't let her. I have to pull it together.

By the time Egan opened the door and beckoned them in, she was ready to do battle with Johnny.

When they entered, Audrey saw Mandy smiling triumphantly.

She'd also taken a seat next to Jeremy.

She thinks that, by doing that, she's messing with my head.

Instead, it galvanized Audrey to do her best.

Because she pulled the blue band, she'd be arguing to keep the Internet free.

When Johnny grimaced, she knew he must have felt better prepared to make her argument.

She was right.

Audrey began by pointing out that the Internet's creation was a joint venture between academia and the U.S. Government—both entities supported by its citizens' tax dollars. She then segued to its global importance, and how eliminating payment for use allowed information to be delivered freely to everyone. "A free press is the First Amendment in our Constitution," she argued.

Although Johnny was well prepared, the strength of her argument and the ease in which she made it took him off his stride. Realizing this, he overcompensated by talking too fast and stumbling over a few of his points.

No surprise: Audrey won.

It was time for her to face off with Mandy. By drawing the blue band, Audrey would argue to keep the vice presidency.

Mandy chuckled, as if she'd already won.

Audrey couldn't wait to prove her wrong.

EGAN SAW IT IMMEDIATELY: MANDY WAS QUITE THE LITTLE FLIRT.

She'd started by asking an innocent question. Her appreciation was delivered with a sultry chuckle. Her big move was the oldest one in the book, but definitely tried and true: she dropped a pen on the floor so that she could flash a bit of cleavage—something she had in abundance.

And, oh boy, Jeremy was enjoying the show.

Ain't love grand, Egan thought. Not always, but it sure as hell was fickle.

Gee, I wonder if I should toss that out as a debate question?

Despite Mandy's antics, Egan marveled at Audrey's ability to stay focused on the task at hand: winning.

Something she did quite handily.

Now for the clash of the titans.

EGAN HADN'T KNOWN WHAT TO EXPECT, BUT IT WASN'T A TIE.

Audrey's opening was eloquent. She based her proposition on the Constitution's brief three-point statement of vice presidential duties. She then explained how, throughout history, the vice president's importance had grown based on the necessities of a working democracy.

In closing, she declared: "In times of a president's impeachment, incapacitation, sudden death, or assassination, the position of vice president has allowed our government to function rationally and immediately."

Mandy's opposition began by shredding Audrey's examples of vice presidential duties, using examples of those who held the office and had ended in obscurity for not making the most of the position. "These supposed statesmen blew their chance to leave their mark on history," she argued.

And so it went on for yet two more rounds, Audrey thrusted with a point and Mandy parried with a counterpoint. Fact was fought with perception; history with observation.

And a few caustic barbs thrown in for good measure. When Mandy declared "There were several deadbeat vice presidents who should have gotten *the boot* for trying to *steal* the presidency," Audrey had countered with "Well, that's certainly one for *the books*—and quite *heart*-felt!"

Her retort left Mandy speechless, but not for long. When it came time for their final replies, Egan was wondering if they'd come to blows.

At that point he noticed the smirk on Jeremy's face. Why, that little shit is getting off on this, Egan realized.

The vote seemed to take an eternity. Before the votes were tallied, Egan had been impressed with the team's extensive albeit silent deliberations. Now, in hindsight, he wondered how much personal bias came into play—

Especially, in Jeremy's case.

Somewhat thrown by the scores, he asked the Kennedy twins to manage the recount. A few minutes later, they replied in unison, "Nothing's changed."

He asked both girls to leave the room while he conferred with the judges.

Mandy and Audrey easily guessed the problem.

And by Jeremy's sheepish face and Mandy's sly grin, Egan realized her plan had worked. Jeremy's allegiance to Audrey had disappeared–most likely to be found between Mandy's cleavage at a later date.

"You'll have to cast the deciding vote," Portia reminded him.

As a senior, Audrey deserves priority. But more to the point, Audrey would make a better leader.

It's the right thing to do.

But Egan wouldn't.

It would be tempting fate. All he had to do was gaze into her eyes to know how she felt about him.

When it's right—and if it's right—we'll know it.

With a heavy heart, he replied, "Please call them in."

HE DOESN'T WANT TO TEMPT FATE.

That was the only reason Audrey could think of for Egan choosing Mandy over her.

If he could just admit that she'd stolen his heart but that their timing was off, or that he owed Lavinia nine months of his undivided attention—at least, not divided by Audrey—she could live with that.

Instead, he said nothing.

Instead, she got the occasional placid glance or an absentminded grin.

But not a word. No indication whatsoever of what her future held.

Her future with him.

Damn! It's just not fair—

Unless it's over.

Unless he likes her better.

Yes, the thought crossed her mind. Like now, as he clapped when Mandy made her winner's speech. The roar of her misery drowned out Mandy's words, so that was one good thing.

She planned to linger after everyone else took off, but she didn't want to seem like a sore loser.

Besides, that might be Mandy's gameplay too: cling to him like some deep-sea barnacle.

No way was she going to act like Mandy! If Egan wanted to explain—or better yet, apologize—she'd let him seek her out.

Audrey gathered her things to go—

And that's when she realized the library book wasn't there.

Mandy hadn't stuck around at all.

Egan, busy at the blackboard, had his back to her as Audrey slipped out too.

"*Boo-yah*, big boy!" Cornell clicked his martini glass with Egan's Scotch tumbler. "Another big win—and against University High this time! AA's Debate Eight is *on fire!*"

Egan guffawed. "So, you'll help me chaperone our trip to the State finals in LA?"

To beg Cornell—and Odette too, after school, he's taken them for drinks at Zuni Cafe.

"You bet I will!" Cornell sighed happily. "As long as there's some play time built in. The hotel is a hop, skip, and a jump from WeHo—"

"And Beverly Hills," Odette declared with a happy sigh. After taking a sip from her champagne flute, she added, "It's been ages since I broke a stiletto on a Rodeo Drive shopping spree!"

"Yeah, well, I hate to be a downer, you two, but I don't remember seeing the words 'free' and 'time' under AA's regulations for field trip chaperones."

"*Merde*," Odette muttered. "In other words, you're keeping us on a leash for the whole weekend?" She thought for a moment, then purred, "On second thought, I find that a tantalizing proposition."

Egan sighed. "Okay, yeah. Since Beverly Hills High is hosting the competition, why don't you take a few hours while our team is waiting to go onstage?"

Odette and Cornell high-fived each other. "Now, what about the sleeping arrangements?" Odette batted her eyes in anticipation of his answer.

"That's easy. There are four male and four female students. They'll bunk in pairs. We chaperones get individual rooms interspersed between those occupied by the students." Egan grimaced. "Hopefully, there won't be a lot of extracurricular activity through the night."

"Not for them or us, either, if we have to stay on guard duty all night," Cornell groused.

Egan chuckled weakly. "Taking shifts playing hall monitor may not be such a bad idea."

Odette frowned. "You're kidding! Right?"

The look on their faces told him he'd better be, or else he'd have to drum up two other saps to make the trip with him.

"I have noticed that they're a pretty tight group," Odette admitted. She raised a brow. "Who knew Debate Team could be so stimulating?"

"Yeah, who knew," Egan murmured as he swallowed the last of his drink. He motioned the bartender for another round.

Frankly, he was pleased with the past few months. They were just now in the middle of the spring semester. His classes were a success with the students, and therefore with their parents, which made Lavinia pleased to no end.

College acceptance letters had arrived last week. From the euphoria enveloping his senior students, Egan realized he'd done well in assisting them on their college essays. While he hadn't graded leniently, he'd challenged them to do their best.

They hadn't let him down.

And yet, at the end of the day, a sense of sadness overcame him. He knew why:

He already missed Audrey.

She was there, but she wasn't. Like the other seniors, Audrey's mind was focused on what lay ahead of her in the coming months. She'd gotten accepted to five universities, including her first choice: Berkeley.

Yes, she still attended his seventh period class. And her papers were exemplary. She wasn't shy in class, either.

As for Debate Team, despite having lost the leadership position to Mandy, she threw herself into every assigned task. And, by sheer personality, Audrey was usurping her rival.

Mandy knew this too.

The junior was peeved about it. Egan could tell by the way she rolled her eyes whenever Audrey got up to give an argument.

And she never failed to fume when Audrey scored higher than her, which happened often.

Like the time, during a tight match against Lowell, when Audrey's rebuttals nudged AA to a winning score by a mere two points. Egan overheard Gemma declaring, "Audrey, girl—you're on fire! How do you do it?"

It's because Audrey puts in the hard work. She makes helpful suggestions to her teammates too, unlike Mandy, who thinks nothing of deriding them with caustic quips.

The question took Audrey by surprise. "We deserve it. It's our last year, so why not pull out all the stops?"

Gemma's head shook with her raucous laughter. "You are *way* too serious about this shit. It's those boots! Admit it. They're magic! Every time you wear them, we win."

Portia nodded solemnly. "I think so too."

"You see?" Gemma insisted. "No shame in that. We all need a little mojo, right?"

Egan's eyes dropped down to Audrey's feet. It was the first time he'd noticed that she was wearing Doc Martens.

Maybe she's like every other girl her age after all.

Even thinking that made him feel disloyal to her. He knew in his heart she was anything but average.

Mandy looked down at the boots. Furiously, she stormed out.

Considering the camaraderie that had developed between Audrey, Portia, and Gemma, Egan assumed Mandy's teammates were now regretting their choice of leader.

As for Egan? Yes, he rued the day he'd cast that tie-breaking vote.

Only Jeremy got applause from Mandy.

Grudgingly, Egan had to admit that sometimes it was deserved. Jeremy hadn't given up on impressing Audrey. Instead, he'd realized that Debate Team was the best way to win her respect. And now that football season was over, he was focusing all his energies there.

His hard work was paying off. Of the team's individual scores, he came in third behind Audrey and Portia.

Anyone can see that Mandy has Jeremy in her sites, Egan thought. *Heck, the way she licks her lips whenever he's within reach, you'd think he was a pork chop.*

Jeremy was clueless enough to appreciate Mandy's syrupy accolades. He always made it a point to turn to Audrey to see if she heard it too.

If Audrey did, she ignored it. To Jeremy's dismay, she ignored him too.

Egan didn't know what exactly had happened between Jeremy and Audrey that day in the locker room. He only knew that whatever it was, it had hurt Audrey.

Since then, she'd disdained her old boyfriend. But she still nursed the pain of the event. Egan wished he could comfort Audrey, with words if not with a hug.

But because he couldn't, he did the next best thing: take Mandy down a notch, whenever possible.

"Mandy, as much as we all admire your ability to think before speaking, perhaps you should consider studying the topic instead of just winging it..." he'd say. Or, "Gee Mandy, don't be so hard on yourself! I'm sure that whatever you did last night instead of working on your arguments was worth it, even if you did let your teammates down."

Thankfully, Mandy's lack of leadership skills didn't stop her teammates from working even harder. Otherwise, Ashbury Academy wouldn't be representing its district in the state finals.

Mandy is darned lucky they want to win so badly, Egan thought. *Otherwise, they'd ask that she be exiled from the team. In fact, maybe I should suggest it before I find out what ounce of flesh she covets from me.*

Egan was quite aware that Mandy's sugary compliments were leading up to something. He wished she'd just come out with whatever it was so that he could only say, "No."

He'd savor that moment.

He hoped it happened in front of Audrey so that he'd see her laugh again.

"Debate Eight: are we ready for this weekend's tournament?" Egan shouted.

"YES, WE ARE!" His team shouted back.

For the most part.

Although Audrey kept her mouth shut, for a second it looked as if her eyes were twinkling at his antics.

"Great!" Egan exclaimed. "There will be six rounds, total. The first two are topics we know, and therefore may prepare for, but the third round is not. Round four also allows for prep, but rounds five and six are impromptu. Here are the debate topics."

When the students had finished copying what he wrote on the board, he continued: "For the impromptu rounds, we only get an hour to prep. For those rounds, your duties are as follows." He tapped the blackboard with each point: "The Kennedy twins will pull raw data, which they will then hand off to Johnny, Gemma, and Mandy. They in turn will assess the pros and cons, then create talking points based on the data team's statistical notes, handing everything over to Portia, Jeremy, and Audrey, who will write the opening arguments."

Egan had thought long and hard about assigning Jeremy and Audrey the final task. When it came to opening arguments, Audrey's strength was evident in her scores, which were the highest on the team. Portia's came in second. Jeremy's improvements had earned him the third highest score.

Mandy bristled.

Egan ignored the signs of an impending tantrum. He anticipated a bigger one with what he had to say next. *It may not be well received, but it was for the good of the team.*

"The tournament takes place at Beverly Hills High," he continued. "We leave on Friday from AA, eight o'clock sharp. Cornell and Odette are joining me as your chaperones. We'll be driving in two cars. I've rented a van for the men. The girls will caravan with us in Odette's car."

"I for one am glad for that," Gemma declared. "I've noticed that men can't control their farts during long car trips."

The Kennedy twins snickered and high-fived each other.

Egan rolled his eyes. "Continuing with more pertinent information, folks: teammates will bunk in twos. For the boys, that's the Kennedys in one room and Johnny and Jeremy in the other. For the girls, Portia and Gemma will share, as will Audrey and Mandy."

Jeremy sunk deep into his seat.

Both girls' eyes grew large. At the same time, they raised their hands and shouted, *"Excuse me?"*

Egan's way of girding for the impending battle was to honor them with a grin. "That's all for now, team. Those of you with questions are welcome to stay behind."

"NO WAY AM I SHARING A ROOM WITH AUDREY!" MANDY'S SQUAWK COULD BE heard all the way down the hall.

Audrey's anger came out in her hands, which were flexing.

At least they're not around Mandy's neck, Egan thought. Well, not yet, anyway.

"Why not?" Egan asked calmly.

Mandy's eyes narrowed. "No reason—other than I have it on good authority that *she snores.*"

Angered, Audrey clenched her fists tightly to her side.

She's doing her best not to blow up at the little bitch, Egan realized. Scoffing, he declared, "Mandy, that's just silly."

Mandy crossed her arms on her abdomen. "I'm serious, Egan! I mean… Well, *come on, already!*"

"I'm serious too," he retorted.

"Cut it out," she countered. When he didn't fold, she grimaced. "How dare you! Just who do you think you are?"

He snickered at her audacity. "Maybe you've forgotten I'm your teacher."

Mandy smiled sweetly. "No. Quite frankly, Mr. Gable, *you are not.*" Her gaze drifted to Audrey as if they shared some sort of secret.

But the look on Audrey's face showed that she was just as appalled by Mandy's behavior as him.

That's it. I've got to put Mandy in her place.

Coolly, he murmured, "You're right. I'm not. But I am running Debate Team. And, as of now, I view you more as a liability than an asset. So, if I were you, Mandy, I'd drop this. *The topic is closed.*" He leaned against the wall as if daring her to argue.

With a toddler's cadence, she pouted, "Well, then I wouldn't want to make 'teacher' mad. He might put me in the corner."

Egan glowered at her. *That's it, you little—*

"Okay, listen, I'm sorry. Truly, I am." Mandy shrugged. "I'm willing to bet that Audrey feels the same way. I mean—us, sharing a room? It's ludicrous! At the very least, it'll shake our confidence. At the very most, it may cost us the tournament. Am I right?"

Audrey acquiesced with an involuntary blink.

"Let me propose an easy fix," Mandy continued. "My stepfather can pay for a room of my own. So, why not let him? That way, it's not an expense for the school, and both Audrey and I get a good night's sleep before the tournament."

She's got a point. Maybe it's the best solution.

Egan nodded slowly. "Okay, sure. That works—as long as you get clearance from Lavinia."

"No problem," she purred.

She turned on her heel and went out the door, slamming it behind her.

IT WOULD BE EASY FORGING LAVINIA'S SIGNATURE, MANDY REASONED. HELL, the woman put it on every school missive, even her personal notes to students congratulating them on their academic achievements and improvements.

Mandy's plan: to either celebrate or commiserate AA's showing with Jeremy.

Frankly, she didn't care about the results. Being the captain of a state-finalist debate team—*in her junior year, no less!*—had already catapulted her to the front of the pack.

Despite Mandy and Jeremy's numerous and robust sexploits (after the book heist in the girl's locker room, Mandy caught on quickly that it might be a perfect place for some afternoon delight), she'd noticed that Jeremy's eye was wandering again.

He certainly had a type: lithe, brunette, and big-breasted.

I'm batting one for three, she thought.

It gnawed at Mandy's ego that he refused to admit publicly that they were an item. She blamed Audrey for that.

He still thinks he can win her over, Mandy seethed. *Well, I know how to kill that dream once and for all.*

Just as galling was Audrey's habit of wearing Mandy's stolen boots to every match. Mandy assumed it was Audrey's way at unnerving her; to take her off her game.

And, if Mandy were to be honest with herself, she'd admit it had worked.

Yet another reason to get Jeremy to profess his love for Mandy to the whole world.

And to Audrey.

Mandy's plan was simple. On the eve of the debate, she'd wait until the rest of the students and chaperones were in bed, and then she'd sneak Jeremy into her private suite. But before they got down and dirty, they'd partake in a few recreational drugs—at a minimum some pot. Little by little, she'd stolen some primo grass from Simon's secret stash—again, in his tighty-whitey drawer. Apparently, the dude was a creature of habit.

She'd also found some hashish. When she rolled the joints, she'd be sure to sprinkle it into them before they lit up.

After Jeremy passed out, she'd pose him on top of her and take an artsy photo that would look as if they were making love. She'd already stolen Simon's new digital camera. Their house was cluttered with all the latest and greatest gadgets. She knew he'd never miss it.

If, after LA, Jeremy still refused to be seen in public with her, she'd show him the picture and threaten to tell Lavinia that he'd raped her while they were at the debate tournament. That would scare the shit out of him. Admissions letters had arrived just last week. The last thing he needed was for the six colleges that offered him a place to withdraw their offers, not to mention his football scholarships.

She'd warn Jeremy he'd have to agree to stay her boyfriend through the summer. By the fall, she'll allow him to tell others she'd kicked him to the curb. By then, her popularity would be sealed.

She could then focus on the recommendation to Berkeley from Egan.

But Mandy would have to move fast. She could see the writing on the wall. Egan was already tiring of her shenanigans. It was all too obvious in his snide observations about her toward her teammates.

Blackmail would do the trick.

Still, everyone had a weak spot. Like a wild hog hunting morels buried deep in some primordial forest, she'd rut out Egan's dirty little secrets and then threaten to expose them if he refused to give her a recommendation letter.

It would be even more fun than making Jeremy come to heel.

But nothing would top the fun of taking Audrey down.

Before the end of the school year, she'd figure some way to accomplish that too.

EGAN HADN'T EXPECTED TO BE LEFT ALONE WITH AUDREY.

With the door closed.

His heart ached to tell her what he was thinking:

That he loved her, but he knew it would be wrong to act on every impulse he had—to tease her, to kiss her, *to love her*—until one of them was gone from AA.

Until both of them were mature enough to handle their feelings.

Because he never wanted to hurt her, ever.

She was the first woman—*girl*—for whom he'd felt that way.

Which was why he kept his mouth shut.

It seemed like an eternity before Audrey finally spoke: "I have something to tell you—"

"No... don't. *Please!*" He shook his head. He couldn't bear the thought of hearing her profess her love to him.

Audrey stammered, "No.. *NO!* You don't understand what I'm going to say—"

"I do, Audrey! Believe me, I do!" Without thinking, he placed his hand on her arm.

The touch of her skin sent jolts of desire charging through him.

She stiffened as if she felt it too.

And then she pulled away. Before she hung her head, she closed her eyes, as if shamed.

No, worse: *revolted.*

What if I'm wrong, he thought. What if she's not professing her love? What if she wants to tell me she hates me?

For toying with her. And then...

Nothing.

It's true, he reasoned. Audrey has every right to hate me. For making her life so miserable.

She can't understand why it has to be this way.

He jerked his hand back. As if to stop feeling her touch—to stop all feeling for her—he shoved it in his pocket.

AUDREY WANTED TO TELL HIM EVERYTHING:

About how she changed Mandy's schedule so that she could take the younger girl's place in Egan's class.

How Mandy had stolen her library book; and how, in retaliation, Audrey had stolen it back, along with Mandy's shoes.

Most of all, Audrey wanted to warn him about Mandy. The heart drawn around his photo worried her. Even scarier was seeing how Mandy had treated Egan just now:

Not as a teacher, but as her equal.

Mandy had acted as if she were spatting with her boyfriend. As if she were looking forward to kissing and making up...

The thought was so revolting that Audrey shivered.

But if I tell him why Mandy hates me, he'll think I'm jealous—or worse!

He'll think I'm just as conniving as Mandy for having changed my schedule to get into his class.

Because I care about him.

But if it's true and he's fallen for her, then he doesn't still care for me.

And I'm embarrassing him…

Oh my God! Egan and…

Mandy?

Fuck it! After all this time…

After all that's happened?

Frustrated, she threw up her hands, and cried, "Why are you doing this to me?"

———

BECAUSE I CARE ABOUT YOU, EGAN THOUGHT.

That was the problem: he cared too much.

Not that he could say that to her.

Not now. Not wondering if she'd already moved on.

Not if she *disdained* him.

Instead, Egan shrugged.

"Okay, right. Got it," Audrey muttered.

As she flung open the door, he flinched, anticipating the door to slam shut again.

But no. What he heard instead was the click of Audrey's heels as she walked away.

She wasn't Mandy. She had too much regard—too much *love*—for Ashbury Academy to abuse the fine old building.

Egan told himself: You did the right thing by letting her walk away.

No matter how much he wanted to believe it, he couldn't.

CHAPTER 12

"*L*adies, which one of you wants to ride shotgun?" Odette's invitation was met with noncommittal mutters from Audrey, Gemma, and Portia. Urban legend had it that the breakneck speed in which Odette took the city's streets had been the reason there were stop signs on every corner of San Francisco's residential neighborhoods.

Gemma and Portia scrambled into the back seat. When Mandy attempted to follow, they blocked her. "You're the captain," Gemma pointed out. "You get the honor of sitting up front."

"And besides, we promised Audrey she could sit in the middle," Portia added.

Mandy knew it was a lie; that they didn't want to sit with her. No problem. For once she hoped the rumors about Odette's driving were true. If Audrey barfed all over the others, justice would be served.

She glanced over at Audrey, who was locked in a farewell embrace with Lavinia.

My God, you'd think we were going to the ends of the earth and never coming back, she thought. It's just LA! Get over it!

At that moment, her eye caught Lavinia's. The headmistress smiled. She raised the hand that was stroking Audrey's hair to wave at Mandy.

Slowly, Mandy waved back.

That Audrey had Lavinia as a mom was yet one more reason for Mandy to hate her.

"I wish you all the luck in the world," Lavinia whispered.

Audrey smiled. "We're excited. I feel we're prepped. We won't let down the school."

Lavinia chuckled. "This isn't about the school. It's about you and your team. For the next seventy-two hours, you are all one and the same. You must look after each other."

Audrey looked skyward. "I wish we all felt that way."

"Let me guess. Mandy?"

Audrey nodded. "How did you know?"

"I didn't. But I suspected." Lavinia shrugged. "She just needs a large dose of kindness—and a little space."

"Well, then it's a good thing you signed off on her private room."

Lavinia pulled back, surprised. "What? I didn't…"

At that moment, she moved her gaze beyond Audrey, toward Odette's car.

Finally, she looked back at her daughter. "Whatever happens, happens. Things have a habit of sorting themselves out."

And that's how Audrey knew Mandy had lied to Egan about getting permission for a room of her own.

"HERE YOU GO: KEYS FOR SEVEN ROOMS, ALL ON THE THIRD FLOOR." THE front desk clerk at the Beverly Rexford handed Egan five bundles of keys, two for each room.

"I know we reserved seven rooms, but really, we'll need *eight*," Egan explained.

"Okay…" the desk clerk tapped her computer keyboard. Satisfied with what she saw, she turned to grab an additional key. "It's on the floor below the others. Room 204."

"That'll do," Mandy replied breezily.

"No, it won't," Egan said firmly.

He was exhausted and hungry. The drive down Interstate 5 was long and tiring—over six hours trying to keep pace with Odette, who drove like a bat out of hell. Not to mention the lunch break at some place renowned for its pea soup (not his favorite), and then the numerous bathroom stops along the way. "Perhaps you can move all of us so that we're on the same floor?"

The Debate Eight groaned. They were getting antsy. "Take the keys already," Johnny muttered in frustration.

The front desk clerk shrugged apologetically at Egan. "No, sorry, sir. The three other rooms on that floor are currently occupied. In fact, the only vacant room in the hotel is this one." She held up the key stamped 204.

Mandy snatched it out of the clerk's hand. "Thanks. The second-floor room is fine."

Egan plucked it from Mandy's fingers. "It'll go to one of the chaperones."

The clerk's mouth dropped open.

Gemma nudged Portia and mouthed, *What the Hell?*

Mandy clawed it out of Egan's fingers. Then, to make the decision final, she dropped it down the front of her sweater, into her bra. "I insist. I'm afraid of heights, so the second floor is perfect."

By now, everyone in the lobby was watching them.

Egan shook his head, resigned to this *fait-accompli*. "Okay. Fine." He turned to the front desk clerk. "I didn't bring a leash long enough, or one of those electronic ankle monitors. But I assume you have video cameras on every floor?"

She nodded.

"Good, then. Hand me an extra key for 204."

The clerk did as ordered.

Egan tossed it to Odette. She caught it with one hand but was frowning.

"Thank you." Egan turned to Mandy. "Expect a call to your room every half hour. And you'd better pick up, or Odette will barge in."

Egan's threat got an eye roll from Odette.

Mandy shrugged.

After Egan handed out the other keys, he explained: "Okay, gang, let's drop our things in our rooms, then grab a bite to eat." He glanced at his watch. "Meet back in the lobby in half an hour. Afterward, let's do a quick rehearsal on the pre-assigned topics." He turned to the clerk. "Is there a small conference room in this hotel?"

She nodded. "Yes. It's where we serve breakfast every morning. It's open until midnight, but after eight at night, it's usually empty."

"Good." He nodded to the students. "When we get back from dinner, we'll meet there."

Everyone nodded then stampeded to the elevator. But too much luggage and too many bodies meant that not everyone could ride up together.

Audrey and Egan were left behind.

Neither spoke as they waited for the elevator, and they rode up in silence too.

When the elevator came to their floor, Egan held back so that Audrey could get her luggage out first. As she made her way down the hall, he realized their rooms were adjacent.

When he entered his room, he saw that they shared an adjoining door.

He groaned.

Then he took a shower.

———

THE FUCKING WALLS IN THIS PLACE ARE PAPER THIN, MANDY GRUMBLED. SHE could hear the guy in the next room chatting—or, to her mind, practically yelling—into his phone.

Like an idiot, she'd forgotten to take her MP3 player. Mandy had no way to tune out the jerk while she laid out the items needed to make Jeremy hers, once and for all: matching black lace panties and bra, rolling papers, a plastic sandwich bag filled with Mendocino Gold, a knob of hashish…

And a square plastic tab of LSD stamped with cartoon dancing elephants.

When she found it in Simon's stash, at first she hesitated to take it. But there were several in there, so she figured he'd never miss it.

Mandy smoked pot. She knew Jeremy toked a joint every now and then too. But LSD would be a new experience for both of them.

Would that spice up their sex? Mandy hoped so. Her plans for greatness depended on her ability to hang onto Jeremy at all costs.

Mandy took out Simon's digital camera and placed it on the dresser facing the bed. She'd read the camera's manual to learn how to use its timer. As a test, she set it and then she fell onto the bed, posing erotically while it snapped away.

When she felt she'd had enough, she flipped through the shots.

Yep, that would do just fine.

She was wondering how she might slip Jeremy into her room when she heard the guy in the next room say, "Yes, tell him I'm one of the other debate judges… the one from Kansas… Thanks, I'll wait."

Mandy froze.

His next sentence included "…the impromptu debate topics? Yeah, they were given to me just before I left for the airport. I'll read them to you. Just give me a second so that I can grab my ThinkPad—"

Mandy noticed a couple of drinking glasses on the room's desk. She grabbed one, along with a hotel notepad and a pen, then ran back to the wall closest to the judge's room. There, she put the glass against the wall, then placed her ear against the glass.

"Yep, got it." The man's voice sounded more distinct. "Are you ready?"

This old spy trick really works, Mandy marveled.

"Round three impromptu topic: 'All US municipalities should install closed-circuit cameras to assist national security…'" The man's voice got louder. "Yes, closed circuit cameras… *national security*. Heard that? Good. Okay, now for round five impromptu: 'Food nutrition labeling should include added sugars and fats'… Yeah, I know, as if that'll stop kids from eating junk food, right?… Ha! Okay, and the round six impromptu: "'If a death sentence appeal is unreasonably delayed, the criminal's sentence should be commuted to life in prison.' Got it?… Okay great! Looking forward to seeing you tomorrow as well…"

Mandy almost squealed at her luck, but then realized if she could hear the judge, he could probably hear her too.

I can't wait to tell Jeremy. We can get a head start on our research and actually win this thing. We'll look like geniuses to the others —

And Jeremy will be so appreciative that he'll finally forget all about Audrey.

Finally.

CHAPTER 13

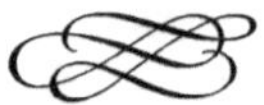

$\mathcal{M}$andy made sure she was the first of their group to reach the lobby. A different desk clerk was there.

Good, Mandy thought.

She held up her key to the woman. "My roommate needs a key of her own. Room 204."

The clerk smiled and nodded. A moment later, Mandy had the additional key. She planned to give it to Jeremy.

She slipped it into her purse and made her way back to the elevator to wait for the others. And just in time too, because when the doors opened, she found herself facing Egan. She saluted him.

He seemed surprised to see her. "How long have you been waiting?"

"Just a minute or two. I didn't want you to think I was dawdling in my luxurious accommodations." She winked seductively. "Come on up and see me some time."

Egan looked at the ceiling as if the right answer were scribbled up there, somewhere. "You seem to enjoy skating on thin ice, Mandy. But a word of warning: don't push me."

Before she could retort, the elevator opened, and the rest of their team surrounded them. Audrey and Jeremy were the last to get off the elevator. Jeremy seemed to be in the middle of saying something to her. The moment they realized they weren't alone, he zipped his lip.

This has got to stop, Mandy fumed.

"We're starving, coach! So, where do we go for grub?" Johnny asked.

"How about Hamburger Hamlet on Sunset?" Mandy purred. Seeing Egan's frown, she added, "My treat! I am team captain after all. And besides, my stepdad invested in it. They'll treat us well."

Odette and Cornell slapped hands.

Egan got the message: Mandy was getting her way.

He only has eyes for her, Audrey thought.

She tried to keep her focus on what Gemma was saying—something about a strategy to unnerve their opponents—but her eyes and thoughts kept shifting to Egan.

Apparently, his gaze and his thoughts were on Mandy.

It's eating at Egan that Mandy is practically climbing into Jeremy's lap, she thought miserably. That's why he's on his third Scotch.

While ordering, Egan had waved off the waiter's question as to what he might like to drink. Nodding toward the others, he replied. "Thanks, but no thanks. We're just here for a quick bite before hitting the books."

"*We* aren't hitting the books." Odette reminded him.

Egan shrugged. "Okay, sure, go for it."

She sighed, relieved. "Dirty martini! A double."

"I'll second that," Cornell added quickly as if he were afraid that Egan might change his mind.

While the other teachers were reminding Egan of his promise of free time, the waiter took the students' orders. It wasn't until the waiter popped a bottle of champagne beside their table that Egan realized it was meant for them.

"Who ordered this?" he asked the man.

The waiter nodded toward Mandy.

"Send it back," Egan commanded.

"But…" The waiter's glance pleaded with Mandy to intervene.

"Really?" she countered. "You don't want us to celebrate that AA's Debate Eight made it to the finals?"

A chorus of protests rose from the table.

"No!… Okay, well…" Egan turned to the waiter. Shrugging, he muttered, "Go ahead, leave it."

The man nodded, placing the bottle in front of Egan, who poured himself enough for a couple of sips and did the same for Odette and Cornell.

Turning to Gemma, he said, "Pass it forward, but only *this* much." He placed two fingers horizontally to indicate an inch each.

The kids groaned.

But when Egan turned his back to say something to Cornell, Mandy grabbed the bottle from Gemma and poured herself a generous portion. She then passed the bottle to Jeremy, who did the same.

In a flash the other students followed suit.

In due time, Egan reached for the champagne bottle to give Odette a refill, only to find it empty. He scowled at Mandy, but it was too late, and he knew it. He had to resign himself to the reality that the students were determined to have little fun.

Or, if Mandy was any example, *a lot* of fun.

Mandy knows flirting with Jeremy is the best way to get Egan's attention, Audrey reasoned.

At that moment, she felt sad for all three of them.

"Have you heard a word I've said?" Gemma grumbled.

"Everything," Audrey lied. "And I think you're spot on." *Might as well join the club,* she thought, as she took a sip of her champagne.

"Wow! Thanks!" Gemma beamed. She lifted her glass. "Well, here's to bringing home the winner's cup!"

"I'll drink to that," Audrey murmured.

It's as big a fantasy as Egan coming to his senses, but hell, why not?

She swallowed her bubbly in one gulp.

Once again, Mandy signaled the waiter to bring another bottle of champagne.

And, once again, he placed it directly in front of Egan.

BY THE TIME THE MEAL WAS OVER, THE WHOLE TABLE WAS TIPSY.

Jeremy's eyelids, half-shut from drink, suddenly opened wide.

Perhaps it had something to do with Mandy's hand in his lap.

His mind was too hazy to convince the rest of him that hardening to her touch was not what he wanted. Not if he were to impress Audrey.

But it wasn't just Mandy's hand in his lap. He looked down to find a key there too.

Mandy leaned in and whispered, "I have a special surprise waiting for you in my room."

His eyes drifted to Audrey. He was surprised to see she was staring back. He knew her well enough to read her face:

Loser.

Oh, yeah? You think so?

Well then, damn it, girl! Fuck you!

Or better yet, fuck Mandy.

He patted Mandy's hand before grinding it into his crotch. "Sure. Can't wait."

Gleefully, Mandy signaled the waiter for the check.

DESPITE EGAN'S PROTESTATIONS, CORNELL INSISTED HE TAKE THE PASSENGER seat. "This time, I'm driving."

The boys, loose-limbed and giggling, stumbled into the van.

Not surprisingly, Odette beat them to the hotel.

When they entered the lobby, it was empty. "I guess the girls went up to their rooms," one of the Kennedy twins deduced.

"Great, then we're off the hook for practice!" The other twin exclaimed. Snickering, he staggered into the elevator.

The others followed—

Except for Jeremy. Seemingly out of nowhere, Mandy was at his side. She shoved him out of the sightline of the elevator doors, shushing him with a kiss.

They waited for the chime that told them the elevator had started its ascent, then took the fire stairwell to the second floor.

Only Audrey, Gemma, and Portia were sober enough to show up for the strategy session in the conference room. After waiting a half hour, Portia asked, "Shouldn't we call Egan to see where he is?"

Gemma snorted. "Where do you *think* he is, silly?"

A horrible thought came to Audrey: Mandy's room?

To rid herself of that possibility, she muttered, "He's sleeping it off."

"If we're going to have half a chance of any sort of showing, maybe we should go to bed too, so that we can get up early," Portia suggested. "After a good night's sleep, the others may be sober enough to review our debate strategy."

Fat chance, Audrey thought.

She rode up in the elevator with the others but waited until they closed their room's door, pausing in front of Egan's suite.

She knocked.

No answer.

Audrey hoped Gemma was right: that he was sleeping it off. But the thought crossed her mind that he wasn't in there at all.

That maybe he was with Mandy.

CHAPTER 14

"So, what's your big surprise?" Jeremy slurred his words. The room was spinning around. He wasn't a big wine drinker. Beer was his libation of choice. He'd always assumed it had more alcohol content. If the goal was to get drunk, sooner was better, right?

He now realized that perhaps overcompensating for any perceived difference may have been the wrong thing to do.

Mandy waved the baggie of pot in front of his face. "I brought us something so that we can have a *real* party. You know, have some fun so that we're mellow and focused for the debate tomorrow. Isn't that what all you athletes do?"

Jeremy snickered. "Bang it out before a game? Nah. Just the opposite. We save all that pent-up energy for when we're on the field." He flopped down on her bed, falling on his back.

"That seems ass-backward to me." Mandy argued. "And besides, we're going to be sitting on our asses, not huffing and puffing out on the field. We want to be *ZEN*." She picked up the LSD tab. "That's what this is for."

Jeremy tried to focus his eyes. "What the hell is that?"

"It's… a sex enhancer." Mandy arched her brows. "What do you say we try some?"

He nodded uncertainly. It took very little to arouse him. A couple of perky breasts coming into view usually did the trick. But the champagne seemed to zap his mojo.

Yeah, a sex enhancer sounded just right. He'd hate for her to spread rumors that he couldn't get it up.

MANDY OPENED THE BAG OF POT. AFTER SORTING THE LEAVES FROM THE STEMS and seeds, she rolled it up, nice and tight.

She lit the joint with a match and took a long drag on it. She held in the hot vapors until she thought her lungs would explode before releasing it with a sigh.

Jeremy was still on his back, oblivious to her attempt to hand him the joint. Mandy looked for somewhere to put it, but since it was a non-smoking room, there wasn't an ashtray in sight. She settled for resting it on the nightstand, hanging its lit end over the edge so that the ashes would flicker to the floor.

Now for that LSD tab.

Mandy reached for it but paused before cutting it open. How much of this should we ingest, she wondered. Since there's two of us, splitting the tab should make it safer.

She didn't really know what she was doing, so she improvised. Grabbing a water glass, she emptied the tab into it, filled it with water, and then stirred it with one of the plastic spoons beside the coffee maker.

Mandy giggled. "Here I come, big boy." Humming, she began a strip-tease: ripping the buttons off her shirt and shimmying out of her jeans. After yanking off her panties, she threw them at Jeremy's face.

They landed on his head. He held them to his nose and sniffed. "Nice," he murmured.

"Hey, look this way! You're missing the show!" To make her point, Mandy unhooked her bra and twirled it over her head.

AS FAR AS JEREMY COULD TELL, THERE WERE THREE MANDYS DANCING IN front of him. "Which one of you should I bang first?"

As she froze, the bra went flying. It hit the wall with a soft thud.

"What do you mean, 'which one of us?'" She shoved Jeremy so hard that he almost fell off the bed. "Who do you think is here with us? Perhaps your crush, Audrey? Is that what you want, a *threesome*?"

Dazed and confused, Jeremy looked around. "Audrey—is here?"

"No, you moron! She's not!" Mandy reached down and cupped him.

He lifted his head to follow her gaze to his crotch. Noting her scowl, he muttered, "Maybe we should try that, um, sex enhancer."

"YEAH, MAYBE THAT'LL GET YOU HARD—*FOR ME*." FURIOUS, SHE ROSE FROM the bed and grabbed the LSD-laced water glass. "Here, drink this."

Nodding meekly, he did as he was told.

"All of it," Mandy barked.

She shoved him back down on the mattress. Naked, she walked to the dresser and flicked on the camera, already set to click continually. It was snapping away even before she leaped onto the bed.

Jeremy's eyes were closed. Had he passed out?

If so, even better.

Mandy straddled him, then placed one of his hands on her ass and the other on her breast. Next, she lifted his head so that it looked as if they were kissing. She then rolled him over so that he was on top of her, entwining his leg with hers. She stared at the camera with a look of terror.

She was moving into different damsel-in-distress poses when Jeremy's eyes flew open. Horrified, he scrambled around the bed, knocking over everything on the nightstand before tumbling to the floor. Leaping to his feet, he shouted, "The colors… so many! And *shit*! *Why are there monsters?*"

"What?… What's wrong with you?" Mandy's fear was real now.

Jeremy ignored her. Frenzied, he dropped to his knees, circling the room on all fours, all the while screaming, "Don't let them eat me! *Don't let them eat me!*"

Suddenly, he came to the open balcony door. Mutely, he rose, mesmerized by the street lamp beyond.

Before Mandy knew what was happening, he rushed out the door and leaped off the balcony.

Mandy screamed as she ran after him. Petrified, she stared down at his broken body on the ground below.

Until she smelled something burning.

Jeremy had knocked the joint onto the sheet.

The bedspread was on fire.

CHAPTER 15

*E*gan groaned and covered his ears. What was that infernal ringing?
It dawned on him that it was the telephone.

He stuck out his hand, but he aimed too low because it smacked into the nightstand.

The pain, coupled with his own scream, sobered him up.

He fumbled for the phone, only to knock the receiver to the floor. At least then he could hear Mandy sobbing, "I think I killed him! And... There was a fire!"

"Killed... *who?... A fire?"*

"Yes! In my room! I managed to put it out, but the smell—"

Egan didn't answer her. Instead, he stumbled to his feet and ran out the door.

By the time he hit the stairwell, he realized he'd slept in his clothes.

At least I'm not naked, he thought.

If only the same thing could be said for Jeremy.

From Mandy's balcony, Egan stared down at the kid. Thank God he'd landed on the lawn instead of asphalt. And he was mumbling incoherently, so at least he was still alive.

Mandy was making excuses quicker than Egan could ingest them. Thank goodness she'd had the good sense to throw on a hotel robe, Egan thought.

He started for the door. "Call an ambulance—*now!"*

"But... *what if they put me in jail?"*

"They won't, but only because he's not dead! Not *yet,* anyway." Egan didn't wait for the elevator but took the fire stairwell instead.

A few minutes later, he heard the ambulance. The night manager must have heard it too because he joined Egan as he went out and explained the situation to the emergency med techs: that Jeremy had somehow gotten drunk and fallen off the balcony.

"Jeez! It's our third drunk-dropping tonight." The lead emergency med tech rolled his eyes. "By the way, we're taking him to Cedars Sinai."

"I'll be right behind you," Egan replied.

But first, he'd have to let Cornell and Odette know what was up so that they could look after the other kids.

And he'd have to call Lavinia and explain everything: how Jeremy and the other students got drunk on champagne. Worse yet, that Jeremy had ended up in Mandy's room and somehow fallen off her balcony.

And how Mandy had set her bed on fire.

Mandy hasn't the decency to ask to go with me, Egan realized. She's some piece of work.

Despite everything else, she was his first order of business.

As he walked back into the hotel, he looked up at Mandy's room. He could see her silhouetted behind the curtain, peeking out.

"THE GUY YOU'VE BEEN CHASING ALL YEAR FALLS OFF YOUR BALCONY AND YOU can't even find it in your heart to check his pulse?"

Mandy flinched at Egan's question. "I can't stand the sight of blood!"

"He could have died," Egan retorted.

"Don't blame me," she screamed. "You're our chaperone!"

Egan looked down at Mandy's bed. He could tell where the fire had started. The veneer of the nightstand was blackened. The bedspread and sheets below it now sported a large burn hole. The remnant of a plastic bag was singed to the scorched mattress. The few twigs in it that hadn't burned up contained what was left of Mandy's stash.

He threw up his hands. "You were smoking pot too? Well, that's just dandy!"

Mandy shrugged. "So I made a little mess. Big whoop! My stepdad will pay for the damage."

"You bet he will," Egan growled. He started for the door.

"Wait a minute, you!" Mandy was nearly hysterical. "I can't sleep here tonight! This place smells like a pot house!"

"Gee, I wonder why?" Egan retorted. "Too bad. The hotel is sold out. You know that."

Mandy shook her head. "Don't start that bullshit about bunking with Audrey."

"You little pyromaniac! I wouldn't dream of putting you in the same room with her!"

"Of course you wouldn't," Mandy spat back. "You wouldn't want to lose your job because you helped me over Lavinia's *precious baby*."

Egan flinched.

Don't show her you care.

Instead, he tossed her his room key. "Room 302. I'll be spending the night at the hospital anyway—with Jeremy."

Mandy huffed out.

Egan looked around the room. He'd have to let the hotel manager know what happened.

Later. Much later. Check-out, for sure.

He threw the bedding into the bathtub and turned on the water. The mattress was salvageable. He'd flip it over so that the scorch mark wouldn't be seen. The sheets, though, were ruined. But it was still possible to mask the smell of pot before checkout on Sunday.

When he got back into the bedroom, he knew he should check around to see if she'd left any drugs lying around.

He went down on his hands and knees, scanning the floor around the nightstand. The culprit—a charred doobie—was under the bed.

So was the torn LSD tab.

Oh…hell.

He didn't want to touch it with his fingers, so he plucked a Kleenex from the box on the desk, folded it around the tab, and stuck it in his pocket.

A hotel memo pad sat beside the tissue box. He glanced at the notes Mandy had written on it:

Round 3 IMPROMPTU: All US municipalities should install closed-circuit cameras to assist national security.

Round 5 IMPROMPTU: Food nutrition labeling should include added sugars and fats.

Round 6 IMPROMPTU: If a death sentence appeal is unreasonably delayed, the criminal's sentence should be commuted to life in prison.

My God, he wondered. Where did she get this?

Just for a moment, the thought of using the intel from her dirty sleuthing crossed his mind, but he shrugged it away. Cheating isn't a victory, he reasoned. It's an opportunity for shame.

He went back into the bathroom, shredded the notes, and flushed them down the toilet.

When he walked back into the bedroom, he noticed the camera on the dresser. It was positioned in such a way that he deduced it had been used to take pictures of Mandy and Jeremy's sexual acrobatics.

Egan clicked through its digital photo archive. It was like fanning a picture book about Mandy's dirty deeds. This didn't shock so much as sadden him.

What was she trying to do, blackmail Jeremy?

If so, why?

One by one, he deleted the photos.

She's done enough damage to the poor kid, he reasoned. To all of us.

Before Egan left the room, he rummaged through Mandy's suitcase to make sure there wasn't anything else that could incriminate her, but only because he knew it would ruin the reputation of the school.

He respected Lavinia too much for that.

THE AMBULANCE'S SIREN ROUSED AUDREY FROM HER SLUMBER. THE CHIME OF the elevator stymied her attempt to fall back asleep. When she heard it a second time, she was curious enough to peek out her door to see who was walking about.

Egan's room was next door. She'd seen him come out of it when they left for dinner. When she realized their rooms shared an interior door, she fantasized about leaving it unlocked just to see if he'd try the knob. If so, and if he were bold enough to open the door, she'd finally know where she stood with him.

And she'd welcome him in.

But now Mandy stood in front of his room. In a bathrobe.

Mandy didn't knock because she didn't have to. She had a key.

Silently, Audrey shut her door.

Now I know the truth.

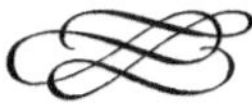

"Jeremy is where?" Gemma exclaimed.

The Debate Eight—now Seven—turned to stare at Mandy.

"You heard me," she sniffed blithely. "The hospital. I guess he couldn't hold his liquor."

"We shouldn't have been drinking anyway," Portia's voice trembled with anxiety. "And where's Egan?"

"He went with Jeremy," Mandy snapped. "So, we've lost our beloved coach. Big deal. Let's just keep our cool. Otherwise, we won't win this thing."

"Someone will have to take Jeremy's arguments!" Gemma pointed out.

"Duh. We can always count on you to state the obvious, can't we?" Mandy rolled her eyes. "As our captain, I say we—"

Johnny snickered. "Why should we listen to you? Seriously, Mandy, if it hadn't been for you trying to impress us—make that impress *Jeremy*—he'd be here now, and the rest of us wouldn't be nursing hangovers."

Bleary-eyed, the Kennedy twins hissed in unison, "Please! Keep your voices down!"

Exasperated, Johnny, declared, "I rest my case."

"Fine! I get it. You want me to be the scapegoat for why we're probably going to screw this up." Mandy stood up. "To hell with that! I'm taking a taxi out of this third-rate dump—"

"You'll do no such thing," Audrey said calmly. "As our captain, you have to lead us to victory...or whatever." She stood up. "We've got just two hours before we have to be at the tournament, so let's get to work." She turned to the others. "Debate rehearsal in Mandy's room, in five—"

"No!" Mandy exclaimed. "I mean..." She glared at Audrey. "You're not sharing a room with anyone either. Why don't we do it there instead?"

"Okay, whatever." Audrey shrugged. "By the way, did Egan tell you when he'd be back?"

"How would I know? You're the teacher's pet, not me," Mandy retorted. Sniffing, she added, "Okay, Audrey's room—*in five.*" She stalked off.

Audrey stared after her. *I'm teacher's pet?*

For a moment, it seemed as if her world had opened up again.

At least, her heart.

Toward Egan.

Where the hell are my notes?

Frantically, Mandy roamed through her room, looking for the sheet of paper with the impromptu debate topics mentioned by the loudmouth tournament judge.

Every drawer was thrown open. Every inch of the floor was searched on her hands and knees. She pulled the desk away from the wall in case it had fallen behind it.

She even upended her suitcase onto the stinky bed.

As a last resort, she looked in the bathroom.

A tiny scrap of something was floating in the toilet bowl. Tissue paper? No, it was lined note paper.

Desperate, she stuck her hand into the water and pulled it out.

Despite being smudged, she could make out one word:

IMPROMPTU

Mandy howled, "*Damn you, Egan!*"

She tried to recollect the impromptu topics: something about junk food... No, but sugar was involved...And national security... And the death penalty.

Mandy's head was hurting. She didn't particularly like champagne, and pot made her dizzy anyway. To make matters worse, whomever was next door to Egan had cried throughout the night.

So much for getting a good night's sleep before a tournament, Mandy groused. I guess football coaches aren't so stupid after all.

Screw it. Even if I'd mentioned the topics to the team, I'd have to lie about how I knew about them... Like, maybe say I'm psychic?

Nah. They're dweebs but they're not stupid.

She realized she'd be better off scrutinizing her room for other detrimental evidence Egan may have found.

Mandy's bedspread and sheets were soaking in the bathtub. The burn hole made her wince.

The bag of pot and the rolling papers were gone. She wasn't surprised, considering the fire. So was the torn tab that had held the LSD dose.

And the camera was in a different place on the dresser.

She grabbed it and tapped into the photo archive.

It was empty.

Damn it! Egan knows the truth about Jeremy!

Mandy didn't even try to stifle her giggles. "Touché, you son of a bitch," she crowed.

Then it occurred to her:

Before he can use it to get me tossed out of school, I've got to get something on him.

It should be easy. He's got such a big ego.

Just in case she had to make a quick getaway, she packed her things and rolled her luggage to the bag-check station.

With each other's help, the team honed in on the three publicly announced topics.

Everyone on AA's team was an orator and could think on their feet. The state winner would be chosen in the eighth round. Should the team make it through the first four rounds, everyone would have a chance to argue a pro and a con and give a rebuttal.

Throughout the practice session, Mandy kept her ego in check. No snide comments. No eye rolls. If she felt she had a stronger point than the ones offered by her colleagues, she spoke up. Otherwise, she listened and took notes.

As she suspected, Audrey filled in the leadership void.

Fine with me, Mandy thought. It's hers to lose. And if we win, I'm still officially the team's captain.

Jeremy's absence would cost them dearly. He had prepped the rebuttals for round one; and if AA were to make it into round five, he'd have been doing AA's pro argument, with Johnny on con, and Portia on rebuttal.

"Who can take his place?" Portia opined.

"Audrey," Johnny replied adamantly. "She's our strongest debater."

Like hell, Mandy thought.

But before she spoke, Audrey said, "I'm flattered. But we all have our strengths and weaknesses. Mandy seems to knock rebuttals out of the park, so she should sub for Jeremy in the first round." She met Mandy's eye. "Are you okay with that?"

Mandy shrugged. "Sure. I'll take Jeremy's place."

"And Audrey, you're our strongest in pro," Gemma pointed out. "If we make it to the fifth round, you'll replace him."

"But I just said—"

"Sure, I'll do it," Audrey declared, cutting Mandy off. Absently, she fiddled with the lace of her boot.

Mandy's boot.

Anger roiled through Mandy.

She did that to remind me how much she hates me. All the more reason I've got to win my match. Then it'll be up to Little Miss Goody Two Shoes to bring it home...

Or everyone will hate her.

Okay, yeah, that works for me.

WE'RE WINNING.

Audrey couldn't believe her team's luck.

Portia's pro argument in round one showcased her classic eloquence and Mandy's rebuttal cut the legs out from under their competitor.

In round two, Ashbury Academy pulled the con argument. Johnny pulled out all the stops, as did one of the Kennedy twins on rebuttal.

Round three's impromptu topic suggested that the country's cities should install CCTV for national security purposes. Considering that they only had an hour of prep time, the team followed Egan's plan in division of duties: the Kennedy twins pulled raw data, which was used by Mandy, Gemma, and Johnny to write first drafts of the pro, con, and rebuttal arguments, which were passed to Portia and Audrey for fine-tuning.

Audrey, assigned the pro argument, was glad to finally make it to the podium. Her statements, made clearly and elegantly, ruffled their opponents.

She was finishing up when Egan walked in. Though the house lights were dim and he stood in the back of the room, she could still make him out.

She'd know him anywhere.

This is for you, she thought.

She watched as his fist punched the air when the judges announced Ashbury Academy had won.

Egan ran up to the stage to make the group hug that enveloped her.

She reached over and took his hand.

It surprised her when he didn't pull away. In fact, he squeezed it tightly.

At that moment, Audrey's life was perfect.

"Tell us about Jeremy," Portia begged. Because round four's topic had been previously announced, she, like the others, was too curious to think about anything else.

"He's alive." Egan's bluntness made clear what he didn't want to say: If barely.

"Thank God," Audrey murmured. She turned to Johnny. "Were you asleep when it happened?'

"I guess so." Johnny paused as he tried to remember his sequence of events. "I was in the Kennedys' room for a couple of hours. They hooked up their Nintendo 64 to the TV. When I finally went into my room, I didn't even look to see if Jeremy was in his bed. I just dropped like a stone the minute my head hit the pillow."

"What does that matter?" Mandy hastily countered. "He had his own key, right?"

"Well, if he fell from our room, he must be a ghost," Johnny replied. "Our balcony door was shut."

Audrey let that sink in. Finally, she mused, "Doesn't your balcony face the parking lot? I thought he was found on the grass, which is on the other—"

"How he got there doesn't matter," Egan interjected. "I take full responsibility. This weekend, his health and safety, just like yours, was on my watch. To that end, Lavinia was informed of his injuries and I stayed with Jeremy until his parents could join him at his bedside."

Mandy smiled slyly at Egan.

She thinks I'm covering for her, Egan thought.

When she realized Audrey was watching, Mandy demurely dropped her gaze to her lap.

Egan frowned. "Round four starts in a few minutes. Let's give Gemma, Portia, and whichever Kennedy is up time for a run-through."

Audrey stood up and walked away.

Ah, hell, Egan thought. Audrey is smart enough to put two and two together.

But she's going to get it all wrong.

He couldn't think about that now. He owed it to the team to keep them on their winning streak.

He had no need to worry. Gemma shined in her con argument, as did the second Kennedy twin in the rebuttal.

Mandy had made it a point to sit beside him. Every time she leaned toward him, he leaned away.

She's practically in my lap, he fumed.

Egan wondered how Mandy's shenanigans looked from Audrey's perspective. He looked around, but he couldn't find Audrey anywhere.

As the judges announced Ashbury Academy as the winners, Egan stood with the rest of the team to give Gemma and Kennedy Twin Number Two a standing ovation, then waited as the judges announced round five's impromptu topic: food nutrition labeling should include added sugars and fats.

As the remaining teams broke into their workout sessions, Egan's team gathered around him. "Okay, who's up to bat?"

"Portia on con and Johnny on rebuttal. But Jeremy was to do the pro," Gemma reminded him. "Since he's not here, we all decided that Audrey would be our strongest player."

"Agreed," Egan declared. He looked around. "Where is she now?"

Portia nodded toward the door. "I think she went out for some fresh air."

"I'll look for her. Get started on the research," he commanded.

"Maybe I should come along too—in case she's throwing up in the lady's room," Mandy offered. "You know, nerves or something. If she blows it for AA, Lavinia won't be happy." She sighed as if she really gave a hoot. "In fact, maybe I should do pro instead."

"Nah," Egan countered. "You're the last person I'd choose, *ever*, to replace Audrey." Egan laughed at the thought. "Besides, you're needed here to do what you do best: rebuttal. You have this uncanny ability to find fault on any issue and make it seem important. Granted, in this case, it's only about nutrition labeling, but don't let that stop you from giving it your all."

As Mandy sputtered angrily, he strolled away.

Egan found Audrey sitting in the school's bleachers, watching a track meet.

She didn't see him until he sat down beside her.

"We won."

She nodded. "Good."

"So, you're up."

Audrey shrugged. "I'm too distracted. Maybe someone else should do it."

"You can do this, Audrey," Egan insisted.

"You don't understand." She looked away, but not quickly enough. He'd already seen the tears in her eyes. "I don't want to let... to let anyone down."

She means me, he thought.

"You could never do that." His voice cracked.

Take a deep breath.

Egan started again: "Audrey, please do it for…"

For us.

"…for Jeremy." That was what she wanted to hear, wasn't it?

Especially now.

Now, when Jeremy needs her most.

Audrey faced him. More tears had fallen. More would fall still when she nodded. "Yeah, sure. If you say so," she whispered. "For Jeremy."

She ran back to the auditorium.

THE KENNEDYS HAD DONE A GREAT JOB. THE DATA WAS ALL THERE.

By the time Audrey reached their workstation, Portia had finished the first draft for the opening argument.

Egan wasn't surprised that Mandy's rebuttal draft was half-assed at best. He could tell she wanted to sabotage the team: if not Audrey, then Johnny.

He prayed AA would win the right to present pro because Gemma pulled some excellent summation points.

And he now knew Audrey would do her best to deliver them.

ASHBURY ACADEMY WAS TO FACE OFF AGAINST BRANSON, A PRIVATE SCHOOL from Marin County. As with each previous match, this one began with the two teams pulling one of two disks from a crystal bowl: one stamped PRO and the other CON.

Audrey pulled PRO.

Her argument was straightforward. It centered on the power of knowledge, and the harm done when it is withheld from the public. It segued to the science of nutrition before driving home the need for governments with open markets to protect its citizens' wellbeing with federally mandated regulations. She closed with a call to action: "A society is only really free when it has the facts to make the right decisions."

She did it, Egan thought.

For him.

IF ONLY JOHNNY HADN'T FALTERED.

The mistake came in his opening statement of his rebuttal. Whatever he read had him pausing to re-read it. Unconsciously, he mouthed, *What the fuck?*

Seeing this, students in the audience giggled.

By the time he got a grip on his argument, it was too late.

Ashbury Academy lost by six points.

Johnny stormed off the stage. Passing a trash can, he tossed his note cards into it.

Audrey was curious enough to stop and see why: When she found the card with Johnny's opening bullet points, she noticed some words had been blacked out with a Magic Marker.

Who would have done that—and why?

Audrey turned to Portia. "Who prepped Johnny's rebuttal?"

Portia thought a moment. "Mandy. Why do you ask?"

She sabotaged us, Audrey thought. Not that she could say that to Portia. She'd be angry and heartbroken, like the rest of the team. And right now, considering Jeremy's condition, they needed to hang together, no matter what Mandy threw their way.

THE DECISION TO SKIP A SECOND NIGHT AT THE HOTEL WAS UNANIMOUS.

While her teammates packed, Mandy collected her luggage at the baggage stand. When the hotel's manager presented her with a bill for the damages to her room, she tossed her credit card at his chest. "Put it on this," she muttered.

When Egan finally gathered everyone together in the lobby, he directed them to hand him their keys.

Odette handed in the two assigned to her. Nodding toward Mandy, she declared, "The second was for her room. Thank goodness I didn't have to use it."

Egan shook his head at that.

"Ooh, speaking of two keys..." Mandy reached into her purse and pulled out a key. She held it up clearly so that Audrey could read the number:

302

She tossed it to Egan.

She laughed when she saw the look on Audrey's face.

If she blabs to Lavinia that Egan and I may have done the dirty, all the better, Mandy thought. But before he gets fired, I've got to get him to write that letter for me.

CHAPTER 17

$\mathcal{I}$t was past eleven at night when the Debate Team finally pulled up in front of Ashbury Academy. The ride home had been glum. Jeremy's critical condition put a damper on the team's exemplary showing.

Seeing the cars pull up, Lavinia ran out to greet them. Most of the parents were there too.

The kids shrugged off the congratulations. They were too worried about their friend.

Jeremy's parents were conspicuously absent.

When Cornell, Odette, the students, and their parents finally dispersed, Lavinia turned to Egan. "Shall we speak in my office?"

He nodded.

Audrey wished she could follow them in, but she knew better than to ask.

Despite his relationship with Mandy, Audrey hoped Egan would tell Lavinia the truth of what he knew about the incident and let the chips fall where they may.

At the very least, he owes that to Lavinia, she thought.

Audrey walked into the school to make three quick calls. She knew Tallulah, Davis, and Bliss were eager to meet up and hear about the tournament.

"No way! Egan? With...*HER?*" Bliss's screech was so loud that the late-night crowd at Tommy's Joynt—mostly cops on break—looked over curiously at her before rolling their eyes and resuming the task of tucking away their mile-high brisket platters and Hofbrau sandwiches.

"I was shocked too." Audrey shrugged. She hoped her friends missed the tremor in her voice.

"First she's all over Jeremy, and now my favorite teacher?" Bliss shuddered. "It's like playing Whack-a-Mole! Each time you smack her out of your life, she finds another hole, and *out she pops!*"

"I guess if you're going to dump Jeremy just because he had the bad luck to fall off a balcony, Egan is a considerable step up," Davis pointed out.

"More like a leap into Outer Space!" Bliss sighed. "And with her being underage and all, couldn't that get Egan into legal trouble? I mean, even if it was consensual, in California, isn't seventeen years old, like, statutory rape?"

"As it turns out, she's already eighteen," Audrey replied. "I saw it on her transcripts. Mandy was held back because her mother quote-unquote allowed her to take an 'early gap year' in the tenth grade when her stepfather's job relocated them to Singapore."

"Well, that takes Egan off the hook legally if not ethically," Davis added.

I was fooling myself. He never really loved me. It was just a flirtation.

"So, what should we do about her?" Tallulah's devious smile scared Audrey.

"Absolutely nothing! I mean that, Tal. We have no right to butt into her business with… anyone."

Tallulah shrugged. "If you say so."

Audrey nodded. "I do. We graduate in two months. Our lives are ahead of us, not behind us. In the big scheme of things, Mandy Blackwell will just be a sad footnote." Slinging her backpack over her shoulder, she added, "And frankly, that's the way I'd like it to stay. Agreed?"

Tallulah shrugged, but then finally nodded.

"Davis, agreed?" Audrey asked.

His eyes moved to Tallulah. Her slight nod took him off leash. "Yeah, sure."

"Bliss, you too," Audrey warned.

"Pinky swear," Bliss murmured through her pout. She held out her hand, pinky extended.

As the friends entwined fingers, they laughed.

"Great. Okay." Audrey forced a smile onto her lips. "We play it smart until graduation, right? Then we get on with the rest of our lives."

She'd miss AA. Because of Lavinia, it was more than just a school to her.

In a bittersweet way, Egan had made it special too. Audrey had hoped he was her future. The sad reality was that he'd soon be part of her past.

She would never again walk the halls of Ashbury Academy without being haunted by the ghost of his memory.

Things will change between all of us, Audrey realized. Bliss was going to Santa Cruz, and Davis had earned a full scholarship to UCLA.

Tallulah, whose goal was to get as far away from her mother and her rotating cast of hangers-on, sycophants, and lovers as possible, had gotten accepted to Oxford. But before going, she planned on taking the whole summer to trek through Europe.

Upon hearing this, Bliss squealed, "Can I go too? Please? Pretty please?"

Tallulah rolled her eyes. "Yeah, okay." She turned to the others. "How about it, guys? A road trip?"

Davis shook his head. "Can't. I'm hitting LA the minute school is out."

Audrey understood how he felt. San Francisco was his past. UCLA was his future.

Audrey sighed. "Sorry, Tal. I've got plans this summer too. Congressman Blanchard has agreed to let me intern for him this summer."

Audrey had known Harris Blanchard all her life. He'd been at Berkeley with Lavinia, where they coordinated the student protests that were his springboard into politics. He'd also been on AA's trustee board since the school's inception.

So, when Harris offered her the position, she readily accepted.

It's time I got on with my life.

Without Egan.

Most definitely without Mandy.

FINALLY ALONE WITH EGAN, LAVINIA GOT RIGHT TO THE POINT: "WHAT happened?"

"One of the kids got out of hand."

"Was it Mandy?"

Egan blinked twice. "That wasn't just a good guess, was it?"

"I've been at this for a few years. I think I know a little something about raging hormones, adolescent acting out, and questionable parenting skills." Lavinia shook her head, awed by the thought of it all. "In Mandy's case she's a triple threat. Add to that a field trip with an overnight in a hotel? My God, Egan, I'm so sorry! I blame myself for sending you into that lion's den with no one to have your back."

"I had Cornell and Odette—"

Lavinia rolled her eyes. "They're the last folks you want in that fox hole with you. I should have steered you toward Berney and his wife, Jean." She winked. "I've seen them in action. Believe me, the 'archeology' thing was a cover. They were Covert Ops at some point."

"I also had… Audrey."

The tension in Lavinia's face eased. "I'm glad to hear she was able to keep her wits about her—considering it was Jeremy."

So, she suspects Audrey still has feelings for him.

Knowing this, Egan felt his chest caving in.

"Was it Jeremy's stash?" Lavinia asked.

"Doubtful. And Lavinia, it wasn't just marijuana."

"I was a child of the sixties. I learned how to read toxicology reports as a volunteer at the Haight Ashbury Free Clinic." Lavinia shrugged. "Jeremy's attending physician says he had LSD in his system. And it would strike me that if the evening took place in Mandy's room and with Mandy's drugs, then Mandy would also have enjoyed a magic carpet ride."

"Unless…" Egan didn't want to say the obvious.

"Unless Mandy didn't tell him about it—and skipped it herself," Lavinia replied. "If so, then Jeremy was coerced into trying it." She reached for the phone. "I'll tell his parents that we are of like mind on the supposition that he didn't take it voluntarily—and that we don't feel it's worth a suspension, let alone expulsion."

In other words, Lavinia had no intention of ruining Jeremy's opportunity to accept any scholarship that still might come his way.

"Lavinia, what do you want to do about Mandy?"

There was no mirth in the headmistress's chuckle. "Wring her neck. But I'll settle for using my time with her next year to help her get over her insecurities. It's the basis of all the harm she's caused. Maybe before she graduates next year, we can help her see the bigger picture: how her deeds have a long-term effect on everyone she knows, including herself. We may yet be able to save her from herself."

Egan's guffaw was genuine. "If you say so."

Audrey is so lucky to have Lavinia in her life.

And so am I.

CHAPTER 18

"Knock, knock!" For a Monday morning, Mandy's sing-song entry knock was too cheerful by half, in Egan's opinion.

And, considering Jeremy was still in intensive care, he found her behavior outright ghoulish.

Right now, it looked as if the kid's injuries were severe enough that he might not be able to play football. Thankfully, his strong math aptitude had allowed him to apply for some academic scholarships too. Stanford had offered him one, but he'd already turned it down when USC came through with a football scholarship. Lavinia was already pulling strings to see if she could get Stanford to reconsider.

Egan beckoned for Mandy to enter.

"I have a favor to ask," she declared.

"Really?" Egan feigned shock and awe.

She shrugged. "What's got you so grumpy?"

"You mean, other than the fact that your actions sent one of my students to the hospital with an overdose, a concussion, and a few broken bones when he should have been studying for a tournament?" Egan shrugged. "Why, nothing at all." He leaned back. "So, tell me, what can I do for you?"

"Write a letter of recommendation."

Interesting. "To whom?"

"Ideally, your very best contact at Berkeley." She ran a manicured finger over his desk. "You graduated in Lit, am I right?"

"Aren't you the little psychic," Egan murmured.

More like "psycho"…

"And your faculty chair—Clive Cunt-Luckinbill—wasn't he that guy who won the Pulitzer?"

"It's *Munt*-Luckinbill. My, my! You have done your homework!"

"Don't tease me, Egan. I'm serious." Mandy pursed her lips into a pout. "Or trying, anyway."

"Okay, I'm now waiting with bated breath."

Mandy frowned. "For what?"

Egan chuckled. "For you to ask, my sweet! Beg. Grovel. Whatever." He brushed the air with his hand. "Anytime you're ready."

"I don't see why you have to make fun of me!"

"I'm not. I'm quite serious."

Anger darkened her face. "Well, for your information, I won't..." Suddenly, she smiled. "Oh, I get it. You want a little quid pro quo."

"Nope. No quid. No pro. And certainly no quo, Mandy. Because, to be honest, I can't even imagine where your quote-unquote quo has been, and I don't want to find out the hard way. You see, I'm allergic to penicillin." Despite her indignant gasp, he leaned forward. "All I want is the truth."

"The truth...about what?"

"About Jeremy's overdose. Was it accidental?"

"Jeez, Egan! Of course, it was accidental! Do you think I'd—"

"Do it on purpose?" he asked. "No. I think that you didn't realize how potent LSD can be." Egan shrugged. "And I'm glad you're willing to admit you tricked Jeremy into taking it."

"I'll admit nothing of the sort!" Mandy growled.

"A shame. Because if you were to admit the truth, then...well, just between you and me—*and I do mean just between the two of us*—the gesture would go a long way toward keeping you at the school. Rumors have a nasty way of following a student around, especially those who are encouraged to transfer elsewhere before their senior year."

He let that sink in.

"So, what you're saying is that my *admission* gets me the letter?"

"Yes. I'd feel you were somewhat contrite for your actions, and I'd have absolutely no hesitation in giving you what you want—*without* any groveling."

She smiled, relieved. "Then... yes. I brought the pot."

"And the LSD," Egan added.

"Yes, okay, that too," she declared.

You little bitch.

"And you took pictures of the two of you *in flagrante delicto*."

"Okay! Yeah!" Mandy looked skyward as if her exasperation had fallen somewhere from above. "So, I get the letter, right?"

"I won't go back on my word. It'll be waiting for you here on my desk in the morning."

Her mouth hardened into a grimace. "Not just any letter, right?"

He kissed his fingers. "It'll be a love letter, albeit a work of fine fiction."

"Okay, then." Mandy's grin went ear to ear.

"Oh, and one more thing: your tenure with Debate Club has ended. Don't bother to try out next year."

He could tell she was seething at the slight. Still, she walked out the door with her head held high—and her middle finger straight up as well.

Egan laughed so hard he almost fell out of his chair.

Then he opened his computer and started typing Mandy's letter to Clive. After the salutation, and a few pleasantries, Egan also wrote:

I still have so many fond memories of Clementine, despite her calling me "thick." (A joke? Frankly, I concede she's right—in more ways than one!) Such a joy, sticking around that incredible woman. You are one lucky guy.

Now, for the purpose of this letter: I want to recommend a student who, I feel, fits right in with your mission for the Lit department...

From there, he made sure to include the sort of buzz words that he knew his old mentor despised: things like, *"Ms. Blackwell has a strong voice for commercial fiction,"* and *"She uses phrases steeped in the vernacular of the time, with none of the mundane adherence to classic narrative structure..."*

He also included this line, knowing it would rankle the celebrated author:

As for Miss Blackwell's drive, she will do whatever it takes to assure editors will sit up and take notice.

And, finally, Egan paraphrased the man's most cutting remarks about his thesis:

Ms. Blackwell will never hear such scoffs as 'derivative,' 'half-hearted,' pedestrian,' or 'false." No one will ever say that she has faltered in developing a unique voice. Her writing has just the right amount of gravitas.

I see so much of myself in her. I hope you do too.

In abject sincerity and regard,

Egan Gable

He then stuck it in an envelope he'd addressed to Mandy.

Egan wished he could tell Audrey about it and watch her laugh.

<h1 style="text-align:center">CHAPTER 19</h1>

There was only one elevator in AA: an old Otis that, from its plaque, informed those who cared to crouch down to read it (through many decades' worth of wear and grime) that it had been installed at the dawn of the Twentieth Century.

Really, there was no need to stoop. Proof of its age came with use.

It rose at a snail's pace. Worse yet, when it went down, it jerked intermittently, moaning and groaning, like a woman in her tenth hour of labor. Those along for the ride either cursed, squealed in terror, or moved their lips in silent prayer. All of these reasons were more than the needed incentive to take the stairs.

This time, however, Audrey didn't have that option.

Tired of watching her daughter mope away the afternoons after school, Lavinia had given Audrey the task of moving some of the discarded textbooks from a fourth-floor closet to the lobby, where the janitor, who started his work at the school around eight at night, would load them onto a truck and haul them to one of the city's recycling centers.

This task meant using a cart, and that by default meant taking the elevator.

Audrey had begun two hours ago, right after school. It was May—a week until graduation. San Francisco was enjoying an unusually hot day, and the sky was a crystalline sapphire hue.

The school had emptied out quickly. San Francisco's rainy season was over, and everyone wanted to enjoy the sunshine while they could. The baseball team, which fielded balls and swung bats every afternoon in Kezar Field, wasn't around either. It was playing a school on the opposite side of the Bay Bridge. The players had carpooled over. The last of the teachers had taken off by four-thirty. Even Lavinia had somewhere else to be: she was wooing a new benefactor.

In truth, Audrey liked the peace and quiet in the building and the busy work because it got her mind off other things.

Like Egan.

That wasn't easy.

As frustrating as the year had been leading up to the debate tournament, every day since that weekend, Egan's demeanor toward her had been gracious but formal.

As if we're strangers, she realized.

It was as if the few magic moments they had shared—when they first met, and he'd teased her about Paris—had been a dream.

And then there was Mandy.

Audrey still wondered what had happened between them.

I might as well give up, she thought miserably.

She shoved the cart down the hall until she reached the elevator, and then pushed the button summoning it.

Finally, she could hear it groaning its way toward her.

Maybe Davis is right, and he's not worth all the time and effort everyone puts into pleasing him. Perhaps he's just the adult version of lame. Maybe we should just all grow up and move on—

It opened, and there was Egan.

"Oh!" Dumbfounded, Audrey stared at him, then looked away, convinced it was a dream. But no, when she glanced back, he was still there.

"I thought—I thought I was alone," she stammered.

"Sorry. Really, I didn't mean to scare you. I had to... to grade some papers." For some reason, Egan seemed ashamed to face her. As if to change the subject, he jabbed at the elevator button. "This thing throws me for a loop every time. I'm sure I pushed the down button."

"I may have pushed first, which would override your push. I'm sorry about that." She took a step back and bumped into the cart.

"Here, let me help you with that." Egan attempted to move out of the elevator. Bad move. Having a mind of its own, the doors were already closing before he had more than a leg out the door. With a hand on each door, he shoved them open again, like Superman. "Get in, quick! I don't know if I can keep this beasts' jaws open much longer."

Audrey grabbed the cart and shoved it into the elevator, running over his toe in the process.

"*Shit! Ouch!...* Oh, sorry. I guess I shouldn't have said that." He tried to hide his grin.

That made her angry. "For God's sake, I've just run over your toe! You don't have to stand at attention," she huffed. "This may surprise you, but I have heard that word before. And 'hell,' 'damn,' and 'fuck' too."

There. That should dispel any presumptions he has that I'm some goody-two-shoes just because I'm Lavinia's kid.

He glanced over, puzzled.

His stare made her blush. *Why wasn't the damn elevator moving?*

She jammed her thumb into the button, but still nothing. Frustrated, she slammed it again and again with an open fist.

Suddenly, the elevator started whining and huffing and jerking its way down to the third floor, all the while shaking back and forth frantically.

Only when it tossed them up in the air, then, again and again, did they realize that what they were feeling was an earthquake.

As the ancient lift shuddered side to side, the cart slammed into the elevator walls, flinging the books in every direction.

Audrey and Egan covered their faces best they could, but the force of the earthquake threw them up and down and into each other.

When it stopped, they were both trembling.

Audrey heard herself groan. With the electricity off, the elevator was pitch black, and she couldn't see her bruises. Instinctively she touched them with trembling fingers. The pain made her moan again.

Hearing her, Egan pulled her close and cradled her in his arms. They were warm and even more muscular than Jeremy's.

To quit from trembling, she focused on stroking his arm.

He said nothing, as if he, like she, were afraid that talking would make it happen all over again.

Would that be so bad?

No, she thought. I could stay here in his arms forever.

They sat together like that for what seemed like ages. Finally, she raised her head. In doing so, her cheek rubbed his. Its stubble felt like tiny pinpricks.

Egan lowered his head, and she felt his warm breath. That's how she knew how close his lips were to hers.

Close enough to kiss.

But they didn't. Instead, he pulled away slightly and whispered the obvious. "Jesus—an earthquake! Are you hurt?"

As she shook her head no, the top of her head scraped against his chin. She didn't want him to pull away again, so she edged into him.

She could feel his heart pounding furiously in his ribcage. She knew if she moved her hand slowly, down into his lap, she'd find him stiffened.

If he chose to move her hand there, she'd already made up her mind she wouldn't pull away.

But he didn't.

A few moments went by, and his heart slowed a bit. He nudged her up somewhat so that he was no longer holding her.

That saddened her.

For the longest time, she didn't say anything. Finally, she just came out with: "Egan, why don't you like me?"

Egan didn't know how to answer that.

Should he tell her that he'd flipped over her, that very first time he saw her?

Or that he was rock hard that very moment?

But he knew he couldn't say that for all sorts of reasons, not the least being that he didn't need some jailbait crush to fuck up his life.

If only she were even a year older —

And it would help if her mother weren't his boss; and if he weren't also Audrey's teacher…

Instead, he opted for another version of the truth. Sort of. "Audrey, seriously, you've got it all wrong." The words stuck in his throat, like gritty grains of sand. "I do like you! I—Okay, *no*. What I mean to say is—"

He sounded like a fool, stumbling around for the right words.

Worse yet, he sounded like some lovesick schoolboy.

No, that would never do. He shook his head, knowing that she couldn't see his anguish in the dark. He had to pull himself together and fast.

He took a deep breath, then cleared his throat. "Okay, the truth? Audrey, listen, this isn't *The Dead Poets Society*. I'm—I'm just a guy looking to earn a living while I write my book."

"Oh." Audrey let that sink in. "Okay, yeah. Gotcha."

She let her hand fall into his lap.

It was there she found her answer:

Yes, he had feelings for her. His hard-on was proof of it.

She'd let that sustain her.

Audrey moved her hand quickly away to give the impression that the contact had been incidental.

They sat there for what seemed like forever.

Finally, as nonchalantly as she could, she inched away.

The silence must have been weighing on her, too, because she started chattering: about the passage from *Madame Bovary* he'd had them read the week before; about her disgust with the stupid war in Afghanistan; about the odds that the Giants would once ever win a World Series in San Francisco.

All safe topics for discussions.

They conversed politely—like a student and teacher should, for what seemed like an eternity.

Enough time for his erection to subside.

She thought she was now safe from his charms when, with heart-breaking casualness, Egan said, "I hear you got accepted to Berkeley."

She nodded.

"And Wellesley too, I'd heard. And Sarah Lawrence, USC, Bennington, Boston U, NYU…" Egan chuckled. "Did I leave any out?"

Audrey felt her cheeks heating up. "No. That pretty much covers it."

"And yet, you chose the school closest to home."

She fought off the urge to declare: *No. I chose the one closest to you. In case you ever come to your senses and realize I'm here for you.*

If he could tear himself away from Mandy.

Audrey was not surprised that Mandy had dropped Jeremy. Around campus, he was now a figure to be pitied: someone who'd seemingly had it all one moment, only to lose it the next.

As expected, the sports scholarships had vaporized after his accident. Thankfully, with Lavinia's connections with AA benefactors who were alumni at Stanford, the private university had come through with a partial math scholarship for him.

Still, the accident had changed him, and not just physically either. Jeremy was no longer the guy whose spontaneous fun-loving attitude had made him so popular with his classmates. His smiles now quickly hardened into grimaces. There was a wariness in his stare. His spirit seemed as broken as the bones which were yet to fully heal.

Since Jeremy's return to school, Audrey made it a point to seek him out. When they were together, she slowed her pace to match that of his walker. She kept all topics upbeat, congratulating him on his acceptance to Stanford, encouraging him on his physical progress.

Most of all, she tried to ignore his jibes that she must have much better things to do than "to hang with a broken gimp like me."

The last time he made that crack, she'd finally responded, "You needed a wake-up call, Jeremy. Hey, your body may have hurt like hell, but bones mend. Hearts take a little longer."

He'd flinched, but then he reached for her hand too. "I'm so sorry we broke up, Audrey."

She chuckled. "I got over it."

It was the first time since the accident that she'd seen him laugh.

Now, she wished she could say the same about Egan: that she was over him.

She couldn't. If anything, being close to him now only heightened her longing for him.

She realized that, over time, the feelings of desire would wane.

Maybe college will change that.

Eventually, they heard Lavinia shouting Audrey's name, so they yelled back. They didn't dare beat on the door because they didn't know how well the elevator would stand up to it.

Ten minutes later they heard pounding and screeching as Lavinia edged a crowbar between the elevator doors and attempted to pry them back. It took her another half hour, and by the time she was through, the space she'd made for them was only two feet wide, but it was large enough for both to slip through, although they had to jump down a few feet since they were stuck between the third and fourth floors.

The flashlight Lavinia placed on the floor dimly lit the hall. Despite being drenched in sweat, she hugged her daughter as if she would never let her go again. The hug she then gave Egan started out clumsy and shy but ended up just as fervent. The tears of relief that followed were justified if what she was relaying about news reports of the earthquake's damages were true.

"The electricity is out in a lot of places throughout the bay! The radio says that, as a precaution they've closed the Bay Bridge and BART's Transbay Tunnel." Under the weight of worry, Lavinia's face caved in on itself. "Until the phones come back online, I won't know if the baseball team made it back over the bridge after the game, or if they're stuck in Oakland." She tried wiping away her tears, but they kept falling, fogging her glasses in the process. "Oh, Egan! I forgot that you live in Berkeley! You won't be able to make it home." She straightened up as she pulled back from him. "We've got a guest room. You must come home and spend the night with us."

"No!... No, really, that's not necessary." Egan felt the edges of his mouth waver from the weight of his shame.

Why should I feel guilty? Nothing really happened! Jesus, we could have died in that old rattrap of an elevator! I was just trying to protect the kid, and we survived, didn't we? My response was natural— adrenaline, I guess... or something like that. Besides, it was Audrey who stroked my arm. It was she who brushed her hand across my lap, not the other way around...

Even as he addressed Lavinia, he locked eyes with Audrey to gauge her response to her mother's invitation.

Her smile was polite, nothing more.

If she hated me because of Mandy, she despises me even more now, he thought sadly.

"Thanks for the invitation, really. But–well, I've still got some papers to grade, and I was going to have dinner with a friend afterward—"

"Oh!… Then, you'll be sleeping over there?" Lavinia's response was more concerned than polite.

"Yes! I'm sure that will be okay."

In truth, there was no friend. He would just have to sack out on the lumpy couch in the teachers' lounge.

And try not to dream about Audrey.

"That's good." But Lavinia seemed genuinely disappointed. She shook her head sadly. "Well, we can all say we came through it in one piece."

Egan laughed weakly. "Now, if you'll excuse me, I'll get back to my papers." He picked up his satchel and headed back toward his classroom, taking the stairs this time.

———

WHEN HE GOT THERE, HE REALIZED THE ELECTRICITY WAS STILL OFF. SO HE JUST sat there, watching out the window as daylight turned into twilight. Eventually, Lavinia and Audrey walked out of the old building toward their home.

Then he closed his eyes.

And cursed his fate.

She's the first girl I've ever wanted that I couldn't have, he thought miserably. In a week, she'll be gone from the school. She'll be getting on with the rest of her life.

Without me.

Fuck it—why didn't I say something?

I'm such a loser.

———

HE MUST HAVE SAT THERE FOR ANOTHER HALF HOUR WHEN IT HIT HIM. SLOWLY he opened his satchel and took out the typewritten pages of his book.

He threw it into his metal wastepaper basket.

Then he struck a match and tossed it in too.

He stared into the basket. As the pages caught fire, he was reminded of the Shakespearean quote Audrey had used as the theme for the essay in which she compared the love of Romeo and Juliet to that of Jay Gatsby and Daisy Buchanan:

Love is a smoke made with the fumes of sighs…

It wasn't as bright as looking directly into the sun, but he knew that gazing directly into the flame was just as stupid.

The loss of his eyesight certainly wouldn't improve his writing.

As the fire brightened the room, he thought of his new novel, which was already writing itself in his head. The story would embody all the love and lust and heartache and youthful exuberance that had been missing in the other manuscript.

Its characters were right there, at Ashbury.

The quixotic Lavinia and her gently worn staff; all the sharp flirty girls and clueless horny boys.

Too handsome but too clueless Jeremy, sad little Davis, true to her name Bliss, and tough-as-nails Tallulah—even scheming, capricious Mandy—would feature prominently in his cast of characters.

But most of all, the novel would be about Audrey.

Or at least, the way he imagined her to be: the savvy, sweet, sexy heart-breaker.

At least in his fiction, she would finally be his.

THREE YEARS LATER

CHAPTER 20

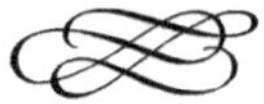

"So, how's life?"

Whenever Audrey and her dearest high school friends got together, that was always the first thing asked.

This time, it was Davis who broached the question.

And, as always, it was a dare to give the most audacious answer.

"Why don't you start?" Tallulah suggested.

"I second that motion," Bliss chimed in.

"Me three," Audrey added, laughing. As antsy as Davis was, she knew he was bursting to tell them something significant. As for herself, long ago, she had resigned herself to the fact that life as a political science major at Berkeley was as mundane as it could get—at least when compared to her friends' journeys.

Granted, she was politically active and had worked on numerous causes that supported society's underdogs. As class projects for her pre-law curriculum track, she wrote white papers that sought to strengthen national health regulations.

She'd also spent the last two summers interning for Congressman Blanchard in DC. Her hard work had impressed him. She planned to do so this summer too.

At the very least, it'll give me a few interesting things to say to the gang when we meet up again in the fall, she thought.

Hopefully, the next reunion would take place then or sooner, but she wouldn't bet on it. She'd noticed that their meetups were fewer each year and further apart.

The only constant was the locale: the Magnolia Brewing Company, near the corner of Haight and Masonic.

"Okay, you twisted my arm." Taking a deep breath, Davis declared, "I've been asked to helm an action flick for Universal."

The girls squealed in surprise and then enveloped him in a hug.

"I love you guys so much," Davis murmured.

Although still a year away from graduating from UCLA's film school, Davis was already making his mark as a movie director. A few months earlier, his student film premiered at South by Southwest. Critics hailed the semi-biographical film about life in San Francisco's seamy Tenderloin district as "the ultimate statement on today's human condition," and "a haunting parable for our time."

In the meantime, he'd been invited to pitch every major film studio.

"Well, congratulations!" Audrey exclaimed. "So, which one of us gets to walk the red carpet as your date?"

"All of you, of course," he promised.

Bliss's jaunt through Europe with Tallulah ended in its sixth week. While in Paris, a professional photographer saw her on Pont Neuf, gazing at the boats drifting down the Seine. Newspapers around the world picked up the picture he took of her, clad in cut-off jeans, stiletto heels, and a gauzy midriff-cropped hand-painted blouse from her parents' shop.

Bliss was an instant celebrity. Offers from modeling agencies poured in.

Additionally, the blouse became a fashion sensation. Its sales were the catalyst for Over the Rainbow's growth into twenty other U.S. cities, with Bliss as its cover girl—just one of her many modeling contracts.

Today's news was that Bliss had just signed on as the new face for an international cosmetics line.

"Wow!" Audrey declared. "Your face will be everywhere—even bus stops!"

Bliss guffawed. "Yeah, well, that can be a curse and a blessing. That just makes it easier for pervs to defile you in public. Just ask Gisele."

Tallulah laughed. "You know, I don't think we'll ever get that opportunity."

"Sure you will," Bliss insisted. "Let's all meet up in New York during Fashion Week and I'll introduce you."

As for Tallulah, her studies at Oxford were curtailed in her sophomore year when it was discovered that Chameleon's financial manager had absconded with all of Maggie's money.

Tallulah now divulged how she'd succeeded on her vow to "chase the son-of-a-bitch to the ends of the Earth, and make him pay back every cent." But sadly, before being caught, he'd managed to punch a massive dent in the Wishart Family Trust.

Reluctantly, Maggie had agreed to give Tallulah her power of attorney. Tallulah was now in the middle of negotiating Maggie's latest contract with her record label and running her mother's next tour.

"I've also been asked to manage another band. In fact, it's the opening act on Maggie's tour. It's called Jammerhead." Tallulah's eyes sparkled with excitement. "Its lead singer and writer is…well, he's a *genius!* He's— so *deep!*"

Davis cocked a brow. *"That's* an interesting metaphor. Are you describing his lyrics or something more interesting?"

Tallulah smiled coyly. "I'd be lying if I said we haven't spent a few late nights discussing things other than the band's song list." She frowned. "I'm just hoping Maggie backs away from the idea of cutting the tour short, which always happens when she thinks she's in love."

"Who is it with this time?" Davis asked.

"Wait, let me guess," Audrey interjected. "Does he play bass guitar?"

Tallulah sighed. "Bingo! And, are you ready for this? He's half her age."

"In other words, he's our age," Bliss pointed out.

"You've been through this drill a dozen times," Davis reminded her. "What are the chances that it's really serious?"

"I'm frightened enough that I want to lock up her estate so that it's cad-proof." She glanced over at Audrey. "That new boyfriend of yours—Daniel, right? Isn't he an associate at some San Francisco law firm with six names?"

Audrey laughed. "Only four. But yes, it is a well-respected firm."

"Good! Because I like the cut of his jib. And since, from the looks of him, he's head over heels in love with you, maybe throwing some business his way will have him seeing additional advantages to wooing you besides the fact that you're the sweetest person in the world."

Audrey blushed. "Frankly, the last thing Daniel needs is more encouragement."

"Finally!" Bliss exclaimed. "If anyone deserves someone who loves them unconditionally, it's you."

Audrey, touched, toasted her friends. As their glasses met, she replied, "I have all of you, and I have Lavinia. I am already blessed."

"Oh, cut the crap!" Davis's eyes twinkled merrily. "We all say prayers that we'll find a guy who's not only a great lay but who only has eyes for us."

Audrey choked on her wine.

She had never admitted to her friends that, at twenty-one, she was still a virgin. And because the subject never came up, she let them assume otherwise.

Dating was easy for her. She was pretty enough that men flirted with her, and her openness made it easy for them to feel comfortable in her presence. But it was when they saw her kindness in action that they fell in love.

Until Daniel McKittridge, she'd never felt that she could reciprocate.

Daniel was tall and broad-shouldered, the result of making the swim team of every school he'd attended. His hair, brown but already graying, curled tightly when he missed his barber appointment, which, with his overloaded work schedule, was much too often. Audrey didn't mind because she liked it when she could brush an errant lock back behind his ear.

His brown eyes squinted naturally. His nose crooked slightly to the left, and his grin rose higher on the right, which gave the impression that this lopsidedness was his mouth's way of overcompensating for genetics' shortcomings.

All of this created the illusion of a man on the verge of handsomeness but somehow missing the mark.

Not that it mattered. His most attractive feature was his laugh, which he did often.

They'd met at the Berkeley Law Library, where she worked three nights a week. He'd come in search of a book on Costa Rican case law. He'd hoped that the antiquated tome, published in 1923, would offer a bit of arcane knowledge that might save one of his firm's pro bono clients from deportation.

She was touched that Daniel offered to climb through the library's dusty old archives with her to locate it. "Your sweater is much too nice for the amount of grime in that joint," he'd pointed out.

She looked up, surprised. "So, you've been inside the library's vault?"

He laughed. "When I was getting my JD, I practically lived in it. I was lucky to work my way through school in this building. Granted, I doubt I'll sustain my feelings of fondness if I end up dying an early death from some disease carried by dust mites."

She handed him a smock, latex gloves, surgical mask, and a shower cap. Donning the same, she followed him into the archive.

"Normally, that's not a sexy look," he murmured. "But somehow, you pull it off."

Lots of men had flirted with her. But Daniel's joke was the first time a thrill ran through her since the day she met Egan and he teasingly offered to take her to Paris.

The search for the book took an hour. By the time they'd found it, Audrey was due to clock out.

"Would you like to join me for dinner?" Daniel asked.

Now, two months later, she wondered how she'd lived her life without him.

She loved the cadence of his voice. She adored him for opening doors for women, even at Berkeley, where any sort of male patronization was disdained. When they walked through one of Berkeley's many parks, his eyes softened when they passed young mothers pushing baby carriages.

Most of all, she loved curling up in his arms at night and listening to him in the dark as he recapped his day.

But now, even after eight weeks of seeing each other every weekend, they'd yet to make love.

She knew he was a passionate man. Had she said yes, they'd have made love that very first night. Since then, on numerous occasions, their heavy petting had brought her to the edge of wanting more; of exploring her sensual side with someone so open with his adoration of her.

As her relationship with Daniel deepened, her desire for Egan seemed to fade away like a half-remembered dream. At these times, Audrey asked herself what she was holding out for.

"Speaking of someone who's come pretty far in the past three years, who'd ever think we'd see Egan Gable on the cover of *Time*?" Tallulah exclaimed.

"Not to mention *People* and *Vanity Fair*," Davis added. He reached down to grab his satchel and pulled out a copy of both magazines. "I couldn't resist buying these at the airport. Our old prof has hit the big time!"

Audrey's friends were right. Egan's face was now everywhere, thanks to his recently released novel entitled *Extracurricular*.

Audrey had only learned about it an hour before. While heading toward the Downtown Berkeley BART station on her way to meet her friends, she passed the campus bookstore. A display of Egan's novels took up the whole front window.

"Yeah, well, I was in *Vanity Fair* first," Bliss sniffed.

Davis snickered. "I said, 'the cover.'"

Bliss smacked him on the arm. "I'll get there—eventually."

The sight of Egan's face may not have been as ubiquitous as Bliss', but it was enough to chip away at Audrey's heart.

"Have any of you read *Extracurricular*?" Bliss asked.

"Not yet," Tallulah admitted. "In fact, I'm almost afraid to! From the description I read in the *Chronicle*'s review, he may have based it on Ashbury Academy."

Audrey's heart lurched in her chest. "What do you mean?"

"It takes place in a private high school in San Francisco and—" Tallulah explained

"Oh, my God! You don't think he..." Bliss's eyes opened wide. "*Did he?*"

"We've got to get a copy!" Tallulah exclaimed. "We may be in there!"

I may be in there.

Audrey felt as if she might faint. To steady herself, she took a sip of her wine. Audrey's friends had no knowledge of her history with Egan. She wanted to keep it that way.

Davis poked Audrey. "When did he leave AA?"

"Right after our senior year," she murmured.

"Well, then, hell yeah, we're in there!" Davis laughed gleefully. "Hey, if it's any good, maybe I'll option it for a movie. Of course, I'd have to pump up my character's role."

"And maybe you'll give me a role in the film," Bliss declared. "Then I will most assuredly make the cover of *Vanity Fair*. And besides, who could play *moi* better than... *moi?*" She pointed at herself with both hands.

"You're assuming too much." Despite Audrey's retort, she had an awful premonition that she was wrong.

"You mean that Bliss can actually act?" Davis teased.

Bliss socked him on the arm for that crack.

Most of AA's instructors stayed a week after the last day of school to get their classrooms ready for the following year. Knowing this, Audrey had made it a point to stay away from the school until she knew Egan had left on his summer sabbatical.

She'd been surprised when, in the first week of July, Lavinia informed her that Egan had turned in his notice.

Audrey couldn't believe her ears. "He's leaving?"

"Yes. But it's the right thing for him to do," Lavinia replied. "At some point, he realized he wasn't happy here. He's moving to New York."

Had I told him how I felt when we were stuck in the elevator, would he have stayed for me?

Now, three years later, she'd never know.

"Hey, what do you think ever happened to Audrey's library book thief?" Bliss mused. "What was her name again?"

"Mandy Blackwell," Davis shuddered. "Who knows? My guess is she'll eventually end up at some L.A. talent agency. Trust me, that piranha would fit right in." He turned to Audrey. "Did she even graduate from AA?"

Audrey nodded. "As I recall, yes. And she got into Northeastern."

Tallulah snickered. "What a joke! Let me guess: Stepdaddy Warbucks slapped his name on one of their buildings. Presto! Instant undergrad."

Audrey shrugged. "Sadly, it happens all the time."

"It may be a legal bribe, but it's unfair to the kids who aren't born with a silver spoon in their mouth," Tallulah retorted. "Audrey, you're a protector of the downtrodden. Work on that, won't you?"

"I'll drink to that," Bliss retorted.

So they did.

THE NEXT MORNING, AUDREY WENT INTO THE CAMPUS BOOKSTORE TO BUY *Extracurricular*, but she couldn't find a copy on the shelves.

However, she did see a poster next to a front table. It announced:

EGAN GABLE, AUTHOR OF THE NOVEL *EXTRACURRICULAR*, WILL DO A READING FROM THE BOOK.
Supplies Are Limited. Buy Your Copy Today!

To encourage attendance, the poster included a few snippets of the novel's reviews:

> "Raw, honest, and moving."—*New York Times Book* Review
> "A heartbreaking parable of unrequited love." —*New Yorker*
> "The must-read of our time." — *London Review of Books*

For a moment, Audrey felt as if she couldn't breathe.

Egan—*there?*

Audrey went up to the sales clerk: another student she recognized from her first-year biology class. "I'd like a copy of..." she couldn't bring herself to say the book's name. Instead, she pointed to the poster.

The clerk clicked her tongue. "*Extracurricular*? Sorry, we're already sold out of our copies." The woman leaned in. "In fact, it's sold out every-where! Apparently, it's pretty steamy."

Audrey blanched. "What do you mean, steamy?"

The clerk cocked a brow. "You know how some books are a love story? Well, let's just say that this one's a *lust* story—and all that implies."

Lust?...

Egan didn't write about me after all. He wrote about Mandy.

Audrey didn't know if she should be relieved or disappointed.

"We still have a few reserve tickets for the event," the clerk was saying. "They come bundled with a copy of the book. If you'd like to buy one, I'd suggest you do it now. I'm sure they'll be gone by the end of the day."

"Sure, okay," Audrey heard herself mutter. "In fact, I'd... I'd like two tickets."

The clerk took Audrey's credit card and rang up the order. "Here you go! Two tickets. When you show them at the front door, the ticket taker will also hand you two books."

Audrey reasoned that she owed it to herself to see Egan one last time.

In fact, she'd take Lavinia with her.

"It's great to hear your voice—and it isn't even Sunday," Lavinia exclaimed delightedly.

"I've got a surprise...sort of." Audrey took a deep breath. "How would you like to accompany me to see Egan Gable speak on his debut novel?"

"Ah, yes! *Extracurricular.*"

"You know about it?" Audrey flinched, ready for the worst.

Lavinia chuckled. "I'd have to be living on a deserted island to miss it." After a pause, she added, "Have you read it yet?"

"No. It's sold out on this side of the bridge."

"Here as well," Lavinia replied. "But I'm sure Egan will have one waiting for me when we see each other on Friday night."

"*What?* You… and *Egan…*" Audrey sat down hard.

"Yes. He's that night's speaker for City Arts and Lectures—you know, at the Herbst Theatre. He called and told me that he saved me a seat. We'll be having dinner beforehand."

"Oh…" Tears welled in Audrey's eyes. "How sweet of him. Be sure to tell him… that I said hello." Audrey covered the phone as she caught her breath.

Think of some excuse. "I've got to run, Lavinia. Class starts in a few minutes."

She hung up, hoping Lavinia hadn't caught the catch in her voice.

She knew that Egan and Lavinia had ended their professional relationship on a positive note.

If he's already reached out to her, then the novel can't be something he'd feel she'd resent, she reasoned.

It must not be about us.

About me.

Audrey felt relieved.

Then sad.

At that moment, she knew who to take to the event, instead.

Daniel.

He'd be proof positive to Egan that any schoolgirl crush she may have had was over.

Because it was.

Surely.

As for Daniel, she'd tell him the truth—sort of. Egan was her favorite teacher in high school. Going to the event was just her way of showing her support.

She was certain Daniel wouldn't mind having Egan sign his copy for Tallulah instead.

"Guess what we're doing Saturday," Audrey exclaimed to Daniel.

"Enjoying a picnic in the park." His answer was confident, almost cocky.

And yes, it would have been acceptable too. Certainly nicer than trying to introduce the man you'd once wanted so badly to the man who now wants *you* with all his heart.

"Um… no," she replied uneasily. "I bought tickets for a lecture by one of my former instructors."

"Oh." Daniel thought about that for a moment. "Maybe I had him too. What course does he teach?"

"He didn't teach at Berkeley—although he did get his Ph.D. from here." Had Egan ever finished his thesis? Audrey couldn't remember.

"What's his lecture about?"

"He wrote a novel. Apparently, it's a big hit: *Extracurricular*."

"Yeah, I've heard of it." Daniel paused. She guessed he was trying to remember why. "What's it about again?"

"A prep school." *No need to go into detail.*

To change the subject, she added, "The tickets come with copies of his book."

"I know authors love signing their books. Since you're a former student, I'm sure he'll appreciate your support."

"You'll get a book too. But would you mind terribly if I gave that copy to Tallulah? She… she had a crush on him, so I know she'd appreciate it."

What a liar I am.

"Sure, no problem. If he intrigues me enough, I'll just read your copy." Daniel laughed. "Saturday, eh? What time does it start?"

"Two o'clock."

"I have to go into the office to work on a brief that has to be filed on Monday, but I should be back in plenty of time."

"Great." Audrey leaned in for a kiss.

She wondered what Egan might write in her book.

All of a sudden, she hoped Daniel would never want to read it.

By eleven o'clock on Saturday morning, Audrey hadn't heard from Lavinia. Although she was dying to hear about her mother's dinner with Egan, she fought the urge to call her and ask about it.

When the phone rang at noon, she leaped for it.

"Hi, honey." It was Daniel's voice, not Lavinia's.

Audrey stifled her disappointment with a weak giggle. "Are you on your way to campus?"

"Well, that's just it." Daniel sighed. "One of the partners walked in. For the past two hours, he's been bending my ear about one of his international cases. He'd like me to be the second chair on it."

"Wow, congratulations," Audrey replied. "Great news, right?"

"Yes and no. Audrey, I'm still stuck here, finishing the brief. You won't mind going without me, will you?"

"Not at all." *Oh. No.*

"Thanks," Daniel sounded genuinely relieved. "I'll make it up to you tomorrow. That picnic I mentioned? I'll pack it. But you're charged with bringing the wine. Noonish?"

"Sure." Audrey hoped she sounded positive.

"Hey, if you want, bring that book along. If it's funny, we can read some of the passages out loud."

As if.

The lecture auditorium was only a ten-minute walk from Audrey's apartment. The tickets included seat numbers, so Audrey had no reason to get there early.

The last thing she wanted was to seem as if she were eager to see Egan again.

She couldn't wait.

CHAPTER 21

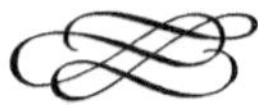

*T*he curtain on the left side of the auditorium's stage had been pulled back just enough that Egan could scan the crowd.

He'd agreed to a signing on the Berkeley campus for one reason: he hoped to run into Audrey.

His dinner last night with Lavinia had gone well. She'd mentioned that her daughter had purchased a ticket, which came with a copy of his novel.

Will she see herself in my heroine, Zelda?

Will the book help her realize why I kept her at arm's length, even as I longed for her? Even knowing she longed for me too?

Well, now there is nothing to stand in our way.

Unless what she reads embarrasses her.

Unless it was just a schoolgirl crush, and nothing more.

Unless—

His thoughts bolted from his consciousness when, suddenly, he felt a hand at the base of his spine.

"I've missed you, Egan."

That voice...

"Tell me you've missed me too."

It was dark enough that had one glanced at them from the wings, one would be able to see how her hand now roamed downward—

Until Egan stopped it.

Holding tight, he lifted Clementine Munt-Luckinbill's wrist to her side.

Even in this dim light, he could see she'd aged. Granted she'd kept her figure. The paper-thin faux-leather pencil skirt stretched tightly enough to leave no doubt about it. And while most of the wear and tear on her face had been tightened and tucked away, he knew it well enough to remember when the skin under her chin didn't sag, the lines on her neck didn't crisscross her throat like railroad tracks, and the hollows under her eyes hadn't needed to be plumped with cosmetic filler.

Or maybe it was always like that but I just didn't care because she was such a great lay, he reasoned.

As if reading at least those last seconds of his thought, his surprise visitor gave a throaty chuckle. "So you have missed me!"

"Ah, Mrs. Munt-Luckinbill—what a wonderful welcome!" Egan gave Clementine a chaste kiss on her cheek. "I was wondering if Clive might release you from his ivory tower to welcome me back." Still holding her wrist, Egan twisted it so that he could kiss the back of her hand.

He'd already been on the book tour a week. Each stop had supplied him with a smorgasbord of women ready, willing, and able to follow him into his room for the night.

But the conquests had been too easy. Out of revenge for her ratting him out to Clive, Egan was curious enough to see how far Clementine was willing to go to make amends to play along.

"It's a shame about Clive's 'head cold.' I was looking forward to sharing the stage with him." In truth, Egan had almost danced a jig when he'd arrived at the auditorium only to be informed that his former mentor was to be a no-show. "Is that the code word for 'in his cups'?"

"You know him so well." Clementine shrugged. "His publisher is balking at our counter-offer to its mediocre advance for his next book. If they don't capitulate by Monday, his agent starts shopping it around."

"Let me guess. The last one never earned out."

Frankly, that was Egan's biggest fear: that *Extracurricular* would die a premature death.

As it turned out, he'd had nothing to worry about. Between the titillating title and the intriguing description, it appealed to all the right readers.

Clementine shrugged. "Prestige has its privileges. Still..."

She didn't have to finish the sentence: *a book's sales are what mattered most.*

It also didn't help that Clive was a passive-aggressive tyrant. No matter how many awards were showered on him, it was inevitable that his publisher would eventually get tired of coddling him.

The university will follow suit, Egan reasoned. One had to work hard to get kicked out of a tenured position, but it was still possible.

"We'll just tell the audience that he's got a nasty cold." She smiled. "But you're in luck! I'm his stand in."

"*You'll* be moderating?" Egan frowned. He'd hoped to avoid both Munt-Luckinbills altogether. Clementine's very visible role in tonight's event could complicate things.

"Sure, why not?" Clementine replied. "As I recall, you enjoyed our sessions of Truth and Dare tremendously."

Egan chuckled uncertainly. "But those were private, and we always ended up naked, albeit in some interesting positions."

"The day isn't over yet." Clementine smiled grandly. "Speaking of which, you arrived so close to the starting time that the university gave the key to your hotel suite to your book publicist."

"Fine, no problem." In fact, the publicist, Kimmy, had handed it to him right before he went backstage. When she mentioned she'd be visiting old friends in the area later that evening, Egan told her she could take off during the book signing.

He too hoped to be spending time with a dear old friend.

Certainly not Clementine. And he had no intention of letting her ruin his mission:

Telling Audrey he loved her.

Who knew where things would go from there?

Clementine's way of abruptly rousing him from his fantasies of all possibilities was to cup him and whisper, "Shall we?"

This is not going as planned, Egan thought.

BY THE TIME EGAN REACHED THE PODIUM, HE'D FOUND AUDREY IN THE crowd: fourth row, just right of center.

He had to pretend to listen to Clementine's fawning introduction. It seemed as if she gushed on about his newfound notoriety for an hour. He'd stifled the desire to tell her to shut up already.

This really wasn't about him. It was Audrey's night.

Egan had to tamp down the urge to rush through the reading so that he could finally get Audrey alone by reminding himself that, through the passage he'd chosen to read, she'd finally hear everything he'd wanted to tell her these past three years.

So he read the passage slowly, as if his life depended on her verdict.

Every now and then he'd look up from the pages and seek her out in the sea of faces dimly lit by the footlights. Since he'd known Audrey, she'd been the judge and jury over his every thought and desire.

From the look on her face, he'd finally earned his reprieve.

IT WAS ALL THERE, IN HIS OWN WORDS.

The passage Egan had chosen took no more than six or seven minutes to read. In it, he'd told their story: the once-upon-a-time in which their paths crossed; the missteps and cross purposes that broke their hearts and changed their lives forever—

But that nothing, not even time, could stand in the way of their happily ever after.

With eloquence, he wove a tale of how he (that is, "Caleb") had fallen in love with her (in this case, "Zelda") from the first moment he'd laid eyes on her.

In just a few sentences, he relayed his dismay for how the combination of his position as her teacher and her age made the romance unthinkable.

But, despite his attempt to shove his feelings aside, he couldn't stop yearning for her.

By the time Egan had finished reading the passage, some in the audience were sobbing.

In Egan's book, Caleb and Zelda's unwitting deeds produce a tragic sequence of events before the lovers end up together.

We end up together.

But it was just a fantasy. Egan's fantasy, Audrey thought.

In real life, he was famous. Beloved.

And she was…

Still Audrey.

In real life, people change, she reasoned.

Everyone she knew—Tallulah, Bliss, and certainly Davis—had zigged and zagged off the path of the life they thought they'd lead.

When confronted with an obstacle, they overcame it. They were quick to recognize an opportunity and take advantage of it. Despite life's twists and turns and detours, her friends had still found the path to success and self-satisfaction.

Only I've stayed constant.

Constant for Egan.

Is Extracurricular *truly an homage to our love—or was it used merely as the novel's plot device?*

If I approach him tonight, will he sign my book with no more than a handshake and a polite smile, or will he finally profess his love for me?

She'd find out soon enough.

"So, tell us, Egan! I'm sure *everyone* is dying to know: who is the real Zelda?" Clementine smirked as if she already knew the answer to that question.

In your dreams, lady.

"Each of us has a Zelda in our life, don't we? An unrequited love? The one who got away?"

From the look on Clementine's face, one would have assumed Egan had broached a question as profound as how to achieve world peace. "If your Zelda is worth loving, isn't she also worth wooing again?"

Egan turned to stare out into the audience. Finding Audrey, he proclaimed. "You're right. And it's why I'm here."

He could have sworn he saw Audrey wipe away a tear.

———

AUDREY HAD DONE EXACTLY AS EGAN HAD HOPED: WAITED UNTIL THE LAST autograph was signed before finally approaching him.

And unlike the acquaintances who had shown up at his signings awed at the spectacle of it all, Audrey didn't attempt an awkward reintroduction.

Instead, true to her nature, with her unflinching gaze she simply declared, "I never knew you'd felt that way about us, Egan."

Tears glistened on her lashes.

He felt his own eyes dampening and thought it best to close them until he could smile again. Otherwise, he'd bawl like a baby.

When he opened them, he replied softly: "Now that you do, tell me, Audrey: what would you like to do about it?"

Instead of answering him, she held out her hand.

He took it, and they walked out together.

He was relieved that Clementine had disappeared immediately after the question and answer session. Apparently, she'd taken the hint that his interests lay elsewhere.

———

"THE UNIVERSITY IS TREATING YOU LIKE ROYALTY!" AUDREY LOOKED AROUND Egan's hotel suite. A sumptuous meal had been set up on a small table for two. A magnum of champagne sat in a silver ice bucket. Chocolate-covered strawberries filled a crystal cake stand. "Does this happen everywhere you go?"

Egan grabbed the champagne bottle and popped it. As the liquid rushed to its head, he put two glass flutes side by side in time to catch the fizzy libation's spillover.

Handing one of the glasses to her, he replied, "No, not quite. But now that I've hit the bestseller list, I guess Berkeley wants me to forgive and forget the Lit department's harsh words toward my thesis."

They clinked glasses. As Audrey drank from hers, Egan reached for Audrey's copies of his books. "Why the second one?"

"It's for Tallulah."

He chuckled. "Okay then. I know exactly what to write."

He scribbled with a flourish and then showed it to Audrey:

Dearest Tallulah,
You'll find yourself throughout the book, doing what you do well—creating havoc.
Enjoy! —Egan

Audrey laughed too. "She so richly deserves that. And frankly, Egan, you've deserved all your success too."

"Coming from you, that means a lot to me." He sighed. "But the truth is, Audrey: my faculty chair was right. The stuff I wrote before I met you… Well, let's just say you were the perfect muse. In fact, I want to memorialize that fact."

He picked up the other book and wrote:

Dear Audrey,
You were the ideal fantasy.
May our reality be just as wonderful.
With all my heart, love, Egan

"Oh…" To hide her disappointment, Audrey slipped the books into her bags then turned her gaze to the window. It faced Berkeley's renowned Campanile, which was just then chiming the hour: four o'clock.

Egan walked up beside her. "You sound disappointed."

"I'd hoped…I'd hoped I was more to you than that." Audrey shook her head. "Not just fodder for your novel."

Egan stared at her, confused. "What I felt for you was very real! I just couldn't… I couldn't let us do—"

Audrey put two fingers on his lips to shush him. "I understood. I knew it then, and I know it now."

When he calmed down, she dropped her hand to her side. "I'd always wondered why you didn't feel the same about Mandy."

He frowned. "What about her? … What do you mean?"

"That you didn't view her as—you know: 'off limits.' I guess it's because she was already eighteen—"

"*What?*… I don't understand…" Confused, Egan shook his head.

"The weekend of the debate tournament I saw her going into your room—in her bathrobe. She didn't knock. She had her own key."

Egan searched his memory. "Oh… My God! You didn't know!"

"Know what?"

He shook his head, awed. "All the stunts she pulled that weekend. The whole ploy for getting her own room was so that she could blackmail Jeremy."

"*Jeremy?* Why?"

"They were screwing. But he wouldn't go public with the relationship, so she wanted to force his hand."

"Oh! Well, I guess I had *him* wrong." Bemused, Audrey sunk onto the sofa. "How is it that you knew about their relationship and I didn't?"

"Because… I was jealous. Like me, he only had eyes for you." Egan sat down beside her. "And, frankly, for a while, I thought the feeling was mutual between him and you. Or, that you were toying with him to retaliate against me for not— well, for not taking you seriously enough."

"I was upset that you were friendly with everyone but me," Audrey admitted. "So, why *did* Mandy have a key to your room?"

"Because she'd started a fire in her own room and needed somewhere to sleep the night before the tournament. I stayed at the hospital with Jeremy." Egan winced. "Really, Jeremy started the fire, when he fell out of Mandy's bed. He was on a psychotic trip. Mandy had given him LSD. It's why he leaped from her balcony."

"I had a feeling she had something to do with Jeremy's accident!" Audrey shook her head angrily. "Why didn't you tell Lavinia?"

"I did tell her! She decided to handle it in her own way—with tender loving care." Egan shrugged. "I didn't stick around to see if her theory would work. I was too busy licking my wounds over the thought that you'd gone back to Jeremy."

Audrey burst out laughing. "*Are you serious*? No way! I was too much in love with you!" Saying it out loud wiped the smile off her face.

"And all this time I thought you hated me." He took her hand. "When we were in the elevator during the earthquake, I told you I was just there to do my job—"

"And to write your novel," she reminded him.

He let loose with a mirthless chuckle. "I misread so many signals."

And that's when she kissed him.

He understood that sign well enough.

They were still locked in their kiss as he carried her into the bedroom.

CHAPTER 22

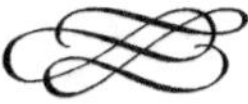

The sweetness of her lips had him craving even more of her. His fingers roamed the buttons of her blouse, undoing one after another. At the same time, his lips moved down to the cleft in her chin, a spot that had teased him for nine months, so many years ago.

In fact, the exploration of every nook and cranny of her exquisite body —every inch of skin, every dimple and pucker—was met with a groan of anticipation or a sigh of joy.

At the same time, Audrey's hands passed lightly over his chest, causing his heart to pound harder. As they floated over his abdomen, his cock, already stiffened, ached to be inside her.

By her moans, he knew she wanted him too. He parted her thighs with his hand.

When he entered her, she was so tight that his gasp was as loud as hers.

My God…I don't know if I can hold out—

Suddenly, Audrey clenched so firmly that it was all he could do to hold on; to keep from exploding.

He couldn't help himself: he came.

Egan collapsed on top of her, spent.

PAIN…

Oh my God—SUCH PAIN—

JOY.

So much joy.

Finally.

FINALLY!

He was worth the wait.

And yet…

It was over so quickly!

… Is it always like that? God, I hope not…

Suddenly she was crying. Yes, from the pain—oh, how her muscles ached down there!—and yes, from the wave of bliss washing over her.

As if reading her mind, Egan reached up to stroke her cheek.

"You're crying," he murmured. "Why?"

"Because…" Audrey sighed. "I waited so long for this."

For us.

A HAZY MEMORY ROSE IN EGAN'S CONSCIOUSNESS: JEREMY'S UNSUCCESSFUL attempt to be Audrey's first lover, and Egan's own dismay that the boy may have succeeded on the day they skipped his class. But when confronted, Audrey had made it clear to Egan: she hadn't gone through with it.

Wait…

Nah. She's now a junior in college—and at BERKELEY, no less! I mean, come on. There's just no way she's still a virgin…

I mean… My God—she knew what she was doing down there…

So…

Tight.

Shit."

Egan had to ask: "Audrey… Are you…?"

How can I put this so that it doesn't seem so ludicrous: "Are you seeing someone?"

OH, GOD! HOW DID HE KNOW?

Caught off guard, Audrey whispered, "Yes."

"Oh."

He sounds almost—relieved.

"I don't mean this very second," she said crossly.

Not until tomorrow. Noonish.

At the thought of Daniel, a volt of guilt charged through her.

I am Egan's fantasy, but I am Daniel's reality.

Egan laughed. "Of course, not. You're with me now."

What did he mean by that? Was he finally ready to make a life with her?

She'd waited so long for him to love her. And now, this was the moment—

"Yoo-hoo, darling! Sorry it took me so long to get here, but I wanted to pick up a little surprise for you…"

The bedroom alcove was positioned so that Audrey could see the woman enter through the suite's front door.

It was the woman who had interviewed Egan: Clementine something or other, hyphenated.

As Clementine stripped out of her clothes, she plucked one of the chocolate covered strawberries and ate it whole, all the while babbling about a particular sex act she'd missed with Egan. Something about his joystick…

She held up a cock ring tied in a pretty bow. "Appropriate, wouldn't you say?"

"What the hell, Clementine!" Egan sat straight up. "How did you—"

"I kept the second key, silly!" She waved it at him. "I'm sure I mentioned it to you…or your publicist." Clementine shrugged. Then, noting Audrey's presence, she exclaimed, *"Peek-a-boo!"*

Mortified, Audrey pulled the covers to her chin.

Convulsing with laughter, Clementine clucked her tongue at Egan. "Naughty boy! You started the party without me?"

Despite the pain wracking her body, Audrey scrambled out of bed.

As she scooped up her clothes, Clementine cooed, "No rush, hon." She shifted her gaze to Egan. "In fact, she can stay, if she likes. I enjoy a threesome every now and then. And if I remember, sweet Egan, it was one of your fantasies, too."

Egan's fantasy.

Apparently, he had quite a few of them.

Audrey ran to the bathroom.

Egan stood outside the door, pleading for her to ignore Clementine, to believe him that he hadn't been expecting the woman, and other things that were just as likely to be lies in the hope to convince her to stay—

And complete another of his fantasies.

As she flung open the bathroom door and rushed past him, she noticed that Clementine was already naked and in the bed.

Audrey was barely out the front door when she heard the woman exclaim, "What is this—*blood*? Since when did you start liking the rough stuff?"

AUDREY STOOD UNDER A STEAMING SHOWER FOR OVER AN HOUR. THE SORENESS had ebbed somewhat, but not entirely.

The condition of her heart was a different matter.

What a fool I am, she thought. All these years, I believed that I was doing the right thing: waiting for love.

Waiting for *his* love.

Instead, she got fucked.

Three years of pining after some guy whose opening line was to tease her about taking her to Paris. What a naïve dolt she was!

Three years of waiting for him to call, just to say, "I've been thinking about you. I have something to say to you. When can I see you?"

But, no. Instead, Egan's way of professing his supposed love—nope, make that *lust*—was to make her some saintly, unattainable heroine in his book!

That bastard!

The phone was ringing off the hook. Audrey's apartment was small enough that, even in the shower, she could hear the messages on the answering machine:

"Audrey, please don't freak out that I have your contact information. I had my publicist beg someone to give it to her because I... I need to apologize. I wasn't expecting Clementine to just appear like that! *I swear!* I mean, yeah, we once had a thing. But that was before I—"

Good, thought Audrey. The answering machine cut him off.

But not for long:

"Listen, Audrey, before this damn thing cuts me off again: please—*I'm begging you*—please let me see you tonight. We've got to talk this out! I know you feel that way too! I'm right... *Right?* In fact, I'm standing right outside your building now. Won't you just buzz me in? *Please?* I swear, had I known you were a... well, *you* know... I wouldn't have... I think you get my drift—"

He's got my address too?

Audrey leaped out of the shower and ran to the window.

Yep, there he was: right outside her building.

Why, that cad is telling the whole world that he just broke my cherry!

Because she needed both hands to open the window, she waited until she'd wrapped her body in the drapes. Through it, she shouted, "I called the police! They are on their way! Unless you want to end up in jail, you better get lost *now!* Boy, I'll bet your publisher would *really* appreciate that!"

Audrey was sorely tempted to bean him with the signed books, but that meant giving him one more look at her naked body. He'd have to settle for watching her slam the window shut.

As for the books, they were too large for the wastebasket beside her desk, so she dumped them beside it instead.

She spent the rest of the evening sobbing her heart out.

———

SOMEWHERE AROUND MIDNIGHT—AFTER AUDREY'S MIND HAD RACED THROUGH all the would-haves, could-haves, should-haves, and might-haves that may have salvaged her relationship with Egan—Lavinia's words about sex came to her:

> *Your first time making love is a special moment. But even more important than the desire or passion you feel now is the issue of trust.*
>
> *When the person you love has earned your trust, then the time will be right to share your love.*

She'd never dared to assume that Egan, now a twenty-nine year-old man, had been pining for her. The assumption he'd gone the past three years without a sexual encounter would have been merely naive. Women were drawn to him like hummingbirds to nectar. His relaxed demeanor around them made his attention all the sweeter. Her attraction to him was proof of that.

Until now.

Their relationship—or, more honestly, lack of one—had given Egan something to write about. But if a mercy fuck was his way showing his appreciation, he could go to hell.

At the very least, he could have scheduled it at a time he wasn't expecting company.

After what just happened, I'll never be able to trust Egan again, she realized. *Certainly not the way I trust Daniel...*

Oh, my God—

Tomorrow.

Daniel.

There was no way she could meet with Daniel. She wouldn't be able to look him in the eye.

Not tomorrow.

Maybe never again.

She couldn't lie to him about losing her head over Egan.

Or for that matter, her maidenhead.

Not that he ever pushed her on the issue. He wouldn't know to push. He just thought she wanted them to take it slow.

Now "slow" was changing status to "standstill."

Audrey dialed his number with trembling fingers. Thankfully, it went to voicemail.

She took a deep breath: "Listen, I..."

I what—lost my virginity to an old crush?

Am no longer a virgin but a fickle whore?

Am I an idiot who let a fantasy go to my head?

All of the above?

"...came down with something that has me tossing my cookies," she continued. "If it's contagious, maybe we should postpone our, um, picnic. I'd hate for you to come down with this too. I'm going to bed now. I'll call you later in the week when I feel better."

She knew she wouldn't.

I don't deserve him.

VOICE MESSAGES

Daniel McKittridge, Monday, 3:32 pm: "Hi, hon. Hadn't heard from you, and I was just wondering how you're feeling. Call me with an update. Love you."

Daniel McKittridge, Tuesday 5:46pm: "Hi, Aud. I have to say, I'm somewhat concerned that I haven't heard back from you. Whatever bug you think you've got... I hope it hasn't put you in the hospital! If you get this, can you call? If I'm in a meeting, leave a message. I love you."

Daniel McKittridge, Wednesday, 9:03am: "Audrey, just to let you know: I called University Health Services. The folks say you haven't been admitted as a patient... So, please, can you tell me what's up? Just... check in. Call my voice mail. I promise I won't pick up. I love and miss you."

If Egan had called too, Audrey wouldn't have known it because she'd asked PacTel to block his call.

Audrey had spent the last few days sleepwalking through her classes. By midnight on Wednesday, she knew Daniel was right: she owed it to him to tell him something, even if it was that she didn't want to see him anymore.

She didn't call him at home. He was an early riser and most undoubtedly asleep. Besides, by calling his office, it would roll over to voicemail—

Only it didn't.

"Hey." Daniel was trying to sound casual, but she knew him well enough to hear the anxious tone in his voice.

"I… I thought you'd be home by now." *I thought you said you wouldn't pick up.*

"I should be," he admitted. "But I've got a case that's working me overtime."

"I'm sorry I've been so hard to get…I was feeling so ill that I slept through a couple of days of classes. I've got to play catch-up myself." *Don't lie. Tell the truth.*

"That's all I need to know—that you're alright."

Audrey felt even worse, hearing the relief in his voice. "Daniel, I think we should take a break."

"Oh?"

He's surprised. But of course, he should be. If the shoe were on the other foot, I'd feel the same way.

"I feel a bit overwhelmed at the moment," Audrey replied.

"Aw, honey, I'm sorry! I forgot. You've got exams in a couple of weeks."

"Yes. Thanks for understanding." *No! What I'm trying to say is that you deserve better than me—*

He laughed softly. "Can I help it if you're the best part of my week? But, hey, been there, done that with the cramming sessions. Call me when you feel human again. You know I'll always be here for you."

The lump in her throat made it hard for her to talk. Finally, she was able to whisper: "I know, dear friend. Goodbye."

CHAPTER 23

For four weeks the copies of *Extracurricular* sat on the floor beside the wastepaper basket—and probably would have been thrown in the dorm's recycling bin had Tallulah not called with an invitation to catch Maggie's show at San Francisco's Bill Graham Auditorium.

Audrey knew how badly Tallulah wanted to read it, so, with great trepidation, she mentioned that not only had she scored two copies of the book, Egan had autographed them too.

Tallulah giggled with glee. "Well, then, lady, get your butt over to this side of the bridge—pronto! I'll leave your name at the Bill's backstage door!"

The concert was sold out. The opening act, Jammerhead, had the crowd hyped into a frenzy.

As Tallulah read Egan's inscription to her, she snorted. "Well, he certainly had *my* number!" She looked up expectantly at her friend. "Hey, so, what did he write in yours?"

"Nothing half as cute. Basically, a one-liner." Audrey shrugged.

"Have you read the damn thing yet?" Tallulah was doing her best to shout over Jammerhead's riffing.

"No—but he read an excerpt to the audience." Audrey exhaled slowly to give herself time to choose her words carefully. Finally, she yelled back: "Davis was right. Egan sensationalized his students—and himself."

To hear over the music, Tallulah pulled Audrey into a backstage corridor. "In what way?"

"We're in there, Tallulah." *What an understatement.* "And—he has a thing for one of his students."

Tallulah's eyes opened wide. "Can you make out who it is?"

176

"Yes," Audrey admitted. "It's—"

"No, no—let me guess: Mandy?"

Audrey frowned. "She was certainly the obvious choice."

"You can say that again! She was one big suck-up—and all that implies."

Audrey shrugged. "Nothing is ever as it seems. That goes double in fiction."

"Quit taunting me! If I wasn't on double duty right now, I'd tear right into it."

"What do you mean, double duty?"

Tallulah smiled. "Don't you remember? I'm also managing Jammerhead. In fact"—she blushed. "I'm especially managing Mr. Jammerhead himself." Instinctively, her hand fell on her belly. "Audrey, you're the first to know. I'm going to have a baby!"

"What?" Audrey leaned against the wall, awed. It was the first time she'd noticed that Tallulah wasn't in her usual attire. Skin-tight jeans and a spaghetti-strap tank top, usually worn braless, had been replaced with a gauzy loose-fitting mini-dress. "When…and…how?"

Tallulah laughed. "I think the 'how' is obvious. As for the 'when,' I found out a few weeks ago. In fact, right after we met up at Magnolia." She blushed. "He's so sweet, and funny—and *fearless!* And most importantly, he knows my world, so he's not in awe of it—or Maggie. It's also why I felt it was so important to convince Maggie to complete the tour. I want her to get to know Jammerhead better before I break the news to her."

Audrey placed her hand on Tallulah's belly too. "Knowing Maggie, I guess the news that she's about to become a grandmother won't go over so well."

"Yeah, you've got that right!" Tallulah shrugged. "Well, too bad. Jammerhead is just as excited as me about this little unexpected surprise."

"Will there be a wedding before the birth?"

"That little piece of paper isn't so important to me. Time will tell if we're the real deal, right? Like you, I never knew my father. Maggie was too much of a tomcat to keep track. Heck, I'm surprised she went through with the pregnancy! My guess is that just being around Lavinia while she was pregnant with you may have convinced her that bringing a life into the world might be the biggest high of them all."

"If that's so, she must thank her lucky stars every day. You're more than just a daughter to her. You're her lifesaver."

Twice, Tallulah had come home from school to find her mother overdosing.

Had she not been there, Maggie would have been yet one more rock and roll tragedy, Audrey reasoned.

Audrey hugged her friend. "I'm very happy for you."

"And I'm happy for you too," Tallulah winked knowingly.

Does she mean Egan? How does she know?

Audrey felt her cheeks grow hot. "I don't know what you mean."

"I meant about you and Daniel!" Tallulah threw up her hands. "Do you know how long I've been waiting for you to get over Jeremy?"

"Jeremy?" Audrey couldn't believe her ears. "All this time, you thought I was pining for Jeremy?"

Tallulah rolled her eyes. "Well, who else could it have been—especially after he started screwing that little slut, Mandy."

I guess I really was the last person to know about them, Audrey reasoned, but only because I couldn't care less.

"By the way, how is lover boy?"

Audrey winced at Tallulah's coy reference to Daniel. "I… I haven't seen him for a while. Exams and all." She hesitated. "In fact, I suggested we take a break. Frankly… I don't deserve him."

Tallulah went nose to nose with her. "Audrey, don't be a fool. Trust me, there are a lot of jerks out there. Daniel McKittridge is smart, funny, kind, and head over heels in love with you. Think hard now: do you really want to let him go?"

She's right. Daniel loves me unconditionally.

"Thank you." Audrey kissed her friend on the cheek.

Surprised, Tallulah laughed. "For what?"

"For putting everything in perspective," Audrey shouted as she ran down the hall.

She'd only been to Daniel's place a couple of times. He had a one-bedroom apartment on Russian Hill. It was small and on the fourth floor of an old Edwardian, but it had an awe-inspiring view of Angel and Alcatraz Islands. And, after the fog burned off, the Berkeley Campanile could be spotted across the bay from his windows.

Because it was after nine at night, she took the risk that he was home from the office.

She wouldn't be able to find out immediately because Daniel's building had a closed garage. He always left a light on in the apartment's front window, so that wasn't a telltale sign either. She knocked twice on his door. Then twice again, harder.

No answer.

She was about to leave when she realized Daniel was walking up the stairwell. He was carrying a bag from a local Thai restaurant. When she was here last, he'd taken her there: just a little hole-in-the-wall place, down the hill, on Polk Street. There, they'd tucked into a feast: spring rolls, shrimp pad Thai, rainbow beef curry, and tofu basil.

The sack of food in his hand was much smaller than what they'd brought back as leftovers. He'd ordered for one.

His eyes opened wide. "Gee, what a pleasant surprise! In fact, I was just thinking about you."

"Were you? What about?"

Instead of telling Audrey, he showed her with his kiss.

She'd missed Daniel's mouth: the way it skimmed hers first before finding its place against her lips, then parting them.

She loved the way his eyes closed sleepily as if the most important thing in the world was the task at hand: proving the depth of his love.

His hard, strong arms drew her in closer.

When her fingers grazed his chest, she felt him harden against her.

"Perhaps we should go inside," she whispered.

She didn't have to ask twice.

ON SO MANY LEVELS, SHE KNEW IT WAS WRONG TO COMPARE HER SECOND experience with the first one.

Sex with Egan—achingly longed for and fervently anticipated—had been a hot, raw frenzy of lust.

Sex with Daniel was more encompassing. His actions made it clear that he wanted to savor every moment with her; to treat her like a precious treasure.

As for Audrey, she strove to capture every second in her mind's eye in the hope that it would erase that tortured afternoon with Egan.

She marveled how Daniel took his time undressing her: gently slipping her shirt over her head, then unsnapping her bra before his hands caressed her breasts.

Once naked, Audrey followed his lead: slowly loosening his tie before pulling it off, flicking each button on his shirt free, and unbuckling his belt, allowing his pants to fall to the floor.

It was harder to pull off Daniel's boxer briefs, what with his erection in the way. Audrey tried not to stare at it. She had no desire to compare it with Egan's.

She saw immediately that his goal was to explore with her a new and deeper sensual intimacy, something they had yet to experience but both desired passionately.

When Daniel entered her, she flinched in apprehension. She was pleasantly surprised at how her body opened to him, to find pleasure in gripping him, in hearing his contented groans.

Every surge was a rollercoaster of bliss. Each stroke thrummed her to her core. When the moment came in which he exploded with ecstasy, her joy was just as intense.

She fell asleep in his arms wishing she could stay there forever.

———

A SHAFT OF SUNLIGHT SOMEHOW SLIPPED BETWEEN THE CURTAINS, WARMING her face and awakening her.

Audrey opened one eye to see Daniel propped up on one elbow, grinning down at her.

"Marry me," he whispered.

"We haven't known each other all that long," she whispered back.

"I think that works in our favor. We can spend the rest of our lives discovering all the great things we love about each other."

"And what about the bad things?" she countered.

"Okay, you start," he challenged. "Name one thing you think will make me hate you."

Audrey teared up. "I can't."

Because I'll ruin us forever.

"I knew it. You're perfect."

She shook her head. "No, that's not true *at all.*"

Tenderly, Daniel traced her nose with his finger. "Don't assume I think you're perfect. I don't. If you need proof, I've found a small pimple." He tapped the side of her face. "Right here."

"Thanks for pointing that out," she retorted.

"I'm sure you'll do the same for me, over the course of time. Hopefully, a very long time." He took her hand in his. "But first things first. You have to say yes."

"And what if I refuse?" she teased.

"You won't. Because you know in your heart no man will ever love you as I do."

When their eyes met, she realized he was right.

"Yes, then. I'll marry you."

They celebrated by making love again.

Afterward, sore but content, Audrey fell asleep, thinking: *Egan may have been my first love, but Daniel will be my last.*

———

AUDREY SPENT THE WHOLE WEEKEND WITH DANIEL IN THE CITY. ON SUNDAY morning, they paid a surprise visit to Lavinia.

Audrey's mother had heard her mention Daniel, but had not pressed to meet him. She knew her daughter well enough that, should he prove right for Audrey, that time would come soon enough. So, when Lavinia opened the door, she looked Daniel over, then said, "It's about time."

Puzzled, Daniel exclaimed, "You know then—about our engagement?"

Surprised and delighted, Lavinia laughed. "I guess that gives us two things to celebrate! A beautiful day and a happily ever after."

———

As Audrey suspected, in the course of the afternoon, her mother and fiancé developed a mutual admiration.

While Lavinia puttered around the garden, Audrey and Daniel made themselves at home in the lounge chairs. Daniel, curious about Ashbury Academy, asked Lavinia about her goals for the school. In turn, Lavinia quizzed him about his legal cases.

They found common ground by trading arcane observations about Audrey that had each other laughing and invariably embarrassing Audrey.

Especially when Lavinia asked, "By the way, were you able to connect with Egan when he was in town?"

Audrey's attempt at a nonchalant nod was a bit wobbly. "Yes. He autographed books for Tallulah and me."

"So, you did find someone for your second ticket after all," Lavinia exclaimed. "I'm so glad."

"Me too, since I couldn't make it either," Daniel chimed in.

Audrey felt uncomfortable for allowing them to think that Tallulah had gone with her, but it was better than admitting she saw Egan alone.

In his hotel room—

Where Clementine What's-Her-Name barged in.

"Audrey, have you finished the book yet?" Daniel asked.

Audrey shrugged. "To tell you the truth, I haven't even started it." *At least that's truthful.*

"I have," Lavinia said.

Audrey felt a sudden chill. "Oh? What do you think of it?"

Lavinia lowered her sunglasses in order to look at her daughter. "Well, let's just say he certainly has an active imagination."

Daniel laughed. "Now you've got *me* curious. I've got a business trip coming up. Maybe I should borrow it so that I can read it on the plane."

Audrey realized the first thing she'd have to do when she got home to her apartment was to hide that damn book.

———

While back at school on Monday, Audrey took her longest break between classes to visit the university's health clinic.

The sex she'd had with Egan had been unprotected. Now, just over four weeks later, Audrey felt relieved she'd dodged a bullet. But with her relationship with Daniel moving into an intimate phase, she couldn't take the risk of a pregnancy.

At some point, she and Daniel would want children. But that would happen much later: after she'd attained her undergrad degree, completed law school, worked for a firm—

Much later. Right now, other things in life were ahead of her.

Them.

"I'd like birth control, please," she told the clinic's nurse.

The woman nodded and handed her a clipboard holding a form. "Fill this out, completely."

A history of her sexual activity? *Well, that was easy enough. Twice only: once, four weeks ago. And once, three days ago.*

The date of her last menstruation? *Hmmm. Shouldn't it be any day now?*

She looked at the clinic's wall calendar and started counting backward on the number of weeks...

Oh, no.

She walked to the nurse's desk. "Excuse me, may I have a home pregnancy test?"

The nurse nodded. She went down the hallway behind her and was back a moment later with the requested item. Pointing to a door marked WOMEN, she said, "You can use this in there."

It took a minute to pee on the stick.

The results took a few minutes longer.

She spent the next half hour staring down at the stick and cursing the fact, in the past seventy-two hours, she'd felt both the happiest and saddest she'd ever been in her life.

IF DEBATE CLUB HAD TAUGHT HER ANYTHING, IT WAS TO LOOK AT THE PROS AND cons of every situation.

> *CON: I'm pregnant before I wanted to be.*
> *PRO: I could abort, or put up the child for adoption.*
> *CON: I'd never do either of these things. Not to some soul who is my flesh and blood.*
> *PRO: I'll have the baby.*
> *CON: I'll lose Daniel because the child isn't his.*
> *CON: I'll put my college on hold or else spend it being pregnant.*
> *CON: I'll raise the child by myself.*

From every angle, there were no more pros, just a long line of cons.

UNLIKE HER GUILT OVER HAVING SEX WITH EGAN, AUDREY FELT SHE SHOULD tell Daniel immediately about her situation, and that she would not hold him to his promise of marriage.

She felt she should tell him in person. The sooner the better. She picked up the phone and dialed his number.

"Hi, beautiful," he said. "Miss me already?"

"Yes, terribly." Audrey wasn't kidding. "When can I see you?"

"A week from Saturday, unfortunately. That trip I mentioned when we were at Lavinia's? It means I fly to Japan tonight, for that new case I'd mentioned a while back. A big international merger with a lot of moving parts."

"Oh!..." Audrey was dismayed. By the time he got back, she'd be almost six weeks along.

"I know. It's driving me crazy that we can't be together."

For the rest of our lives.

"Look, Audrey, I've got to go into a deposition. I'll call you tonight, okay?"

"No... no, don't, Daniel. Just... have a safe journey. We'll talk when you get back."

PRO: Daniel will make a wonderful father.
   PRO: My child won't grow up fatherless.
   PRO: My child will have two parents who love him or her.
   PRO: I can spend the rest of my life with Daniel.
   CON: He'd hate me if he ever found out that I'd lied about my child being his.

THE NEXT TWO WEEKS WENT BY TOO QUICKLY FOR A WOMAN WITH AUDREY'S honest nature, but not fast enough for a woman in love.

She was there to meet Daniel when his return flight arrived at SFO.

They took a taxi back to his place. He couldn't stop kissing her.

The taxi driver seemed to enjoy playing voyeur. But when he had to swerve to avoid the car in front of them, Audrey shook her finger at Daniel. He got the message.

When they arrived at his place, she tried to stop him from taking her to bed. But then she realized that perhaps the rumors about break-up sex were true, and since it was probably the last sex she'd ever have (probably the rumors about single mothers' love lives were also true) she decided she should take advantage of the opportunity being offered.

All was great until their mutual climax was interrupted by her first bout of morning sickness.

"Audrey... are you... ill again?" He stood at the door to the bathroom while she heaved into the toilet.

"I'm... pregnant," she admitted between heaves.

There. Now he knew.

What she couldn't understand was why he was hugging her. And kissing her. And proclaiming that he was the happiest man on earth.

And that he'd be fine if she wanted to move up their wedding before her graduation.

"But... but..." Audrey was speechless.

I have to tell him the truth.

PRO: He's happy about being a father.
    CON: Egan wouldn't be. He'd feel resentful.
    PRO: Daniel makes me happy.
    CON: Egan doesn't.
    PRO: My child deserves a father who loves his or her mother.
    CON: I was infatuated with Egan.
    PRO: I need a husband I can trust.
    PRO: I love Daniel.
    PRO: I am marrying Daniel.

Daniel hugged her. "I've never been happier in my whole life."

"Me too," Audrey whispered.

RIGHT NOW

CHAPTER 24

*Rule #6: Parents, please note: student attendance to Magic Circles is
mandatory.*

*Ashbury Academy recognizes the present and future need for students to become
keen problem identifiers, problem solvers, critical thinkers, and creative innovators.*

*Since its inception some twenty-five years ago, AA has used its "Magic Circle"
conflict resolution technique to teach students how to consciously work on their
decision-making process, and on their interactions with others.*

Why? Because it works!

So yes, attendance to Magic Circles *is mandatory.*

—Ashbury Academy Admissions Handbook

"The twins will laugh if they see you crying."

Daniel was right, of course. Charlene and Charles—Charly
and Chuck to their friends and family—were in the stage of their young
lives where they covered their own embarrassment by snickering at the
foibles of others.

In other words, they were typical teenagers.

"Crying about the first day of their senior year in high school is silly, I
know." Audrey's attempt to blot both tears and trepidation from her lashes
without smearing her mascara was futile.

The kitchen had no mirrors for her to scrutinize any cosmetic damage.
She pulled a hand mirror from the satchel.

She shuddered at what she saw. Besides the muddy puddles in the
hollows above her cheeks, mascara had seeped into the tiny web of lines
around her eyes, making her look even older than she felt that day.

186

I wonder if this year will change their lives, as it did mine. If so, here's hoping that any transformations are for the best.

"Honey, you'd better hurry or you'll make them late for school." Daniel wrapped his arms around her waist. As his lips nuzzled her neck, he breathed deeply, enjoying the scent of her hair.

She resisted the urge to lay her head on his broad chest and sob away her silly melancholy.

Or, more honestly, her guilty regrets.

He wants to comfort me, but there is no way he can.

Instead she put on her sunglasses. They were wide enough to hide her smudges until she could fix her face in AA's parents lounge, where she was due to meet the two parents who would replace her this year as Ashbury Academy's PTA chair.

Now that the twins were in their senior year, Audrey wanted to leave the *sturm* and *drang* of the school's politics behind her. It had been a constant in her life since the Ashbury Academy's inception.

She was handing the reins to two of her dearest friends who also happened to be alumnae: Tallulah and Bliss.

Bliss' career as a fashion model had put her in front of the man who swept her off her feet and was now her husband: the celebrated Italian couturier, Raffaele Belluci. These days Bliss only stepped onto a runway to promote her husband's line of clothes or for a favored charity.

Their daughter, Sienna, was now a junior in the school. The girl, blessed with her mother's willowy figure and stunning face, was already following in her mother's footsteps. Through Snapchat and Instagram, she was building an army of avid followers, and she'd signed with a modeling agency. However, her father insisted that her photo shoots take place during weekends or school breaks, or the summer months.

"He's always telling Sienna, 'You're not just a model. You're the heir to a dynasty!'" Bliss fretted. "I wish he'd just let her do her thing."

As for Tallulah, she and her common-law husband, Jammerhead, had a son in the school. Quest was a senior, just like Chuck and Charly. The kid, sweet but clueless, had one love: music. Even as a toddler, it was his first and only interest.

This, plus the fact that he sang like an angel, had convinced his grandmother, "Mimi Maggie," to get off the drugs that had haunted her since the early days of her success.

Her belief—that a family who toured together stayed together—was the impetus for the annual summer tour of both Chameleon and Jammerhead. Quest had grown up on the road. Now seventeen, he felt he had to live up to his musical legacy. To his parents' dismay, his studies suffered because of it.

"Hey, why don't I drive the twins to school today?" Daniel's question was proffered with studied nonchalance.

"You're hiding out from Lavinia, remember? If she sees you, she'll twist your arm until you commit to joining the school's trustee board."

"Maybe it's time I said yes," Daniel countered. "It's Chuck and Charly's last year of school, and you've had all the fun up until now."

Audrey laughed. "Your plate is already full, my love. You're the managing partner of your law firm, remember?"

"And you're Congressman Blanchard's speech writer," Daniel countered. "He makes over a hundred speeches a year, and tosses out at least three times that in the sound bites you write that make him the darling of his district. He owes every reelection to your eloquence. So, isn't it time that I tend to this home fire?"

Audrey sighed. "Daniel, trust me. Sitting on the school's board won't be a cakewalk. As the parent liaison, I know it firsthand. All those humongous egos in one place, jockeying for a chance to mark their children's school with their Grade-A liquid gold piss–"

Daniel guffawed. "I doubt Lavinia would appreciate your urinal metaphor for her school."

"Don't be so sure," Audrey countered. "She's seen them all at their worst! Remember, since the board's inception, she's had to play referee; tamp down all their ludicrous expectations for what they think the school should do and be." She sighed. "Lavinia has singlehandedly turned AA into the most desirable private school in the San Francisco Bay Area. Why don't they just leave her alone to do what she does best?" She hesitated, then added: "Frankly, Daniel, I think it's finally wearing her down. She seems so tired lately."

Daniel nodded. "I've noticed that too. But 'retirement' is not in Lavinia's vocabulary. In this case, the school wouldn't be the same without her. She's been its heart and soul since Day One. This is, what, its twenty-fifth anniversary?"

"Silver, yes. And to celebrate, AA's PTA is pulling out all stops with the annual spring fundraising gala. In fact, it's taking place over the whole weekend. Not only will it include the parent gala, there will be a carnival brought in on Saturday for the students too—*and* a concert with big-name headliners."

"Let me guess: Tallulah has somehow convinced Maggie to come out of retirement."

"Yep. And Jammerhead will also be on the bill. As will a slew of other acts."

Awed, Daniel shook his head. "Just between those two names, there are two dozen platinum albums, not to mention Maggie is in the Rock and Roll Hall of Fame."

"And there's talk of Jammerhead being inducted this year," Audrey pointed out.

"Well, the alumni are certainly pulling their weight!"

"I wish I could say the same for the Titans." Audrey rolled her eyes. "Titan" was the nickname the alumni used for wealthiest parents whose children made up the school's second generation. "The stuff Lavinia's done to appease them is mind boggling. Frankly, I think it's doing more harm than good to the school's reputation. Why, just the other day, I overheard two Town School moms at Whole Foods, comparing notes on private high schools for their eighth graders. One of them called AA 'the Crystal Cruise Line of San Francisco prep schools!'"

Daniel laughed. "But it's true, isn't it? What other high school has a Michelin-rated chef and hot tubs all over campus to relax the kids?"

"The chef is an alumnus himself, remember? And by the way: he approached Lavinia," Audrey argued. "He insisted he'd never been happier than when he was at AA, and he wants to find that bliss again. It's a win-win for him *and* the school."

"Okay, I'll concede that—but only because he makes some of the best grub in the city. Still, Audrey, I mean come on! Just last summer, the whole junior class went on a field trip to Antarctica!"

"The best way to learn about the history of a time or place is to experience it in person," Audrey countered. "They went to Ernest Shackleton's expedition site—"

"Yeah, okay, sure." Daniel looked at the ceiling so as not to laugh out loud. "Then tell me this: what other school's 'Family Fun Fridays' feature fireworks and Cirque de Soleil? Admit it, babe: Ashbury Academy is no longer the little hippy school run out of a dilapidated Victorian."

Audrey frowned. When she was a student at the school, the Friday night gatherings were merely potlucks initiated by the students' parents. To offset this fond remembrance, she shrugged. "Perks like that come with the territory. The parents who pay full freight at the school have…well, I guess you could call it a sense of entitlement."

"That's putting it mildly," Daniel muttered. "Heck, my old high school had an ancient gym. We studied off photocopied pages from the few school books allotted to each class, and I came out alright."

"You've always been the exception to the rule," Audrey teased. "Believe me, Daniel: *I hear you.* When it comes to bells and whistles, AA is practically in a class by itself. But its real selling points are an average class size of only seventeen students, and a teacher-to-student ratio of one-to-eight; and the thirty-one Advanced Placement courses it offers its students. And the best part of all: Ashbury Academy has an eighty-three percent college acceptance rate to its graduates' first-choice schools."

She reached for her keys. "It's why those parents who pay the full freight of $51,000 are here in the first place."

"And why those parents—as you call them, the 'Titans'— resent the fact that half of AA's students pay nothing at all, or, based on a sliding scale of their household family income, no more than five thousand dollars."

A quilt embroidered with Ashbury Academy's mission statement, created by the school's first graduating class, was now encased in the glass frame that hung over the school's reception hall. It stated:

We, the students, teachers, staff, administrators, and parents of Ashbury Academy, vow to uphold our mission of individual honesty and institutional integrity. Students seeking intellectual engagement and a pure pursuit of knowledge will be welcomed with open arms, despite any social or economic barriers they must overcome.

"In the meantime, if the Titans are slowly taking over the trustee board, Lavinia's vision may not stand for long." Daniel continued.

Deep down in her heart, Audrey knew he was right.

"From what Lavinia told me, this year's board president, the fund manager Seamus McCoppin, doesn't seem to have an altruistic bone in his body," Daniel added. "Did you know he actually suggested that the school should quote-unquote 'quit footing the bill for some deadbeats' kids'? And that most of the board would prefer that their fees and donations go toward, say, a grander gymnasium designed by a renowned architect, or maybe hiring Lady Gaga to sing at the junior-senior dance?" He shook his head in disgust.

"The alumni won't let that happen," Audrey insisted. "For some of them, it's the only way their children will have a chance to have the same sort of education they had."

"Audrey, why do you think Lavinia wants me on the board?" Daniel put his arms around her neck. "Honey, with your resignation, she's lost her majority. I'm serious when I say I'd love to do this for Lavinia. It would only be a one-year commitment. The trustee board has just one meeting a month. I'll be taking part in votes and giving legal counsel on pertinent paperwork. That wouldn't be so bad."

Audrey sighed. "For the past three years, our lives have revolved around that school. And it starts all over again next year, when Noah enters as a freshman."

To his credit, the youngest McKittridge favored Daniel—not just in looks but in demeanor. He was sweet and kind; funny, but soft-spoken. And like Charly if not Chuck, he took his studies seriously.

"I for one am ready to give it a break," Audrey insisted. "Seriously Daniel, take my word for it: run fast and far."

He nodded forlornly. "Okay—but only because you're so adamant about it." He looked at the kitchen clock. "We'd both better get going. But I'll drop Noah at Town School while you take the twins to AA." He smiled slyly. "Oh, and while you're there, break the news to Lavinia that you've forbidden me to join her board."

Audrey's frown warned him that she wanted to slap that knowing grin off his face.

But, instead, she kissed him—*hard*.

"*Gross*, Mom! Quit pretending you guys still know how to get it on and let's move it. Otherwise, we're going to be late for school."

Chuck's voice, coming from behind Audrey, roused her from the safest place she knew: her husband's arms.

"Is your sister still upstairs?" she asked.

Chuck rolled his eyes. "Are you kidding? She's queen of the nerds and it's the first day of school. She's already in the car." He plucked the car keys from Audrey's hand. "I'll drive, okay?"

Before Audrey could protest, he added, "Otherwise, that's two things I'll have to bring up with my shrink: the vision of you sexing up Dad, and the fact you're a helicopter mom."

Audrey punched her oldest son's arm as a warning that he was about to go too far.

But she didn't take away the keys.

Despite Audrey's insistence that all three of her children were her favorites, Daniel teased her that Chuck—the kid who knew no barriers, broke all the rules, and could talk his way out of any situation—had his mother wrapped around his little finger.

She'd never admit he was right.

Or why, for that matter.

CHAPTER 25

*E*xcept for one time that Chuck forgot to stop at a crosswalk and when he rushed through a yellow caution light in front of a police car, the ride to school was uneventful.

"You drive like you eat—as if the house is on fire," Audrey scolded.

Charly giggled. "Yeah, well from what I hear, that's not all he does fast."

Chuck eyed her through the rearview mirror. "Oh, yeah? What's that supposed to mean?"

"If you must know, the scuttlebutt in the senior girls' lounge is that you're a bit quick on the draw—"

Audrey's head whipped around to stare at her daughter. "Are you telling me that my son has loose morals?"

"Let me put it this way," Charly retorted. "If 'his morals,' as you call them, were any looser, they'd be hanging down to his knees."

"Hey, watch it," Chuck growled.

"No, *you* watch it," Audrey exclaimed. "You almost hit that motorcycle in front of us!"

"Charly's distracting me, Mom," Chuck grumbled.

"No, it's *Fawn McCoppin* who's distracting you," Charly replied.

Oh, now, that's just great, thought Audrey.

Since the twins' earliest years, one of Audrey's greatest fascinations in life was listening to the patter that Charly and Chuck had developed between them.

But by the time the gibberish they shared as toddlers gave way to actual words, Audrey responded with awe, laughter, or concern.

At four, they processed their curiosity in the world around them in very different ways. Chuck took everything at face value. Charly questioned everything.

By seven, while Charly was journaling her observations in her diary, Chuck reveled in being an enthusiastic participant in the world around him. He was active in soccer, baseball, and most enthusiastically, basketball.

This led to a pattern that held to this day. Whereas Charly saw trouble as an iceberg to avoid, Chuck threw caution to the wind, consequences be damned.

As they grew into their teens, like her mother at her age, Charly's circle of friends was small, but choice. They shared quick wits and a love of learning. Charly studied hard and was dependable.

And, like the man who sired him, Chuck was a fun-loving bon vivant: widely admired by guys, and strongly desired by girls.

Charly's taunt was proof of that.

As Chuck pulled into one of the school's guest parking spaces, Audrey tapped his arm. "Chuck, I raised you to be a gentleman at all times. Please remember that."

"I'll try, Mom! But it ain't easy when the girls are practically throwing themselves at you."

"Give it a go. Just… *pace yourself.*"

Chuck rolled his eyes. "It's not like back in your day—you know, when everyone stayed a virgin until they were married."

"This may come as a surprise to you but I wasn't born in the Victorian era," Audrey retorted.

Chuck grinned viciously. "Next you're going to tell me that Charly and I weren't immaculate conceptions either!" He nodded toward Charly. Seeing his mother's shocked look, he added, "Hey, Miss Brainiac there did the math, so we know better." Chuck kissed his perplexed mother's cheek then leaped out of the car.

Charly was about to follow when Audrey stopped her. "What did he mean by that?"

"Oh, Mom, please! We've known since we were twelve." Charly raised a brow. "We were born less than nine months from your wedding day."

"Twins are known to come early!" Audrey protested.

Charly guffawed. "Mom… *really*? Not *that* early!"

Oh, God…

Audrey stammered, "Honey… I would hope that if you were… you know. I mean, if you were inclined to—"

Charly patted her mother's shoulder. "Mom, *please*! Seriously, do you think I'm stupid enough to let some idiot man-boy take advantage of me? When I do 'it,' it'll be with someone who's mature enough to love and respect me—like you did with Dad."

"Yes, but…" Audrey stuttered, "We were in college—"

"People can be stupid in college too," Charly pointed out. "It's not when, it's with whom, isn't it? You don't have to worry about me. Whoever my 'he' is, I know for a fact I won't find him while I'm at AA!" With a quick kiss, Charly was out of the car too.

Audrey was making her way to the parent lounge when Clare, Lavinia's assistant, called out to her from the reception desk. "Do you have a moment to meet with Lavinia?"

"Of course," Audrey replied. She detoured to her mother's office.

The door was shut, so Audrey knocked.

My mother looks so tired, Audrey thought.

Slowly and cautiously, Lavinia raised from her chair to greet her daughter, but Audrey waved her to sit again.

Kissing her mother's cheek, she pulled up the closest chair. "Happy first day of school!"

"Same to you!" Lavinia smiled. "Are Charly and Chuck excited to be back?"

"Charly, for sure. Chuck—well, he's ready for basketball season to begin."

Both women laughed.

"You and Daniel will bring the children over on Sunday?"

"Of course. Family tradition, right? We wouldn't miss it."

Since the children were toddlers, everyone—children and adults alike —spent Sundays helping out in Lavinia's garden. At first the children learned to pick out the weeds. Next they were taught when to pluck tomatoes or strawberries or any other task for which they could better appreciate the garden's delicious bounty.

"Good." Lavinia nodded absently. "I've been lax in my gardening lately." She shrugged. "It was one of the things I wanted to talk to you about."

"If you need help, we can always hire a gardener to pitch in," Audrey suggested.

"Eventually..." Lavinia's smile faded. "Audrey love: I've been diagnosed with breast cancer. Stage Four."

For a moment, Audrey felt as if the world had stopped spinning.

No, no, no...

God, no.

"Your doctor... Is she suggesting surgery? Chemo? What does she—?"

"Surgery is an option, yes. But I won't lie to you. She isn't hopeful. As for radiation or chemo at my stage of life..." Lavinia leaned forward. "I'm sorry, my love. I've made you cry."

Audrey blinked away her tears.

I should be thinking of her, not the other way around. I have to be strong...

"Eventually, I'll be stepping down as Head of School. I'll give the board enough notice that it can conduct a search for my replacement." Lavinia took a deep breath. "As for the board, a couple of members are already pushing to alter the school's core mission, especially as it pertains to our fifty percent scholarship mandate."

"You expect a fight," Audrey murmured.

"Unfortunately, yes. Seamus McCoppin in particular has made no bones about it. I'm sure he spent the summer rallying some of the others to his side." Lavinia's face hardened with resolve. "Before I leave this world, I will prove him wrong. Besides you and the beautiful family you've created, Ashbury Academy is all I leave behind."

Sadness surged through Audrey.

"I respect your decision to stay off the board," Lavinia continued. "But I hope you'll reconsider your reticence about Daniel joining in your stead. It would be a great comfort to me."

"Of course. No problem!" Audrey heard herself say the words, but she didn't remember opening her mouth. "If you want, Lavinia, I'll stay on the board too."

Her mother shook her head. "Unfortunately, by state law, the number of trustees who can be family members is dictated by the board's size. In this case, we're allotted only two seats. As a lawyer, Daniel will hold his own against Seamus. And with both Tallulah and Bliss taking your place as PTA co-chairs, they'll also vote to hold steady on the mission. We'll have Harris' support too. Unfortunately, the rest of the board is a toss-up, but between all of you, I know you'll keep AA safe." Lavinia sighed. "Audrey, at this point, only you know of my condition, and I want it to stay that way."

"But shouldn't we let Daniel know too?"

"Daniel in particular should not be made aware of it. Otherwise, he'll have a fiduciary responsibility to tell the board. I'd prefer to wait for a final prognosis. In the meantime, I'll be interviewing for a Dean of School in the hope that this person can step in quickly should I"—Lavinia took a deep breath—"should I become incapacitated."

Audrey nodded. "Okay, I'll keep it a secret for now. But you'll let me know when the time is right to tell Daniel."

"Thank you, darling." Lavinia hesitated. But before she could continue, her phone buzzed. She picked it up. "Yes?... Oh yes!... Audrey is leaving now, so do send her in."

Reluctantly, Audrey got up. "I'll check in with you after school."

"Not to worry, dear. I'll be leaving for a meeting with one of our bene-factors—"

She was interrupted by a knock on the door.

A woman peeked in. She was stately, blond, and dressed in an exquisite belted sheath. "Lavinia, may I enter?"

"Yes, Miranda, please come in!" Lavinia rose. "My daughter, Audrey—"

"Ah, yes—but of course!" The woman's tall heels clicked loudly as she made her way across the floor to shake Audrey's hand. "So good to see you!"

"Thank you, my pleasure as well." Audrey did her best to muster a smile.

"Miranda D'Arcy is now AA's new college admissions consultant," Lavinia explained. "She comes highly recommended. Quite an impressive track record in private school administration! And of course, her biggest asset is that she's also an AA alumna."

"Always a plus. Well, I'll leave you two to talk business." Audrey was too stunned for niceties. Right now she wanted to go home and curl up in her bed, and cry. It didn't help that she still had to meet with Tallulah and Bliss.

I have to keep Lavinia's secret from them too, she realized miserably.

She steeled herself to put on a good act.

CHAPTER 26

*A*s the door closed behind Audrey, Miranda winked at Lavinia. "I don't think she remembered me."

"Perhaps not. Then again, it's been, what, two decades or more?" Absently, Lavinia waved away the years. "And we all change, don't we, Mandy? You, for example. I'm so proud of you! What a success you've made of yourself! And in the field of academia, no less!"

"Thank you for that," her guest purred. "But Lavinia, I don't go by Mandy anymore. It's a childish name. And to be honest, I never really liked it." She shrugged. "It was my stepfather's name for me."

"I understand." Lavinia nodded. "I've noticed you changed your surname too."

Miranda shrugged. "A marriage that didn't work out. At least I got a pretty name out of it."

"Then, Miranda D'Arcy it is." Lavinia turned to the credenza and picked up a sheaf of papers before turning back to her guest. "I've got your contract right here. I must say, I'm surprised you'd rather consult than go on staff full time. I know the fee works out to be the same, but the school does have marvelous benefits."

"Trust me, it works out best this way. You, your students, and their families get my full attention during school hours. At the same time, the few client families who still count on my services for the siblings of children I've already successfully placed in their first-choice colleges won't be left in the lurch. It's a win-win for everyone."

"Agreed." Her question answered, Lavinia signed the contract, then handed it back. "As you know, we have one hundred and twenty-five seniors and the same number of juniors. This first semester, of course seniors must take precedent. But don't be surprised if some of the juniors and their parents are anxious to get into your good graces."

Miranda chuckled. "That's always the case, isn't it? Rest assured I don't play favorites."

"I appreciate that," Lavinia replied.

"In fact, Audrey's children—you previously mentioned that they're seniors this year." Miranda closed her eyes as if the memory of their names escaped her. "They are twins, right? Charlene and Charles?"

"Yes," Lavinia confirmed. "With Charly, you'll have no problem. She's a dream student." Lavinia's smile dimmed. "Chuck will be more of a challenge."

Miranda laughed. "I do love a challenge! And considering that private schools live and die by their Ivy League acceptance rates, I'll make him my pet project."

"That's kind of you, but remember: no playing favorites."

Miranda nodded contritely. *We'll see about that,* she thought.

"And, do remember one of AA's longstanding tenets: that each student must devise his or her own path beyond high school, which may or may not include immediate college admission—or, for that matter, college at all."

Miranda shrugged. "Yes, I remember it well. I just thought…you know, with tuition fee increases and all—doesn't the thought of their children skipping college worry AA's parents?"

"Initially, yes. Still, this philosophy has had great success. Those students who are ready to continue their academic journey are encouraged to analyze their options based on their life goals. Ninety-two percent of our graduates are college bound. Of these, eighty-three percent end up at their first-choice school. But not all our graduates see college as the best path to their happiness or professional success. For those who go without, I assure you: their successes in their chosen fields are almost one hundred percent."

Miranda grinned and nodded, all the while thinking, *Well, that will change once I take charge.*

Out loud, she replied. "For the college-bound, I'll make it my goal to best the current record."

"I love your enthusiasm. Miranda, with all my heart, I'm glad you came home to us."

Miranda tried not to snicker out loud at that.

"Clare will show you to your office while I move on to my next task." Lavinia sighed. "We've just learned that our literature teacher must take an emergency leave. Poor dear Mercy's pregnancy has been more difficult than she anticipated. And after two miscarriages…well, she feels it best to take the year off. I'd like you to head up the interview process for her replacement."

Miranda smiled. "On it. I'll go through the usual channels." She paused, as if a thought had come to her. "In fact, have you considered reaching out to Egan Gable?"

"Egan?" Caught by surprise, Lavinia blinked. "Considering his literary success, why would this position appeal to him?"

Miranda shrugged. "From what I've heard, sadly, his subsequent novels never caught fire like the first. And there was a recent blurb in Leah Garchik's *San Francisco Chronicle* column that he's now back in the Bay Area. His father recently passed and his mother, poor thing, is in a care facility. Egan is taking care of his parents' estate."

"So sad about his loss." Lavinia shook her head sadly. "And I know he had high hopes for his writing. At least he had one huge success."

"Yes, it certainly put him on the map," Miranda murmured. "For a short time, anyway." *Son of a bitch.*

His fictional depiction of her was galling. Even if the character had been a truer rendition, Miranda would never admit it because she found the character's name appalling: *Fanny.*

"You're right. It's a good idea to reach out to Egan. Thank you for following up," Lavinia exclaimed. "Heaven knows, in the brief time he was here he was popular with the students."

"Yes, we found him charming." Miranda smiled. "I'll see if I can find a telephone number and reach out to him."

OF COURSE, HE'LL DO IT, MIRANDA REASONED.

He's a failure. A loser. An egotistical louse who lives to impress those who don't know better. Like clueless teens and their wannabe parents who consider has-beens the next best thing to actual celebrities.

AA is perfect for Egan.

She reveled at the opportunity to make the call. To play his savior.

And more to the point, to get back at him for screwing her over with her Berkeley application.

It wasn't until she became a college admissions counselor that she discovered the truth about his dirty trick. As part of her job, she made annual pilgrimages to all the top-tier schools, Berkeley included. Over drinks with one of the school's recruitment specialists, she'd casually asked what was the *worst* thing an otherwise perfect undergraduate candidate could do in the admissions process.

"You mean, besides getting arrested for a felony?" He chuckled. "Well, let me think…" Suddenly, his eyes opened wide. "Ha! We once had a letter of recommendation from a former Ph.D. candidate—he'd also been a teaching assistant in the department." The man took a gulp of his beer and then stifled a burp. "Anyway, this guy had the audacity to write a letter recommending an admissions candidate to his faculty chair, whose wife he'd been caught boinking!" He winked at Miranda. "Here's the real irony: when the chair found out, he'd fired the guy. No way would he take the Lothario's recommendation!" He shook his head in disbelief. "In fact, the letter was written as if Lover Boy *knew* he'd be screwing over the poor kid who asked him for the recommendation."

"That's disgusting," Miranda muttered.

And now, years later, Miranda knew just how to get back at Egan.

He's down on his luck. His last six books flopped. His editor has retired. His agent dumped him.

I'll bet he's low on money. Why else would he be living in his parents' old house?

Egan's cell number wouldn't be easy to find, but his parents' phone number was easily Googled.

EGAN PICKED UP THE PHONE ON THE FIFTH RING. "YEAH, WHAT IS IT?"

He knew he should be polite—especially if the family's lawyer was on the other end of the phone line. The old coot was claiming it would take at least six months to settle his parents' estate. Until then, Egan wasn't allowed to sell their house, let alone salvage what was left of his father's savings for his mother's nursing care.

This realization had eviscerated whatever pride he'd had.

I can't support myself, let alone Mom.

If he sounded rude, so be it. Six scotches on an empty stomach made him ornery.

Sleeping in his old bedroom didn't help his mood either.

"Egan?"

"Yeah, speaking."

The voice sounded familiar. Maybe it belonged to one of his parents' friends. Those who were still alive had been calling all week, expressing their condolences. A few had even stopped by with casseroles and asked after his mom, not that they'd get off their duffs to visit what was left of her in the geriatric facility a mere two miles away.

In some cases, they brought copies of *Extracurricular* for him to sign.

A few times he'd noticed a bookseller had stamped REMAINDER on it. When that happened, he longed to throw the book at the culprit and shout, *Fuck you! Oh, and seriously? Do you think anyone will actually give you a dime for it on eBay?*

But by now he'd learned his lesson about keeping his cool. All it took was being tossed in jail for cold-cocking an off-duty cop in some New York Upper West Side bar for eyeing some woman's ass so longingly.

The woman was Egan's date.

Well, almost. He'd been in the middle of making his move.

Popping the cop in the jaw may have seen chivalrous at the time, but it had cost him too much, and not just the woman. It led to his publisher deeming him more of a liability than an asset.

Other publishers took that at face value.

The money went fast.

Fame was just as fleeting. These days, pick-ups occurred less frequently.

He prayed the call wasn't from some old bat with yet another casserole.

"Egan, I'm calling on behalf of Lavinia Thorpe of Ashbury Academy…"

Lavinia…

Audrey.

He hadn't thought of either of them in years.

Not in a conscious state, anyway. But with the amount of liquor he drank these days, those hours were fewer and far between.

Egan stammered, "Lavinia?… How is she?"

How is Audrey?

"You know our fearless leader—indomitable as always." The woman chuckled softly. "She would have called herself, but she is stepping into a meeting and asked me to do so in her stead. You see, an emergency has left the school without a literature teacher. She'd heard of your loss, and she sends her condolences, of course. It had her wondering if perhaps you'd be available to step into the position."

"Would I teach again at AA?" Emotions surged through him: curiosity, nostalgia, excitement, anxiety, hope—

Desire—

Shame.

Finally, he muttered, "I don't think that's a good idea."

The Miranda woman sighed longingly. "You were Lavinia's last hope. But she knew it was a long shot. And it would be quite an honor for the school, to have a *New York Times* best-selling author on the academic staff. That would mean a lot to parents! They seem to give more generously when underwriting chairs for prestigious instructors—"

The money.

If he were to get a cut of it above and beyond a teaching salary…

But I'm Egan Gable, damn it! I can teach at any university—

Okay, maybe not after the assault and battery charges…

"You know, I'd hate to let Lavinia down. Tell her I look forward to it."

"Wonderful! We'll look forward to seeing you tomorrow! Perhaps you can come in an hour early? You know. Get the lay of the land, as it were. At AA, some things never change, but a lot has too." The woman giggled at her poor attempt at a joke.

God, what a horrible laugh.

"Yeah, well, it'll be good to see some of the old crew—if they haven't all retired." He hesitated. "And, I guess Lavinia's daughter, Audrey, still lives in the area?"

"Oh, yes. In fact, she just retired from the board. But she shows up on campus intermittently. Who can stay away from the place that gave us the best years of our lives?"

"True." For once, he wasn't being sarcastic.

We're sure to run into each other.

Does she still hate me?

No, it's not possible. Otherwise, Lavinia would never have reached out to me...

Having convinced himself of that, he exclaimed, "Tell Lavinia I'll get there by seven to give myself time to settle in."

"Splendid!" Miranda Whomever gave a sigh of relief. "Oh! I forgot to add: the position entails heading up Debate Team as well. Lavinia hopes you won't consider it too much of an imposition since you already know the ropes. It'll be just like old times, right?"

"*Debate?*" Egan flinched at the thought.

His desperation for money stiffened his back again.

"Sure," he murmured. "Just like old times."

CHAPTER 27

The tip line to the FBI's San Francisco office rang incessantly before the only person in the bullpen, Lionel Porter Polk III, finally picked it up.

It was very early in the morning—just after six o'clock. Lionel had been reviewing the final summary of a case he and his partner, SallyAnne Jagger, had recently closed. It involved a stockbroker who had been making fraudulent trades to cover up his client's losses while he lived *la vida loca.*

SallyAnne had stayed until one in the morning, typing it up before leaving it on his desk. Despite her late night, Lionel had no doubt she'd be back in her cubicle at eight sharp. Her dedication was one of the things he found most endearing about her.

Well, that, and the fact she had no qualms speaking her mind, sometimes sprinkling in a few salty phrases that left him admirably slack-jawed along with anyone who might be the object of her ire, be it a suspect or their boss.

He'd often wondered if she also talked dirty in bed.

As much as he'd like to find out personally, he respected SallyAnne too much to jeopardize their three-year professional partnership. Instead, he settled for admiring her from the mere few feet between their adjacent cubicles. Or even better, as they sat side by side in a stakeout vehicle. It was an imperfect compromise for a man married to his job and afraid of rejection.

The tipster refused to identify herself. No issues there. All calls to the bureau were instantly traced. Her ID came up as a Los Angeles area code. If her lead panned out, he'd have a way to follow up.

"I'm not sure, but I think what I have to report is illegal," the woman insisted. "You see, my husband sits on the trustee board of a private prep school. The trustees recently discovered that an administrative employee —the college counselor—was guaranteeing admissions placement into top Ivy League schools."

Lionel's ears perked up at that. "Which prep school?"

"I can't tell you that! My husband swore me to secrecy. I shouldn't be talking about it at all! But I'm just so angry—as are several other parents— at the increase in our tuition fees because of this debacle!"

Whether the counselor could or couldn't deliver, the situation had the distinct odor of fraud. "Were the fee increases tied to the counselor's success?" Lionel asked.

"If only!" The woman sighed longingly. "What parent *wouldn't* pay to have that sort of guarantee?"

Lionel was tempted to answer "A smart one," but he'd learned long ago to keep his mouth shut and let the informant rattle on.

"No," the woman admitted. "I mean, yes, she delivered, alright! For a pretty penny, I might add. But, as one of the board members informed the others, there actually is no way to ensure acceptance unless"—here, the informant lowered her voice to a whisper—"bribes were somehow offered to the colleges."

"And, if so, fraud has been committed," Lionel replied.

The informant sighed mightily. "That's why I called you! But to save the school from embarrassment, the trustees offered her a severance package to keep her lips zipped and go away quietly. The severance was five times her annual salary!"

Her. So the alleged suspect was a woman.

"And here's the kicker: they even gave her a letter of recommendation before she went on her merry way!" The tipster's voice shook with anger.

"You're right. It's B.S." Lionel words were strong, and his tone was fervent. Yes, he felt her pain. "I'll need the names of the parents who used the counselor's services in the past and got the college acceptances they'd anticipated."

The woman gasped. "I really don't want to name parents whose kids go to school with mine!"

"Ma'am, it's the only way we can build a case against the alleged suspect. And since your tip is anonymous, the parents will never know our source." This woman is lucky that SallyAnne didn't pick up the phone, Lionel thought.

Had the informant balked to SallyAnne, she would have threatened to charge the woman as an accessory after the fact. Lionel's technique was more velvet glove and less hammer, albeit SallyAnne's hard-nosed tactics never failed to get results.

The tipster was silent for so long that Lionel wondered if she'd hung up. Finally, she whispered, "Okay, then. I guess we should meet."

Heck, yeah, we'll meet, Lionel thought. "Ma'am, to get this moving, I'll need the college counselor's name. And do you know if the counselor got a job at another school?"

"It's Miranda D'Arcy," the informant declared. She even spelled it for him. "I heard our Head of School mention she's now in San Francisco. The school is Ashbury Academy."

Lionel scribbled that down. He couldn't wait for SallyAnne to get back into the office.

Their next case had just fallen into his lap.

BOOK TWO

FALL SEMESTER

CHAPTER 1

y mother is dying.
The thought that one day, very soon, Lavinia Thorpe would no longer exist beyond her family's cherished memories or in a few fading photos of the many that lined Ashford Academy's halls numbed Audrey so thoroughly that she stopped cold in the middle of the private high school's entry rotunda.

Students streamed around her, oblivious to her grief. Although Audrey felt them breeze past her and saw their lips moving in earnest discussion or whispered gossip or gushing flirtations, her brain blocked out all sound except that of her pounding heart.

So that her sadness wouldn't blind her to the here and now, she forced herself to focus on something—anything. That was when she noticed a slim ray of sunshine had somehow found its way beyond the umbrella of leaves shielding the rotunda's tall windows.

The bright beam intersected Audrey's wrist, creating the illusion that her hand had been severed.

The symbolism was not lost on her. When Lavinia died, a part of her would be lost forever.

To escape this unbearable thought, Audrey shifted her gaze to the window instead. Through it, San Francisco's celebrated Haight Street was partially obscured by the early morning dew, which still glistened on the ancient panes of glass.

During the month prior to the school's founding—Audrey's freshman year, some twenty-five years ago—she'd helped her mother, the school's founder and headmistress, scrub every pane to a sparkling brilliance. It was one of many tasks mother and daughter performed side by side to ready the careworn Victorian mansion for the thirty-six teenagers who would find themselves amongst its first four graduating classes.

Only six seniors had graduated that first year, three of whom were from impoverished families. All had received multiple offers from Ivy League universities.

As the school's reputation for hands-on learning, exemplary test scores, and high acceptance rates into the country's top-ranked universities grew, so did its student body and academic staff.

Today, four hundred students were enrolled. Still, its mandate was unchanged:

> **Students seeking intellectual engagement and the pure pursuit of knowledge will be welcomed with open arms, despite any social or economic barriers they must overcome.**

For now, anyway.

Ashbury Academy is Lavinia's legacy, Audrey thought. For that reason alone, the values that led to its creation need to survive beyond her.

Despite what some of the school's newer trustee board members might attempt to do to decimate those founding principles.

I swore to Lavinia I'd keep her illness a secret. I must hold to that.

Audrey had made her mother another promise: to allow her husband, Daniel McKittridge, to take a seat on Ashbury Academy's trustee board.

But because Daniel was an attorney, she couldn't divulge Lavinia's secret to him. Otherwise, it would be his fiduciary duty to alert the other board members of her failing health.

She wished Daniel was there to hold her. Instead she made up her mind to call him.

Before doing so, she walked outside.

Under the tree, out of reach from the morning sun, those few moments of reflection faded to a mere glimmer.

Everything in life is fleeting.

"YOU'VE BEEN CRYING." AFTER EIGHTEEN YEARS OF MARRIAGE, DANIEL KNEW Audrey well enough to pick up on the gruff catch that only affected her voice when she was upset.

"You're right. The kids found my first-day-of-school sentimentality something to scoff at." She attempted a chuckle, but it too got stuck in her throat.

"I'm sorry about that, babe."

Hearing his concern, Audrey winced. She'd always hated lying to Daniel.

Then again, she'd never been able to top the first one, almost nineteen years ago.

It was a doozy.

Well, at least this one is in Lavinia's honor.

"Aren't you in the middle of your PTA meeting?" Daniel asked warily.

"I've got a few minutes." Another small lie. In fact, she was already late. On the agenda: introduce her dear friends, Bliss Thackeray Belluci and Tallulah Wishart, who had jointly agreed to replace her as Ashbury Academy's Parent-Teacher Association chair.

As such, they'd also take her place on the trustee board.

"Listen, Daniel, I've been thinking. You were right. If you're keen on taking Lavinia up on her offer to join the board, you should do it. I've had all the fun these years. Now it's your turn."

"I think that's great!" Daniel laughed. "And after duly warning me this morning of all the reasons I shouldn't want to be on the board, I promise I won't complain, no matter how contentious I find it. I also promise it'll be a one-year stint, tops."

"I'll hold you to it." Yet another lie. She prayed that, like her, Daniel would want to stay on the board until the perfect replacement could be found for Lavinia: one who would stand up to the board's ever-increasing demands.

She knew she could count on Daniel. He too revered Lavinia and would do what he could to protect her legacy.

"My mother will appreciate it greatly, Daniel. Thank you, and... I love you." She hung up before he could respond to her fervent whisper.

Whoever said that each subsequent fib got easier was dead wrong.

Or was lying.

MIRANDA D'ARCY, ASHBURY ACADEMY'S NEWLY HIRED COLLEGE ADMISSIONS consultant, always kept a to-do list on her cell phone. Continuously updated, its line items—taking calls with parents who were current clients, returning calls to parents who wanted to beg her to work on behalf of their children, and making calls to her network of contacts at various Ivy League schools—were ranked in an order of importance that rose and fell like the frenzied trading of stocks.

Even on this very first day of school at Ashbury Academy—her sole in-house consulting retainer—Miranda's most pressing task wasn't rubbing shoulders with AA's parents at the PTA's Back to School parent kaffeeklatsch that was already going on. Nor was it wooing new private clients with deep pockets and under-achieving children to her private college admissions concierge program.

Instead, it was reminding her somewhat forgetful and usually belligerent freelance test proctor, Winslow Jennings, that two students had appointments with him on this coming Saturday, and another two on Sunday.

She let his private phone ring until it rolled to voice mail. After hanging up, she did the same thing again.

And again.

Finally, he picked up. "What is it, Miranda?"

"That's a fine howdy-do for your boss," she growled.

He sighed. "I view our relationship more like a partnership. I mean, I am the Director of Testing at University Prep & Test."

The testing facility—a subsidiary of a shell company owned by her—was a necessary evil that allowed her to make good on her promise to her clients: that, under her tutelage, none of their children would score below 1400 on their SAT tests—a grade that put them in the running for their first-choice universities.

To keep that assurance, she desperately needed Winslow.

So she bit her tongue at Winslow's impertinence, declaring instead, "Speaking of which, check your online calendar. You'll note that you have clients coming in this weekend—four of them, two each day."

"Not too early, I hope," he whined.

"Yes, early," she warned him. "The first test appointments are nine o'clock, sharp! The second appointments are scheduled for two o'clock."

"Why do they have to show up at all?" Winslow countered.

"Because the students have to take the test!" she shouted.

Winslow snickered. "Not really. I take it for them."

"But they don't know that. They think they've earned their scores fair and square." She added with a snarl: "And that's just the way their parents want it."

Usually, SAT tests were taken at the students' schools, and the tests were timed. However, with their school's permission, students with learning disabilities were allowed to take untimed ACT and SAT tests, and they could do so at an accredited location, like UP&T.

As it happened, most—make that *all*—of the students in Miranda's program were given a disability waiver by a Special Education consultant: in this case, Winslow.

After these students took their exams at UP&T, the final test papers sent to the national testing companies weren't the students' versions, but ones filled out by Winslow, who also acted as the tests' administrating proctor.

It was the only way Miranda could hold to her assurance: that the students would score that magic number of 1400 or above.

Miranda's guarantee came at a very steep price. But, for parents who were desperate to see their children enrolled in a top-tier university—and were willing to do so by any means possible—no price was out of bounds—

An obsession that was making Miranda very wealthy.

"You scheduled them over both days?" Winslow fumed. "No, Miranda! Sorry, but I'm not going to let you kill my whole weekend!"

"*Pshaw*! It works for my clients, and that's all that matters. You're being paid handsomely for your time, Winslow. Not to mention that you have the rest of the week to surf, or play video games, or any of the other ridiculous folderol."

"'Folderol'?" Winslow snorted. "You don't even know the proper usage of the word! Otherwise, you'd have sung some witty ditty."

When Miranda had first considered hiring Winslow, she'd been warned against it by the referring source: a professor who'd mentored him during his Ph.D. program in Mathematics. "Winslow is that most exotic flower in the wild, overgrown garden of academia: a delicate genius," the professor had told her. "But, sadly, he is also a savant, and all that implies."

"Meaning what, exactly?" Miranda had asked.

"You know—on the spectrum, as it were. Obsessed with arcane trivia. Parses every word. But of course, he would. He memorized the Merriam-Webster dictionary before the age of three. Book smart, but not street smart. I guess that's why he's such a great test taker."

That's all Miranda needed to hear. She shrugged off the professor's warning. "I'm not asking him to cover me in a knife fight. So, where will I find this savant?"

The man chuckled. "He could be in any casino between here and Las Vegas. He makes his living as a professional gambler. He's one of the best card-counters in the world."

Now, having worked with Winslow for two years, Miranda realized it was the professor's delicate way of warning her that Winslow was an idiot savant.

No. Just a damn idiot.

But because he delivered the requisite scores, Miranda put up with his periodic tantrums.

Like this one.

She took a deep breath. When she exhaled, she muttered, "You want a 'witty ditty?' Okay, how's this?"

Then, in a mezzo-soprano voice to the tune of *Mary Had a Little Lamb*, she crooned:

"If you want to be an ass,
You will soon be out of cash.
I will cut you off LIKE THAT.
Cross me, and you'll FEEL MY WRATH.
I won't take your ands or buts

Rather, I'll chop off your nuts!"

"Not bad for off the cuff," Winslow admitted grudgingly. "Although, I'm sure you'll agree with me that the first two are slant rhymes, and therefore somewhat of a cheat —"

"You're testing my patience, Winslow!"

"And you are testing mine," he answered calmly.

Miranda realized it was time to cut to the chase. "Let me guess: there's some big gambling shindig you want to make this weekend."

"Yep. And I'll be honest with you, for what you're paying me, I don't see why I shouldn't take the whole weekend off."

"You're scoffing at five thousand dollars per test?"

"Yes. Admit it, Miranda: your clients pay you at least ten times that."

"You're dreaming if you truly think that," she lied.

Silence.

Winslow made a handsome living by bluffing. Suddenly, she wondered if he could smell fear, even through the phone.

"How much?" she muttered. It was a big gamble. Then again, she wrote a lot of fat into her clients' fees, just in case little emergencies arose.

His pouting was a perfect example.

"Fifty thousand each."

"*WHAT?*" Miranda sputtered. "NO... *NO!* Forget it! I'll find someone else."

"Not in time for Saturday."

"I'll reschedule their tests until I do." Miranda was bluffing now. Hopefully, she was just as good at it as him, although his Vegas outings had undoubtedly given him plenty of chances to hone his chops.

"Forty, then."

"Ten thou each."

Silence.

"Forty K, Winslow! Unlike Vegas, UP&T is a sure bet. Take it or leave it."

More silence.

She wondered if he'd hung up. And if not, she agonized if she should do so first, as proof that she meant business.

"Okay," Winslow muttered, finally.

"Thank you." The tremble in Miranda's voice was real.

She wanted him to hear it, to think he'd bested her.

In truth, he hadn't.

Miranda's concierge fees ran six figures. Sometimes as high as seven, if the parents were bound and determined to shove their child, even kicking and screaming, through the heavy oak doors of a prestigious university.

And Miranda was right there beside them to give their little darlings that final shove.

CHAPTER 2

"So, Boss, you agree with us, right? That we should at least meet with this woman, who knows about this counselor and these parents who are bribing college administrators to accept their kids into their schools?"

FBI Special Agent SallyAnne Jagger may have broached her comment as a question, but in truth, it was a declaration.

She was daring him to tell her she was wrong.

FBI Division Director Vance Melamed acceded with a nod and a sigh.

SallyAnne and her investigative partner, Lionel Porter Polk VII, considered themselves lucky to have snagged Melamed's very first appointment of the day. After placing the follow-up report of the anonymous source on his desk, SallyAnne had been pacing his office for the past half hour, railing on about the injustice of this potential crime.

How such incidents usually went under the radar because the perpetrators were invariably privileged;

How these crimes were wrongly labeled victimless when in fact the victims were those who had played fair in a supposedly chaste admissions system but then got sidestepped in favor of the cheaters' children;

Moreover, how the perpetrators were wealthy enough to play by their own rules.

"Not this time," SallyAnne vowed.

As she continued to make her case, Lionel sat silently, but his eyes followed the petite brunette's every step, and not just because her legs looked so great in that new skirt. (At least, that's what he told himself.)

Whenever SallyAnne went to the mat for a cause that she believed in, she was an indelible force of nature that always left him in awe. Lionel loved the way her dark eyes smoldered with resolve. When she paused after making a crucial point, her dimples deepened beside her pursed lips.

She's smart. She's fearless. She's adorable—

"Do you agree, Special Agent Polk?" Director Melamed barked.

"Do I…" Because Lionel always sat ramrod straight, there was no telltale clue in his posture that he'd been fantasizing.

He prayed that he hadn't torpedoed SallyAnne's argument for taking on the case. His declaration followed an attempt to clear his throat: "Agree? Emphatically? Oh, yes, sir!"

His cough caused a ghost of a smile to alight on SallyAnne's lips. She knew he'd been daydreaming. After three years as partners in San Francisco's white collar crime division, she knew all of his quirks and tells, just like he knew hers.

If not, he hoped he'd have many more years to discover them.

"What Special Agent Polk means to say, Sir, is that, as a Harvard man, he too is offended by the audacity of this illegal enterprise and hopes you'll agree with us that we should pull out all the stops to shut down the scheme before it defrauds more deserving students out of their fair chance to enter the school of their choice."

Lionel nodded vigorously.

Like him, SallyAnne had been intrigued when Lionel played back the recording of the anonymous source claiming proof that some college counselor was offering to help parents of graduating high school seniors attain admission to certain upper echelon universities through some fraudulent "side door."

Lionel did not doubt that even mediocre students were given a leg up if they were children of alumnae. The same reality could well apply to major donors, regardless of their previous affiliations with the university, if even any at all. However, in this case, where money changed hands for a guaranteed admission? Well, that certainly merited a detailed investigation.

"Special Agent Jagger, you're coming in loud and clear," Director Melamed conceded. "But the anonymous call came from Los Angeles. If what the tipster says is true, a lot of the case will be made down there. Why not just hand it off to that office?"

"Because the purported suspect has relocated here, Sir," Lionel explained. "And, unlike the Boston bureau's case, this time we can catch the purported suspect in action."

"And, just like the Boston case, if we flip the suspect into a cooperating witness, we can indict her clients and her network of on-campus co-conspirators," SallyAnne added.

Melamed stood up. "Okay, you two, then you better get on it. If we're lucky, it'll be as big as Boston's case. Just make sure the evidence is as tight as a gnat's ass." Nodding to SallyAnne, he added, "Excuse my French."

SallyAnne's grin was proof she was not bothered in the least.

When the agents got back to their cubicles, Lionel took on the first task: calling the anonymous informant to set up a meeting with her as soon as possible—that afternoon, in fact. There were flights to LAX almost hourly. The call had been traced to a home in LA's Bel-Air neighborhood. It belonged to a couple named Robert and Helene Edelson.

Lionel and SallyAnne had a lot to do between now and their departure.

It was a shame that the hour-long flight between San Francisco and Los Angeles didn't merit an overnight. Lionel always looked forward to an excuse to spend a few more hours with SallyAnne. His partner's ball-busting demeanor softened after a meal and a glass of wine. She cracked a few jokes and even laughed at his feeble attempts at humor.

He had good reason to trust her with his heart.

CHAPTER 3

"esting—one, two, three! Testing, one, two, *THREE!*" Bliss Thackeray Belluci tapped the microphone in her hand. "Can you hear me from the back of the auditorium?"

Tallulah Wishart, perfectly positioned in the back, nodded enthusiastically, as did some of the parents who had already taken their seats, now that the first hour of class was in session.

A few seconds later, Tallulah was on the stage with Bliss.

Whereas Lavinia would be giving her opening day address to the students in the larger of AA's two auditoriums, the students' parents were welcomed into the smaller auditorium—really, the mansion's old ballroom —to attend the school year's first PTA meeting. There, they could enjoy coffee, tea, and juice, along with fresh-cut fruit and pastries (including gluten-free, dairy-free, sugar-free, and high fructose corn syrup-free options).

The first item on the agenda was for Audrey to pass the gavel to Bliss and Tallulah, the incoming PTA chairpersons.

"I'm sorry that I'm so late!" Audrey ran up the steps to the stage, all the while unbuttoning her coat—

Until she realized it couldn't come off unless she dropped her satchel first.

Instead, she flung it at the closest table—

Only to watch it skid off the other side and onto the floor.

As it landed with a plop, the latch gave way, and everything fell out. The pages from Audrey's welcome speech slid into the notes for a speech she'd written for her boss, Congressman Harris Blanchard, and a white paper she was due to review with him later that afternoon.

"*Damn! Damn!*" Audrey mumbled as she bent down to pick up the fallen sheets.

Immediately, Bliss and Tallulah scrambled to help—

Only to bump heads.

The parents in the almost-full auditorium chuckled at their antics.

Like Audrey, they kept their heads bent and grabbed for everything.

"Oh...Thanks!" Audrey, flustered, added, "Just stuff everything else back in here." She opened the satchel wide.

"We're not making such a great impression, are we?" Bliss muttered.

"They're almost all Virgins. Trust me, because they're so anxious to fit in, they'll kowtow to our every beck and call," Tallulah predicted.

She has a point, Audrey thought.

"Virgin" was the nickname Tallulah and other parents who were former alumni had given the new parents at the school.

"There are plenty of Titans out there too," Bliss warned her.

This was the name alumni gave those who felt that their wealth and additional school donations should provide them and their children special privileges.

"In fact, Gretchen McCoppin has already asked me what Tallulah and I are doing up here," Bliss continued.

Tallulah guffawed. "What did you tell her?"

"All I said was that Audrey was detained and asked us to test the microphone before the meeting. Little did I know I'd be telling the truth!" Bliss chuckled, then turned to Audrey. "Got a late start, eh?"

"Yes, something like that." Audrey winced. "Ha! And I thought handing over the reins to the school's auction would keep her too busy to stick her nose in PTA business too. Boy, was I dreaming!"

"That's okay," Bliss countered. "According to PTA bylaws, if you resign because of a personal emergency, you have the right to appoint interim successors. And since there has to be a semester moratorium before another election, Tallulah and I will have plenty of time to prove we're worthy of the position."

Audrey laughed, "I'm impressed at how well you know the bylaws!"

"Modeling is a lot like the Girl Scouts. It teaches you to always be prepared," Bliss replied primly. "At least, now I'll get to leave my bear spray at home."

"What did you need *that* for?" Audrey asked.

"Oversexed photographers and billionaire man whores." Bliss shook her head at the thought. "Tell you what, Tallulah: what say we split up our new PTA duties? The way I see it, I'll be the brains, and you can be the muscle."

Tallulah murmured, "I never thought I'd agree to that. But in this case, it makes sense. Heck, twisting the arms of parents to help out with the teacher appreciation days—not to mention AA's twenty-fifth-anniversary gala, will be a cakewalk compared to keeping music executives and concert promoters in line."

Tallulah managed two world-famous bands: Her mother, Maggie, was the lead singer for Chameleon, one of the Summer of Love's legendary rock bands. She also managed Jammerhead whose namesake and lead singer was her significant other.

"Don't be so cocky," Audrey warned her. "Last year, two moms almost came to blows when their daughters showed up in the same prom gown. Each thought they'd purchased a designer original. Guess who had to step in and pull them apart?" Audrey pointed at herself. Frowning, she added, "Maybe Bliss should lend you her bear spray. It may come in handy."

That sobered up her friends.

Audrey looked at her watch. "We'd better get this show on the road."

"Oh, listen," Bliss exclaimed. "Before you head to the podium, Clare mentioned that Lavinia wanted you to add one other item to the agenda: an introduction to AA's new college admissions consultant. Her name is…" She frowned, distressed at her own forgetfulness.

"Miranda D'Arcy," Audrey replied. "Yes, I've just met her. She's an alumna."

Tallulah shrugged. "Never heard of her."

"I hadn't either…" Audrey looked out into the audience. "She just walked in—the blonde in the suit and Louboutins."

Bliss and Tallulah followed her nod.

"Well, what do you know?" Bliss exclaimed. "Her suit is from our Spring collection." Her husband, Raffaele Belluci, was an internationally renowned couturier.

"Then I guess she has your seal of approval," Audrey replied.

Bliss shook her head. "You can't sway me with a pretty face. Actions speak louder than words." She hugged her friend. "If you're going to sell us to this anxious mob, you'd better put on a smile."

Easier said than done, Audrey thought.

DESPITE HAVING TO WING HER OPENING REMARKS, AUDREY STAYED ON POINT.

First, she welcomed the parents. Then she recognized the hard work of those who had been active the year before—specifically pointing out Gretchen McCoppin, who had broken all previous auction fundraising records.

Gretchen preened grandly.

Finally, Audrey broke the news that some unexpected personal and professional commitments would keep her from completing her third consecutive term as PTA president.

As expected, the crowd moaned its regrets.

Also, as expected, Gretchen McCoppin wasted no time in asking, "Audrey, will we be voting immediately on your replacement?"

"Per AA's PTA bylaws, the vote will take place next semester after candidates have declared themselves and have had time to campaign for the position. In the interim, I've appointed Bliss Thackeray Belluci and Tallulah Wishart as co-presidents."

"I object!" Gretchen huffed.

"That may be the case, but this isn't a court of law," Audrey replied. "Frankly, Gretchen, if you'd attended any of the PTA steering board meetings, you'd have known that I'm only following the bylaws."

"It's a blessing she doesn't. Otherwise, I'd have jumped off the steering committee," Tallulah muttered just loud enough for Audrey and Bliss to hear her.

Audrey stifled the urge to laugh. When she knew she could talk again without giggling, she added, "Now, for the final issue on today's agenda, I'd like to introduce Ashbury Academy's new college admissions consultant who also happens to be an alumna—Miranda D'Arcy."

She beckoned Miranda to the stage.

Miranda seemed to glide down the auditorium's center aisle before floating up the stage steps like a queen at her coronation. When she reached Audrey, she took both her hands and then kissed her.

Audrey was so stunned at the gesture that she froze.

Had Bliss and Tallulah been on the other side of the stage, they'd have been able to warn Audrey of the blood red lipstick mark that now branded her left cheek.

———

"IT EXCITES ME BEYOND WORDS TO ONCE AGAIN BE A PART OF THE ASHBURY Academy family." Miranda made eye contact with at least five parents before opening her arms wide to the rest of the room. "As our school's college admissions counselor, first and foremost, my mission is to make your children happy with their choice for the next part of their life's journey. I'll do this by making sure that their time here at Ashbury Academy has paid off—*by acceptance to a college worthy of all of their hard work.*"

Parents nodded happily, obviously pleased with her determination.

"My second mission is just as important." She paused and leaned in as if she were about to divulge a vital secret. "To make you ecstatic—wait, dare I say *delirious?*—that you chose AA as your children's school."

Everyone chuckled.

"But we're all quite aware that in this day and age, even students with exceptional grades and excellent skills that are showcased by the right extracurricular activities can still miss the target by *that* much." Miranda held up a hand, its thumb and index finger a mere inch apart. "Last year,

Georgetown, UCLA, and USC only accepted between fifteen and seventeen percent of the students who applied." Miranda frowned. "As for Stanford, Harvard, and Yale, it was between four and seven percent. With those kinds of acceptance rates, what else can a parent do to catapult their student into these elite schools?"

Miranda's smile faded along with her sigh. "We used to believe it takes a village. In fact, it takes cunning, guile, and the guts to do anything and everything needed to reach that lofty goal."

She paused to let that sink in. "Case in point: I'm sure you've heard that odious urban legend whispered by parents on San Francisco's playgrounds over the past couple of years. You know, the one about the mother who jumped off the Golden Gate Bridge when her son was passed over for admission by all the Ivys?"

The parents sat up ramrod straight, like marionettes whose strings have been pulled by their puppet masters. Some nodded, albeit hesitantly, as if thinking, I'm sure I've heard it…Wait…have I?

Setting the stage for her tale, Miranda leaned into the microphone conspiratorially. "Her son was a star athlete all throughout high school—it was public—having lettered in basketball, baseball, and lacrosse. He'd also been tutored six days a week, sometimes in shifts. But the results were worth the sacrifice! He aced all of his classes, and he placed in AP Math, Science, and English courses."

An awed murmur rose through the audience.

"To top it off, not only had the young man mastered the cello and the tuba—he was a dance-battle winning krumper, too!" Here, Miranda's voice rose to a crescendo.

"But…why?" The question, exclaimed in a strangled panic, was proffered by one nervous father, one of the Virgins.

Miranda's glare relayed her annoyance for his having interrupted her riff. "This last skill had been honed at the suggestion of one of the city's most expensive educational consultants," she explained.

Duly chastised, he hung his head.

"All this, and what was supposed to have made him a shoo-in was his volunteerism: he'd spent not one, but *two* summer vacations, doling out condoms to disease-ridden natives in some third world country…" Miranda thought for a moment. "Or perhaps it was Lodi, California. Sorry, but some of the details are hazy." she shrugged. "In any event, acceptance letters arrived—for all of his classmates. But his never did." She shook her head. "Not one."

The parents' alarmed murmurs were a wall of sound that would rival any on a Phil Spector album.

Miranda waited for silence again before delivering the *coup de grace*: "Ironically, this young man's acceptance letters—*all six of them*—arrived the day after his mother jumped. Apparently, the mailman had delivered them to the *wrong address*. Go figure."

Dead silence.

"The upshot of this rumor," Miranda continued, "is that each subsequent year, the number of applications to San Francisco's private high schools have risen twenty-three percent." Once again, she held out her hands to her audience, as if embracing them. "Welcome to a very elite club! As in all of life, you get what you pay for. Ashbury Academy is a proven commodity—and so am I. It's why Lavinia wants me here for you and our precious students. My promise to you: that I'll encourage your children to aim high. I will inspire them to be their personal best. Most importantly, I'll assess them as if I were the admissions director of their first-pick school. To do so, I'll first have to discover their strengths, which I'll place front and center in their applications. As for any weaknesses..." Here, Miranda paused just a nanosecond. "Well, if I discover any, it'll just be our little secret, okay?"

The parents laughed as if she were wise to them.

Hell yeah, she was. She knew that the last thing they'd want is for any of their children's character blemishes to be exposed.

It was a promise she'd make—for the right price.

They'd find that out soon enough.

The rest of the audience soon joined the first few parents who stood up and clapped.

As if touched by this show of respect, Miranda placed both hands over her heart with index fingers and thumbs touching, to mimic sending her love back to them.

She made a specific point to hold the gaze of that Gretchen person who was so obviously a thorn in Audrey's side.

If her pockets are deep and she's got a kid who's as dense as her, she may be a perfect candidate for my concierge program, Miranda reasoned. At the very least, if there's bad blood between her and Audrey, I can make that work to my favor.

"LOOK AT THAT LINE TO SHAKE MIRANDA'S HAND AND GRAB A BUSINESS card!" Tallulah exclaimed. "You'd think she was running for president!"

"I'm just glad Raffaele isn't here. Between her suit and the speech she just gave, he'd have hired her on the spot and thrown in a new wardrobe to boot, just to get her to sit on Sienna twenty-four-seven. He's determined that she get a business degree from Harvard, Yale, Columbia, or Wharton. He feels it's the best way to position her to our stockholders as his successor."

"Granted, she is a junior. And if she's interested in college, yes, she should be touring schools this year," Audrey conceded. "But Sienna never struck me as the biz school type."

Bliss rolled her eyes. "My point exactly! Sienna is fine just being herself: a teenage girl who loves fashion, great causes, and cute boys. If that means passing on the best business college—or any college at all—I'm fine with that. Neither Raffaele nor I have college degrees. But he'll blow a gasket if she fights him on it."

Tallulah laughed. "Too bad, because her online presence is certainly paying off. Her Instagram and Snapchat followers are through the roof! Let me tell you, Jammerhead is jealous of her."

At that moment, Audrey turned her head, revealing Miranda's lipstick mark on her cheek. "Talk about being catty!" She took a tissue from her purse. "Keep still. It looks as if your new friend branded you!" Frowning, she turned to stare at Miranda. "What year did you say she graduated?"

"I didn't. Lavinia never said," Audrey rummaged for the hand mirror in her satchel. "But she can't be that much younger than us."

"You're right," Bliss chimed in. "She's had some work done on her face, and God knows where else."

Tallulah smirked. "I'm willing to guess: say, those perky tits, that perky ass, and that flat as a pancake gut, for starters."

Audrey shook her head, dismayed. "Now, now, ladies, no need to be catty."

"Spoilsport," Tallulah groused.

"I'll have to ask Lavinia," Audrey admitted. "In fact, since you're seeing her at the board meeting tomorrow afternoon, feel free to ask her then."

"We will. Trust me," Tallulah muttered. "By the way, who is the teacher trustee this year?"

"Last year it was Berney. But he just retired." Audrey shook her head sadly. "I have no idea who'll be his replacement. I guess the staff will have to vote on it."

She already missed the school's geography teacher and his sweet wife, Jean, but she knew they were happy to be traveling the country in their Silver Airstream trailer to his favorite archeological digs throughout the Mountain West.

Audrey shrugged. "Tallulah, Bliss—I can never thank you enough for taking me up on my offer to co-chair the PTA. You have full-time jobs and lots of employees who depend on you, not to mention that you must travel all over the world..." Audrey allowed her voice to fade rather than to choke up with gratitude. "I guess what I'm trying to say is thank you for having Lavinia's back."

"Of course we'd say yes!" Bliss exclaimed. "We love this school! It was our home, our sanctuary."

"We became the people we are because of AA," Tallulah added. "And besides, you and Lavinia are our family."

Bliss and Tallulah leaned into Audrey for a hug. "Always and forever," they promised in unison.

Audrey left before they could see the tears glistening in her eyes.

———

THE REST OF AUDREY'S DAY WAS SPENT FIELDING CONFERENCE CALLS WITH Harris and various members of his staff: fine-tuning a speech to the state's teachers' union, discussing a position paper on California's homelessness, and tweaking talking points for an upcoming town hall debate. All of this Audrey welcomed, as it kept her from fretting over Lavinia's failing health.

She tried to make it back to the school before Lavinia left for her benefactor's meeting, but missed seeing her mother anyway.

Maybe it was for the best. Her eyes were still red from crying.

She put on her sunglasses before the twins bounded into the car.

On the way home, Charly drove while Audrey asked about their day.

To her first question—if they shared any classes—Chuck declared, "Unfortunately, yes. Math and Lit."

"You jest now, but you'll miss having your sister at your side if you go off to different colleges," Audrey warned him.

"Heck no, Ma! I'm sticking to her like glue—but only because I know if I beg, she'll help me with my homework."

Charly snickered. "As if you could get into Berkeley with your grades!"

"You just wait," Chuck retorted. "We're both legacies, not just you. Remember?"

"That doesn't necessarily make you a shoo-in," Audrey warned him.

"I was joking." But Chuck's disappointed tone proved otherwise. He rallied by exclaiming, "I can't wait to prove you wrong, Charlene Lavinia Thorpe McKittridge."

"Now, that's my boy. A positive attitude!" Audrey turned around to grasp his hand and shake it. "Do you like all your teachers?"

"So far, so good," Charly replied. "Although we haven't yet met our Lit teacher. We'll have a substitute until Mercy comes back from maternity leave."

"Lit is which period?" Audrey asked.

"Seventh." The twins said in unison.

Tomorrow evening was AA's parent-teacher open house. That meant Comp Lit's session would be the last one of the night.

Hopefully, Audrey asked, "Does that mean Dad and I can skip your Lit class at the parent and teacher open house tomorrow evening?"

"Nope. Lavinia told us that the sub will be there. Since Mercy's sabbatical might run through both semesters, she expects the parents to be there," Charly assured her.

"I had Mercy for tenth-grade English," Chuck retorted. "This new teacher means I can start with a clean slate."

Audrey tried hard not to wince. Chuck was right. When it came to grades, his sophomore year had not been a stellar one.

Still, to show her support, she replied, "Agreed. And this year, do yourself a favor. Stay on top of all your assignments and ask questions if you're stumped. It's okay to be teacher's pet."

"Don't have such high hopes for him. Fawn is also in our class," Charly warned her. "It should be interesting to see if hearing you talk in iambic pentameter is going to make you any sexier to her." She stuck her tongue out at Chuck through the rearview mirror.

Intrigued, Chuck's brows went up. "Whatever that is, it sounds dirty. I look forward to proving you wrong."

Audrey laughed at that.

Charly too was giggling so hard that she almost ran a red light.

This is going to be one heck of a year, Audrey thought.

Suddenly, she realized that Lavinia might not live to see the twins graduate.

She forced herself to forget that sad possibility as they picked up Noah from private all-boy Town School.

To her relief, she was able to hold back her tears until she could cry in the privacy of her shower.

By the time Daniel got home, her composure was stable enough that she could smile while asking about his day, fill him in on the children's antics, and answer his questions about the other board members.

Later that night, while wrapped in her sleeping husband's arms, she grieved silently.

CHAPTER 4

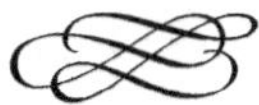

"$\mathcal{M}$rs. Edelson—*Helene*. May I call you that? Thank you for taking the time to meet with us," Lionel began. "I'm Special Agent Lionel Polk, and this is my partner, Special Agent SallyAnne Jagger."

They held out their badges for her inspection.

Having been Helene's initial contact (and the more diplomatic of the team at that), it was a given that Lionel would start the interrogation.

SallyAnne didn't mind this at all. As the saying went, you catch more flies with honey than vinegar. Since her approach was more like a flyswatter—make that a sledgehammer—it was best to leave it as a last resort.

Helene hesitated a long minute before stepping aside and waving them into her home: a stucco-and-glass post-modern behemoth at the end of a narrow lane that zigged and zagged its way up a pinnacle hill in Los Angeles' Bel-Air neighborhood. Lionel and SallyAnne hadn't had time for lunch before the flight. In hindsight, it was a good thing. To keep from spewing the coffee she'd drunk on the plane, SallyAnne had stared at the horizon as Lionel willed the rental car up the windy road.

The reward for making the climb was the spectacular view from the two-story floor-to-ceiling wrap-around windows in the Edelsons' living room. It extended from Los Angeles' downtown cityscape in the southeast to the Pacific Ocean to the west, with Beverly Hills in between.

"Mesmerizing, isn't it?" Helene murmured.

SallyAnne nodded.

What Helene didn't know was that SallyAnne's eyes hadn't lingered long on what was outside the Edelson's living room. Instead, they lighted on the personal items interspersed between the white modular furnishings.

Books filled suspended shelves (mostly classic novels and histories). There were numerous family pictures as well. Formal portraits were interspersed among candid photos of Helene, her husband Robert, and their two children.

In many of the photos, the children wore sports jerseys. Soccer seemed to be the sport of choice for both. The trophies were displayed in a glass case on one of the higher shelves.

SallyAnne pointed to one photo: a boy, kneeling near a goal post, a soccer ball in hand. "Is this your son?" she asked.

Helene nodded. "Yes. Rob Junior—Robbie—is now a freshman at USC."

Lionel pointed to another photo: a teen girl, in a period costume, onstage. "And this is your daughter?"

"Yes. She's a junior this year at Bobbitt-Hennings Prep School."

Lionel nodded. "Is that the school where the incident happened?"

Helene frowned. "Yes. Robbie graduated from there last year. It's just down the hill and a few miles from here. Across the 405, in Brentwood."

Lionel and SallyAnne already knew this. After tracing Helene's phone call to the bureau, they'd pulled up what they could about her and Robert, including all social media postings and online photos. A picture from the school's latest fundraiser had popped up.

"Helene, Special Agent Jagger has read the transcript of our call," Lionel explained. "But, for the record, I'd like you to reiterate the key points—also recorded, for our records."

The woman's lower lip quivered at the thought. Still, she motioned for them to have a seat on the sofa, taking its twin across from them.

SallyAnne pulled out her phone, hit a recording app, and then noted the date, time, and that the interview being recorded was with Helene Edelson.

"Okay, well, as I mentioned, one of the members of the trustee board divulged his knowledge of Ms. D'Arcy's activities with another school parent."

"You mean, she had approached the parent about some contacts she had at a university, and that she could facilitate students' admissions?" SallyAnne asked.

"Frankly, it was blunter than that. She boasted that she's built a network of contacts with several universities: five or six elite choices on both coasts."

"The trustee who brought it to the board's attention—who was he, or she?" Lionel asked.

"I was curious, but Rob wouldn't tell me. He felt he'd already said too much. Everything the board discusses must stay confidential, for obvious reasons." Helene shrugged. "He just said many of the trustees were stunned. Others just rolled their eyes. They'd heard the same scuttlebutt." She paused. "Then one trustee admitted he too had been approached by Miranda. He had seriously considered her offer after another parent boasted she'd done the same for him the year before. It was at a pool party. The man was tipsy. For that reason, at first, the trustee didn't believe him." Helene shook her head in disbelief. "But then he asked one of his children. The boy was a friend of the student involved. His kid laughed. He thought it was funny that the boy got in as a crew coxswain! Our school doesn't even have a crew team!"

"Did the trustee in question approach Ms. D'Arcy after learning this?"

"Yes. He admitted doing so." By Helene's tremor, it was apparent she sympathized with him. "But apparently, he found the fee for her services outrageous."

"What was it?" SallyAnne asked.

"He was quoted one hundred thousand."

Lionel's eyes grew large. "That's more than the first year of tuition at many universities."

Helene nodded. "I'm sure that's why he passed on the offer."

"He'd have done it if it were cheaper?" SallyAnne asked.

"Probably. Private schools attract a lot of parents with more money than brains. To them, finding a side door into the college of their choice may not seem like a crime. Wealthier parents will offer to pay for a building, so why not?"

SallyAnne's eyes narrowed with disgust.

Lionel's cough warned her: *Behave.*

"The bigger crime is that a proper education is so expensive in the first place." Helene looked around the room. "It may not be a stretch for some of us, but many parents with kids at our school are barely scraping by. They make the sacrifice because they hope their children can get into a top flight college. And think of those children coming out of public schools! Talk about having the deck stacked against you!" Frustrated, Helene shook her head.

"We can understand your anger, Helene," Lionel murmured. "I mean, you work very hard to get your son into USC. Then, to hear some of the other parents would gladly pay for the privilege of having their children gain acceptance under fraudulent circumstances? That's got to hurt!"

"It hurts all right," Helene retorted. She scrutinized SallyAnne, then Lionel. "Are you married?"

Lionel's eyes widened. "You mean, to each other?"

SallyAnne blushed a deep red.

Helene smirked. "Sorry! I didn't mean to hit a nerve."

Lionel's face suddenly felt flush too.

"My question was meant in a general sense. Are either of you married? Do you have children?"

"No." They answered in unison, and as if there were shame in it.

"We're quite aware that college tuition has skyrocketed," SallyAnne countered.

Helene guffawed. "Who said anything about college? Let's start with the fact that private preschool tuition now rivals what your parents shelled out for your senior year in college. Now, couple that with the reality that applications to your preferred preschools—and do note the use of the plural pronoun here: as in, have at least *five* safety schools!—should take place sometime during your second prenatal trimester—and you've got some idea of what you're facing, both financially and compet-itively—"

She paused here, for emphasis: "*For the next twenty-two years of your life.*"

Lionel and SallyAnne flinched in unison.

"Metaphorically speaking, whatever belt-tightening was necessary for private kindergarten is merely pinching an inch compared to how you'll suck it in for private elementary school. You can double that figure for a well-regarded prep school," Helene added.

"Around ten thousand dollars? Maybe closer to twenty?" SallyAnne asked.

Helene arched a brow. "You're joking, right?... No? Well then, I'm glad you're sitting down." She leaned in. "We're talking thirty or forty thou."

SallyAnne's eyes grew wide.

"Don't worry. You'll find the money somewhere. Go ahead, take out a second mortgage on your house, or sell a few bonds, or break into that 401(k) you were hoping would get you through your golden years." Helene smirked. "Better yet, beg your spouse's parents for it! A recent survey shows that one very successful ploy is to convince them that retiring to Florida is *so* last generation. Instead, convince them that extended family living is back in fashion and that you've already started converting your basement into an in-law suite so that they can move in the day you've shipped your child off to his Ivy of choice. To seal the deal, invite them to choose their own wallpaper. It's the least you can do, now that you know that the kid's tuition has sucked the yolk out of their nest egg."

SallyAnne blanched. She remembered her parents insisting that they pay for her college tuition. Knowing it would come out of their retirement savings, she opted to work and go to night school instead. They never said it, but she knew they were relieved that she never took them up on the offer.

"And you wonder why parents will lie, steal, cheat, and beg, to get their kids into college? Now you know." Helene shrugged. "Sorry I got so carried away. It comes from growing up with two public school teachers as parents."

It took a while before Lionel could find his composure. Softly, he asked, "Previously, you stated that the board fired Ms. D'Arcy."

"Yes, at Rob's recommendation. He was quite disconcerted about the matter."

"You also mentioned the board paid her a severance," SallyAnne pointed out.

"Yes. Six hundred thousand dollars." Helene grimaced. "And to add insult to injury, the board also gave her a letter of recommendation!"

"What a disgrace!" SallyAnne's voice rose in frustration. "But no one thought to inform local law enforcement?"

"There was only hearsay. There was no proof to back it up. If the rumors were wrong, she could have sued the school and taken it under! Either way, our school's reputation would have been ruined. The bitch knew that. Better to just let her go on her merry way." Helene shuddered at the thought.

"Thanks again for your help, Helene," Lionel said.

"Any time...I guess." She stood up. "By the way, did you find her at that San Francisco school—you know, Ashbury Academy?"

"We're not allowed to discuss an ongoing investigation," Lionel replied.

Helene's face went slack. "By that, I take it you're at least investigating her. Good. Miranda is ruining lives. She shouldn't be able to get away with it." She looked Lionel in the eye. "Listen, if Rob knew *I* was the one who turned you on to Miranda's scheme—"

"We'd never reveal an anonymous source," Lionel insisted.

Helene's lip quivered.

"I'm sure there are many other parents just as disgruntled with the turn of events," Lionel pointed out. "The last person he'd suspect is you."

Her silence spoke volumes: she didn't believe him.

"Odds are we won't have to interview him," Lionel assured her.

Finally, Helene nodded.

Lionel caught SallyAnne's smirk at this outright lie. Rob Edelson sat on B-H Prep's trustee board. He was an attorney. Of course they'd follow up with him.

And as an officer of the court, he'd answer their questions truthfully.

Thankfully, Helene missed SallyAnne's tell because she was wiping away a tear.

"DO YOU WANT TO HAVE KIDS?" LIONEL'S QUESTION CAME WHEN THEY WERE halfway down the hill.

It was all SallyAnne could do not to turn and stare at him, and not just because she might throw up, what with the way he was hurtling down the hill. "I… I guess I would. With the right person."

"Even after what she said about that whole school situation?"

"It's not the kids that have made education a mess. It's the parents! They do too much to shelter their children from reality. They don't allow them to grow and discover and make decisions on their own." SallyAnne shrugged. "They don't do enough to support their public schools."

"Not all parents," Lionel countered.

"But enough of them," she argued. "Enough to make this kind of behavior—this disregard for fairness—a thing." She gave him a sidelong glance. "How about you? Do you want children?"

"With the right woman, yes."

I'm the right woman.

Someday, she hoped to prove this to him.

And face the consequences.

She winced at the thought that he might say, *Sorry, SallyAnne, but you've got it wrong. We're great partners, and we should leave it at that…*

No, better to keep things just as they were. Right now, they were together eight, sometimes ten hours a day. If she were lucky, there would be an out of town trip that allowed them to stay in each other's company into the long hours of the evening.

Putting a case together was hard work. However, it was also an adrenaline high. Especially when the last thing you wanted to do was sleep.

When all you could think of was being with him.

It was always harder when the investigation meant an overnight stay. It was all she could do to keep from banging on his door and hoping he'd open it naked. At which point, she'd—

"Interviewing Rob Edelson is a must," Lionel was saying. "But I don't think we should tackle it today. We'll walk in unannounced to Edelson's law office first thing in the morning. I'll call Melamed and get it cleared with him."

"Okay," SallyAnne murmured. *YES! YES!*

"When Rob comes clean with the trustee who was compromised and the parent who took Miranda up on her offer, we'll track them down too." Lionel glanced over. "We may be down here for two or three days. Are you fine with that?"

SallyAnne prayed her voice didn't quiver when she replied, "It's part of the job, right? We're down here now, so let's make the most of it."

CHAPTER 5

*A*ll night long, Egan Gable had tossed and turned over the decision to take Lavinia up on her offer to come back to Ashbury Academy as its Upper Grades English instructor.

Even before the alarm went off, he was already awake. Egan felt like a convicted felon who had lost his last appeal and was now minutes from being strapped down for lethal injection.

Yes, I need the money, he'd reasoned. And yes, it'll only be temporary. Still, the world will see me as a loser to be back where I started before I was published.

Yeah, okay, so this is where I am in my life at this very second. I should make the best of it, right?

I mean, I'm a good teacher. The kids looked up to me. Heck, a few even idolized me. I made an impact on their lives.

Damn it, suck it up and just do it already!

He rose to shower, shave, and eat a cold bowl of cereal while gulping down his coffee. It was early, so congestion on the Golden Gate Bridge shouldn't be too bad. The city's traffic into the Haight was another beast altogether.

The sooner he left, the better.

When Egan got to the school, he was surprised by its many physical improvements. It was the same Victorian mansion, but it was no longer shabby. Fresh paint in a bright multi-hued pallet now accented the school's unique architectural details: turrets, gables, porch spindles, and fishtail shingles.

The decrepit storefronts and townhouses that had shared its block had been replaced by various structures that extended Ashbury Academy and complemented the architectural integrity of the original building. An ornate wrought iron fence connected the buildings, creating a private park between them. From the curb, one could see that the gravel paths intersecting the mossy lawn in the center of the campus were dotted with ornate benches.

These changes left Egan dismayed. He thought that, even some twenty-two years later, the school would have somehow stayed just like he remembered it. That, as in *Brigadoon*, the whole of it—building, students, and faculty—had gone into a deep sleep after he'd departed, only to be awakened again in his presence.

The school's future was very bright, whereas his star had fallen into a black hole.

Somehow, he had to climb out of it.

"*Yoo-hoo!* You're Egan, aren't you?"

Before he could answer, the woman reached out to shake Egan's hand.

He hesitated to take it, if only for a moment. When he did, she grasped it firmly and leaned forward. "I'm Miranda D'Arcy. Remember?" Her voice had a seductive tone to it.

He had to admit he liked it.

In fact, from what Egan saw, there was much about her he found pleasing. The blonde—slim, perhaps a decade his junior—was dressed in a suit that hugged every curve. The top two pearl buttons on her sheer blouse were open. A pearl pendant hung just above the V between her generous breasts.

Nice, he thought.

When he shifted his eyes to hers, she winked as if to say, *Gotcha.*

He didn't mind that at all. "Yes, of course I remember. We talked yesterday. So kind of you to be my welcoming committee." It was Egan's nature to hold any attractive woman's gaze and smile as if she'd already done something to please him. Experience taught him that, eventually, she'd want to.

And by Miranda's throaty chuckle, he knew she wouldn't want to disappoint.

This, above all, put to rest the niggling qualms he had about being back at Ashbury Academy.

Miranda placed her hand gently on his back as she guided him down the hall. "You'll have a full day, I'm afraid. Of your three courses, two you'll teach twice. You do have a period off, for lunch."

He nodded resignedly.

"Lavinia is already in the teacher's lounge," Miranda continued. "She is very excited to see you again! By the way, she took the liberty of reviewing and approving Mercy's syllabus, but she's open to any changes you may want to make. She trusts you implicitly."

Egan's grin wavered as he nodded mutely.

Even after all these years.

Even after what I did to Audrey.

But of course, Audrey would never have mentioned the incident to her mother.

Had she done so, he wouldn't be here now.

Miranda stopped in front of a door marked TEACHERS' LOUNGE. "I'll leave you in good hands."

Egan stared up at the sign and sighed. "I wonder if anyone I knew back then are still here?"

"Let's see: you were here for just one year, and it was over twenty years ago?" Miranda clucked her tongue. "I hear that there are still one or two of the original staff around."

"So, you're new here too?"

Miranda nodded. "I'm an alumna. But yes, I'm also new to the staff."

Noting his disappointment, she patted his arm. "Not to worry. I'm a friend, too, right?"

"I hope so," Egan murmured. He meant it. In a sea of doubt, she'd tossed him a lifeline. He wasn't about to let go anytime soon.

"Of course, we are!" Miranda chuckled. "We're old friends already, you and I."

She's quite a tease, he thought. Okay, two can play this game. "I feel that way too. Old souls, former lives."

Miranda winked playfully. "Yes, eons ago."

"I look forward to playing catch-up."

"No more than me," she assured him. "And we'll have plenty of opportunities to do so. As AA's in-house college admissions consultant, I seek out the teachers' opinions as to which seniors are excelling in their classes. In your case, perhaps their preferred college has a literary program that's a good match."

"I'm at your disposal," he promised.

"I'm sure you are," she purred. "And to return the favor, I'd like to make a suggestion. If the opportunity presents itself, volunteer to join the trustee board as the teacher representative."

Egan frowned. "That means staying later to attend the meetings."

"Just one night a month," Miranda reminded him. "It also means you'll be endearing yourself to the board members who are likely to underwrite your chair here at Ashbury Academy. Trust me. It will pay off handsomely." She winked seductively. "Not to worry. If you find yourself too tired to cross the bridge, I'm sure *someone* will be happy to let you sleep over."

She waved as she walked off, only to turn around after a few steps—

At which point, she caught him admiring the view.

Shaking her head at his audacity, she laughed all the way down the hall.

ALTHOUGH MIRANDA WASN'T A MEMBER OF THE TRUSTEE BOARD, JUST THAT morning she'd suggested to Lavinia that she attend its first meeting of the year. "As an administrative asset and sounding board, if you will," was how she had positioned it to the headmistress. "The school's crowning achievement is the number of students who have been accepted by their first-choice school. I've been hired to play an integral role in building on this success. Meeting with the board as soon as possible gives me an opportunity to answer their questions."

"I think it's a great idea," Lavinia agreed, albeit she then added firmly: "But remember, Miranda, the school's—and therefore the board's—first and foremost goal is to provide the students with the skills that allow them to make the best choices for their lives, now and into the future. If an academic path is what they decide, then yes, of course, you'll be a wonderful resource for them. But college isn't necessarily right for all students. We must respect their choices."

Miranda noted the gentle rebuttal with a meek nod.

In fact, she knew AA's bylaws by heart. It was the best way to protect herself should any of her illegal activities go awry. It had almost happened in her last position.

At least she had accomplished her immediate goal: an introduction to the trustees.

The endgame: a permanent seat on the board.

"YOU HAVEN'T CHANGED A BIT." LAVINIA BECKONED EGAN CLOSER FOR A HUG. There was no standing at attention with her.

She felt frail in Egan's arms; noticeably smaller somehow.

Instinctively, he looked down at her head. Where gray strands could once be glimpsed in its formerly thick curly brown mane, now only a few dark threads stood out in the almost sheer drape of white hair pinned primly to the nape of her neck.

The naïvete of her statement pierced his heart. He sighed. "If that were true, it would be a travesty."

"Would it?" As if surprised that she may have offended him, she laid a hand on his arm. "When you were here, you thrived! Ashbury Academy was the start of so many great things for you!"

His laugh was fierce and joyless. "'Was' is the operative word there. Whatever greatness I had, Lavinia, I've since failed it."

"Your life isn't over, Egan. Granted, our circumstances are in constant flux. But our mistakes create detours on our journey, not dead ends."

"Apparently, my road has turned into a cul-de-sac." He looked around the teachers' lounge. Despite new furnishings and walls now painted crisp beige as opposed its former dingy taupe hue, it was the same room he remembered. "Lavinia, you know I adore you. And I meant no offense to Ashbury Academy because my time here was special in so many ways. I guess what I'm trying to say is that being back where I started… Well, I feel like Dante: stuck in some soul-sucking circle of Hell."

Lavinia chuckled. "I read your novel, Egan. It strikes me that your time at AA was more like *Vanity Fair*."

He laughed. "Did you hate *Extracurricular*?"

Did Audrey? Does she hate me as well?

Lavinia shook her head. "Each person's perception of the same incident is going to be unique." She raised a brow. "And it was fiction, after all."

He let that lie.

"Although, Egan, I must say: until I read your book, I hadn't known you'd placed Audrey on such a high pedestal."

"As you said: it's fiction." Egan shrugged. Before he'd lose his nerve, he asked, "How is she, anyway?"

"You can ask her yourself." Lavinia winked. "She's no stranger to AA. In fact, she'll be here tonight. She wouldn't miss it."

"Does she know I'm back?" His heart pounded heavily at that thought.

Lavinia laughed. "I'm sure she will, before tonight's open house…Oh, didn't Miranda tell you? It's at seven. We're all in for a long day! Speaking of which, before the other teachers start filtering in, we should go over the syllabus Mercy prepared for her—that is, *your* classes…"

CHAPTER 6

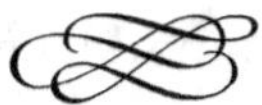

*B*y nine the next morning, Lionel and SallyAnne had entered the lobby of the Century City law firm that bore Robert Edelson's name along with those of three of his partners.

According to the receptionist, Edelson had been there since at least eight. And yet, he kept them waiting almost an hour.

Finally, an assistant arrived to show them to Edelson's office.

It was on a corner and almost the size of a ballroom. Like his home, it boasted floor-to-ceiling windows that afforded him a westerly view of Santa Monica and the ocean.

It's the office I would have chosen, given the opportunity, Lionel thought. The alternate corners—staked out by the other partners, he supposed—would have looked directly east onto the regularly traffic-congested Santa Monica Boulevard, or southeast toward amber-hazed downtown Los Angeles, or north toward the stark Hollywood Hills.

I wouldn't have lasted as long as that sun-baked potted plant in the corner, he realized. Corporate law offices like this one made him happy he'd chosen the FBI instead.

Rob stood as they entered and motioned to the chairs facing his massive desk as opposed to the more comfortable leather Corbusier couch and side chairs that made a conversation pit in the middle of the mammoth office.

We are the enemy, Lionel reasoned.

The goal now was to find out why.

"What can I do for you, Special Agents"—Rob nodded to SallyAnne first—"Jagger? Great name! My favorite rock-and-roller." His eyes shifted to Lionel. "And, um, Polk, right?" He chuckled. "Not such a great president. No relation, I assume."

"Yes, as a matter of fact." Lionel admitted. "Great uncle, six times removed."

Rob seemed taken aback by that. "Well then...I guess we're all related to someone."

Lionel and SallyAnne let that sit. They knew Rob wasn't really trying to make small talk.

"Mr. Edelson, we're investigating a case of potential fraud," SallyAnne explained. "A woman by the name of Miranda D'Arcy is currently a person of interest. If you have any evidence that, in her capacity as a college admissions counselor, she established a network of university administrators who are willing to, for lack of a better word, 'facilitate' admissions of students for a fee, it would help us establish that she is, in fact, a prime suspect in our case."

The color drained from Rob's face. "I see."

"Additionally, Ms. D'Arcy's illegal activities may have included tampering with, or falsifying, standardized test scores," Lionel explained.

Rob nodded slowly. "How did you get my name?"

Lionel shrugged. "Our sources are confidential."

"I still don't understand why you're here talking to me."

Lionel and SallyAnne exchanged glances. Lionel knew they were thinking the same thing: *something is not right here.*

SallyAnne pulled out her cell phone, clicked on an audio recording app, and laid it on Rob's desk. After stating the date, the time, the agents present, and Rob's full name, she began: "Rob Edelson, you sat in a trustee meeting in which felonies were discussed. As an officer of the court, you had a fiduciary responsibility to bring these matters to the attention of the appropriate authorities. Not doing so makes you—not to mention the other trustees—suspects in a criminal conspiracy."

"Wait... *Wait just a minute!*" Rob stood up. "How do you know what was discussed in the meeting?"

"For the record, are you telling us that you do not know of anyone, including Ms. D'Arcy, who may have committed illegal acts such as fraud, or bribery, or cheating to facilitate student admissions to U.S.-based universities?" SallyAnne asked.

"I...I didn't say that!" Rob stammered.

"Then, exactly what are you saying?" Lionel countered.

Rob glared at him. "Level with me. It was that bitch who sent you here, wasn't it?"

Bitch?...

Is he referring to Helene? Did we give her away?

Lionel and SallyAnne's stares met. Apparently, she was confused too.

Rob's lip curled into a smirk. "Agents, I'm no fool. I know how this plays out. I become a felon! My law license gets suspended—or worse, I lose it for life! My wife divorces me, and my children are shunned. Robbie will hate me because I didn't believe he'd get into USC on his own. And all because that bitch flipped first—"

Oh, I get it now.

"Sir, please…*Calm down,*" Lionel's voice was soft but firm. "We've yet to talk to Ms. D'Arcy."

As Lionel's words sunk in, Rob dropped back into his massive captain's chair.

He stared out the window: two minutes at the most, but it seemed like an eternity. Finally, he looked up at Lionel. "Well, then, I guess that works in my favor doesn't it, being the first up to bat?" His attempt at a smile was weak at best. "You'll note I'm a cooperating witness, correct?"

"Yes, absolutely." Lionel glanced at SallyAnne.

She nodded. "As an officer of the court, you're sworn to tell the truth. Not to mention, as a possible suspect yourself, any misstatement will be seen as obstruction of justice and dealt with accordingly."

Rob sighed. "Alright. Let's move forward then, shall we? So, what is it you want to know?"

Thank God for cooperating witnesses, Lionel thought.

SALLYANNE BEGAN: "MR. EDELSON, FOR THE RECORD, CAN YOU NAME THE individual perpetrating the college admissions fraud?"

"Her name is Miranda D'Arcy. She was formerly the college placement counselor at Bobbitt-Hennings Prep School here in Los Angeles."

"How were you made aware of these acts?"

"She approached me with an offer to attain acceptance to a top-tier university of my choosing for my son, Robbie. She named other parents who had had success with her, um, methods."

SallyAnne nodded. "Did she explain these methods to you?"

"Yes. And there are numerous opportunities for fraud. In many cases, the students' standardized tests are taken by, or substituted with others provided by a professional test taker. This is done by getting approval from the school to take the test off-campus, at a certified testing center. In this case, it was University Prep & Test." He shrugged. "Additionally, false narratives about a student's extracurricular activities are established to give the student a non-academic advantage over others."

"Was Ms. D'Arcy paid for these services?"

Rob scoffed. "Yes. Serious money."

"How much?" SallyAnne asked.

"The fees varied substantially, depending on what Mandy—that is, Miranda—thought she could get."

Mandy…? That sounds cozy, Lionel noted.

From the way SallyAnne's brow lifted, she also caught the nickname. "Can you give us a range?" she insisted.

"Yes. Fees ranged as small as ten thousand dollars. But those were rare. As Miranda put it, she'd cut some slack for the desperately poor."

"How generous of her," SallyAnne muttered.

Rob flinched at the jibe. "Yeah, well, that's Miranda for you. To answer your question, most parents paid in the mid- or high six-figures. A few paid over a million, if you can believe that."

Lionel's eyes opened wide.

SallyAnne paused, then asked: "Mr. Edelson, how much did *you* pay to have Robbie's SAT test falsified?"

"One hundred thousand." Just admitting this, Rob deflated like a hot-air balloon stabbed with a cold knife.

Lionel remembered Helene's pride in her children's accomplishments, both in and out of the classroom. "Why do it?" he wondered aloud. "Robbie's grades were better than good. And he had at least one solid extracurricular. He was a soccer champion."

Rob looked up sharply. "How do you know that?"

Damn it, I may have just outed Helene.

Lionel was relieved when Rob muttered, "Never mind. I know you guys don't bother asking a question unless you already have the answer." He looked down at SallyAnne's phone and shrugged at the recording. "Robbie… well, he's a lousy test taker. Just freezes. His real SAT score wouldn't have been enough to get him into my alma mater."

"But he would have gotten into other good schools," SallyAnne countered.

"Maybe," Rob conceded. "But it wasn't worth risking. Not for such a paltry fee." He grimaced when he saw SallyAnne's eyes narrow.

This case rubs her raw, Lionel realized.

So that Rob wouldn't just close up, Lionel knew it was time he jumped in: "How were the fees paid?"

"The testing center was paid directly, but I wouldn't be surprised if Miranda took a cut of what it got." Rob shrugged. "As for the counseling fees, they were paid to a non-profit corporation called the Best Face Forward Club. That way, parents get to write it off as a tax-exempt donation. It's a win-win."

The IRS would surely be interested in this revelation, Lionel thought.

Annoyed, SallyAnne clenched her fists. When she finally released them, she asked, "How and when did the Bobbitt-Hennings trustee board discover her actions?"

"Mid-July. Someone made a formal complaint. I couldn't let the other members know I was one of her so-called 'concierge clients,' so I suggested that, as the school's legal representative on the trustee board, I negotiate a settlement with her."

SallyAnne shook her head in awe. "As opposed to telling the authorities about her illicit activities?"

Rob shrugged. "As far as the board was concerned, it was all hearsay. It wasn't the board's place to prove or disprove the allegations. In the meantime, to maintain its stellar reputation, it was best that the school quickly distance itself from her."

"You said that Miranda D'Arcy's average fee was the mid- six-figures," SallyAnne pointed out. "And yet she charged you only one hundred thousand. Why is that?"

Rob's face turned bright red.

Suddenly, Lionel knew what Rob was trying hard not to say, so he asked: "How long had you been having an affair with Ms. D'Arcy?"

Rob muttered, "It wasn't like that! We...we only did it once." He shrugged. "I told her we had to meet because the board was onto her. At her suggestion, we met at her place. She insisted she didn't want to make trouble for the school. She was upset and worried about the possible consequences of her actions." He shook his head. "One thing led to another... You know."

SallyAnne allowed a minute to pass before asking, "And, for that, she walked away with a severance five times her salary—and a reference?"

"No—not for *'that!'*" Rob retorted. "She knew her reputation was in tatters. If she tried to Me-Too me, it would be her word against mine." He frowned. "She needed insurance. She made a video of us—*together!*"

SallyAnne looked from him to Lionel and back. "A sex tape?"

Rob nodded. Then, remembering he was being recorded, he murmured, "Yes."

"You're saying she blackmailed you?" Lionel asked.

Rob's response was so soft that Lionel wondered if the recorder picked it up.

"Again, please, Mr. Edelson," he prompted him.

"Yes! She told me if I couldn't convince the board to pay up, not only would she take the school down with her, she'd send the video to Helene." Shamed by his confession, Rob closed his eyes. "As it turned out, Miranda didn't need the video anyway. The board gladly gave her what she wanted to put the incident to bed without a scandal."

Lionel waited until Rob opened his eyes again to ask, "Can you name any others who were also... you called it, 'concierge clients,' right?"

"Yes. Janna and Eric Calisher. They live in Beverly Hills. He's in financial management. The firm is Dewey-Calisher. Their kid, a boy, isn't the sharpest tool in the shed," Rob rolled his eyes. "The other client is Tanner Simpson."

SallyAnne perked up. "Tanner Simpson, the director?"

"Yeah. He doesn't let anyone forget it, either. If he could, he'd carry around his Oscar to remind the rest of us." Rob's scorn was evident in his tone as well as his words. "His daughter—Lacey, is her name—skirts by on his reputation."

"Are there any others?" Lionel asked.

"Probably, but I can't think of anyone else. My guess? It's just the tip of the iceberg for Miranda." Rob opened his hands wide. "Agents, I'm doing what I can to earn brownie points. Consider me part of the team."

"I'm glad you put it that way, Rob. And, as part of your agreement to cooperate fully, we'll need all correspondence between you and Ms. D'Arcy," SallyAnne explained. "By the way, within the next twenty-four hours, an FBI tech team will be at your office and home with subpoenas to go through all your computer and other electronic devices."

"Understood."

"In the future, we may also ask you to make a call to Ms. D'Arcy and ask her specific questions. The conversation will be recorded."

"No problem." Rob nodded. "Agents, I know I have no right to ask you this, but… if my wife finds out…" His voice trailed off.

Lionel nodded. "Like you, we're sworn to keep our findings confidential. Remember, we've only just begun the investigation. At this point, we can't say how long it will take to build the case and issue subpoenas for Ms. D'Arcy and her network of bribed administrators."

"A year, maybe?" The hope in Rob's voice made SallyAnne grimace.

"Even so, eventually the parents who participated in Miranda's scheme will be named in court documents and have trials of their own," Sally-Anne replied. "How a judge may rule in your case…well, it's hard to predict. You know that better than most."

Rob sighed. "I just pray whomever is appointed is not someone I've already pissed off."

Division Director Melamed agreed with Lionel and SallyAnne that they should spend the rest of the week in Los Angeles, perhaps even longer, checking out the leads that had come their way via Rob Edelson.

Melamed also approved the search and seizure of all of Edelson's devices, and the wiretaps on all of now prime suspect Miranda D'Arcy's communication devices. As soon as these could be analyzed and assessed, the deep dive into Miranda's background would begin.

"I'll send Riley Kemp down there to facilitate on tech," he promised.

In larger markets, the bureau had travel accounts with Marriott. Because it was spending taxpayer dollars, whenever possible agents were encouraged to take the less expensive brands within the chain. With this in mind, for this trip Lionel had chosen the Marriott Courtyard in Century

City beside Beverly Hills, which was within ten miles of most of the Bobbitt-Hennings Prep School parents who were currently potential suspects.

After returning to their rooms, Lionel joined SallyAnne in hers. Their task: create a profile on Miranda from anything they could pull up on their suspect from public records and online sources, such as social media, news clippings, college transcripts, and her company's website.

SallyAnne watched as Lionel's eyes perused every photo they could find on Miranda D'Arcy, née Mandy Blackwell. They felt they'd struck gold when they located an online version of her high school yearbook.

As a teenager, Mandy had been pudgy and pimply, with a tightly coiled mass of bright red hair. But from what SallyAnne could see from the pictures of Miranda D'Arcy on her latest driver's license, passport, and company website, the once ugly duckling had grown into a slim, blond swan.

By seven, the agents were famished. Lionel suggested that they use their allotted per diem to eat at a casual Italian restaurant.

SallyAnne gave him an immediate thumbs-up. She loved spending time with him when they were officially off the clock. When fatigue and a glass of wine kicked in, she gleaned a few more touching tidbits of the man behind the badge.

That night, they spent the balance of the meal discussing the approach they'd take with the potential suspects: the movie director, Tanner Simpson, and Janna Calisher and her husband Eric, the financial manager.

"Perhaps tomorrow's first stop should be Simpson," SallyAnne suggested. "We could approach him when he's leaving his home for the movie set. That way, we won't have to be announced by studio security."

"Sound theory," Lionel murmured. "Later that morning we can then interview Eric Calisher at his office."

"He'll tell his wife immediately afterward," SallyAnne pointed out.

"Probably. But by getting Eric on record first, we can then explain to her what he could be facing so that she makes the best decision for herself and their children. They've got two others who are currently in middle school."

In other words, Janna may want to cut a deal to avoid or reduce her jail time.

SallyAnne held up her wine glass. "Here's to securing our first witness willing to turn on Ms. D'Arcy, and, hopefully, three more to come."

Lionel tapped his glass to hers. "I can't wait to meet her in person."

SallyAnne raised a brow. "Why is that?"

Lionel met her question with a shrug. "I'm always fascinated to see what it is about our suspects that beguiles their victims. Or, in this case, co-conspirators. She must be quite a smooth operator to have convinced these parents to secure her services regardless that they'd be skirting the law."

SallyAnne knew him well enough to realize he, too, felt Miranda should do jail time for creating this enormously profitable scheme.

Once again, she tipped her glass toward his. "I'll drink to that."

It made her proud to have him as her co-worker.

How she wished they were much more than that.

CHAPTER 7

I'm the man.

This declaration had been reverberating through Egan's mind all day.

At first, it was the mantra he needed that morning to propel himself out of the house and into his car—really, his father's ancient Camry—for the trek over the Golden Gate Bridge and through the city to Ashbury Academy.

But then Miranda D'Arcy's flirtatious greeting (make that her obvious come-on) bolstered the phrase into an honest-to-God possibility.

Any doubts still lingering faded in the very warm welcomes he received from the two former colleagues still on staff.

Odette Pettigrew's rib-bruising hug was accompanied with an alarming whisper: "When I read *Extracurricular,* I was touched to learn I was your muse! Perhaps we should explore that role in depth, on our off time?"

Egan covered his horror at that thought by chuckling benignly. Apparently, she hadn't recognized the character he'd based on her: Lilliane Canard, a frowzy, flirtatious tippler with a heart of gold.

Far be it from him to correct her.

Cornell Rothchild's response was even more surprising. Egan had fully expected the slight, effete chemistry teacher to chide him for leaving him out of *Extracurricular* altogether since any actions that could have been attributed to him went to an über-masculine hulk who went by the name of Oscar. Instead, Cornell nodded toward the exclusive blend of beans now steeping in his private portable French press.

"Stay away from that swill in the communal coffee urn," he warned

248

Egan. "In fact, I've got enough of this for another cuppa or two, if you care to join me."

Egan winced at the thought of having to drink from one of Cornell's prissy little cups. He was relieved when the brew was presented in a mug engraved with Ashbury Academy's logo.

As Egan sipped the excellent coffee, Cornell pulled out a copy of the book and asked Egan to autograph it. With a broad wink, he added, "Please make it out to 'Oscar.'"

As Egan signed, it brought to mind the most famous stanza from Robert Burns' poem, "To a Louse, On Seeing One on a Lady's Bonnet at Church":

O would some Power the giftie gie us
To see ourselves as others see us!

Burns was spot on, Egan thought. Most people are blind to any truth about themselves.

Egan's version of their truth, anyway.

EGAN'S ANXIETY WAS FURTHER ASSUAGED BY LAVINIA'S HEARTFELT introduction of him to the rest of the teaching staff: "In the solitary year Egan's presence graced Ashbury Academy, he was an eager volunteer for school events, a true friend to his fellow teaching colleagues, and an inspiration to his students."

His twenty-eight new coworkers instinctively turned to peruse the recipient of Lavinia's praise. All were younger than him, some by two decades.

To cover his chagrin, he did the one thing that never failed him in anxious times: he grinned broadly, then sought out the prettiest woman in the room and winked at her.

As in every other incident, the chosen one blushed even as she returned his wink.

This was not lost on the others. Curiosity abounded. Nonchalant glances hardened into outright stares.

One of the male teachers in particular—tall but wiry, a twenty-something sporting hipster chin scruff—scowled outright. When he caught Egan's eye, he glared. Egan held his gaze until the man finally looked away.

Egan imagined what he must be thinking: *Has a new pecking order been established?*

Hell, yeah it has, Egan thought.

I'm the man. And don't you forget it.

"...AND REMEMBER, STAFF: A CATERED DINNER WILL BE PREPARED FOR teachers who won't have time to go home prior to the parent open house, which begins at seven tonight." Lavinia's tone was gentle, but firm. "The parents will be following their student's class schedule, so there will be a total of seven meet-and-greets. Each will run only fifteen minutes. I'd suggest structuring your time so that you give a short introduction to your course—no longer than five minutes. Take their questions for the balance of the time. The parents have only five minutes to get to the next class. Any questions?"

Lavinia waited a moment. Hearing none, she added, "We have one last bit of business before we join the students in the auditorium. Berney Neufeld's retirement leaves the academic staff without representation on the trustee board. We'll need a replacement." Lavinia scanned the room. "The board meets once a month, in the evening: usually on a Wednesday. The position means presenting the collective faculty issues that merit the board's attention. As you can imagine, diplomacy is of the utmost impor-tance, as is the ability to appreciate the opinions of the parents who sit on the board. They have a tendency to..." Lavinia hesitated as she struggled to find the right phrase.

"Be complete assholes?" Someone grumbled.

Egan noticed it was Hipster.

"Forget all that we do to keep their kids from turning out like them?" Another declared—this time, a female instructor. From her shorts and tee shirt, Egan deduced she was a PE teacher.

Lavinia's eyes shifted from Scuff to the woman and back again. "Ike, Candice, if that was your audition for the position, you missed the mark."

Nervous chuckles resonated through the room.

"What I'm trying to say is that these parents feel the school's wellbeing is important enough to take the time to meet and offer their unique skills on its behalf. They come from all walks of life. They help us with legal issues that may arise. They help us balance our books. They raise funds from outside sources for AA's scholarships and other important programs. And they donate. *Yes, we need them.* But have no doubts: it is a symbiotic relationship. They need us too. More to the point, their children need us to work together so that we have a school that makes each and every one of us proud." Lavinia's voice seemed to fade away.

She seems so tired, Egan thought.

Finally, Lavinia took a deep breath. "Any takers?"

No one raised a hand.

Egan kept still too.

Today's drive from his parents' house in Greenbrae had taken him an hour. The main vein of the county, Sir Francis Drake Boulevard, was always a traffic nightmare during rush-hour. When he'd finally reached US-101, there was still the issue of getting over the Golden Gate Bridge, not to mention the stop-and-go traffic through town as he drove toward the Haight.

Suddenly, he remembered Miranda's advice: that getting onto the board would be the best way to curry favor with those who could underwrite his position.

And besides, I'm sure Lavinia will appreciate having another board member advocating her vision of the school.

He raised his hand. "I'd be happy to sit on the board."

Lavinia beamed gratefully. "Thank you, Egan. You'll be a welcomed addition."

He waved away her appreciation. Suddenly, he felt guilty for being selfish at her expense.

"That guy Lavinia just introduced—our seventh-period teacher—he's the one who wrote that book!" Manya Patel nudged her pals, Charly McKittridge, Sienna Belluci, and Zina Sisley-Calder, so that they'd quit gossiping and take notice.

The girls followed their friend's gaze at the man now making his way to the podium.

Charly was particularly interested in him. She was ecstatic when she learned that, like her friends, she'd been accepted into AA's advanced placement Shakespeare Comparative Lit class. It would look great on her college transcript. The scuttlebutt from AA alumni was that the course had prepared them well for similar classes on the university level, especially those who went on to post-graduate degrees in Literature, Fiction, or Creative Writing.

The new teacher, Egan Gable, looked to be about the same age as her parents: in his mid- to late-forties. He wore a navy blazer over a gray tee shirt tucked into his slim-cut jeans. Caught in the beams of natural light slanting through the auditorium's high windows, the silver strands entwined with his dark hair flickered like tinsel.

There was a confident air about him. His grin grew wider as his eyes scanned the crowd. When he took a deep breath, it was as if he were drinking in the energy bouncing around the room.

Quest Wishart-Jammerhead, who sat right behind the girls, stuck his head between Manya and Charly. "Yo, so, what book did he write?"

Manya sighed as she rolled her eyes. "Why do you care? You can barely read."

"Oh yeah? I've read...um...*Lord of the Rings*!" he retorted.

"Read it, or saw the movie?" Charly teased.

Quest's blush made his freckles pop even more. "I...read it. Really, I did."

"Okay, then what's the name of the elf?" she asked.

Quest thought for a moment. "Arwen."

"You're right—*in the movie.* In the book, it's Glorfindel." She wagged her finger at him.

"*Shhhh!*" Odette glared up into the bleachers to see who was talking. Satisfied with the pending silence, she turned back to Egan.

"Seriously, what's the name of his book?" Charly's lips barely moved as she asked the question.

"Don't tell me you haven't heard of it!" Zina put her hand over her mouth as if she were shocked. "It's called *Extracurricular.* It's a novel about a private prep school."

Sienna squinted. "I've heard of it too—through Mom. All I know is that it came out before I was born...so it's *ancient!*"

Quest shoved his head back between them. "He must have written other stuff since then."

"That would just mean more stuff you haven't read." Charly shoved him back into his row.

"The guy sounds like a one-hit wonder," Quest mumbled.

Charly glared at him. "So was J.D. Salinger."

Quest stared blankly at her.

She shook her head, amused. *"Catcher in the Rye?"*

He frowned cluelessly.

"Remember? We read it in the ninth grade," Charly insisted.

Quest winced. "That was, like, a lifetime ago."

Charly sighed.

"Extracurricular was considered racy back in the day." Zina raised a brow.

"Seriously, how much could doing the dirty have changed between then and now?" Charly asked.

Zina snickered, "If you were doing it, my sweet little virgin, you wouldn't have to ask."

Charly stared back at the podium. Zina and Manya had relationships with their boyfriends that began in their junior year. When the girls broke the news to her, it was quite matter-of-fact. They seemed relieved that their virginity was no longer an emotional burden.

Charly doubted their folks knew any of this. Manya's mother, Nira, was a single parent who was determined that her daughter follow in her footsteps and become a physician. Had she known that Manya was already playing doctor with Theo Dempsey—now a freshman at Stanford —she'd put her in a convent or something.

Zina's parents knew she and Sven Jorgensen were dating. They weren't pleased by it. "You're too young, and he's too white," Gemma had warned her daughter. "If Grandpa Sisley knew, he'd hit the roof!" Gemma's father was a renowned civil rights attorney who had made his name defending Black Panther activists.

"If we want an inclusive world, it has to start somewhere," Zina had argued.

"Honey, I don't see it starting with you," Darius responded.

He backed off, albeit warily, when he heard Sven in last year's county debate tournament defend the legitimacy of W.E.B. Du Bois' statement: "The price of culture is a lie."

Now, listening to Egan, Zina sat up straight. "Hey, did you hear that? This Egan guy just said that he taught here before."

"Does that mean the book is about AA?" Manya wondered out loud.

Sienna and Charly's eyes grew large at this possibility.

"If so, I'll bet my mom has a copy," Zina mused. "I'll ask her."

"Mine would too," Charly murmured. "I'll do the same."

"And the school would have it in the library, wouldn't it?" Sienna asked.

"If not, there's got to be a few copies floating around the public library system," Manya countered.

Quest whispered in Charly's ear: "You're seeing this dude in seventh period. Before you get all hot and bothered about the darn book, why not just ask him if it's about AA?"

He was right.

For once, she didn't swat him away.

When introducing Egan to the student body at its morning assembly, Lavinia again spoke from her heart as she lavished praise on the latest addition to the teaching staff.

Although she mentioned his previous tenure at AA and his bearing as a "celebrated published novelist," Egan had no expectations that the students would find yet another middle-aged instructor the least bit intriguing. He was pleasantly surprised that her introduction garnered some impressed nods and curious murmurs.

As he took the podium, Egan realized that the last thing he wanted to do was disappoint his newfound audience. After thanking Lavinia for her kind introduction, he vowed to keep his classes interesting and entertaining. ("Not on a *Game of Thrones* level, but I'll do my best to come close...") He then sprinkled in a few humble brags. ("I haven't felt this appreciated since my editor called to tell me I'd made the *New York Times* Bestsellers list..." and "For those of you who grew up reading Harry Potter books, I can assure you, J.K. Rowling is every bit as whip-smart as Hermione Granger—even after a cocktail or two...")

Egan's words had the hoped-for effect: a few outright chuckles, murmurs of excitement, and finally enthusiastic applause.

Undoubtedly, for someone with Egan's pride, publishing offered a tantalizing prize: fame and fortune.

Having achieved this in his first book, he'd garnered his fair share of acolytes: mostly awed readers, although every now and then another author would grace him with a grudging compliment. And he could always count on his publicist to stroke his ego.

But as a novelist, Egan had felt he was constantly in competition. The expectation of success for his next book—from his publisher, his editor, his agent, his readers, and himself—was stratospheric and therefore unrealistic. Not only were its sales to be measured against those of *Extracurricular,* it would also be compared to the novels of every other best-selling author — debuting and established.

In his case, a second chance at the brass ring never happened. Egan's fear of failure had him second-guessing every plot point, every line of dialogue, and every turn of phrase in his second novel. His uncertainty proved to be his undoing. The manuscript missed its submission deadline by three years: just in time to catch a recession that wiped out many of the independent bookstores that had championed *Extracurricular.* Without the enthusiastic support of his publishing house, his second novel lost its way in a vast, endless universe of digital releases.

Egan was no longer the "shiny new thing." In time, as far as the publishing industry was concerned, he wasn't a "thing" at all.

How he longed to prove them wrong.

As a teacher, his role wasn't to compete, but to lead; to inspire.

If he stayed the year, he'd have time to regroup; to plot out his comeback novel. Ashbury Academy had inspired him once. Perhaps it would do so again.

Being here isn't so bad, he thought.

For the first time all day, Egan was okay with admitting this to himself.

———

By Egan's last class— his second course of *Advanced Placement Shakespeare Comparative Lit* for seniors and juniors—he realized what he missed most about teaching: sharing what he knew with students who were eager to hear what he had to say.

As with the earlier Comp Lit class, Egan began by making a simple request: "Write down one line from William Shakespeare. It doesn't matter which play. You've got five minutes."

Before the gentle clack of keyboards went silent again, Egan got up and strolled down the center aisle. His game plan: choose a student at random.

He scanned their faces until one caught his attention. The girl was slim and by the height of her torso, he could tell she was also tall. Her hair, the color of young mahogany, was mussed and cut pixie short. This accentuated her wide green eyes in a perfectly heart-shaped face.

"What's your name?" he asked.

"Charly," she replied with a blush.

Perfect, he thought. It was the name he would have chosen, had he conceived her as a character in a novel.

He grinned down at her. "Hello, Charly. Would you be so kind as to read me your quote?"

She nodded, then cleared her throat: "'Everyone can master a grief but he that has it.' It's from *Much Ado about Nothing*."

"Correct. Now, tell me: what does it mean to you?" Egan leaned in as if hoping to divine some grand secret.

"Well..." Charly paused as she collected her thoughts. "We may tell someone we feel their pain, but the reality is that unless you've experienced a similar tragedy, you can't really understand another's grief."

Egan nodded, as if intrigued. "I take it you would agree with Shakespeare on this premise?"

Charly thought a moment. "Yes, certainly. It's why people at a funeral will say, 'Sorry for your loss.' Even someone who's never experienced the death of a loved one feels obliged to say it. But then, during the reception or wake, they converse and laugh without any thought as to how it may affect the grieving family."

"An excellent example. Have you read a book recently that epitomizes Shakespeare's contention?"

Charly thought for a moment. "One that comes to mind is Edith Wharton's *House of Mirth*."

"Why is that?"

"The main character, Lily Bart, is running out of money. Although her so-called friends pity her, they're willing to let her starve, to fall from grace, while they gossip about her."

"Great choice. Then your first assignment shouldn't be too challenging: turn your contention in an essay of, say, a thousand words." Egan scanned the room. "Tell me, Charly, would you say that anyone you know exemplifies Shakespeare's quote?"

Charly rolled her eyes. "Like, here at school?"

"That's a good place to start."

"Well, then yeah—probably everyone."

The other students laughed at that. Seeing that Egan was grinning too, Charly smiled shyly.

Suddenly, someone yelped: a girl, who then whined, "*Chuuuuck*—shhh! Cut it out!"

It wasn't a desperate plea. More like a taunt; a dare.

If there was any doubt of this, the plea's theatrical delivery—the seductive tone in which the girl crooned the boy's name, allowing it to linger deep in her throat—robbed it of any sincerity.

Charly's smile faded. Instinctively, she turned toward the commotion.

So did Egan and the rest of the class.

Apparently the kid named Chuck—broad-shouldered, with light brown hair, his long legs stretched far in the aisle—had been flirting with the girl in front of him.

Granted, she was a stunner: fair-haired, big blue eyes, full pouting lips, generous breasts under a form-hugging tee shirt.

Both looked up when they heard the room grow silent again. When the girl's eyes met Egan's, she held his gaze as if pleased to have his undivided attention.

Chuck saw the look too. He didn't seem to like it.

Good, thought Egan.

Frankly, he was annoyed that the girl even assumed that, like the boy, he'd be enticed by her all too obvious simper. They were disrupting his class, undermining his authority.

This was his domain. Here, he was the master.

Time to prove it.

He nodded at Chuck. "I'm not interrupting anything, am I—*Chuck?*" Egan's deliberate emphasis of the boy's name hadn't had the same drawn-out cadence as the girl's. Still, it had the desired effect: the other students snickered.

Chuck grinned as he leaned back in his seat. "No, sir, not at all. We're enjoying the class immensely."

"Good to hear." *Smart-ass.* "Tell us—*Chuck*: which of Shakespeare's many passages will you be honoring us with today?"

Egan was prepared to be underwhelmed with one of the more common quotes; say, "Romeo, Romeo, wherefore art thou, Romeo..." or "To thine own self be true..." or "To be or not to be, that is the question..."

Had that been the case—and worse yet, had Chuck failed to identify the chosen phrase's origin—Egan was prepared to use the boy's ignorance as a warning to him and any other slackers: if they didn't take the class seriously, they'd receive a grade that would kill their GPAs.

And if that unnerved Chuck into requesting a transfer from the class, Egan would gladly accommodate him.

Instead, Egan was dismayed when Chuck responded, "'A fool thinks himself to be wise, but a wise man knows himself to be a fool.'" He then added, "It's from *As You Like It,* by the way."

Surprised, Egan nodded. "And your thoughts on its meaning?"

"If you have any real intelligence, you'd realize that you're never as smart as you'd like to think you are."

Egan's approval was grudging at best. "A decent analogy. Tell me, *Chuck*, do you agree with Shakespeare?"

Chuck squinted as if he were taking the answer seriously. "Not necessarily. But I know my mom does because she says it every time I sass her."

To Egan's dismay, the class broke out in a fit of giggles.

Great, I've got a class clown on my hands.

"Yes, well, I for one certainly feel *her* pain," Egan declared. "Tell me, *Chuck*: does any book come to mind that may exemplify your quote?"

Chuck grinned. "Does a comic book count?"

Laughter roiled through the room.

"I think you know the answer to that. Tell you what, since you're at a loss to come up with one, I'll assign it: *The Beautiful and the Damned.* There's a character in it who always thinks he knows it all. You'll identify with him, I'm sure."

Chuck's grin disappeared. "But...but..."

It was Egan's turn to smile. "Oh, and by the way, although Disney has yet to make an animated film of it, there are other cinematic versions. Should you be tempted to use one as a shortcut, I'd prefer you drop the class instead. It will save your poor mother another heartache when your report card comes out."

Egan's tone put everyone on alert: *Don't fuck with me.*

So that the others understood that he much preferred handing out carrots as opposed to sticks, he exclaimed, "Class, now that you have the gist of your first assignment, take another five to ten minutes to write down a novel with a plot you feel embodies the phrase you've just chosen. I'll call on a few of you, to see if you're on track. By the way, you'll have until Friday to turn in a paper. I'll expect footnoted excerpts that help you make your case."

The rest of class time went just as Egan had hoped: the students brought their A game.

He was glad about that. He'd be seeing Lavinia at the trustee board meeting and he wanted to be able to tell her that his day had been a love fest between him and his students.

Some smart ass wasn't going to ruin that for him.

DAMN YOU, CHUCK!

Her brother's wisecracks made Charly want to crawl under her seat.

All this, just to impress Fawn, she fumed.

Charly had felt she'd established a real connection with Egan. He seemed to appreciate her thoughtful choice and the insight she had into its relationship with Lily Bart's plight.

Why must Chuck always be the center of attention—and at my expense?

It was not lost on Charly that, amongst their three children, each of her parents had a personal favorite.

In both cases, it wasn't Charly.

She knew her parents loved her dearly. And that they appreciated the hard work and determination she put toward her studies. They were verbal in their admiration of her dutiful nature. They always took her at her word, no matter the issue. They showered her with gratitude, never once withholding their affection for her.

At the same time, their actions toward her brothers spoke volumes.

For her mother, Chuck was the clear choice. He never failed to make her laugh at his silliness. Whenever Chuck got in trouble, if he couldn't convince Mom that the crime was one of ignorance or impulse, eventually he'd sweet-talk his original sentence down to a misdemeanor. She'd never understood why her mother allowed Chuck such leeway.

Charly had always modeled her behavior on her grandmother and mother: work hard, do your best, be gracious, and think of others.

It would mortify Charly to disappoint Audrey. But should it ever happen, no doubt her mother's dismay would come with consequences.

For Dad, the favored child was Noah. This was to be expected, considering the twins shared a natural closeness and buoyant personalities: traits their mother felt best fell under her watchful eye. Add to this the fact that the younger boy's thoughtful deliberateness mirrored their father's, Noah was the natural choice.

It helped, too, that Noah was just as passionate as their father about cycling.

As soon as the McKittridge kids learned to maneuver a two-wheeler, they ecstatically joined their father in what became a weekend tradition: exploring the rugged trails and old fire roads that coiled around Marin County's Mount Tamalpais.

Before Noah was old enough to join them, the family would drive over the bridge and start their trek from the nearest town: Sausalito. At first, toddler Noah was their mother's excuse for passing on the excursions. But when even he was ready to join the others, she gave a somewhat weaker rationale: without them underfoot, she'd have time to prepare the picnic that would be waiting upon their return.

When the older children reached high school age, the four McKittridges cycled over the bridge. Afterward, they'd enjoy a meal in Mill Valley, one of the small towns nestled at the foot of the mountain.

Occasionally, their mother would drive in to join them. They'd ride back into town with her, the bikes tethered to the extended rack on the back of the family's SUV.

Eventually, Charly realized what their mother was really doing: gifting them precious time with their father during his much-deserved respite from a long week spent managing his law firm.

Charly now wondered if Chuck or Noah had also figured this out. Maybe Noah. He seemed to have been born wise. His actions bore this out.

Chuck was the opposite. The universe revolved around him and no one else.

His behavior in Comp Lit was proof of that.

Charly was still steaming over her brother's antics when AA's bell tower chimed the end of the school day. As her classmates rose to their feet, Egan's next words succeeded in breaking through her tortured thoughts:

"…and by the way, Debate Team tryouts are in three weeks. If you're interested, feel free to take the handout on the corner of my desk. In the year I was here, I was proud to coach AA's very first team to the state quarterfinals. I'd like to best that record with some of you."

Manya nudged her. "What do you think? Should we go for it?"

"I'm in!" Zina exclaimed. "I know it helped Sven get into Stanford."

"Me too," Sienna declared.

Charly shrugged. "Sure, sounds like fun."

Despite her nonchalance, she was determined to do one more thing that might set her apart from her brothers—especially Chuck.

Not that a jock like him would dream of trying out for Debate Team. And even if he did, after today's incident, there was no way he'd make the cut.

That was fine with her.

CHAPTER 8

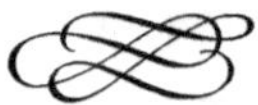

ell, well, who is this handsome devil?
More to the point, why is he here?

Miranda had caught sight of the tall, dark stranger just as he'd entered the parents' lounge, where Ashbury Academy's trustee board meeting would soon take place. She had long ago tuned out Egan's humble-bragging about his first day back at the school. He hadn't noticed because she'd been *oohing* and *ahhing* in all the right places even as she scoped out the rest of AA's board members.

In one corner of the room, that pompous fool—the investment fund manager, Seamus McCoppin—held court with his allies: Warner Crawford, Jess Smallwood, and Darius Calder. All were superb golfers and always part of Seamus' foursome at the gold-plated Olympic Club.

Miranda had spent the past evening memorizing their names and faces. She'd researched their work histories, wives, and university alma maters. She'd perused their presence on social media.

Like Seamus, Warner and Jess were financial titans who rode roughshod over other people's money: in Warner's case, union pensions. For Jess, it was limited partnerships created for angel investors interested in tech start-ups.

As for Darius, he was a lawyer. And although the firm he'd started with his wife—Miranda's old Debate Team nemesis, Gemma Sisley—was renowned for defending the civil rights of underdogs and death row inmates, its cash cow was another sort of clientele, handled solely by Darius: drug kingpins and other shady entrepreneurial clients looking for creative ways to shelter their undeclared earnings.

All of this intel was to give her some idea whether they'd be potential concierge clients.

If their newsworthy endeavors and social media accounts were to be believed, the answer was a resounding yes. Everything about the men and their wives oozed status and privilege.

Miranda had also looked up their children's names and GPAs. Sadly, for Warner, Jess, and Seamus, their children's grade point averages were lower than the acceptable standard for topflight universities, but would get them into a mediocre technical school or a junior college that fed into a state university.

The great news for Miranda: neither option would be acceptable to men with their inflated egos.

Warner's son, Buck, was a handsome devil. But be it sports or academics, he'd never applied himself at either, and it showed.

In the dictionary, the boy's picture could appear beside the word *sloth*, Miranda thought.

In her opinion, Jess' son, Hugo, was less of a loser but only by a thin margin. The best thing he had going for him was his entrepreneurial skill: he was the school's go-to drug dealer.

Only Darius and Gemma's daughter, Zina, could be a shoo-in. First off, she was an excellent student. Being a person of color would also work in her favor. Had she also participated in sports, she would have been a slam-dunk for an elite university. But, from looking at Zina's test scores, Miranda could tell that the girl's Achilles heel was math.

Maybe that's my way in with Darius, she thought.

One thing Miranda knew: after her shameful incidents during the Debate Team tournament, she certainly had to stay away from Gemma.

If Egan, Audrey, Tallulah, and Bliss don't remember me, maybe Gemma won't either, she reasoned.

Bottom line: she'd have to win the men's trust, which meant playing to their egos.

MIRANDA WATCHED AS THE STRANGER MADE HIS WAY TO LAVINIA. AT FIRST, the headmistress didn't notice him because she was deep in discussion with the trustee who had been on the board since the school's inception: US Congressman Harris Blanchard. Despite a slight stoop inherent with surviving seven decades of life, the revered statesman towered over the headmistress.

When the stranger offered her his hand, she pulled him in for a quick hug instead.

Interesting.

Then again, Lavinia was touchy-feely with everyone. For all Miranda knew, the guy was her accountant.

Tallulah and Bliss stood on the other side of Lavinia. After shaking hands with Blanchard, the stranger offered pecks to the women.

A spark of jealousy charged through Miranda. It was disappointing how little either of them had aged. Instead, they'd become sleeker, posher versions of themselves.

They wear their success with such ease, she thought enviously.

When they'd arrived, the two women had nodded hello to Miranda. Other than that, they ignored her. It was high school all over again, what with the two of them murmuring animatedly between chuckles.

Like that idiot, Audrey, they haven't put two and two together as to who I am, Miranda realized. *Otherwise, they'd probably spit on me.*

All the more reason to keep them clueless as long as possible.

Periodically, Bliss and Tallulah's eyes scanned the room but didn't linger on anyone, not even the men. Not surprising. Considering their personal success and the size of their bank accounts, they certainly weren't in the market for breadwinner husbands.

And with how quickly my wealth has grown these past few years, neither am I.

Miranda smiled at that realization.

"What, did I say something funny?" Egan asked.

She stifled the urge to roll her eyes. *He's such an egomaniac!*

Instead, she batted her lids and simpered, "If I could, I'd follow you around all day. I wouldn't want to miss any of your scintillating *bon mots.*"

Gag me, please!

Egan puffed up at that. He must have taken this as her invitation to continue because his blathering began again.

She'd had enough. Miranda had just devised an excuse to sidle over to Seamus and his cronies when Lavinia proclaimed, "Now that we're all here, shall we get started?"

Miranda didn't need a second invitation. As if regretting the intrusion, she murmured, "Excuse me, Egan. Time to sing for my supper," then made her way to the circular conference table.

She waited until Seamus took his seat before choosing her own; to his right.

As it turned out, the handsome stranger chose the chair to her right.

Perfect.

Egan grimaced at this turn of events. So as not to look silly, he took the chair to the stranger's right.

This put him across from Tallulah and Bliss.

Tallulah eyed him curiously.

The guileless Bliss couldn't resist: "You look familiar."

"You do too." Egan's smile went full wattage. "But up until recently, I've lived in New York. Do you have occasion to go there?"

"Occasionally," she replied coolly.

He nodded. "I'm a member of the Metropolitan Club."

Bliss shook her head.

"Core Club?"

"Sorry, no."

"Let me guess. Soho House?"

"Nope. Wrong again," Bliss replied. "With all your friends back there, I suppose we should be honored to have you all to ourselves!"

Egan's face warmed with embarrassment.

Tallulah turned her head so that Egan wouldn't catch her smirk.

Oh my God, how emasculating for that horn dog, Miranda thought.

She pursed her lips to keep from laughing.

LAVINIA GOT RIGHT DOWN TO BUSINESS. "FIRST OF ALL, I'D LIKE TO INTRODUCE our newest members and a guest." She nodded at Daniel. "When Phillipa Garner resigned, AA's board lost its legal advisor. As the managing partner of one of the city's largest international law firms, I'm grateful Daniel McKittridge accepted my invitation to take Phillipa's place. I'm sure you'll agree that he'll be an integral and appreciated addition to the board."

Though Miranda's hopes for the vacancy were dashed, she was more determined than ever to gain access.

No better place to start than Audrey Thorpe's husband.

"It's also with great pleasure that I introduce Bliss Thackeray Belluci and Tallulah Wishart as this year's PTA co-chairs." Lavinia nodded toward the women. "As you're already well aware, Ms. Thackeray Belluci is an iconic face around the world and a leader in the fashion industry. Ms. Wishart manages two of the most celebrated musical artists of our time. Thank you, ladies, for making the time for us too."

Daniel winked at his friends.

When Egan's jaw fell open in shock, Miranda had to stifle a snicker.

The board members nodded appraisingly. They were well aware of Bliss's fashion celebrity and Tallulah's standing in the music industry. That both were now on its trustee board gave Ashbury Academy additional bragging rights.

"It will be a pleasure to work with you, gentlemen. One suggestion: I won't believe all your bad press if you'll do me the same favor." Bliss' honeyed-tone request was met with chuckles and preening.

Tallulah added: "Because this is the school's twenty-fifth anniversary, the PTA is playing a critical role in fundraising for the scholarship program, which supports fifty percent of the student body, either partially or fully. This is also AA's edge over the city's other private schools." She looked each man in the eye. "As much as Bliss and I admire each of you for your many accomplishments, we're all sitting at this table because we understand one simple rule: money talks. We look forward to your support in this endeavor."

Seamus scowled at Tallulah's audacity.

The other men shifted uncomfortably in their seats.

"Thank you, ladies, for your candor." Lavinia then nodded toward Egan. "There are several new programs offered this year. Our more generous parents will be asked to underwrite them. In fact, the accomplishments of our new academic trustee"—she nodded toward Egan —"merit a special chaired position in his honor." Lavinia was practically beaming at him. "Once again, AA is lucky to have on staff the *New York Times* bestselling author, Egan Gable."

JESUS...BLISS AND TALLULAH ARE...

Women.

Egan forced himself to gaze at a spot on the wall beyond Warner's bald pate so that he wouldn't be tempted to stare at his former students. Instead, his mind created a double exposure: here they were in Technicolor, superimposed over his sepia memories of them.

Bliss had always been a stunner. Egan was impressed to see that two decades of maturity hadn't dimmed the innate charm of the leggy, wide-eyed wild child of his memories. Back then, her stream-of-consciousness exclamations had been like a handful of Skittles thrown up in the air, its sugar-coated innocence falling willy-nilly on confounded ears, albeit its sweet logic hard to swallow. This new Bliss voiced her opinion sparingly with a savory sultriness that left listeners longing for seconds.

As for Tallulah, the halo of bright red curls was now tamed into a blunt auburn bob. Chic designer skinny jeans and a sheer blouse worn under a fitted jacket had replaced her slip dresses and bulky denim vests. Louboutins now took the place of her standard-issue army boots.

Her tart bluntness is still intact, Egan thought wryly.

And now that he'd been singled out, he noticed that they too were surprised to see him.

Really? Do I look that different?

He knew the answer to that.

It was inevitable that muscle and flesh would soften and sag after twenty-two years of gravitational pull, abetted by too much fine dining, heavy drinking, and summer fun in the Hamptons. With each passing year, the tiny lines etched around his eyes, nose, and mouth had deepened with the seismic events that shook, rattled, and rolled through his life.

When he'd had the money, personal trainers and hairstylists helped greatly to stave off life's cruel vagaries. As his funds dwindled, Egan had convinced himself that jogging and push-ups would fight off the pounds just as quickly. But all it took was one clumsily administered at-home dye job to accept the silver creeping through his hair.

Glancing at Warner, he thought: At least I still *have* hair.

And now it was time for him to turn on the charm, to impress all these movers and shakers; these pillars of the Ashbury Academy community.

Including two of Audrey's dearest friends.

Had they read his book? And if so, had they been flattered or appalled at his depictions of them?

Hard to tell. Now that the shock of seeing Egan again had worn off, their benign smiles were back in place.

Time to find out. "It's a pleasure to be back at Ashbury Academy. It holds a special place in my life, having been the inspiration for my debut novel."

Whereas the men murmured their approval, Egan noticed Tallulah and Bliss exchange grimaces.

Ah, heck, he thought, they hate their characters.

He forced himself to keep his voice on an even keel: "Today was my first day back as an educator, and I'm already impressed with the skills and determination of my students."

"In fact, Seamus, your daughter, Fawn, is in Egan's seventh-period Shakespeare Comparative Literature class," Lavinia pointed out.

Seamus leaned over Miranda to scrutinize Egan.

Egan groaned inwardly.

The blond fembot is this guy's kid? Great. Just…great.

Egan hadn't had time to look over the class rosters let alone memorize his students' names. Hell, he'd barely had time to review the lesson plans.

Despite this, he forced himself to grin. "Ah, yes! She is quite the charmer, that one."

He panicked for a quick moment over the thought that Seamus might ask him to elaborate.

Lavinia saved him by adding, "And Daniel, Charly is also in that class—"

"Charly is your daughter?" Egan cut in excitedly. "She certainly knows her Shakespeare! She made quite an insightful comparison with one of my favorite Edith Wharton novels, *House of Mirth.* I was very impressed."

"Yes, Charly is a great kid. She never ceases to amaze me too." Daniel smiled appreciatively, adding, "I won't play favorites, but I feel blessed."

Perhaps blessed enough to donate generously for the Comp Lit chair?

I'll be seeing him in the last open house, Egan remembered. Before this meeting breaks up, I'll ask him if he has time to go out for a drink sometime soon and discuss it.

"WE ALSO HAVE A VERY SPECIAL GUEST WITH US TODAY," LAVINIA POINTED out. "Miranda D'Arcy is Ashbury Academy's new college admissions consultant. Besides being one of the most sought-after professionals in her field, Miranda has been retained by our school to assess each student's admissions criteria and guide them to the university that's best suited to their unique talents and interests."

"Based on that criteria, my kid may end up in my basement for the rest of my life," Warner muttered.

Jess Smallwood shrugged in solidarity.

No argument there, Miranda thought.

Instead, she said, "Don't sell him short! I know I won't. I'm proud to say my track record for getting my clients' children in at least one of their top five schools rivals that of AA's." Miranda smiled winningly. "My goal here is to beat both records with this graduating class."

Warner nodded grudgingly. "I would imagine the easy cases take care of themselves. Does that give you more time to work on those who are harder to place?"

"Each student, no matter their GPA, receives equal attention. Obviously, the seniors are my initial priority. I'll be scheduling a session with each of them to discuss their admission goals, and to assess their grades, standardized test scores, and extracurriculars before they tackle the applications under my watchful eye." Miranda sighed. "We have over a hundred seniors, so I have my work cut out for me. I've already started scheduling meetings with the more—for lack of a better term, *ambitious* students and their parents—"

"I'll be blunt," Jess interjected. "Can you work a miracle for a lazy student?" From the anxious look on his face, she knew he was only half-joking.

"For those students who have been sitting on the fence for some reason or another—I call them late bloomers—I will be meeting with their parents first. For their children, I may suggest a more aggressive plan of attack."

Jess nodded vigorously.

"You called yourself a 'consultant,'" Seamus pointed out. "Does that mean you're not part of the administration?"

"Very perceptive of you, Mr. McCoppin," Miranda replied crisply. "I accepted the position as a consultancy because my practice includes private clients as well. Most of them have two, sometimes even more children. I've placed their eldest in their dream schools. They want assurance that I'll do the same for their siblings."

"In other words, you're filling in your schedule with our kids," Seamus argued.

"Hardly," she countered. "My retainer agreement with AA puts me here on campus every hour the school is in session, and it calls for me to be available by appointment after school hours as well. In other words, I'm at your beck and call." When she leaned forward, it had the desired effect: his eyes went to her cleavage.

He nodded grudgingly.

At least that shut him up, she thought.

"Any other questions?" Lavinia asked.

"Do you walk on water too?" Jess joked.

The others chuckled.

"Since we'll only have a half hour to enjoy our catered dinner before the parent-teacher open house, I'd like to call for adjournment."

"I second the motion," Darius declared.

The others quickly exclaimed, "Aye!"

As Miranda rose from her seat, Jess waved her down. "Do you have a minute to chat?"

Ca-CHING!

EGAN TURNED TO SHAKE DANIEL'S HAND. "IT WAS A PLEASURE MEETING YOU."

Daniel smiled. "Likewise."

"And I meant what I said about Charly. She's a gem."

"I appreciate your saying that."

"Daniel, listen, if you can take the time some night, perhaps we can meet for a drink soon. Lavinia views my return as a viable fundraising opportunity. I want to do everything I can to help her make that happen, and I'm sure you do too. Since you have a far better lay of the land, maybe you can suggest a couple of likely candidates."

"Sure, anything I can do to help." Daniel looked at his watch. "We get done tonight at, what, nine? Nine-fifteen?"

"Yeah, about that," Egan replied. "And since Charly's in my seventh-period class, you're in my last open house. We can walk over to Magnolia Brewing Company afterward, if you'd like."

"Works for me. My wife and I are in separate cars, so I won't be holding her up if she needs to get home to help our youngest with his homework."

Before Egan could say any more, Lavinia tapped him on the shoulder. She was holding a covered plate. "I didn't want to interrupt you, Egan dear, but you'll barely have time to make it to your classroom for your first open house." She handed him the plate. "Take this with you, so that you have a little sustenance between meet-and-greets."

Reluctantly, he got up. After nodding goodbye to them, he headed for the door.

Maybe it was for the best. Egan noticed that Tallulah and Bliss were heading his way. He wasn't ready to answer their questions about his fall from grace. Or about his book, for that matter.

The last thing he wanted was their pity.

He'd much prefer information on Audrey.

Not that he could ever ask for it.

CHAPTER 9

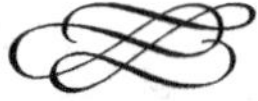

*C*ross-town traffic was so bad that Audrey made AA's first period parent-teacher meet-and-greet with only ten minutes to spare.

As promised, Daniel had waited for her at the classroom's door. His kiss was quick, but as always, passionate.

When he pulled away, Audrey sighed. His lips always had that effect on her.

She murmured, "So, how was the board meeting?"

She hoped she'd kept the anxiety out of her voice even as she wondered: *Did Lavinia seem ill?*

She was afraid that if it were apparent to Daniel, the others would have noticed too.

"It was interesting and uneventful," Daniel replied. "You'll be happy to hear that the Tallulah-and-Bliss tag team made quite an impression."

"Thank goodness!" Audrey pretended she meant that about her friends, but in truth, she was relieved that he hadn't started out by mentioning Lavinia. Had Daniel noted anything unusual about her, it would have been the first thing he'd have mentioned.

Daniel grimaced. "By that, I gather you expected a death match between Seamus and Tallulah."

Audrey sighed. "It may not have happened today, but I know them well enough to say it's inevitable."

"I wouldn't take that bet," Daniel conceded. "The one time Tallulah showed her claws, Seamus bristled like a porcupine."

"Well, you know what they say about pricks," she muttered.

Daniel laughed. "What a naughty remark, Ms. Thorpe! In most schools, it would merit a trip to the principal's office."

269

"Thankfully, corporal punishment has never been acceptable at AA." She wiggled her brows. "However, I'm sure all kinds of dirty deeds have played out in the many nooks and crannies of this old building."

"If you're offering a tour, I'll happily take you up on it—"

Daniel's quip was interrupted by the chime of the school's clock tower, announcing that the first open house would commence in five minutes.

"Ah well, I guess that little excursion will just have to wait." Audrey pretended to pout. "This year, Charly and Chuck only have two classes together. As in the past, we'll have to split up for the others." She handed Daniel a notecard. "Charly's classes are on this card. You were very kind to take on the board, so I figure you deserve to hear glowing reviews all night long as opposed to the winces and sighs that come with examples of Chuck as class clown."

"That's very generous of you." Daniel rolled his eyes. "Still, maybe it's best that I take Chuck's schedule. You know, in for a dime, in for a dollar. And besides, if anyone is going to scare the kid straight, I think it's going to be me. You've got too much of a soft spot for him."

"Now you're beginning to sound like Charly," Audrey huffed.

"Sorry, but it's true, whether you want to acknowledge it or not," Daniel countered. "Letting him slide isn't doing him any favors, Aud."

She plucked Charly's schedule out of his hand and replaced it with Chuck's. "Okay, then, by all means, run roughshod over him."

"Not to worry. I won't let you down."

"You never do." This time, Audrey initiated the kiss.

When they came up for air, she added, "The twins share this first class: Trigonometry. A guy named Ike Melton teaches it. He's been on the staff a couple of years, but our two scholars haven't had him before. I hear he's a real taskmaster and a hard grader." She frowned. "Chuck can do the assignments, but that doesn't mean he will. You'll have your work cut out for you."

Daniel shrugged. "Duly noted."

"We'll join up at the last class of the day, Comp Lit. Wait outside if you get there first. I'll do the same."

Daniel nodded. "Speaking of which, you'll be happy to hear I already received a compliment about one of our children. From the Comp Lit teacher."

"Really?" Hope rose in Audrey's heart. "About Chuck?"

"Guess again."

"Ah! So Charly's already made an impression on her new teacher! What did the woman say, exactly?"

Before Daniel could answer, the warning chime sounded. He nodded toward the class. Ike Melton was closing the door.

Instead of answering her, Daniel ushered Audrey inside.

She'd meet the twins' instructor soon enough, she reasoned. Even one accolade about her daughter would make up for all the winces that would greet her when she introduced herself as Chuck's mother.

———

If Cornell hadn't been scolding Audrey about Chuck, Audrey would have been on time to the twins' seventh-period class. "It doesn't take much to memorize the Periodic Table," he pointed out to her. "By Chemistry II, he should know it!"

"If he doesn't, why do you keep passing him?" Audrey asked, defensively.

"Trust me, if he weren't so charming, I wouldn't."

At least Cornell is honest, Audrey thought.

She ran up the stairs to Comp Lit. Reaching the door, she had a déjà vu moment. It awed her that, even with all of AA's renovation and additions, twenty years hence the course was still being taught in the same classroom.

As they'd agreed, Daniel had waited for Audrey outside the door. They had a second for a peck but then Daniel's phone rang.

He stared at the Caller ID. "It's our Kyoto office. I should take it. Go on in. Save me a seat."

Audrey nodded and hurried through the door.

———

The teacher, a man, was writing something on the white board. Embarrassed at her tardiness, Audrey scurried toward the only two adjacent empty seats: in the back of the row closest to the window.

At this point, the teacher made some joke about wishing Lavinia had let the teachers set up full bars in their classrooms. "It might help us be candid with each other—you'd be more forthcoming about what I've gotten myself into, and I'd be honest about what they've really been up to." He paused. "As if you'd really want to hear that, right?"

The parents laughed heartily.

He's got a nice voice…

Hmmm, sounds familiar…

Just as she'd reached the empty seat, she realized where she knew it:

Egan…

She whipped around:

Yes, there he was.

Audrey felt faint. As the blood rushed to her head, her pounding heart drowned out all sound. She forced herself to sit down very slowly.

Get ahold of yourself! Breathe!

BREATHE.

Even as her heartbeat steadied, emotions surged through her:

Excitement. Rage. Shame—

Sadness.

OPEN YOUR EYES.

She forced herself to look at Egan; to see that he was real.

Physically, age had blunted the sharpness of his features. The angle of his jaw was somehow softer. His shoulders were rounder. His once slim girth was now fuller, just as his hair was graying.

But his wit was still as crisp and dry as ever. His audience drank him in like an Oakville sauvignon blanc, savoring each tart aside, every nuanced rejoinder.

He lets them in on the joke, she thought. *It's what makes him so desirable.*

But not to me.

Not anymore.

Not after that afternoon.

As her heart stilled, Egan's voice seemed to grow louder: "...and the joy of having your children in my class—"

The children...

Our children.

Oh my God...Chuck and Charly...

It dawned on Audrey that Egan was now glancing around the room. She would have ducked, but he'd have seen her anyway. The seat in front of her was empty.

It was the one she was holding for Daniel.

Oh my God—Daniel!

At that moment, Egan's eyes met hers.

Jesus...

She's here.

Egan had been scanning the room, doing a headcount, trying to figure out if his chatter was getting enough laughs; hoping that it seemed meaningful to the parents, perhaps inspirational, maybe even life-changing for their children.

Otherwise, for what AA charged as its annual tuition, why not buy a Tesla instead?

Granted, it would be the cheapest one in the showroom—the mid- five-figures Model 3—but a Tesla nonetheless.

Then again, considering the average household income of the AA families paying full-freight, odds were that most of them already had a garage filled with Teslas—

And that's when his eyes lit upon Audrey.

The desire to linger on her face was a visceral one: it was pretty and therefore pleasing. But what caused him to want to scrutinize it further was that it seemed familiar as well.

When recognition finally snapped into place, his eyes widened and his voice faded away.

Audrey.

She's here.

She came.

For me.

Egan forced himself to say something, anything; to remember the patter he'd come up with; the jokes that seemed to be working.

He was just about to go back into his rift when, behind him, the door opened.

Annoyed, he turned to berate the intruder.

It was Daniel.

Having caught Egan's eye, he apologized with a contrite nod.

By rote, Egan waved him in and waited politely for him to take a seat.

Daniel strolled to the aisle where Audrey was seated. But before taking the seat in front of her, he bent down to kiss her.

In that quick, sweet second their lips met, Egan felt himself deflate as if she'd punctured something deep within him:

His purpose for being.

Wrap it up — now.

"Any questions, folks?"

A couple of hands went up.

Including Daniel's.

Fuck you. How dare you!

Egan pointed to a woman sitting front row center. She was too tanned, with skin that was tight and brittle like wrapping paper. He forced himself to tune her in: to hear her blather some nonsense about *Titus Andronicus*: "...perhaps encouraging the students to compare such a timeless play to some of the Serbian and Bosnian authors who have emerged after their civil unrest in the 1990s?"

Really, lady? THIS is what you want to ask?

Egan hated show-offs. Still, he forced himself to smile. "Interesting analogy...and quite sound! I'll take it under advisement, for sure. But if anyone whines, 'That was *soooo* last century,' I'm sending them your way." He shot her with his index finger as if to say, *Right back atcha!*

Everyone chuckled.

"Anyone else?"

A guy in the third row on the left, shouted out: "Do you grade on a curve?"

Another joker, like that Chuck kid.

Egan took a closer look to see if there was a resemblance. Nah. The dude looked like an overripe toad. Chuck's father was probably some high-testosterone braggart already on his third wife, who indulged his son because the kid was a chip off the old block.

He chuckled, as if in on Toad's joke. "Yeah...right. Quick answer: *NO.* This is an AP course. And before anyone asks, I don't grade in iambic pentameter either."

Again, a spate of laughter.

"Any other questions?" Egan gazed down at his watch in the hope that they'd all take the hint: *It's time to wrap things up.*

He waited a beat—just long enough to ignore any hands that may have been raised. Then, clapping, he exclaimed loudly, "Wow, folks, congratulations on making it through seven open houses—without a *single cocktail!*"

They fell for it. Applauding his cleverness, they rose en masse.

Acquaintances hugged farewell. Others made their way to the front to shake Egan's hand, hoping to make some impression, perhaps because they knew their children weren't going to leave much of one, or worse yet, the wrong one.

That is, everyone except Daniel and Audrey, their heads together deep in discussion.

About what? Me?

Is she telling him—

NOW?

At that moment, Daniel caught his eye and waved at him.

Then Egan remembered why: Oh, hell—I invited the asshole out for a drink!

Shit—is Audrey joining us?

He could see it now. Audrey would hate every minute of their little gathering. Every glance in his direction would sting like a pinprick. He'd be smarting from hurt and jealousy, whereas she'd be reliving the shame of trusting him to be her first lover.

If only she'd told me that was the case. Things might have been different...

I'd be him—Daniel.

If she came along, there would be deadly silences between small talk that hit every topic except the ones that mattered most:

How they felt about that fateful night.

How they feel about each other now.

Instead, they'd pretend that nothing happened.

But something did happen. It was the end of the beginning.

I wanted to spend the rest of my life with you.

Instead, you're spending your life with him.

It angered him that she never gave him the chance to tell his side of the story, let alone apologize for…

It.

Okay, yeah, I broke your cherry. But to be fair, you broke my heart…

So, can we call it even?

He guessed the answer to that was *NO*.

Oh, shit, Daniel's an attorney. Can he sue me for that?

…No. I'm being…ridiculous…

Right?

He suddenly realized they were making their way toward him. Trying not to panic, he swiveled to make eye contact with one of the few parents still lingering in the classroom—

Too late. Daniel tapped his shoulder. "Egan, sorry I interrupted that great song and dance." His apology came with a shake of his head.

"No problem. It was bound to happen. Seven times up to bat. Got to hit a foul every now and then." Egan shrugged. He forced himself to keep his eyes solely on Daniel. If he dared to glance at Audrey, he didn't know what he might do.

Kiss her?

Curse her out?

Slug Daniel?

Cry?

Maybe.

"Understandable response—especially on an empty stomach." Daniel nodded toward the dish Lavinia had made Egan. It was still covered and obviously untouched. "You've got to be starving by now. Listen, are you still up for that drink and maybe a burger? I don't think Audrey would mind. Would you, hon?" Daniel's hand went to the small of Audrey's back as if propelling her forward.

"Audrey…" Her name tumbled out of Egan's mouth as if finally freed from the prison of his shameful memory.

To his own ears, it sounded like a choking cat that had fallen down a well.

Instinctively, Audrey looked at him, her eyes opened wide in panic. What Egan saw in them made him sad:

Fear.

Pleading.

"Audrey…Thorpe?…as in my former student?" Egan smiled blandly. "What a pleasure to see you again."

"Thank you," she murmured. "It's good to see you too, Egan. Congratulations on all your success."

Our success.

I couldn't have done it without you. You know that.

You hate that.

You hate me.

He knew they expected a response. But none of what he was thinking was appropriate. Finally, he answered, "So, you're Charly's mother."

As if shocked, she bolted upright. Finally, warily, she replied simply, "Yes."

"And we're Chuck's parents, too," Daniel added with a grin. "But don't hold that against us."

"Chuck...is *your* son?" Egan's eyes roamed from Audrey to Daniel and then back to her.

She nodded defiantly. "They're twins. You didn't notice the resemblance?" Her tone was as cold as ice.

Egan laughed weakly. "Now that you mention it."

She mesmerized him with her stare. "Daniel just told me you've joined the trustee board as the new academic liaison." Audrey's voice took a softer tone. "I'm sure Lavinia appreciates your support."

"Thank you. I think so." Egan was relieved they'd shifted to a safer topic. "She's been a lifeline to me...now, and...then."

When we fell in love.

But now you love him.

He couldn't just stand there, staring at her like a love-starved puppy. He blurted out: "Will you be joining us?"

Audrey stiffened, then shook her head. "Our youngest, Noah, is waiting up for me. He likes it when I check his homework."

"How old is he?"

Audrey shifted her gaze to Daniel, but her attempt at a smile died before it reached the corners of her mouth. "Thirteen. He'll be here at AA next year."

"I look forward to teaching him someday." Egan was lying. He'd be long gone.

If he could, he'd resign now, this very second.

I can't keep letting you break my heart, Audrey Thorpe.

"Enjoy your chat, gentlemen." She held out her hand to Egan. "I'm sure I'll be seeing you around school."

He took her hand and pressed it firmly, taking in its warmth and softness a tick too long as if daring her to break away first.

Egan was disappointed when she lived up to his prediction and pulled away.

He felt bereft.

Angry.

Daniel nodded toward the door. "Let's go. I'm buying."

You're living the life I wanted. Hell yeah, you'll pay, you son of a bitch.

CHAPTER 10

*A*udrey staved off her panic attack until she got into her car. Once she was in the driver's seat, she allowed herself to gasp. But soon her gasps turned into sobs, which became wails, which morphed into screams accompanied by her fists pounding on the steering wheel.

It was inevitable that she'd accidentally hit the horn.

Those parents still in the parking lot jumped nervously, craning their heads to see if a car was barreling in their direction.

One woman was close enough to make out Audrey's face: Nira Patel, whose daughter, Manya, was one of Charley's closest friends. She had also been in Egan's last open house. She waved. Concern etched her brow.

Audrey waved back, and quickly started her car's engine. It was the best way to keep Nira at bay; to send the universally understood non-verbal message, *there's nothing to worry about. Everything is fine and dandy.*

Nothing could be further from the truth.

Slowly, she inched her way out of the lot and onto the street.

He will soon know, she told herself. My God, how could he not?

Even a mere hour a day, five days a week, would be enough time to recognize his scratchy chuckle in the twins' laughter. To catch himself in their profiles and notice the similarities to his own: their height; their wide-set eyes the shade of seafoam.

She'd rue the day he'd make a panicked call begging her to meet him so that she could look him in the eye and tell him to his face:

Yes, they are yours.

And, no, I'm not sorry.

Not for keeping them from you.

Not for marrying Daniel.

Not for the one time we spent in the frenzied rapture that created those two precious beings.

Then she remembered all the things Egan had gotten wrong about their relationship—heck, about himself!—and her fear subsided.

I guess that's one good thing about being a self-centered son of a bitch. You don't see beyond the nearest mirror.

IT WAS LATE ENOUGH THAT DANIEL AND EGAN COULD GRAB ONE OF THE PUB'S tall-back booths.

Until and after the waiter took their orders for beers and burgers, they made small talk: the Giants' chance at another pennant, if the Warriors could bring home another NBA title, the cost of living in San Francisco—safe topics for two men who should be getting to know each other and were supposed to be allies for the same cause.

Egan ached with hate.

Eventually, he mentioned that he commuted from Marin County.

Daniel perked up at that. "We live on this side of the bridge, but I love Marin for the trails. The kids and I bike to Mount Tam on most weekends."

"Audrey doesn't go too?" Egan asked.

Daniel shook his head. "She's always been welcomed. And she's certainly fit enough. She won't say it, but I think she really wanted it to be 'our thing'—you know, just mine and the kids'."

"That sounds like Audrey," Egan muttered.

"Yeah, she's always thinking of others," Daniel acknowledged. "I'll bet she was like that even when she was the twins' age."

"She was…" *…perfect.* Egan gulped his beer. "How did you two meet?"

"At Berkeley. We met in the law library. She was working there in her junior year. I was already a lawyer, but I was looking for a particular case law book. She helped me find it." He paused as if transported back to there and then. "It was love at first sight." He munched a fry. "Before then I'd never believed such a thing was possible."

Egan shrugged. "I know what you mean."

"Hey, believe it or not, you and I almost met a few years back," Daniel exclaimed.

Warily, Egan looked up. "How?"

"You did a reading at Berkeley when your book came out, right?"

As Daniel motioned the bartender for their tab, Egan nodded cautiously.

"Audrey went to it. You signed a couple of books for her. Remember? I was supposed to be her date, but I got held up at work." Daniel drained the last sip from his glass.

"Yeah, I do remember that." *As if I'd ever forget that day.*

Egan gulped his Pilsner for the courage to ask, "Did you get a chance to read it?"

Daniel shook his head. "Sorry, no. But now that I know you, I'll make it a point to do so." He thought for a moment. "I'm sure we still have it...."

Egan frowned. "You don't sound too certain."

Daniel laughed. "Only because it could be anywhere. Our house is filled with books. Like Audrey, the kids are avid readers." He shrugged. "Well, two of them anyway. We're still working on Chuck." He smiled. "Speaking of scholastic miracles, consider your chair underwritten."

Egan choked on his beer. "I...I appreciate that. But ...shouldn't you talk it over with Audrey first?"

"Not necessary. If you've got Lavinia and Audrey's *Good Housekeeping* seal of approval, you've got mine too." Daniel clinked his mug against Egan's. "The prodigal son is always welcomed home."

Egan sat there, stunned.

If only you knew.

BY THE TIME AUDREY GOT TO THE HOUSE, THE KIDS HAD COMPLETED THEIR homework assignments and were huddled together on the couch, watching *Stranger Things.*

The boys, caught up in the show's bump-in-the-night suspense, barely mumbled their hellos.

Charly waved at her mom, albeit distractedly. "So that Noah could watch with us, we triple-checked his homework. Not to worry. He aced it." Lovingly, she tousled her little brother's hair.

"Thank you," Audrey kissed her forehead and then did the same for each of her sons.

Chuck smiled, but teasingly brushed away the dampness with an "Ew, yuck!"

Anxiety had parched Audrey's lips. What he'd felt were her tears.

LIKE THE CHILDREN, AUDREY WAS ALREADY IN BED WHEN DANIEL ARRIVED home.

She pretended to be asleep, rolling over on her side, away from his part of the bed. Better that he not read the anxiety in her face.

If Audrey had asked, she knew he would have relayed his conversation with Egan. But asking would make her seem concerned, which was the last thing she'd want him to think about her.

Besides, if Egan were to say something stupid (in the back of her mind, she imagined him boasting, "I had her first, you know...") Daniel would flip on the light and awaken her so that they could discuss it.

Instead, she breathed a sigh of relief as he washed up and changed before coming to bed.

Audrey felt his body curl around hers. An arm folded snugly around her waist.

Feeling his warmth, she scooted back against him. This is what she lived for: those pitch dark hours when they held each other, seemingly far away from the rest of the world. She couldn't see him, but the touch of his skin never failed to make her tingle.

And it never failed to have an arousing effect on Daniel.

Behind her, Daniel's cock hardened. Instinctively, his hand curled around her breast. His index finger barely touched her nipple, but it stiffened nonetheless.

Audrey turned her head, her lips hungry for his. He was just as voracious for her. While his kisses wandered down her neck and over her breasts, his thumb and finger strummed her: gently then deeply, stirring an insatiable desire to feel him inside of her.

She stroked his cock with her fingers before her hand tightened around it. When she released him, they were both ready.

He plunged so deeply within her that she gasped.

Ecstatic with desire, she tightened around him. His moans set the tone of their rhythm: steady and slow at first. But then an urgency took hold, elevating their mutual pleasure to a fevered pitch.

When he burst within her, she had to clench her lips to keep from screaming out.

No one can take this away from us.

AFTERWARD, HE STROKED HER CHEEK AS THEY LAY IN EACH OTHER'S ARMS.

"Hey, um, this isn't exactly pillow talk, but because I have to be at the office at five this morning for a confab with our European offices, I do have to mention something before we both drift off to sleep."

"I'm all ears," Audrey purred.

He chuckled appreciatively. "Oh no, you're much more than that. Having just taken a complete inventory, I can vouch for the fact that you have other body parts just as delectable."

"Thank you, kind sir. Now, what's so important that you've stopped mid-snuggle?"

Daniel rested his head on his elbow so that he could gaze into her face. "If you remember, right before my mother passed, she told me she wanted me to use a portion of her estate for our children's education. I know she felt guilty that I had to do all kinds of jobs while getting my undergrad.

The partial scholarships helped, of course. Still, Mom was so concerned about my student debt that she did her best to talk me out of law school. She suggested that I teach instead." He winced. "She was so proud that I got a job offer from a prestigious law firm. But she knew that an associate's salary wasn't going to make much of a dent in my debt—not with the twins still in diapers and all."

"I wish she were here to see you—and them—today." Audrey wiped away a tear. She'd loved Ruth and appreciated all the traits Daniel shared with her: patience, kindness, and a wonderful sense of humor.

Soon, Lavinia will be gone too, Audrey realized.

How she longed to tell Daniel of Lavinia's plight.

"Since the kids' college fees are now funded, I've been trying to come up with the perfect use for Mom's legacy," Daniel continued. "Lavinia provided it at the trustee meeting. She's looking for benefactors to underwrite specific academic chairs. The first one starts this year."

"Sound interesting What does it entail?"

"The sum goes toward covering the salary of the prestigious recipient —an instructor of some renown—who will serve as an inspirational role model. It also allows for a very generous stipend toward their living expenses."

"How generous?"

"A quarter of a million."

Audrey whistled. "Well, that should attract some great press, and yet one more reason for parents to fight for their children's acceptance to AA. Not to mention a few qualified applicants!"

"This year's chair is already filled."

Audrey stared blankly at Daniel. "Really? Who?"

"Egan, of course." Daniel chuckled as he kissed her nose.

Had he not then snuggled back around her, she would have leaped out of bed to—

To do what, pace the floor while she cursed Egan for coming back into her life?

Or, perhaps explain to Daniel that his mother's life savings shouldn't go to the man who was the twins' real father?

It would kill Daniel if he ever found out. But I have to say something—

"I can't wait to tell Lavinia tomorrow," he whispered.

A moment later, he was snoring softly.

I can't do this to him.

Or to Lavinia.

Everything would be perfect if it weren't for Egan.

CHAPTER 11

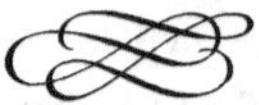

$\mathcal{A}$t five-thirty the next morning, SallyAnne and Lionel were parked across the street from Tanner Simpson's sprawling Spanish hacienda overlooking Benedict Canyon.

Within fifteen minutes, a black luxury sedan had pulled in front of the movie director's long, gated driveway. Five minutes later, the gates opened, and the director—dressed in his signature attire, a black tee shirt and jeans—stepped out of his house.

The driver got out of the car to open the back door. Lionel and Sally-Anne also jumped out of their vehicle. By the time Tanner reached his driver, they too were standing beside the town car.

Tanner looked over at his driver. The man's crestfallen face reflected his shock.

Lionel and SallyAnne pulled out their badges. "Mr. Tanner, we're with the Federal Bureau of Investigation," Lionel announced. "We'd like a moment to discuss your knowledge of a possible act of fraud."

Tanner grimaced. "I'm on my way to my movie set at Paramount Studios."

"We can talk out here, or inside the house, if you prefer," SallyAnne suggested.

Instinctively, Tanner looked up toward his home. "No! My daughter is there..."

"We can ride along with you," SallyAnne offered. "Fair warning though: this regards a confidential matter." She'd already glanced into the town car and noted it had no privacy screen between the front and back seats.

"Or you can go along with us," Lionel suggested. "Your driver is welcome to follow behind."

"Yeah…okay." Tanner nodded to the driver.

SallyAnne let Tanner and Lionel walk ahead of her. Tanner's gait—slow and hesitant—was that of a guilty man. When he got to the agents' car, SallyAnne was surprised when he opened the back door for himself: another telltale sign of guilt.

She startled Tanner by sliding in beside him. It was the best way she'd be able to assess his answers while Lionel drove.

Their opening remarks were almost identical to what they'd said to Rob Edelson: that they were investigating Miranda D'Arcy for the fraud she'd committed in her capacity as a college admissions counselor.

Tanner leaned against the backseat's headrest. "What did she do?"

"So, you know her?" Lionel asked.

Tanner thought a long moment, then sighed. "I guess you already know I do, or you wouldn't be here."

"Then the question is, Mr. Simpson, exactly what services did she provide for you?" SallyAnne asked.

"Um… Well, she was my daughter's college admissions counselor."

"I'll be audio recording this conversation, Mr. Simpson." SallyAnne pulled out her phone, clicked onto her audio app, and placed it between them.

Tanner inched away from it. "I have nothing to say except that I want to call my lawyers."

"Sure, feel free," Lionel replied casually.

Tanner treated that as a dare, jabbing his index finger on a saved number in his frequent contacts. "Artie… Yeah, sorry for the early hour. Listen, I'm sitting with a couple of FBI agents…. No, not for a picture, nothing like that. I'm—I'm being questioned about my, er, involvement with someone they're investigating… regarding Lacey's college application…." Tanner glanced furtively at SallyAnne. "Um…. yeaaahhhh." He frowned. "Yes."

There it is, SallyAnne thought. His admission of guilt.

The muttering on the other end of the line stopped. When it started again, Tanner's eyes got glassy. Turning to SallyAnne, he muttered, "He asked that I put the call on speaker."

She nodded.

Artie Abrams barked out an introduction. SallyAnne responded with her name, and Lionel did the same.

Then in the expected tone—that is to say, brusquely—Artie Abrams launched into the anticipated questions:

Was his client under investigation?

"Currently, he's a Person of Interest," Lionel answered.

Did they have any evidence against him?

"I'm sure a search warrant, which we'll have in hand within twenty-four hours, will bear more light," SallyAnne replied. "We'll also be searching the electronic devices belonging to Mr. Simpson's daughter, Lacey, as well as those of his ex-wife, Cassandra."

Tanner's eyes went wild. "My ex? Why her? She didn't know about Miranda's..." His mouth snapped shut.

"Miranda's illicit activities on Lacey's behalf, that were sanctioned by you?" SallyAnne prodded.

Artie barked, "Don't say another word, Tanner!"

All the color left Tanner's face.

"Listen, Tanner. It's gentlemanly of you to admit that your ex-wife knew nothing of your activities. I'm sure she'd greatly appreciate it if we got that on the record," Lionel suggested gently. "Lacey would too, for that matter. Having only one parent arrested for fraud is better than two."

"The DOJ will ask for leniency from the court for parents who have hired Miranda and are willing to cooperate quickly and fully," SallyAnne added. "It's already happening. No one wants to be out on that limb when Miranda is sawing it off."

"What do you mean by that?" Tanner stammered.

"Ask Mr. Abrams. He'll be the first to tell you that the moment we arrest Miranda, she'll be looking for ways to get the judge to reduce her sentence," Lionel replied. "She'll surely turn on those parents who haven't already decided to give evidence against her. How ironic it would be for her to turn on you when you've been protecting her."

Tanner barked, "Artie, is that true?"

Artie's silence went on a beat too long. "It's certainly a consideration, yes. But if you were to plead 'not guilty,' a jury might be more receptive to your position than a judge."

Tanner's celebrated dimpled chin jutted out. "I'll take my chances that a jury will find me not guilty."

"Seriously? Do you want to take the chance you'll walk, just because you've got something the jurors don't—money and celebrity status?" Lionel asked. "Don't you think they'll resent that you did something they couldn't: buy your daughter's way into a great school by cheating and lying?"

"Worse yet, what if they hated your last movie?" SallyAnne muttered.

She knew she hit a nerve when Tanner winced. His last film was eviscerated by movie critics.

SallyAnne's jibe crumbled Tanner's stony gaze. Broken, he stared down at his hands. "If I go to jail, it'll ruin me! I'll never be able to work in the industry again!"

"We're truly sorry about that." Lionel's sincerity was real. "But Tanner, fraud is a serious crime. If you have any realistic hope of a lighter sentence, help us put Ms. D'Arcy behind bars."

"Okay—*Okay!*" Tanner croaked. "What do you want to know?"

SallyAnne's eyes caught Lionel's slim grin in the rearview mirror. Like her, he was ecstatic. They were now two for two.

"So, my daughter's math scores were sub-par," Tanner explained. "Miranda had a separate program for her private students. She called it 'concierge college admissions counseling.'"

"How much did you pay her, and how?" Lionel asked.

"Half a mil. I have the dough, so I thought, sure, why not?" Tanner shrugged. "Miranda asked that it be paid directly to her non-profit—the Best Face Forward Club."

SallyAnne frowned. "So that you could take the fee as a tax deduction?"

Tanner hesitated, but finally, he nodded.

"What did she do for her fee?" SallyAnne asked.

"Well, the very first thing was to connect Lacey with a tutor. The guy also ran some sort of testing center."

"University Prep & Test," Lionel replied.

"Yeah, that's the one," Tanner acknowledged. "And, as Miranda promised, Lacey's SAT Math score was significantly higher than when she took the test at her school."

"By how much?" SallyAnne asked.

"Enough to earn a score of 1440 overall." Tanner shrugged. "Lacey isn't much of an athlete, so Miranda suggested she play a game or two of volleyball—you know, at the beach. Her mom took the Malibu house, so she could easily catch a game there. Miranda took a few photos, and it went in with the application." He rolled his eyes. "Miraculously, Lacey ended up on the team—for all of five minutes. She was sort of disappointed when the coach told her she wasn't up to the team's standards. But hey, it got her on campus..." His voice drifted off.

SallyAnne could guess what he was thinking: *until now.*

"I paid for the testing center separately."

Just like Rob Edelson, SallyAnne thought.

When they reached the studio, Tanner stuck his head out the window. Recognizing him, Paramount's security guard motioned them through the gate.

Tanner directed Lionel through the lot's maze of narrow streets to the studio's warehouse-sized stage where he was shooting his latest production, *Beyond Heavenly.*

As Tanner opened the car door, Lionel reminded him, "We'll have a search warrant by the end of the day."

"Yeah, whatever. I'll call the housekeeper and tell her to expect someone." Tanner shrugged. "Hey, listen, seriously: at this stage of the game, do Lacey and Cassandra need to know about this crap?"

"Sorry, but yes—if you want them cleared as suspects," Lionel replied.

"Of course I do! I just don't want them to…you know, hate me!"

Lionel grimaced. Sally realized he didn't want to lie.

Of course, they would. Tanner's ex-wife would hate him for smearing the family's reputation. His daughter would be hurt that he didn't trust her to make it into such a great school on her own.

For some reason, SallyAnne felt compelled to say, "Your daughter may be upset at first, but in time, she'll forgive you."

Tanner looked up at her. Hope filled his eyes. "You really think so?"

She nodded. "Yes, because she'll realize you acted out of love."

He nodded and then shuffled off.

When SallyAnne got into the front passenger seat, she noticed that Lionel was smiling at her.

She blushed. "What is it?"

"I …I didn't know you had that in you."

SallyAnne cocked a brow. "Had what in me?"

"Such…kindness." He patted her hand.

His touch charged through her. She didn't pull away.

He didn't either. That is, not immediately.

By the time his hand went back to the wheel, she'd made up her mind. She didn't always have to be the hard-ass.

CHAPTER 12

"You'll never guess who we saw last night!" Tallulah's voice boomed through Audrey's car's speaker.

Oh, no, Audrey thought.

There is no way I'll allow the kids to hear this conversation.

"Can't talk now, Tallulah! We're driving to school!" So that Tallulah would take the hint, Audrey tooted the car horn, causing an elderly man strolling in the crosswalk with his teacup poodle to bolt upright. He grabbed the dog, wrapping the pooch in his arms protectively.

As the tiny poodle yelped hysterically, the man raised his hand in a one-finger salute.

The kids burst out laughing.

"Oh, my God! Is everyone okay there?" Tallulah asked.

"Ma just scared the bejeezus out of some poor old guy, is all," Chuck proclaimed. He tapped his mother on the shoulder. "Want to pull over so I can drive?"

Charly scoffed, "Like heck! I'm the safest driver in the family—"

"No way!" Noah piped up. "It's Dad by a long shot!"

"Tallulah, I'll call you back." The only thing good about the conversation was that it gave Audrey an excuse to hurry off the phone.

"Don't bother, love! Just meet Bliss and me for lunch—Rose's Cafe, one-ish! We've got to tell you how—"

Immediately, Audrey tapped her phone off the speaker.

"Mom...*MOM!* You're passing the carpool line!" Through the rearview mirror, Audrey saw her youngest son smack his head with the palm of his hand. She skidded to a halt.

The car immediately behind her honked its horn. She sped up again and swerved to the curb, just beyond the drop-off point. The carpool monitor gave her a scowl.

Audrey's mea culpa was a wave.

She caught her youngest son's eye in the rearview mirror. "You've made your point, sir. Now, give me a kiss before your walk of shame."

Noah's smack on the cheek was too quick for her to corral him for a kiss of her own.

Never mind, she thought. I've embarrassed him enough.

Anxious to find out what the twins thought of their seventh-period teacher, Audrey wracked her brain for some way to raise the subject. She need not have worried. Five minutes into the fifteen-minute ride from Noah's school to theirs, Charly paused the twins' usual verbal jousting to declare, "Hey, guess what, Mom? I'm going to try out for Debate Team. Our seventh-period teacher is the coach."

Chuck scowled. "And that's why I'm not."

Audrey gripped the steering wheel so hard that her knuckles turned white.

"The teacher? Who is it again?" To her own ears, Audrey's voice sounded like a squeak.

"His name is Egan. And he thinks he's hot shit," Chuck muttered.

"He's not the only one. Everyone thinks he's hot—*especially Fawn*," Charly taunted. "In fact, she's trying out for Debate Team too."

Chuck's jaw fell open. When he caught his mother's eye in the mirror, he shut it and shrugged. "Then, maybe I will too," he declared.

"Ha!" Charly crowed. "After how you sassed Egan on his very first day, what do you think your chances are of making it?"

"You got into an altercation with your teacher—*on his very first day of school?*" Audrey exclaimed.

This time, Chuck avoided the mirror and looked out his window instead. "I was asking Fawn something—"

"She squealed while Egan was making his point," Charly corrected him.

Chuck retorted, "Well, I proved to Mr. Big Shot Gable that you weren't the only one in the class who could quote Shakespeare, Little Miss Show-Off." To prove his point, Chuck nudged his mother. "You see, Mom? All those times you quoted the Bard to put me in my place finally paid off!"

This time, Audrey turned red. "Wow, I'm so proud," she murmured sarcastically.

Chuck nodded vigorously. "Yeah, well you would have been if you'd seen his face." Chuck slapped the back of Charly's head. "Don't worry, you'll be the teacher's pet in no time, just like you are in all your classes."

The blush that crawled up Charly's neck was not lost on Audrey. She felt as if the pit of her gut was on fire.

That's why Charly wants to try out for Debate Team — to impress Egan. History is repeating itself.

I can't let that happen.

Audrey glanced at Charly. "Honey, do you even have time for Debate Team? You have so many other extracurriculars! And almost all your courses this year are APs. Isn't it more important to focus on your grades?" She took a deep breath, then added: "In fact, why don't you drop Comp Lit and do something fun like… I don't know, Glee maybe?"

Charly looked at her as if she'd lost her mind. "*Glee?* Are you kidding me?"

"She's got a point there, Ma," Chuck exclaimed. "Haven't you heard her sing?"

Charly turned to pound Chuck's arm. He inched away just in time to avoid it.

"I will not be dropping out of the AP class I've waited two years to take," Charly growled. "And as far as Debate Team goes, I'm not trying out just because it'll quote-unquote look great on my college apps. I'm doing it because it'll be fun. So, if you want me to have more fun this year, mission accomplished."

Audrey's heart dropped into the pit of her stomach. Still, she nodded silently.

Don't push it. Don't make her suspect anything.

"And besides," Charly continued, "don't you want me to follow in your footsteps and lead the debate team to victory?"

"I?…Oh…well…" Audrey stammered. "How did you know about that?"

Charly rolled her eyes. "I saw the trophy in AA's display case. There was an *LA Times* article attached. It said, quote, Audrey Thorpe argued succinctly yet poignantly, leading her team to its next win, end-quote." Charly grinned. "Mom, I get it: you've set the bar pretty high. But I'm going to do my best to beat your record."

"To be frank, it was a team effort," Audrey insisted. "And it was a lot of hard work, believe me." *Yes, it was exhilarating — but for all the wrong reasons.*

"Mom, since you already know the ropes, you can help me make the team too," Chuck declared.

Audrey panicked. "But…Why would you even go out for it? Between basketball and baseball, don't you have enough on your plate?"

Charly snorted. "Because of Fawn. He's afraid he'll lose her to Egan. At least, that's how Fawn's playing it."

"She isn't 'playing' anything," Chuck shot back. He caught Audrey's eye in the mirror. "I need an academic extracurricular. Something like that will look great on my college apps. Isn't that what you keep telling me? So, you'll help me—right?"

Chuck's gaze said it all: *You love me. Of course, you will.*

How could she say no?

As far as Audrey was concerned, they couldn't reach Ashbury Academy's student drop-off queue soon enough. While their car idled in line, Charly's peck on the cheek goodbye came with a question: "Since you were on Debate Team, you had Egan too, right?"

"'Had'… him?" Audrey stammered.

Shit… SHIT.

"For Comp Lit. Isn't that why you're such a Shakespeare nerd?"

"Oh! Yes, of course! I mean, that one year Egan was here, I was in his class."

"Then you must have been excited when his novel came out. It's called *Extracurricular.*"

"Everyone was." Even to her own ears, Audrey sounded defensive. She turned her head to hide her frown.

"Do we have a copy in the house?"

"No…" Technically, she was right. Her copy was buried in the back of the closet of her old bedroom in Lavinia's house.

"Oh," Charly shrugged. "That's okay. Zina thinks her mom may have a copy because he taught her too. If not, I'm sure there's a copy in the school library."

"Why do you want it? So that you can impress Egan by giving it a glowing review in class?" Ignoring his sister's glare, Chuck grabbed his book bag. "Or do you just want to read the sex scenes?"

Charly's eyes went wide. Turning to her mother, she asked, "Are there sex scenes in *Extracurricular*?"

Audrey's answer was a flushed face.

Chuck hooted with laughter. "Wow, Mom! Really? His porn is that hot?"

"I wouldn't know," Audrey huffed. "Frankly, I never opened it."

I didn't have to. Egan read it to me—along with an auditorium filled with others just as moved by his erotic fantasy of…

Me.

"I'm sure they'll have a copy in the school library," Charly reasoned.

Oh my God—she's right!

Hearing the honks behind her, Audrey lurched the car forward before squealing to a halt in front of the school's entrance. "Out, kiddos. Make your mama proud today!"

The twins took the hint and scrambled out of the car.

After pulling away from the curb, Audrey took the first parking space she could find. She waited for AA's clock tower to chime the final bell announcing the start of the school day and then rushed through the campus to the library.

THE LIBRARY'S ORIGINAL BUILDING WAS STILL ITS ENTRANCE, BUT A NEW WING had expanded it considerably. There, the bookcases were tall enough that a rail holding a rolling ladder was needed to reach the highest shelves.

The students were in their first period classes, so the library was empty. Audrey waved at the librarian—Suri, a woman in her twenties, who was tattooed from her wrists all the way up to her shoulders. There were several earrings in the younger woman's nose and ears.

Suri smiled and waved back. "Great to see you, Audrey! Call me if you need anything." As the PTA chair, Audrey had helped raise tens of thousands of dollars for the books that now filled the newly renovated library.

Audrey nodded casually, then sat down in front of one of the online catalog monitors and put in the title she sought. Yes, a copy of *Extracurricular* was in the system, and it was currently on the shelf.

Audrey easily found it. She slipped it into her valise. But as she made her way toward the front door, she noticed the security arch.

I can't just walk out with this. And I certainly don't want to be seen checking it out!

I've got to hide it somewhere…

Casually, Audrey strolled back toward the library's non-fiction section, in the library's new wing. She glanced around. Suri's desk was too far away for the librarian to see her.

Audrey scanned the shelves, wondering what topic would interest the students the least. Architecture, perhaps? Maybe Mathematics or Science. For her, it would be Technology and Engineering, but that might not be the case for the AA students whose parents saw Silicon Valley as the right career path for them.

In any case, she started there, climbing the closest ladder as high as it would take her. She found a row of books on the topic of Fracture Mechanics and opened one.

Perfect, she thought, it's about concrete. Dull enough.

The books were tall, whereas Egan's novel was only nine inches in height, and relatively slim. If she pulled out four of them and put *Extracurricular* behind them and on its side, it would likely never be found.

In seconds, the deed was done.

She hurried down the ladder but slowed her pace by the time she reached Suri's desk. The librarian, engrossed in a book, looked up. "Did you find what you were looking for?"

Audrey shook her head. "It was already checked out, so I roamed around a bit to see if something else might strike my fancy. But I just realized I'm late for a coffee date and I've got to run. I'll be back later in the week."

Had Audrey waited even a few hours to hide the book, she'd have failed in her mission. As it turned out, Charly stopped by the library at lunchtime.

After perusing the online catalog and seeing that *Extracurricular* was indeed listed and on the shelf, she headed to the fiction section, where the books were shelved in alphabetical order by the authors' names. She found a gaping hole where the book should have been.

On the off chance that it had been misfiled, Charly eyed each shelf above and below, then through all the authors filed under G. Still not finding it, she went through the Fiction section shelf by shelf.

Finally, she stopped at Suri's desk. After greeting the librarian with a welcome-back hug, Charly explained, "I'm looking for Egan's novel, *Extracurricular*. The catalog says it's checked in, but I can't find it."

Suri's brow knotted with concern. She tapped a few keys on her computer screen and nodded. "You're right. It should be back there."

"Could it have been misfiled?"

"Maybe. The last time it was checked out was last February."

"Could it be in the return cart? Maybe someone could have walked it up here and then changed their mind?"

Suri shook her head. "Doubtful. But you're welcome to take a look."

It took no more than a few seconds to see that it wasn't there either. "Ah, well. I'll check the public library after school." Charly waved as she walked away.

"Oh, Charly, I forgot to mention to your mom that if she calls me with the name of the book she was looking for, I'll be sure to hold it for her."

Charly stopped and turned around. "My mom was here?"

Suri nodded. "Yes. She was in Non-Fiction looking for some sort of science book."

Charly shrugged. "Oh… Probably for her job. I'll be sure to tell her."

CHAPTER 13

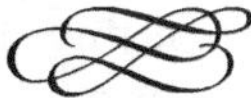

*S*allyAnne and Lionel's next stop was the Wilshire Grand Center, where Eric Calisher's brokerage office was located.

The firm took up three floors of Los Angeles' tallest building. One of its three receptionists, all of whom were wearing wireless headsets, stood up from behind a desk that looked as if it were modeled after the flight deck of the latest *Star Trek* movie. She greeted them the moment they walked into the lobby.

In a town of gorgeous women, she—all three of them, really—ranked up there with some of the supermodels who graced the fashion magazines that stared out at SallyAnne during her late-night runs to the local Mollie Stone's Market.

Was the woman a failed actress or an aged-out model? Perhaps her role was that of a human work of art? In any event, her presence relayed the message to Calisher's clients that his firm provided them with the best of everything—even waiting room eye candy.

The receptionist stared when they declared they were with the FBI but didn't flinch when they presented their badges. Instead, she whispered so low that SallyAnne couldn't hear what she said to the person at the other end of the phone line: presumably Eric.

Finally, she turned to them and murmured, "Follow me, please."

Their path began through a pair of double doors paneled to fade into the wall. There were no handles. Instead, the doors slid open the moment the receptionist was within a few feet. SallyAnne deduced the woman emitted a security clearance signal.

The hall was long, and doors within it were recessed. They weren't

293

taken to an office but to a conference room adjacent to where they'd entered.

There was a surveillance camera in the corner of the room. SallyAnne wondered if the conversation would be audio-recorded as well. If so, by California law, this would have to be disclosed upfront. Not that it mattered. What the agents would say to Eric followed the letter of the law anyway.

Eric kept them waiting ten minutes. He was a tall man, impeccably dressed, with the lean muscular build of someone who worked out religiously. Although mid-fifties according to his birth record, he'd had enough nips and tucks to fool anyone into believing he was a decade younger.

They rose to shake hands and show their badges. The brief second their palms touched, SallyAnne noted that Eric's was dry.

"So, agents, what can I do for you?" No pleasantries. Just right to the point.

Lionel's introductory remarks were the same: their investigation was into Miranda's activities as a college admissions consultant, and that Eric, as a client, was a Person of Interest.

They expected him to interrupt them at that point to ask how they knew this, but he didn't take the bait: to either confirm or deny their allegation. Instead, with no emotion whatsoever, he replied, "If that's the case, I'll be contacting my attorney. Feel free to do the same. It's Phillip Isaacson, at Conley Bell & Brownwell. Good day, agents."

He stood up to leave.

"Mr. Calisher, we'll be back with a search warrant," SallyAnne said matter-of-factly.

He waved that tidbit away as he walked out the door.

Lionel glanced at SallyAnne. As she stood up, her eyes moved to the security camera.

He got the hint and silently followed her out the door.

SallyAnne waited until they were outside the building, then asked, "Next up, the wife, right?"

Lionel nodded. "Yeah. But like you said, he's probably calling her right now and telling her to lay low. In which case, if she's home, she won't answer when we ring the doorbell. We have to prepare for that."

"We may be in for a stakeout," she countered. "Still, eventually she'll have to leave to pick up the kids or return home with them. And she may not want to play this his way."

"We'll know when we get there," Lionel replied. "At least we know what she looks like, so we won't miss her."

As with Miranda, they'd pulled photos from online sources, mostly social media. In the case of the Calishers, the fact that they gave significant donations to a number of charities made them regulars in the society columns.

When they're indicted, I wonder how many of their friends will stand by them, SallyAnne wondered.

THE CALISHER HOME WAS A POST-MODERN MANSION ON A CORNER LOT IN Beverly Hills. An ornate wrought iron fence ran the home's full perimeter.

A gate opened onto a circular driveway in front of a grand portico. There were no cars out front.

Lionel parked the car in front of the home. He and SallyAnne walked to the gate and rang the security buzzer.

No answer.

They rang a second time, leaning on it longer.

Still, no response.

"I guess we have a wait ahead of us," Lionel grumbled.

SallyAnne shrugged. "Late lunch, then. If we get hungry in the meantime, I took some apples, bananas, and a couple of granola bars from the hotel breakfast buffet."

Lionel chuckled. "You think of everything."

To get her mind off his compliment, she murmured, "There's got to be a garage. Perhaps in the back?"

Lionel drove the car around the corner. SallyAnne was right. An alley ran behind all the houses on the Calishers' block.

He pulled the car across the street from the alley and up a few feet. "This way, we can watch if anyone comes out of the front or the back of the house," Lionel explained.

While they waited, SallyAnne called in the search warrant requests for the Simpson and Calisher homes. She then asked to be transferred to Riley to learn if anything had been found on the Edelsons' computers.

"There was no correspondence between D'Arcy and the wife or the son," Riley confirmed. "And we've downloaded all correspondence between D'Arcy and Edelson, including the payment to the Best Face Forward Club. We also found an electronic receipt to University Prep & Test."

"Thanks, Riley. Call with updates."

"Will do."

SallyAnne had just hung up when Lionel nudged her. A car was pulling into the alley. It stopped in front of the Calishers' garage and idled.

A man was driving. A woman sat beside him.

"Hey, the woman in that car is Janna!" Lionel tapped the photo sitting on the dashboard. It showed a stunning redhead—as beautiful as the receptionist, but about fifteen years older.

SallyAnne craned her neck. "But that's not Eric…is it?"

Lionel pulled out a pair of binoculars for a closer look. Suddenly, his mouth dropped open. "Nope," he murmured. "And they're kissing!"

"If she's been quote-unquote indisposed, maybe Eric hasn't reached her with the news that we might be on our way over." SallyAnne took out her cell phone and took a picture of the car's license plate. In answer to Lionel's quizzical stare, she declared, "Leverage. It may come in handy."

He laughed. "Janna is opening the car door," he noticed. "We'd better storm the castle now before she pulls up the drawbridge."

Spoken like a true knight in shining armor, SallyAnne thought.

THEY PASSED THE CAR AS IT PULLED OUT OF THE ALLEY. THE DRIVER DIDN'T look twice. In fact, he made a point to turn his head: a clear indication that he didn't want to be noticed by a couple who might be Janna's neighbors.

By the time Janna tapped the garage's security code, they were at her side. "Ms. Calisher, FBI. May we have a moment?" Lionel asked.

Startled, she froze even as the garage door rose slowly in front of her.

"Who…me?" she stammered.

"Yes, thank you." Lionel smiled down at her. "You see, we're investigating a case involving an acquaintance of yours: Miranda D'Arcy."

"Miranda?" Janna frowned. A faint buzz emanated from her purse. Instinctively, she opened it to reach for her phone. Reading the caller ID, she said, "Oh! I…I have to take this! It's my husband. He's been trying to reach me all morning."

"You mean that wasn't him in the car?" SallyAnne asked. "The man you were kissing?"

Janna froze. She stared down at the phone's screen as if it were radioactive. Finally, the call rolled into voice mail.

No one moved.

At long last, Janna muttered, "What do you want?"

JANNA CALISHER TOOK THEM INTO AN EXPANSIVE, BEAUTIFULLY APPOINTED living room. As was the usual procedure, SallyAnne made it a point to mention that the conversation would be recorded and then placed her phone in plain view.

Janna nodded silently, and listened as they explained the situation:

That they already knew about Miranda's crimes;

How they knew Miranda had worked with Janna and her husband for their son David's application to USC.

And why she needed to be truthful about her role and that of her husband.

"You still have two children at home, don't you?" SallyAnne nodded toward the large family portrait on the wall behind the sofa.

"Have you already talked to my husband?"

Lionel nodded. "He wasn't forthcoming."

Janna shrugged. "Then I suppose I shouldn't be either."

"It won't matter," SallyAnne warned her. "We'll have a search warrant by early evening. When we do, the texts, emails, and photos on your husband's cell phone—and yours—will tell us a good deal."

Janna blanched at that thought.

She's thinking of how Eric will react to the news of her lover, Sally-Anne realized.

"Janna, was hiring Miranda your idea or Eric's?" Lionel prodded.

She grimaced. "It was Eric's. He'd heard from some of her other clients that she always delivered. He wanted a sure bet. Heaven knows our son, James, isn't exactly a shoo-in to the schools Eric would have liked to see him attend."

"Had you known about the tactics used to get your son into the university of his choice?" SallyAnne asked.

"I...I guess I suspected. It sounded too good to be true." Janna grimaced. "But Eric's response was, 'don't ask, don't tell.'"

"Janna, I must warn you: if you follow your husband's lead and hold out for a jury trial, like him you're chancing jail time. You'll also be doubling down on whatever verdict it delivers," Lionel explained. "And don't expect any leniency in your sentence. A judge won't appreciate that you attempted to skirt the law. Now, are you sure that's what you want?"

Janna dropped her head. "I...I don't know! I just know that it'll be worse if I cross him." She wiped away her tears.

"Janna, listen: you strike me as a woman who doesn't like to take chances," SallyAnne said. "If Eric wants to take the fall, so be it. But if you cooperate, you'll put this behind you more quickly and can get on with your life sooner than later."

Janna shrugged. "One way or another, this is over, isn't it? This life, I mean."

"Just the things that are wrong about it," Lionel murmured.

"If you say so." She stood up. "Yes, okay, I'll cooperate. In fact, if you'll wait here a moment, I think there's something that will help make the case even easier for you."

"Providing crucial evidence will go a long way with a judge," Lionel murmured.

Janna nodded sadly. Then she stood up and walked to the staircase that led to the home's second story.

"Did you see the relieved look on her face?" SallyAnne whispered. "Whatever she's got, it must be important."

The answer came with a single gunshot.

"Holy shit!" SallyAnne exclaimed.

She was on Lionel's heels as he ran up the stairs.

CHAPTER 14

*T*here were three more copies of *Extracurricular* in different branches of the San Francisco Public Library. Audrey barely had the time to track them down and check them out before her luncheon with Bliss and Tallulah.

She was the last one to get there. Bliss and Tallulah had already snagged an outside table. They waved her over.

She'd barely had time to sit down and unfold her napkin before Bliss exclaimed, "Guess who's back in town?"

"Egan." Audrey replied bluntly.

"Darn it!" Tallulah exchanged disappointed pouts with Bliss. "Let me guess. Charly told you because she's in one of his classes."

Ha! If only she'd mentioned it before I walked into the seventh-period open house...

"Nope. Daniel mentioned that Egan was the board's teacher liaison," she reminded them.

Bliss slapped her forehead. "How could we have forgotten that!"

"I know someone who would have remembered," Tallulah winked playfully. "That college counselor —Miranda D'Arcy."

Audrey frowned. "Why is that?"

Bliss arched a brow. "Let's just say she perked up when Daniel entered the room. For a moment there, I thought she was going to throw Egan over for him."

Audrey felt her cheeks heat up. "What do you mean, 'throw Egan over'? Were they doing something other than talking?"

"Not during the meeting," Tallulah admitted. "But there was some heat between the two of them. I'd be willing to bet lunch that she didn't go home alone."

Bliss patted Audrey's hand. "By that, she means Egan, not Daniel."

At least that gave Audrey something to laugh about. "Good to know. But in either regard, lunch is on Tallulah. After the last open house, Egan went out with Daniel for a burger and a beer."

Tallulah shrugged. "I'm still banking on Egan and Miranda becoming an item."

In a way, I hope she's right, Audrey thought.

Should Egan be struck with a sudden crisis of conscience, a lady friend would give him added incentive to keep his mouth shut about their first and only outing.

As if devastating my marriage wouldn't be reason enough.

Audrey waited for their waiter to take their order before asking, "How did Egan react to seeing you?"

"He remembered us, but he didn't recognize us," Bliss replied.

Tallulah giggled. "Yeah, it was quite a thrill seeing his jaw drop on the table, especially after his attempted come-on—to Bliss, anyway."

Audrey ignored the remark. Still, it bothered her, although she knew it shouldn't. It had been eighteen years—plenty of time for Egan to ruin a lot of women's lives.

Bliss shrugged. "In his mind, Audrey was the intellectual, you were the renegade, and I was the airhead. I took great pleasure in letting him know how successful we'd become." She turned to Audrey. "And how did he react to you?"

"He was polite, nothing more. If Daniel hadn't introduced us, I don't think he would have recognized me." Audrey truly believed that.

"Poppycock! Just look at you. Lean, firm—and more muscular than when we were teens," Bliss argued. "It's all that cycling you do."

"I thought you never went out riding with Daniel and the kids," Tallulah interjected.

Before she could answer, Bliss replied, "She doesn't. Last week I just happened to be walking by one of those indoor cycling studios, and there she was"—she pointed a thumb at Audrey—"pedaling away furiously."

Audrey held up a finger to her lips. "It was supposed to be our little secret."

Tallulah shook her head, awed. "I don't get it. Your whole family spends almost every Saturday morning cycling over the bridge, up a mountain, and back, and you don't want to join them?"

"They see too much of me and too little of Daniel. I can spare them those precious few hours a week together," Audrey insisted.

Tallulah looked skyward. "This, from a woman who never keeps secrets from anyone, let alone her husband."

If only you knew, Audrey thought.

She spent the rest of the lunch listening to her friends chitchat about PTA business and their work.

Bliss was proud that Sienna had suggested the net proceeds from her favorite pocketbook in the Belluci fall collection be earmarked for Ashbury Academy's scholarship program.

The generous offer left Audrey speechless. When she found her voice again, she murmured, "What a great idea!"

"I thought so too. In fact, I suggested to Raffaele that since it was Sienna's idea, she would be the perfect person to walk it down the runway during Fashion Week. But he's adamant that she participate only on the business side of Belluci," Bliss explained. "Instead, I'll take it onto the runway. Still, Sienna insists on mentioning it on every vlog post she does between now and then. She's so close to many of the kids who get scholarships to AA." Bliss beamed proudly. "Hanging with them has been a reality check for her. I know that's true for many of AA's well-off students."

For Tallulah, the news was that Maggie was all in for headlining the twenty-fifth birthday gala for Ashbury Academy, and not just because it would raise money for her dearest friend's life achievement.

"She also wants to do new recordings of all the songs from the album that came out the year AA was established," Tallulah announced. "You remember: *Make Lust, not Love*. All proceeds will go to the school."

"Oh, my God!" Audrey exclaimed. "That would be incredible! Have you mentioned it to Lavinia?"

It was a perfect message to take her mother's mind off her illness.

Tallulah shook her head. "I suggested that Maggie break the news to her in person. Bliss did the same with Maude and Reggie. Her parents will be carrying the handbag in all their boutiques. They've arranged to take Lavinia to dinner tonight so that they can tell her together."

Audrey blinked away her tears. "Lavinia and I don't have dearer friends than you and your parents."

"Group hug!" Bliss exclaimed.

The three friends threw their arms around each other. Audrey sighed. "I wish Davis were here too!"

Tallulah's eyes sparkled. "Let's call him now! He'll flip out when I tell him about Egan."

She didn't wait for permission.

Davis picked up on the fifth ring. "Wow, I was just thinking about you guys!"

Tallulah guffawed. "Sure you were—in between taking meetings with studio suits, right?"

"In fact, I'm on my way to Netflix now, which means sitting in traffic for at least another half hour. So, what gives?"

"Bliss and I are sitting here with Audrey. I told her you may have something to tell her."

"I sure do! Hi, sweet cheeks!"

Despite the noise level in a busy restaurant during lunch, those at nearby tables glanced over at them.

Audrey blushed. "Hey, this is on speakerphone! I don't need the whole restaurant knowing about our love affair."

"Too bad. You have that effect on everyone, lassie. In fact, to stay always in your heart, my latest random act of kindness will be premiering my next indie film there in San Francisco to coincide with Ashbury Academy's gala fundraiser. All ticket proceeds will go to the scholarship program."

Audrey's eyes glistened with tears. "Oh my goodness, Davis! Lavinia will be so touched."

"I was just one more kid kicked to the gutter when she found me and invited me to our school. I owe her everything, Audrey. You know that." He sighed. "And by the way, I'll also have a private screening for AA students in the school auditorium. The stars and some of the tech crew will be with me to answer the kids' questions."

"They'll be over-the-top ecstatic!" Bliss declared.

"No more than me. I can't wait to give all of you—and Lavinia—a great big kiss."

Audrey turned her head to wipe away a tear. *The tribute may be coming just in time.*

"Speaking of big deals at the school, guess who's back at AA?" Tallulah teased Davis.

He chuckled. "Don't leave me in suspense."

"Egan Gable. He's teaching again."

The silence on Davis' end went on for so long that, finally, Audrey asked, "Are you still there?"

"Yes! Sorry. It blows me away to hear that," Davis admitted. "I have to tell you: my first reaction is 'my, how the mighty have fallen.' But, frankly, like us, the best thing that ever happened to him was because of Ashbury Academy, so maybe it's not such a wrong move on his part."

Audrey bit her tongue to keep from shouting, *It's awful!*

She finally managed to say, "So, you liked his book?"

"Yes, of course! Didn't you?"

"Frankly, I never got around to reading it," she murmured.

"It was a real tearjerker, as I recall," he replied. "I do remember he made me look swell, so I have no complaints. Ah, good times."

She waited for the other shoe to drop: for him to ask her what went on between Egan and her that had inspired such sensual prose—

But nothing.

So, Davis didn't recognize me in the book either, she realized.

If Egan had had the good sense never to return, she might have been disappointed about that.

"Yeah, well, you were one of the lucky ones," Tallulah pouted. "I came off looking like some kind of rebel without a cause, and he wrote up Bliss as some clueless love child."

What about me?

As if reading her mind, Bliss replied mournfully, "And poor Audrey..."

"What do you mean by that?" *SO THEY KNOW.*

"Well, it's just that..." Bliss winced. "I guess you didn't make much of an impression."

"Are you kidding me?" Audrey turned to Tallulah. "Is she kidding me?"

Tallulah raised her hands in surrender. "Hey, don't shoot the messengers! We just figured he didn't find you interesting enough. And since you never mentioned it, we certainly weren't going to bring it up."

Davis whistled. "Yeah, boy—but that thing he had for Mandy! Talk about love being blind!"

Audrey's relief was so intense that all she could do was laugh hysterically.

Bliss, shocked, murmured to Tallulah: "At least she's not crying."

CHAPTER 15

he gun Janna Calisher shot herself with was an S&W M&P Shield. The Beverly Hills Police Department's CSI unit appeared just minutes before the FBI unit tasked with the search warrant showed up.

BHPD deduced what SallyAnne and Lionel already suspected: she'd been sitting at the foot of her bed when she pressed the gun firmly against her chest. In order to pull the trigger, her hand had to be at an awkward angle. Still, she succeeded in hitting her heart directly. The force propelled her backward onto the bed. The blood, thick and crimson, had washed over her torso before spilling onto the duvet.

Had SallyAnne not seen Janna prior, she would have never guessed that the dead woman's silk blouse was white.

She found it strange that Janna was smiling.

Having received Lionel's call, Eric came in just as the FBI's search and seizure was concluding. He was accompanied by another man.

The lawyer he mentioned, Isaacson, SallyAnne deduced.

Ashen and silent, Eric stood in the middle of his living room, his eyes darting at the activity around him: the swarm of federal agents going through all the electronic media devices they'd found; BHPD CSI cordoning off the crime scene; its sister unit, Forensics, wheeling away the body.

The sight of the body bag containing his wife infuriated him.

He glared at Lionel. "What the hell did you say to Janna?"

"All we did was explain why we came here to meet her," SallyAnne explained. "She agreed to let us record her."

"As his attorney, I want a copy of the recording." The man at Eric's side

304

handed her his business card. As she suspected, he was Phillip Isaacson. She handed him her card as well. Lionel did the same.

"I'd been calling Janna since you left my office. Are you the reason she wouldn't pick up my calls?" Eric snarled.

"No," Lionel replied. "Janna ignored an incoming call in our presence, but it was a decision she made on her own."

SallyAnne was glad Lionel didn't feel the need to elaborate.

"By the way, Janna acknowledged your involvement with Miranda D'Arcy," Lionel added.

Eric opened his mouth. But before he could say anything, Phillip put his hand on his client's shoulder. "Just because she said it doesn't make it so. In fact, Eric claims no knowledge that Ms. D'Arcy's activities on his son's behalf were illegal."

"Eric's correspondence with Ms. D'Arcy may prove otherwise," Sally-Anne countered. She nodded toward a man standing behind Eric: Riley was there now too.

"In fact, we've discovered several email addresses for Mr. Calisher," Riley piped up. "And one was used exclusively for correspondence between Ms. D'Arcy and him, including the one in which a fee was paid to a non-profit controlled by her."

"What is the email account name?" Isaacson asked.

"It's a Gmail account: the name Calisher followed by the numbers zero six zero six," Riley replied. "It's a desktop computer in the upstairs office, off the master bedroom."

"Even if there was correspondence between this account and Ms. D'Arcy's, it doesn't mean the correspondence was conducted by Mr. Calisher—especially if *Mrs.* Calisher also had access to the office, the computer, and that specific email account. And considering Mrs. Calisher's state-of-mind—especially as it concerned David's anxiety about the college admissions process, all of the dealings with Ms. D'Arcy may have been conducted by her instead." He turned to his client. "Isn't that true?"

SallyAnne frowned. *Damn him—he's leading his client.*

Eric got the message. He nodded vigorously, insisting, "I don't remember ever opening, let alone using, that email address. Did I meet Miranda D'Arcy? Sure, a couple of times at David's school. Did I know about her work on David's behalf? Yes—but I was only told what my wife must have wanted me to hear: that Miranda's process was legal and above board." He opened his hands wide. "To put it bluntly, my job was to bring home the bacon. The kids and their schooling were Janna's domain."

Noting SallyAnne's scowl, Isaacson added, "Look, agents, my client wants to cooperate fully. He'll tell you everything he knows about your suspect. But that doesn't make him complicit in his now-deceased wife's actions."

"That's very good of him," Lionel muttered. By his tone, SallyAnne knew he wasn't buying their bullshit either.

Eric's smirk proved he couldn't have cared less. "My younger children will soon need to be picked up at their school. If you'll excuse me, agents, I've got to break the news to them and to David about their mother's death."

"We're sorry about your loss, Mr. Calisher," Lionel murmured. "Our IT forensics analysis should take a week or two. Afterward, I'm sure we'll be back in touch."

WHEN THEY GOT INTO THEIR CAR, LIONEL DIDN'T START THE ENGINE immediately. Instead, he stared down the street.

Three houses away, a gardener was using a leaf blower to clear away fresh grass cuttings. Another gardener was across the street, trimming a hedge. Workmen were coming out of a house farther down the street. The only pedestrian foot traffic was two au pairs wheeling baby carriages.

"Where are the people who live here?" he wondered out loud.

SallyAnne rolled her eyes. "Working, I guess. Or shopping. Or eating lunch out with the girls—or the boys."

"Exactly. This isn't a neighborhood where people talk across fences to each other while their kids play in their yards. Beverly Hills is a collection of *Architectural Digest* showrooms! These homes are entertainment write-offs."

"So, what's your point?"

"Janna was lonely. It's why she was disconnected from her husband. It's probably why she was having an affair."

"I can't say I blame her. Talk about Mr. Freeze! I got frostbite just being in the same room with that cold fish!" SallyAnne shivered. "But if she was unhappy, why not just leave?"

Lionel shook his head. "Not everyone is strong like you."

SallyAnne laughed weakly. "I'll take that as a compliment."

"Good, because it is."

She shrugged so that he wouldn't know how touched she felt by it. "Speaking of Janna's lover, shouldn't we have a talk with him?"

"Agreed. I'll call in the car's license plate to get his name and address."

A few minutes later, they were on their way to Santa Monica to talk to someone named Van Pierce.

THE CAR, AN OLDER MODEL PRIUS, WAS PARKED IN THE DRIVEWAY OF A STUCCO duplex located just a few blocks from Santa Monica's beach.

SallyAnne and Lionel's knock was answered by a man in his mid-thirties: the one whose driver's license matched the name attached to the car registration. Van Pierce's hair was dark, thick, and on the longer side. The hair on his face was scruff more than beard or goatee. He was slim and almost as tall as Lionel.

Van wore sandals, cargo shorts, and a loose *Game of Thrones* tee shirt. On it, the words WINTER IS COMING was emblazoned in a circle.

He wasn't exactly who SallyAnne was expecting. Like Lionel, she held up her badge. "Are you Van Pierce?"

"Yeah." He nodded, surprised. "What can I do for you?" he had a soft Southern drawl, more Georgia than Texas.

"You have an acquaintance—Janna Calisher," SallyAnne stated.

Van's smile faded. "Yes. We're friends."

"May we come in, Mr. Pierce?" Lionel asked. "What we have to say is somewhat personal in nature."

Warily, Van stepped aside so that they could enter.

The place was a typical man cave: a leather couch, a matching leather easy chair, a big screen TV, and not much of anything else. It wasn't exactly tidy, but it wasn't a pigsty either.

To encourage Van to sit down in the chair, they took the couch.

"Coffee? Water?" Van asked.

"Thanks, no," Lionel replied. He said no more until Van finally plopped down in the easy chair.

"Mr. Pierce, what I have to say isn't easy. You see, earlier this afternoon, Mrs. Calisher took her own life."

Van leaned back in the chair. All color left his face. He moaned as if he'd been punched.

When he finally talked, it was to whisper one word: "Why?"

"We were hoping you could shed some light on that very matter," SallyAnne replied. "In our very brief conversation with her, we got the feeling she was an unhappy person."

"Yeah, well, that's an understatement! Frankly, I don't think she and I would have...I don't think we would have connected like we did if she were happy." Van shrugged. "I mean, I'm not exactly her type."

"What type do you think that is?" Lionel asked.

Van scowled. "The guy she married thinks he's Master of the Universe."

Lionel leaned in. "Was it a happy marriage?"

Van snorted angrily. "Are you kidding? She hated that asshole! He'd had affairs on her—sometimes with her friends! He didn't think twice of flaunting it in her face. Heck, Janna wanted out of it, badly! But she knew if she divorced him, she'd lose everything: his money, their house, her social standing...maybe even the kids. He's a winner-take-all asshole."

The perfect M.O. for Miranda D'Arcy, SallyAnne thought. "How did you meet Janna?"

"I was David's tutor. Since his freshman year and up until his senior year. Then Eric insisted David go to some bogus testing center instead: University Test & Prep." Van rolled his eyes. "David wasn't a great student. That drove Eric up the wall. The sad thing was we were finally making progress."

Lionel frowned. "The test center was *Eric's* idea?"

Van nodded. "I mean…that's what Janna told me. She was upset about it. More than me. She even insisted on taking me out to dinner to break the news." He attempted a smile. "It was the first time we really talked—not like client and vendor, but like two people. Afterward…we had our first kiss. She was a sweet person. Sad, but sweet." He shook his head, sadly. "I'm going to miss her."

"Van, you called the prep center 'bogus.' What did you mean by that?" SallyAnne asked.

"Frankly, that was Janna's word for it. She felt David wasn't improving at all. Just for the heck of it, I wanted to see if she was right, so I dropped in to see if they were hiring. The more successful places always are, especially in the more affluent areas. Lots of parents want their kids tutored, and there are only so many after-school hours for that to happen; less if the kids have lots of extracurriculars. But University Prep & Test is a one-man band, if even that. I went three times in the after-school hours. No one was there! Only once did someone open the door—some guy. He must have been expecting a client."

"What did the place look like?" SallyAnne asked.

Van grimaced. "He wouldn't let me get through the threshold. But I peeked over his shoulder. All I saw was a couch, a coffee table and a couple of desks." Van rolled his eyes. "When an operation is that small, usually the private tutoring takes place at the student's home. A private tutor certainly doesn't need the overhead of an office in a high-priced neighborhood."

"Thank you for your time, Van." Lionel stood up. SallyAnne rose too.

Van nodded. "I'm stunned—just blown away! I knew she was unhappy, but this…Poor David!"

SallyAnne paused. "One last question: what were David's extracurriculars?"

"Other than video games and TV?" Van forced a grin. "Nothing I can think of. He wasn't really into sports." He looked at his *GoT* shirt. "This was a gift from him. I watched enough of the show to pass as a gray worm."

"A what?" Lionel asked.

"It's a *GoT* fan who thinks Stannis is the true King of Westeros. It was how I connected with David."

From the car's speaker phone, Director Melamed declared, "A bird in the hand is worth two in the bush."

"With all due respect, sir: what the heck does that mean?" SallyAnne asked.

"It means that we've got a cooperating witness willing to give evidence against our prime suspect. The fact that Eric Calisher's hands aren't dirty in this case doesn't matter."

"But it does—because *he's the perp!*" SallyAnne insisted. "He's the one who hired Miranda, not his dead wife!"

"From what Riley says, there isn't any evidence that Calisher ever talked to her directly, let alone met her. And the emails on the shared account aren't signed by either of the Calishers."

"But Van Pierce just told us that hiring Miranda was Eric's idea!"

"Unless Mr. Pierce has proof, what he told you was hearsay," Melamed interrupted. "And for that matter, a disgruntled, unfaithful wife who was depressed enough to kill herself isn't exactly a reliable resource, even alive and first-hand. Wrap it up down there, agents."

Melamed clicked off.

"I need a drink," SallyAnne muttered under her breath.

"Food first," Lionel countered. "Neither man nor woman can live on bananas and granola bars alone."

"Sure. Absolutely." She knew he was right. Besides, if she drank on an empty stomach, she might say the wrong thing.

She might even tell Lionel how she felt about him.

"Maybe we shouldn't be doing this," SallyAnne blurted out.

"What? We can't leave now!" Lionel looked down at his watch. "Our food will be out any minute. At least, that's what they keep telling us."

They'd ended up at the lounge at the Hotel Casa del Mar. From their oceanside table, high above the walkway that catered to the continuous flow of walkers and cyclists, they'd spent the past half hour staring out at the waves lapping at the beach.

"No! I didn't mean leave here. I meant, leave *this case.*" Really, Sally-Anne couldn't have left even if she wanted to. She'd barely touched her salad. To top it off, somewhere along the line she'd switched from wine to martinis.

Now she was feeling tipsy. And guilty. "If we hadn't approached Janna, she'd still be alive," SallyAnne stared down into her empty martini glass. "If I hadn't told Janna we'd be looking at her phone messages and texts, maybe she wouldn't have gone upstairs and…and…" She slumped down in her seat.

"Hey, listen: *Janna's death wasn't your fault.* She was a very sad person. Van told us that." Lionel laid his hand over SallyAnne's. "And besides, who kills themselves over a college admission crime?"

"That's my point!" SallyAnne straightened up. "Miranda preys on parents who are insecure enough to take her up on her offer. They have money, and they'll use it to do anything for their kids—even illegal stuff! Even stuff that no one in their right mind would do if they weren't egotistical, or paranoid for their kids—or depressed!" She waved her fork at Lionel to make her point. "People are out there murdering. They're selling and transporting drugs! They're robbing banks! They're committing acts of terror! And what are we doing?" She smacked the table with the fork. "We're arresting parents who have more money than brains! It isn't even a crime of passion! It's… It's a crime of *privilege!*"

Lionel grabbed SallyAnne's wrist with one hand. With the other, very gently he pried away the fork. "You're right—about one very important thing: *it's a crime.* Period. Bribery to create fraud is illegal. Paying by interstate commerce is illegal. And don't forget: universities receive taxpayer dollars for their programs. We, the taxpayers, are paying for the education of these fraudulently admitted students. And as for those who missed out on that university seat: what would you say to them? That what was stolen from them wasn't as important?"

SallyAnne meekly shook her head.

"Good, because the course of their lives was changed too. They missed out on jobs, and experiences—maybe even friendships that may have changed their lives."

SallyAnne nodded silently. "You're right. I'm sorry."

"So, you're not going to ask for a transfer to the Domestic Terrorist unit?"

The worried look on his face sobered her up quickly.

She shook her head. "No. You're not getting rid of me that easily, Mr. Polk. Partners forever."

"I'll drink to that," he murmured.

Thank goodness, when he raised his glass to his lips, he was grinning again.

Jesus, I almost blew it, SallyAnne thought.

For just a second, she thought she saw a haze of longing in his eyes.

Now I'm imagining stuff? Jesus, Mary, and Joseph—no more booze tonight!

awn McCoppin stood in front of her closet's full-length mirror, scrutinizing every inch of herself.

Her make-up had been applied as meticulously as a supermodel's, and with the same effect: polished perfection that emphasized her large eyes, sharp cheekbones, and generous mouth.

As always, she'd placed a small beauty mark on the left side of her lips. Her hair was loose, its long locks gently teased into a messy mass.

She wore a cheerleader's uniform: not the one she used while leading shout-outs to Ashbury Academy's football and basketball teams, but one of several she'd had custom-made and wore exclusively when uploading new content to her premium-subscription erotic website, CheerFullyY-ours.Club.

The uniform she chose for today's video was a hot pink little number, except for the material inside the pleats of its tiny skirt, which was Easter Egg blue—the same hue as the letter "F" sewn below the cleavage created by the uniform's skintight, low-cut shell top.

Under the skirt, Fawn wore blue "spankies"—Spandex briefs, cut high on the thigh. To complete the outfit, she accessorized it with hot pink and pale blue pompoms.

This particular outfit had never been worn before, but Fawn already knew it would be a crowd-pleaser. A daily analysis of the viewing habits of the website's subscribers—primarily males between the ages of thirty-five and sixty-four, with household incomes of over two-hundred thousand dollars—hinted at this by what they'd enjoyed previously on the site.

It wasn't just the website's clicks and views that Fawn assessed. Besides knowing who watched which video and when, she also knew how many times the viewer had done so. Just as important, Fawn could see when a subscriber lingered on a certain portion of the video in order to enjoy a particular part of her sensual routine.

As always, Fawn dressed quickly and off-camera. But when she disrobed, it would be on-camera and at a snail's pace: a slow, languid striptease that intercut regimented gymnastic moves with the slower, sensual undulations of an experienced pole dancer. She scripted every camera angle, every action, every word, every inflection.

Cameras were hidden behind the mirrors placed throughout the room —not just the mirrored closet doors and the mirror over her makeup table, but the ones hanging behind and over her bed as well. This allowed her to watch her performance, assuring her that she was amping up the heat at the right time and in the right place.

The cameras were controlled by a miniature remote control secured in the palm of Fawn's hand. Her greatest skill was found in the tip of her index finger. With a single tap, she could manipulate a specific camera to turn on or off; to zoom in or out.

To follow her every move.

By trial and error, she'd learned that her audience—her "sugar daddies," as she called them—craved fantasy and sensuality; dirty talk and primal action. Her video vignettes were erotic, yes; but no more salacious than what you'd see while watching a well-choreographed burlesque show.

Certainly not porn.

Still, her cosplay came close enough to keep her almost half-million subscribers panting and heaving for their weekly dose of Fawn.

In her post editing sessions, the real thrills were added. A mere glance at bare skin—a peek-a-boo freeze shot of the top of her thigh below her skirt, a close-up of a fully covered breast, a slo-mo zoom-in on her cleavage, or something as simple as allowing the camera to linger on her pouting lips—was why her sugar daddies watched her videos over and over again.

Afterward, the spankies worn in the routine would be auctioned off to the highest bidder. Of all the ancillary items Fawn sold on her website— sex toys, blow-up dolls in her image, even cheerleading attire—the biggest money-makers were things that had actually touched her body.

Fawn had no doubt her clueless parents would blow their tops if they knew what went on under their very roof.

Well, too bad. CheerFully Yours was Fawn's way of breaking Seamus and Gretchen's chokehold on her life.

Heck, they didn't even know that she'd skipped every class today up to AA's lunch break. On Friday mornings, her mother met with her tennis foursome. Afterward, the ladies got massages and indulged in a long, liquid lunch. By the time her mother returned, Fawn would be back at school.

Skipping her morning classes was worth it. What CheerFully Yours had earned her to date wasn't just pin money. It was giving her the financial arsenal she'd need to combat Seamus' dictatorial edict:

That she waste the next four years of her life as a college student.

It wasn't because he thought she was smart. Far from it. Seamus made no bones of his contention that she was too flighty, too lazy, and too dumb to make anything better than just a passing grade in any of her classes.

Realizing he had no other expectations, Fawn lived down to them.

Seamus did have one mandate. She should do what other pretty girls had done before her: marry well.

When she was fourteen—already a willowy budding beauty catching the eye of every male who crossed her path, he explained it this way: "A beautiful girl is catnip to boys who know how to make money. They find the girls they want to marry in college. And not just any university, either, but the *créme de la créme* schools. That's why you've got to focus on what counts."

"My grades?" she asked.

He laughed heartily at that. "Yeah, well… Look, no one is telling you not to try your best. But let's face facts, Fawnie. Life deals each of us just an ace or two. Yours wasn't brains. It's *your looks.*" He patted her on the head. "A man who has made his way in the world has earned the right to have a pretty wife by his side. I'll get you into the right college. Once you're there, set your cap on some MBA student at the top of his class and you're home free. If he has a trust fund, all the better."

She'd smiled blandly and nodded to indicate she understood: *Be that girl. Marry money.*

NOT.

No way was she going to end up like her mother, Gretchen: an arm charm to a vainglorious man.

Granted, Fawn owed her parents a lot. Her beauty, now in full bloom, had been Gretchen's genetic gift. Seamus' legacy was the Machiavellian cunning that drove every relationship she'd ever had.

And, like him, her God was the Almighty Dollar.

Someday, her parents would be proud that she showed such entrepreneurial ingenuity. In the meantime, her goal was to keep the clicks coming and the money flowing.

It's why each of CheeryFully Yours' posts was a work of cinematic art; not just its production values but the stories too. Each ten-minute video had a provocative beginning, a middle ramped up with a series of subsequent actions, and a very satisfying ending. If Fawn's only interest in school—literature—had taught her anything, it was that these criteria were the essence of every great story.

Fawn worked hard to build her persona; to create her *brand.*

But she knew she couldn't play the role of the provocative cheerleader forever. If her mother's numerous cosmetic surgeries had taught her one thing, it was that within a decade—maybe fifteen years, if she stayed out of the sun and cut all sugar from her diet—she'd have to segue to some other business.

A natural career choice was to produce pornographic films. Fawn had already learned a lot about erotic cinematography. By the time she was ready to pack her cheerleading outfits away once and for all, she would have earned enough to finance a porn studio.

But as quickly as that idea came to her, she dismissed it. By their nature, actors were temperamental creatures. She couldn't even imagine the amount of cajoling needed to get a few well-endowed porn actors to perform sex acts under the camera's glare with the same realism she put into her own mini-movies. Right now, Fawn was the producer, the director, and the star. Whatever she did next would have to further embellish her brand—not someone else's.

Before choosing her senior year school schedule, it had occurred to Fawn that a better use of her storytelling skills would be writing erotic books. She'd done a happy dance when learning she'd been accepted to Ashbury Academy's Advanced Placement Comparative Lit class. She looked forward to studying the works of master storywriters.

All the more reason to create a strong impression on Egan. As a best-selling author, he'd hacked the code to success in the publishing industry.

Fawn's mission was to compel him to share it with her. She wouldn't be too obvious about her quest to become teacher's pet. But to do so, she knew she had to dump Chuck McKittridge, and pronto.

A shame, too, because he was actually great in the sack.

And boy, did he appreciate her for all her talents.

In fact, every time the cameras rolled, Fawn's thoughts went to Chuck. She pretended it was him she undressed for; that it was Chuck who coveted every inch of her.

But it was obvious that Egan abhorred Chuck. And since Fawn had no intention of associating with anyone who rubbed the teacher the wrong way, she'd have to drop him—and fast.

She'd do it this afternoon, in fact.

Perhaps, in Egan's classroom. That way, Egan would realize how serious she was about Comp Lit.

Chuck's sister presented a different problem. Intuitively, Fawn could tell Egan was intrigued with Charly; that he'd been impressed with her knowledge and insights on the course's topics.

If Fawn weren't so jealous, she'd actually admire Charly for it.

She noticed that Charly's friends—Manya Patel, Zina Sisley-Calder, and Sienna Belluci—were cut from a similar cloth. They seemed as true-blue to her as she was to them.

Fawn had never had friends like that. Her entourage was made up of sycophantic wannabes who stroked her ego and played yes girls to her.

Needless to say, none of them knew of her side business. She planned on keeping it that way. She vowed she too would someday have friends she could count on; friends who were her equal. More than likely they'd be pop stars and supermodels; a few Famechangers, maybe—if they were at least in the Mega-Influencer category, like Sienna Belluci, whom she despised almost as much as Charly.

The second she turned eighteen, Fawn would thumb her nose at Seamus' grand plan for his little girl: to be his bartering chip in his corporate playground.

She chuckled softly when she thought of how many of his colleagues and clients were actually her subscribers.

Unfortunately, her eighteenth birthday was still a full year away. Until then, she'd have to play along. Sure, she'd do his bidding and enroll in some elite college. She was certain he'd be good to his word and make sure her entree was as easy as possible.

In the meantime, she'd build up her getaway stash.

With that in mind, she clicked on Camera One's button. Under its watchful eye, slowly and seductively, she picked up her pompoms. Then in a Kewpie Doll voice, she shouted out this cheer, choreographed to a bouncing bump-and-grind that, by the end of it, left her naked and panting:

You think you're bad? You think you're hot?
You think you'll score? Not till I show you what I've got!
Say, what? You want to come again?
Not so fast. Not 'til I say when.
You say you're uptown? Let me take you down…
Down!… Down!

"Congratulations!" Miranda's slap on Egan's back was hard enough to make him wince.

But what she said next, delivered with a gleeful giggle, had him cringing: "I just heard that Daniel McKittridge is sponsoring your chair! How fortunate is that?"

Egan felt his face warm up. "I don't know why you find that so amusing," he retorted. He glanced around the teachers' lounge to see who else might have heard her.

Turns out it was everyone.

By pretending to be seemingly engrossed in his class's Comp Lit textbook—ironically, one written by his former college mentor, Clive Munt-Luckinbill—he'd hoped to spend his lunch hour working through the conundrum he'd now found himself in because of Daniel's generosity.

He could only imagine what Audrey thought when she'd heard the news: that somehow Egan had coerced Daniel into funding his honorary chair; that it was payback for the horrible way they'd split up;

That he had done so to make a mockery of her.

By taking his lunch in the teachers' lounge as opposed to hiding in his classroom, he'd hoped to catch Lavinia to suggest that Daniel's donation go to a different purpose and to promise that he'd work doubly hard to secure another gift in its place.

But Miranda's declaration proved it was much too late for that.

Where was Lavinia anyway?

Egan stood up. "If you'll excuse me, I have some tasks to do in class before the bell."

"Oh…I'm so sorry!" Her smirk puffed outward into a pout. "I would have thought you'd think it great news. It was one of your goals in taking the position, wasn't it? Making sure it paid to make it worth your while?"

Heads turned. Brows arched. The math teacher, Ike, rolled his eyes.

"With or without the sponsorship, I find it an honor to be here at AA," Egan huffed.

"I'm sure you do," Miranda murmured.

She didn't sound convinced.

The snickers of some of the other teachers echoed that sentiment.

Egan was too upset to sit there any longer. He headed out the door and up the staircase.

Egan was already at his classroom's threshold when he realized Miranda had followed him. With a sigh, he asked, "Is there something else you wish to say?"

She nodded contritely. "Only that I'm sorry. And, frankly, I'm confused as to how I upset you."

He shrugged. "Miranda, seriously…it's not you. It's just that…well, I don't feel comfortable taking Daniel's money."

"You mean, you don't want the chair?"

"Yes!…I mean, *no!*…I mean, yes, certainly, I *want* the chair."

I want the money. I need the money.

"And I feel honored to have been given the gift. But I just don't want *the McKittridges* to be my sponsors."

She frowned, perplexed. "Why not?"

"It's…" He was about to say, *it's personal,* but that would lead to even more questions—all of which had embarrassing answers. "It's just not right. Not with their children being in my class. Someone may assume they were buying my favors. You know, a better grade or something."

Miranda scoffed, "Doubtful! In the first place, Charly's grades are impeccable. Granted, Chuck's are a bit—well, shall we say less than stellar? But from what I hear, he talks his way out of all sorts of shenanigans." She winked. "He is quite the little charmer. Our female students certainly think so, anyway."

"Yeah, well, that's what I mean. I don't want it to seem...*odd*."

"A shame! Lavinia was ecstatic to hear that Daniel stepped up—and so enthusiastically too. You'll break her heart if you turn down the gift." Miranda poked him with her finger. "Look, Egan, in academics—especially in schools like this one—no one looks twice at donations, especially for such a great cause." She put her hand on his chest. "Do yourself a favor: *just take the money and run*."

"I don't know..." Maybe she has a point, he thought. If it's chickenfeed to Daniel, who was Egan to assume anyone would take it the wrong way —even Audrey?

Miranda leaned in. "Are you at all concerned because of Audrey?"

Egan did a double-take at the thought she'd read his mind. Warily, he asked, "Why would you say that?"

"Oh...nothing." Miranda shrugged. "I guess I shouldn't be talking out of school. It's just that...Well, from what Lavinia mentioned you'd made quite an impression on her."

"What? You mean, last night at the open house?"

"No, silly! *Back in the day*. You know, when you first taught here." Miranda grinned slyly. "I guess she had a little crush on you." Suddenly her eyes widened. "I hope I didn't make you uncomfortable, pointing that out."

"No, not at all." Egan smiled uncertainly. If Lavinia knew about it and it hadn't bothered her, she would have never asked me back if she thought it would make Audrey uncomfortable, he reasoned.

Suddenly, he felt very silly about the whole thing.

And intrigued at the thought that Audrey still cared about him.

"Okay, since you put it that way, I'll graciously accept it. Why look a gift horse in the mouth, right?"

Miranda giggled. "I won't tell Daniel about your almost change of heart if you don't. I'd hate for him to get jealous."

Egan muttered, "There's nothing for him to be jealous about."

Miranda raised a brow. "Oh, I wouldn't say that, exactly. From the way Tallulah and Bliss reacted to you, I imagine there might still be embers in that old flame." She glanced down at the book in his hand. "I've taken up too much of your time. I'd better let you get back to work."

As she sauntered out, he wondered, *Could she be right?*

He smiled at that thought.

THAT NARCISSISTIC HORN DOG LAPPED IT UP!

The whole time Miranda was stroking his ego, she'd had a hard time keeping a straight face.

She'd seen how Tallulah and Bliss had reacted to him: first with disdain, and then with pity.

Good. To Miranda's way of thinking, Egan deserved both.

Her instinct had told her that even if Audrey had outgrown her crush, Egan's pride wouldn't let him believe it.

Especially if someone else confirmed it.

And since he trusted her, she was that perfect someone.

No woman in her right mind would see Egan for anything less than what he was: an egotistic asshole.

Certainly not one who had a man like Daniel wrapped around her finger.

So now, if Egan acted on his worst instincts—those instincts being to flirt with the prim and proper Mrs. McKittridge—he'd be sure to repulse her *and* lose her husband's donation in the process.

And Lavinia would have no other recourse than to ask him to resign.

The thought of engineering Egan's imminent downfall sent a thrill through Miranda.

Still, trifling with Egan was *petite amusement.* At happy hour today, real business was at hand. At the board meeting, she'd piqued Jess Smallwood's interest in her private consulting services.

They were to meet for a drink at six, at Palmer's on Fillmore. She'd already reserved a private banquette.

In the meantime, she had only a few hours to review the intel she'd pulled up on Jess' son, Hugo. What a piece of work! She found easily decoded messages on SnapChat and Instagram that bore out the rumor he was the school's busiest drug pusher. If she could sniff this out, so could a savvy university admissions officer.

If Jess's goal was to erase all traces of Hugo's illegal activities as well as pump up his SATs and extracurriculars, it would cost him a pretty penny.

CHAPTER 17

Chuck had waited all day for seventh period for one reason: Fawn was avoiding him.

She hadn't shown up for Ike's trigonometry class. And when she came in during lunch period, she took great pains to avoid Chuck.

Nor had she responded to his texts, and she let his calls roll into voicemail.

By the seventh period, anxiety had set in. Fawn had played the tease all summer long. But then, right before school, when she knew her parents would be out for the whole day, she'd invited Chuck to the McCoppin's Presidio Heights home.

Located on a high hill adjacent to the historical national park that gave the neighborhood its name, the imposing Beaux-Arts mansion commanded an incomparable view of the Golden Gate Bridge.

Fawn's bedroom—cotton-candy pink, its round bed lined with plush stuffed animals—was nothing like his sister's small, prim attic garret room that overflowed with books, its walls papered with maps of the world.

But there was nothing juvenile about Fawn's approach to sex. He didn't need to cajole her into foreplay. And from how she responded to his touch, he had no doubt that she appreciated his handiwork.

In no time they moved beyond the usual slap and tickle to prodding and probing, and finally to the main event.

Other girls had told Chuck he was, like, hung. *Hugely*. It didn't faze him to hear that except for the fact that he felt it came with the expectation of a worthy performance.

Before Fawn, he'd had enough practice to pace himself. So, between her initial moans and her final gasp, he was sure he'd satisfied her.

319

Why else had she smiled and commanded, "Yummy! Again, my noble steed!"

By their third go-round, she was sated.

He was in love.

Chuck envisioned their senior year as an alliance. Every second together would be badassical.

Every moment apart would suck.

But now, in only the first week of school, something had changed. Why?

What the hell had happened?

The second he walked into his seventh period classroom, he saw who was to blame.

Egan.

The teacher was leaning against Chuck's desk. Fawn was chuckling at something he'd just said. She was in her seat—well, sort of. Really, she was sitting on her desktop. With her arms placed behind her, she was partially reclining. The top two buttons of her blouse were open, exposing her generous cleavage.

What ...the hell?

So, that's how it is!

By now, other students were meandering into class—Charly, Manya, Sienna, and Zina included. Like some of the others, instinctively their eyes fell on their teacher. Curious, they tuned into the conversation.

Angrily, Chuck walked over. Egan, who was listening intently to Fawn's animated dissertation, hadn't realized someone was beside him until Chuck declared, *"Do you mind?"*

Though still intrigued by whatever tale Fawn was spinning, Egan nodded distractedly. As he moved from the desk, he patted Chuck's shoulder.

Chuck shrugged off his hand and then slammed his backpack on the desk.

Fawn frowned. "Gee, seems someone sure woke up on the wrong side of the bed!" She winked knowingly to Egan.

Egan shrugged.

Chuck was glad Egan didn't attempt some clever rejoinder. Otherwise, he might have socked him.

He was relieved when the final seventh-period warning bell chimed because Egan strolled to the front of the classroom—

Only to turn back to Chuck. "By the way, I never told you I was very impressed with how you were able to come up with the *As You Like It* quote so quickly."

Taken aback, Chuck muttered, "It was easy enough for me. As I told you, it's been thrown in my face enough times."

"I'm sure your mother says it only because she loves you, and she believes you can accomplish anything you set your mind to."

The audacity of this guy!

Incensed, Chuck grinned at Egan. "You taught my mother too, right?"

The question seemed friendly enough.

Egan nodded hesitantly. "Yes. Audrey was a conscientious student."

Chuck smirked, "That's nice of you to say, considering the stuff you put in your book about your students."

Egan frowned. "What do you mean by that?"

"Wasn't your novel based on Ashbury Academy?"

Egan's back stiffened. "It's a work of fiction."

"Fiction..." Chuck wiggled his brows. "Like, what...*porn?*"

"Critics consider it contemporary literature," Egan countered coolly. "But, yes, there is sex in the book, if that's what you're hinting at."

"Let me guess: between a teacher and his student?"

At that very second, every other conversation in the room ceased.

Everyone stared at Egan.

"I take it you haven't read it. Otherwise, you'd realize that's an asinine question." He smiled as if the joke were on Chuck.

"I haven't," Chuck admitted. "Still, I'll take that as a yes. Am I right?"

"Tell you what. If you take the time to actually read it, we'll have an honest discussion as to the plot, the characters, and my inspiration."

Fawn licked her lips, fascinated by Egan's rejoinder.

Chuck could have kicked himself. *Fuck! Fuck! Now she'll read it for sure. And she'll want to be his next inspiration.*

"Sure," Chuck muttered. "Looking forward to it."

When Chuck's gaze met Fawn's, she rolled her eyes. Then she grabbed her books and moved to an empty seat—beside Charly, of all places.

Charly's reaction cut the deepest: she closed her eyes tightly and shuddered as if watching a baby seal getting clubbed to death.

Fuck Chuck!

Egan fumed silently, even as he called on various students to read aloud their homework assignments;

Even as he pretended to listen, then gave bland atta-boys before calling on the next student.

Egan had wanted to give Chuck a clean slate. Really, he did. But if the kid was stupid enough to jibe him because he was jealous—and over a silly simp like *Fawn McCoppin, of all people!* —then so be it.

As soon as Egan's sixth-period class had cleared out, Fawn had made her entrance. She was juggling a stack of books that just so happened to slip from her hands as Egan noticed her—

Allowing her to bend over seductively to pick them up.

By then, Egan knew the game she was playing: Easy A.

To put an end to it, he walked over, knelt down, and picked up the books she'd missed.

That would have been the end of it, but she then mentioned that she felt confused by the debate pamphlet he'd left for those interested in the tryouts. She'd perched herself on top of her desk then leaned back seductively so that he'd be sure to notice that her breasts had somehow breached the top two buttons of her blouse. Then, in a kittenish purr, she asked to meet him after class so that he could explain the debate rules and definitions to her.

He'd said no—firmly—and recommended instead that she buddy up with another contender and become critique partners to sound out their arguments and rebuttals. "You know, like your boyfriend, Chuck," he pointed out.

Fawn giggled at that like it was the funniest thing she'd ever heard.

That's when Egan knew she'd already decided to dump Chuck.

She was still laughing when the poor kid walked into class.

Chuck, kiddo, you reap what you sow.

In Fawn's case, Egan could only imagine how many others had plowed that field before Chuck. Maybe he should warn Audrey to have the kid checked for STDs...

Oh, hell—*Audrey!*

Egan had almost freaked out when Chuck prodded him if *Extracurricular* was about a teacher-student tryst. He was glad he thought of asking Chuck outright if he'd read it.

He'd felt a wave of relief when Chuck said no.

No doubt, though, that the first thing Chuck would do when he got home was to ask Audrey if they had a copy of her former teacher's book, *Extracurricular.*

At first, she'd be taken aback. Then, cautiously, she'd ask. *Why do you want to know?*

Chuck would tell her that Egan had assigned him the book for a report.

Audrey would be horrified, Egan realized.

She'll trash it, or burn it—

If she hasn't done so already.

In any regard, Audrey would assume Egan had assigned Chuck the book to humiliate her.

She'll hate me all over again, Egan thought miserably.

Then he remembered what Miranda had said: "The way Tallulah and Bliss reacted to you, I imagine there might still be embers in that old flame."

If she's right...

Then what?

Then maybe I'll have a chance to show Audrey how much I love her.

And do what—break up her marriage? Wreck a seemingly happy home?

Egan glanced over at Chuck. He wasn't surprised to find the boy still scowling at him.

No. Never. It's not worth it.

But maybe…

We can be friends?

Reality charged through him like a blast of frigid air:

As if.

JUST AS THE SCHOOL CHIMES RANG OUT THE END OF CLASS, FAWN TAPPED Charly on the shoulder.

Charly turned around. As Fawn anticipated, she was surprised to see who'd summoned her. Because Fawn ignored those she considered a waste of her time, she was used to this reaction. For guys, it was a shock. For other girls, it was awe. Go figure.

She fully expected Charly to stutter something that indicated she was flustered and flattered by Fawn's attention. Instead, Charly, bemused, replied, "What do *you* want?"

For once, Fawn was taken aback. "Well…Okay, see, I was thinking…" *Damn Charly! Why was she always acting so superior to everyone else?* "I guess you're going out for Debate Team. Am I right?"

Charly nodded warily.

"Well…so am I. And…I wondered if you'd like to be, you know… critique partners?"

Charly glanced over to the classroom door, where Manya, Sienna, and Zina were waiting for her.

Fawn followed her gaze. Charly's friends, relaxed and confident, gossiped and chuckled together, totally oblivious of the exclusive offer she'd just made to their bestie.

They are all so damn smug. Well, wait until Charly dumps them—for me.

Charly would do it too, because it was an honor to be included in Fawn's inner circle. The girls already there—Kaylie, Sophie, and Mackenzie—met a certain standard. They were pretty enough, but not gorgeous like her. They were smart, but no geniuses and had none of her cunning.

And like Fawn, they were snobs.

Better yet, their greatest fear was being banished from her posse.

Just then, Chuck, still stunned at being humiliated so publicly, was shuffling out the door.

Charly nodded toward her brother. "Wouldn't you rather partner with Chuck?"

Fawn sniffed, "*Are you serious?* Do you actually think he's going to try out too?"

Charly shrugged. "He claims he is."

Fawn frowned. "Either way, the answer is no."

"Why not?"

Fawn studied a nail. "I'm sorry if this hurts you to hear it, Charly, but your brother is a loser. Plain and simple, he doesn't have your smarts."

Charly tilted her head as if she hadn't heard Fawn correctly. "Wait, let me get this straight. You enjoy fucking my brother, and you love that he's head over heels crazy in love with you. But because you're angling for a better grade and you think Egan will hold it against you that you're dating Chuck, you dumped him?"

Fawn stiffened. "It sounds cruel when you put it that way."

Charly snapped her fingers in Fawn's face. "Earth to Fawn: *that's because it is cruel.* You used Chuck, and now he's not important to you anymore. *So, you're ghosting him.*" Charly stood up. "You know, there should be a word for a female who acts like a player. Until someone comes up with it, I guess 'bitch' will have to do."

Charly left to join her friends.

At first, Fawn was too incensed to do anything but stare after her.

Why, that little nobody! How dare she talk to me that way!

In Fawn's world, only she had the right to turn down an offer of friendship. Just the thought of this slight made her furious.

She grabbed her books and headed for the door.

As she passed Egan's desk, she noticed he had his back to her. Still, she could tell he was chuckling about something. It mortified Fawn to think that he might have heard Charly put her in her place.

She quickly dismissed that thought. Egan was enthralled by her. Perhaps even smitten. It was why he'd found it necessary to put Chuck in his place.

Now more than ever she wanted to take something away from Charly: Egan's respect.

She knew how to do it too: she'd impress him at the debate tryouts.

CHAPTER 18

 $\mathcal{M}$ iranda arrived at Palmer's fifteen minutes earlier than the designated time for her appointment with Jess Smallwood. She'd pulled up everything she could from AA's files on his son, Hugo.

No doubt about it, Hugo was a smart boy. When he was a freshman, his grades were exemplary. But sometime in the middle of his sophomore year, he dropped two grade-points on average for each subject.

This was bound to happen when his only purpose for going to school was to distribute drugs to his clients—that is, a few trusted AA students, Miranda reasoned.

Some teachers included a few insightful notes for other faculty and staff:

Hugo keeps a low profile.

(Teacher-speak that meant he didn't participate well in classroom discussions).

Hugo is constantly tethered to his phone.

But of course he was. It was how he procured orders. Miranda was willing to guess that the code for his various products—weed, coke, Ecstasy, whatever—was simple enough code to crack.

Miranda looked forward to hearing Jess' take on his kid. She wondered if he actually knew anything about his son's lucrative side business.

Her guess was no.

But if Jess were aware of it, she was willing to bet it simply didn't matter to him.

It was worth bringing up if only to gauge how much he was willing to pay to make his son squeaky clean.

She didn't have to wait long. Jess walked in promptly at six o'clock. As they waited for their cocktails—martinis for both—they made pleasantries: about her take on AA's students; and his upcoming trip to Bangkok.

Once the drinks arrived, Jess got right to the point: "You mentioned some sort of private concierge service. What does that mean, exactly?"

"A student's best attributes aren't always apparent via a university's standard admission criteria: you know, grades, extracurricular activities, awards and other achievements."

"In Hugo's case, his GPA stinks, he's not on any teams, and he's not exactly a do-gooder." Jess rolled his eyes. "So, how would you enhance his, for lack of a better phrase, 'best attributes?'" He took a swig of his martini.

"Do you mean the fact that he's a successful drug dealer?"

Jess spewed his drink. "Well, you certainly come right to the point."

"So, you do know about his extracurricular activity. Good! We won't have to beat about the bush." Miranda leaned in. "But in order to make him appealing to college admissions officers, I'll need complete honesty from you—and him."

"Sure, okay," Jess murmured cautiously.

Miranda smiled broadly. "Believe it or not, you've given me a lot to work with."

"Are you serious?" He motioned the waiter for a second round.

"Yes—depending on how we spin it, Hugo's triumph over substance abuse—and his desire to help others fight it too—could make for an inspirational essay."

"Stop it. You're giving me a woody," Jess murmured. "Oh…Wait! I just went soft at the thought that Hugo is an awful writer. Not to mention he doesn't preach against drugs. He *sells* them." Jess gulped his drink.

The sexual innuendo annoyed Miranda. Still, she was willing to ignore it if he accepted the price tag for her services. "Not to worry. I'll get Hugo a private tutor who will help him write a gripping saga of his triumph over cocaine."

"Marijuana—but, yeah, from the way he's talking, he wants to take that on too, as a secondary product line," Jess replied. "He's like a capo—you know, got to keep the troops marching."

"He has a battalion of foot soldiers to do his bidding? What an industrious overachiever! How does he deliver his, er, product?"

"It's really quite creative! Only edibles—lollipops, in fact. Great high, but no smell. And he sells them in airtight sealed metal containers: like the kind used to sell mints, only larger."

"Genius! Unobtrusive and raid-proof!" As if awed by Hugo's ingenuity, Miranda applauded slowly. "Now, about your son's SATs: *abysmal.* He'll need a tutor."

"Yeah, no shit. Or more importantly, a miracle," Jess muttered.

"They do happen, you know." She grinned mischievously. "With the right tutor. Mine. How does a score of fourteen-fifty sound?"

"I think I just came! This is better than phone sex." He leaned in and put his hand on her thigh.

"Do tell," she muttered. Although if she were to be honest with herself, he was looking more desirable after a second martini. "Was Hugo ever a substance abuser?"

"He was, but he's clean now." Jess grimaced. "He's got an entrepreneurial bent. He saw a way to scratch an itch. Big deal. Besides, most kids his age are only recreational users, right?"

Until they're not, Miranda thought. "When Hugo got clean, did he do it in rehab?"

Jess nodded again. "Yes. Two months, the summer between his sophomore and junior years. One of those fancy airy-fairy dry-out spas."

"Has Hugo ever been arrested?"

"Not yet. But worrying about it keeps me up at night." Jess' face seemed to fold into itself like a fallen soufflé. "So how much do these so-called miracles cost?"

"One million dollars," she purred.

This time he choked on his olive. "You're kidding!" he gasped.

"I never joke about money," she huffed. "Put it in perspective, Jess. You've already paid much more than that for twelve years of private schooling. Am I right?"

Jess nodded grudgingly.

"All of it has been leading up to this: *admission into a top-drawer university,*" Miranda added. "You don't want to fumble the ball on the five-yard line, do you?"

Jess thought for a moment. Finally, he muttered, "I'm a sucker for whores. But despite the *Pretty Woman* reference, usually when I dole out that kind of money, at the very least I get a blowjob."

"This isn't Bangkok, Mr. *Smallwood.* The fee is non-negotiable."

Miranda's emphasis of Jess' surname made him wince. He sat silently.

"Shall I continue?" she asked.

He nodded.

That's when she knew he was hooked.

"We'll make sure to tick all the boxes. That starts with getting him into the *right* university—that is to say, one in a state that has already passed laws that make it legal to sell marijuana."

"Like here in California," Jess pointed out.

"Bingo! Home of Berkeley, Stanford, UCLA, and USC. Do you think he'd be interested in any of those schools?" Miranda batted her eyes at the obvious.

"Jeez, I'm hard again," Jess declared.

"We'll narrow the choice further to universities with Business Administration programs underwritten by Big Pharma." Miranda tapped the table as she thought. "Which is all of the above—oh, except for Berkeley." A shame, she thought, considering that once upon a time mind-blowing recreational drugs were practically part of the curriculum.

Jess grimaced. "Does your million-dollar fee come with a guarantee?"

"First of all, it's a 'donation,' so you get an IRS write-off," she pointed out. "And an SAT score in the mid-fourteen-hundreds or higher means serious consideration by every university. Now, top that with the right extracurricular or two, and he's a shoo-in."

"He can't very well join Future Business Leaders of America," Jess scoffed.

"In fact, the specific purpose of the non-profit you'll be donating to— The Best Face Forward Club—is to align graduating seniors with an inspirational mission. For Hugo, I would imagine a few photos of him and his distribution crew—those he's helped get on their feet financially by selling his colorful candy tins for a great cause—will do the trick."

"What's the 'great cause'?"

"Why, the Best Face Forward Club, of course!" Miranda patted his wayward hand, but she didn't move it.

Instead, she used her other hand to motion the waiter for another round. She had one more pitch to make. Another drink might help him see the advantage of agreeing to it. "Now that we've gotten Hugo's conundrum out of the way, I'd like to talk a little board business."

Jess looked up, surprised. "You're on the board? But I thought you only sat in that one time, to introduce yourself and make a quick presentation."

"My point is that I *should* be on the board—for a couple of reasons. First of all, despite Lavinia's contention otherwise, the most important mission of our school is really how well our students get placed upon graduation. Shouldn't it be a board imperative to have my ongoing insights on this?"

"Yes, certainly!"

"Secondly, the way the board is set up now—with eight members, since there are now two PTA representatives—there can never be a voting majority. Should push come to shove on the issues important to your little clique —say, reducing that illogically enormous budget for scholarships, or some student perk that Lavinia may balk at—I imagine you boys would find a tied board to be a bit cumbersome."

"I see your point," he said gravely. "I'm sure Seamus will too."

"I thought you would." She tipped her glass to his. "Here's to Hugo's success."

As he tapped hers, he murmured, "And yours."

Miranda was sipping the last of her martini when she felt his fingers crawling higher between her legs.

Ah, the quid pro quo.

Miranda had already made up her mind that she was up for Jess' antics. She'd need a powerful ally on the board. Of all its members, he was the most desirable.

As she'd done with Rob Edelson, she'd be video-recording their trysts. She saw it as an insurance policy. Jess Smallwood's first marriage had already cost him dearly. He couldn't afford for his second to implode as well.

"Why don't we take this celebration back to my place?" Miranda murmured. To make her position clear, she cupped him firmly.

To her dismay, what she felt there came up short. Apparently poor Jess lived up to his name.

CHAPTER 19

*W*ithin minutes of learning that they were back from their weeklong Los Angeles fact-finding investigation, Director Melamed summoned SallyAnne and Lionel to his office. Then, for the next hour, he sat, stone-faced, throughout their briefing session.

Granted, he'd been ecstatic that they'd secured three cooperating witnesses against Miranda D'Arcy. But like them, he was disappointed when they acknowledged having hit a stone wall.

Or as he put it: "So, your LA-based cooperating witnesses had no leads on other possible parent suspects?"

"That doesn't mean more aren't out there," Lionel replied. "It's just that most of them knew better than to talk about it in public."

"University Prep & Test also came up empty," SallyAnne admitted. "Janna Calisher's boyfriend—the private tutor, Van Pierce—was right. It's a shell company. In the three days we staked it out, no one went in or out of the place."

"We left a detail on stakeout. Eventually, someone has to show up," Lionel added.

"The building's leasing agent must have a contact," Melamed countered.

"Yes, it's someone who calls himself 'John Smith,'" Lionel replied. "The agent took that at face value. I guess he felt it wasn't worth questioning, considering the guy paid a full year's rent in advance."

"When we called the facility's phone number, it prompted us toward three different departments: Consultation Requests, Test Appointments, Test Results." SallyAnne explained. "We called each one to see if someone would actually pick up. All of our calls rolled into a voice mailbox."

The agents never left a message. There was no need to alert Miranda and any employees of the FBI's interest in her activities.

"We also checked state business license records and the IRS as to whether University Prep & Test filed with either," Lionel added. "We came up blank. The company must be pocketing the fees from the parents, or funneling it through the Best Face Forward Club, which isn't even registered with the California Secretary of State as a non-profit."

"No surprise there," Melamed muttered.

"Sir, we suspect it's nothing more than a virtual voicemail service. Still, we'd like to get a trace initiated on the calls coming in and out of it," Sally-Anne suggested. "At the very least, they'll lead us to parents whose children are using UP&T. Some—maybe even *all* of them—will be tied to the prime suspect, Miranda D'Arcy."

"And when she calls into it, too, we've hooked our whale," Lionel added. "Metaphorically speaking, that is."

"You'll have it by Monday, along with one for Ms. D'Arcy's phone," Melamed promised.

Lionel smiled. When he noticed SallyAnne's congratulatory nod, he winked at her.

"Go home and enjoy your weekend." Melamed nodded toward the door.

As they walked out, he muttered, "Too bad the testing facility was a bust."

As far as the case was concerned, Melamed was right. Still, Lionel wouldn't have called it a total waste of time.

He'd gotten to learn a lot about SallyAnne.

University Prep & Test occupied one of three suites on the top floor of a low-rise office building in Beverly Hills with a private gated garage. The other two suites were empty. The agents spent three days camped in the hallway outside UP&T's door.

The whole time, not a single person crossed their path.

To bide their time, they talked through every angle of the case. Then they gossiped about their colleagues. When they ran out of small talk, SallyAnne had suggested a game called Never Have I Ever.

"Sounds…intriguing," Lionel admitted. "How did you hear about it?"

"It's one of those things people play at parties. You know, as part of a drinking game." She shrugged. "But you don't need to drink to play—like now, I mean."

Right then and there, Lionel learned something he never knew about SallyAnne: she actually made time to go to parties.

He wondered what it would be like to run into her at one.

He wanted to—so badly.

Noting his grimace, SallyAnne quickly added, "Look, we don't have to. I just said it to, you know, pass the time."

"No! ...I mean, yes, let's do it," Lionel insisted. "Okay, so, how does it work?"

"I ask you a question—a daring one." SallyAnne's face reddened. "And I'll preface it with the words, 'Never have I ever.' Now, the key is that you have to answer truthfully, 'Yes' or 'No.' If you elaborate, you get to ask the same of me. If you want to keep it to yourself, you have to come up with another question."

"Sure," he murmured.

Heck, what will I ask?

Is there anything I shouldn't ask?

My God, there's so much I want to know about her...

"Do you want to go first?" He wanted to see how far she'd take it.

"Okay..." SallyAnne thought a moment. "Never have I ever farted in the office?"

"Um...No. In fact, I have."

Lionel admitted it so sincerely that SallyAnne snickered, "I guess I've been lucky enough to be upwind!"

"Lucky you. I'm sure it's because I eat too much fiber...but hey, the stuff's good for you."

This time, she doubled over with laughter.

When she finally got ahold of herself, he asked, again in all sincerity, "Too much information?"

"I'll let you know if it ever comes to that," she replied solemnly. "Okay, your turn."

"Wow. Okay, let me think..."

There were so many questions he wanted to ask—

Play it safe. Don't scare her away with something too personal.

"Never have I ever, um...tattled on a sibling?" Did she have brothers or sisters? They'd never discussed stuff like this. She was so damned buttoned up and by the book.

It was another thing he loved about her. One of many.

She grinned. "My brothers are older than me. They were a couple of scamps, for sure. Teased me unmercifully! But I got back at them." Her eyes twinkled. "One had a girlfriend who lived just around the corner. They used to make out on her front porch. I took a picture of an intentional nip slip with his hand around it." She rolled her eyes. "Let's just say my mother was so appalled that he was grounded for a month. From then on, the girl was known around our house as 'the harpy.'"

Lionel laughed.

She joined in.

And on it went, just like that:

Questions about family, close friends, pets;

Favorites—colors, flowers, teachers, travels, books, sports, cars, so on and so forth;

Hopes were divulged, fears admitted, and secrets revealed via questions couched playfully, but nuanced with more than a mild curiosity.

On the first two days, a little after six, they reluctantly threw in the towel. His disappointment was more about leaving the game than missing out on anyone who could shed light on their suspect.

Lionel wondered if SallyAnne felt the same way.

On their last day in LA, Friday, the stakeout was cut short so that they could make it back to the San Francisco office in time to catch Melamed before his weekly jaunt north to his Russian River cabin.

On the flight home, Lionel wondered if their little cross-examination games meant as much to her as they did to him.

No. Ridiculous thought. Surely, she saw it as no more than a distraction from boredom.

As for him, her responses were like childhood treasures: each one tucked away in an old shoebox to be scrutinized periodically, cherished secretly, and always remembered in context with every blush, grin, and errant touch that accompanied it.

There would be other stakeouts. If SallyAnne again suggested playing Never Have I Ever, he'd be up for it.

CHAPTER 20

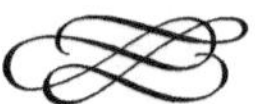

*A*shbury Academy's monthly Friday Fun Nights were something the entire school community looked forward to with anticipation.

From what Egan gathered from Odette, this AA tradition had started a couple of years after he'd resigned. "Initially, its activities were simple: a potluck and a sing-along or improv skits put on by anyone who wanted to get involved—students, staff, or parents."

"But in the past five years, everything about it went from the ordinary to the *extraordinary*!" Cornell added. "Granted, it's great to have a gourmet chef on campus. But that gives it the feel of a must-see, must-attend event."

Tonight's catered buffet featured organic roasted chickens and grilled wild salmon; a harvest bounty mélange made of vine-ripened tomatoes, fresh chickpeas, and fingerling potatoes; and for dessert, apple pie and homemade ice cream.

A student jazz trio would play during the buffet. Afterward, AA's full student orchestra would accompany a laser light show designed by the physics club.

Because the teachers had a few hours off before the event, Egan allowed Cornell and Odette to talk him into joining them for an off-campus happy hour.

Apparently, their favorite hangout was a place called Barvale, on trendy Divisadero Street in San Francisco's NoPa neighborhood.

They walked over after Egan signed the lease on a small one-bedroom apartment located just a few blocks from the school—something he could now afford, thanks to the additional stipend provided by Daniel's endowment.

Leaving his parents' old house would be a relief—not just because of the torturous drive into town but because it held too many memories of his failed dreams. Whereas his position at AA wasn't ideal, it was a step in the right direction—

One that had put him back in Audrey's world, if only as an uneasy acquaintance. As long as he was at the school, he'd have to live with that.

But just as they snagged a table and ordered a round of drinks, Egan realized his cellphone was buzzing.

It was his literary agent, Chastity Blunt. Since the bar was much too noisy, he excused himself and went outside.

In the grand old days, when *Extracurricular* had soared to the top of various bestseller lists, Chastity was sure to touch base daily: if not to read him sales numbers or drop the names of editors jumping over each other to work with him, then to prod him toward the completion of whatever current work-in-progress she hoped to sell on his behalf.

But when each subsequent sale brought in a smaller advance or failed to earn out the advance she'd wrangled from his current or even a new publisher, Chastity's calls slowed to a trickle.

He realized the worm had turned when he did all the dialing.

On the few occasions when Chastity deigned to take one of Egan's increasingly desperate calls, invariably a client whose sales were higher would ring up. At that point, Chastity would leap off the phone with less grace than a streetwalker turning her back on one john in order to wave down another whom she knew paid more.

In the past year, whenever Egan called Chastity, it was inevitable that her assistant would inform him that her boss was on another call and would have to get back to him.

Naturally, the callback never came.

Seeing her name now on Caller ID, Egan tamped down the desire to sneer out something he'd regret. Instead, with as much pleasantness as he could muster, he proclaimed, "Well, well, Ms. Blunt! To what do I owe this pleasure?"

"I wish it were something that would make us some money, Egan. Really, I do. Unfortunately, I've got bad and even worse news. Which do you want to hear first?"

Egan felt a cold chill run down his spine. "Start with just plain bad."

"In that case, you should know that your publisher, Signal Press, has been slapped with a defamation of character lawsuit for publishing *Extracurricular*. Some woman is claiming that one of your characters—the one called 'Fannie'—is based on her."

"Let me guess—her name is Mandy Blackwell."

"Oh… So, it's true?" Before he could answer, Chastity quickly added, "No, no, don't tell me! I'd rather not know in case I have to take the stand." She paused, and then added, "And by the way, you're named as a co-defendant. Since my agency represents you, the subpoena was served here. So you better lawyer up."

"I wrote the damn book twenty years ago! Isn't there some sort of statute of limitation?"

"Depending on the state, one year; maybe two. However, her attorneys are making the case that since the novel is still in print, each subsequent purchase, print or digital, makes the suit valid—that is, until it's out of print entirely."

"Why, that's absurd!" Egan exclaimed.

"I agree," Chastity replied mournfully. "Believe me, Egan, I do."

"You know what they say: no news is bad news, right?" Egan countered. "Why doesn't Signal Press use the publicity of the lawsuit to stoke sales?"

"Frankly…" Chastity paused. Egan guessed she was dragging on a cigarette. "That brings me to worse news. Just in case some judge agrees with Ms. Blackwell's contention, as a way to placate her Signal Press felt it smarter to halt publication immediately."

"Does that mean digital copies too?"

"Sadly, yes. In fact, Signal has already sent takedown orders to all the online bookstores—as well as the public libraries. To motivate the latter, those libraries that do so within twenty-four hours get a free replacement: anything else from Signal's extensive catalog." Chastity paused, then added: "Additionally, they extended an olive branch to the plaintiff."

"What does that mean, 'an olive branch'?" If the term were literal, he'd offer to deliver it himself—and soundly lash his nemesis with it.

Chastity sighed. "A cash settlement."

"Signal Press isn't going to put up any sort of fight?" Egan couldn't believe his ears. "They're just going to let Mandy set some bogus precedent for future suits?"

"Apparently so. And the settlement is substantial—a quarter of a million."

"Oh, well—hell." He massaged the ache in his forehead. "Let me guess what's next: they want me to write another book for them, gratis, to pay for the loss."

"Um…No. In fact, there's even more bad news: because of how your contract is written, Signal Press is suing *you*."

"Wait, wait…"

This is all a bad dream!

"You've always made sure I was indemnified from any lawsuits deriving from my books!"

After a frosty silence, Chastity growled, "You forget, Egan. You were a very eager, very desperate debut novelist. You insisted that any clause that got in the way of the sale of *Extracurricular* be jettisoned—including your indemnification."

"It was your job to warn me against that!" Egan shouted. "Maybe I should countersue Mandy, Signal Press, and *YOU!*"

As soon as the diatribe left his mouth, he regretted it. Chastity was his lifeline to the only thing that still mattered to him: his writing career.

"Oops! Sorry, Egan! My phone system put you on mute because another call just came in. I'm sorry but I really have to take it. The author —a debut novelist—just hit the *USA Today* list and is simply *overjoyed—*"

Egan clicked off.

Then he threw the phone at the wall, breaking it.

Damn, he thought. *I can't afford a new iPhone…*

Dismayed, he threw up his hands and stormed back inside.

Then he proceeded to belt down a double Scotch.

"Whoa, cowboy!" Cornell warned. "Don't you want to wait for the tapas we just ordered? Lavinia won't like it if you set some parent's hair on fire with your breath."

Lavinia.

Shit.

Cornell was right. And not just because Egan couldn't afford to get fired, either.

To sober up, he gulped water, lots of it, with his tapas.

As the fog of Scotch dissipated from his brain, he thought about the few times in the past week that his path and Lavinia's had crossed. He'd noticed a difference in her. The headmistress' naturally rosy complexion had paled. The quickness of her response to questions was off, if only a beat. When around those she loved unfailingly—her students—there was still a buoyancy in her demeanor, but an unmistakable scrim of sadness had darkened her eyes.

Egan was worried about her.

He wondered if Audrey was too.

But he knew she'd be the last person he could approach with his concerns.

I'm sure I'm just imagining it anyway.

"Fawn!…*FAWNIE!* Where the hell are you? The damn driver is here!" Seamus' bellow came through the home intercom. It was as loud as a cargo ship's horn while sailing through the Golden Gate passage on a fog-shrouded night.

Fawn's response was a litany of curses—one she knew no one could hear from her wing of the three-story twenty-room mansion. It had nothing to do with her father's obnoxious summons and everything to do with Fawn's frustration at her inability to pull together some semblance of a debate argument.

It wasn't for lack of trying either.

For the past week, she'd gone back and forth on which two subjects she'd choose from a list of four that each contestant was to argue, both pro and con:

• *Is the current approach to illegal immigration too harsh or too lenient?*

• *Are there ramifications for teens in the "hook-up culture," and if so, are they emotionally or physically harmful?*

• *Does the death penalty constitute a cruel and unusual punishment?*

• *Should scientists be allowed to clone humans?*

She'd finally decided to tackle the cloning question (the research should be easy enough, she reasoned) and the one on teen hookups. (A subject that everyone would assume she was an expert in it anyway. For once they were right,)

Making arguments for cloning was harder than she'd anticipated. There were lots of ethical cases already prepared for the con part, but it seemed as if no one agreed with her that making carbon copies of those revered by others—celebrities, the wealthy, the powerful—might actually save humanity from itself.

"I don't really have time for this shit!" Fawn shouted. "I have a dynasty to run!"

She was right. Her website had shot into the stratosphere. And to keep it there, she had to feed the beast, as it were.

When her parents were home, they pretty much left Fawn to her own devices. Despite this, posting even one video a week was an arduous process for someone who was also a real cheerleader enrolled in a competitive prep school with several AP courses on her schedule.

It dismayed her to no end that her ploy to secure Egan's attention had backfired. She'd dropped Chuck to give their teacher the message that, like him, she saw Chuck as a loser. Instead, Egan ignored her ploys to get his attention. If anything, it seemed as if the animus Egan had previously felt for Chuck was now directed at her.

At the same time, Chuck was repositioning himself as a good student. By participating in class discussions, making decent grades on tests, and showing interest in trying out for Debate Team, he was earning Egan's grudging respect.

When did they kiss and make up? And why hadn't she been invited to do the same—figuratively if not literally?

But of course, she already knew the answer to that. She'd shamed Chuck in front of the whole class. Because of that, now he wouldn't even look in her direction.

To top it off, she'd then gotten her comeuppance at the hand of his caustic nerd of a sister—in front of Egan, no less.

Instead of being grateful for the invitation and falling into line, Charly had insulted her. First, she'd called Fawn out for dumping her twin. Then she'd called her a bitch.

Fawn couldn't have felt more humiliated.

It wasn't supposed to happen that way. A summons by Fawn for friendship was as rare as the Queen of England granting a Dame Grand Cross. Those who received it were honored to do so and showed their appreciation with total submission.

Knowing Charly, she's already gotten her debate arguments all worked out. And if not now, soon...

At that moment, it occurred to Fawn that if she could confirm it, she'd have the perfect way to get back at Charly.

Steal her arguments.

It would surely be easier than going through the time-suck of creating her own.

But to do it, she'd need Chuck.

He'd spent the past week stewing in the misery of being dumped, Fawn reasoned. By now, he'll be more than ready for a reconciliation.

And no better time than tonight—when everyone could see that their spat was over; that she'd finally forgiven him.

Yes, Chuck would be so grateful.

Even if it meant selling out his sister.

And the makeup sex would be awesome.

She smiled at the thought.

Fawn fairly flew down the floating staircase and out to the grand foyer to the limousine waiting in the McCoppins' circular driveway.

Her parents were already in the backseat. Seamus grumbled, "About damn time! If you'd taken any longer, we'd have missed the damn laser light show—which my firm has sponsored!"

Although a steady regimen of Botox made it impossible for Gretchen's anxiety to show in her face, Fawn heard it in her voice as she hissed, "Your father almost left without you!"

Fawn shrugged. She knew this would never have been the case. Without her, neither of her parents would have had any reason to go to Friday Fun Night.

She was their trophy child.

CHAPTER 21

"You know, it would have been okay for you to miss one Friday Fun Night." Audrey's admonishment to Lavinia was delivered with a hug.

Her mother didn't know it, but Audrey's hugs were how she gauged her mother's condition. Although Lavinia's flowing tops made it difficult to see the subtle changes happening to her body, by wrapping an arm around her mother's waist Audrey could tell that, in just a few weeks' time, Lavinia's body was in full retreat.

Since being sworn to secrecy, Audrey had made it a point to spend as much time with her mother as possible. Dropping the twins to and from school gave her a reason to stop by her mother's office with some make-believe excuse: tidbits about Lavinia's grandchildren, a reminder about some public discussion that might be of interest to her, a quick chat about current events, or, say, the latest news about what project she'd currently initiated for Congressman Blanchard.

If no other excuse presented itself, Audrey would drop off a bouquet of flowers.

On Saturdays, while the rest of the family biked over the Golden Gate Bridge and into Marin County, Audrey cycled over to her mother's house.

Whether it was to return a borrowed book or to drop off fresh fruit from the farmer's market, Lavinia always saw through her excuses. "You'll be here on Sunday, with the rest of the family, helping me in the garden," she reminded her daughter.

"That's different, and you know it. Sometimes I like it when it's just the two of us."

Their time together was more precious than ever before. They both knew that.

They'd sit on the back porch and talk. Lavinia would give updates on her prognosis. If there was none, they gossiped about school business.

Other times, they simply reminisced. It never seemed to surprise Audrey how the prism of time bent their perspectives in different directions. One subject neither had yet to bring up was Egan's departure after Audrey had graduated, nor his triumphant visit three years later.

Audrey wondered if Lavinia had suspected the attraction they'd shared.

Not that it mattered now.

Audrey warned Lavinia that Daniel was working late at the office but had promised to get to the school before the laser light show started. Although it was late September, the days were still warm until the sun set beyond San Francisco's seven hills and the evening's crisp chill set in.

The crowd milling around on AA's central campus green was thick and animated. Chuck was nowhere to be found, but Audrey spotted Charly sitting on a picnic table with Manya, Zina, and Sienna, laughing and talking.

Like moths drawn to a lamp on a dark night, a few boys hovered nearby. Audrey recognized Quest among them. His parents were on tour through the weekend. Just a month older than the twins, the three had grown up together like siblings, along with Sienna and Zina.

They'll always be there for each other, Audrey realized. Just like Bliss, Tallulah, and Davis are for me.

As it should be.

Sensing her daughter's pride, Lavinia murmured, "There is so much of you in sweet Charly. And her father too, of course."

At the thought of Egan, shame flamed in Audrey's cheeks.

Lavinia didn't see it because she leaned into her daughter. Her sigh indicated what Audrey already suspected: Lavinia's regimen of chemotherapy was sapping her vitality.

Not that she'd ever admit it.

Additional evidence of this: the note card in Lavinia's hand with prompts for the announcements she'd make before the light show. In the past, Lavinia had always been able to ad-lib in front of audiences.

Lavinia has to tell the school. They are her family. They are her community.

Now, having noted the concern in her daughter's eyes, Lavinia answered Audrey before the question was even out of her mouth:

"Yes, I'm tired. And yes, sometimes I tend to forget a thing or two. But no, my sweet Audrey. *Not yet.* I can still fight this."

Audrey nodded. It broke her heart that Lavinia had chosen to battle her cancer in silence. But she also knew that she had to honor her mother's wishes.

To the very end.

Lavinia scanned the crowd. "The McCoppins are finally here. Good! Now I can thank Seamus for underwriting this event. Excuse me, dear." She pecked Audrey on the cheek and then made her way to the stage to address the happy, unsuspecting crowd.

"She's quite a lady." At the sound of Egan's voice, Audrey's heart raced.

She didn't turn around. She hoped—she prayed—that if he didn't get a response, he'd just figure that she hadn't heard him. Then, instead of repeating it—instead of making a fool of himself, of them both—he'd slink off into the night, burying himself in the crowd.

It would be just like Egan to run away again, she reasoned. He always looked for the easy out.

But no, that wasn't fair: damning him whether he did or didn't finish what he'd started.

In this case, a mere attempt at a conversation.

It was a long time ago. Daniel is funding Egan's chair.

Egan is teaching the twins.

Our children.

For everyone's sake I need to be civil.

I need to keep my cool.

She turned to face him. "Thank you for that. It's been a mutual admiration society, hasn't it?"

"Us?" His question seemed hopeful.

"Yes, of course!" She hoped to put him at ease by nodding. "Lavinia has always had such a high opinion of you too. You proved her right."

"Good to know." Despite his words, he sounded disappointed. Immediately, he tried to hide it with a smile. "Audrey, I was overwhelmed by Daniel's generosity! Shocked, frankly."

Audrey's guffaw was involuntary. Embarrassed by it, she added, "To tell you the truth, I was too."

"I see." He looked away, dismayed.

Her reaction had been honest. But she could see how he could have interpreted it as also being cruel.

Audrey shook her head. "By that, I meant to say it was *unexpected.* But Daniel loves Lavinia and the school. The money was a legacy from his mother for the children's education. They both see it as a worthy cause."

Her words seemed to put him at ease. "Thank you for that. Speaking of Chuck and Charly—"

Does he suspect? Her heart pounded at the thought.

"I'm truly impressed with their diligence in my class. They're both excellent essay writers and they have no problem with grasping some of the Old English nuances."

Realizing her fears were for naught, relief flooded over her.

A wave of surprise hit her next. Incredulously, she asked, "Chuck too?"

Egan laughed. "To be honest, he had a rocky start. Some male posturing. You know, playing the cock of the walk—"

Gee, I wonder where he gets that from...

"But he's fallen into line. He split up with the girl he was trying to impress. That helped tremendously." Egan took a deep breath: "Listen, Audrey, there's something I need to ask you."

Oh no, she thought, here it comes! He's going to bring up that awful day...

Suddenly he stopped. Apparently, something had caught his eye.

Audrey followed his gaze.

He was staring at Chuck and Fawn.

Arm in arm, laughing, they were slipping away from the crowd, but then paused beside the largest tree on the green—an ancient live oak. They looked around. Then, assuming no one was watching, they kissed.

Deeply.

Too long.

Chuck's hand slipped under Fawn's top.

She stopped it from reaching her breast. Instead, she held onto it, pulling him with her toward one of the school's buildings: the old gym.

The blood drained from Audrey's face when she realized where they were headed, and why.

"At least, I thought he'd come to his senses." Egan scowled. "Don't worry. I'll take care of this before things get out of hand."

He took off after them.

THE ROOMS THAT ONCE HELD THE OLD GYM'S LOCKERS WERE NOW USED FOR storage: mostly desks and chairs that had yet to be given away or junked.

The first door, to the old boys' room, was locked. Fawn giggled when Chuck hooted upon discovering that the second door's latch was broken.

The only light in the room filtered in through its high windows. Long shadows danced about the clutter.

Fawn pushed Chuck through the door and then shoved him down onto an empty backless bench. In no time, she was straddling him.

Her mouth was voracious for his. Their kisses—endless and sweet— concluded with hungry groans: Chuck's.

"I can't hold back much longer," he warned her.

"You'll have to," she declared. "I'm in charge here. Now"—she cupped him so hard that he grunted—"and forever. Do you get that?"

"Yes m'am," he murmured.

"That's better."

Before Chuck could stop her, Fawn yanked his tee shirt over his head. Next she went for his belt buckle. After pulling the leather strap from his jeans, she grabbed his arms. Flinging them over his head, she used the belt to tether them to the bench.

She then yanked off one sneaker and then the other, throwing them over her shoulders.

Finally, she slowly unzipped his jeans and pulled them to his knees. Chuck moaned, "Fawn...*please*...I'm busting here—"

"I said, shut up!" To make her point, Fawn tweaked his nipple.

Chuck yelped.

They both screamed when the lights went on.

WHEN THEIR EYES ADJUSTED TO THE LIGHT, THEY SAW HIM:

Egan. He was standing at the doorway.

Fawn leaped up too quickly, toppling to the floor with a thud on her hands and knees. "Ouch! *Shit!*"

Egan ignored her. He was too fascinated with the belt knot she'd contrived. Clapping slowly, he murmured, "Wow! I don't think a horny psycho sailor could have done any better!"

"What the hell are you doing here?" Chuck muttered.

"Saving you both from a suspension—I hope." He picked up one of Chuck's shoes and tossed it at him.

Unfortunately, it landed on Chuck's erection.

The boy groaned. Reflexively, his legs curled up toward his waist.

Catching Fawn's eye, Egan nodded toward Chuck. "Untie the poor kid."

Fawn smirked, "Is that really what you want? I mean, you followed us, right? Admit it. Wouldn't you rather watch?"

"What, you think I'd get off on some sort of teen porn amateur hour? I'll pass." Egan shrugged. "How old are you anyway?"

"Seventeen," Fawn looked up from the task of undoing her handiwork in order to wink at him.

"How about you, Chuck?"

"The same," Chuck growled. "What does it matter to you?"

"I'm trying to assess who between the two of you would end up in prison, and what kind of sentence you'd get, is all."

Chuck's shackle was loose enough that he could wrench away from it and sit up. "What the hell are you talking about?"

"In this state, even consenting teens under the age of eighteen can be tried for statutory rape. It would probably be considered a misdemeanor, but it would still carry some penalties: up to a year in a juvenile detention facility. Oh, and up to a thousand-dollar fine. Depends on the judge."

Fawn took Chuck's hand in hers. Solemnly, she declared, "I would never say you raped me. Cross my heart."

"That's really touching, Fawn." Egan pretended to wipe away a tear. "But the real question is whether Chuck feels the need to press charges against *you*." He pointed to the belt in her hand. "You lured him into this prison and tied him up. Hey, if Chuck's mom hadn't seen you coerce him down here, who knows if I'd have stopped you in time?"

Chuck stared at Egan. "*Shit! Shit!* My *mom* knows I'm down here?"

"She suspects…something." Egan shrugged. "But, hey, no one wants to get you"—his eyes went from Chuck to Fawn—"or you kicked out of school. So here's the deal. This sort of extracurricular activity doesn't happen on campus anymore. Understand? From now on, if you treat AA with the respect it deserves—that is, hallowed ground, considering all the time, effort, and money your parents give it—I'll pretend I didn't find you together down here." He pointed toward the door. "Fawn, you take off first."

He didn't have to ask her twice.

"Put your pants on," Egan muttered to Chuck. "If your mom asks, I never found you."

Mollified, Chuck did as he was told. But as he zipped up, he stammered, "So…so you're not going to tell her you saw me like—you know, like this?"

"And embarrass her?" *Yet again? Hell no.* "I have too much respect for her," Egan muttered. "And I know you do too."

Chuck nodded. He glanced around for the other shoe.

Spotting it, Egan picked it up and tossed it to him.

This time, Chuck caught it with one hand. "Thanks." His tone was sincere. "Mom…she has a lot on her mind these days."

"Oh? How can you tell?"

Chuck snickered as he untied the second shoe. "I've known her all my life! I can tell when something is bothering her."

I wish I'd known her all your life too…

For a second, Egan wondered what it might have been like to have a child with Audrey.

Now, knowing Chuck, he shook his head at the thought of all the drama he'd avoided.

And all the love he'd missed.

"Turn off the light when you leave," Egan muttered gruffly as he walked out the door.

EGAN REACHED AUDREY JUST AS THE LASER LIGHT SHOW WAS BEGINNING. As each beam flared and pulsed to the syncopated music, the cheers grew louder.

Audrey leaned in close to ask, "Did you find them?"

"Yes!" He had to shout for her to hear him. "They were headed over to the buffet table. But just in case the chef's special works as an aphrodisiac, I checked all the doors to the building. They were locked, so I don't think—"

"Wait! I don't know if I heard you!" she shouted.

He moved in so close that their eyes were only inches away.

Their lips too.

Egan fought the urge to kiss her. And yet, he wondered if Audrey would have been shocked or upset by it.

Or if her mouth would have accepted his eagerly, willingly.

If Chuck were right and she was anxious about something, a kiss would tell him what he'd suspected:

It's because of me.

Egan looked into her eyes, hoping to find his answer there. Instead he found relief.

She was smiling again.

This was verified when she shouted, "Did you say the *buffet table*? And that the building was all locked up? Thank goodness! That's all Lavinia needs—some reason for Seamus to pull his little princess from the school!" Audrey grimaced. "Not with...everything else Lavinia is going through." The moment the words were out of her mouth, she pursed her lips as if daring anything else to come out.

There were so many lasers beaming up in the sky that Egan could see the single tear that had fallen onto Audrey's cheek.

How he longed to touch it.

But...why is she crying?

He then remembered that just before they'd seen Chuck and Fawn sneak off, he was going to mention his concerns about her mother.

She's not worried about me. She's worried about Lavinia.

"Audrey, before I went after Chuck, I wanted to ask you something. Remember?"

Her smile faded as she nodded solemnly.

"It's about Lavinia. Is she...well?"

Egan had seen such deep sorrow in Audrey's eyes only once before: the afternoon they'd made love.

She hung her head so low that he had to bow his head to hear her say, "Lavinia...has cancer. But no one knows about it yet." Audrey turned slightly so that he could see her lips as if assuring that he couldn't mistake what she said next: "You're the only other person who knows. I can't even tell Daniel because he's on the board, and he'd have a fiduciary responsibility to inform the others. Some of them would want to force her out!" Suddenly, Audrey clasped her hand to her mouth. "Oh my God! I forgot— *you're also on the board!*" The tears were now falling furiously. "Egan, please...I'm begging you..."

So that she'd calm down, Egan held tight to both her hands. "Audrey, it's okay! I'll do anything you ask! You know that. I... I love her."

And I love you.

Audrey was so grateful that she kissed his cheek.

Egan looked skyward, feigning awe of the colorful beams flaring over their heads. In truth, he was memorizing the soft touch of her kiss.

ALL NIGHT LONG, MIRANDA HAD BEEN WATCHING EGAN FOR TELLTALE SIGNS that word of the Mandy Blackwell lawsuit had finally gotten to him. Unfortunately, he never had time to break away from the throng of fawning parents surrounding him—Gretchen McCoppin included—so that she could sidle over and wean it out of him.

Finally, when Egan had broken clear of the parents, he'd walked over to Audrey.

Old emotions surged through her:

Hate. Spite. Retaliation.

She'd vowed to destroy them. To that end, tonight couldn't have been scripted any better.

At the same time, Seamus cornered Miranda to gripe about the dearth of Easy-A classes offered at the school.

Or, as he put it: "With all the AP-class overachievers out there, how else is a normal kid supposed to get into Yale these days?"

When Daniel strolled onto the campus green, Miranda realized he was the perfect foil for both conundrums.

Seamus was the type who resented knowing someone else was a bigger priority. To interrupt his bellyaching, she declared, "You'll have to excuse me. I promised to take Daniel McKittridge over to Egan the minute he came in. It was so smart of him to underwrite our celebrity teacher, what with the twins taking Egan's AP Comp Lit class and all. Don't you agree? Not that I'm inferring that it'll guarantee A's to either Chuck or Charly. Why neither of them is *half* as clever as your Fawn..."

Seamus' scowl was proof she'd hit her mark.

And how convenient for Egan to be wooing Audrey at the very second her husband spotted her!

"Oh, gosh—*is that Audrey and Egan?* Looks like they're having a ball, catching up on the good old days!" Just in case Daniel missed the view of his wife through the clearing in the crowd, Miranda thought it worth pointing them out—

Locking lips, no less!

At least, it looked as if that were happening.

Granted, it was nighttime, and the light show was creating all sorts of shadows. Still, their body language was unmistakable:

Concern. Trust. Intimacy.

My God—they still feel something for each other!

To be heard over the band, Miranda cooed in Daniel's ear, "That's so Egan! Ever the flirt! He's been at it all night long!"

"Really? With Audrey?" Daniel squinted for a better look.

"Well, I don't want to speak out of school, but of all the moms, he's certainly sweet on her in particular—"

"Look, Miranda, you don't have to be so concerned." He put his arm around her. Then, leaning in so that she could hear him above the crowd and music, he added, "I mean, look at all you've got going for yourself! Any man would be proud to have you at his side. You're the full package: sharp, beautiful, and confident—"

Miranda let that sink in. *He's so jealous that he's coming on to me? My God, breaking up Audrey's marriage will be easier than I thought!*

And so much fun!

"—which is why there's no need for you to feel the least bit insecure. I'm sure Egan realizes that too. If not, hey, I'll be glad to give him a subtle heads-up."

What the hell? He thinks I'm pining over Egan?

"Frankly, I think you'd make a cute couple. All he needs is a little nudge in your direction." Daniel nodded toward Egan. "Oh, hey, look! Audrey's spotted us." He waved at his wife. "We should walk over."

"Sadly, I'm still on duty," Miranda purred. "You go ahead."

She didn't know what made her angrier: that he assumed she thought so little of herself, or that he had an unshakable trust in his wife's fidelity.

On both counts, she was determined to prove him wrong.

---

*R*ELIEF.

That was what Audrey felt when Egan reassured her that Chuck and Fawn weren't up to anything that would embarrass Lavinia.

She felt it too when, to her shock, Egan's solemn query hadn't been about the secret she feared he'd one day guess—that the twins were his—but the secret that now haunted her every waking moment: Lavinia's illness.

I can trust Egan.

Audrey saw it in his eyes. He too loved Lavinia and would do anything to protect her.

Exuberance had driven Audrey's desire to kiss him: chastely, on the cheek. With the appreciation one friend felt for another.

She knew he'd understand; that he wouldn't mind her taking such a liberty. Lavinia had brought them together. Now, Lavinia's secret was what bound them.

That, and the twins.

The thought that she'd never be able to share that with Egan—with anyone—had the weight of a boulder tossed into an ocean and always tumbling through the black water of her shame.

Would its fall ever hit rock bottom? Could it ever find its way back to the surface?

Shamefaced, she turned away from Egan.

Her eyes fell upon a familiar figure: Daniel.

He had his arm around a woman—

Miranda.

The way their faces were angled, she could tell they were talking earnestly.

Or maybe they're…

Kissing?

Misplaced guilt, Audrey warned herself.

Or was it?

Just then, Daniel looked up. Having noticed that she was staring at him, he gave her a wave.

Whatever he said next had Miranda smirking. Her eyes followed Daniel as he walked to his wife.

The look on Miranda's face sent a chill through Audrey.

What did Daniel say to her?

She was still shivering when Daniel reached her side. Putting his arm around her, he declared, "You two look as if you're enjoying the show."

Audrey forced herself to smile before turning to him. Taking his arm in hers, she declared, "Just a couple of old friends, playing catch up."

She couldn't believe how normal she sounded.

She'd become such a casual liar.

Secrets do that to a person, she reasoned.

For the first time since they'd married, Audrey wondered how many secrets Daniel had kept from her as well.

CHAPTER 22

"*W*e're live!" Riley shouted to Lionel and SallyAnne.

Hearing that, his team leaders high-fived each other. They then picked up their earphones.

Their court order not only allowed them to monitor Miranda's incoming and outgoing calls, but it also gave them the right to track text and emails sent out of, and going into, all of her devices, and to review previous messages.

Upon discovering that Miranda used a virtual assistant app—and that she also recorded every conversation, either on the phone or live—her cell phone also gave them a way to use it as a real-time listening device.

"Gotta love Siri!" Riley crowed. "She and Alexa are law enforcement's BFFs!"

"Where's Miranda now?" Lionel asked.

"She's still at the school. She has to stay late for some sort of board meeting," Riley replied. "But, hey, great news! Lover Boy will be there too." He wiggled his brows.

"Ha!" SallyAnne snickered. "This is better than a soap opera."

"So, who wants to wager whether Smallwood will do what he promised and get her voted onto the trustee board?" Lionel asked.

"With all the blowjobs she's given him to—well, shall we say 'pump him up'—I'd say it's a done deal," Riley retorted.

Lionel grimaced. "Ladies present," he muttered.

SallyAnne felt her cheeks warm up. Had Lionel just laughed, she would have too. She'd worked in law enforcement far too long to be offended by a high-testosterone quip. Still, she appreciated Lionel's sensitivity on her behalf.

Riley rolled his eyes. "SallyAnne's no lady. She's one of us."

To change the topic, SallyAnne snapped, "*Shhh*—listen! She's meeting with someone *right now...*"

TODAY'S THE BIG DAY, MIRANDA THOUGHT.

After what she'd observed on Friday Family Fun Night, she knew how it would go down:

Those who would vote to add her to the board would be Jess and Seamus, along with Darius and Warner.

If Lavinia was against it, those assured to vote her way were Tallulah, Blanchard, Bliss, and Daniel.

Egan was the wild card.

Maybe Blanchard would pull a no-show. True, his name added gravitas to the school and to the board. But after perusing minutes from the past two years, odds were fifty-fifty that he'd be absent.

And if not, the vote could deadlock at four against four.

No matter what happened, the only chance she'd have to get on the board was to flip one of them.

Egan was the likeliest choice.

Damn it, Miranda thought. I wasted my time flirting with Daniel on Friday Family Fun Night! If only I'd walked over to Egan and Audrey with him. It would have been so easy to flirt with him instead of trying to turn Daniel's head.

One thing would have led to another. Maybe he'd have suggested they christen his new apartment.

A disgusting notion, but hey—she would have said yes.

Anything to lock up his vote.

There was still time to do it.

Egan would be in his classroom, killing time before the meeting.

She knew exactly what to say.

MIRANDA KNOCKED ON EGAN'S DOOR AND WAITED FOR HIM TO CALL OUT, "Enter at your own risk."

She peeked in. "Hey, got a minute?"

"Sure. What's up?"

Melodramatically, she looked down the hall—first one way, then the other—before stepping over the threshold and closing the door behind her. "I need someone I can trust. You were the first person who came to mind"—she forced a blush—"well, except for my mother."

"I guess I should be flattered," Egan muttered.

"If you knew her, you would be," Miranda dabbed away an imaginary tear from the corner of her eye. "Listen, I overheard something I shouldn't —about school business— and it concerns me! But it's not something I feel comfortable bringing up with the Trustee board because"—Miranda sighed mightily—"some members of the board are involved."

That got Egan's attention. "What are they doing?"

"They want to usurp Lavinia's policies! Can you imagine? I mean, her philosophy is why this school was founded in the first place! It's also why the school has been so successful! But here's the problem: right now, the way the board is made up, Lavinia is at risk of losing the majority vote."

"From what I can tell, Lavinia is usually opposed by Seamus McCoppin, Darius Calder, Warner Crowley, and Jess Smallwood. That's four members," Egan pointed out. "On the other hand, those who vote with her are lock-solid: Congressman Blanchard, Tallulah, Bliss, and Daniel are on her side on every vote. And, of course, me too. So that makes six. She's got a clear majority."

"Thank goodness for your loyalty," Miranda murmured. He confirmed what she'd suspected: Seamus could never win—

Unless she were on the board too.

And she controlled Egan's vote.

"But you're wrong about one of her lock-solids." Miranda made her lip quiver, then added: "Daniel."

Egan's eyes opened wide. "But...he's her son-in-law!"

"He's also the senior partner of a firm that counts Seamus, Jess, and Warner among its clients."

"Jesus!" Egan frowned.

"Tell me about it! Even if Daniel votes with Seamus' block, board rules call for a *supermajority*. That means sixty percent or more," Miranda explained. "To get it, tonight Seamus is going to ask the board to eliminate one of the two PTA representatives on the board. His rationale is that the bylaws only allow for one representative from the PTA. If he succeeds, he'll wipe out Lavinia's majority."

"I'd never vote against Lavinia. Neither would Harris and whichever PTA representative was left on the board," Egan declared. "With Lavinia, that's four votes."

"Still, she needs another lock-solid ally. That's where I think you can help." Miranda perched herself on Egan's desk: better to lean in and make her point, not to mention position her breasts at eye-level. "To counteract Seamus' ploy, why don't you suggest adding another member from the staff? In fact, if you suggest me, they may actually go for it since I play such a valuable role in helping their children." She rolled her eyes. "It's embarrassing, the things they'll say or do to coerce me into giving their kids special attention!"

"Well, sure! Anything to keep the status quo."

Miranda reached over and put her hand over his. "I knew I could count on you!" Her fingers stroked the back of his hand. She leaned in, so close that their faces were only inches apart—

Until Egan eased back. "Listen, Miranda...I'm flattered. Really, I am! But..."

He's turning me down? How dare he!...

Because of her:

Audrey.

So, I'm right—he still lusting for her.

Bingo!

"Forgive me!" Miranda forced her lip to quiver. "It was wrong for me to—to assume you might feel anything..." She bowed her head, as if shamed. "Look, I get it. The last thing you need is...is *another* rejection."

Egan frowned. "What are you talking about?"

"You...and Audrey." She shrugged. "What the two of you shared. It was beautiful."

Egan's hand stiffened under her touch. "How...do you know about that?"

So Audrey and Egan did have an affair!

"I was in the women's restroom in the teachers' lounge—in one of the stalls. Audrey walked in. She thought it was empty so she called someone. From what I could tell, she was on with her shrink. She was upset about...*about running into you.*" Miranda paused dramatically. "She said... she said it broke her heart to see you again after...after what had happened between you."

Egan hung his head.

It's true, alright.

"At that point, I couldn't just come out of the stall, could I? I was stuck in there until she hung up and walked out!" Miranda forced a sob. "You won't tell anyone I overheard, will you?"

"Of course I won't say anything! I mean—I certainly don't want anyone to know—" Egan put his hands on her shoulders so that she had to look him in the eye—"and neither would Audrey. Please, Miranda. Do you understand what I'm saying?"

"Daniel doesn't know, does he?" She stared back at him.

Egan eyes darkened with his sadness. "No."

Even if Egan hadn't said it, she could read it in his eyes.

"And...I promised myself he'd never hear it from me." He dropped his hands to his side. "So...I'm begging you..."

"You don't have to do that, Egan. Your secret—yours and Audrey's—is safe with me." She winked. "We'll always have each other's backs. Deal?"

"Deal." He held out his hand.

As if sealing their promise, Miranda pulled him in close—
But this time, it was for a chaste kiss on the cheek instead.
She slid off the desk. She knew his eyes were on her as she smoothed her tight, short pencil skirt back into place.
And she was sure his eyes were following as she walked out the door.

BY THE TIME EGAN MADE IT TO THE MEETING, MOST OF THE OTHERS WERE already there, including Miranda.
She was standing between Seamus and Jess, and probably playing the suck-up, he reasoned.
She returned his wave with a smile and a wink.
Certainly, having Miranda at the meetings would make the damn things more palatable, Egan thought.
He remembered how she'd stroked his fingers. Obviously, she was open to moving their relationship beyond mere co-workers.
Maybe we can go out for drinks afterward. And if one thing leads to another…
I can't keep pining after Audrey. I have to open my heart to other possibilities, other women.
Maybe Miranda's the one.
Daniel was there too, of course. He was in another corner of the room, talking to Tallulah, Bliss, and some guy he'd never met but somehow looked familiar…
I know him…the rocker, Jammerhead. He's Tallulah's husband!
Jammerhead was dressed in the standard uniform for aging rock stars: a black tee-shirt, slim-cut tight black jeans, and boots. His long, graying hair was pulled back into a ponytail.
Tallulah was scowling. She had her arms wrapped around her waist as if shielding herself from assault.
The way she was shaking, Egan realized he had it wrong. She was holding herself back from doing something she'd regret.
And from the way she was glaring at Seamus, Miranda, and Jess, Egan guessed one of them was the culprit of her distress.
For some odd reason, Cornell had also shown up at the trustee meeting. Egan waved at him and walked over. "What, are you a glutton for punishment?"
"Not this kind, that's for sure." Cornell frowned. "Believe me, I wish I were here to beg for a grant for AA's robotics team. As it turns out, I've got a serious issue to report." He leaned in and hissed, "Student related."
Cornell was interrupted when Seamus barked, "Where the hell is Lavinia? This meeting was supposed to start fifteen minutes ago!"
"I vote we begin without her," Jess declared.
"I second the motion," Warner Crowley harrumphed.

"All in favor?" Seamus thundered.

"Excuse me, but I'm Lavinia's proxy until she arrives," Daniel reminded him.

Seamus waved his hand through the air as if shooing a fly. "Well, then get on with it, McKittridge."

Ah, great. This is going to be a hell of a night, Egan thought.

After Daniel called the meeting to order, he declared, "We've got several items on the agenda that need our immediate attention. First off, Miranda has an update on the senior students' college admissions process." He cleared his throat, then added, "We also have a student disciplinary issue to discuss."

"I called in with an agenda item too," Seamus said. "Why isn't it being noted?"

Daniel glanced down at the page on the table in front of him. "I don't see it here, but we can add it at the end."

"No. After Ms. D'Arcy's report, perhaps," Seamus countered. "It's short and sweet, and I'm sure everyone will agree."

"I'm glad you feel so confident about it." Daniel's sarcasm earned him a frown from Seamus. He ignored it. Instead, he glanced over at Tallulah, who shrugged.

Daniel nodded. "Okay, no problem. Miranda, why don't you begin?"

Miranda smiled sweetly. "I'm happy to report that eighty-four percent of our seniors did as well, or better, on their most recent SATs than on prior attempts. As for those who did not score as hoped, I've already sent emails encouraging them to attend the practice drills being held twice a week up to the last SAT date before the college admissions deadline."

"Great idea," Darius declared. "Zina will be signed up for it, that's for sure. She freezes during that damn test."

"That is certainly something I may be able to help her with," Miranda murmured. "Feel free to see me after the meeting so that we can discuss it further."

Darius nodded.

"Anything else, Miranda?" Daniel asked.

"Yes." Miranda pursed her lips. "Frankly, like Darius just pointed out, there are many reasons for tepid SAT scores. It's one of the reasons I'd like prep sessions to be compulsory as opposed to optional."

"Just do it," Seamus huffed.

"That's just it..." Miranda grimaced. "It goes against school policy."

"Maybe it's time for a new policy," Jess replied.

"But Lavinia's philosophy is that students shouldn't be forced to do anything; that they should be allowed to come to their own decisions," Miranda explained. "That includes prepping for college—or not."

"Bullshit!" Seamus retorted. "If that were the case, they'd all be parked on our couches watching reality TV twenty-four-seven! Let's put it to a vote, right here and now! I move that SAT prep sessions be compulsory for seniors."

"I second that motion," Jess added.

Daniel frowned. Finally he declared, "Those in favor?"

Jess, Seamus, Darius, and Warner raised their hands.

"Opposed?"

Daniel, Tallulah, Bliss, and Harris raised their hands.

Daniel turned to Egan. "What about you?"

Egan shrugged. "Here's a hypothetical: A student comes up to you and says, 'I know English I is mandatory, but I don't feel I need it because I already speak English, so I'm not taking it.' AA wouldn't allow him to graduate until he did. Am I right?"

Everyone nodded.

"We make certain classes compulsory because, at this time in their young lives, our judgment may be better than their own. Agreed?"

Again, the others nodded.

"Then I have to say that Miranda has a good point. AA students excel because we give them every opportunity to succeed. To that end, we hired the best college admissions consultant we could find, and she's doing everything she can to prepare them for the next stage of their lives—including ongoing SAT Prep." He nodded in Miranda's direction. "No one is saying that every AA student has to go to college, or when. But even if they never go, having taken the SAT when they were at their best and brightest will be yet another accomplishment. And if within five years they've changed their minds and want to further their education, *the test score is still valid*. They'll have one fewer admissions hurdle to worry about." He let that sink in. "So, yes, I vote that SAT test prep should be mandatory for those who score below a certain threshold. It's just as important as English I, or Algebra I, or any compulsory History class. It is the best skill preparation for the next stage of their lives."

The table was silent.

Finally Daniel said, "Then the motion passes."

For the first time all night, Seamus broke out into a smug grin.

Across the table, Miranda caught Egan's eye and mouthed the words, *thank you*.

For the first time in a while, he felt he'd done something right, and for all the right reasons.

"Thank you, Miranda, for your report," Daniel murmured. "Now, for our next new business item. Seamus, you're up."

Noting that Miranda was gathering her notes to leave, Seamus said, "Ms. D'Arcy, if you wouldn't mind staying."

Miranda froze, wide-eyed.

"I'm very impressed with the initiative Ms. D'Arcy has taken on AA's behalf. In fact, I'm so appreciative that I'd like to like to move we expand the trustee board to include Miranda D'Arcy as a permanent member instead of a periodic advisor."

"I second that motion," Jess declared.

Egan noticed Cornell and Jammerhead exchanging flabbergasted stares. Blanchard's face lost all its color.

Instinctively, Egan's eyes moved to Miranda. Her face reflected similar shock and awe.

Well, what do you know! She's impressed Seamus enough that he's deluded himself that she'll be another of his trustee board pawns.

And now I don't have to bring it up, thank goodness.

"Wait...*Expanding the board*...without Lavinia's input?" Tallulah exclaimed. "That's not just audacious, it's obnoxious!"

"I agree, Tallulah. In fact, I refuse to put that to a vote without Lavinia present," Daniel replied.

"There is nothing in the bylaws that says Lavinia has to be present for every vote," Jess pointed out.

Realizing he was right, Daniel frowned. He turned to Miranda. "If offered, would you take the position?"

She glanced around the table as if considering the suggestion for the first time. Finally, she murmured, "It would be an honor! Yes, of course, I will!"

"The motion has been made," Seamus insisted. "We must vote on it."

Reluctantly, Daniel nodded. "Those in favor?"

Not surprising, Jess, Darius, and Warner voted yes along with Seamus.

And, as expected, Tallulah, Bliss, and Harris voted no.

Egan was surprised that Daniel also voted no.

Miranda was wrong about him.

Daniel pointed to Egan. "It's a tie. Which way are you voting?"

Instinctively, Egan looked at Miranda. She was staring down at the papers in front of her.

He remembered her earlier words: *We'll always have each other's backs.*

She'd already vowed to cover his—regarding his tryst with Audrey. Even if mere friendship was as far as their relationship were to go, at least his yes vote now would prove he too was as worthy of her trust.

And it certainly wasn't the worst *quid pro quo.*

"I'll always welcome another AA administrator to the board, especially someone with insights to the momentous task of running a school and whose life is dedicated to the students' success," Egan murmured softly. "I vote yes."

For Lavinia.

"The motion passes." Daniel cleared his throat. "Miranda, welcome to the board."

DANIEL THEN MOTIONED TOWARD CORNELL AND JAMMERHEAD.

"Cornell is here because of a student disciplinary issue that happened in his classroom." He turned to Cornell. "Do you wish to explain?"

Cornell nodded. "I intercepted the sale of five grams of cocaine between"—he nodded toward Jammerhead—"Quest Wishart-Jammerhead and Hugo Smallwood. I caught them in the middle of the act. Unfortunately, I couldn't tell who was selling and who was buying. And neither student will admit to bringing it into our school."

As if watching a three-way tennis match, the others shifted their gazes from Tallulah's scowl to Jammerhead's stare and then to Jess' smirk.

Jess pointed a finger at Jammerhead. "How dare your kid try to get my kid hooked on snow!"

Jammerhead's back stiffened. "Are you crazy? Drugs are forbidden in our home!"

"Bullshit!" Jess replied. "You rock stars are all the same—sex, drugs, and groupies all over the place!"

"Are you kidding me?" Tallulah stood up, glowering. "Everyone at school knows your son is one of the biggest high school dealers in the city!"

She stared pointedly at Seamus, who was smirking.

Tallulah guffawed mirthlessly. "See what I mean? Gee, Jess, if you really didn't know about it, I guess Hugo doesn't trust you enough with his revenue to make you his investment advisor."

Jess snickered. "Since when does the queen of the groupies care that her kid snorts, anyway?"

Tallulah leaped up.

Daniel placed his hand over hers. "Tallulah, please."

Still glaring at Jess, slowly she sat down.

"Let's continue, folks. Now, as we all know, the school's policy on this issue is strict: no illegal drugs on campus. If caught, it means formal expulsion." Daniel let that sink in. "Considering the severity of the offense, the board is entrusted to note for the record its adherence to school policy. Tallulah and Jess already know they must recuse themselves from the board's decision."

"Wait," Jess interjected. "If you have to vote on it, does that mean the board can vote *against* it too? You know, make an exception?"

Daniel shook his head. "AA's handbook is very clear on the subject. The vote is merely a formality."

Miranda raised her hand. "May I make a suggestion?"

"Yes, sure," Daniel replied.

"Quest and Hugo are seniors. Expulsion will ruin their chances for college." She scanned the faces around the table. "Is that truly what we want to happen for them?"

The room was silent.

Of course not, Egan thought. It might just as well have been one of their kids.

Finally, Harris spoke: "If word gets out that the trustee board made an exception for two of its own children, we'll have to do so for the next student who breaks the rule; and the one after that. And parents will expect leniency on other infractions as well."

"He's right," Tallulah muttered.

Jammerhead nodded as if accepting his son's fate.

"I'm not suggesting that we *don't* punish the students," Miranda explained. "Perhaps a suspension—say, two weeks—and two months of community service."

"I second the motion!" Seamus barked.

"You're jumping the gun again, Seamus." Daniel sighed. Turning to Miranda, he asked, "Is that a motion?"

She nodded uncomfortably. "I move that we offer these students a two-week suspension, along with two months of community service. Everyone makes mistakes, right?"

"Yes. And sometimes the consequences have an irreversible ripple effect." Despite this admonishment, Daniel added, "Okay, then, all in favor?"

Seamus, Warner, and Darius raised their hands along with Miranda.

"Opposed?" Daniel added.

His hand went up, as did those of Harris and Bliss.

Egan didn't know how to vote. The right thing to do was expulsion. Still—

"Please forgive me for being so late. I had to take care of a ...an emergency." Lavinia stood at the door.

She looked around the room. Noting the number of guests, she smiled quizzically as she took her usual seat. "Now, tell me. What did I miss?"

To Daniel's credit, his narrative of the meeting was both concise and positive.

Lavinia blinked twice at the news that the board had voted to make the

SATs mandatory and testing below AA's historic average the litmus for mandatory prep as well.

"Egan had an interesting point about it." Daniel nodded toward the man in question. "Testing and prep are wonderful services that the school provides. However, considering the school's mission, it should be as compulsory as, say, English or Math. It doesn't mean the student has to actually *apply* to any university upon graduation or afterward. But it does assure them an easier acceptance should they decide to do so, either immediately or within five years."

"I see," Lavinia murmured. When she shifted her gaze to Egan, he couldn't help it: suddenly, he felt like a sellout.

He felt even worse when, resignedly, she shrugged.

She turned back to Daniel. "Go on."

"Cornell is here to report a disciplinary problem. Two students engaged in a drug purchase during class. Cornell confiscated the item —cocaine."

Lavinia sighed. "The school handbook is clear. AA enforces a strict policy for such matters."

"Yes, well..." Daniel hesitated. "The majority felt that, since two seniors were involved, we should lessen the punishment to a two-week suspension and two months of community service. That way, the punishment would have no effect on their college applications."

"The point of punishment is to teach a lesson," Lavinia replied.

"Why such a harsh one—for just one stupid mistake?" Jess countered.

"Was the student's mistake in selling an illegal drug, or selling it and getting caught doing so?" Lavinia asked. "And had it been off campus— say, across the street in the park—and the sale had been to an undercover police officer, wouldn't the consequence be even worse?"

"Of course, it shouldn't have taken place at all, either off or on campus," Jammerhead insisted.

"Says the guy who writes songs about his highs," Jess retorted.

Jammerhead smacked the table with an open palm. "Like I said before, asshole—*I don't sell drugs, and neither does my kid!*"

Jess shrugged. "In either case, Ashbury Academy isn't the police. And if it were, a donation to the Police Benevolent Society or our illustrious mayor's re-election campaign would get the matter taken care of with a hell of a lot less fuss."

"I'm sorry you find me harder to bribe than our local law enforcement," Lavinia replied.

"Some of us cover the costs of those who might have ended up as juvenile delinquents if they weren't here!" Jess snarled. "With all due respect, Lavinia, it should count for something!"

Lavinia closed her eyes.

She looks so tired, Egan thought.

Knowing her plight, his heart went out to her.

When Lavinia's eyes opened again, she said, "Yes, thank you, Jess. Having our scholarships covered by the families of those students who don't receive them is very much appreciated. Now, about the situation at hand: I take it that this motion for a more lenient disciplinary action is to be the exception, *not* the rule?"

"Yes," Daniel glared at Seamus, as if to say, *don't push it further.*

Seamus nodded once.

"Good," Lavinia said. "Anything else I should know about?"

Daniel nodded. "Well… It was suggested that we add an additional board member—Miranda."

Lavinia looked over at her.

Miranda nodded and smiled.

"And why is that?" Lavinia asked.

"Isn't it obvious?" Jess replied. "The board is evenly divided in its philosophies on how to run the school, which increases odds for a stalemate," he smirked. "I for one hesitated to vote for yet another staff person who may use it to curry favor with you, Lavinia. But considering it's in the school's best interests, I did so."

"How magnanimous of you," Lavinia murmured dryly. She turned to Miranda. "It's a big commitment. Considering you have private clients as well, will you have time for the board too?"

Miranda nodded fervently. "As I said when Daniel asked the same question, I'd do anything for this school."

Lavinia smiled wanly. "I appreciate your dedication, Miranda." She glanced around the table. "I'd like to add my vote to the minutes. Please let it reflect that I too wish to expand the board and that I also vote to include Miranda D'Arcy in this new trustee position."

Egan leaned back in his chair.

Thank God, I did the right thing.

"Since there is nothing else on the agenda, the meeting is adjourned." Lavinia knocked the gavel softly.

Egan watched as Miranda stood up. Jess was also on his feet. In fact, he was standing so close to her that it looked as if they were joined at the hip.

Make that joined at the hand—Jess', anyway. It had found its way to the center of Miranda's back as if she were some sort of life-size ventriloquist's dummy.

No, actually, Jess's hand was positioned lower.

A lot lower.

That son of a bitch…

So, it was Jess who'd divulged Seamus' Machiavellian scheme to Miranda.

Well, thank goodness he blabbed it to someone who has Lavinia's back.

Egan had met Jess' ex-wife, Lizbeth during the second-period meet-

and-greet at AA's open house. She was the petite brunette with skin like leather. Too many tennis foursomes, Egan figured.

During Egan's short conversation with her, Lizbeth's eyes had darted fervently about the room as she searched for the man who had dumped her.

Although Jess usually brought his current, much younger wife—their son Hugo's former *au pair*—to the school's social functions like the Friday Family Fun Night, he'd come solo on the night of the open house. When Lizbeth finally spotted him, her one attempt to beckon him over was met with outright hostility.

During Egan's open house patter, Jess had done little to hide his boredom, preferring to spend the time continually texting.

Egan wondered if the asshole texted during sex too.

For a brief moment, the thought crossed his mind that Miranda might know the answer to that.

Immediately, he dismissed it.

Miranda is in a hard position. She has to pretend to like all parents, even the obnoxious ones.

Even the ones who cup your ass.

We're very much alike, he reasoned. We're strong people. We'd never let others use us.

"Jeez, that teacher guy is a sap!" Riley exclaimed.

"She played right to his ego," Lionel added.

Riley snorted. "Yeah, just like she played to Smallwood's joystick!"

Lionel frowned. Again, he nodded toward SallyAnne.

She shrugged off his attempt at chivalry. "Riley has a point. Miranda D'Arcy is devious, to say the least. Besides wrapping a few members of the board around her finger, she's now on it herself—thanks to that teacher."

"Did anyone catch his name?" Lionel asked.

Riley and SallyAnne shook their heads. But SallyAnne thought she'd heard his voice before—

But from where?

"Anyone want to take the bet that she'll be able to keep him in play without jumping in the sack with him?" Riley asked.

Neither answered.

"Nah, I didn't think so." Riley sighed. "If she keeps it up, she'll have to hire an air traffic controller to keep her lovers from colliding!" He put on his earphones and waved them away. "Okay, back to the porn portion of our drama."

SallyAnne was glad neither she nor Lionel were tasked with listening or transcribing Miranda's sexploits. She doubted whether Lionel was turned on by Miranda's boudoir shenanigans. She could tell, however, he was certainly intrigued by how Miranda operated.

He likes strong women, SallyAnne realized.

She felt she met that criterion. But she also knew of agents who'd had relationships with co-workers. It always ended badly.

Better to admire Lionel from afar, she reasoned.

CHAPTER 23

"Can you believe that woman? The way she talked her way onto the board—with Egan's help, no less!" Tallulah's heels clicked fiercely on the floor as she paced in front of Audrey and Bliss.

Always a stickler for client confidentiality, the version of the meeting that Audrey heard from Daniel was less detailed and certainly much less emotional. Although, to Audrey's mind, the message was the same:

The fix was in to get Miranda D'Arcy on the board.

Now, the question was whether that was a good thing or a bad thing.

It hadn't helped that Lavinia had given her approval on the record.

"You know, if Lavinia had been there when Miranda's scam was going down, she wouldn't have bought into it," Bliss pointed out. "She'd have slapped it down *tout de suite.*"

Audrey didn't dare mention she'd been with her mother, at her doctor's appointment. Lavinia's chemotherapy was tiring her out. Still, she insisted on doing everything she could to stop the spread of her cancer.

And she insisted that Audrey say nothing to anyone. Not yet, anyway.

"If you could have voted on it, would you have voted to expel Quest?" Audrey asked.

"Hell, yeah!" Tallulah insisted. "I said as much too! Quest has seen how drugs can wreak havoc on a life! He was too young to remember how hard it was on our family before Jammerhead got clean, but, hey, he was old enough to see how it affected his own grandmother—Maggie!" She threw up her arms in dismay. "Thank goodness she's clean now too, but it took her half his life to get there! Why would he do something so stupid now?"

"Because he wants to fit in," Audrey explained. "You know, had he been at a public school, both boys would have been arrested."

364

"Maybe it would have been a wakeup call. Some of the AA kids are shielded from too much. And we, their parents, are enablers," Tallulah retorted. "I only wish Jammerhead felt the same way."

"He did look relieved when the board voted for leniency," Bliss admitted.

Tallulah frowned. "That's because my bullheaded husband thinks our son is ready for college. He's wrong. Quest is a musician. It's all he's ever wanted to be since he was old enough to strum a guitar. But no matter how many times I remind Jammerhead that *he* didn't need college to be a successful musician, he says we should view college as Quest's 'back-up plan.'"

"Jammerhead has a good point," Bliss countered. "Few musicians, with or without a college degree, attain his level of success. And with a kid like Quest, the right college could turn him onto a passion in a different field while giving him some additional skills that might be useful for a music industry career, if that's where his future lies."

"I'm not against Quest going to college. I just don't think *he* wants to go—at least, not right now," Tallulah explained. "Heck, if my son were more academically inclined, I'd be pushing him on his grades like every other mom. But he's a natural musician! He needs to follow his passion, hone his chops with a band, on the road in front of audiences. If not now, then when?" She threw up her hands in frustration. "But Jammerhead's big fear is that Quest will always be in his shadow and Maggie's. He insists if Quest goes to college, he'll be able to manage the business better."

"That's not such a bad idea," Bliss pointed out. "At least, that's the way Raffaele sees it for Sienna."

Tallulah raised a brow. "And we all know how Sienna feels about it. Frankly, she's right. She's already on her way to being a brand."

Bliss nodded resignedly.

"You can start college at any age. If the time comes when Quest feels he needs it, he can always enroll," Audrey pointed out.

"Exactly! Now, if Jammerhead would just let Quest do his thing—*play music*—the kid may prove him wrong," Tallulah muttered.

"Maybe that's what Jammerhead is afraid of," Audrey pointed out.

"I hope not." Tallulah blinked away her tears. "Jammerhead's father never told him he was proud of his success. It would be a shame if he did the same to Quest."

Audrey put her arms around her friend. "Stick to your guns on this one."

Tallulah nodded. "You better believe it." She leaned her head on Audrey's shoulder. "Speaking of the academically inclined, how are your two scholars?"

"Frantic!" Audrey sighed. "Sadly, between their studies and now

Debate Team tryouts, I'm worried they've both taken on more than they can chew."

Bliss grimaced. "I hope Charly makes the team. Otherwise, she'll be heartbroken."

"Why do you say that?" Audrey asked.

Bliss laughed. "Because she idolizes you, silly! She won't be satisfied until she follows in your footsteps and becomes the team's captain."

Audrey shook her head. "I never had that title. It belonged to Mandy What's-Her-Name…Blackwell."

Tallulah snickered. "Bullshit! Don't try to rewrite history. You were why the team succeeded, and don't you forget it. In any case, that's how Gemma Sisley tells it—and she was there during that whole sordid weekend." She rolled her eyes at the thought. "By the way, I hear Chuck is also trying out for Debate Team."

Audrey nodded. "And, no surprise, he's approaching it as if he doesn't have a care in the world. I asked him if he was serious about making the team. I even offered to critique his arguments, but he insists he and his critique partner"—she made quote marks with her fingers—"have it down pat."

"Who is it?" Tallulah asked.

"Fawn McCoppin." Audrey stifled a shiver.

"Well, then, don't hold your breath for Chuck. That girl is nothing but trouble," Tallulah warned.

"Believe me, I already know it," Audrey retorted.

"He does seem to have a talent for charming his way out of things." Bliss chuckled. "Except with Charly. She's onto him. I pray for his sake that he never crosses her."

MIRANDA HAD BEEN EXPECTING DARIUS CALDER'S CALL.

She remembered how, at the trustee board meeting, he'd bemoaned his daughter Zina's, lousy test-taking.

And despite his acceptance into Seamus' boys' club, she could tell their relationship was one based merely on convenience (they were members of the same golf club) and strategy (Seamus needed his vote on Ashbury Academy's trustee board).

She also knew that, after almost twenty years of marriage, Darius and Gemma shared a "don't ask, don't tell" policy. Perhaps it had developed over the differences in their legal clientele, but Miranda guessed it covered many other issues as well.

So, when Darius suggested they meet for a drink to discuss Zina's college placement concierge program, Miranda knew the score.

She also knew his hot button: Zina was to follow in her grandfather and parents' footsteps in becoming a lawyer.

The girl had big shoes to fill.

And to do so, she'd first have to get into an elite college, and then follow up four years of exemplary grades in order to get accepted into a top-flight law school.

Miranda arrived precisely on time at their rendezvous locale: the tony Pied Piper Lounge at the Palace Hotel. Three men were sitting with Darius in the deepest corner of the lounge's wood-paneled anteroom.

One was a slim twenty-something man with the mien of a cherub: pouting lips, full cheeks, and ice blue-eyes. A highway of tattoos crawled up both arms bared by his sleeveless tee-shirt. This manboy's strawberry blond hair was shaved tight on the sides but spiked into a tall flattop.

Miranda recognized him immediately: a pop star who went by the single hyphenated name, Plug-Ugly. Despite his mobster swagger, he'd been raised in the heart of well-heeled and wealthy suburbia: Woodside, California. His latest song was blasting the airwaves—something touting big guns, big mansions, big-bootied women, and big bank accounts.

The two men on either side of him were scowling hulks twice his size. Plug-Ugly didn't look so happy either. Whatever Darius said had made the pop king somber and silent.

Seeing Miranda, Darius waved her over. Plug-Ugly and his security goons took this as their cue to vacate the booth, but it didn't stop them from staring and smirking at her as they walked away.

As she held out her hand to Darius, Miranda murmured, "So, *he's* one of your clients?"

Darius nodded. "You look surprised."

Miranda shrugged. "I guess…I guess I envisioned your clients as…"

"Let me guess—the stereotypical hip-hopper or gangster. Am I right?"

Miranda conceded with a nod.

Darius smirked, "Ms. D'Arcy, let me assure you, those who make their living on the outer banks of the law come in all shapes, sizes, *and colors*"— his eyes to roam over her—"and for that matter, genders."

"Good to know," she murmured coolly. "I now officially feel like a piece of meat."

Darius let loose with a deep-throated chuckle. "I'm sure you're used to it. You're a beautiful woman."

Miranda smiled. "Flattery will get you anything."

"Including admission to Yale?"

He goes straight to the point.

"That depends," she replied.

He listened intently as she made her pitch: how the best universities had an abundance of students to choose from, "…even those students from diverse populations."

Darius snickered at the term.

How some students were almost the full package but not entirely. And acceptance was based solely on the subjective decisions made by the admissions staff's criteria for that year.

She admitted that the game was rigged for children of alumni. And opening one's wallet for, say, a building or curriculum program bearing your name was no longer the awesome sauce for consideration for a non-alum's child. "The worm has turned on that little game."

"Bullshit!" Darius scoffed. "There's always a way of gaming the system."

"You're right. And that's why you called me, correct?" She looked him in the eye. "Let me guess: Jess suggested you call me."

Darius nodded. "He mentioned you have a failsafe system."

Miranda stymied the urge to frown. The smaller the dick, the larger the piehole, she thought.

Word of mouth was a double-edged sword. Tell the wrong person, and the Feds would be swooping down on you. It was why Miranda liked to do her own recruiting.

As if reading her mind, Darius added, "I have a lot of clients whose business practices are creative, to say the least. Through the years, I've made sure to put systems in place to mitigate their worst instincts."

"I'll remember that in case I ever need an attorney with your skillset," she replied dryly.

"So, let's talk about your side door," Darius said. "Does it work with, say, Yale?"

"It's on the list," Miranda assured him. "Zina has great grades, so that's no problem. As for her SAT scores, I can arrange a prep session or two, followed by the test—which, this time, she'll take with a disability pass, so that she has all the time in the world with her proctor."

Darius grimaced. "For that, won't she need a doctor's note, or something?"

She waved away his concern. "The tutor will take care of that."

"If only all of life were that simple," he retorted. "So, be honest. What else does Zina need to be a slam-dunk?"

"Does she play a sport?"

He shook his head. "She'll hit a few tennis balls with her friends or play two-on-two basketball with her cousins. But, as she puts it, she doesn't want to be a stereotype."

"In this case, that's a shame," Miranda admitted. "Sports recruits are allowed to bypass the extremely competitive process set up for regular applicants. Instead, the university's student-athlete admissions committee would have reviewed their applications."

Miranda had some of the coaches in her back pocket. They added her client's children to their initial rosters and then cut those with what was officially called "limited ability" a few weeks later—just long enough for them to have formally settled into campus life.

"No need to worry." Miranda assured him. "Does she have any academic extracurricular activities, like, say, chess team or Spanish club?"

Darius paused in thought. "I know she's trying out for Debate Team."

"Perfect! If she makes it, that's a plus."

"Yeah, well, from what I hear, so is every junior and senior in the school. Even Smallwood's little delinquent is going for it!" Darius chuckled. "I guess he figures it's a way to expand his distribution channels into the other schools." He shrugged. "When the kid pulls that stuff on some university campus, he'll be stepping on some big toes."

Miranda couldn't care less. Jess had already paid in full, and she had a no-refund policy.

"I'll see what I can do to help Zina's cause," she promised.

Darius grinned. "I'm sure you will."

"What's that supposed to mean?" Miranda huffed.

"Hey, I'm not blind. Egan knows a pretty woman when he sees one." Darius arched a brow.

"You do know how to flatter a girl," Miranda simpered. She could tell Darius would be fun in the sack.

Until that situation presented itself—and she had no doubt it would—Darius did have a point: should Hugo and Zina make the team, it would certainly make them easier to place at their chosen universities.

The best way to influence Egan was to judge the tryouts with him. Piece of cake. She'd played him well thus far.

"Let's get down to brass tacks," Darius said. "How much are we talking here, to get Zina to Yale?"

"Half a million." She said it firmly and without blinking.

Darius laughed so hard you'd have thought she'd told him the best stand-up line in Vegas. "You're aiming too high. As you just said, Zina's almost the full package. Your job is to just tie a pretty little bow around her so that those admissions folk see it too."

Miranda frowned. "I can go as low as four hundred thousand."

"You'll go a quarter-million," Darius told her. He handed her his business card. "Half up front, half on delivery."

"Everyone pays my fee upfront," Miranda huffed.

Darius shrugged. "I'm not 'everyone.' I'm the furthest from 'everyone' you'll ever meet. And if you're willing to do business my way, I'll be the best friend you'll ever have."

"What's that supposed to mean?"

"I'm just saying if you scratch my back, I'll scratch yours—metaphorically speaking, of course." Darius winked knowingly.

Damn it! Is that loudmouth, Jess, telling everyone I'm an easy lay too?

Seeing the concern in her face, Darius burst out laughing. "Don't worry, Miranda. I take everything that blowhard Smallwood says with a grain of salt." He looked her up and down and smiled. "And even if it were true, I'd like to spare you any unnecessary grief that might befall either of us, should my darlin wife even suspect anything you did was untoward, be it business or pleasure."

"That's quite chivalrous of you," Miranda murmured. In a way, she wished it weren't the case.

"I'll have a hundred and a quarter, in small bills, delivered to your doorstep tomorrow."

"I'd prefer it through the Best Face Forward Club. It's a non-profit that I support."

Darius snickered. "I'll bet you do."

Miranda slid a business card his way. "Here's its online address for donation information."

Darius reached into his pocket and pulled out a slim wallet from which he extracted a card. "And here's mine. Just in case your world ever comes tumbling down."

His words sent a chill through her.

She shrugged it off. "It won't. By the way, I'll call Zina in tomorrow and let her know I'm setting her up with an SAT tutor for a full assessment."

"Good. But mum's the word on any special treatment," he warned her. "Like I said, our arrangement is just between us."

"No problem there."

"By the way, I overheard Manya Patel's mother, Nira, talking to Gemma. Apparently, Manya also has test anxiety. Nira is a single mother—an MD. She insists that Manya follow in her footsteps. She feels it's the only way that Manya won't get burned in a relationship, like, apparently she did. Nira's ex gets half her earnings." He snorted. "Even divorce is an equal opportunity outcome."

"If you say so," Miranda muttered. Nothing new there. She had first-hand knowledge. "Well, thanks for the heads up on Nira."

"What are friends for, right?" Darius' eyes moved beyond her, to the front of the room. "Ah, my next appointment is early. I suggest you go so that you don't collide with Public Enemy Number 44. He's sure to have an undercover cop or two trailing him."

Miranda took the hint, nodded, and headed for the door.

The man walking in as she stepped out had countless gold chains around his neck, and a gold grill on his teeth to match.

The eye that wasn't covered by a patch followed her out the door.

———

"OH, MY GOD! WE'VE GOT *DARIUS CALDER*!" SALLYANNE EXCLAIMED.

Dumbfounded, Lionel nodded. "Hell yeah, we've got him! The lawyer for every drug-dealing badass in the Bay Area! Melamed will be over the moon about it!"

They slapped palms.

SallyAnne would have rather they had chest-bumped.

Better yet, if they'd held hands.

"So, when we arrest him, we'll suggest he sing about his clients to get some leniency with our charges," SallyAnne crowed.

"Boy, Miranda will be pissed when he throws her under the bus," Lionel predicted. "She's attracted to him."

SallyAnne frowned. "How could you tell?"

Lionel shrugged. "There's a different cadence to her pitch when she's truly interested in a guy, versus playing at it. It shows in how she nuances certain words."

"Does it?" SallyAnne sniffed. "I'm impressed. You've done quite a study of her voice."

"Thanks!" He sighed, "Yeah, makes me wish we had video too."

"I'll bet you do," SallyAnne muttered. She grabbed her purse. "Have a great night."

Lionel looked up, surprised. "Wait…what say we grab a bite to eat? Like me, I'll bet you have a few ideas on how we can use what we just heard—"

"Sorry, but I'm late for a date." She waved as she walked out the door.

In truth, she had no plans except go to a really nice hotel bar.

She needed a drink.

No—she needed *a man*. It had been a while since SallyAnne had had sex. If she picked up some guy and went back to his room with him, all the better.

For the past few years, most of her intimate liaisons had been one-night stands, usually initiated at some bar and with civilians who never knew what she really did for a living.

There was a reason she kept her job to herself: she'd learned early on that most civilian men were uneasy dating female agents. She could never understand why. Odds were that they weren't involved in illegal activities.

Even so, everyone has something to hide, right?

Mr. Lucky wouldn't know it, but they'd both be role-playing. While he assumed she was some out-of-town corporate lawyer who'd just finished a meeting with a locally-based client, and she'd close her eyes and pretend he was Lionel.

And unlike the real Lionel, he'd be one satisfied customer.

CHAPTER 24

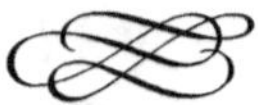

"Mom! Dad! Read it and weep!" Charly ran into the dining room, her SAT score held high.

Her parents and brothers paused as she handed the official paper to her mother first.

Seeing it, Audrey's eyes opened wide:

Evidence-Based Reading and Writing: 782
Math: 719
TOTAL: 1501

She handed it to Daniel.

Reviewing it, his eyes grew wide. "Excellent!" Daniel gave his daughter a hug. He glanced over at Chuck. "Was yours in the mail too?"

Chuck frowned. "Yeah." He leaned forward to pull something out of his back pocket. He handed the paper to Audrey.

Her heart sank. Because I'm a soft touch, she realized.

Cautiously, she opened it:

Evidence-Based Reading and Writing: 486
Math: 713
TOTAL: 1199

Audrey winced. As she handed it to Daniel, she murmured, "Isn't this total less than your last try?"

Noah leaned toward his father for a glance. "Wow, you didn't even make it to twelve-hundred!"

Chuck's middle finger shot up in Noah's direction.

"Don't do that!" Audrey cautioned him.

"Your brother has a point," Daniel muttered. "What happened, Chuck?"

The boy shrugged. "Yeah, well, you know. With basketball season and all."

"Granted, your math score is decent. But how could you blow the reading and writing?" Audrey asked.

"I don't know! I mean, it wasn't like I did it on purpose."

"Apparently, it was," Daniel countered. "You're better than that. You got into AP Comp Lit, for Pete's sake!"

Charly snorted. "That's only because he kissed up to Mercy—you know, the instructor who would have been teaching it if she hadn't gone on maternity leave."

This time, Chuck tossed a middle finger salute in his sister's direction.

"Enough of that!" Audrey warned him.

"Look, Mom, Dad—maybe I'm just not college material. Or maybe I'm just not ready for it *now*—right out of high school. The Brits and the Aussies have the right idea: you know, take a year off—"

Charly interrupted: "It's called a 'gap year.'"

"Yeah, okay—*whatever!*" Chuck threw up his hands. "Like I was saying, if I took a year off to think about it, maybe I'd know better what's right for me."

Audrey shook her head adamantly. "Chuck, true: you can always go to college. But why drop out before you've even given it a try? Some people do, and…and they never go back. I did, granted—but almost two years later. With twins in tow. You see, real life gets in the way."

When Chuck and Charly exchanged startled glances, she wished she'd never said it like that.

"We all know you can do better," Daniel added. "Listen, guy: maybe you should resign from all sports to prove it."

"*Are you nuts?* I'm the basketball team's captain and starting forward! And I'm the starting pitcher on the baseball team!"

"Yes, you are—for teams that consistently place third or less in their division," Daniel argued. "That doesn't necessarily guarantee you a scholarship to any college." He leaned in. "Chuck, we're your parents. It's our job to make you buckle down. If you can give one hundred percent for your coaches, you can do it for us too."

All color went out of Chuck's face. "Dad, please! Don't make me quit!"

Audrey laid her arm on Daniel's wrist to caution him. "Your father is making the point that something's got to give. Something that gives you more time to study. So give us a solution, Chuck. What's it going to be?"

"I'll try harder on the next SAT session! I promise!"

Daniel rolled his eyes. "That's what you said before the last test."

"And there's only one SAT exam between now and when our college applications are due," Charly pointed out.

"Okay—*ALRIGHT!* Listen…" Chuck ran his fingers through his hair—something he did whenever he was at the end of his rope. "I'll raise my GPA!" His chin jutted forward. "I'll… I'll ace Comp Lit!"

"Egan did mention you were trying much harder in class," Audrey conceded.

Satisfied he'd made his point, Chuck nodded to his father. "See?"

Daniel shrugged. "That's a step in the right direction. But it won't help your SATs."

"I'll…I'll get a tutor."

"Okay, good." Daniel smiled. "We'll get a referral from Miranda."

At that suggestion, Audrey pursed her lips.

"I dunno. That lady scares me." Chuck rolled his eyes. "Hey! Maybe Egan won't mind helping me out."

Daniel frowned. "I would think he's got enough on his plate."

Chuck smirked. "He'd do it—if *Mom* asks him."

Audrey felt a blush creeping up her throat. "Why do you say that?"

Chuck shrugged. "He likes you. He sees you as some kind of…I dunno —*nun* or something."

Daniel choked into his water glass. When he recovered, he declared, "Well, then, by all means, ask him. It can't hurt."

"He'll say no," Charly declared coldly. "He's got Debate Team tryouts. And once the team starts up, he won't be able to make the time for you."

"Gee! Sounds like Teacher's Pet may be a bit jealous!" Chuck retorted.

"I have nothing to be jealous about," Charly replied smugly. "I have the highest GPA in the class—*because I care!* I work my ass off."

Chuck leaned out from his chair to examine his sister's backside. "Ha! Could have fooled me."

Charly tossed her bread roll at him.

Chuck caught it with one hand—quite a feat considering how hard he was laughing.

Incensed, Charly lifted her father's glass—

But Daniel grabbed her wrist before she could toss it on her brother. To his dismay, Daniel got back-splashed instead.

"Oh, shit! Sorry, Dad!" Charly yelped.

Audrey glared at Chuck. "You need to apologize to your sister!"

"Hey, I'm not the only one who thinks so. Fawn claims Charly's got some sort of daddy complex—"

Charly's jaw dropped open. "Why that—*bitch!*" Her eyes glazed up with tears.

"*Fawn?*…" Audrey frowned. "What does she know about…about something like that?"

"I would say it takes one to know one," Daniel muttered.

"Fawn knows *nothing* about Charly!" Audrey shot back.

Daniel raised his hands in mock surrender. "Calm down, folks! All I was saying is that everything Fawn does is to grab Seamus' attention."

This time it was Chuck who gagged on a gulp of water. When he recovered, he scoffed, "Ha! I wouldn't exactly put it that way."

Daniel raised a brow. "No, I guess *you* wouldn't." He shook his head. "Look, Chuck, I'm not telling you who to choose as your friends—"

"Good! Because as far as Fawn goes, I'm not dumping her." Chuck's voice shook. "We almost broke up once already."

"That's because *she* dumped *you*—and very publicly, too," Charly retorted. "What kind of girlfriend is that?"

"The kind who knows how to say she's sorry," Chuck declared. "In fact, she wants to help me succeed. We study together. And she's my debate team critique partner."

Charly guffawed, "Wow! I can't wait to see how *that* plays out!"

"All those snide little remarks you make—just like that one—are the reason our parents think I'm stupid." With as much dignity as he could muster, Chuck rose from the table.

But before he could take off, Daniel reached over and grabbed his arm. "Let me make this clear: we've always judged you and your sister and your brother by your actions only. Only you can prove Charly wrong."

Chuck jerked his arm away and stormed out of the house.

Charly wiped her damp cheeks with the back of her hand. "What you said isn't really true, you know."

Daniel stared at her. "What do you mean by that?"

"You guys play favorites! We all know it too."

"That's not true!" Audrey protested.

"Sure it is," Charly insisted. She turned to Noah. "Kiddo, of the three of us, who would you say is Mom's favorite?'

Noah guffawed. "Duh! *Chuck.*"

"How about Dad?"

Noah blushed. "I'd say...Me."

Charly's gaze went from her mother to her father. "I rest my case." She ran from the room.

They could hear her bedroom door slam.

Noah frowned. "I was going to tell her that she was the only one that both of you loved equally." The boy sighed. "May I be excused too?"

His parents nodded.

Audrey waited until Noah was out of earshot to whisper, "Doesn't Charly realize we love her?"

Daniel shrugged. "She knows it. But now we know she doesn't believe we love her *as much* as we do her brothers."

"We have three kids! There's no way we can—or should—have a favorite! We love them all equally!"

"Obviously, that's not how they view it. And if, like Charly, you believe you're the odd child out, it's got to hurt. Especially if the others see it too."

Audrey crossed her arms at her waist. "Exactly what do they think they see?"

"Well, in my case, since Noah was just an infant, he was my charge whenever you had to run shotgun over the twins. You know, when you ferried them to and from their big kid activities."

"I offered to swap duties," Audrey pointed out.

"I know," Daniel conceded. "But so many of their play dates were with Tallulah, Bliss, and Gemma's kids too. I didn't want you to miss out hanging with your best friends."

She nodded.

"As for you and Chuck..." Daniel sighed. "No matter what hot water he finds himself in, he can charm his way out of it"—he hesitated—"with you."

"Ha!" Audrey scoffed. "I take it you view yourself as the bad cop!"

"Wasn't that the pact we made at the parent open house? And even tonight, you didn't exactly back me up when I gave him the ultimatum about sports and the SAT."

Audrey had nothing to say because he was right.

Daniel stood up and walked over to her. Wrapping his arms around her, he murmured, "It's not as if we've taken a course in parenting. We both have made mistakes."

"I don't remember things being this complicated with Lavinia and me."

"She was one parent with one child. She adored you, and you felt the same about her. You never had to share your love with another sibling." Daniel chuckled. "I guess that means we'll have to scare up another parent somewhere."

Audrey couldn't laugh at that.

If only you knew, she thought.

"*Slow...down!*" Fawn's demand was adamant.

"I...I'm doing the best I can!" Chuck muttered.

But, sweet Jesus, it was hard!

So hard, what with the sight in front of him: Fawn's backside, rising and falling, again and again, on his cock.

Her reverse cowgirl was squeezing the Kickapoo joy juice out of him. She must have known that.

Not that she gave a hoot. He knew she was there for her own satisfaction. The longer he could hold out, the longer he could hang onto her.

She's my little filly.

At least, that's what he told himself.

This was his mantra although she insisted on riding him as opposed to the other way around.

It was his mantra whenever he denied his parents' contention that she wasn't right for him.

It was his mantra whenever his sister arched a brow upon hearing Fawn's name.

And it was most definitely his mantra as he climbed over the high thick wall that separated the McCoppin estate from the Presidio—the best way to avoid the security camera aimed at their front gate, all the while fighting off his vertigo as he scurried up the lattice arbor next to her third-story bedroom suite.

When Chuck called Fawn, fuming over his fight with his family—about Charly's cruel taunts about his chances of making Debate Team—she cooed sympathy and promises to make him feel better.

She didn't have to ask twice to get him over there.

Even so, Chuck wouldn't have come over if Fawn's parents hadn't been out for the evening. After Egan's reality check about the legal consequences for underage sex, Fawn knew that Chuck was skittish about running into Seamus and Gretchen.

Ironically, Egan's warning had only whetted their appetites for each other. Suddenly, it wasn't just fun and illicit, but illegal too.

So yes, sex was on the agenda. But first things first: Fawn insisted that they look at the debate questions and decide together which ones to tackle.

"Which ones are Charly interested in?" She'd asked nonchalantly.

Chuck shrugged. "I forget."

"Well, Silly, it would help us develop our arguments if we could see how it was done," she pouted. "Where does Charly keep her classwork?"

"In our family iCloud account," Chuck admitted.

"Do you know her password?"

"Maybe. I mean, I can guess at it. But—"

"Listen, Chuck—tryouts are on Monday! *We've got less than three days to pull something together!* It'll take us a second to log in, copy her notes, and then log out again. But, hey, if you're too lazy, you can just leave because I'll have to pull an all-nighter." As if in anticipation of a long night, Fawn stretched toward the ceiling. (And, yes, he'd noticed that she wasn't wearing a bra.)

"Alright," he muttered.

Fawn handed him her iPad. "Use this to pull it up. We'll review it —*afterward*."

Reluctantly, he went into the account. After a few tries, he rightly guessed his sister's password:

LisaSimpson6*

"Um… Sorry but that is too frickin' weird," Fawn muttered.

"Yeah well, it's the cultural icon she most identifies with, plus her favorite number. She once told me the star was her favorite keyboard character," Chuck admitted.

Remembering the same could be said of her own password—Kardashian5$— Fawn realized she should change it immediately.

Just like that, she had both Chuck's and Charly's passwords. Quickly, she downloaded Charly's DEBATE NOTES file.

Chuck couldn't see it, but while he was admiring Fawn's undulating ass, she'd grabbed the iPad again and had logged back into the McKittridges' iCloud account.

With a click, she deleted all the documents within Charly's DEBATE NOTES file.

Best. Multitasking. Ever.

CHAPTER 25

It was the best of days.

It was the worst of days.

Over the next twelve hours, the day's ecstasies and agonies rose and fell like a seesaw commandeered by two very rambunctious preschoolers.

Miranda's first disappointment was Egan's response to the suggestion that she help him judge Debate Team tryouts.

"To celebrate our coup against Seamus' evil empire," as she put it, Miranda had come bearing gifts: a thermos of Blue Fog coffee and a canister of peanut brittle, which she claimed was her grandmother's recipe.

(In fact, she'd bought it off a clearance shelf at the local Safeway. It was right at its expiration date, but that didn't matter, since she wasn't going to touch it.)

Egan nodded, pleased. "Very kind of you—both the brittle *and* the brew." He opened the thermos and poured a generous portion of its contents into his mug. "But I've had the judges lined up for weeks. Thanks anyway."

"Even so, it would mean so much to me," Miranda purred. "You scratched my back—for Lavinia, I mean. I want to return the favor."

"It's a chore. Trust me. Besides, Cornell and Odette know the ropes already."

"I love learning new tricks, believe me," Her voice was husky with nuance.

By the way his eyes dropped to her breasts, she knew he'd picked up on it. "Look, Miranda…I don't want to step on any toes."

She frowned. "What are you saying?"

"I mean…you and Jess."

Jesus! First Darius, and now Egan?

Who else thinks that slime-bucket and I are an item?

If Lavinia hears rumors…

Miranda shook her head, angrily. "*Jess Smallwood?* Trust me, there's no 'there' there!"

"He seems to think there is," Egan pointed out.

"Well, he's wrong," Miranda insisted.

"Even so, I just don't think we're—"

The buzzing from Miranda's phone cut him short.

Miranda looked at the screen. Clare had texted her:

Jammerhead is here to see you.

Well, whattaya know! Tallulah's husband…

"Must run! Duty calls." She didn't wait for Egan's reply. She'd just have to pray that, by some miracle, at least a few of her new AA clients made the team.

JAMMERHEAD WASN'T WAITING OUTSIDE HER DOOR.

In fact, her door was wide open.

It steamed her to see that he'd made himself comfortable on her office couch.

Not that she could bitch about it to anyone. All of AA's staff was at every parent's beck and call, so why bother?

And besides, here at AA, Jammerhead was royalty.

She knew that because of his touring schedule, he rarely attended school functions. When he did, it was a big deal to the other parents. San Francisco wasn't as star-struck as many other places around the country. At the same time, it wasn't as blasé about its local celebrities as Los Angeles. Having seen the other parents gawking while in his presence, it was apparent to Miranda that old idols die hard. And despite Quest's lackadaisical study habits, she knew some of the parents with sons in the kid's class pushed them to hang out with him.

Miranda's eyes swept over Jammerhead. His black tee shirt hugged him like a second skin. Despite being on the far side of forty, he wore his hair down to his shoulders, as he did, what, twenty years earlier. And those skinny leather pants: had he used a crowbar to get into them?

Admittedly, as a teen, his *Bad Boy* album poster had hung over her bed, stirring up all sorts of fantasies.

And yet, life had not necessarily been kind to him. His face was pocked. He had bags under his eyes. Silver had threaded its way through his frosted locks. The Lycra in his shirt allowed it to cling to his biceps, but it also outlined the hardened pouch that had once been taut abs.

He looks as if he's going to a retro costume party as an aging rock star, she thought.

Playing at it was an apt analogy. Miranda had read somewhere that his last album had barely squeaked into the Top 100. His audiences were aging out. These days when he toured, fans sat in their seats during his new songs. The lighters only came out for the golden oldies, his classic hits.

Soon he'll be like all the other rock burnouts, she thought, resting on his laurels and nudging his stockbroker for better market calls.

"What can I do for you, Mr... I'm sorry, is Jammerhead your first name or last?"

"It's my only name. And you can drop the mister."

"I get it. Like Madonna." Miranda grinned slyly. "What can I do for you?"

"Pull another miracle for Quest. Get him into college."

BOOM! Just like that...

Jammerhead leaned in. "I have to be honest. I'm pissed—*outright pissed!*—at the accusation by those trustee board jackasses that it was my kid who was selling coke!"

"Is it perception, or reality?" Miranda challenged.

"What the hell are you trying to say, lady?"

Miranda had every intention of speaking her mind.

The world considers Jammerhead a legend. The city touts him as an honored son. And in the AA universe, he's married to an alumna. But despite his wife's do-gooder intentions for their son, this jerk is just like Seamus and his smug buddies. He thinks he deserves special treatment.

I'll give him the treatment, alright.

Miranda smiled encouragingly. "I'm asking you to look inward and ask yourself: 'Has my public persona given my son the wrong message of what he should be doing with his life?'"

Jammerhead frowned. "We are different people at home. Not freaks. Just everyday folk."

"In other words, you help Quest with his homework. You discuss colleges with him. You push him to raise his GPA, which now stands at..." She turned to her computer and tapped a few keys. Then, grimacing, she murmured, "Yikes!"

"So, um, no to all of the above," he conceded. "Okay, I get it. I'm shit as a parent! But now I want to make good on all that—*for Quest's sake.*" Jammerhead leaped up, pacing the room like a caged animal. "Look, don't get me wrong. Quest is one hell of a good guitarist—amazing, in fact! And he's got a great ear for lyrics too. But the industry is changing. Just to tread water you've got to spend more—and you still make less. Songs are pennies per download. Touring costs are through the roof! If Quest wants to survive, he'll need the business smarts to do it. Granted, it takes the fun out of it. But, shit—that's today's reality in the music business."

So, that's why he's worried, Miranda reasoned. To keep up the appearance of success, people like JammerJerk here run through their money at a quick clip. In case his next album sinks and his lifestyle burn rate leaves his son with nothing, he wants to make sure the kid can stand on his own two feet.

As if. Quest is clueless.

Miranda nodded sympathetically. "I feel your pain. But if we're going to pull this off, it'll call for some drastic measures. A full-court press!"

She got up, walked around to the front of the desk, and perched on it, crossing her legs demurely. "Recently, I initiated a special counseling program for those who are, um… stressed for help on admissions testing." Noting his interest, she thought it best to lean into the phrase. Quickly, she pulled together its acronym: "Or, as I call it, SHAT."

He guffawed. "'Shat'? What…*themselves?* Over getting into college?"

Miranda frowned at the irony of it. She shrugged. "Sure. I mean, a rose by any other name."

"Would smell *much, much* sweeter!" Jammerhead chortled.

"Yes, well, everything about the program is still in Beta," she huffed. "Rest assured, there is nothing like it anywhere."

"In what way? I mean, you all do the same things: practice tests, academic coaching, blah, blah, blah—"

"That is not *our* approach. I mean, yes, of course, we will offer those methodologies too—well, except for the 'blah blah—'" raising her frosty lips a few millimeters let him know it was a joke—"but we will…how shall I put this? Let me be blunt: we will be *reinventing* the student. *Including his SAT answers.*"

Jammerhead stared blankly at her. "What does that mean exactly?"

"We assess his SAT scores with a tutor—one I've already vetted—who will focus our efforts on correcting Quest's specific test errors. Down to each test answer. Do you understand what I'm saying?"

Just then, a ringtone on Jammerhead's cell phone howled through the room.

Miranda yelped, "What the hell is that?"

Jammerhead tapped a button to stop it. "Sorry! It's a riff from a song I'm working on." He stared down at the screen and grimaced. "Tallulah is texting me."

"Shall we include her in this conversation?"

"Hell, no! She'd hit the roof if she knew!"

"And that doesn't make you opposed to my unorthodox methodology?" Miranda's brow arched.

Jammerhead grimaced. "You're saying some shill will be taking the test for him, right?"

"To be clear, the tutor at my disposal is a very competent and well-proven test taker."

Jammerhead nodded. "Yeah, sure. Whatever it takes."

In your face, Tallulah!

Once again, the ring tone shrieked through the room.

Jammerhead sighed as he tapped it off. "Can you guarantee you can get a student into one of his top five schools?"

"Yes...and one in particular, for sure." She winked slyly. "It just so happens to have a great music program with a dual academic track: Composition and Music Business. And it's in Los Angeles, in fact, so he'll be right in the heart of his chosen industry."

"And which university are we speaking about?"

She reached for a pad and a pen. With a quick almost indecipherable scrawl, she wrote it down and handed it to him. She knew Jammerhead would leap at the opportunity to get his deadbeat spawn into it at any cost.

He peered at the note. His eyes grew large. Grudgingly, he gave a curt nod.

Time to go in for the kill.

Miranda steeled herself by placing both hands flat on her desk as she leaned forward. "Be duly warned, Mr...I mean, just Jammerhead"—the silliness of such a name was cringe-worthy. She shrugged it off with a sigh—"SHAT is exclusively for my concierge clients." She pursed her lips as if warning him not to get his hopes up. "And because it's still in the Beta phase, only a small number of students will be accepted."

"So, what will it take to move my kid to the front of the line?"

Miranda chuckled. "You're a funny one—as is every other parent who is begging for a slot in...*SHAT*."

Note to self: change that damn acronym, SHAT, to something more appealing!

Jammerhead shrugged. "The way these parents jockey over every little thing for their kids? I can only imagine."

"Frankly, I'm at the point where I'll need to hold a lottery to fill the slots equitably."

"How many slots are there?"

"Just, er...six."

"What do you say about making seven your lucky number?" He didn't even wait for her to answer. Instead, he pulled a checkbook from his jacket, scribbled away, then ripped out the check for her to see. "Will this cover it?"

Miranda stared down at it. *Seven hundred thousand dollars? Well, hell yeah!*

She was roused from her stupor by Jammerhead's impatient sigh. "Not enough, eh? Jeez, you people! Okay then, I'll round it up to a mil."

NO SHIT! A million dollars—for his kid's acceptance to some made-up malarkey program...

"Well, ...okay." For once, Miranda's deadpan tone was from shock as opposed to disdain.

Not that Jammerhead could tell the difference. "When does he start?"

"During Quest's free period. Have him see me then."

"He'll be there. Or else the Tesla I just ordered for his graduation present is canceled."

Well, that should light a fire under the boy's ass, she thought.

Jammerhead whistled as he went out the door.

A million forking dollars...and from Tallulah's husband no less!

Payback was sweeter than she'd ever imagined.

Shit, she thought. Quest's math grade and his SATs *SUCK!*

I'll be earning every penny of it.

Dammit, maybe I should have asked for more...

The thought peeved her to the point of missing the soft purring of her phone: not her regular cell phone but the one she used to access remote messages for University Prep & Test.

Apparently, it had been buzzing off the hook with calls from desperate Los Angeles-based concierge parents. To a one, their messages said the same thing:

Why has Winslow rescheduled my kid's SAT test?
If we wait any longer, we'll miss the deadline!

What the hell was happening? Where the hell was Winslow?

Miranda was frantic. For the next two hours, she'd had her office door shut so that AA staff and students couldn't hear her assuaging her concierge clients over their distress that their children would miss the testing deadline in between frantic calls to Winslow's private number.

But he wasn't picking up.

Apparently, Winslow had gone AWOL.

Her lie was simple: Winslow had a family emergency. If they insisted that she elaborate, she gave some cock-and-bull story about his father getting run over. "Winslow is devastated," she'd say, faking a sob. "Not to worry, though! We'll call later with an update and a date to reschedule."

Her next course of action was to call every casino between LA and Reno to find him. Winslow always registered under an assumed name: usually the Henry James character named Caspar Goodwood from *Portrait of a Lady.* She knew this because he'd once asked her to cover his marker with a casino by wiring it under that name. "They'll jail me if I don't pay it," he'd pleaded.

At the time, Miranda had no recourse but to follow through.

She was sure he'd have the same excuse this time. She was fed up with it. She'd have to replace him. The sooner the better. Otherwise, the lawsuits would start flying.

If he wasn't already dead in a ditch, she might put him there herself—after the SATs, of course.

Miranda was about to call her eighth casino when she realized Winslow was finally calling back. Immediately, she answered. "Where the hell are you?"

"Macau." The phone connection was awful. He sounded as if he were underwater. "Listen, Miranda, I'm in a jam! I owe these thieves twenty-thou! Do you think you could—"

"Are you crazy? Twenty thousand dollars?"

"Euros, really."

"Jesus, Winslow! …How much is that in dollars?"

"I don't know! And seeing that I've got two goons ready to break my thumbs, I'm currently not at liberty to pull up a currency exchange app! I was about to board an EVA flight back to LAX when they caught me at the airport. I can still make the flight if you send the dough. I've just texted you the bank account number—"

Just then someone rapped on Miranda's door. She stifled the urge to shout, "Get lost!" Instead, she settled for "Enter!" in a tone that gave fair warning of her mood.

Egan stuck his head in the door. "Okay, yeah, I accept your offer," he declared.

Distracted, Miranda frowned. *"What?"*

"What the hell do you mean, 'what'?" Winslow's primal howl roared through her Air Pods. "I told you 'what'! Listen, Miranda—*OW! That hurt, dude!… Seriously, Miranda, I don't have a lot of leeway here! It's dismember-ment…or…or worse! Please! Send the money! PLEASE!"*

Egan also assumed she was speaking to him. "Just what you said—you know, about scratching my back? That you want to reciprocate? Metaphor-ically speaking only, of course." He grinned as if tantalized, if regretful. "Cornell bit into your peanut brittle and broke a tooth. He's already on his way to the dentist. Needless to say, he's ditched on judging Debate Team tryouts this afternoon, so you're up to bat—"

With Winslow blathering in one ear and Egan yammering in the other, the only thing Miranda could think to do was to nod vigorously and exclaim, "Sure! No problem!"

"Thanks! See you after school then. In the auditorium." Egan gave her a thumbs-up, shutting the door behind him.

"Oh, thank God!" Winslow was blubbering so hard that Miranda could barely make out what he was saying.

"Don't miss that EVA flight," she hissed. "Or I'll kill you myself!"

The line went dead.

She sighed, checked her text messages, and followed the instructions Winslow had sent.

"Now he's my bitch," she muttered.

Exhausted, she laid her head down on her desk.

Until she heard her phone buzz again.

It was Clare, with another text:

Can you make time for Nira Patel? In lobby now.

Hell yeah, I can. Miranda thought.

Darius was already working his magic.

"So now, what you're saying is if I sign Manya up for your client concierge program, she will be assured entry into one of her dream colleges?"

From the look on Nira Patel's face, Miranda could tell that Manya's mother still couldn't believe her.

She's not leaving this office until she does, Miranda vowed silently.

"Face it, Nira. Getting into a topflight med school is *much* more competitive than when you got into Stanford."

Nira frowned. "I had the second-highest GPA in my high school class. Stanford was lucky to have me."

"You were a product of a *public* school. Had you been at a private prep with much higher standards—say, Ashbury Academy—that may not have been the case. Isn't that why you have Manya here at AA as opposed leaving her in public school—so as not to take any chances in today's competitive environment?"

That same thought must have crossed Nira's mind because she nodded slightly. "But, it's not just the student's grades they take into consideration, is it? Manya has been working as a hospital volunteer since she was fourteen. She has an excellent bedside manner. Her biology grades are exemplary—"

Miranda interjected, "And yet, she has never scored above 1240 on her previous SAT exams. At the same time, if her aim is Yale, Stanford, Georgetown, UCLA, or USC's pre-med programs, she'll be competing with every other applicant of diverse origins. And you know this better than anyone—especially when you toss in the international student applicants."

"Her ethnicity wouldn't—*and shouldn't*—be the only reason for them to consider her," Nira insisted.

"You're right. But, fortunately, putting that card in the deck is what broke the chokehold of all white and all male applicants. And now, by a mere eyelash, women physicians are the majority! That's because of women like you, Nira!"

Nira preened proudly at Miranda's display of sister solidarity.

"All the more reason to make this happen for Manya." Miranda placed both hands on the desk in front of her. "Let me be blunt. College admissions are a cutthroat process. We—Manya, you, and I—can't afford to be timid. When the opportunity presents itself, we should be gaming the system *just like countless others.*"

Reluctantly, Nira nodded. "What do you mean by 'gaming the system?'"

"Like you, I believe Manya is *almost* the complete package: bright, personable, and caring—all of which works in her favor. However, there are some criteria in Manya's application that need to be massaged to make her an even more obvious pick." She walked around to the front of the desk, taking the seat beside Nira. "Our best bet for Manya is raising her SAT score. I can make it happen—and I do, for my concierge clients. Its results are proven. It guarantees that Manya will attain an SAT score of 1440 or higher."

Nira's eyes brightened at the thought. "How does your concierge program work?"

"As Manya's college admissions counselor, I can position the result of her low SAT score as a learning disability caused by emotional anxiety. It is an accepted prognosis that will enable Manya to take the test away from the school and untimed, with the help of a certified proctor who can explain the questions in a way that lessens her anxiety." Miranda paused to take a deep breath. "However, the program is a bit unorthodox.

"In what way?"

"The proctor will actually be taking the test for her."

Nira said nothing.

Jesus, did I blow this?

Finally Nira whispered, "I understand."

Miranda hid her relief with a stiff nod. "Good! I'll call Manya in for a one-on-one appointment with me so that I can start her assessment immediately. And of course, we'll look at other ways to enhance her application." Miranda gave Nira a reassuring smile. "I've noticed that Manya doesn't partake in sports, music, or drama."

"I've kept her focused strictly on math and science," Nina declared.

"It would help if she broadened her profile in other ways—"

Nira interjected, "She's trying out for Debate Team."

"That's a plus," Miranda assured her. Silently, she cursed Egan for once again stymying her success.

"And...the cost of your program?" Nira pursed her lips.

Miranda hesitated. She remembered what Darius had said to her: that Nira's ex-husband had secured half her earnings as alimony, and that she was still paying off her med school loans.

Even if Manya was on partial scholarship at AA, whatever was left in Nira's paycheck couldn't be much.

Finally, Miranda replied: "Fifty thousand."

Nira dropped her head in defeat. "That's...a little rich for my blood." She stood up to leave.

"Are you on scholarship here?" Miranda asked.

Nira nodded almost shamefully. "I know what you're thinking: 'She can't afford to pay for her daughter's tuition on a doctor's salary?' Sadly, that's my reality." Her head shook with anger. "I've made some mistakes in my life. Despite the lazy oaf I married, Manya wasn't one of them. She was the best thing that ever happened to me." Nira stared defiantly at Miranda. "I've raised her alone. She's seen me work hard. And when she's a doctor, she won't need to rely on...*on anyone.*"

Miranda shrugged. "Look...why don't we say...ten thousand?"

Nira clasped her hands to her cheeks as if she'd won the lottery.

Miranda reached over the top of her desk and plucked a business card from an open box. "Your payment will be made to this non-profit."

"Ah! So it's tax-deductible too!" Nira reached over and hugged her.

Miranda never felt so good.

And so bad.

And so angry with herself for being so foolishly generous.

Miranda closed the door gently behind Nira.

———

IT SUDDENLY DAWNED ON HER THAT SOMEWHERE BETWEEN JAMMERHEAD AND Winslow and Nira, Egan had popped in to ask her something—

No, to demand something of her—

AS IF!–

And she had stupidly agreed to do so if only to get him out of her hair.

What was it again?...something about...

DEBATE TRYOUTS.

He wants me to help judge them after all!

Two new clients, University Prep & Test crisis averted, and a way to get three of my clients into a great academic extracurricular? It was the BEST of days!

———

RILEY TOSSED HIS HEADSET ONTO THE DESK. "MY IDOL HAS CLAY FEET," HE groaned.

"What do you mean by that?" Lionel asked.

"I grew up listening to Jammerhead," Riley declared. "He was *THE MAN*. Now he's just some anxious *helicopter dad!* How pathetic is that?"

"Snowplow," SallyAnne corrected him. "Helicopter parents hover and nudge their kids. Snowplows actually do the work so that the kids never get a chance to learn from their mistakes."

"Gotcha." Riley saluted her. "Whoever thought that one of the most rebellious teen rockers of our generation would turn out to be such a pussy of a parent—sorry, SallyAnne."

"You're turning into Lionel," she muttered.

Lionel frowned. "Is that a bad thing?"

SallyAnne shrugged. "I…meant it as a compliment."

"Oh, no! The parents are fighting!" Riley put his hands over his ears. "On that note, I'm outta here. When I get home, I'm burning all my old Jammerhead LPs."

"That should cause quite a stink," SallyAnne warned him.

"No more than the bad publicity when Jammerhead makes his perp walk." He waved as he went out the door.

Lionel turned to SallyAnne. "We've confirmed that Winslow made it onto the plane flying out of Macau. The EVA flight makes a stop in Taipei before heading to LAX. It'll be in by five o'clock tomorrow afternoon. We should meet it."

SallyAnne nodded. "Agreed. With all the gambling bridges he's burned, he'll flip like a pancake. We'll get the names of all of Maleficent's clients."

Lionel frowned. "*Who?*"

"That's my new nickname for Miranda. Because she's so evil." Sally-Anne shivered. "Just like the evil queen in *Sleeping Beauty.*"

"Oh, I don't know." Lionel shrugged. "She just cut Nira a break on her fee. That wasn't so evil."

SallyAnne snickered. "Yeah, right, keep telling yourself that! Have you forgotten that she's just convinced a single mom who worked her way through medical school to commit fraud?" She stalked the room. "You know, Lionel, if I didn't know better, I'd say you have a blind spot for our suspect!"

"Not everything is black and white," he argued. "And not everyone is all good or all bad."

"You are." SallyAnne could have kicked herself for letting that comment slip out.

"I'm…*what?*"

"You're…all good. Always by the book, I mean." SallyAnne stared down at her feet. "You'd never do anything wrong."

"In other words, I'm predictable," he muttered.

"Yes. But in a *good* way." She picked up her valise. "Unless you let it cloud your judgment."

Like now, she thought.

She could tell he'd read her mind.

Good. Fair warning.

Lionel let her walk out by herself.

CHAPTER 26

"**A**re you sure the file is gone?" Manya asked Charly.

"Yes, of course, I'm sure!" Charly's heart was palpitating.

"When was the last time you looked at it?" Zina asked.

"I don't know…about three weeks ago?"

Sienna slapped her forehead. "Damn, girl! That was practically when Egan handed out the debate topics!"

"What can I say?" Charly wailed. "I did my arguments really quickly. I wanted to get them out of the way of homework!"

"It's 'out of the way,' alright!" Zina declared. "It is *so* far out of the way that now you can't find the file."

It was lunchtime. The girls were in one of the group study rooms located on the top rotunda of Ashbury Academy's library.

"With Debate Team tryouts today, when and where you going to go over your arguments?" Manya asked.

"Now—and here." Charly shrugged. "I wanted it to be fresh."

"If you can't remember any of your research, it'll be more like improv," Zina muttered.

Charly winced at her friend's chiding.

In truth, she'd been fretting about it all weekend. But between juggling her school reading assignments with the family's Saturday bike excursion and their traditional Sunday gardening and dinner with Lavinia, she hadn't had time to look at it.

These days, Lavinia was uncharacteristically tired. The chuckles brought on by her grandchildren's joshing came a beat later than usual. And while Lavinia had come up with a few quips of her own, her tone was more wistful than lively.

Audrey's tender silence around Lavinia proved she was also concerned.

Last night, the family stayed until almost ten o'clock. When they realized Lavinia's eyes were closing, Charly had an overwhelming desire to linger. "Why don't I stay here tonight?" she pleaded to her grandmother. "Tomorrow morning, we'll walk to school together."

Lavinia shook her head. "The minute you leave, I'm going straight to bed." She tweaked Charly's nose. "You'd be bored watching me sleep."

Charly had reasoned she'd have plenty of time during lunch break to study the arguments she'd prepared. Now, to find the digital folder empty, she felt like crying.

I'm so stupid! I should have opened it long before now!

Where could those darned files have gone?

Sienna plopped down in front of Charly's laptop. "Maybe it's still retrievable. Let me take a look."

Charly buried her head in her hands. "Be my guest."

Sienna clicked some buttons. A moment later, she asked, "Hey, um… have you accessed the file from anywhere other than your home or the school's IP addresses?"

"What the hell is an IP address?" Zina asked.

"Every computer has one," Sienna explained. "It identifies the computer, its location and the service provider that it uses for its web access."

"Do you think I was hacked?" Charly asked.

"From what I can tell, yes." Sienna frowned. "I've got an Instagram fan who's a white hat hacker. I'll ask her to look at your browsing history to see if my guess is right."

"In the meantime, we should get cracking on recovering as much of your research as possible so that you can rebuild your arguments," Manya said. "What topics did you choose?"

"Human cloning and illegal immigration," Charly replied. "How about you?"

"I chose hook-ups and the death penalty," Zina said.

"I've got the death penalty and human cloning," Sienna added.

"For me, it's illegal immigration and hook-ups," Manya replied. "My mom almost had a cow when Miranda told her I'd chosen the last one."

The other girls snickered.

"Miranda is critiquing your debate?" Charly asked.

Manya nodded.

"Mine too," Zina added.

"That's nice of her," Charly murmured.

"Okay, so Charly, since I chose human cloning too, why don't you and I do the research on that?" Sienna suggested. "And since Manya has already researched immigration, she and Zina can research that topic. We'll have to leave after the lunch break, though. Charly, what do you have after lunch?"

"Odette, for French IV," Charly replied.

"Skip her class. I'll tell her your PMSing," Manya promised. "She'll understand."

"Hey, the research will go a lot faster if you check your browsing history from three weeks ago," Zina suggested. "Split up the links between us and we can pull them up and make PDFs for you."

"Brilliant!" Charly exclaimed.

The girls high-fived.

By the end of the lunch hour, they'd cobbled enough research on Charly's topics for her to make her arguments again.

"You're the best friends in the world," Charly declared.

"Don't get all sappy on us," Sienna warned her. "You can't afford to short out your computer with tears. Now, write your arguments and make us proud!"

She still got a peck on the cheek from Charly.

So did the other girls.

"SO, TELL ME HOW THIS WORKS EXACTLY," MIRANDA COOED TO EGAN.

She flirting with me again, he realized. I wish…Nah. I can't.

He knew he was a fool to still be hung up on Audrey.

Miranda's come-on was appreciated nonetheless.

Because of the number of contestants, Egan had to change his grading system somewhat to choose the top eight who would make up the team.

"It's simple," Egan replied to Odette and Miranda. "We have about eighty or so contestants out there. You're to grade them on a scale of one to ten, on three criteria. Category One is organization and clarity. Category Two is argument support. And Category Three is cross-examination and rebuttal. This allows for a high score of thirty. That would make ninety a perfect score from all three judges."

"Easy-peasy," Miranda purred.

"I hope so," Egan admitted. He handed both women the pamphlet listing the four questions:

- *Is the current approach to illegal immigration too harsh or too lenient?*
- *Are there ramifications for teens in the "hook-up culture," and if so, are they emotionally or physically harmful?*
- *Does the death penalty constitute a cruel and unusual punishment?*
- *Should scientists be allowed to clone humans?*

"Each student was asked to choose two of these questions for debate," he continued. "The students are waiting for us now, in the main auditorium. They've divided themselves into four groups: one for each question they wish to debate first. They'll be called into this room randomly, two by two, prepared to present both sides of the argument, which will be determined by the flip of a coin."

"Got it," Odette said.

"Don't score brutally, but do score fairly," Egan insisted. "And please! *No playing favorites.*"

Odette rolled her eyes.

Miranda chuckled. "I'm too new here to have any favorites. I guess you could say that too, Egan."

Except, perhaps Audrey's kids…

She'd be watching to see how high he scored Chuck and Charly.

It's so obvious that he's still got a thing for that nitwit, Miranda fumed silently.

The way he had pointedly teased her about Jess, she wondered if he'd be wondering the same about her regarding Hugo.

Over the past couple of weeks, she'd already had two "tutoring" sessions with Hugo. From his broad wink, she'd quickly and angrily deduced that his loudmouth father had let him in on her scheme. "Anything to get me on a fat-cat campus," Hugo crowed. "Somewhere I can *really* clean up."

Miranda had made Hugo write a few test essays. She then placed all the writing samples in the University Test & Prep iCloud account. There, Winslow could access them. He'd copy the handwriting samples for the tests that would eventually be sent to the SAT's grading division.

She'd done the same with Manya, Quest, and Zina, all of whom were clueless as to how far Miranda's handholding would go on their behalf.

And all the more reason that, no matter how badly they choked on their debate arguments, they'd receive the highest grades possible from her.

CHARLY'S HEART LEAPED IN HER THROAT WHEN SHE SAW HOW MANY OTHERS had shown up for Debate Team tryouts.

There must be seventy, maybe eighty, other students milling around, she realized. It's practically half of the senior class and at least a quarter of the junior class.

As Charly signed in, a student volunteer asked her to write her name on two cardboard disks and place them in the bowls designated by the name of the argument topics she'd chosen.

She winced when she saw Quest sitting with Sienna, who, like Charly, had chosen "Immigration Arguments" as her first debate question. The competition was going to be stiff. She loved him as a brother. She didn't want to see his heart broken by a low score.

Zina and Manya waved at her from across the auditorium. They were sitting in the "Death Penalty Arguments" section.

Charly was dismayed to see that Chuck and Fawn were also sitting in the Immigration Arguments section. Fawn was practically sitting in his lap. Charly waved at her brother, but he barely nodded back. Since the argument at dinner two weeks ago, they'd scarcely said two words to each other.

If I make the team and he doesn't, he may not speak to me all year.

The thought saddened her.

Egan came out to say a few words. After thanking everyone for being there, he added, "As you read in the pamphlet, each round should take five minutes. If you win your first round, you move onto the second. If you don't, you've been eliminated."

The contestants grimaced.

"The top eight scorers make up the team. If there are ties for eighth place, the lowest-scoring contestants will be asked to face off with their second argument. Got that?"

This time, the contestants nodded.

"We'll start with the topic of immigration. To compete, two names in that bowl will be chosen randomly. We'll keep drawing until there aren't any more competitors. At that point, we'll move onto a different topic, then another, and finally the last one," Egan explained. "When you hear your name called, walk to the front table again. There, you'll pick from the bowl holding a pro and con disk." He clapped his hands. "Okay, the first category is 'Immigration.'" He reached down into the bowl and called the first two names.

Sienna was called before Charly, in the third Immigration argument team. She drew the pro argument.

When she came out, she was smiling and gave Charly a thumbs up. She had her arm around her opponent, a senior girl, who was in tears.

Fawn was also called before Charly. She showed her triumph with a happy dance that caused her opponent to storm out of the auditorium.

Charly's name was the first one called for the eleventh pairing. When she stood up, Sienna whispered, "Break a leg!"

Quest was too nervous to say anything. When Charly patted his shoulder, he said, "I'm just glad I didn't have to debate you!"

Me too, Charly thought, as she headed down the bleachers to the front table.

Hearing the next name—"Chuck McKittridge"—stopped her in her tracks.

Chuck froze too.

Instinctively, the twins' eyes went to each other.

Their stares reflected their sadness at this anomaly.

Chuck pulled the pro disk, leaving Charly with the con argument.

Following the lead of the other contestants, they shook hands before entering the judges' room.

CHUCK IS MAKING MY PRO ARGUMENT.

The thought that her own brother stole her debate files felt like a punch to Charly's gut.

She forced herself to stay calm as he spoke her previously planned lines verbatim. He'd always been great at rote memorization.

He'd make a great actor, she thought, or a thief. He's well on his way to being either or both.

When it was her turn, she kept one thought in front of her:

I won't let Chuck rob me of my place on the team.

It drove her to make eye contact while making her opening remarks.

It gave clarity to the critical points in her argument.

She closed with an eloquence she never knew she had.

From the look on Egan's face, she could tell she'd wowed him.

From Odette's smile, she could see her French teacher was proud of her.

Miranda was smiling, too—also a good sign.

Chuck wasn't. He looked worried.

Good, thought Charly. That will teach you never to screw me over again.

WHEN CHUCK AND CHARLY WALKED INTO THE ROOM, MIRANDA HAD ALMOST crowed at the situation before her:

The chance to make Audrey's life miserable, even in this small way.

With that in mind, Chuck got tens in all three categories.

On the other hand, she graded Charly with a six, a five, and a four.

Seeing her score sheet, Egan did a double-take. He whispered, "Wow! Don't you feel you graded Charly pretty harshly?"

Miranda shrugged. "She seemed too...I don't know, practiced, or something."

By Egan's frown, she knew he wasn't buying her answer.

Miranda was chagrined when Charly's overall score came in at seventy-five. That meant Egan and Odette had given her tens across the board.

She was dismayed when Chuck's score came in precisely the same.

"What do we do when there's a tie?" Odette asked.

"Both contestants are allowed to go through," Miranda muttered. She remembered this from past experience.

Egan looked sharply at her. "Yes! How did you know that?"

"Lucky guess," she replied.

<hr>

CHUCK AND CHARLY WERE RELIEVED TO KNOW THEY'D AT LEAST MADE IT INTO consideration. But both were thinking the same thing:

Is my score high enough to make the team?

The rest of the afternoon was just as dramatic.

The good news was that Manya and Zina also won their debates.

Even better, albeit surprising, was that Quest had as well.

But the best news of all was that Sienna, Manya, Zina, and even Quest had all made the team.

Surprisingly, so had Hugo Smallwood and Fawn.

When the eight top scores were called, Charly and Chuck were on the team—if barely.

"Gee," Quest exclaimed to Charly. "How did I score better than you?"

It was a great question.

Chuck walked over to his sister. Fawn was wrapped around him.

He looks as if he's being squeezed by a boa constrictor, Charly thought.

"Hey, looks like we're going to be teammates," Chuck declared.

"You sound as if you're proud of that," Charly retorted.

Chuck frowned. "Why shouldn't I be?"

"*Really?* You're proud of stealing my research and my arguments?" Charly poked his chest with her finger.

"I...we ...didn't steal anything!" The color went out of Chuck's face. "Did we?"

"*We?*" Charly looked from Chuck to Fawn and back again. "Why are you asking her?"

The smirk on Fawn's face told Charly all she needed to know.

Fawn clicked her tongue. "I heard in French class that you were feeling a little under the weather. Instead of taking it out on your brother, take a Midol or something."

To keep his sister from clawing out his girlfriend's eyes, Chuck leaped between them. As he hustled Fawn out of the auditorium, he looked back at Charly.

He's a clueless idiot.

Charly waited until everyone left the auditorium before going back into the judge's room. The score sheets were still on the table.

Miranda's scores were what had brought her down.

Ironically, Egan and Odette's scores for Chuck had pulled him even with her.

Fawn had only scored a point higher than the twins, as had Hugo. Again, Miranda had championed them with the highest scores possible.

Charly stuck the sheets into her backpack.

Then she changed her iCloud password.

CHAPTER 27

"What do you mean, Winslow Jennings wasn't on the flight?" Melamed was practically bellowing into SallyAnne's phone.

She moved the phone away from her ear. Lionel winced when he heard their boss too.

They'd delivered the news while standing in an alcove off of LAX's international concourse.

Finally, when they could tell he'd quit talking, she replied, "He was booked through to Los Angeles, but he must have gotten off in Shanghai."

Lionel indicated for SallyAnne to put the phone on speaker. When Melamed's cursing subsided over this new bit of information, Lionel suggested, "We can put a tracer on his passport."

"He could be anywhere in the world," Melamed grumbled. "So, yeah, do that. It's not like we have a choice. When it comes to Miranda D'Arcy, he knows where all the bodies are buried."

"Don't we have enough to take her down now?" SallyAnne asked. "She's lining up new clients every day!"

"This is much bigger than just her college admissions fraud. She's a guppy, and there are bigger fish to fry," Melamed countered.

"You mean Darius Calder," Lionel deduced.

"You betcha. We have to keep her in play at least until she's delivered for him, not to mention the others," Melamed explained. "Once we have him dead to rights, he'll flip on a few of his clients to lessen his own sentence." He rang off.

SallyAnne turned to Lionel. "In other words, we can't make any arrests until after her clients get their acceptance letters?"

He nodded. "Frankly, it may make sense. Once they accept the offers, it

399

goes from being conspiracy-to-commit to a lock-solid fraud case. To pull off a scam like this, Miranda must have a number of co-conspirators on the college campuses. We'll need the extra time to round them up." Lionel looked at his watch. "If we hit the United terminal now, we can stand by for the SFO flight. It leaves in about an hour—if air traffic delays don't stretch it even longer."

SallyAnne nodded. "Sure, let's do it."

The memory of their last LA trip was still fresh in her mind. She wondered how he'd feel about a game of Never Have I Ever as they waited to board their flight.

She never imagined he was thinking the same thing.

WHAT THE HELL IS ALL THAT BANGING?

Miranda woke with a start.

Glancing at her clock, she saw it was only three o'clock in the morning. She was sorely tempted to ignore the pounding, but her gut told her she shouldn't.

Slowly, she got out of bed. Wrapping her bathrobe around her, she walked to her front door and looked out the peephole.

Winslow was standing in the hallway.

Before the racket woke her neighbors too, Miranda threw open the door.

"Why aren't you answering your phone?" he hissed.

"Because I turn it off at night!" Miranda sputtered. "What the hell are you doing here?"

"I came to warn you!" he hissed. "Something is fishy at the UP&T office. I've got a couple of hidden cameras in there and around the place—"

"You do?" Miranda was livid. "And you never told me?"

"It's insurance, trust me," he declared.

"Insurance against what?" Miranda asked. "Have you been recording me and our conversations?"

"No!... Okay, *yes*—but that goes with the territory." Winslow shrugged. "What, you don't trust me?"

He snickered. "Tell the truth. Do you trust *me*?"

"You have a point there," she muttered. Suddenly, she was angry she hadn't thought of surveillance herself. "So what did you see that has you so concerned?"

"I had a stopover in Shanghai, so I thought I'd kill time by scanning the surveillance footage. It's a good thing I did, too. Someone was staking out the joint."

From his cell phone, he showed her some of the footage: a man and a woman, in suits, knocking on University Prep & Test's office door. After doing so several times and getting no answer, they hung out in the hall—for a long, long, time.

Three days, in fact.

"Wow! Talk about a couple of desperate parents," Miranda murmured.

"I thought so too—at first. But then I realized they could be a couple of goons from… I don't know, one of the casinos."

"Jesus! Did you get caught again, counting cards?"

"It's an occupational hazard—like broken legs." Winslow shrugged. "Listen, Miranda, what I'm trying to say is that, for whatever reason, UP&T is too hot right now for either of us to go back there."

Miranda took a closer look. "They don't look like mobsters."

"Don't be an idiot. These days, most of the casinos hire ex-cops. Not only do they know how to play rough, many of them still use their law enforcement connections to track down the bad bets." Winslow frowned. "In case they were tracking my passport, I ditched it in the Shanghai airport men's room."

"How did you get back into the states?"

He rolled his eyes. "What…you think I travel with only one?"

She jabbed him in the chest with a finger. "I've got *you* to thank for this! What the hell am I going to do with all the parents who've already paid me to get their kids into the college of their choice?" She paced the floor. "You'll have to set up shop somewhere else. Maybe Brentwood—"

"Are you kidding me?" Winslow snorted with laughter. "If they've already paid up, what do *you* care? Do you think they're going to run to the cops and say, 'Woe is me, I gave a crook a ton of money because she promised to illegally get my kid into some college, and now she's disappeared off the face of the earth'?"

"You're right!" Her eyes glistened at the thought of her great fortune. Her clients had already paid upfront. They couldn't implicate her without taking themselves down too.

"You should set up here instead," Miranda insisted. "I've already secured several new clients—"

He frowned. "To hell with that! You're on your own, lady. I'm plowing new pastures."

"But—you can't leave me, just like that…without notice!"

Winslow stared at her as if she'd lost her mind. He laughed all the way down the hall.

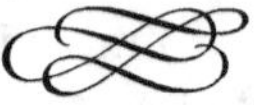

"*I*'m sorry…what was that again?" Lavinia looked at Daniel, and then at Seamus.

The November board meeting was not going well. From what Egan could tell, Lavinia's mind was elsewhere.

If Harris hadn't been stuck in DC, she might have seemed more like her usual self, he reasoned. Seamus seemed to try harder to be an obnoxious prick when the congressman wasn't there to protect her.

Thank goodness for Daniel and me, Egan thought.

He was surprised, though, that Daniel hadn't noticed this too. Some of the other teachers were picking up on it. Egan could tell by the way they exchanged concerned glances when her thoughts drifted off mid-sentence.

And yet, no one said anything.

Were they afraid of seeming disloyal? Or, like him, did they prefer to be in denial of what was happening to the school's beloved headmistress?

Egan was tempted to divulge Audrey's promise to Lavinia and Daniel, but then he thought better of it. Audrey's trust in him was one of the few reasons for what little pride he had these days.

"We were arguing over Tallulah's budget for the damn anniversary gala," Seamus grumbled. "I told her that if she wanted to cut corners, instead of doing away with the ice sculptures, we should hire some of the scholarship kids as waiters. That way, the rest of us can see them earning their keep."

Lavinia blanched at the thought. Turning to Daniel, she murmured, "And you agreed to that?"

"No! Of course not!" Perplexed that she'd even think such a thing, he shook his head. "Since this has devolved into a discussion over ice sculptures and yet one more way in which we can shame our scholarship students, I'd like to call for an adjournment."

"I second that motion," Tallulah declared. "But first let me add that we've already promised *every* student a free ticket to the gala anyway—even our scholarship students. So, if any parents wish to volunteer as cater-waiters to defray costs, I'm sure everyone would appreciate it."

She stood up and stomped off.

Bliss was right on her heels.

"Well, that went well," Jess murmured. He looked around the table, but his gaze froze on Miranda. "Anyone up for a drink?"

Egan grimaced. But, yes, he was curious if Miranda would take Jess up on his offer.

He was surprised when she feigned a yawn. "Not for me, thank you. It's been a long day and an even longer night." Miranda stood up but was taking her time gathering her things.

Chagrinned, Jess walked out with Seamus, Warner, and Darius.

"I, um, should go too. It's been a very long day." Lavinia murmured. As she lumbered to her feet, Daniel reached over to steady her.

"Would you like a lift home?" he asked her gently.

Lavinia managed a chuckle. "Of course not, dear. I'm practically around the corner. But thank you for the offer." She pecked him on the cheek and waved to the others as she walked off.

Egan was going to ask Daniel if he'd like to stop off for a beer when he realized Miranda was whispering something in Daniel's ear. He pretended not to notice when Daniel nodded to whatever she was saying, or that they walked out together.

By the time Egan made it outside, Daniel was already driving off.

Miranda was in the car with him.

"I appreciate you giving me a lift." Miranda shifted so that she was angled closer to Daniel. "I'd forgotten how long these meetings can run! Otherwise, I would have never left my car with the mechanic today. He closes at six on the button."

The truth was she had Ubered to work and could have Ubered back home too. She knew Daniel was too polite to turn down her request for a lift.

To accomplish her next goal, she needed Daniel on her side.

"No problem," he assured her. "You're close enough to us—the Summit, right? On Russian Hill?"

She nodded. "Hey, I want to thank you again for your diplomacy with Lavinia about my addition to the board. I'd hoped she would approve."

Daniel grimaced. "She proved it with her own vote, wouldn't you say?"

"I'll always appreciate her vote of confidence." Miranda faked the emotional quiver in her voice. "Which is why I'm finding it very hard to bring this up."

Daniel glanced over at her. "Is something wrong?"

"Frankly, I was hoping you'd tell me." She sighed. "I've noticed some odd behavior from Lavinia."

"Like what?" Daniel's question was stilted.

"I can't put my finger on it, exactly. She seems tired. And then there's the weight loss—not that it should be an issue! Heaven knows we could all afford to lose a few pounds." She paused: "I guess it's the forgetfulness that is the most concerning. I'm just wondering…is there something I should know?"

Daniel shook his head. "I'm sure it's just the stress over AA's twenty-fifth anniversary events."

Miranda laid her hand on Daniel's shoulder. "I'm here for her. I hope you know that, Daniel. That being said, if there is any way you feel I can help—you know, to make things easier for her…or for the good of the school…" She let her fingers linger.

Until Daniel veered the car to the curb, at which point both hands went to the dashboard to brace herself. "We're here. Let me get the door for you."

Before she knew what was happening, he was out of his side of the car and beside hers. He opened the passenger door.

"You're such a gentleman," she muttered.

"Yes, I am," he said crisply. "Look, Miranda, if your questions are at Seamus' bidding, please make it clear to him that Lavinia is fine. She'd probably seem less haggard if, like most heads of school, she had a trustee board that did their best to support her as opposed to tear down what she has spent a lifetime building."

So that she took his hint the conversation was over, he drove off without saying goodnight.

Daniel waited until he and Audrey were in bed to say, "Lavinia was odd tonight."

Usually, Audrey's concern would cause her to flip on the light. Instead, she murmured, "In what way?"

"She was listless. Tired. Forgetful. Surely you've noticed her weight loss!"

"Yes, I asked her about it," Audrey's tone was casual enough. "Lavinia told me she's on a new diet. Apparently, it's working."

"Too well! Maybe she's not getting—oh, I don't know—enough nutrients or something!" Because Audrey hadn't flipped on her light, he turned on the one on his bedside table. "Honey, I'll be honest—*I'm worried about her.*"

Audrey didn't turn around. Instead, she said, "People change as they get older. I'm sure she's fine!"

Look me in the face and tell me that, he thought.

Instead, he turned off his light.

A few minutes later, Audrey turned over so that she could spoon him, wrapping her arms around his chest.

When he pulled her in even closer, he felt the dampness of her cheeks on his back.

If anything were wrong with Lavinia, she'd tell me, he reasoned.

As Daniel drifted off to sleep, he chided himself for making her worry; for causing her to cry.

That Miranda is such a bitch.

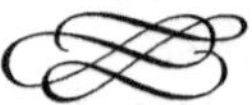

*A*udrey hadn't realized how hard it would be to juggle three bags of groceries on her bicycle, even while going the short distance of the few blocks between the Haight Fillmore Whole Foods and Lavinia's cottage.

It was a week's worth of food for her mother. Audrey had also purchased the ingredients needed to prepare the meal Lavinia usually made every Sunday: pasta, an artisan bread, and peppermint ice cream, along with a salad from her garden bounty.

The family wouldn't know that it was Audrey's handiwork.

Before her illness, Lavinia had always made her own pasta and bread. But the effects of her chemotherapy put an end to that.

It was a bright, cool Saturday morning in mid-October. As always, Daniel and the children had biked over the Golden Gate Bridge, where they'd spend the day trekking over Mount Tam's many dusty trails.

Since learning of her mother's illness, Audrey's Saturdays were now spent with Lavinia. She wondered how many more they'd share.

Audrey carried the heavy bags onto the porch. The front door was locked, so she rang the doorbell, then waited nearly a minute before ringing it again.

Silence.

By balancing the grocery bags between the door and her hip, Audrey used her key to unlock the door and then slowly opened it.

She called out to her mother.

Again, no answer.

Not surprising. Lately, her mother's energy had been so low that

Lavinia had taken to sleeping on the back sunporch or lounging in the backyard.

Instead, Audrey found her mother comatose on the kitchen floor.

She dropped the groceries. She didn't care that the eggs cracked and a jar of olive oil broke. All that mattered was that Lavinia still had a pulse despite not responding to Audrey's attempt to revive her.

When Audrey's hysteria finally subsided, the 911 operator was able to get her to verify Lavinia's address and answer a few questions about her mother's condition,

While they waited for the ambulance, Audrey patted her mother's face and arms. She ran to her mother's bedroom for a pillow and blanket with the thought of putting the former under her head for comfort and the latter to put over her body for warmth, but then she worried that perhaps it would have the opposite effect. Would the pillow angle her head in such a way that it would block her windpipe? Would the blanket make Lavinia so hot as to set off cardiac arrest?

Finally, Audrey heard the ambulance's wail. She ran to the door, flung it open, and waved the med techs into the house.

Lavinia moaned as they strapped her onto the gurney.

Audrey insisted on riding with her mother. She didn't want to navigate the city's busy streets and hills on her bike, and she didn't want to spend precious time looking for Lavinia's car keys.

It may have seemed as if it took the ambulance an hour to get there, but when it reached the hospital, Audrey realized it wasn't even lunchtime yet.

DOCTOR VIOLET JIMENEZ'S RESPONSE TO WHY HER MOTHER HAD REACTED SO violently to her chemotherapy left Audrey reeling: "I'd warned her that no two patients respond exactly in the same way to their specific cocktail."

"So you stopped her chemo?"

"No," Doctor Jimenez explained. "But we have had to change her regimen and attempt more aggressive treatment. As you can see by today's development, Lavinia's response to this change in protocol has not been good."

"My mother never told me any of this!" Audrey exclaimed.

The knot in her throat made it impossible for Audrey to continue asking questions. She knew from the beginning that Lavinia might not make it through her illness, but for the first time she felt the cold reality of living the rest of her life without her mother's love to buoy her.

Sensing her dismay, Dr. Jimenez took Audrey's hand. "Your mother has a lot of fight in her. We're going to do all we can to help her get through this. We'll keep her here overnight, for observation. Leave your number with the nurse, and you'll be called with a time to pick her up tomorrow."

"Thank you, doctor," Audrey whispered.

Audrey stared down at Lavinia. Despite the tubes tethered to her at one end and the monitors at the other, she looked peaceful.

Audrey closed her eyes for a bit. When she opened them again, she found her mother gazing at her.

Lavinia's lips were parched, and her eyes were damp. "So...you know?"

Audrey nodded. "I wish you'd told me your treatment wasn't going as well as you had hoped."

"Several times this past week, I was on the verge of telling you. But I couldn't bear the thought of causing you more worry."

Audrey wanted to cry, but she couldn't.

Not in front of Lavinia.

She saw her mother as never before: vulnerable.

Lavinia closed her eyes again.

For the next two hours, Audrey listened:

As the monitors chirped softly like crickets.

To her mother's gentle breathing.

To her own pounding heart.

Every half hour, a nurse would stop by the room to get a monitor reading or to write something on the chart at the foot of Lavinia's bed. Audrey finally dared to ask, "What is in the drip?"

"A little something to help with her pain, but mostly it's fluid to keep her hydrated," the nurse answered.

After the woman left, Audrey heard Lavinia say something, but it didn't make sense.

Audrey wondered if what was pouring into her mother's arm might act like a truth serum. If so, maybe now she'd get the answer to the one question she hadn't asked her mother since she was old enough to understand that it was something Lavinia felt, for whatever reason, should die with her.

But no, Lavinia. I need to know. And I want to hear it from you.

She took a deep breath. Then, softly she asked: "Lavinia, who is my father?"

Lavinia answered her with a gentle snore.

Audrey kissed her mother's cool forehead and left the room.

She took a cab back to Lavinia's house so that she could clean up the mess in the kitchen.

The melted ice cream, the carton of broken eggs, the olive oil, and the now soggy loaf of artisan rye created a surreal, colorful tableau: pink, brown, and yellow goo on a black and white checkerboard floor.

It took half a roll of paper towels to sop it all up. Then Audrey mopped the floor. When she finished, there were no remnants of the sticky, smelly concoction. But Audrey wouldn't need to smell it to remember this day.

The sight of Lavinia, lying on the floor so helplessly, would stay with her forever.

WHEN AUDREY GOT HOME, DANIEL WAS ALREADY THERE. NOTICING HOW SHE looked around, he read her mind. "The kids walked down to Fillmore Street for sushi and ice cream. They were famished. Did you have a good day?"

How could she answer? Was this the time for yet another lie?

Or, should she tell the truth—and in doing so, break her promise to Lavinia?

Audrey said nothing.

Instead, she grabbed Daniel's arm and led him, running, upstairs to their bedroom, shutting the door behind them.

Slowly, she undressed him and watched his face intently as he did the same to her.

They made love silently. She let her mouth and her fingers and her sighs tell him all he needed to know:

She never wanted to lose him.

She *could not* lose him too.

CHAPTER 30

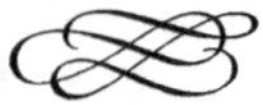

*A*shbury Academy's second debate, against University High School, was to take place on Wednesday.

And after handily defeating Marin Academy, the team was pumped for another win.

Well, most of the team, anyway.

To Chuck's eye, Manya, Zina, Charly, and Sienna worked together like a well-oiled machine. Even Quest—who would do anything Charly asked of him—proved to be a whiz at finding the necessary research on the four topics to be debated:

Should jobs be subcontracted into developing countries?
Do celebrities get away with more crimes than non-celebrities?
Is it appropriate for adolescents to be sentenced to life without parole?
Should more people choose adoption as opposed to having biological
    children?

Quest's research was then passed forward to Charly and her pals. Their tasks were to extract the relevant information that would best help the team form their own pro and con arguments, along with the necessary rebuttals.

Like Chuck, Fawn was watching the process from the sidelines. "Call me when you have my argument written," she chided callously.

"You're supposed to write your own arguments," Charly argued.

Fawn snickered. "Why should I do that when you'll do it so much better?"

"It's why you supposedly made the team," Charly retorted. "Oh,

410

wait…you're right! The only reason you're here is that *you and my brother stole my arguments!*" She glared at the two culprits.

Chuck felt his face heat up.

He was determined to succeed and prove Daniel wrong: that he could in fact manage basketball and Debate Team with equal skill.

But Fawn had put him in an awkward position. He'd only hacked Charly's debate argument folder at her insistence.

Okay, granted, it was much easier to memorize her argument than to build one from scratch. And he genuinely thought no one would find out.

Except Charly did. Up against Chuck, his sister had heard her hard work repeated verbatim.

This one act of thievery had severed their relationship. Charly no longer adored him.

In fact, she now ignored him entirely.

Oddly, Charly hadn't yet told their parents. Was it because she thought they wouldn't believe her? Chuck couldn't imagine it was because she was protecting him.

Because Charly had stated her accusation against Fawn loudly enough, Egan stopped mid-conversation with Manya to ask, "Charly—what did you say?"

Charly shrugged. "I think Fawn can explain it better." She nudged Fawn with her elbow—*hard.* "Go ahead."

"I was just saying that I thought it would be better for the team if those who were more adept at writing arguments could do it for those who weren't," Fawn huffed.

"And I told her that wasn't fair," Charly countered. "I mean, supposedly, that's why we're all here in the first place. We beat out others who actually took the time to create their own arguments."

"I've seen it work both ways," Egan admitted.

"See? Egan says it's best for the team!" This time Fawn nudged Charly —hard enough that Charly stumbled.

"That's not what I said at all," Egan countered. "In fact, Debate Team is supposed to help you look at both sides of a situation. If all you're doing is memorizing someone else's argument, it defeats the purpose."

"Is that so?" Charly pushed Fawn so hard that she stumbled forward.

Fawn shoved back.

Charly slapped her.

Everyone gasped.

Except for Hugo, who crowed, "Catfight! *Meow!*"

Enraged, Fawn's fist went for Charly's nose.

Chuck stopped it by grabbing it with his hand. When it slammed into his open palm, he yelped from the pain.

"You three!" Egan growled. "In the hall with me—*Now!*"

"Okay, who wants to start?" Egan was doing his best to stay calm. The last thing he needed was for Lavinia to find out that her grandchildren were at each other's throats, thanks to Seamus's evil spawn.

The teens eyed each other warily.

Charly shrugged. "The team should vote as to whether it's necessary to carry those members who won't do their own research, let alone write their own arguments."

Fawn scowled at her.

When she balled her fists, Chuck moved between them again. "Charly is right. We're not all pulling our weight equally."

Fawn glowered at his betrayal.

"But we're all proud to be on the team, so those of us who are holding the others back will just need to try harder," Chuck continued. "That won't necessarily make us a winning team, but it will teach us some important lessons about ourselves—and each other, if we're willing to share what we've learned." He looked from one of the girls to the other. "I'm willing to work harder. And if others need my help, I'm there for them too."

Jesus, Egan thought. This kid sounds as if he's running for class president or something!

Egan nodded. "Okay, sure, with one caveat. Those who do research for others get help on their arguments. And for that matter, the whole team critiques all arguments. That way, building the strongest argument will be a team effort."

Charly, Chuck, and Fawn shrugged in agreement.

"Chuck, why don't you explain it to the others?" Egan suggested.

Chuck nodded enthusiastically—but then replied, "I'd rather Charly tell them. She's sort of the team leader anyway."

Charly's eyes grew large.

"Sure, works for me," Egan said. "But just a heads up. I'll be choosing the team's captain—and it will be someone who demonstrates leadership and fairness. If you want to be in the running—and I'd imagine you all do, considering how it would look on your college applications—start acting the part. *Capisce?*"

To make his point, he looked each of them in the eye.

As Egan watched them trek back inside, he wondered what had precipitated Chuck's peace offering to his sister.

For a brief moment, he felt such tremendous pride in both of them.

I guess this is what it's like to be a parent.

In good times, anyway.

No one expected the debate between Ashbury Academy and University High to be such a nail biter.

Certainly not Miranda.

AA was the home team. The audience reflected this: not just in the number of students and teachers present, but parents too.

Including Jess. As always, he'd somehow seen Miranda before she had a chance to see him first and hide.

"Hey, my kid did okay, right?" he exclaimed.

"A chip off the old block," Miranda cooed.

Far be it from her to point out that Hugo's score was the lowest on AA's team. But now that she'd burned her bridges in the Southland, it was essential to keep every San Francisco-based parent in play.

After this year, I can retire, she reasoned. No more lazy kids to coddle. No more sucking up to their snotty over-privileged parents.

After Winslow's visit, Miranda had checked out countries that didn't have an extradition treaty with the US. None of them were appealing. Ruling out war zones like Afghanistan or Third World countries like the Congo, she was left with a few European dictatorships or some Middle Eastern monarchies in which the *couture du jour* began and ended with whatever color burka was in season.

Thank you, but no thank you.

Until then, she'd continue to build her war chest.

With that in mind, she scanned the seats for her next victim.

Seamus was there with Gretchen. They have me to thank for Fawn's inclusion on the team, Miranda thought. I'll be sure to let him know that.

Gemma and Darius were also there, as were Bliss and Raffaele; and Tallulah and Jammerhead. To the crowd's delight, even the infamous Maggie Wishart had made an appearance.

Quest's family is just thrilled to see him on any stage, even if it's to stutter through a debate, Miranda reasoned.

Daniel was there too, with their youngest—the boy, Noah. They sat on either side of Lavinia. Blissfully, she held both their hands in her lap.

So, where was Audrey?

Miranda didn't have to look far. As she suspected, Audrey was standing next to Egan. Although they were looking at the stage, their heads were tilted toward each other as they exchanged comments.

He's still in love with her, Miranda realized.

The thought enraged her.

I have to kill his obsession with Audrey.

To do that, I'll have to make him fall in love with me.

Once, a long time ago, the idea of inciting Egan's lust had held some appeal, if only as a means to an end.

But now it merely seemed vile. Miranda's hatred for Egan went back to the day she'd learned how he'd successfully sabotaged her admission to Berkeley by writing a letter of recommendation that was anything but that.

And yet, were he to fall for her, Miranda would then have the votes she needed for her endgame: control of the trustee board, which was necessary if, sometime in the future, she needed to make a clean getaway, just as she had in Los Angeles.

The decimation of Audrey's mother's school—with Egan's unwitting help, no less—would be the ultimate triumph.

Out of the corner of her eye, Miranda noticed someone was waving at her: Seamus. He nodded for her to follow him out of the building.

What the hell does he want? Miranda wondered.

MIRANDA WAS PREPARED TO MAKE SMALL TALK—ABOUT THE DEBATE MATCH, the board, whatever—but Seamus shut her down bluntly: "What the hell is wrong with you?"

"*What?* I don't know what you mean—"

"Cut the bullshit! Listen, missy, the only reason I supported you for the board was because—"

"Seamus, please—*calm down!*" Miranda huffed. "I have no idea what you're talking about!"

He leaned in so that they were nose to nose. "Your exclusive college admissions concierge program! Why didn't you tell me that I could *buy* my daughter's way into any school I wanted?"

Miranda slapped her hand over his mouth. "It's exclusive for a reason, as you just now so boisterously pointed out. *And I'd like to keep it that way.*"

Seamus's eyes darted up and down the street. Noticing something, he nodded slowly.

She saw them too: a couple of men, idling across the street, watching her and Seamus.

Shady characters, indeed. But it was the Haight, so shady was to be expected.

"Tell you what," Miranda whispered, "I'll call you, and we'll talk. *Privately.* Okay?"

"Yeah, okay. Just…make it happen! My Fawnie deserves it!"

"No problem, I'm on your side," she assured him. "How do you think she got on Debate Team anyway?"

His eyes widened at her revelation. "Thanks, then," he muttered.

"You're welcome. Fair warning, though: besides my fee, you'll need to do something for me, too."

"Name it," he muttered.

"Call an emergency board meeting for Friday. Ask for Lavinia's resignation."

He frowned. "We won't have the votes! Remember, Darius' wife is best friends with Audrey Thorpe."

"Sure, we will. Lavinia is going senile. I'm not the only person to notice it. Heck, Seamus, you saw it yourself in the last board meeting!"

He frowned. "She did seem distracted."

"Now is the time to push it through. And while you're at it, you can recommend me as her replacement—temporarily. Until a nationwide search proves I'm the best candidate anyway." Miranda grinned. "So, which university do you want?"

"The best, of course!"

"But of course." Miranda chuckled. "Perhaps your alma mater? What is it again? ...Yale, right?"

"Why, er... yes." His winced as if dubious of such a pipe dream: Fawn at Yale.

"I may be able to arrange that," she assured him. "But first things first." She leaned in so that he'd have to look her in the eye. "Lavinia is out. Understood?"

"Okay, sure. You're on." Delighted, he chuckled as he strolled off.

After a minute, Miranda followed Seamus back inside.

Through the reflection of the auditorium's windows, she noticed that the men at the end of the street had never moved.

ASHBURY ACADEMY WON BY A MERE TWO POINTS.

The team, ecstatic, went into a group hug, pulling Egan in with them. "I'm proud of all of you," he declared, shaking hands all around. When he got to Charly, he winked his approval too.

But it was Chuck to whom he said, "Thanks for keeping everyone focused this week on the prize."

Chuck beamed at the praise.

He deserves it, Charly realized.

She reached over and squeezed her brother's hand.

Seeing her mother's happy face, Charly shouted: "Mom, tomorrow and Friday are teacher workdays, so we're off from school! Can I invite the girls back to our place for a sleepover celebration?"

Quest looked hopeful. "Boys too?"

Charly rolled her eyes. "You know better than that. No boys allowed!"

Chuck added, "Fawn too—right Charly?"

Charly pursed her lips. Finally, she shrugged. "Sure...if she wants."

IF SHE WANTS.

Fawn could hear the disdain in Charly's voice.

Up until that moment, she'd been so proud of herself. She'd killed her argument!

And just seeing the look in her father's eyes made it all worthwhile. For once, he saw her for who she really was: not only pretty, but brilliant as well.

Perhaps college was a viable option after all. And not just college, but anything she chose to achieve beyond it. Brains and looks made a heady combination, so why not?

She had to admit, having others critique her honestly had made her argument only that much stronger. In fact, it was Charly who'd come up with Fawn's killer closing line.

At the time, Fawn felt Charly might actually have wanted to be a real friend, not just someone who had to be nice to Fawn for the team's sake.

But now the look on Charly's face stopped this fantasy in its tracks. Apparently even giving a great argument wasn't enough to gain acceptance into Charly's little clique of nerdy girls.

It occurred to Fawn that there would always be nerdy girls—certainly in college—who would think they were superior to her. And, like her father, they would always judge her on her looks, not her smarts.

I'd better learn now how to deal with them; to hurt them before they hurt me.

Fawn knew just how to do that.

She'd seen how Charly sought out Egan's attention; how sullen Charly had been when Egan accepted Chuck's resolution to their spat.

She's got a crush on Egan, Fawn realized.

Right then, she knew what she'd do—and tonight, too.

She leaned into Chuck and purred, "Honey, tonight let's make it just you and me, okay?"

That certainly put a smile on his face.

"I've got to go home with my parents, but why don't you pay me a visit…say, midnight?" she suggested.

Chuck's answer was a kiss. As he pulled away, he whispered, "You were awesome."

She shrugged off her guilt as she left the auditorium.

But instead of following her parents to their waiting car, she ran upstairs to Egan's classroom.

EGAN'S COMPUTER WAS ON HIS DESK.

She took a guess at his password. It was easy enough to hit it on the first time.

Extracurricular#1

Men are so predictable, she thought.

Through the school's open browser, she could access his private Gmail account, and wrote down its mailbox name.

She was out of the classroom in no time.

WHEN FAWN GOT HOME, SHE WENT UP TO HER ROOM, LOCKED THE DOOR, AND opened her computer to set up two new Gmail accounts:

Egan.Gable
Charly.McK

THE MESSAGE FAWN SENT FROM THE FIRST ACCOUNT WENT TO CHARLY'S REAL email account, and would undoubtedly pique her enemy's interest:

Dear Charly,
I know it seems strange to you that I'd reach out in this way, but I can tell
you've got something very important on your mind.
Your feelings are important to me. I hope you feel the same about mine.

I guess Shakespeare said it best:
"Love looks not with the eyes, but with the mind."

If you're free, why don't you stop by my classroom at the end of the teacher
workday tomorrow. Say, four o'clock? It would mean more to me than
you'll ever know.

With tremendous respect, always,
—Egan

Of course Charly would show up. She salivated every time Egan threw a compliment her way.

Since Fawn controlled the password to Egan's fake account, she'd check it later to see if Charly had responded.

From the Charly.McK email account, Fawn wrote to Egan's genuine private email account:

Hi, Egan,
Look, I know it seems strange to you that I'd reach out to you in this way,
but there's something that's very important on my mind. You seem to

*care deeply on so many levels that I feel I can talk to you about it
without feeling awkward.*

I guess Shakespeare said it best:

"Love looks not with the eyes, but with the mind."

*If you're free, would you mind if I stopped by your classroom after the
teacher workday tomorrow? Say, four o'clock? It would mean more to
me than you'll ever know.*
With tremendous respect, always,
—Charly

Fawn imagined Charly would show up and make a fool of herself.
Then, having done so, she'd be so embarrassed she'd drop out of Debate
Team.

As it should be.

The others would wonder why. But Charly would be too ashamed to
explain.

Fawn would never tell Chuck. If he ever found out what she'd done to
Charly, he'd hate her for it.

She didn't know when Chuck's feelings started meaning something to
her, but admittedly, they did now.

CHAPTER 31

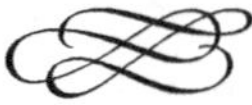

*L*ionel was always the first one into the office, which was why he was at his desk when the call came in that Darius Calder's Mercedes-AMG S65 had been shot to smithereens while crossing the Bay Bridge last night.

Immediately, Lionel put in a call to Sally Anne. The news broke through her sleepy "Hello" and was followed with the anticipated alacrity by "Holy shite! It must have happened after the debate match! So, his wife and daughter—"

"As it turns out they weren't with him. The girl went to a sleepover, and the wife went out to dinner with old friends. Darius was on his way back from a business meeting. The musician, Plug-Ugly, is under suspicion for Darius' murder. By the way, SFPD is keeping the murder out of the press until they've notified the deceased's next of kin."

"We need to tell the boss!"

"Agreed. I'm making that call next," Lionel promised.

"I'm on my way in," Sally Anne exclaimed.

"Two suspects dead—first Janna Calisher, and now Darius Calder!" Director Melamed fumed. "Not to mention that Winslow Jennings has disappeared off the face of the earth!"

"Maleficent is like a black widow," Sally Anne replied. "What piss-poor timing for us!"

"You can say that again," Melamed said. "And timing is everything.

Since we can't afford to lose any more suspects, I say go ahead and arrest Miranda D'Arcy."

"Aren't we jumping the gun?" SallyAnne asked. "I mean, none of D'Arcy's promises with the AA parents come to fruition until this spring. If we arrest her now, even if D'Arcy were to get a guilty verdict, it would be for 'conspiracy to commit fraud,' which comes with a much lighter sentence than if the fraud were perpetrated."

"She may walk, anyway. She's very convincing with parents. A jury may believe her too," Lionel pointed out.

SallyAnne scoffed. "Are you suggesting we drop the case?"

"Not at all," Lionel replied. "But without a full list of the Los Angeles-based clients whose kids she got into some university by fraudulent means, the case is pretty thin. And the fact that Winslow has yet to return to the UP&T office suggests he might suspect it's under surveillance. Or else he flew the coop for reasons unknown to us. So I doubt we'll be getting the list from him."

"He's right," Melamed muttered. "We've got more cooperating witnesses who've flipped on Miranda than we've got parents who we can convict alongside her!"

"But what about the parents she's cultivating now?" SallyAnne asked.

"There are, what, only four of them here in San Francisco?" Melamed frowned.

"A fifth one came online last night—Seamus McCoppin," SallyAnne reminded him.

"I heard the recording," Melamed replied. "Miranda didn't exactly pitch him, nor has she closed the deal. And no money has changed hands —*yet*."

"Another thing that may hurt our case is that one of those parents—Jammerhead—is a rock star with a huge following, and beloved because of his numerous charitable causes," Lionel pointed out. "If a jury lets him walk, it could soften the cases against other parent suspects, not to mention Miranda."

"If that's the case, one would think that the single mom, Nira, who paid only ten thousand dollars, could garner jury sympathy too," Sally-Anne added. This particular exchange had saddened her.

"So, we're caught between a rock and a hard place," Melamed retorted. "If Winslow warned D'Arcy that University Prep & Test was under surveillance, she may also fly the coop. However, if we arrest her now, we can still make the case—especially if she's willing to turn on her LA-based clients we haven't already flipped."

"And if we let it play out through this school year's college acceptance period, we can convict her San Francisco clients of fraud too, as opposed to merely 'conspiracy to commit,'" SallyAnne added.

Melamed nodded. "Okay. You've got your marching orders."

THANKS TO MIRANDA'S ONLINE CALENDAR, LIONEL AND SALLYANNE WERE already in the lobby of Epic Steak Restaurant when Miranda walked in for her lunch with one of her university co-conspirators.

"What does this guy do again?" Lionel asked.

"Phil Brantley calls himself a 'Medieval games coach.' He's at USC." SallyAnne rolled her eyes. "Maleficent agreed to take the meeting because he claims he's got something golden to pass forward."

Lionel grimaced.

SallyAnne wondered if it was the nickname that made him wince, or that someone was willing to make Miranda's job that much easier.

She guessed the former.

When Miranda walked in, the agents purposely turned their backs on her. They waited until the hostess seated her before asking to be seated as well. They requested a table close enough to Miranda's that their listening devices could pick up every word.

Miranda and Brantley made small talk until their lunch courses were set in front of them. Brantley's pitch was simple: A week from Friday he'd have the answer key to the SAT test questions. "It's being sent to me by a contact in Beijing."

Ironically, Miranda's response was what SallyAnne would have asked: "The Chinese have hacked SAT headquarters?"

Phil chuckled. "Who knows? Maybe. But in this case, it's last year's international version of the test. It will be the version taken in the US this year."

"How much do you want for it?" Miranda asked.

"A million."

Miranda guffawed. "In your dreams." She glared through him. "One hundred thousand. Take it or leave it."

He choked as if his steak were stuck in his throat. Eventually, he shrugged. "One-fifty, and I won't go a penny lower. And I want it in small bills. Delivered to my hotel room by seven tonight. I'm catching the late flight back to LA."

"Done. I'll send it to you in a doggy bag." She picked up one of the bags left on the table for less ravenous patrons.

Miranda got up. She didn't bother to shake his hand. For that matter, she didn't bother to say goodbye. But she did toss down cash for the meal.

SallyAnne and Lionel followed her out the door.

"OH, MISS… MISS!" THE MAN WHO TAPPED MIRANDA ON THE SHOULDER HAD a pleasant enough voice: gentle, but persistent.

When she turned around, she found herself looking into a broad chest clad in bespoke Brooks Brothers.

The face above it was appealing: blued-eyed and square-jawed. His fair hair was cropped shorter than she liked, but she could work around it.

"May I help you?" she purred.

"You're Miranda D'Arcy, am I right?"

She hadn't noticed the woman standing off to the handsome stranger's side: short and slim, her dark, curly hair cropped short.

Miranda's simper faded. "Yes. And you are?"

They flipped open slim wallets holding small shields that clearly read:

Federal Bureau of Investigation

The rest of the odious woman's statements echoed in Miranda's ears but barely connected with her brain.

She deduced that she was being arrested.

The charge was fraud in relation to her college admissions counseling practice.

She could call an attorney, or the court would appoint one—

Darius.

"I want to call my attorney now!" she growled. She pulled out her phone and punched in his name—

Only to hear that his voice mailbox was full.

"Excuse me," the bitch beside her asked. "Were you trying Darius Calder just now?"

How did she know that?

Miranda was too surprised to stop herself from nodding.

"I'm sorry to be the one to tell you, but Mr. Calder was murdered late last night."

Darius... Dead?

Fuck...

The bitch—what did she call herself? Oh yeah: *Special Agent SallyAnne Jagger*—added: "Is there another person you'd like to call?"

Miranda scoffed. "Which son-of-a-bitch lawyer will make your lives the most miserable?"

The agents exchanged pitying glances.

"Wouldn't you prefer to be a cooperating witness?" Handsome suggested. "It would make everything much easier."

Easier? Nothing in life was easy.

Still, it would be great to know all the angles. Why not hear their pitch?

"Okay, let's talk," Miranda declared.

D ESPITE HAVING THE DEMEANOR OF A MILQUETOAST ACCOUNTANT, M IRANDA'S new lawyer, Gerald Breslin, was touted as the best balls-to-the-wall criminal defense attorney in the state, second only to the dearly departed Darius.

As if trying to prove this were the case, he held her hand as they listened to Lionel, SallyAnne, and Vera Gott—the U.S. attorney for the Northern District of California, who'd be heading up the prosecution.

"Right now, we've gotten testimony from three of your Los Angeles-based clients," Lionel explained.

Vera added, "Considering the number of multiple criminal fraud counts—including bribery, blackmail, as well as mail, wire, phone fraud, and IRS fraud—you could be looking at over fifty years in prison, and a fine of two million dollars."

Miranda almost chuckled at the fine.

However, the prison term was no laughing matter.

"And if Ms. D'Arcy is a cooperating witness?" Breslin asked.

Lionel shifted his gaze to Miranda. "How many families are involved?"

"Close to sixty," she admitted.

Breslin grimaced.

"Should you agree to be a cooperating witness—that is, name your co-conspirators at the various colleges, as well as give us a full list of your clients who have already paid you to commit fraud on their behalf—we will certainly take that into account when recommending sentencing," Vera promised.

"What would Ms. D'Arcy's role as a cooperating witness entail?"

"Besides a full list of her clients, she should indicate which of those had successful placements in a university, and which are to be accepted this spring." SallyAnne replied.

Miranda shrugged. "Sure, I'll provide it."

"If your contact with them happened before our surveillance subpoenas went into effect, you'll need to contact them again," Lionel added. "You'll explain that you want to curtail any flags that may pop up from the IRS on their quote-unquote donations to the Best Face Forward Club. For our recordings, you'll get them to admit that their donation was really a payment for the placement of their child in the specific schools they requested, and to reiterate the amount paid."

"Got it," Miranda muttered.

"We know you're already getting word-of-mouth referrals on your special concierge college counseling here in San Francisco," SallyAnne explained. "We will have surveillance on you at all times. Should anyone approach you about your fraudulent services, we'll expect you to let the conversation take its course."

Miranda's lips rose into a smirk. "Are we talking entrapment?"

"Only if you actively solicit a potential client is it entrapment," Lionel explained. "Otherwise, if they approach you and agree to your stated terms, they formally become suspects."

"Potato, po-*tah*-to. I call them 'marks.'" Miranda leaned back and smiled as if enjoying their conversation. "By the way, a business like mine has expenses. For example, I've just agreed to pay a contact for a copy of this year's SAT test."

SallyAnne nodded. "You mean the one hundred and fifty thousand dollars you agreed to pay Phil Brantley before seven o'clock tonight?"

Miranda frowned. "My, my! Little pitchers have big ears!"

SallyAnne glared back at her.

"Posing as a courier, one of our agents will drop off the money to Mr. Brantley," SallyAnne replied. "He'll then be arrested. For a lighter sentence, no doubt he'll offer up your name. Another reason it's good that you've decided to play ball."

"I'm also expected to wine and dine my clients," Miranda added. "And considering their wealth, we're not talking the sort of tab you'd get at a taco joint. Who will be picking up my expenses?"

SallyAnne rolled her eyes.

"The FBI has an expense budget," Lionel explained. "If you can keep it in line, we won't charge it against your reparations."

Miranda snickered as if he'd made a joke. "In fact, I'm to set up a meeting with a parent who approached me just last night—"

"Yes, we know. Seamus McCoppin," SallyAnne interjected. "Since he's approached you, take the meeting."

"Gladly," Miranda murmured. "I'll set it up for this evening."

But the card she'd leave with him with instructions for his donation would go to an account the Feds weren't aware of. Nor would any other fees going forward.

And she'd make sure that Seamus kept spreading the word.

CHAPTER 32

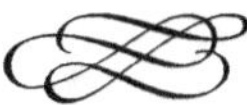

When Charly got Egan's email, she was both surprised and pleased.

The way it was worded, she knew whatever he had to tell her was important. She could also tell that it wasn't something he felt like sharing with any of the others on Debate Team.

Did his cryptic message have anything to do with the fact that Debate Team hadn't chosen its captain?

Frankly, Charly would be thrilled if Egan chose her.

But after the argument she'd had with Fawn, Charly realized she might have blown her chances.

Maybe that was the news Egan wanted to deliver privately; that she'd somehow disqualified herself by her silly, petty actions, and that he was dismayed she'd done so.

Charly groaned. She'd just remembered that Egan had been standing next to her mother when Chuck had asked if Fawn could hang with the other girls at the house. Surely Egan had noticed that Charly's tepid response had made it clear the other girl wasn't welcome.

Fawn had certainly gotten the message. Charly could see it in the girl's glassy-eyed glare.

Had Egan noticed it too?

Charly was willing to admit to him—and to Fawn too—that she'd made a mistake. She would explain that she'd already tried to make it up to Fawn by helping her with her arguments.

She'd make it clear that she would do anything he could suggest to make it happen.

EGAN HADN'T NOTICED THE EMAIL FROM CHARLY UNTIL HE WAS BACK AT THE school for Thursday's Teacher Work Day.

The gracious but strident way in which it was worded reminded him of Audrey at Charly's age.

He wondered what she wanted to discuss...

Egan chuckled at the thought of what he would have done had he ever received a similar missive from her mother those many years ago. Most likely, he'd have assumed it was her way of reaching out to express her feelings for him.

Would he have finally given in to his own longings for her?

With what he knew now, he realized the answer was yes.

Well, too late.

Whereas Audrey's feelings for him had once glowed hotly with desire, he'd missed the opportunity to prove himself worthy of her love.

Now he was willing to settle for the friendship she offered—one based on mutual trust and the memory of what they'd once shared.

Charly was so much like her mother. He looked forward to some one-on-one time with her; to hear what she had to say.

CHARLY'S KNOCK CAME RIGHT ON TIME.

Egan put down the paper he'd been grading and waved her in. "Having a good day?"

"Better than yours, I guess—since you had to work today, and tomorrow too." Charly walked in slowly as if deciding where to sit.

To make the decision easier for her, Egan moved out from behind his desk and leaned against it. He pointed to one of the front desks, indicating that she should feel free to do the same.

"Frankly, without you students here to harass me, I'm actually getting a lot of work done," he admitted. "Lavinia was only in for the first hour—" Egan stopped because he remembered Audrey's words of caution:

No one knows about Lavinia's illness yet...

"—which means when the cat's away, the mice will play," he concluded. "Some of the teachers left early, or are taking tomorrow off."

"So you hung around *just for me?*" Charly blushed at that thought.

So that she wouldn't feel so guilty, he replied playfully, "You're worth it."

Her smile is Audrey's.

Realizing this, he felt his face grow flush.

Charly saw it too. Embarrassed, she stammered, "Listen, Egan...I know

I haven't been…well, I haven't been completely upfront with…with you… about…about how I feel about…"

As Charly formed her thoughts, she twisted her fingers.

It was a familiar gesture. Egan tried to remember when he'd seen Audrey do the same.

He chuckled to himself. *She's her mother's daughter, that's for sure: heart-felt, self-assured, passionate…*

Wait…

Is Charly trying to tell me that she…?

Oh…

Shit.

No.

Just…no.

SHE'S COMING ON TO ME!

If he was right—if Charly was professing some sort of *crush*—he knew he'd have to head it off at the pass.

He stood up. Nervously, he paced the floor. "Look, Charly…I…I know what you're trying to say…because…Well, let's just say, I've felt that way too."

"You have?" Charly looked relieved.

"Yes…I mean, *no!*" He wondered if he were making any sense. "What I'm trying to say is that I've done things I've regretted. Who hasn't, right? But whatever feelings you feel right now, at this specific moment…well, regret shouldn't be one of them."

"Wow! Hearing you say that…I feel so much better!" She almost seemed relieved. "Because…well, I was just hoping…that you'd—"

He moved away, shaking his head. "Charly—*I can't.*"

"But you just said…" Charly frowned. "So now you *don't* feel I'm—"

"Of course, I feel you're…" He held his hands in front of him as if that would stop the hurt she'd feel when he let her down. "Listen, I think we should just…*drop it.*"

Charly's face crumpled with defeat. So that he couldn't see her cry, she bowed her head.

Oh hell—I broke her heart.

Just like I did to Audrey.

He went over to her. Before he knew it, she leaned in.

Gingerly, he put his arms around her as she wept.

"I'm sorry," Charly sobbed. "I guess…I guess I didn't think it would affect me this way! But…*I just want it so badly!*"

Holy shit!

It took Charly awhile to collect herself. The moment she reached for a tissue from the box on his desk, Egan inched away.

Wiping her face, Charly sniffled, "You must think I'm an idiot because I care so much about it. Silly, isn't it?"

"No, it's not silly at all. It's life." Egan sighed. "And, frankly, I'm somewhat flattered."

"So then...you don't want me to quit Debate Team?" Charly asked meekly.

"Of course not! Charly, you're the team's heart and soul!"

She was so relieved to hear him say this that she did the unthinkable: impulsively, she hugged him again.

Stunned, he didn't dare put his arms around her.

When Charly pulled away, she was smiling sadly. But when she reached the door, she stopped and turned around. "Are you sure you won't reconsider?" she asked shyly.

He forced a chuckle and waved her out.

Shit.

SHIT!

This can't happen again.

I've got to tell Audrey.

CHARLY FELT TERRIBLE AND WONDERFUL, ALL AT THE SAME TIME.

She'd found it harder than she'd thought to speak her mind to Egan about her screw-up with Fawn. Then she'd fumbled her opening statement so awfully. She never even got out her pitch about why she should still be in consideration for Debate Team captain!

To her own ears, she'd sounded like a blithering idiot.

When Egan interrupted her and tried to put her at ease with his sweet "everyone makes mistakes" speech, she thought he intuitively understood that she was apologizing for her silly behavior. But when he adamantly told her he could never consider her for the position—that they should drop the topic immediately—she was heartbroken.

I can't believe I cried over it.

Egan was sweet to hold her until she'd quit blubbering. And it was kind of him to admit how touched he was by the depth of her feelings.

And when he declared she was the heart and soul of the team, she knew there was still hope that he might choose her for the team's captain, even if he'd refused to admit it at that moment.

That's okay. Charly was bound and determined to prove she was the best person for the job.

AUDREY WAS STILL AT HER CUBICLE INSIDE HARRIS BLANCHARD'S CAMPAIGN offices hashing out the topics for his next town hall meeting when her cell phone rang from a number she didn't recognize—one with a 212 area code.

Knowing Harris was in New York City for the day, she picked it up.

"We need to talk." Egan's voice sounded ominous.

"What…Why?" Cold dread surged through Audrey. "Is it…Lavinia?"

"No! It's about *Charly.*"

Audrey felt relieved and concerned all at once. "What about her?"

"I don't think we should talk about it over the phone. Can you meet me…maybe for a drink, or something to eat?"

He knows.

"Okay, sure, if you can give me an hour," she murmured. "Where?"

"I don't know… Osteria, on Sacramento at Presidio."

"I'll be there in an hour."

EGAN WAS ALREADY AT THE RESTAURANT WHEN AUDREY ARRIVED. HE'D secured a small banquette in an alcove against the back wall.

Thank goodness, it was nowhere near a window, she thought. She'd never seen him so upset.

Egan stood when he saw her. He didn't sit back down until she slid in beside him. When he beckoned, a waiter came over with two glasses of wine, and Audrey indulged Egan by taking a sip.

He did the same.

The waiter left them with menus.

Audrey said nothing until she couldn't stand the suspense any longer. Then she whispered, "Egan…please tell me what happened."

"Charly… Well, to be honest, I think she has a crush on me."

"*What?*" Audrey's shriek turned a few heads. She ducked. Finally, she hissed, "What…what did you do to her?"

Before he could answer, she realized her phone was buzzing. Audrey looked down at the caller ID: *Charly.*

Does she know I'm here—with Egan?

I'm being silly, she reasoned. Still, Audrey fumbled to turn off her phone altogether.

"What do you mean, 'what did *I* do to *her?*'" Egan huffed. "*I did nothing!*" Indignantly, he added: "How could you say such a thing?"

"Oh, bullshit, Egan! *You* know how you are!"

Frowning, Egan sat up straight. "What exactly is that supposed to mean?"

"Charming. Flirtatious. You live for our attention! Women eat it up!" The words flowed out of her as if a dam had broken in her heart. "Hell, I ate it up…once, a long time ago."

Egan bowed his head. "I never came onto her, Audrey, if that's what you're implying!"

"That may be the case," she conceded, "but girls that age can misinterpret the slightest action or phrase. And Charly is ...she's vulnerable. Unlike some girls her age, she's still—she's still ...*innocent*."

Audrey's thoughts went to the dinner she'd had with Gemma, Tallulah, and Bliss after the debate match last night. While talking about their children, Gemma had divulged that Zina had confessed to having sex with her boyfriend, Sven. "If Darius finds out, he'll hit the roof!" Gemma opined.

Noticing Audrey's sudden grimace, Gemma then patted her friend's hand. "Hey, you've got nothing to worry about with Charly. Zina let it slip that she's still a virgin—for now, anyway." She'd then chuckled. "But that Chuck and Fawn...*Oh, my God!* Did you know that Fawn is into making sex videos?"

First there's Lavinia's health, and then there's Chuck's infatuation with Fawn, Audrey thought. And now I have to worry about Charly too—

Because Egan is egotistical enough to play into it.

Her worst fears were reaffirmed when he retorted: "Quit trying to make me out to be the bad guy, Audrey. If you're so in tune with your seventeen-year-old self, you should respect Charly's feelings. I know I do. I proved it by—"

"By what? What did you do?" Audrey's eyes opened wide. "Egan...*what did you say*?"

"Gee, now, what would be the one thing I could say to break a teenage girl's heart?" He glared back. "What do you *think* I said?"

So, he told her...about us.

"You *fool!*" She was too ashamed to look him in the eye. Instead, Audrey stared down at the glossy white plate on the table in front of her. "Egan...the twins... *You're their father.*"

THEY'RE MINE.

Chuck and Charly—

How could he not have seen it?

The cadence of Chuck's laugh.

The way Charly tented her fingers when she was thinking her way through an argument.

They had his height, his crooked grin.

His ease with others.

Yes, they were his children.

Had they felt it too?

Maybe that's why Charly was so desperate to see me.

And I pushed her away.

What a stupid fool I am.

He leaned across the table. "Audrey…do they know?"

"No! Of course not!" Audrey looked shocked at the notion.

"Well…we *have* to tell them!"

Adamantly, Audrey shook her head. "No! No, we cannot!"

Egan couldn't believe his ears. "But they need to know! *They'll want to know!*"

"You're wrong!" Audrey hissed. "They already have a father, remember? Daniel! Quit being so—*so selfish!*"

"Me—*selfish?*" How audacious of Audrey to even think such a thing, let alone say it! "And you weren't selfish to keep it from me all these years —the news that I have a daughter and a son—*who have grown up without me?*"

"You didn't love me!" Audrey retorted. "What would ever make me think that you could love them?"

"I loved you with all my heart!" The same heart now beating so fiercely in his ears.

"You certainly had a stupid way of showing it—screwing anything that moved in the three years since I'd last seen you. It's been two decades, Egan! No—*longer!* Did you once call me? Did you once reach out to me?"

"Why would I? To have you shout out to the world how much you hated me?" He laid his hand on top of hers as if his grasp might make her realize she couldn't run away from him yet again.

"I had every right to hate you," Audrey spat out. "I wasn't important enough for you to stick around." She jerked her hand away. "Forget whatever fantasy you have about Chuck and Charly. They are Daniel's reality. *He* is their father."

"So he knows too?"

"No! Of course not!" She shuddered at the thought. "Daniel was so excited when I told him I was pregnant that I couldn't find the nerve to break his heart about…what I'd done *with you.*" Her words, strangled by her emotions, came out in a whisper. "Daniel believes the twins are his flesh and blood. He lives for them! And I've encouraged that," Audrey admitted bitterly. "It's why I don't partake in the family bike ride on Saturdays. After keeping such a big secret from him, I never felt worthy of taking away this precious time he spends with them!" Audrey used her napkin to dab away the tears clouding her eyes. "Why do you think I kept the name Thorpe? *Because I never felt I deserved his name.*" She raised her head defiantly. "But Charly and Chuck do, even if I don't."

Seeing her like that—so sad, so broken—and yet, so determined…

Egan tilted her head up so that she had to look him in the eye. "Audrey —*okay!* If that's what you want, I won't say anything to…to anyone. For now, anyway." He sighed. "But it's only right that they know, eventually."

"I know. When the time is right." Elated, grateful, Audrey kissed his cheek.

But she missed because Egan had been so startled that he'd lowered his face.

Their lips met instead.

Just an instant.

Just enough for him to savor their warmth.

Ah, Audrey! If only…

He felt her pull away. When he opened his eyes, the sadness in her gaze cut deep into his soul.

Shaking, Audrey stumbled to her feet. "Don't ever do that to me again." Grabbing her purse, she whispered more to herself than to him: "How can two supposedly bright people be so stupid about love?"

YOU MUST REMEMBER THIS...

Only now, it's from Egan's point of view...

CHAPTER 33

Egan hadn't realized how awestruck Audrey's confession had left him until he found himself wandering Sacramento Street in a stupor.

The double scotch he'd downed after her revelation might also have had something to do with the daze, he now reasoned.

At some point, Egan paused in front of one of the shops: a children's store called Dottie Doolittle. Its large window showcased a dainty pink Victorian dollhouse. It had been placed in the center of a moving train set amid a diorama of a town, a thicket of woods, and an antique railroad station.

I'll bet Audrey once bought the twins' toys here, Egan thought.

Had Audrey just let him explain away that awful day in Berkeley, he would have been around to help her pick them out.

He blinked away his tears.

How stupid of me to have kissed her just now!

The last thing Egan wanted was for Audrey to despise him. Now that she did, he wondered if he'd ever win back her friendship, let alone her trust.

I have to keep my vow to her, he realized. I can never tell our children who I am.

My children.

A montage of the moments he'd shared with them raced through his mind:

When his eyes first alighted on Charly, and how he thought she looked familiar;

Chuck's cocky attitude, especially when Egan had embarrassed him in front of Fawn;

How finding Chuck in the basement of the school's old gym had brought out some instinctual urge to protect the boy from himself;

The pride he felt at the twins' desire to please him, both in class and on Debate Team;

And when push came to shove, the allegiance they shared.

They are both so much like me, he realized.

I'd do anything for them.

Except that, right now, he wasn't in a position to do anything at all for them. Hell, he could barely keep his own head above the financial whirlpool swirling around him.

Throughout Egan's life, there had been many one-night stands. Every now and then, he'd enjoyed a particularly memorable lay. But he'd never had a long-term relationship.

Instead, he'd held onto a dream, a fantasy.

Audrey.

For far too long.

During that time, Audrey had created a life with a different man: Daniel.

And together they'd created a loving family.

They should have been my family, he realized.

The twins lived in Daniel's home. And Daniel's salary as a corporate attorney allowed them to live privileged lives.

What could he offer them instead?

Not much, he conceded miserably. Just debt—my parents' and mine.

And now, with those damn lawsuits he'd have to fight off—

That alone would eat up Daniel's gracious donation.

Daniel!

It had humiliated Egan when Audrey's husband had taken it upon himself to underwrite Egan's academic chair.

I wonder how Daniel would feel to know the truth about his children?

No—my children.

But he can never know because I promised Audrey.

She'd made a promise to Egan as well: That when the time was right, the twins would know the truth.

And when that time came, he'd be ready. He'd have written them into his will. He'd have a legacy to leave them—

I have to write again.

And it's got to be a bestseller.

It was the only way Egan knew to make money.

The toot of the toy train broke through the thick fog of his resolve. Realizing its engine had jumped off its track, instinctively Egan reached forward to nudge it back on—

Only to slam his fist into the shop's plate-glass window.

Fortunately, it didn't break.

Startled, the shop clerk looked up and frowned.

Egan waved in apology.

She shook her head as if to say, *loser.*

Of course, she was right.

His publisher hated him. His agent had kicked him to the curb. And no other pub house would touch him.

I need to eat something before I start blubbering like a baby.

I need another drink.

A block away was a restaurant called Spruce. He'd heard of it from Cornell. "Its duck sumo ditalini is *to die for,*" he'd rhapsodized. "And they've got a drink called the 'Sneaky Pete'—just absolutely yummy!"

I hope the joint lives up to its hype, Egan reasoned.

THE HOSTESS RAISED A BROW AS HE SLURRED OUT HIS REQUEST OF A TABLE FOR one. "You'll be served more quickly at the bar," she suggested.

"Sold!" he exclaimed. He shooed away her offer to show him the way, declaring, "I can spot a bar a mile away."

"I believe it," she muttered under her breath.

He was in luck. Although the bar was filled, there was still one stool left.

Even luckier, it was next to a pretty woman: a petite, sloe-eyed brunette. Because she was perched facing away from the bartender, Egan got a good look at her slim, shapely legs.

Pretty, he thought. Like a sprite–a pixie.

Was she saving the stool for someone?

He tapped her on the shoulder to ask.

When she didn't turn, he realized it was because something happening in the closest banquette had caught her attention. Gently, he patted her again.

She swiveled around and tilted her head to one side, allowing her gaze to sweep over him.

If we don't know each other now, something tells me she wouldn't mind making my acquaintance.

He pointed to the empty stool. Grinning, he asked, "Is this seat taken?"

Pixie's eyes grew larger. "No, not at all—*Mr. Gable!*"

She said it loud enough that the man on the other side of her—tall and broad-shouldered, a blond Teutonic god clad in Brooks Brothers —turned and scowled at Egan. Like Pixie, he was also angled for a clear view of the banquette.

So this is Pixie's date? She can do much better.

Ignoring the man's glare, Egan dropped onto the seat anyway. Then, leaning in toward Pixie, he asked, "Do we know each other?"

She reeled back a bit.

Oh, hell! Maybe she's an Ashbury Academy parent. If so, and I'm flirting with her in front of her husband—

But then Pixie gushed, "I read your book, *Extracurricular*. In fact,"—she paused—"it's my favorite."

"Thank you for that." Egan chuckled, relieved. "In fact, *THANK GOD* for that! I thought you were another infernal AA parent!" He scanned her appreciatively. "But of course, you're much too young to have children of your own."

Pixie blushed at the compliment.

Not the Teutonic twit, though. He was still frowning.

"Um...AA?" Pixie stammered. "You... you mean Alcoholics Anonymous?"

"In this case, no," Egan guffawed. "Albeit, many of AA's—that is, Ashbury Academy's teaching staff are chip-carrying members—"

Unable to stop himself, he let out a burp.

Waving away her concerned stare, Egan added, "Not me, mind you." He nodded toward the bartender. "Speaking of which, may I buy you another"—he looked down, to see what she was drinking—"wine? Or, perhaps something a bit more adventurous? I can vouch for the fact that the barkeep makes a mean Sneaky Pete: whiskey, coffee liqueur, and just a splash of milk—"

Just then, Teutonic Twit leaned over and growled, "Sir, do you mind? The lady is on a date!"

Pixie did a double-take. Then she blushed.

Jesus, he's got nerve! The whole time they've been seated here, he's been staring over there, at the blond bitch in the banquette.

And now, he dares to stare me down?...

Oh...

Nope. He's staring at Pixie.

'Bout damn time he took notice of her!

Incensed for her, Egan declared, "Well, you've got an odd way of showing it, sir! Not only are you ignoring this, this"—

Egan burped again—even louder this time—

"—this *beautiful* young woman, the whole time I've been chatting her up you've been staring *over there*"—he pointed to the banquette—"at that over-inflated Barbie doll!"

He threw his arm open toward the object of Teutonic Twerp's fascination—

What the Hell...

That's Miranda.

With Seamus and Gretchen McCoppin!

Suddenly it all made sense:

Miranda's snide, backhanded remarks about Ashbury Academy's gentle, beloved headmistress.

The way Miranda put up with Jess's public manhandling.

Why she wangled a ride with Daniel after the last board meeting.

And why she finagled her way onto the board to be its deciding vote.

With my help, no less.

Stupid, stupid, me.

The realization that he might be having a hand in his mentor's downfall—*the grandmother of his children*— quickly sobered him up.

Does Miranda know about Lavinia's illness? If so, she may be positioning herself as the next Head of School...

Egan's eyes narrowed at the thought.

He realized his fan and her boyfriend were staring at him. To cover up his shame, he declared, "Well, well! It seems I know Barbie—and for that matter, her plasticine friends too—Ken and Midge."

Egan knew he hardly looked his best. The least he could do was straighten his tie, maybe tuck in his shirt again. "If you kind gentlefolk will excuse me, I think I'll mosey on over and pay my respects."

He walked off—not as steadily as he'd hoped, but that didn't matter.

For Lavinia's sake, he had to find out what Miranda was up to.

Egan reached the table just in time to hear Miranda say, "Mum's the word..."

Interesting, Egan thought.

But what he exclaimed out loud was: "Well, I'll be damned! Small world, isn't it?"

The McCoppins met his unexpected salutation with shock and awe.

Jesus, they look as if they're seeing a ghost, Egan thought.

Miranda glowered.

Yep, apparently, I've interrupted a really important hootenanny.

Miranda tempered her frown into a simper, declaring, "Ah, well, look who's here too—AA's illustrious literature professor, Egan Gable!"

When Gretchen realized who he was, she actually gave him the once-over and a wink.

Jesus, now I know where Fawn gets it!

Just the thought that the mother of his son's girlfriend had just come onto him made Egan shudder.

"By the way, Mr. Gable is my top candidate for SAT proctor. I know how much Fawn dotes on him," Miranda cooed coyly.

Huh?... What the hell was she talking about?

"Oh? Well, ...that's great, I guess." Gretchen deflated a bit.

Egan was surprised that Miranda seemed to enjoy Gretchen's dismay.

Seamus nudged Gretchen. "We'd better take off." As Gretchen scooted out of the booth, Seamus muttered, "See you at the next board meeting" to Egan and Miranda.

———

As Egan slid into the banquette, Miranda declared, "Fancy seeing you here." She nodded toward the bar. "Slumming?"

For some odd reason, Pixie and the Twit were still staring at them.

Egan winked at Pixie. "What, with that pretty little damsel at the bar? Are you jealous?" He whistled low. "Surprise, surprise! Not that I blame you. She struck me as smart and beautiful—*and kind.*"

"She is also a…" Miranda stopped herself. "Jesus! Never mind! Enough of this bullshit—and enough of your little head games, Egan Gable!" Incensed, she added, "Oh, and as far as I'm concerned, our little deal is off!"

The deal…

Miranda was going to renege on her vow never to tell anyone about his affair with Audrey.

Egan's blood ran cold.

She could easily hitch another ride with Daniel. If she says something to him about Audrey and me out of spite—

"No… *NO!* You can't renege on what you promised!"

"Says who?" Miranda retorted.

"But-but…" Frantically, Egan grabbed her arm. "Please… *don't!*"

———

Miranda leaned back in the booth and smiled. "Well… Since you're begging. Perhaps we can work something out."

Egan sighed. "I told you twice already. I'm just not that into you—"

"Don't be a fool!" she sputtered. "I don't mean sex, you imbecile! I'm giving you back what you so desperately want."

She paused—not just because she hoped it would make the offer sound more enticing to Egan but because she needed her FBI tormenters to believe what she'd declared was true: "If you'll agree to be the proctor for Ashbury Academy's SAT test."

Egan frowned, perplexed. "Are you joking?"

"Not at all," Miranda insisted. "But you must do everything the job entails—*to the letter.*"

Egan shrugged. "How hard can it be?"

"Just the usual," she replied. "Of course, the most challenging task concerns the seven special needs students. Their math portions must be substituted. Will you have a problem with that?"

"Why should I? As you say, they're special needs, and all that implies."

Egan's response could not have been more ideal. Whereas he presumed a different test, the Feds would interpret it as she meant it to be: exchanged for a version already filled out with the correct answers.

"I thought not," she purred. "There's something I hadn't mentioned before. It is a necessary evil. It involves the essay portion." She sighed. "You're also to provide substitute essays for those students."

Egan frowned. "How is that even possible?"

"It probably means pulling an all-nighter, but, unfortunately, it goes with the job."

"Wait... I'll be staying up all night *with the kids*?"

Miranda's chuckle was devoid of any charm. "Don't play stupid, Egan. It doesn't suit you."

She counted silently to five as the reality of what she meant sunk in.

With each passing second, a different emotion shifted Egan's usual placidity. Incomprehension morphed into realization, which gave way to shock, then concern, and finally anger.

He growled, "You've got to be kidding me!"

"Suddenly, you have a conscience?" Miranda clucked her tongue. "I assure you, the pay will make it worth your while."

Egan's wary silence didn't concern her. She knew he was hard up for cash. In fact, the longer he stewed over his dilemma, the better.

Finally, he asked, "Oh yeah? How much?'

"Fifteen thousand," she replied.

Egan snorted. "Knowing you, you're pocketing at least a hundred thou."

"You arrogant bastard!..." Miranda paused. Then: "Alright then! Thirty-five thousand. Take it or leave it!"

Asshole.

Still, he had her over a barrel.

She took comfort in the thought, however, that if she were going down, Egan would too.

SO THAT'S HER GAME — PARENTS ARE PAYING HER TO CHEAT ON THEIR CHILDREN'S SAT tests!

It sickened Egan to think he'd allowed her to drag him into her scheme.

I'll do it because I have to.

For Chuck and Charly.

He shoved Seamus's plate out of his way but thought nothing of downing the last of the blowhard's wine. "So, how does this little scheme of yours work?"

"A week from Friday, I'm to get the SAT answer key for both math and reading, as well as the essay questions. That night, I'll drop them by your place along with the names of the students involved. After they take their tests, you're to substitute the math and reading portions with ones that you've already filled in correctly—especially the math portion, although, so that the tests look valid, you're to miss one or two answers in the reading questions. And Egan, just make sure they are different mistakes on each student's test, okay?"

Egan frowned. "Yeah, yeah, okay, whatever. And what about the essays?"

"The way the SAT board scores the test's sections, a well-written essay is merely icing on the cake," Miranda explained. "I know you well enough to appreciate your bullshitting skills. I'm sure elevating the students into the literary stratosphere should be child's play for you. And since you already teach these students, matching the essay topics to their voices shouldn't be that difficult for you."

Egan sighed. "If you say so." He was too weary to argue with her. Bone tired. Suddenly, he felt twenty years older. "One caveat, babe: I'll want my money a week before the test, or it's no go."

Miranda chuckled. "That's the easy part. In fact, tonight. Say, nine? I'll even give you the cash with a receipt for—let's call it 'services rendered.'"

He let that sink in.

Suddenly, he remembered something she'd said that had confused him. What was it again? Oh yes:

I'm giving you back what you so desperately want.

What did she mean? His writing career?

Audrey?

Right now, he was too tipsy to decipher her scheme. All he could do was shrug. "Sure, why not?"

Yes, he'd make love to Miranda. Keep your friends close, and your enemies closer, right?

But he'd pretend it was Audrey.

And tonight of all nights, he needed to be with someone, if not her.

Afterward, Egan swore, he'd figure out an even better way to screw Miranda D'Arcy.

The last thing he'd let her do was to take him down with her.

CHAPTER 34

$\mathcal{A}$udrey drove home, lost in a tumult of emotions over finally having revealed to Egan the terrible secret that bound them forever.

Daniel should have been there already. Strangely, though, his car wasn't in the driveway. At that point she remembered she'd turned off her cell phone.

She flipped it on again before going into the house. Seeing that, in a mere hour, she'd received eleven messages, she stopped dead in the driveway and scrolled through Caller ID:

Charly - Gemma - Charly - Bliss - Charly - Tallulah - Davis - Daniel - Chuck - Charly - Daniel -

What the heck was going on?

It was Audrey's natural instinct to play the voicemails in order. However, she flinched at the thought of listening to Charly's pained dissertation as to why she felt it necessary to drop Egan's class and Debate Team.

Not that she would blame her daughter in the least, having gone through precisely the same heartache with Egan.

The egotistical jerk!

That he tried to kiss her proved yet again how insensitive he was to others' emotions.

Audrey was sure that her girlfriends' calls were to follow up on the innocuous gossip that had them laughing into the early morning hours, so not something that merited an immediate callback. Seeing Davis' name intrigued her, but his good news took a back seat to the drama happening in her own life right now.

She imagined Chuck's call was one long groan about how hungry he was and chiding her for the fact that there was nothing to eat in the house. If she had the time, she would have responded by texting him a map outlining the mere ten blocks from their home to Trader Joe's.

She knew she had to take Daniel's call.

She doubted Charly would have divulged to Daniel her talk of shame with Egan. Still, Audrey braced herself as she scrolled to Daniel's cell number.

Just hearing his voice would remind her that there was some normalcy to life.

Afterward, she'd have the nerve to deal with Charly's frantic calls.

"Audrey—finally!" Just those two words relayed a depth of fear and sadness she'd never heard before in Daniel's voice.

"I—was at a meeting!" she stammered "I'm sorry... Why? What happened?"

"It's Charly—"

Oh no...Oh, my God...

She must have told him about Egan.

"She was in the Haight when she got a call from Zina...about Darius."

"Darius?" Audrey was confused. "What about him?"

"You haven't heard yet? He was murdered!"

"Oh, my God! I've got to call Gemma!" Guilt at not taking her friend's call surged through her. And of course, that was why Bliss and Tallulah had tried to reach her as well.

"Audrey, that's not all." She could hear Daniel breathing heavily. "Charly didn't know if Lavinia had heard the news, so she went over to her grandmother's house and...and..." Daniel paused. "She was passed out. Thank goodness Charly was there! Otherwise..." His words stuck in his throat. "She called an ambulance. We're at UCSF now—"

"I'll be right there!... But where do I go? Oncology?"

"What?...*No!* She had a heart attack! We're in the ICU." Urgently, he pleaded, "Audrey, hurry! Lavinia is fading."

I love you so much.

You can't leave me. Please don't leave me.

I need you.

Audrey longed to say this to Lavinia, but she couldn't. Not in front of her children, who were already shell-shocked with grief.

Charly, always the stoic one, had done the best in holding back her tears, but she held her hands cupped at her chest as if that might stop her heart from hurting so badly.

Chuck sobbed openly. Whereas he used the back of his hand to wipe away the tears rolling down his cheeks, he'd placed one hand over Lavinia's as if willing his life force into her.

Noah's tears flowed freely down his face, but his fist, held to his mouth, stifled his sobs. He leaned into Daniel, whose eyes were hazed with tears. Seeing Audrey, Daniel nodded, as if beckoning her to Lavinia's side.

Chuck stood up so that his mother could take his seat. Audrey hugged him dearly before inching the chair as close as she could to her mother's bed.

"I'm here, Lavinia," she whispered.

Her mother gave a slight nod. She gulped hard. Then, through parched lips, she whispered, "Love you…always."

"I'll always love you too." Audrey's words came out between sobs.

"Daniel…"

"He's here. The kids too."

"Yes. They'll…all be fine." Lavinia's voice faded away. Her attempt to open her eyes succeeded, if barely.

Audrey held her breath until Lavinia added. "You too." She released a sigh. "The school…my life's work…"

"It's your legacy. I'll make sure it will always stay that way! I swear!"

A smile rose on Lavinia's lips. "Family first. Always."

"Yes, of course. But—"

"Closer…" Lavinia's hands grasped her gently as if willing Audrey into silence.

As Audrey leaned in, Lavinia's eyes fluttered and then shut.

Her last words whispered to her daughter were: "Tell Daniel…about Egan."

BOOK THREE

CHAPTER 1

The official time of Lavinia Thorpe's death was Thursday at 7:55 in the evening.

The hospital's paperwork took an hour. During the process, Lavinia's doctor had assured Audrey Thorpe that her mother's body would be taken to the hospital's morgue until the family's designated funeral home retrieved it.

Audrey, her husband Daniel, and the McKittridge children—seventeen-year-old twins Charly and Chuck, and twelve-year-old Noah—were home by ten. Stunned by grief, their daughter Charly and her brothers went up to their rooms.

Audrey dreaded the next task: breaking the news to Lavinia's closest friends—Maggie and her daughter, Tallulah Wishart; Maude and Reggie Thackeray and their daughter, Bliss; and Harris Blanchard and his wife, Tracy. Bliss and Tallulah were Audrey's dearest friends, as was Davis Wong, who viewed Lavinia as his surrogate mother since she'd found him living on the streets. By providing him a full scholarship to Ashbury Academy—the private school she'd founded and served as its head-mistress—his life had been forever altered. He was now one of the world's most sought-after film directors.

But Audrey's very first call went to Gemma Sisley. Her father, Grayson Sisley, would have wanted to know about Lavinia's passing, but Audrey knew Gemma would best know when to break the news to him, considering that both would still be in shock over their own tragedy: Gemma's husband, Darius Calder, had been murdered less than twenty-four hours earlier.

Like Audrey, Gemma was consumed by her grief. Together, the dear friends sobbed over their losses.

After these initial calls, it dawned on Audrey that the staff at Ashbury Academy should also be informed as soon as possible. Lavinia had been the institution's heart and soul.

"Let's split up the list," Daniel suggested.

"I'd appreciate that." Audrey's words were weighted with her pain. "Let's ask them to call the parents of students in their first class with the news."

"Will do." Daniel hesitated, then added, "We should also inform the trustee board."

"I'll let you do that. In fact, you should start with them, I guess. I'll leave it to your discretion whether or not to mention Darius as well."

"I think I should," Daniel replied. "It's my fiduciary responsibility since he sat on the school's board."

Audrey stifled a wince. It's why she'd kept her promise to Lavinia and never mentioned her mother's illness to Daniel. Had he disclosed it to the board, Lavinia would not have had the bittersweet pleasure of avoiding the inevitable pity and tears of AA's staff and students during those final months of her life.

I know because my grieving dismayed her.

Audrey stared down at the staff directory, but her eyes couldn't focus through the haze of her tears. Finally, she sighed. "I'll take everyone whose last name begins with A through L. You can take M through Z." She made a screenshot of the directory with her phone and texted it to him.

Miranda D'Arcy was the third name on Audrey's call sheet. She skipped it, though, knowing that AA's college admissions counselor would also be on Daniel's list of board members.

However, when she realized Egan Gable's name was on her call sheet, she decided he should hear the news from her, not Daniel.

After all, he was the twins' biological father.

And the last person he'd want to hear about Lavinia's death from was the man who was raising them as his own.

———

"FASTER.... HARDER.... *DEEPER!* COME ON, BIG BOY—BREAK ME IN HALF! *YES! YES!*" Miranda D'Arcy barked out her commands like a Visigoth general during the sacking of Rome.

When it came to sex, Egan didn't like taking directions—let alone from a woman he despised.

He'd been dismayed when, almost two hours after he'd left her, she actually followed through on delivering the check she promised—from a non-profit company called The Best Face Forward Club. Until then, he'd anxiously been staring out the window, hoping that, by some miracle, she'd have second thoughts about it.

Heaven knows he'd had them.

Buena Vista Park was directly across the street from Egan's apartment. Her car had pulled up into one of the parking spots abutting the greenbelt. As she got out of the car and crossed the street, he'd noticed another auto pulling up as well: a Camry, but a much more recent model than his parents' car. It pulled into an empty space two away from hers.

The driver turned off the engine but sat in the car. Only the streetlight illuminated the figure inside.

Whereas Egan had once considered Miranda a possible love interest, the revelation of her connivery toward Lavinia and Ashbury Academy had killed any inkling of attraction he'd briefly felt toward her, let alone friendship. He had only acquiesced to the tryst as a way to assure her that he would play along with the scheme she'd roped him into while threatening to tell Daniel about Egan and Audrey's one-night stand, now so many years ago.

If Daniel found out, he'd confront Audrey about it.

Immediately, she'd realize that Egan had blabbed their secret to Miranda. She'd panic that Daniel would recognize the truth about the twins. And Audrey would hate Egan even more than she did now—if that were possible.

Caught between two undesirable outcomes, Egan had made up his mind that this tryst with Miranda would be a swift and unmemorable slam-bam-thank-you-ma'am. That way, she'd never suggest a second go-round. Better to have her think of him as a lousy lover.

To his dismay, Miranda had other ideas about the evening. Immediately, she took the lead: yanking off his jeans, shoving him down against the couch, and mounting him without even bothering to strip off anything other than the thong she wore under her designer dress.

Egan had never been into rough sex. He was a romantic at heart. Besides, he liked to please women, both in and out of the bedroom. To him, flirtation was an art form. He strove to create a multi-sensory experience with words, gazes, smiles, and a well-placed hand—say, the mere stroke on a woman's arm. Should the woman respond positively (and odds were she would), he took consummate care in each step of their lovemaking. The foreplay was gentle and thorough. Any words spoken were husky with yearning or filled with desire. When their eyes met, his gaze vowed the depth of his desire.

He never forced, he coaxed. His climaxes weren't quick, and his lover was assured of many.

He left his conquests satiated of their shared lust.

Or so he believed anyway.

But Miranda was another story. Throughout the love bout, her naughty talk was taunts tainted with filth and innuendo, each one more despicable than the last. It sickened him to the point that he felt like throwing up, but he resisted the urge, should she find it a turn-on.

And despite his vow to hold back on any orgasm, as she tightened around his shaft, inevitably, nature took its course.

Thankfully, his orgasm came simultaneously with hers. Had it not, Egan had no doubt she'd be cruel enough to leave him blue-balled.

With a gasp, Miranda collapsed, "Well, now you are certainly earning your keep!" She raised her face to his. Batting her eyes, she added, "You're ready to go again, right?"

Aw, hell...NO. "Look, it's...been a long day. Maybe you should take off—"

He stifled a groan as she cupped him.

"Oh, look!" Miranda giggled, delighted. "You're not tired at all. You're rarin' to go!"

As she leaped off the couch, she grabbed her purse. "First, I've got to make a pit stop. You know, freshen up." She sauntered off toward the bathroom.

And not a second too soon. Egan's phone buzzed. The caller ID showed one letter:

A

Audrey.

It was silly, he knew, to identify her on his phone that way. But considering their secret—especially after what he'd heard tonight—he was too ashamed to claim their relationship, even in the privacy of his phone.

Why is she calling—now, of all times?

As quickly as he could, he tapped open the phone and whispered, "Hi."

"I wanted you to be the first to know. Lavinia died tonight." Audrey's voice reeked of bleakness.

Her words hit him so hard that he had to stifle a groan.

"How..."

"Heart attack." Audrey's sigh was part sob too. "But I'm sure that all the stress over the trustee board gamesmanship and her cancer and its treatment played a hand in it."

Egan flinched at the thought of the role the board had played in Lavinia's demise.

She's right. And things will only get worse if Miranda gets her way.

I have to tell Audrey about Miranda's scheme.

Urgently, he whispered, "Audrey, listen—"

"Egan, sorry, but I really can't talk now. I have to call others on the staff. Daniel is helping me in this endeavor—and he's calling board members too." Egan could hear her choking back her tears. "I...I just wanted you to hear it first, and from me."

She hung up before he could say anything to stop her.

———

THERE WAS A TIME MIRANDA WOULD HAVE NEVER ASSUMED THAT EGAN GABLE would see her *naked*. Then again, who'd have thought that egotist would live up to his own hype?

It took Miranda all of five minutes to wash up. The next five were spent admiring her tits and ass in the bathroom mirror. If her mother had taught her one thing, it was that men abhorred naughty bits that sagged. Both body parts had undergone extensive plastic surgery, but it was worth it. Diet and exercise only went so far.

Thank goodness, she'd done so before pitching Lavinia on hiring her as Ashbury Academy's college counseling consultant.

Even before her divorce—in fact, it's why her husband left her—for Miranda, sex was usually a random pickup: quick, down and dirty, no commitments. These past two months, her tepid trysts with Jess Smallwood had only been a means to an end. It got her on AA's trustee board. From there, she could contain—and better yet, *control*—any issues that might arise from her illegal acts involving her college admissions concierge program.

And now that the FBI was involved, undoubtedly the shit would soon be hitting the fan.

When it did, she planned on being far away.

Too bad she couldn't take the best lay of her life with her—

Egan.

Sadly, she'd have to leave him behind so that he could take the fall for her.

The thought of visiting him in prison for conjugal sex made her all hot and bothered again.

That fantasy was still rolling around in her head when she realized her cell phone was buzzing. The caller ID read:

D McKittridge

Interesting. What could he possibly want this late at night?

"Daniel? How may I help you?"

"Hello, Miranda. Thanks for picking up so late." To her ears, he sounded defeated.

It would be too delicious to hear that he was covertly calling her about helping him get his deadbeat boy, Chuck, into her concierge program.

In anticipation that this was the case, she cooed, "No problem."

"I'm calling all board members as well as the staff with the sad news that Lavinia passed away tonight."

Emotions roiled through Miranda. Shock was replaced by guilt.

Not for long, though. Relief quickly took its place.

Lavinia's trust had been misplaced, but it had worked in Miranda's favor.

Finally, Miranda was filled with elation. With Lavinia's demise, she could be bolder in courting parents gullible enough to buy into her illegal college admissions scheme.

Granted, she'd still have to be cautious about it so as not to alert those who could call it into question publicly—

Like Daniel.

"I'm stunned," Miranda murmured. "Truly, Daniel… Your news—well, it cuts me to the quick."

"I'll pass along your regrets to Audrey," he replied.

He sounds as if he means it, the fool. "Yes, please do. And tell her that if there's anything I can do…" For effect, Miranda let her voice trail off.

"Thank you. Have a good night."

Hell yeah, I will.

Jubilantly, she tossed her phone in her purse. She was about to walk out of the room when her phone buzzed again.

As she suspected, it was a text from Seamus McCoppin. As Lavinia's prime nemesis on the trustee board, he'd be raring to go on a scheme to take control—not only of the board but the school as well. He wrote:

**Lavinia RIP. Must meet to discuss the school's need to transition.
Zingari: 1pm tomorrow.
BTW I have a client referral for you.**

Miranda wrote back:

See you there.

Forty-eight hours ago, Miranda planted the seed that Seamus should oust Lavinia and put her in the headmistress' place—at least, temporarily.

Doing so would have made for the ideal set-up: Miranda could recruit new clients and control the trustee board. No need to have a replay of the Bobbit-Hennings fiasco.

But since then, Miranda's life had changed drastically—and for the worst.

The FBI was now her constant companion.

Miranda needed that coverage now more than ever: to cover her tracks, what with the Feds onto her, and thinking they'd turned her.

Lavinia's sudden death relieved Seamus of the need for a vicious power play.

But no way was she going to let him position her as Ashbury Academy's permanent Head of School. When they meet at lunch, she'd inform him that her private consulting business was too lucrative to give up; that she wouldn't mind stepping in as Lavinia's temporary replacement so that a search committee could take its time to find just the right fit for his vision of AA.

That way, I can manage the board while I plan my exit from everything: the business, the country even.

I'll just disappear with all my money.

Maybe Egan would like to go with me.

It would beat the alternative: a perp walk in front of the whole school.

Not that he knew that. Nor would she tell him—not yet, anyway.

———

EGAN WAS USED TO LEAVING WOMEN WITH SMILES ON THEIR FACES, SO HE wasn't surprised when Miranda returned with a smug grin on her face.

What did perturb him was the casual way in which she snapped her fingers at him. "Time for a change of venue, big boy."

Before he had a chance to respond, she yanked him to his feet, dragging him with her toward his bedroom.

The thought of having sex again with the bitch who was bound and determined to dismantle Lavinia's legacy—and doing so in his bed, no less —so revolted Egan that he actually thought he'd never sleep a wink in there again.

I just moved into this apartment, he thought miserably. I'll have to move again. Worse, she'll do the same thing in the next apartment...

I'm trapped! Miranda is my inferno...

Like hell, I am.

Egan stopped short, taking her by surprise. Before she could object, he growled, "Okay, sure. But this time, we do it my way."

She frowned at his tone. But before she could respond, he grabbed her by her shoulders and turned her so that she faced the wall. He forced her forearms against it. Then he kicked her legs apart.

Annoyed, she declared, "What the—"

But then he walloped her ass, and she took the hint she'd better brace herself. "Ready to play *really* rough?" he murmured in her ear.

Miranda's eyes widened. "Frankly, I didn't know you had it in you," she cooed. "Sure! *Bring it on.*"

As he entered her from behind, she squealed delightedly. He was tall enough that she had to stand on her tiptoes.

Let's get this over with...

Each thrust compounded his anger. Once again, he held off as long as he could—

Until nature took its course.

Exhausted, he collapsed onto her.

Miranda, too, was spent.

As soon as he could, he staggered to pick up his clothes.

Miranda frowned. "Wait—where are you going?"

"Away—from you," he retorted as he zipped up his pants.

Hotly, she exclaimed, "But I'm not finished with you!"

Egan snickered. "Let me make myself clear, Miranda: *being with you repulses me.* If you insist on making it part and parcel of our so-called 'deal,' I'll tear up the check, and that will be the end of it. I will also deny any lies you spread about Audrey or me. In fact, I'll stand up on Ashbury Academy's bell tower with a megaphone and announce your scheme to the world. Do you understand me?"

She glowered back, but she kept her mouth shut.

In no time, he tossed on his shirt and jacket and was through the front door, slamming it behind him.

Why you son of a bitch!

Miranda was still shaking as she snatched her clothes off the floor and then walked over to Egan's desk, where he'd tossed the check.

He did it to taunt me, she fumed. He wants me to pick it up and tear it into tiny little pieces.

But doing so would get him off the hook with the Feds.

Back at the restaurant, when she'd made her deal with Egan, she'd delighted at having him at her beck and call—emotionally and physically. On the drive over to Egan's house, she'd crowed at the thought that the FBI might be listening in. Despite Special Agent Lionel Polk's tough talk about seeing right through her, she could see it in his eyes: she intrigued him. While in the throes of lust, it thrilled her to know Lionel had heard every word—and every grunt.

No doubt, he also heard Egan's cruel put-down.

That son of a bitch humiliated me, Miranda fumed.

She had some consolation. To that extent, she'd already put a very large nail in the coffin of his professional life: Just that morning she—that is, Mandy Blackwell—had signed, in triplicate, the settlement papers for her lawsuit against Egan and his publisher, Signal Press. It had brought yet another half a million dollars to her fly-the-coop account.

To keep the FBI off my back as long as possible, I have to keep Egan in play.

Then, when the time is right, I'll take him down.

And at the same time, I'll ruin Audrey's perfect little world.

In case Miranda was looking out the window, Egan walked into the park, only to detour onto another path that circled around, putting him back in front of the apartment building.

From behind one of the park's behemoth live oaks, he watched as, ten minutes later, Miranda left too.

As she drove off, the car that had arrived immediately after her now started its engine.

Egan watched as it followed her path: north on Buena Vista Avenue, making a quick left westward onto Haight, and then a sharp right onto Central Avenue.

Interesting, Egan mused. Apparently, the driver never got out of the car.

If Egan were lucky, maybe the mysterious car's driver shared Egan's fantasy: doing away with Miranda.

One could only hope.

He went back up to his apartment. When he walked by the sofa, he pointedly turned his head to look away, disgusted by the thought of what had transpired less than an hour before.

I'll have Goodwill tow it out of here as soon as possible, he thought.

Egan walked over to his desk. He stared down at Miranda's check:

Two hundred and forty-five thousand dollars.

Thirty-five thousand times seven students.

Depending on the schools Charly and Chuck chose, it would almost cover two four-year college tuitions—

One for each.

This is to be the legacy I leave my children, he thought.

And knowing Miranda, there will be other parents buying into her program until the final SAT deadline.

Jesus—what if Miranda pitches her scheme to some parent who decides to tell a cop?

She'll take me down with her.

What will Chuck and Charly think of me then?

The thought shamed him.

Still, it could not deter him from what he knew he had to do, first thing in the morning: deposit her check into his bank account.

Egan signed the back of it and then slipped it into an envelope.

I have to spend the money. I have no choice.

To this end, he filled out a blank check from his account and put it in the envelope too, which went in the pocket of his favorite jacket.

Exhausted, Egan went to bed, where he spent the night tossing and turning.

FINDING HIMSELF UP AT THE CRACK OF DAWN, EGAN WENT AHEAD AND GOT dressed. His destination was Ashbury Academy, but first, he stopped off at his bank's ATM machine to deposit the check from the Best Face Forward Club. His heart dropped into the pit of his stomach as the check rolled through his fingers and into the machine.

When Egan reached AA, he found the front door locked. He'd never been the first teacher on campus. But since all teachers had keys to the front door, he let himself in.

He had a hard time passing Lavinia's office without glancing over. Unless she'd been in a private meeting, her habit was to leave the door open. Instinctively, he looked to see her smiling face.

No more, he realized.

He stopped at the receptionist's desk. Clare, who had been at the school since its inception, would soon be in, he knew.

He took a blank sheet of paper from the scrap bin behind her desk and scribbled a quick note. He knew the words he wrote would be small solace for her grief, but perhaps it would help to some extent.

Folding it, he slipped it into the envelope and placed it partially under her keyboard.

He headed for the teachers' lounge. The unwritten rule was for the first one through the door to make the coffee.

He knew where Cornell kept his French press and stash of private label beans. He doubted the chemistry teacher would balk just this once at the notion of sharing it with the rest of the teachers, considering the sadness and gravity of the occasion.

Because it was a Friday teachers' workday, Egan made up his mind he'd nudge the teachers into a discussion of how to handle their grieving students come Monday. Beyond that, he couldn't predict what might happen to staff morale.

Lavinia had been the school's heart, soul, and mind. Now that she would no longer walk through the teachers' lounge, eyes glistening with humor and a broad smile on her face, there was no one there to inspire AA's teachers.

He hoped the trustee board would do a thorough search to find someone who would at least do their best to fill Lavinia's shoes.

And more importantly, make her vision the school's permanent mission.

Somehow, he doubted it.

Still, he'd do his best to make it happen.

He owed Lavinia that much.

CHAPTER 2

FBI Special Agent SallyAnne Jagger arrived at the bureau's San Francisco office just as the sun rose over the horizon.

She too had spent a sleepless night.

She was still in shock over the kiss that she and her investigative partner, Lionel Porter Polk VII, had shared the night before while transcribing their report from the sting that Miranda had set up at the chic Presidio Heights restaurant, Spruce.

What had precipitated the kiss—and Lionel's immediate apology for overstepping such a personal boundary—was what SallyAnne could only deduce as jealousy on his part. A stranger had tried to pick up SallyAnne as they were surveilling Miranda and her clients, Seamus and Gretchen McCoppin.

The man had been persistent.

Granted, he'd also been drunk.

Still, SallyAnne had been flattered—especially when she realized he was Egan Gable—the author of her favorite book, *Extracurricular*.

On the other hand, Lionel had been rude in his attempt to shoo Egan away.

Unfortunately, Egan had picked up on the fact that they'd been eyeing Miranda and the McCoppins.

Such irony! Egan knew them well because he was now teaching at Ashbury Academy. And as it turned out, he was also the teacher liaison to AA's trustee board—one of the reasons his voice had sounded so familiar to SallyAnne, since the FBI had been listening in on the meetings.

Before they could stop him, he had tottered over to their table.

The good news: as promised, Miranda set up the McCoppins to implicate themselves.

The bad news: Miranda was successful in recruiting Egan for her illicit activities.

Although he'd initially balked at her offer to act as proctor for the students in her concierge program—in other words, take their tests for them—he'd finally agreed. Apparently, Egan was desperate for money. Not only that, Miranda was holding some threat over his head. Their conversation didn't reveal exactly what.

Because of SallyAnne's nostalgia for Egan's book, she despised Miranda even more for the hold she had over Egan.

As she rounded the corner to her cubicle, she caught sight of Lionel in the break room. He was deep in discussion with the tech agent also assigned to the case, Riley Kemp.

At that moment, Lionel looked over and saw her too. He smiled.

SallyAnne felt a blush creeping up her neck. She forced a smile onto her lips and strode over. "I guess if I'm ever to make it in earlier than you, I'll just have to put a cot in my cubicle."

"I…couldn't sleep," he admitted.

Because of what happened between us last night?

She longed to ask him that.

"Yeah, well, it seems that none of us is going to get much sleep over these next few months," Riley crowed. "This case is heating up by the nanosecond!"

SallyAnne frowned. "I can only imagine, from what you texted Lionel last night."

"Oh, you ain't heard nothin' yet," he assured her. "Besides the X-rated sexfest, they were alerted that AA's headmistress passed last night!"

"What?" Lionel and SallyAnne exclaimed in unison.

Riley nodded toward the conference room. "I've got the whole audio cued up so that you can hear it yourself."

As much as SallyAnne ached for a cup of coffee, she followed Riley down the hall.

She hadn't realized Lionel was still in the break room until she sat down. A moment later he walked in, carrying two mugs of coffee. He placed one in front of her. The coffee was light, just as she liked it. One sip told her he'd somehow picked up on the fact that she doctored her coffee with two cubes of sugar.

"Thank you," she stammered.

He grinned shyly. "My pleasure."

Don't read anything into this, SallyAnne warned herself. It's nothing more than a random act of kindness.

But she knew better.

Her previous partner, also male, had automatically assumed she'd bring him a cup whenever she got one for herself. Immediately, she cured him of that expectation by substituting salt for sugar.

When she and Lionel had first partnered up, she'd never offered to get his coffee. He'd followed her lead in forgoing beverage requests. Still, she too had watched him order coffee numerous times over the past few years and knew he took his black.

One good turn deserved another, she thought.

But something much bigger than a coffee run. As with his gesture, it had to be something implicit of how she hoped the kiss hadn't ruined their friendship.

In fact, it would express the opposite: that the intimacy they'd shared had strengthened their relationship.

That she thought of him as more than just a friend.

I guess I have Egan to thank for motivating Lionel to show his feelings for me, SallyAnne reasoned.

All the more reason it pained SallyAnne that the FBI sting had embroiled Egan in Miranda's illegal activities.

She didn't know what Miranda had on Egan, but whatever it was, she hoped it wasn't illegal.

If it turned out it wasn't, SallyAnne vowed to do what she could to help Egan get out from under Miranda's thumb.

THE AGENTS LISTENED AS MIRANDA ECSTATICALLY MOANED THROUGH HER first sex bout with Egan. At one point, SallyAnne had to smack Riley on the shoulder to stop him from snickering.

They also listened to Miranda's conversation with Daniel. Although Miranda's words were drenched in sympathy, SallyAnne muttered, "She's putting on a show."

Lionel looked surprised. "How can you tell?"

SallyAnne shrugged. "Because whenever she talks to, or about, Audrey, she has a distinct edge to her voice."

Lionel thought for a moment. "You know, you're right! Why do you think that is?"

"It might have something to do with the fact that Audrey is everything Miranda isn't: kind, thoughtful, and morally sound."

Riley, who'd kept his eyes closed through the cacophony of ecstatic moans, opened one long enough to declare, "I'll bet she's hated Audrey since they were in high school."

SallyAnne and Lionel exchanged glances. That thought had never occurred to either of them.

"That would mean she was also in school with Tallulah Wishart and Bliss Thackeray Belluci," Lionel pointed out. "As of yet, none of these women seem to have warmed up to her, let alone mention the good old days."

"If it's because they can't stand her, I'm sure that drives her up a wall," SallyAnne retorted.

"By the way, Melamed left word that the surveillance subpoenas came through on Jammerhead, Nira Patel, and Jess Smallwood," Lionel announced. "We should have the ones for the McCoppins by tomorrow. Miranda gets the SAT key next Friday. Until then, we're to babysit her as she makes calls to her SoCal clients so that we can record her reiterating the terms."

Riley added, "Tech will start monitoring these witnesses, as well as their college-bound children, for messages and conversations with Miranda."

"Great," Lionel replied. "And after Melamed reads our report about Egan Gable crashing yesterday's meeting between Miranda and the McCoppins, he'll ask for a surveillance subpoena for him as well." Noting SallyAnne's frown, he added, "I have to give your boy Egan some credit for at least one thing. Despite the fringe benefits, he shut down Miranda quick enough."

"He's not my boy," SallyAnne sniffed. "And he certainly didn't appreciate being sexually abused by that conniving *felon*."

As soon as the remark was out of her mouth, SallyAnne regretted it. The last thing she needed was for Lionel to think she had a soft spot for Egan. He was jealous enough as it was.

On the other hand, maybe that was a good thing.

"Sure, okay, if you say so." He looked at his watch. "I'll call her attorney at eight so that he can inform her to expect us by nine." Lionel grimaced at the thought.

Miranda is just as deplorable to him as she is to me, SallyAnne realized.

It was comforting to know.

AFTER FLINGING OPEN HER FRONT DOOR, MIRANDA BECKONED THE FBI AGENTS to enter. "Sorry, just got up. I had *such* a busy night! But you know that already, don't you?"

Seeing SallyAnne's blush, she added, "*Ooooh*, I hope you're not too jealous. I mean, it doesn't bother *me* in the least that Egan tried to pick you up. His douche-bag lounge lizard come-ons are part of his charm, don't you think?" Before SallyAnne could respond, Miranda nodded toward Lionel. "Don't answer that. No need to get Handsome here all uptight over it." Sauntering ahead of them, she cooed, "Haven't even had my coffee yet, but it's percolating. It's the only thing that wakes me up."

To make her point, she turned around and stretched her arms toward the ceiling. Her sweet pink baby doll silk robe rose high enough for a peek of the heart-shaped trimmed nether region of her naked body.

Noting the red creeping into Lionel's face, Miranda giggled. "Oh…*I'm sorry!* I didn't mean to embarrass you." She shrugged. "But it's not as if you haven't seen one before, am I right?" She nodded toward SallyAnne. "Like hers, maybe?"

Fists clenched, SallyAnne took a step forward.

Lionel moved between them. "Why don't you get dressed, Miranda? You've got a long day ahead of you."

"I'll say I have!" She reached for her phone. Pointing to the screen, she exclaimed, "Seamus McCoppin texted me last night. Wants to meet for lunch. Says he has a recruit for me." She shrugged. "But you know that already, don't you, since you have my phone bugged? I guess my car is as well."

Neither agent said anything.

"Hey, no fair," Miranda pouted. "Just by 'fessing up about Seamus I opened my kimono to *you*." To make her point, she untied her robe and flung it open, then giggled as Lionel's jaw dropped open. "Shouldn't you do the same?"

Lionel grabbed her by the shoulders and goose-stepped her down the hall. When he came to what looked like the master bedroom, he tossed her in there, slamming the door shut.

"You've got five minutes to put on something decent," he declared. "If not, your immunity is null and void."

"You can't do that!" Miranda shouted.

SallyAnne detected the panic in her voice. Her guess was that Miranda was straining to hear if they felt she stepped over the line.

She had, and they were tired of her antics. SallyAnne retorted, "Yes we can—*and we will.* We already have you on audio recruiting AA parents for your so-called concierge program. And we also have your list of Southern California concierge clients. Granted, having you call and confirm their participation would have been icing on the cake, but if you're not willing to play ball, so be it. They'll fold like a house of cards, with or without your cooperation. And as far as we're concerned, the more time you spend behind bars, the better."

Silence.

Lionel and SallyAnne's eyes met. Miranda's apartment was on the building's penthouse level. *Surely, she hadn't jumped…*

Lionel tried the doorknob. It was locked.

He had just positioned his shoulder against the door to ram it when it opened. He stumbled through the opening. Luckily, he righted himself before sprawling onto the floor.

Miranda was standing far enough to one side that she avoided a collision.

She'd changed into brown leather pants, a beige cowl-neck sweater, and beige Louboutins. Her makeup was minimal, and her hair was swept into a chignon.

Lowering her eyes, she whispered, "I'm sorry. My behavior was uncalled for."

Neither agent said anything. Finally, Lionel muttered, "Just don't let it happen again."

Meekly, Miranda nodded.

Satisfied, Lionel turned toward the living room.

SallyAnne allowed Miranda to walk past her, which was how she was able to catch Miranda's ever-so-slight triumphant smile.

CHAPTER 3

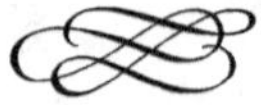

That her mother's death had occurred during a two-day student recess for a teacher's workday adjacent to a weekend seemed right to Audrey. Perhaps it was existentially planned on Lavinia's part: as if she instinctively knew her family, friends, and school community would need these extra days to process their shock over her loss.

When Audrey woke up, the sun was just peeking up over the East Bay hills. Daniel must have felt her stir because his arm went around her waist, pulling her closer to him.

She nestled in for a moment, but then sighed. "I should get up. I have to take care of Lavinia."

By that, she meant setting a time to meet the director of the funeral home regarding the cremation; getting an urn for the ashes; arranging a time and place for Lavinia's private memorial; and inviting the school community and others who loved Lavinia to the public Celebration of Life service.

Daniel sat up in bed. "Of course. I'll go too."

"But…what about the firm?"

"I think the partners will understand. They loved Lavinia. Heck, half of them have, or had, kids at the school."

Audrey nodded. "Great. While you shower, I'll make breakfast."

He nodded. "By the way, when I called Harris to tell him Lavinia passed, I asked if he'd give the eulogy, and he agreed. I hope you don't mind."

"She would have wanted that. Thank you."

He kissed her gently and then rolled out of bed.

She waited until he was in the shower before steeling herself for the day. A prayer—that she could hold her tears in so as not to exacerbate their children's profound grief—gave her the strength she needed to rise from the bed, wrap her robe around herself, and head downstairs.

By the time Daniel came downstairs, the coffee had been brewed. Audrey put up the toast and began the task of cracking eggs to scramble. To her surprise, Charly, Chuck, and Noah entered the kitchen. Unlike her, they were dressed.

"It was perfectly alright for you to sleep in today," she reminded them.

Noah shook his head. "I really didn't sleep at all last night."

"Me neither," Chuck added. "Mom, we want to go with you."

Audrey's eyes shifted from Chuck to Charly. "That's sweet of you. But, really, it's not necessary."

"We know that," Charly assured her. "But she is...*was* our grandmother. We loved her too." Audrey understood Charly's reluctance for the past tense use of the endearment.

It's proof we've accepted she's gone.

"Wherever you need to be, we want to go with you," Noah insisted.

Audrey nodded reluctantly. "Lavinia should already be at the crematorium. After breakfast, we'll go to Lavinia's house. I need to pick out something to put her in for the cremation. The process should take a couple of hours, maybe three." She blinked away her tears. "You don't have to stay the whole time. Dad can take you to lunch."

Noah nodded slowly. "Will you be staying there?"

She nodded. "I think someone should."

Noah put his arms around his mother's waist. "Then we'll wait with you."

As Audrey kissed the top of his head, she caught Daniel's eye. There she saw a mix of sadness and appreciation.

Only Lavinia can make me feel this beloved.

Could make me feel.

She couldn't stifle her sobs at the realization that her mother would now always be thought of in the past tense.

When her family's arms embraced her, she thought she heard Lavinia whisper, *Always and forever.*

<h1 style="text-align:center">CHAPTER 4</h1>

By the time Miranda had to leave for her lunch with Seamus, she'd tracked down five of her former Southern California concierge clients and got them to implicate themselves on the record by reiterating, and effusively at that, just how much they appreciated her illicit shenanigans on their behalf.

When SallyAnne told her to skip Tanner Simpson, Rob Edelson, and Eric Calisher, Miranda realized they'd been the clients who had flipped on her.

Two can play that game, she reasoned.

She was willing to guess that Eric, ever the hard-nosed businessman, would plead not guilty. As innocently as possible, she'd asked Lionel if this were the case.

He frowned. "When we confronted his wife, she committed suicide. And because the email account he used for his correspondence with you had only been accessed at their home and in her name, we have no way to tie him to an indictment."

She nodded slowly. "What if I gave you evidence that he was my sole contact?"

Lionel's eyes widened. "Our deal with him would be voided, and he'd be indicted."

"And it would count as one of my Girl Scout badges, right?"

Lionel sighed. "Yes, of course."

An hour later, she handed him a thumb drive. It contained the proof they needed: an audio file of Miranda's meeting with Eric, in which his son's rate was negotiated.

She hoped it bought her some of Lionel's respect, but she doubted it.

She guessed Tanner and Rob would plead guilty. When that happened, the reporter covering the story for the *Los Angeles Times* would receive the video of her and Rob making love.

For his betrayal, she owed him that much.

Those Miranda chose to call did not include the eight parents who had circled back to her this year with a second child whom they felt also needed her illicit help. After Winslow Jennings—the proctor she'd hired and set up at her fake testing subsidiary, University Prep & Test—disappeared on a gambling spree, he'd convinced her to abscond with their fees.

Miranda saw no need to let the Feds in on *that* little debacle. Why have grand theft added to her already long list of crimes?

These parents were on the list she'd turned in to the FBI. Eventually, she'd have to call them. By then, she prayed any deal her high-priced attorney made with them would be set in stone.

As she hung up from the final call, Lionel asked, "What kind of food do they serve at Zingari?"

"Expensive food." Miranda clicked her tongue in mock apology. "Probably off the charts when it comes to my FBI per diem. But it's one of Seamus' usual hangouts. I couldn't say no to him, now, could I?"

"There are food trucks on practically every corner of the Financial District," SallyAnne muttered.

Miranda chuckled, as if her nemesis had told a funny joke. "My clients don't do business with pikers."

Lionel still had the FBI-issued purse that Miranda had been instructed to use last night—one that had been customized with a video camera.

Miranda frowned when she saw it. Whereas yesterday she'd scoffed at its off-brand label, this time she shrugged. Picking up a compact, she pouted into the mirror as she ran a wand over her lips. "Am I to be on camera again?"

"Yes," Lionel replied firmly.

"That damn thing is black, and I'm wearing brown."

Lionel guffawed. "I'm sure Seamus won't even notice. He didn't strike me as a fashion maven."

Haughtily, she pulled out everything from her real purse and dumped it into the government-issued knock-off. Then, glancing at SallyAnne, she declared, "I suppose you'll be sitting this one out."

SallyAnne scoffed. "What gave you that idea?"

"Seamus knows what you look like." Miranda snapped the compact shut. "It's okay to wait in the van. Handsome can keep an eye on things." Her eyes studied Lionel from head to toe.

"Seamus saw Lionel too," SallyAnne reminded her.

Miranda shook her head. "I doubt he even noticed him. He was too busy staring at your legs. Or hadn't you noticed?"

SallyAnne turned bright red.

"Thought so." Miranda's eyes widened, as if a thought had just occurred. "Perhaps you can make yourself useful by tailing Egan! But don't let him spot you. He's already smitten. Who knows what he'd do if he saw you?" Miranda smirked. "I guess I could say the same for you. You heard his performance, didn't you?"

SallyAnne had to purse her lips to hold herself back from cursing her out.

"Unless you think it's a bad idea." She slid her gaze to Lionel, as if the decision were his to make.

Lionel's face was impassive. Still, SallyAnne guessed what he might be thinking: Miranda had a point. Seamus might indeed remember her. And if Melamed was able to fast-track Egan's surveillance subpoena, having SallyAnne review the calls, emails, and texts monitored by Riley's team might not be a bad idea—

Despite Lionel's personal preference that she stay away from Egan.

Lionel's nonchalant shrug was proof that SallyAnne had guessed right: he thought Miranda had a point.

As Miranda tucked the compact into her purse, she asked, "Agent Polk, since you're tailing me anyway, wouldn't it make sense that we ride over together? That way your *partner*"—she lingered on the word a second too long—"can take the car back to the office." Seeing his surprise, she added, "It was just a thought. Not to worry. I'd return you in one piece."

SallyAnne saw no need to wait for his response. She walked out without a word.

AT LIONEL'S INSISTENCE, THEY ARRIVED A GOOD TWENTY MINUTES BEFORE THE scheduled meeting, which gave them plenty of time to park in a nearby garage and secure tables close enough that he could video record her.

Miranda went ahead and ordered a bottle of wine. She knew Seamus would expect it, and besides, she needed a drink after the past forty-eight hours. Had it been that long since she'd first been arrested?

Jeez, it seems like a lifetime, she thought.

Seamus came ten minutes late—plenty of time for her to drink half the waiter's generous pour of a very expensive cabernet sauvignon.

Jess Smallwood and Warner Crawford were with him.

Oh, bloody hell.

Miranda caught Lionel's eyes opening wide at the sight of Seamus' entourage.

Seamus chuckled as he squeezed into the booth on one side of her, confident in his supposedly secret mission.

Miranda would hear it soon enough.

"A shame about Lavinia." Jess also slid into the booth on Miranda's other side. He thought nothing of squeezing her thigh under the table.

Miranda was tempted to dig her nail into the back of his hand. But his yelp would alert the other men as to what had just happened. Instead, she murmured, "Yes, isn't it?"

If Jess truly wants to sound sincere, he should take that shit-eating grin off his face, she thought.

"I guess AA will now go into the crapper," Warner fretted. "The kids really liked her. Even my son, Buck, minded his P's and Q's around her."

"Not to worry," Seamus huffed. "The new Head of School will keep him in line."

A new head of school...

Oh, bother.

Seamus' big plan was to fast-track some new administrator!

If the new schoolmaster were power-hungry (and most were, Miranda reasoned; seriously, who wouldn't get a high lording it over a teaching staff, a bunch of sniveling students, and fawning parents who considered themselves lucky to be one of such a highly regarded school's chosen few?), she could find herself sidelined from any activities that took her outside those she'd committed to the school.

Which means she'd have less leverage with the FBI.

I've got to make sure the trustee board draws out the search as long as possible.

"She is irreplaceable indeed," Miranda declared. "That being said, I would hope that the trustee board takes its time in finding someone who comes close to filling her shoes—"

"To hell with that!" Seamus bellowed. "We're going to fill it immediately—and permanently. In fact, I've got just the candidate."

"Mustn't be too hasty," Miranda cautioned. "We may end up with another bleeding heart do-gooder."

Seamus raised a brow. "I doubt that very much"—he poured wine into his glass, then raised it toward her. He waited until she raised hers too, then declared—"since it'll be *you*."

What...

Oh, hell!

Miranda almost dropped her glass. "What? I can't! ... *I won't*—"

Not in a million years.

"Sure you will," Seamus growled. "We put you on the board for one reason: to assure it lives up to our standards." He shrugged. "Quit worrying."

She could see it now. As the FBI dragged Miranda away in handcuffs, the parents would fight them off, if only for the honor of stringing her up from the bell tower.

I will have ruined their children's futures. Even those whose kids weren't involved will know the school will be tarnished by the scandal.

I have to nip this in the bud—NOW.

"As honored as I am by your confidence, I don't feel it would be a good fit," Miranda insisted. "You forget, Seamus. Beyond my current obligation to Ashbury Academy, I've got a private practice as well."

She picked up the purse and rose from her seat. As far as she was concerned, the topic was closed.

Seamus put his hand on her arm. "Believe me, Miranda. Our interests are well aligned."

She frowned. "How so?"

He tugged her back down into her chair. "As headmistress, you are perfectly positioned to recruit new parents to the school whose philosophy aligns with Warner's, Jess', and mine. Parents who would do anything —*and pay anything*—to get into the universities of their choice." He leaned in so close that she could smell his breath. "Miranda, imagine a whole school willing to pay your fee—all because you've guaranteed getting their kids into the universities of their choice!"

Miranda's glare shifted from Seamus to Jess to Warner and back again. "I think you're forgetting, Seamus. Our arrangement was *strictly confidential.*"

Seamus chuckled. "Quit being so paranoid! You don't have to worry about Warner here. He's the client referral I mentioned. Trust me, he's all in!"

He jutted his chin toward Warner, who nodded vigorously.

She set the purse back onto the table, the clasp turned toward Warner, so that its camera saw him fully. "What you're telling me, Mr. Crawford, is that you don't mind in the least that my college admissions concierge program may include some illicit acts?"

Warner guffawed. "Buck is the laziest kid at the school. And no matter how many times I've warned him that he can't just send a headshot to get into the school of his choice, he insists he can just skirt by on his looks." He sighed mightily, proof he was resigned to this fact. "So yeah, I'm in. Otherwise, my retirement fund will go to supporting a spendthrift party animal for the rest of his life."

Seamus jabbed Miranda's arm. "See? What did I tell you? He's all in! In fact, he knows at least two other parents who are just as anxious to get their kids into one of their top school picks."

As long as Seamus and his friends were doing the hard work, why not just lean back and enjoy the ride?

Lean back, she did. "Are you suggesting that we build my fee— including the pass-along costs—into the tuition?"

"Eventually, yes," Jess replied. "After this year, like their children, parents will be vetted differently—*to see if they're a good fit with the school's new philosophy.*"

The more desperate, the better, Miranda thought.

"We have two legacies on the current trustee board, a high-profile member who was Lavinia's closest and dearest friend, and another board member who is married to Lavinia's daughter. How do you think they'll feel about this?"

"They'll hate it. Maybe so much that they'll quit the board." Seamus smiled at the thought. "Look, Miranda, if I don't go in asking for the whole hog, they won't even settle for giving me the tail, let alone the squeal. Let me play hardball. Interim Head will be our fallback position."

"Works for me," she murmured.

Prayerfully, the search would go on long enough that she'd never have the title permanently, and with it the wrath of the Ashbury Academy community.

"Once you're installed as Interim Head of School, you'll be tasked with heading up the New Family Acceptance Committee."

Miranda nodded. "My criterion is simple: anyone who is desperate enough to contribute, minimally half a million dollars per student, will automatically be enrolled in the concierge program."

Warner sputtered on his wine. "You want me to cough up *half a mil*?"

"Hardly! As you've just admitted, Buck is dumb as a post. That warrants a fee of *a million dollars.*" Miranda turned to Seamus. "Which brings us to what I'll expect for the salary as Head of School." She leaned in. "If minimally, I'm to work my magic for six more students next year, I'll need an additional three million."

Seamus shrugged. "And for a whole graduating class?"

Miranda took a moment to think. Finally, she declared, "Each successive year, my salary will be predicated on the number of new families who are accepted due to the change in our mission. By the fifth year, the salary will be…oh, say, twenty million."

Jess smirked. "That should fatten the quote unquote 'endowment fund.'"

"Tuition will be raised too," she warned.

Jess frowned. He was thinking of his daughter from his second wife, who would graduate in three years.

"Look at it this way. It's a pittance as to what I'd charge them individually," Miranda countered. "These assurances don't come cheap, you know. Not to mention each *new* family's fee is spread over the four years their child is in school. And besides, the parents who fit our philosophy will be able to afford the increases." She shrugged. "I know you well enough to figure out you are looking for a deal and want to spread the investment. Well, those are my terms, gentlemen. Take it or leave it."

The men exchanged glances. Finally, Seamus growled, "Done—with one exception." He puffed up. "Until the school is at a point where every parent has bought into this new programming feature, those who have done so will prove it by their donations to the newly established 'Lavinia Thorpe Memorial Endowment Fund.'"

Knowing him, it'll be anything but, Miranda realized.

Still, she murmured, "And let me guess who will be controlling this fund—you. Am I right?"

Seamus shrugged. "I'd be honored to increase its corpus with sound investments."

Miranda's laugh rang through the restaurant. "My God, Seamus! You're shameless!" Studying her nails, she added, "Do me a favor and save the motion until after Lavinia's funeral. That way, you don't look like a complete Machiavellian overlord. Besides, we don't need a civil war breaking out."

Seamus scowled, then nodded grudgingly. He raised his glass to her. "Here's to Ashbury Academy finally becoming the school worth our investment."

"I'll drink to that," Jess declared.

As he picked up his glass, Miranda glanced directly at Lionel and winked.

I should get a medal for this—right, Handsome?

Instead, I'll end up in some cell—one I'll probably share with Gretchen McCoppin.

Maybe that wouldn't be so bad. At least, there would be no question who'd be the alpha in that relationship.

As previously instructed by Lionel, Miranda allowed the men to leave first.

Jess tried to linger, but his suggestion of some "afternoon delight" was met with a harried sigh.

"My afternoon is booked with client appointments. And by the way, from what we've just discussed about my fees, maybe you should be shaking your magic money tree so that you're not so stretched by the time your daughter, Elowen, is in her senior year. Last I heard, she's got her eye on Yale."

Jess turned white, mumbled some vague answer, and then did as he was told.

"What a dolt," Miranda muttered.

That was for Lionel's sake.

Lionel followed a few yards behind Miranda until they reached the garage.

Instead of dropping her off at her apartment, he drove straight to FBI headquarters, where SallyAnne, Riley, and Director Melamed were waiting for them in one of the conference rooms.

Miranda smirked. "Wow, what a welcoming committee! I guess I did well."

"Behave yourself, Miranda." The disemboweled voice of her attorney, Gerald Breslin, came in over the speaker on the conference room table. "Seamus' scheme moves this investigation into a whole different league. We can add money laundering to the list of indictments."

Riley started counting them off on his fingers: "Bribery, racketeering, criminal conspiracy, honest services mail fraud—"

"I get the picture," Miranda retorted. "I'll do it—but only if it means I walk without jail time."

"That depends on how successful his scheme is," Melamed countered. "I seriously doubt he has the votes to make this happen."

Miranda shrugged. "We'll see about that." Egan was still her ace in the hole. Metaphorically speaking, anyway.

"By the way, you've just received a text from Daniel McKittridge," Riley declared. "The memorial service is being held at the school on Wednesday, at eleven o'clock."

Miranda glared at him. "You're a wonderful private secretary. Did you RSVP for me as well?"

"Yeah," he admitted. "I mean, I knew you'd want to attend…"

His voice faded when he realized Melamed was glowering at him.

"We'll be your ride to the memorial service," Lionel added.

Miranda frowned. "Why do I need an entourage? It's not like I'll be hustling parents while everyone is bawling over Lavinia."

"Seamus has no filter," Lionel pointed out. "And now he has a vested interest in you. He may actually recruit a few other parents during the service and walk them over to you at some point."

She couldn't argue with that.

"We'll be discreet, so no need to worry. Unless you're going with your boyfriend—*Egan*." SallyAnne's remark had Miranda flinching—proof it had hit its mark like a poison dart.

Lionel's brow rose in consternation.

Ignoring him, SallyAnne paused, as if a thought just came to her. "Oh, wait…he broke up with you, didn't he?"

Miranda stiffened. "As far as you're concerned, Egan is serving his purpose."

"As long as you keep him in play," Melamed reminded her. "Otherwise, you'll never be able to deliver on your promise."

"He cashed the check, didn't he? Then he's in play," Miranda huffed. "Although, I'll admit having sex with him was a mistake."

"So sorry it didn't work out, since you obviously enjoyed it," Sally-Anne murmured.

Lionel shot her a look that was meant to silence her, but it was too late.

Miranda scowled at SallyAnne. "Oh yes, I forgot—the FBI is now my constant companion." She shrugged as if to say, *so be it.* "If you really want to get up close and personal, you should attend as my date," she cooed to Lionel.

"He may run into Egan—who may remember him." SallyAnne countered.

"I doubt it," Miranda muttered. "He only had eyes for you."

SallyAnne's cheeks pinked up.

Miranda's attention shifted to Lionel. "Don't you agree?"

SallyAnne knew Miranda's game: divide and conquer.

But proof Lionel wasn't falling for it was his reply: "Of course I do. We're all going—Riley included."

"But…" Miranda's jaw jutted out in anger. "No one in Lavinia's circle knows you. You'll stick out like sore thumbs."

"It'll be a large crowd—easy for us to blend in. It's what we do for a living," he reminded her. "If you're that concerned, we'll put on disguises. Look, here's the thing, Miranda: until the indictments are served, we're going to be on you like white on rice. Get used to it."

The message was clear: he didn't trust her.

She could live with that—at least until she was free of the FBI.

CHAPTER 5

$\mathcal{T}$he public Celebration of Life for Lavinia was to take place at the school on Wednesday at eleven. As was her wish, at dawn, Audrey, Daniel, and the children spread her ashes off Fort Point, below the Golden Gate Bridge in a private memorial ceremony.

They were joined by those who knew Lavinia best: Bliss and her parents, Reggie and Maude Thackeray, as well as her husband, Raffaele, and their daughter, Sienna. Tallulah was also there, with her husband and son, Jammerhead and Quest. Her mother, Maggie, sobbed inconsolably. Lavinia had been her oldest and dearest friend and confidante.

Davis had also shown up.

Harris was there too, although his wife, Tracy, was still in Washington, having committed to head the fundraiser for a national charity.

Each took a teaspoon of Lavinia's sifted ashes before saying a few words about the woman who had touched their lives so profoundly. They then released the ashes into the frigid, fast-flowing current which marks where the turbulent Pacific Ocean meets the calm wake of San Francisco Bay.

Audrey took her turn last. She did so without saying a word. There were too many things she wished she had said to her mother when she was alive. Too many questions she wished she'd asked.

Would Lavinia have answered?

Now she'd never know.

CLARE HAD INSISTED THAT AUDREY DELEGATE THE SET-UP OF THE EVENT TO her and the teaching staff. By the time the McKittridges arrived, a stage had been placed in the center of the quad.

Rows of white chairs stretched out from it, like the spokes on a wheel. Hanging from the trees throughout the park were laminated poster-sized photos of Lavinia: with staff, students, and parents, tracing her life at the school. Each image had been selected and signed by a student.

As it should be, Audrey thought. *The school was no less a part of her life than me.*

Immediately, Audrey and her family were wrapped in consoling hugs by mourners. Grief was etched deeply into their faces.

Audrey tried to respond to their gently murmured condolences, but the words stuck in her throat.

Lavinia was always the one to console others, Audrey thought. She always knew the right thing to say.

I'll never be like her.

I don't have her strength of character.

As if reading her mind, Daniel whispered into her ear, "I'll speak for the family, if you want."

Relieved, Audrey nodded. She took Daniel's hand. He led her to the front row seats reserved for them.

It was fitting that Harris, Lavinia's oldest and closest friend, deliver her eulogy.

Through his candor, the students who dearly missed the headmistress were introduced to a much younger Lavinia. One who questioned her professors at Berkeley with the verve of a prosecuting attorney. Who never thought twice of inviting down-on-their-luck friends to crash on her couch. And whose Sunday open houses were more fondly recalled for her homemade soups and bread than for the dreams, schemes, and political discourse espoused by the multitude of students in attendance.

Quite a few Ashbury Academy parents teared up when Harris recalled the day Lavinia told him why she was determined to start her own school after spending almost fifteen years teaching, both in private and public institutions: "'The greatest joy is the students,' she explained. 'But despite what anyone says, the administrative vision isn't *student-driven*. If it's not controlled by a union, it is micromanaged by parents. That should never be! The students show us what they need. We must guide them to reach their and society's goals. This school will do just that.'"

The parents in the audience nodded even as they laughed uncomfortably. They saw themselves in her declaration.

After leaving the stage, Harris walked through the crowd. Arms reached out to him with hands ready to shake or grasp him in appreciation for his touching words.

SallyAnne and the rest of her team were scattered within the crowd. She'd always liked Harris as her Congressman. But now, for the first time, she appreciated him as just another person.

Because Miranda was wired, the agents could hear her mutter, "Bravo, Harris! Looks like you locked up a few more votes and donors."

What a bitch, SallyAnne thought.

CLARE RUSHED ONTO THE STAGE. BUT BY THE WAY THE SCHOOL'S SWEET BUT shy receptionist shook, it was evident she was nervous about being there.

In her palm, she held a smooth rock: one of the many that were placed throughout the campus' flower beds. Her voice was so soft that the crowd leaned in to hear what she had to say. "As most of you are aware, Ashbury Academy has a tradition: it's called 'magic circle.'"

Waves of knowing nods rippled through the crowd. "By passing around a river rock, we are encouraged to speak up and talk through our feelings when the rock comes our way. Lavinia felt that honest conversation was a path to resolution." Clare wiped away her tears with the back of her hand. Her voice cracked as she added, "I know we won't resolve our grief, but it may help us process it."

Taking the hand-held microphone with her, she left the stage. She handed the rock to the first person she saw—a junior student, a boy—while holding the mic for him.

JESUS, I NEVER FELT THAT WAY ABOUT A TEACHER, LET ALONE A PRINCIPAL, Riley thought.

Thus far, six mourners had reached out for the river rock and spoke from their hearts about the revered headmistress. Three had been students, two were parents, and one was the seemingly ancient French teacher— she'd given her name as Odette Pettigrew—who had been with the school since the day it opened.

As Madame Pettigrew's voice rose and fell dramatically, Riley stared up at the school's clock tower. He couldn't help but envision this none-too-beauteous Schéhérazade as a gargoyle perched on the peak of its witches' cap roof.

Admittedly, each mourner's memory of Lavinia had been more touching than the last.

The girl speaking now sat across the aisle from him. In a halting voice, she recalled fretting over an oral book report. As she passed Lavinia on her way to class, the headmistress intuitively sensed her anxiety.

In no time, she got the girl to divulge her fear.

"Lavinia suggested I imagine talking to my best friends about the book. That I summarize the story and then tell them all the things I loved about it, but also the things that didn't ring true." The girl smiled. "It worked! I got an A! I was so happy that I stopped into Lavinia's office later that day to tell her about it. She hugged me and said, 'I knew you'd do well. Only we can hold ourselves back from accomplishing our goals.'" The girl's eyes grew misty. "I can still hear her voice in my mind. Can't we all? Because what she said to us resonates in our hearts." As if weighted down with her sorrow, the girl's head dropped to her chest. "She lives on through all of us."

Everyone seemed to be wiping away their tears. Those around the girl comforted her with pats on the back. The ensuing silence was filled with the sobs of a few mourners unable to contain their grief.

Suddenly realizing she still held the river rock, the embarrassed girl thrust it toward Riley.

SHIT! ... SHIT! WHAT DO I DO NOW?

Like all FBI agents, he'd been trained to be as unobtrusive as possible. He was there to observe, not to participate.

But now all eyes were on him.

To his horror, Clare stuck the microphone in his face.

Riley was the center of attention.

"I…. I…" the stammer was to buy time; to think through how he could blend in.

As if.

"I was only here a short time. Not even a semester," he murmured.

A strangled voice, somewhere from another side of the campus, yelled, "Louder, please!"

Riley nodded. In a stronger voice, he added, "Every day, I'd come home, in awe of my classmates, my teachers—and of course, Lavinia."

He buried his head in his hands. *Stall…. STALL.*

Finally, he let out a long sigh. "Still, I didn't feel as if I belonged there… I mean *here*."

Watch it. You're blowing your cover!

"I was sitting by myself—on that bench over there, in fact—when she walked past me. It was as if she knew the turmoil I was feeling. She sat right down beside me and asked, 'How are you?' And it all came out! All my anxieties, my fears. My hurt."

Those closest to him reached out to touch his arm, encouraging him to continue.

Ah, hell.

"She was so...*so kind!* Insightful. And inspiring!" he continued. "She told me I could be anything I wanted, that I could do anything I set my mind to." He dropped his head. "And she was right. In fact, that night, I informed my parents that when I graduated, I wanted to go to...*to mime school.*"

A murmur went through the crowd

Shit! Was that too unbelievable? Say something that sounds real—now!

"They were so upset that they pulled me out of school. They'd decided the school was too...well, in their words, 'too liberal'"—

The mourners gasped.

"—which is why none of you remember me." He didn't know if that was a great cover, but it was all he could think of. "It's why I'm here now. Because of Lavinia, I became the best mime in...err...*Bolivia!* There, I'm known as 'the Mime King.'" He laughed weakly. "Or as they say in my new country, *'El Rey Memo.'*" For once, Riley was glad his high school Spanish paid off.

Elated, he wiped away a tear of relief.

Suddenly, he was enveloped in hugs.

Wow...this feels AWESOME...

EGAN HAD BEEN STANDING IN THE BACK OF THE CAMPUS, BEHIND ALL THE chairs. He'd seen Audrey come in with her family, only to be swallowed up in the crowd.

After our meeting the night of Lavinia's death, the last person she wants to see now is me, he realized.

Miranda was also there. Luckily, the crowd was thick enough that he'd succeeded in ducking out of view whenever she glanced in his direction.

Right now, everyone's eyes were on the goober, whose tale about Lavinia had turned the celebration of her life into a big cryfest.

Egan dove through the crowd until he was at Clare's side. Pointing to the sobbing stranger, he hissed, "We've got to do something, Clare! The crowd is drowning in its own tears! Go up there! Say something that's *uplifting!*"

Clare's eyes grew large with fear. With a shaky whisper, she pleaded, "I—I can't! Please, Egan, do it for me...*for her!*"

He knew she meant Lavinia. Still, instinctively, his eyes went to Audrey. She was crying harder than anyone. Daniel leaned over her helplessly, trying to comfort her.

Egan frowned. "You knew Lavinia the longest! Wouldn't it be better coming from you?"

Clare shook her head, adamantly. "No—please! *I don't like speaking in public.* I'm a behind-the-scenes person. And for you—it comes so naturally!"

Egan nodded, but he wasn't happy about it.

He stooped down and picked up another of the palm-sized stones.

This one's for you, Lavinia.

CHAPTER 6

*E*gan leaped up onto the stage, holding the stone high.

"My name is Egan Gable, and I teach Comparative Literature here at Ashbury Academy." He nodded to the crowd. "I, like you, am here because Lavinia Thorpe touched my life. I'll go further and say she was such a force of nature that she changed the fate of many—me included. I'd like to share the one act that impacted me the most."

Egan looked down at the mourners, all the while steeling himself from the natural inclination to look at Audrey. "It was the day I met her. The school was entering its fourth year. I told her I was a thesis candidate at Berkeley in Creative Writing. That was true—but barely. In fact, I'd just gotten word that the committee considered my thesis—a novel—mediocre at best. To top it off, my parents made it abundantly clear that they weren't going to support me financially as I wrote my version of the great American novel in various and sundry New York coffee shops—"

He got a chuckle with that remark.

"—so, I needed a job and fast." Egan sighed. "As fate would have it, Ashbury Academy needed an English teacher. And *voila!* —a match was made in heaven." Letting loose with a broad grin, he looked skyward but then shook his head. "I wish I could say it was that easy, but we all know Lavinia much better than that. No way was she going to entrust her precious students to *just anyone.*"

Throughout the crowd, heads bobbed. Giggles filled the air.

"Instead," he continued, "she wants to know *everything* about you. Not the just the stuff you think she wants to hear, either—*but the stuff you really don't ever want anyone to know.*"

By now, the chuckles were outright guffaws.

"She wanted to know where I'd grown up. And what I'd done for fun as a kid. And the most important lessons my parents had taught me." He let that sink in. "She wanted to know why I chose to be a Lit major, and if there were anything I'd change about my academic journey."

The crowd froze, enthralled.

"So, of course, I lied."

Now the crowd was laughing outright.

"I created the backstory I wished I had lived, minimizing my heartache and failures. I did so because I was sure she'd think worse of me had she heard the truth, never realizing—at least, not yet—that one of Lavinia's hidden talents was that she could read minds. And that her ex-ray vision easily pierced the armor our egos forged from the tiny fibs we must tell ourselves to hold up our heads; simply to survive another day."

His audience nodded as if seeing themselves through his tale.

"So, no, I didn't fool her. Not in the least. And yet, she chose to see the best in me." Egan looked skyward as if seeing his friend and mentor there. "I had a pancake-flat vision of myself. But like some great chef, Lavinia added those few missing ingredients—a dollop of inspiration, a sprinkle of kindness, and heaps of responsibility garnished with just enough account-ability to make me realize my potential—and turned it into the flavorful, satisfying soufflé that is my life." He paused. "We are all fortunate to have had her in our lives." He paused, then added, "But no one knows that better than her family."

He pointed to the McKittridges—

To Audrey, specifically.

HE LOVED LAVINIA TOO.

Audrey saw that immediately.

And he is right. Lavinia saw right through him.

This realization caused her to laugh through her tears.

She saw through me too. She knew I'd been infatuated with him.

But it didn't matter. Lavinia let fate take its course.

At that moment, her mother's final words came to her: *Tell Daniel about Egan.*

It had been almost a week since her mother's death—plenty of time to try to convince herself that she'd misheard Lavinia.

But she knew better. Somehow, Lavinia had deduced the secret Audrey had kept for eighteen years: that the twins' father was Egan.

All that time, Audrey had lived with the shame of keeping her secret from Daniel.

Oh, how Audrey wished she could have convinced herself that Lavinia's declaration was murmured through a fog of delusion! But no.

Even as Death beckoned her forward, Lavinia had summoned the energy to open her eyes one last time.

They say that the eyes are the windows to the soul, Audrey thought. Her mother's last clear-eyed gaze had put all doubts to rest.

I can't tell Daniel yet.

The thought that day would eventually come had her suddenly sobbing uncontrollably.

Daniel put his arm around her and whispered, "Honey, are you alright?"

At that moment, she realized that Egan had stopped talking and that his arm was held out to her.

Why? What had he just said?

Daniel, too, must have realized she'd just been singled out because his back stiffened. "Do you want to say something?"

She shook her head. "*No!* I can't ...not now—"

He patted her hand. "I'll speak for the family then."

Daniel rose and walked to the stage.

<hr>

"He's such a blowhard."

Seamus had sidled so closely to Miranda that his breath felt warm on her neck.

Still, he'd said it loud enough that several mourners glanced over, shaking their heads in dismay.

He then tapped her arm with something—an envelope.

She stared down at it. "Is that what I think it is?"

"What do you think it is?" Seamus smiled supremely. "It's your pay-off for fixing my beautiful-but-dumb daughter's SAT test."

She glowered at him. "You fool! You were supposed to make an electronic funds transfer to The Best Face Forward Club!" she said in a hush.

Seamus' face fell. "What the hell does it matter?"

"It matters a lot, you dolt! It makes the transaction a legitimate donation!" she shoved the envelope at his chest. "*Just do it.*"

Mollified, he slunk back into the crowd.

She didn't realize Lionel was right behind her until he muttered: "It wasn't necessary. We could take it and pull his fingerprints off the bills to make our case."

Miranda didn't turn around but growled, "I wanted to kick his ass. I don't need him cutting corners and screwing up my deal with you."

"Good point."

Then, silence.

She didn't need to turn around to know Lionel had already slipped away.

BEAUTIFUL BUT DUMB DAUGHTER?

He's paying her to fake my test?

Why that son of a bitch!

Neither Miranda nor Seamus had realized Fawn was standing right there behind them—

Close enough to hear how little he thought of her.

He doesn't believe I can get admitted to college on my own—let alone get accepted by his hoity-toity alma mater, Yale.

Great. Fine. No surprise there.

Seamus may have changed the rules of the game, but she could still win: by raking in as many acceptances as possible—

And then turning them all down.

Including Yale.

Game on, she vowed.

LIKE EGAN, DANIEL CHOSE AN UPLIFTING ANECDOTE.

And like the rest of the crowd, Egan had been listening to Daniel, which is why it took him a while to realize that someone had moved beside him.

He gave the man a sidelong glance, taking note that he was younger. He was also vaguely familiar.

As if reading his mind, the man said, "Egan, it's me—Davis Wong. Long time, no see."

Egan did a doubletake. Yes, the face was the same, but now that he was thirty-nine—forty, perhaps—there were a few lines around his eyes and his forehead. Although his torso was still slight, he'd bulked up, but in a good way.

He held out his hand. "It's great to see you, Davis."

Taking it, Davis declared, "I have to tell you, *Extracurricular* was a great book. I read it when it first came out."

"Why, thank you." Taken aback, Egan shrugged. "And it's been wonderful following your success in LaLa Land."

Davis chuckled. "Maybe I can spread some of my fame and fortune your way. In fact, recently, I picked up *Extracurricular* again. I loved it even more. Laughed in all the right places, cried in a couple too." Davis hesitated. "In fact, I'd like to option it for a television series."

Egan's heart seemed to leap in his chest. "I'm…flattered, to say the least. More so because it's you." He hesitated. "I hate to sound so ignorant about your industry, but tell me: what does this mean in monetary terms?"

"There will be option money, in the mid to high six figures. And if a network wants it, that will double the option I've paid for. If it goes to pilot, even more." Davis shrugged. "Or it could go straight to series, and that's when the big payoff happens."

Egan's eyes grew wide. "Big? What are we talking about?"

"Depends on the terms that your agent can get."

Egan frowned. "I don't know if my lit agent has my back. The publisher recently pulled it from publication because of a lawsuit."

Davis shook his head, awed. "Jesus! Whatever for?"

Egan sighed. "Remember Mandy Blackwell? She rightly guessed the character based on her and threw a lawsuit at me. 'Defamation of character.'"

Davis snorted. "Frankly, I thought what you wrote was a love letter. Ah, well, no accounting for taste." He looked around. "I don't see her here. But the crowd is pretty thick, and it has been over twenty years."

Egan looked skyward. "Don't remind me."

Davis patted his shoulder. "You look great—for an old man."

Egan laughed.

Suddenly, he remembered where he was and pursed his lips. He need not have bothered. Everyone around them was suddenly talking and moving. A few were also laughing. Apparently, Daniel had brought the proceedings to a close on a high note.

Thank goodness, Egan thought.

At that moment, he realized Audrey was staring at him.

Bliss and Tallulah were beside her.

Davis must have noticed, too, because he declared, "My sweet, sweet Audrey." Without a second thought, he waved them over.

Audrey hesitated, grimacing.

She doesn't want to come over because of me.

But a moment later they were at his side.

CHAPTER 7

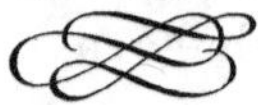

"Hi, Doll. How are you holding up?" Watching as Davis kissed Audrey's cheek gently, Egan yearned to do the same.

Her lips rose unsteadily into a treacly smile. "I'm okay. The kids ...it's a big blow to them."

More so because they hadn't known how ill Lavinia was, Egan reasoned.

Audrey held out her hand to Egan. "Thank you for those very kind words about Lavinia. And for lifting everyone's spirits." She managed a weak smile.

Tallulah craned her head for a better look at Riley. "Who was that mime guy anyway?"

"I didn't recognize him," Audrey admitted. "Although he couldn't have been that much younger than us. And although we had a few students come in mid-year, I certainly don't remember anyone leaving in the middle of the school year, or for that matter, parents being angry at Lavinia for being too progressive. It's what you buy into at AA."

Bliss raised a brow. "Well, at least the dude got into the school of his choice."

Egan snickered. "I've got to write that into a novel."

Davis turned to him. "Speaking of novels, if you're interested in my offer for *Extracurricular,* I can recommend a couple of talent agencies that have literary divisions and might represent you in the deal. Neither reps me, so they'd have, as they say, clean hands."

Egan felt his cheeks flaring. He hadn't expected Davis to bring up their conversation in front of anyone there, let alone Audrey.

"You want to produce *Extracurricular* as a movie?" Bliss asked.

"No," Egan said quickly.

"A TV adaptation," Davis explained.

Egan noticed that all the color drained from Audrey's face.

"Ha! Yeah, now that you mention it, I could see that," Tallulah exclaimed. "It's got that whole *This is Us* vibe going for it! You know, retro and touchy-feely at the same time."

"More like *Clueless*," Audrey muttered as she glowered at Egan.

"Except that it's got that great love story," Bliss pointed out. She looked sideways at Egan. "Although, for the life of me, I can't understand why you based your protagonist on Mandy Blackwell, of all people!"

"*Mandy?*" Egan couldn't believe his ears. He was about to set her straight, but he felt a jab to his back and he turned around.

It was Audrey. Her glare warned him to hold his tongue.

She's right, he thought. Better they should assume it was Mandy than Audrey.

"I don't know who you'd get to play me," Tallulah continued. "...Oh, wait! Maybe Kate Hudson. She married a musician, so she knows the life."

"No model-actress will play me," Bliss warned Davis, "unless I play myself."

"Okay! I promise! There's this new CGI that allows us to make you look twenty years younger. So, yeah, I think we can pull that off." He raised his hands to his face as if buffering any blows that may come his way.

"How about you, Audrey? Who would you want to see..." Tallulah turned, only to find that her old friend was gone.

Egan caught sight of Audrey disappearing into the crowd.

If I let Davis option it, she'll hate me.

But by doing so, I can get out from under Miranda's thumb once and for all.

"I think Daniel waved her over," Egan lied. Nodding to Davis, Bliss, and Tallulah, he added, "In fact, I think Clare needs me. Please excuse me."

He set out after Audrey.

EGAN ROAMED THROUGH THE THRONG OF MOURNERS UNTIL HE FOUND Audrey. She was sitting alone on a bench. It was in an alcove that, miraculously, had not been overtaken by some of the other mourners milling close by.

As he approached, Audrey shook her head as if to say, *please leave me alone.*

Instead, he sat down beside her.

"I didn't broach the idea of bringing *Extracurricular* to the screen with Davis. I swear!"

Audrey sighed. "I believe it. When we told Davis you were teaching here again, he made it clear he'd been impressed by your book."

He snickered. "Who are 'we'?"

"Tallulah and Bliss…and me." Audrey blushed. "They knew he'd be interested in the fact that you're back at AA."

Egan grinned. "I guess I should be flattered that I merited the call."

"Yeah, well, believe me—it wasn't my idea. I knew it would dredge up *Extracurricular.*" She looked down at her hands. "They will guess, Egan! My children—*my husband*—will know you were in love with me! And I'm sure Daniel will put two and two together about…the timeline of it all."

As he watched a tear roll off her cheek and fall into her lap, the crack he felt in his heart now seemed a vast crevice. "I want you to know this, Audrey. If I say yes—and that's a really *big* if—it's because—"

"Egan!"

Recognizing the voice, Egan shut up. Out of the corner of his eye, he saw Charly trotting toward him.

She had Noah with her.

The boy was the spitting image of Daniel. Now, knowing what he did about Chuck and Charly, Egan wondered how obvious the twins' resemblance to him might be to others when they stood next to him.

Would Daniel one day see the resemblance?

A part of him wished he would.

But no, it'll never happen, he reasoned. When Daniel looks at the twins, he sees them through eyes brimming with love, pride, and devotion.

We only see what we want.

"Egan!" Charly shocked him when she threw her arms around him in a tight hug. "I was so touched with what you said about Lavinia."

"I…I loved your grandmother." He said it to Charly, but his gaze took in Noah too.

Charly attempted a smile through quivering lips. "Have you met my brother, Noah?"

Egan patted the boy's shoulder. "Nice to meet you finally."

Noah scrutinized Egan with one eye shut. "You taught Mom too?"

"Yes. She was my favorite student."

Audrey frowned at the compliment.

Charly snickered. "You mean until you had *me.*"

"You've certainly come in a close second—*thus far,*" Egan warned her. "Your mom is a hard act to follow." He glanced over at Audrey. "Listen, would you mind if your mom and I took a moment to—"

"Ah, here you all are!"

The sound of Miranda's voice made Egan flinch. He turned to find her behind him.

Daniel was with her.

Chuck was with them too, and he was grinning from ear to ear. As he gave Egan a quick hug, he exclaimed, "Wow, you said some pretty great things about Lavinia! I guess you couldn't fool her either."

Egan laughed. "By that, I take it you tried yourself a few times?"

Chuck nodded. "Yep. She saw right through me too." His voice grew softer as he added, "I want to be more like her."

"We all do," Audrey murmured.

As they stood silently with that thought, Egan glanced over at Miranda. She'd managed a placid smile. She'd also made it a point to avoid looking at him.

Fine with me.

"With that in mind, I've followed up on Dad's suggestion to use Miranda's help with my college submissions." Chuck nodded toward the college counselor. "In fact, she's placing me in her concierge program!"

Miranda took Audrey's hand. "I'm so glad Daniel suggested it. I'd already reviewed Chuck's grades and his teachers' notes on his study habits, and I was concerned he was showing signs of ADHD or some other learning disability. With Daniel's approval—and yours too, of course—we start our assessment as soon as possible."

"If he's agreeable, then yes, by all means..." Audrey's voice trailed off. Consternation was etched on her brow.

Egan couldn't believe his ears: *Miranda had convinced Daniel to pay for Chuck's test to be forged.*

"Not to worry," Miranda assured her. "Even if it turns out I'm right, Chuck will be able to take the test privately and untimed—with AA's teacher proctor, of course," Miranda continued.

Chuck slapped Egan on the back. "Miranda mentioned you volunteered to coach those in the program and be its test proctor too."

"Did she, now?" Egan hoped they hadn't picked up on the edge in his voice. His eyes moved to Miranda.

But before he could say anything, Miranda added, "I'm so appreciative that Egan leaped at the opportunity! I'm sure he'll work it around your other activities—Debate Team, basketball, whatnot. But we don't have much time. The final test takes place just a few weeks away—the last Saturday in November."

"Well, then, we'd better get cracking," Daniel said. "Whatever assignments Egan gives you in preparation for it, you'll be on top of it, right?"

Chuck nodded. "I'll do my best."

I'm supposed to help my son cheat just because his so-called father doesn't believe in him.

Just the thought of it made Egan sick to his gut.

Lovingly, Daniel put his arm around Audrey's waist.

She leaned into him, then turned up her face.

He kissed her on the lips.

As Egan looked away, he caught Miranda's eye. Beaming, she had the audacity to wink at him.

He quelled the urge to slap her. Instead, he walked away.

———

THE WOMAN LOOKED FAMILIAR—

Well, sort of.

The hair was different: longer, and blonde.

But she was petite. And those beautiful dark almond-shaped eyes. Even her glasses couldn't hide the gentle intent he found in them.

Yes, she was staring right at him.

Intrigued, Egan walked over to her. "Do we...do we know each other?"

"No." Her reply, short and curt, was disappointing.

No more so than her way of dismissing him: by turning her back on him and walking away.

Maybe it was for the best. As attractive as she was, the last thing he needed was to get involved with an AA parent...

But she's not. She told me that...

But when?

Where have I seen her?

He turned around when he heard Miranda's laugh. She was staring straight at him. Apparently, she'd seen it all.

God, I hate her.

CHAPTER 8

"Audrey! I wasn't expecting to see you here today!" Harris rose from the couch in his district office in order to give her a hug, then beckoned Audrey to sit beside him. Some of his upcoming position pages were spread out on the coffee table in front of him.

"I just came in to get a couple of things from my desk." Audrey hesitated, then added, "And to tell you that I'll be taking a leave of absence from work."

"Getting over a parent's death is…it's a big thing. Take as much time as you need—a month, two if necessary."

"It may be longer than just a couple of months." Audrey walked over and sat down beside him. "Lavinia was the only parent I knew. But I also have a father somewhere—at least, I hope he's still alive. Lavinia never revealed his name, not even at the end. I…I think it's important to find out." Misty-eyed, she sniffled, "I guess I'm not ready to be an orphan."

Before her eyes, Harris seemed to collapse.

Had he not already been seated he might have fallen to the floor. He covered his face with his hands as if he was too ashamed for her to see his tears.

His deep heaving sobs startled Audrey. "Harris, I'm so sorry! It was cruel of me to spring this on you this way. You were Lavinia's closest, dearest friend! Of course, your grief is just as deep as mine."

Harris raised his head. Because they were only inches apart, she could hear him as he whispered, "Audrey, *I* am your father."

Harris.

Of course.

Other than Lavinia, he'd been the one constant presence in Audrey's life: for her birthdays and graduations, at many of Lavinia's summer open houses and Thanksgiving gatherings, even on most Christmas Eves.

"But...then, why didn't you and Lavinia marry?"

"We always loved each other. But I saw my destiny as serving in public office—something that frustrated your mother to no end." He sighed. "The thought of being merely a politician's wife—to smile sweetly, say nothing, and keep to the background—was anathema to her. She wanted to change the world her way—one child at a time. I understood that, and I respected it. But that didn't lessen my love for her—or for you."

"Still, you never acknowledged me," Audrey pointed out.

"I would have! Please believe me when I say that! But by the time Lavinia told me she was pregnant, I'd already married Tracy—on the rebound, I guess." He shrugged. "You were a dream come true for Lavinia. Still, she insisted she didn't want her pregnancy to end my dream, my goals. She knew if our secret ever got out, I'd be pilloried by my opponents and by the press. I'd be 'the Congressman with the love child.' It wasn't something she wanted for any of us. Certainly not Tracy. My wife could never have a child. Lavinia insisted she was never going to tell and urged me to keep silent about it as well."

Just like I'm urging Egan to keep quiet about the twins, Audrey realized.

She remembered the night, those many years ago, when Egan made his triumphant return to Berkeley to read excerpts from his bestselling novel. How he and she had finally talked through all their misunderstandings and missed opportunities. How he'd declared, *I misread so many signals.*

It was the same night he'd gotten her pregnant.

How many misunderstandings, how many missed opportunities, had Lavinia and Harris shared? Did they regret that their paths had diverged at such a significant milestone—the birth of their child?

Despite this, my mother and father did what they felt was right at the time.

And so did I.

Harris' pain is Egan's too.

"Tracy..." Audrey murmured. "Does she know?"

"Tracy has always suspected. But she's never asked. I don't think she wanted to know the truth. She's always embraced the perks of the office." He grimaced at the thought.

Harris' wife had always been kind to Audrey, if distant. Now she knew why.

"I should have played a much bigger part in your life. For that, I ask for your forgiveness." Weighted with regret, Harris' head fell to his chest. "I'll accept anything you want to do about it. In fact, Lavinia and I had one set rule: once you knew about this, the decision would be yours. If retiring from Congress will rectify this, I'll do it."

"Lavinia wouldn't have wanted that, and neither do I." Audrey placed her hand on his cheek. "Knowing you're my father gives me one more reason to love you, Harris."

Hope filled Harris' eyes. "If Lavinia's death proved one thing, it's that we are all pawns of Fate. I want to spend more time with you, Audrey, and your family. I hope you'll allow me to make up for some of the time we've lost."

"Being in public office doesn't mean we won't be in your life. And besides, look at all the good you've accomplished while in office!"

"Thank you for that." He rose, nudging her to do so too. "You've been a part of my life's work for a long time—twenty years now. Please take as much time off to grieve as you need. But I do hope you eventually come back here."

"I will," she promised.

The soft buzz of Harris' cell phone alerted him to a text. He stared down at the caller ID. He frowned, but it was important enough for him to read the message. "Seamus has called for an emergency meeting of AA's trustee board for tomorrow."

"I'm not surprised." Audrey shrugged.

Little by little, the safe, sweet haven that had been her mother's world was turning to ashes.

She hugged Harris before taking her leave.

INVARIABLY, EGAN'S SEVENTH PERIOD STUDENTS EBBED INTO HIS CLASSROOM like choppy waves: slowly and singly at first, but when the warning chime rang out, swells of students came in closer together, rolling in several at a time, laughing and gossiping.

Since learning his real role in the twins' lives, Egan's heart swelled at even a glimpse of Charly or Chuck on AA's campus. Usually, Charly's entourage included her closest friends: Sienna Belluci, Manya Patel, and Zina Sisley-Calder. As for Chuck, if he wasn't surrounded by his basketball or baseball teammates, he was locked arm-in-arm with his girlfriend, Fawn McCoppin.

Before, Chuck and Fawn's closeness had been a mere annoyance. Egan knew Fawn was using Chuck as a pawn in one of her mind games, but to what end? Egan wondered when her motive would be revealed.

Knowing that she was one of Miranda's concierge clients didn't help his opinion of her.

And now, thanks to Daniel, Chuck was also ensnared in Miranda's web of corruption.

It would not be easy for Egan to honor his promise to Audrey—that he keep her secret from his children. To do so, he'd have to treat Chuck and

Charly like any other student: resist the urge to stare at them in wonder, or to talk to them exclusively. He'd have to tamp down the urge to question them about their childhood, their hopes, dreams, and fears.

He'd have to force himself to look away when they were upset about something, despite the paternal urge to take charge of their young, naïve lives.

I must do this because I promised Audrey.

Egan had every intention of keeping this vow.

But then, when Chuck walked up to him after class and proclaimed, "Miranda said that you can tutor Fawn and me together, since we're both in her concierge program and your free period and our lunch time coincide."

Egan cocked a brow. "Miranda said that, did she?"

Fawn nodded. "Yep. She said you'd make it easy-peasy too."

Egan had been lucky enough to avoid Miranda since their tryst. But the emergency trustee board meeting scheduled for that evening meant he'd be face-to-face with her sooner than he'd hoped.

Coolly, he muttered, "Well, she's wrong. I'm not getting paid to coddle you. I'm helping you pass your most important test this year. I expect you to give it your all."

Chuck saluted, adding, "Hey, no worries! I'm bringing my A game."

On the other hand, Fawn frowned. Confusion was etched in her face.

Had Seamus given her a heads-up about the cheating?

If so, it would be a shame. Miranda hadn't said so, but her scheme had to include more than cheating on SATs to guarantee admission to a top pick university.

No kid should feel that their parent doesn't believe in them, Egan thought.

Because Debate Team practice ran late, Egan made it into the trustee board room just in time to hear Bliss exclaim, "Seamus, explain to me why you think it's so important to have a board meeting tonight, despite there not being a full roster of board members to vote on anything!" Her voice seemed to be cracking under the weight of the past week's events.

Egan looked around the room. Tallulah and Daniel were missing, but Warner was there, as were Jess and Harris.

All heads were turned to Seamus and Bliss.

Miranda was there too. When she nodded to him, he ignored her.

"Bylaws state that any trustee can call a meeting in twenty-four hours if seconded by another." He nodded at Jess, who smiled. "Look, I can't help it that your friends are shirking their duty!"

"My friends are grieving," Bliss retorted. "I'm sure Daniel is doing what he can to hold Audrey together—"

Hearing that made Egan's heart ache.

"—and Tallulah is at the hospital with her mother."

Egan stuttered, "What…what happened?"

"Maggie…she's had a relapse."

"By that, do you mean 'overdose?'" Seamus sneered.

"You…*you monster*!" But Bliss' stutter was proof he'd guessed right. "Her dearest friend died suddenly—or have you forgotten that?"

"Tallulah isn't here to hold your hand. Big deal!" Seamus argued. "Since we last met, Ashbury Academy is in a shambles! One board member was murdered in cold blood and the school's headmistress is dead and buried!" Seamus leaned across the table as if his looming hulk could cower her. "We also have to choose Lavinia's replacement."

"Sorry I'm late." Daniel stood in the doorway. There were dark shadows under his eyes. Where he'd always attended in a suit and tie, today he was in jeans, a sweater, and sneakers.

Bliss was right, Egan thought. He'd stayed home to comfort Audrey.

Daniel took a quick glance around the room. "Since we now have a quorum, I'd like to call the meeting to order."

SEAMUS WASTED NO TIME IN MAKING HIS CASE: "WE NEED TO FIND LAVINIA'S replacement as soon as possible."

"I think we're all in agreement on that," Daniel murmured. "I move that we hire a couple of headhunters to line up some appropriate candidates. At the same time, we'll form a search committee made up of staff, parents, and board members. The committee will vet at least three possible candidates before the board interviews them and takes a final vote."

Seamus snorted. "To hell we will! We have great talent on staff, so why not utilize it?"

Bliss frowned. "You mean, hire internally?"

He nodded. "Sure, why not? It'll save a lot of time—something that's in short supply these days."

"Our most important function is the wellbeing of AA's students," Bliss snapped. "The Head of School is AA's guardian, leader, and biggest draw for attracting new families. If you don't feel you have the time for a national search, perhaps you shouldn't be on the board to begin with."

"If you believe so strongly in Lavinia's so-called 'mission,' you should trust in the team she's put together," Seamus retorted. "Our graduates are proof of that. Would you not agree?"

Bliss merely shrugged. She couldn't argue the point.

Seamus grinned smugly. "That's why I recommend we make Miranda the new Head of School."

Egan almost fell out of his chair.

No fucking way!

Whereas Jess and Warner's heads bobbed in agreement, Bliss and Harris' faces mirrored Egan's concern.

Egan couldn't read Daniel's reaction because his head was down as he scribbled notes on the pad in front of him.

As for Miranda, she stared demurely at her clasped hands. Still, her slight grin was the telltale sign that she was in on Seamus' scheme.

And probably Warner and Jess too, Egan deduced.

Seamus is giving her coverage so that she can get away with her college admissions shenanigans, he realized. I won't—I *can't*—let them.

"Big mistake!" Egan exclaimed. "She's too new. And she works primarily with seniors and juniors, so half the kids don't even know her!"

"Their parents do, either by her interaction with them directly, or by reputation—and they think she hung the moon. Her track record speaks for itself," Seamus countered. "So if, as Ms. Thackeray so eloquently put it, the damn kids come first, why screw up the rest of their school year searching for some clone of Lavinia when what we all want is right here already?"

Egan snorted. "By 'what we all want,' you mean someone you feel will guarantee your child is accepted into a prestigious university?"

"Of course, you fool!" Seamus bellowed. "Why do you think we're all here?"

Bliss glared back. "Not necessarily. Most of us are here because we love the school for achieving what Lavinia set out to do with it: teaching students to think for themselves, follow their dreams, and attain their goals—with or without attending a prestigious university."

Silence thickened the tension in the room.

Daniel turned to Miranda. "I assume you've already discussed your interest with Seamus"—his eyes scanned Warner and Jess—"and others as well."

"They approached me, yes," she acknowledged. "I told them how much this school means to me. It molded me into the person I am! But to be honest, giving up my client base will mean a pay cut for me, so there is that to consider." Miranda's sigh made Egan flinch. "As long as I can honor my commitment to my private clients, I'll accept the position of Interim Head of School while a national search is conducted."

No shit.

"I assume Miranda will also feel free to put her name in the hat for the permanent position?" Seamus barked.

Daniel shrugged. "Of course she will."

"Then yes, Daniel. In fact, *I'd be honored* to be Interim Head of School."

Egan marveled at how easily Miranda could make her eyes mist up.

Miranda added, "After all, Lavinia's purpose in hiring me in the first place was to groom me as her successor."

Like Egan, Bliss gawked openly at this revelation.

Daniel frowned. "Funny, she never mentioned that to me. Or to Audrey for that matter."

"*Really?*" Miranda shook her head in disbelief. "Are you sure Audrey has been completely honest with you?"

Daniel stared back.

Finally, shaking his head, he muttered, "Let's put it to vote—specifically, that we offer Miranda the position of *Interim* Head of School while we conduct a national search for Lavinia's permanent replacement."

Reluctantly, Seamus huffed, "I second the motion."

Daniel shook his head in disgust. "All in favor?"

As anticipated, Warner's and Jess' hands went up along with Seamus'.

"Opposed?" Daniel asked.

Harris and Bliss raised their hands.

Miranda's gaze went to Egan.

When he also raised his hand, her crocodile tears seemed to vanish in the heat of her glare.

Bliss murmured, "Daniel, how do you vote?"

Daniel shrugged. "I support the motion for Miranda to step in as Interim Head of School."

Egan leaned back, aghast.

So, Daniel has paid Miranda to cheat on Chuck's behalf.

It was the only rational reason for Daniel to vote for Miranda to take his beloved mother-in-law's place, even on a temporary basis.

Audrey doesn't know.

She can't.

She would never allow him to do that to her son…

Our son.

Egan tamped down his anger.

It wasn't easy, not with Seamus smugly crowing: "Congratulations, Miranda. Now, I guess we should talk about replacements for the open positions on the trustee board…"

I CAN DO IT NOW, BEFORE THIS WHOLE THING COMES DOWN AROUND ME, Miranda realized.

I can ruin Egan and Audrey.

Daniel had hesitated when he handed her the gavel. That didn't bother her. She knew she'd be getting her revenge on him and his wife when Egan substituted Chuck's SAT test.

I'll be getting the SAT answer key tomorrow. Afterward, I'll order Egan to meet me at my place, perhaps on Saturday night.

He won't dare say no—

Not now that I control every source of his income.

If Miranda ever got angry enough with Egan, she might even tell him she was Mandy. She'd crow about the pleasure it gave her to have his publisher pull his book from the shelves. She enjoyed that even more than the settlement money.

Well, almost.

While relishing this thought, she'd tuned out the bickering around her, which had begun when Seamus and Egan volleyed suggestions for the staff member who would replace her. It was finally decided that Cornell would do. Seamus saw him as innocuous and controllable. Miranda could tell that Egan thought the same.

She relished the opportunity to prove him wrong.

By now the bickering was *sooo* damn loud that it was distracting from her jubilation. Apparently, Seamus was going nose-to-nose with Bliss as to who should take over as the new parent board member candidate.

"My wife, Gretchen, is perfect!" Seamus insisted. "And besides, she has been the best fundraising chairperson this school has ever had."

"I want to nominate Gemma Sisley," Bliss insisted. "We should do it out of respect for the loss of her husband, who served the board admirably."

Egan was surprised she could state that with a straight face.

"I disagree," Seamus countered. "If anything, she's probably all torn up about it—too much so to consider being on the board—"

Miranda interjected, "I'd like to propose a compromise candidate."

The room went silent.

I could get used to this.

Too bad I can't—unless it's in some Federal prison yard.

She closed her eyes to erase that horrifying vision from her mind. "I think Nira Patel would make a wonderful trustee."

Bliss shrugged her approval. Seamus did the same.

"All in favor?" Miranda asked.

The vote was unanimous.

Only Egan caught the wink between Seamus and Miranda.

CHAPTER 9

"*N*ormal," Audrey insisted to Daniel. "The sooner we get back into our routines, the better."

It was Friday—only two days since Lavinia's funeral. Still, Audrey had insisted that the children go back to school.

And that Daniel go back to work.

His nod was reluctant at best. "I know you're right. It's just that..." Daniel looked away. "Lavinia's death was so sudden, and it happened only a week ago. I don't feel we've had a chance to process it."

"By 'we,' you mean me, specifically." Audrey glanced away. She'd yet to tell him that Lavinia had told her about the cancer on the very first day of the school year.

She certainly wasn't going to do so now. What would it matter anyway?

"Okay, we'll honor your wishes," Daniel conceded. "But 'normal' should mean doing something fun as well. Why don't we have dinner out as a family? Say, Little Star Pizza. The one on Divisadero."

He knew it was her favorite.

Audrey shrugged. "Sounds good to me." She didn't mean it. She hadn't had an appetite in over a week. Between Lavinia's death and her admission to Egan about the twins, she'd been too upset to even think about eating. "I'll pick up Noah after basketball practice. Then we'll swing by AA and pick up the twins. See you there."

Daniel kissed her. "Stay in bed as long as you like. I'll get the kids to school."

"I will. But...at some point, I have to go over to Lavinia's house and... and start clearing it out."

She hated the thought of putting the house on the market. She was born and raised there.

"Not today," he insisted. "Do it tomorrow. The kids and I will meet you there after our bike ride."

Audrey nodded. She was fine with that. She'd need the day to force herself out of her fear that life as she knew it was at an end.

By the time Audrey and Noah got to AA, it was already past six o'clock.

They found parking one block from the school. Originally, Audrey thought they might wait for the twins in the car, but Noah nixed that by complaining of the cold.

"Look! Even my words are freezing," he insisted, pointing to his chilled breath. "Can't we go in? *Please?*"

Reluctantly, she got out of the car and followed him into the school.

Because it was late on Friday, the school was practically empty. The lobby seemed to have been decorated. Colorful cards filled its large Palladian windows.

For Thanksgiving perhaps? It was only a week away…

When she got close enough to read them, she realized the students had written down fond memories of Lavinia.

"Mom—they're talking about Lavinia!" Noah pointed up to the intercom.

Audrey realized they were listening to students relaying their memories about her mother.

This tribute must have been going on all week, she realized.

As she wiped away a tear, she made a mental note to ask Clare for copies of everything—the notes, the photos, and the audio tribute.

Egan was right when he said Lavinia changed the world of everyone she touched, Audrey realized. She lives on through all of us.

Had the Debate Team practice been held in Egan's classroom, he would never have run into Audrey.

As it turned out, he'd secured the smaller of AA's two auditoriums so that the team could practice on a stage and at a podium.

After seven matches, the team was undefeated. As opposed to playing favorites with the twins, he found himself being even harder on them than their teammates.

Well, harder on Chuck, anyway. Unlike Charly, who always came prepared, Chuck's habit was to review the research for his topic at the last minute. He also played to the audience as opposed to sticking to his talking points.

"You'll be judged by how clearly you make your case. Winking to some hottie in the front row isn't going to win over the judges," Egan warned him.

"Unless she happens to *be* a judge," Quest countered.

His interruption earned him Egan's glare. "Don't encourage him," Egan snapped. Turning to Chuck, he continued: "Look, I know you don't want to let your team down. So do us a favor: *pull your weight.*"

"Wow! That's harsh, Egan," Fawn exclaimed. But by the way she winked at him, she must have appreciated being called a hottie.

"No harsher than his teammates will be if he blows AA's chances to win the regional tournament," Egan retorted.

Chuck nodded stoically. "Okay, yeah, I get it! I'll treat it like a test instead of like...fun."

Egan rolled his eyes. "That's the spirit."

The team's titters at Chuck's exclamation roiled into belly laughs at Egan's sarcasm.

Shaking his head, Egan glanced at the auditorium's clock. "What say we call it a night? But please be ready again on Monday. Remember, it'll be the last practice before our next match. Have a great weekend, everybody."

As the others filed out, Egan fell into line behind Chuck and Fawn. Tapping Chuck's shoulder, he asked, "May I have a word in private?"

Surprised, Chuck nodded.

Fawn pouted but took the hint and stalked up the aisle without him.

Egan waited until she was out of hearing range to say, "I think you have the potential to be anything in this world you want. But if you keep selling yourself short by getting lazy—you'll blow it, plain and simple."

Chuck shrugged. "You sound like my dad."

Egan blinked away his compulsion to blurt out, *that's because I am your father.*

Instead, he muttered, "All that proves is that we both believe in you."

Mollified, Chuck murmured, "Gee, thanks, Egan. I...I appreciate that."

"Good, because there's something I wish to propose. Although Tuesday is a half day because of the Thanksgiving break, I'd like you to hang around an extra hour or so to do some SAT drills. Are you up for that?"

"Yeah sure, I guess." Chuck's eyes followed Fawn out the door. "Are you asking Fawn too?"

"I was under the impression that the McCoppins head down to Laguna Beach every Thanksgiving." He'd heard Seamus discussing that with Warner. "It's not like you two are joined at the hip or anything, is it?"

"No...of course not!" Chuck shrugged. "I doubt she would have wanted to waste the afternoon doing it anyway. She seems to think she has it in the bag."

I'll bet she does.

Egan wanted to ask Chuck to elaborate but he noticed Noah was walking toward them.

Audrey and Charly were heading down the aisle as well.

Audrey's face was placid, but shadows still darkened her eyes. Other than that, she was as beautiful as always.

Egan gave her a slight wave. She nodded back.

When Noah reached Chuck's side, he high-fived his older brother.

"Hey, are you ready to go?" Noah asked. "We're meeting Dad at Little Star."

A pang of jealousy pricked at Egan.

"Sure." Chuck turned to his teacher. "We're done here, right?"

"Yep." Egan forced a smile onto his face. "Enjoy your dinner."

But before he could walk away, Charly tapped him on the arm. "Egan, I was just telling Mom that you came up with the idea for the students remembering Lavinia with the pictures and audio tribute."

Audrey smiled up at him. "I want to thank you for that. I'm touched that you suggested it."

Egan deflected her thanks with a shrug. "I thought it would be a good way for the students to process their grief. I'm glad the other teachers agreed with me."

Chuck reached for the car keys dangling from his mother's hand. "I'll pull the car around, if you want."

Charly grabbed the keys from him. "Um—*NO*. It's my turn to drive! Remember?"

Chuck snatched them back and then held them up high so that Charly couldn't reach them.

She tickled him so that he'd drop his hand. Instead, he ran up the aisle with them.

She took off after him.

Noah was on her heels—

Leaving Audrey alone with Egan.

"How are you holding up?" he asked.

"I'll be better after…after the holidays, I guess." She sighed. "I'll wait to tackle Lavinia's house afterward."

"You're selling it?"

"We have to." Audrey's eyes grew damp. "I grew up in that house. But it was her wish. And it will go a long way in establishing the endowment.

It's worth close to two million dollars." Suddenly, her tears were falling fast and furiously. "The kids are upset. They'd rather I didn't."

"Oh, Audrey, I'm so, so sorry!" Egan put his arms around her. "Cleaning out a parent's home...it's not easy. Every item in it comes with some memory."

He knew this from experience. When his father died, his mother refused to get rid of any of her husband's belongings.

When she was moved into the care facility, the sale of the house was necessary to keep her there. Egan had to tackle the task of cleaning out the home himself.

The worst part was his parents' closets. Their scents lived on in his father's business suits and in his mother's cocktail dresses, bringing to life his memories of them as younger, vital people.

It struck Egan that when his time came, there would be no one to do the same for him.

Without thinking, Egan stroked Audrey's hair.

At first, she sighed at the tender act.

But too soon, she stepped away.

It was for the best, Egan reasoned. *Not with what I need to mention next.* "Listen, Audrey—we have to talk."

Warily, Audrey murmured, "What about?"

"I can't say in front of the children," he insisted.

"Egan please! You're not going to insist again that I tell them...and... Daniel—"

"This has nothing to do with that," he promised, he motioned for her to walk with him. "Did Daniel mention what went on during the trustee meeting last night?"

Perplexed, Audrey shook her head. "I was worn out and went to bed early. And this morning, with getting the kids ready for school and all..." She shrugged. "Daniel didn't mention it, and I forgot to ask."

"Lavinia's successor was named."

Audrey shook her head in disbelief. "But...a search would need to be conducted first."

"Half the board would agree with you—at least, the half that voted against it and lost."

Obviously Daniel wants to keep it from her. But she has every right to know. Just tell her.

Egan paused, wondering if he should just come out and tell her whom. Finally, he added: "Seamus and his contingent pushed for Miranda."

Audrey frowned. "Miranda D'Arcy—*the college admissions counselor?* Why her?"

He shrugged. "They feel she is best positioned to get their children into the colleges of their choice. And"—Egan took a deep breath—"they may be right, but for all the wrong reasons."

"What do you mean?"

"Before I answer that, let me ask you a question. Did Lavinia ever indicate to you that she was grooming Miranda as her successor?"

Audrey shook her head. "Not in the least! I mean, she thought Miranda was a good hire. And as you know, at the time, Lavinia already knew she was sick. But she would never have just handed over the reins to someone who didn't have the approval of the school community, let alone someone who didn't fit her philosophy for the school."

Egan snorted. "Trust me. She doesn't. Which was why I was just as dumbfounded as Bliss and Harris when Daniel voted to go along with Seamus' cockamamie plan—as Interim Head, anyway."

"*Daniel* voted for her too?" Audrey's shock at this revelation revealed itself with a shudder. Noting his concern, she murmured, "Egan, what are you trying to say?"

Tell her. Everything.

He would have, too, if a car horn hadn't blared just then.

They looked up to find that Chuck was parked in front of the school.

"Ask Daniel how much he paid for Chuck to be in Miranda's concierge program, okay?"

"But...her counseling services are supposed to be gratis to AA's students. It's why she was hired in the first place."

"I said ask him what he paid for her concierge program—which is altogether different, trust me." He moved in close to make his point. "Please Audrey, just ask."

Audrey frowned. "Okay, I will." Waving at her children, Audrey ran out the door.

"Isn't that nice! You've had a few precious moments alone with your heartthrob!"

Startled by Miranda's voice, Egan took a step backward before turning to face her.

She almost laughed at the pained look on his face.

"No need to be jealous," he retorted. "We were discussing Chuck's progress."

"If that's what you call those loving strokes to her hair, I'm surprised every mother in the school isn't lining up at your door to get an update." She laughed. "As for Chuck, don't you mean 'lack thereof?' Not that it will show up on his SAT score." She moved closer in order to stroke his cheek. "Speaking of which, I'll have the test's answer key for you later tonight, along with the final list of my clients. Why don't you drop by my place and pick it up—say, eight o'clock?"

Egan took a step back. "We've already had this discussion. My duties as your concierge program's SAT coach and proctor don't come with fringe benefits. Just hand it off to me on Monday, here at school."

Miranda clicked her tongue in mock shock. "As of last night's vote, I'm your boss here at AA too. Remember? And, as such, you're at my beck and call—*including tonight.*" Her palm brushed against his bulge. "And don't think I wasn't hurt when you voted against me. I should fire you over it."

"Is that a threat?"

"You bet it is," Miranda declared. "Quit playing games, Egan. We both know you're strapped for cash. When I offered you the position of proctor, I offered you a lifeline. The money is plentiful and easy. *You don't want to fuck this up.*" Her hand cupped the bulge in his jeans.

Suddenly Egan's open palm came toward her face—

Stopping a mere inch from her cheek.

Instinctively, Miranda reeled back, as much from fear as shock.

Egan lowered his arm, but he was still seething with anger. "Don't ever touch me like that again," he growled. "Fire me, if you want. But if you do, I'll walk from both jobs."

He waited until she nodded.

"Just leave the information in my staff mailbox," he said, slamming the front door behind him.

THAT SON OF A BITCH.

And all because he's still in love with her.

By the time Miranda reached Lavinia's office—*her* office—her heart had quit pounding in her chest. Still seething with anger, she took the only photo on the credenza—one of Lavinia in the loving arms of the Thorpe-McKittridge clan—and hurled it to the floor.

Shards flew everywhere as the frame's glass crashed into pieces. As she reached to pick up the mess, one pierced her palm.

Miranda cursed "BLOODY HELL—" at the top of her lungs.

It's all Egan's fault.

His—and Audrey's.

Time for payback.

She walked into Clare's office and over to the massive file credenza behind her desk. Finding the drawer labeled DONATIONS, she pulled out the file folder earmarked:

TEACHER CHAIR - ENDOWMENT

It went into the shredder.

She had several offshore bank accounts. One was an emergency account that contained a mere three hundred thousand dollars.

From that account, she transferred $250,000 to The Best Face Forward Club.

It was earmarked

Donation - McKittridgge D. (Chuck)

The last fifty thousand dollars was transferred from the personal account to another she had registered to one of her fake names: Pucci Tedeschi. That way, there would be no trace of where the so-called donation had come from.

However, when the FBI discovered it, she'd reluctantly admit it was from Daniel.

On Monday, when the announcement that she'd been selected as the new Interim Head of School would be made public, everything and everyone would fall in line.

Including Egan.

Miranda would have access to the school's bank accounts. She'd shuffle funds into new ones set up and controlled by her.

Seamus would only be given some of the account information.

The FBI would be given a different story.

She didn't know how—*yet*—but hopefully, when the money trail went cold, she'd be long gone—

Along with the missing funds.

Audrey and Daniel would have a heck of a time explaining away the contribution. And by the time they did, Daniel may have lost his law firm partnership, perhaps even his license to practice law.

And when it came out that Egan had substituted Chuck's test—at the behest of Daniel, in fact—Mr. McKittridge and Ms. Thorpe would have reason to hate each other.

Their family would live in disgrace.

If I have to go down, they're going down with me.

"Miranda's assessment and tutoring for Chuck—is that something we're paying for?" Audrey waited until they were home from dinner and were reading in bed before doing as she'd promised Egan.

Daniel put down the brief he'd been studying. "Nope. Why do you ask?"

"During the first PTA meeting, Miranda mentioned some sort of 'concierge counseling program' she has for her private clients. I was wondering if she'd talked you into it."

Daniel shook his head. "All she offered was what we wanted: that Chuck be given extra attention on his SAT drills. But if her special program could help Chuck buckle down before he takes the test, should we consider it?"

"I don't think there's time to schedule it. The final SAT test takes place in two weeks. And besides, Chuck mentioned in the car that his first coaching session with Egan is on Tuesday. Why don't we see how that goes first and then panic?"

Daniel guffawed. "I guess you're right. By then, it would be too late for Miranda to pull off a miracle anyway—although Seamus and Jess seem to think she could under any circumstances. Warner too."

"No wonder she has the trustee board wrapped around her little finger," Audrey muttered.

"What do you mean by that?" Daniel asked.

"Egan mentioned that the trustee board voted her as the interim replacement for Lavinia until a nationwide search can take place."

Daniel shrugged. "It did indeed."

She turned to him. "Did you vote for her too?"

Daniel grimaced. "What, Egan didn't tell you?"

"No, but I didn't ask either." She frowned. "I thought the answer would be obvious."

"I guess it isn't, since, yes, I did vote for her."

"But why? If Harris and Tallulah and Bliss thought a search would be a better solution–"

"You forgot to include Egan," Daniel snapped back.

Audrey felt her cheeks warming up.

"By the way, Tallulah wasn't there," Daniel continued. "Maggie is in rehab. She took Lavinia's death pretty hard."

"Oh! I didn't know." Audrey's shoulders slumped. "Look, Daniel, I guess the point I'm trying to make is that obviously, my friends felt uncomfortable with just handing over the reins of the school to someone who is still learning the AA community."

"Anyone brought in from a nationwide search will be in the same position," he pointed out. "In that regard, Miranda has a head start—and at least the confidence of half the board." Daniel tossed the brief to the floor. "I suppose this is your way of telling me that your 'proxy' made the wrong choice."

"You aren't my proxy," Audrey protested.

Yes, you were. THAT WAS THE DEAL.

"You're right. I'm not," Daniel retorted. "I took the position under my own free will—and with your blessing, I might add. So it would be nice if you—and Egan—didn't second-guess me."

"This has nothing to do with Egan!" Audrey retorted hotly. "It's just that...well, I've been skeptical of Seamus' motives since he enrolled Fawn. You know that. And for that matter, there's something about Miranda that's a bit off-putting as well. And I'm not the only one who's noticed."

"If you mean Bliss and Tallulah—"

"And Harris," Audrey added.

"Okay, yes, and Harris—then I guess I screwed up. But I felt that, at the very least, Miranda—as a stop-gap measure—was the most viable and least traumatic option."

"But that's just it! Seamus ultimately wants her as Lavinia's permanent replacement—and *you* were okay with that!" Audrey's tears flowed now. "As if that...that woman could ever replace Lavinia!"

"No one can replace Lavinia! Everyone—even Seamus—knows that!" Daniel reached for Audrey's hand. "Lavinia's death was so sudden. You—and I, and the kids—are still processing it!" He pulled her close. "I didn't want you to have to worry about the school too. I told Seamus and his group Miranda was only a temporary fix."

Audrey nodded. "I appreciate that. Truly I do. But even on an interim basis, I hope it was the right decision."

"Believe me, I do too," Daniel murmured.

<h1 style="text-align:center">CHAPTER 10</h1>

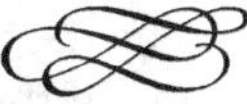

On Monday morning, waiting in Egan's school mailbox designated for Egan was a large manila envelope.

It contained the SAT answer sheet, along with the final names of the students whose tests were to be substituted:

Chuck McKittridge
Buck Crawford
Hugo Smallwood
Zina Sisley-Calder
Fawn McCoppin
Quest Wishart-Jammerhead
Manya Patel

On Tuesday, to Egan's great relief, after the school let out at noon for the Thanksgiving break, Chuck showed up on time for his SAT coaching session.

He would have been disappointed if Chuck had let him down.

Granted, on Chuck's first drill, a language test, he barely made an acceptable score. However, he did a lot better on the math test.

The essay test was passable too.

After the initial drills, Egan declared, "Okay, let's start with some simple tips for the language portion."

Chuck nodded.

"First off, use the process of elimination. Since only one answer can be right, immediately eliminate the three that are the weakest."

"Gotcha," Chuck murmured.

"Also, skim first. You do this by starting with the first and last paragraphs and then reading the first and last sentences in each paragraph. Then see if you can answer the main question first. The other questions will reference smaller details, so their keywords will be reflected in what you've just read."

"Okay."

"And all answers will be backed up by evidence presented in one of the paragraphs. If not, it's wrong."

Chuck nodded slowly. "Can I try one?"

Egan handed him another language test question. "Go at it."

This time, he answered all but one of the questions correctly. But on the next three drill sheets, all were correct.

Hearing this, Chuck leaped out of his seat, triumphant.

"Calm down, cowboy. We still have a long way to go," Egan warned. "Okay, now let's address your math score. Granted, from your math grades these past couple of years, you have a good comprehension of geometric and algebraic principles. The questions you missed were incorrectly calculated because you went for the wrong value. I'd suggest revisiting as many formulas as possible. You can do that now. Then you can try your hand at a few practice questions."

"On it."

They took the next half hour reviewing a list of formulas. Then Chuck tackled a few more problems.

After handing them back to Egan to grade, he waited anxiously for the results.

Finally, Egan declared, "Correct, on all of them."

"*YESSSS!*" Chuck exclaimed proudly.

The next hour was spent going over the weaknesses in his essay.

"You have no issues with grammar or spelling. Your weakness is making your case succinctly, then backing it up with evidence."

Chuck snickered. "Just like on Debate Team."

"Ironically, yes." Egan grinned. "Now, knowing this, use the rules I've tried to pound into you during debate practice: come up with three facts or examples. Save the strongest for last. Got it?"

"Yep." Chuck cracked his knuckles. "Let's do this thing."

After four test questions, Egan declared that Chuck had nailed it. He glanced at the clock. It was almost three-thirty. "Now that you've got the hang of this thing, what say we call it a day?"

Chuck nodded. "It seemed to have gone by pretty quickly. Wow, can you believe we've been here three hours?" He grabbed his backpack and stood up. "Hey, Egan, what do you do for Thanksgiving? I mean, like, is your family back in New York?"

No. My family is right here.

You are my family.

Chuck hesitated, then added somewhat bashfully: "I'd hate for you to spend it by yourself. I mean…you're welcome to hang out with us."

Thanksgiving with Chuck and Charly—

And Audrey.

"Thanks. That's very kind of you, but… I'm covered," Egan muttered. "I'll be at my mother's house."

Eating something from the Greenbrae Mollie Stone's deli after spending an hour watching her nurse feed her while I remind her who I am.

Chuck nodded. "Oh! Good, then." But he seemed disappointed.

At least, that's what Egan wanted to believe.

He consoled himself with the thought that Chuck was ready for his test; that when his son saw his grade, he'd believe he did well on it because he'd studied hard for it.

THE FOLLOWING WEEK, EGAN ALSO ARRANGED ONE-ON-ONE AFTER-SCHOOL coaching sessions with Miranda's other concierge students.

Hugo and Buck skipped their appointments. Egan realized they were in on their parents' schemes.

For their turns, Zina, Manya, and Quest showed up promptly.

Manya's issues were not with the test subjects, but with her fear of failure.

"I can't let my mother down!" Manya explained. "She has been working so hard to pay for my tuition—even if I'm lucky enough to get accepted to her alma mater, Stanford." Her anxiety was accompanied by tears. "If I don't earn a scholarship—especially to there—she'll be so disappointed."

"You've gotten straight A's every semester you've been at AA. You've taken every Advanced Placement course the school offers. You're brilliant, Manya!" Egan insisted. "If you're freezing when you take the SAT, it's because you're psyching yourself out. Today, we'll go over some tips that should help you focus on the questions, as opposed to your fears. Okay?"

She nodded.

"Afterward, we'll do a few practice tests in each section. I'm not going to time the drills, so take as long as you like."

She took a deep breath. "Okay."

He lied.

So, when he gave her the test scores—the first one was 1408, while the second was 1466—he also let her know she turned them in well under the time usually allotted.

Hearing that, she burst into tears of joy.

Egan was also elated—

Until she anxiously exclaimed, "I wish these had counted."

Egan shrugged. "You can take it as often as you like. In fact, why don't you first take the last one offered with the rest of your class on Saturday? Then you take the test I'll be administering on Sunday. That way, you'll have two chances at a great score. The highest one will be counted."

Her eyes opened wide. "Great idea!"

She hugged him before going out the door.

How he wished Nira had not fallen for Miranda's line.

LIKE MANYA, ZINA SUFFERED FROM TEST ANXIETY. BUT UNLIKE HER FRIEND, she also had low math test scores.

"I feel like an idiot," she muttered. "I know this stuff! Really, I do."

"Just remember, process of elimination is an important strategy when taking the SAT. Three answers will always be wrong. You just have to determine the *right* one. By knowing the formulas, you'll figure it out."

As he did with Chuck, he went over math formulas that would be used on the test, then drilled her on them, again and again.

After each drill, her scores inched up.

Every time she squealed with joy.

As with Manya, he suggested that she take the timed test that was to be given to AA's students. "Use it as another drill. It'll give you even more confidence for the untimed test on Sunday."

She nodded, but he could see she wasn't excited about the idea. Her doubts were creeping back.

During the final drill, Zina's phone chirped. Looking at the caller ID, she frowned. "That's my mom."

"It's okay if you take it," Egan assured her.

She hesitated a moment. When she finally took it, she turned her back and murmured, "Hi, Mom... With, um, Charly... In the library. Can I call you when we get out? ...Sure, see you then."

Seeing Egan's bemused stare, Zina blushed. "Mom doesn't know I'm here."

Egan nodded slowly, perplexed. "Why not?"

"With Dad's death and all, Mom's got enough on her plate." Zina shrugged. "Look, I know the type of clients my dad had. And I know he kept a lot of secrets from her. I didn't want to tell her that this was yet another one. He knew Mom wouldn't approve of Miranda's special concierge program."

"If you don't have your mother's permission, I'm sure Miranda wouldn't hold her to your father's commitment."

"I asked. But Miranda told me that I'd be dishonoring Dad's dying wish, that I should take advantage of his generosity." Zina sighed. "I guess she's right."

That money-grubbing bitch.

"He was very proud of you, Zina. You must believe that! As far as this test goes, if you do well, it's just icing on the cake."

She hung her head. "No, Egan, it's more than that." A tear trickled down her face. "He wanted me to get into *Yale*. So... I'll do my best. Miranda says that together, we're going to make it happen—*for him*."

And that's how Egan discovered how much more he hated Miranda.

"So, um, what do you think? Is it better than the last drill?" Quest winced as if he didn't really want to hear the answer to that.

Egan shrugged. "It's, um... passable."

The truth was Quest was a hardworking student doomed to mediocre grades.

It took Egan almost three hours and nine drills to accept this reality.

From the hopeful look on Quest's face, saying so would crush the poor kid.

I just can't do it, Egan realized.

"We're all set." He hoped he sounded encouraging, but he doubted it.

Jubilant, Quest leaped up. "Awesome! Can't wait to tell my dad. Have a great night, Egan. And thanks." Instinctively, he grabbed for the guitar that never left his side.

He strummed a few chords before going into a melodic jazz riff that filled the room.

Egan listened, mesmerized.

This kid is terrific.

Egan clapped. "Wow, that's really beautiful, Quest." He hesitated, but he had to ask: "I know your mom has such great respect for your musical skills. And I would think that a working musician with your chops wouldn't necessarily need a four-year college degree to ply your trade. Was it your idea to go on to college?"

Quest paused mid-riff. "Hell no! And trust me, it wasn't Mom's either." His head shook with his frustration. "My dad says I need a good fallback position in case I don't—you know, make it. He wants me to get into USC's music program. He says that at the very least, I'll be able to teach, or maybe take over the business side of things." He stared down at his guitar. "I can't let him down."

Why that son of a bitch Jammerhead! I have half a notion of telling Tallulah—

But Egan knew it wasn't his place.

Besides, he was just as complicit as Jammerhead. He'd taken the money.

With any luck, Tallulah would never find out. His friendship with her was built on the shifting sands of admiration and antipathy.

Should Miranda's scheme ever be revealed, his role in it would certainly tip the scale far beyond the latter—to animosity.

The silence sat between them until, finally, Egan said, "You won't. You'll be fine."

Quest's relief was shown in a sustained guitar lick that followed him out the door.

Why can't parents accept their kids the way they are, Egan wondered.

Right then and there, he vowed to always do just that with Chuck and Charly.

EGAN WAS SURPRISED WHEN FAWN SHOWED UP FOR HER ALLOTTED TIME SLOT.

He was also impressed with her scores on her initial test drills.

"You already test over 1400," he informed her. "And you've turned these in before the allotted time. Your essay was exemplary."

"Are you asking me if I know I'm smarter than my parents give me credit for?" Fawn smirked. "Like, *duh—yeah!*"

"You also have the cheerleading squad and Debate Team going for you." He threw up his hands perplexed. "So, explain to me. Why again do your parents feel you needed to be placed in Miranda's concierge program?"

Fawn's laugh was venomous. "Because they don't believe I can do it on my own—get into Daddy's alma mater, Yale."

"Fawn, do you believe that too?"

"Who cares what I believe? They're paying for Miranda's guarantee." She shrugged. "Even if I get in, I may not go."

"Out of spite?" Egan murmured.

"Yeah. Exactly." Fawn grinned. "Seriously, though, Egan—what do you care? You get paid, either way, right?"

That's when he realized:

She knows.

And she doesn't care.

ON SUNDAY, ALL SEVEN OF MIRANDA'S CONCIERGE STUDENTS SHOWED UP FOR their SAT test session in AA's small auditorium.

Egan told them to take as much time as they needed on each of the three test sections. Should they finish before the others, they were allowed to wait in the school's lobby.

After completing each of the three test sections, Hugo and Buck were the first out the door.

Buck's attempt was half-hearted at best.

Hugo simply wrote:

Go for it!

Egan wasn't surprised at either boy's actions.

Zina, Manya, and Chuck seemed to take his drill advice to heart. They were excited but not anxious. They worked diligently and carefully. And, had the exams been timed, they would have turned in their tests under the wire. He noted that all had at least attempted every question.

Fawn breezed through each section. However, she left a few questions blank in each section. She turned in the last part, the math portion, with a note:

I left the ones I didn't know blank, to make your life easy. —xoxoxo Fawn

Thanks for nothing, Egan fumed silently.

Only Quest seemed to struggle to complete the test.

By the time he finished the final section, the others were long gone. He seemed relieved, albeit far from happy. "Well, at least I did my best," Quest muttered.

Egan realized he'd have his work cut out for him.

It took four hours to finish the job of doctoring the tests.

Hugo and Buck's real tests were useless. Egan's version gave Hugo a score of 1406. Because of Buck's half-hearted attempt, he scored him around 1401.

He tackled Quest's next. Egan was tempted to give the kid a score of 1430 just because he was so nice, if clueless. He decided it was too big a stretch for anyone who knew him to believe, so he nudged it to 1411 instead.

All three of the boys had lousy handwriting. Still, Egan did his best to copy it, but it was a painstaking endeavor.

The essay portion of the tests for Fawn, Manya, and Zina needed no changes, thank goodness.

Fawn only answered the questions she knew were right. But to get her over a score of 1400, Egan needed to fill in about eighteen more questions: eleven in the math portion and seven in the language section. He estimated that her score would be around 1501.

Manya reached a score of 1508 on her own. Egan left it that way.

He massaged Zina's math answers so that she'd come in at 1436.

He left Chuck's test for last.

Only after Chuck left the room had Egan made a decision: he wasn't going to touch Chuck's test or replace it.

He opened it to look at it, but he didn't touch it otherwise.

I'm turning it in just as it was, along with the others, he vowed. Let the chips fall where they may.

What could Miranda do to him anyway? She'd already paid him the cash. She wouldn't dare ask for it back.

So what if she told Daniel about it? No matter what Chuck scored, Daniel would have to live with the result.

Daniel wouldn't sue Egan. It would be admitting fraud.

If he did, Audrey would know. And in Audrey's eyes, Daniel would be a liar and a cheat.

I have a right to make any decision affecting my son.

LIONEL BENT DOWN TO LOOK AT RILEY'S MONITOR. "THAT'S THE VIDEO FEED OF the test session?"

Riley nodded. "I watched it in real-time. It's boring as hell. I'm just adding a few notes."

Because the auditorium was already set up with video cameras, Lionel had secured a subpoena. Riley then hacked into it so that they could watch Egan administer the test.

"Yeah, well, the fun starts after the students leave. That's when Egan tosses their tests and substitutes them with ones he's already filled out," SallyAnne reminded him.

There was no glee in her voice, for good reason: she was genuinely disappointed in him.

It was at that point that the last student—Quest Wishart-Jammerhead —walked out.

Egan sat silently for a moment, sighed, and then pulled out one of the student's tests: From a different camera angle, the agents noted that it was the essay portion of Buck Warner's test.

By the time he'd done the same for Hugo, SallyAnne couldn't stomach watching any longer. She picked up her valise. "It's been a long night. I think I'll head out."

"No worries." Riley waved Lionel away too. "You can both take off. I got this."

SallyAnne guessed Riley was still feeling guilty for almost blowing his cover at Lavinia's memorial service.

She'd felt guilty too. When Egan saw her at Lavinia's memorial service, he'd walked up to her and asked if they knew each other—in front of Miranda, no less.

Thank goodness he hadn't remembered her.

Still, Miranda had no qualms telling Lionel about it.

Had Egan not been drunk the night they'd met, would he have remembered?

For that matter, would he have accepted Miranda's offer to fix her clients' SAT tests?

I'll never really know, SallyAnne realized.

And yet, she desperately wanted to believe he'd have threatened to expose Miranda, but she knew better.

Even if he had regrets, he would have done so since that night, she reasoned. At least that's what Lionel would argue.

And not just because he's jealous of Egan, either.

That thought put a slight smile on her lips.

"What are you grinning about?" Lionel pushed the elevator button.

Since the cage was already there, it opened immediately. He nodded for SallyAnne to enter first.

"Nothing, really," she answered. "It's been a long day and I'm glad it's over. Until the crack of dawn tomorrow, anyway."

"Hey, want to stop for a bite to eat?"

SallyAnne nodded. "My car is in the shop, and I took the bus. Can you give me a lift home?"

"Sure, no problem." Now Lionel was grinning.

Suddenly SallyAnne realized why. She huffed, "Unlike Miranda's fib to Daniel, I'm telling the truth."

"Frankly, I wouldn't be offended if you weren't," he admitted.

They decided to eat on Polk Street, which was the halfway point between their apartments.

Because it was a Sunday and already after eight, they easily scored a table at Fiorella. They ordered a pizza, a salad, and a glass of wine each.

After a second glass of wine, Lionel found the nerve to come out and ask: "You like him, don't you?"

SallyAnne snickered. "Who…*Riley?*"

Lionel shook his head. "Egan."

SallyAnne took a deep breath. "Let's just say I'm disappointed in him. I guess…my idol has clay feet."

Lionel stifled a grin. "That's truly…well, *biblical.*"

"You're laughing at me," SallyAnne muttered.

"No, not at all. But I am worried about you."

She frowned. "What does that mean?"

"It's just that…" Lionel realized right then that he should have chosen his words with greater care. "We're in this for the long haul—when the acceptances come in and the parents involved lay down money with the schools. That way, we tie everything up with a nice little bow before it goes in front of a jury. I just don't want your…your appreciation of Egan—*as a writer*—to…" He winced, because he didn't know how else to say it: "Well, to cloud your judgment."

I don't want you to fall in love with him.

I want you to fall in love with me.

"How—how dare you!" she sputtered. "After all those little mind games you and Miranda play on each other—"

"'Mind games?'" Lionel couldn't believe his ears. "You have the nerve to accuse me of that? Why, you become a different person around Gable!"

"Is that so? Well then, who am I?" Her question was more than a dare.

"You're a… a lovesick fan! When he came onto you at Lavinia's memorial service, you practically melted!"

"I did no such thing!" Incensed, she added, "And you're a… *A TEASE!*"

As SallyAnne leaped up, her valise fell off the chair beside her, spilling its contents on the floor: file folders, her cell phone, and two spare 9mm magazines for her Sig Sauer.

When they scrambled to retrieve it, Lionel's forehead slammed into the back of her head.

"*Dammit!*" They exclaimed at the same time.

But when they righted themselves, he saw it for himself: the concern in SallyAnne's eyes.

No, it was pure unadulterated love.

And that's when he kissed her.

At first, she didn't pull away.

But then she did.

Oh shit, he thought. Oh shit.

Shit!

She shoved everything back into her valise and then stumbled out of the restaurant.

He ran after her. "Wait!" he implored.

Now crying, she shook her head. "I'm just a few blocks away! I'll walk!"

"Please, SallyAnne—"

"Lionel, no! I…" She couldn't finish her sentence because she was sobbing so hard.

He wanted to hold her in his arms. But he knew if he did, he'd never want to let her go.

Ever.

So instead, he let her walk away.

SECOND SEMESTER

CHAPTER 11

"$\mathcal{M}$ ail!" Noah shouted.

He tossed it on the foyer table with one hand, while grabbing an apple from the bowl placed in the center with another.

The rest of the family was plucking ornaments off the Christmas tree. Usually, it stayed up until Epiphany. The fact that it had browned out more quickly than usual was no surprise, considering that Daniel had insisted on getting the tree the weekend after Thanksgiving in the hope of boosting the family's spirits.

Instead, it had the opposite effect. Although Lavinia wasn't there in person, she was always in their thoughts.

It was the family's tradition that she'd accompany them to get the Christmas trees that would grace their respective homes. The larger of the two trees stood in the Thorpe-McKittridge's picture window. A much smaller tree was placed beside the fireplace in the tiny living room of Lavinia's cottage.

Whereas Lavinia's tree was decorated with the homemade ornaments she'd made with Audrey in their time living together as mother and daughter, each year Lavinia gifted each member of the family a unique ornament—something memorializing an experience she'd shared personally with the recipient.

One year, Charly's ornament was a tiny fishing rod holding a trout, commemorating their grandmother-granddaughter fishing trip when Charly was twelve. At the age of six, Noah's ornament was made of a shell they'd found walking along Ocean Beach. Chuck's decoration for the year he turned eight came from a Giants game that Lavinia had attended with

520

the family. He'd sat beside her and named all the players then regaled her with their stats.

It was Lavinia with whom the children designed and baked a gingerbread house. And her contribution to the Christmas Eve meal was her homemade orange spice cookies, egg nog, and sweet potato soufflé.

But now, with Lavinia gone, the family's attempt at gathering around the piano to sing Christmas carols ended after five minutes. Memories of Lavinia sitting side by side with Charly teaching her *Silver Bells* on the piano and then showing Chuck how to strum along on the guitar while Noah sang along in his angelic contralto left them choking back tears.

Lavinia was everywhere, and they missed her terribly.

So yes, the sooner the tree came down, the better.

"Anything of importance?" Daniel asked.

"This sort of looks official. It's for Chuck." Noah handed his older brother an envelope from College Board, the organization that administered the SAT.

Chuck's eyes grew big.

Everyone froze except for Charly, who ran over to him. "Don't keep us in suspense," she prodded.

Chuck ripped open the envelope's seal and stared down the sheet inside of it.

"Well?" Audrey's voice quivered with anxiety.

"Fifteen-twenty-two," he murmured. He waved the sheet at his mother. *"Wahoo! Fifteen-fuckin' twenty-two!"* His shouts were accompanied by a moonwalk that morphed into a hump dance.

"Watch your language!" Their parents shouted in unison. But soon their screams were just as loud as his.

Rolling her eyes, Charly muttered, "You are *such* a homie wannabe!"

"You're just pissed because I scored higher than you," he retorted.

He was right, and Charly knew it. The fact that she took each test seriously and that she studied long hours to maintain a high grade point average had been the one thing no one could take away from her.

Until now.

Daniel's hug lifted Audrey off the floor. When he set her down again, he high-fived Chuck. "See? I told you! If you focused, you could ace it!"

Suddenly, Chuck's cell phone hummed. He glanced at the screen. "It's Fawn!" he exclaimed. As he walked away toward the foyer, Charly heard him say, "Yeah! I just got mine too!... Fifteen-twenty-two!...What? Fifteen-oh-one? Awesome!"

Fawn tied my score?

Great. Just... great.

I have to get out of here.

No one noticed Charly had left the room.

CHARLY HAD JUST STARTED UPSTAIRS TO GRAB HER HANDBAG WHEN SHE HEARD Chuck's voice behind her. She looked down to see him pacing in the foyer.

I'm silly. The very least I can do is congratulate him.

She was about to start down again when she heard him say: "What do you mean, the whole thing's a sham?"

Charly froze.

"Our parents...they paid to do *what?*....I don't believe you! I mean, Egan drilled with me—for hours! *He worked me hard.*"

Silence.

Then:

"Yeah, well, believe whatever you want." Chuck's voice cracked.

He's angry, Charly thought. What the heck did that girl say to him? What's a sham?

Chuck's footsteps sounded as if he'd turned around and was now coming her way. Charly flattened herself against the wall.

Chuck was scowling. But before he walked back into the living room, he set his mouth into a grin.

She could hear her parents welcoming him back and peppering him with questions.

About his study habits.

About revisiting his college applications to make sure they were current.

About touring a few more campuses.

About his future.

Charly grabbed her coat from her room. When the coast was clear, she tiptoed downstairs and out the front door.

THE LINE AT THE KABUKI THEATER FOR THE LATEST *SPIDERMAN* MOVIE WAS SO long that Charly, Sienna, Zina, and Manya decided to skip it altogether and hit one of Japantown's karaoke bars instead.

The driver's licenses they showed the bouncer claimed they were over twenty-one. He didn't look closely—a sure sign he probably knew better.

The fake IDs were courtesy of Hugo. He sold them for a hundred dollars apiece.

When Chuck got one, he insisted that Charly do it as well. In fact, he ponied up the cash for it—his way to keep her from tattling about the forgeries.

Although she'd had the ID since last summer, this was the first time she'd used it. In fact, she was so paranoid her parents would somehow come across it that she hid it in a broken seam of her wallet.

Today, it came in handy.

Zina insisted on paying their way into the bar. She also paid for their cocktails—Moscow Mules. She was still on a high from learning she'd scored 1436 on her SAT test.

"Mine was fifteen-oh-eight," Manya exclaimed proudly.

"I'll bet your mom is still floating on a cloud!" Sienna had to shout over a college-age couple who were crooning *I've Got You, Babe.*

"Why do you think she let me break curfew tonight?" Manya shouted back.

"Damn! You beat me by *seven points!*" Charly muttered. "And Chuck scored fifteen-twenty-two."

Zina's eyes went wide. "Jeebus! I guess Egan is officially a...oh, I don't know—I guess he's some sort of 'dumb-ass whisperer'!"

Charly scowled. "Chuck isn't dumb! He's just lazy."

Zina thought a moment, then nodded. "Point taken. But I'm not just talking about him. I ran into Buck Warner. He claims he scored over fourteen hundred! Seriously, what are the odds of that? That dude could make a lamppost look like a Rhodes Scholar!" She shook her head in dismay. "He told me Hugo scored over fourteen hundred too."

If Egan had coached me, I might have scored over fifteen-fifty. Maybe even the full sixteen hundred...

Suddenly, Charly wished she'd insisted on being in Miranda's special program too.

Manya's smile, caught in each flicker of the bar's pulsing strobing lights, morphed into a frown. "That can't be! Hugo and Buck walked out halfway through each session of the test—"

Suddenly, Charly felt her cell phone buzzing in her pocket. She looked down to see who was calling.

Her mother had tried to reach her eight times.

Well, too bad.

For once, she didn't mind that Audrey was worried about her. If being in trouble was the only way to get her parents' attention, then so be it.

"The next round is on me," she exclaimed. She headed to the bar to get four more Mules.

* * *

SHE DIDN'T REMEMBER HOW SHE GOT HOME, OR WHY SHE'D SLEPT IN HER clothes, for that matter.

She'd never felt so dizzy in her life either.

At least she'd somehow taken off her shoes. She realized this when she rolled over into something sticky...

And smelly:

Vomit.

"Ugh!" she groaned.

"Ah! You're finally awake."

Charly flinched at the sound of her mother's voice. She opened one eye, then the other. "Do you have to be *so loud?*" The question inched out of her mouth in a hoarse croak.

Audrey sighed. "I just seem loud to you because you're hung over." She held out a glass. "Here, drink this."

Charly stared at the glass, then shook her head. "But it's...*green!*" Just the thought of it touching her lips sent her into dry heaves.

"Trust me. You'll feel much better."

Adamantly, Charly shook her head.

"I'm not leaving until you do."

Finally, Charly groaned, sat up, and did as she was told.

"Good!" Audrey grinned. "Darling, are you really all that upset that Chuck did well on that darn test?"

"No! ... Yes..." Charly stared at her bedspread—not such a smart idea considering the psychedelic colors in its retro print were making her dizzy again. She closed her eyes. "Of course, I'm happy he did well. It's just that I didn't expect him to do *so* well—even better than me." She sighed. "Now, Chuck officially does everything better than me."

"We both know that's not true," Audrey replied. "For once, this time Chuck put all his energies into it—"

"Even so..." Charly muttered.

"What do you mean by that?"

"Mom, Chuck isn't the only one who scored well. All of Miranda's concierge students scored at least fourteen hundred—even the ones who barely studied—or left early!" Charly shrugged. "At least, that's what Manya and Zina said."

Audrey frowned. "Were they also coached by Egan?"

"Yes. Granted, they say he was a real taskmaster—"

"Well, then, there you have it. You know as well as I do that AA students have been taught comprehensive learning techniques. Isn't that why you've spent the past four years at the school?"

"Yes. But—"

"Egan was successful in motivating them to channel their energies and skills into the test. That says a lot about his abilities as a teacher."

"Yeah...I guess." She looked away. "Why don't you ask Chuck what he thinks?"

"Okay, I will. But not at the expense of bruising his ego. Chuck worked hard for that grade. He should know we're all proud of him—you, especially."

Charly snickered. "If you say so."

"I do. He respects you more than anyone in the whole world."

Charly wondered, does he?

Of course, she already knew the answer to that. The bond between the twins had always been forged in love and loyalty.

"Okay," she murmured.

Audrey looked at her watch. "It's already noon. The others left at ten."

"On a ride?" Charly was disappointed she'd missed it. Then again, the thought of riding at breakneck speed on Mount Tam's bike trails made her want to hurl again.

"No, they aren't cycling today. They're at Lavinia's house, packing it up. I told them we'd be there as soon as you woke up."

Charly groaned again. "Do I have to go? I feel awful."

"Unfortunately, yes. It's all hands on deck." Audrey stood up. "One of Lavinia's wishes was that it be sold and the proceeds go toward establishing a scholarship endowment in her name. The house is worth close to two million dollars."

Charly's heart lurched in her chest. "Wait!... Does that mean we don't own it? *That none of us can ever live there?*"

"I know how you feel, Charly. And trust me, I feel the same way." She took Charly's hand. "Until it sells, we can go there as often as we like. And we can take whatever belongings we want to remember her by."

Charly tried to protest, but no words came out.

She was glad her mother walked out the door before she threw up again.

CHAPTER 12

*D*espite having a three-hour head start, Daniel, Chuck, and Noah had barely made a dent in the chore of cleaning out Lavinia's house.

A U-Haul truck sat in the driveway, along with Daniel's car.

Daniel was waiting for Audrey and Charly. As they walked onto the front porch, he handed each of them a small pad of Stick-It notes. Audrey's was pale pink, whereas Charly's pad was bright orange.

"Today, we're boxing up stuff to give to the Salvation Army, which will pick it up sometime next week," Daniel explained. "There are boxes in every room. If you want to hold onto something, put your name on the box, toss in anything you want, and take your filled boxes down to either of the cars. If it's too big to box up, put your name on it with a Stick-It note. Tomorrow we'll fill the U-Haul and move the bigger pieces to our house." He nodded at Audrey. "Chuck is working in the living room. And since the garden is still filled with produce, I asked Noah to pluck anything that we can take home with us. Quite frankly, I think we'll also be able to drop a few boxes of produce at the Delancey Street Mission."

"They'll appreciate it," Audrey murmured. "I guess I'll start in Lavinia's bedroom, and then I'll move on to the kitchen."

"Good." Daniel turned to Charly. "Why don't you take the two smaller upstairs bedrooms?"

Charly nodded. She was glad he didn't mention her night out clubbing. She was sure to hear enough about it from Chuck before the day was out.

———

THE GUEST ROOM WAS THE EASIEST OF THE TWO SMALLER BEDROOMS TO BOX UP, so Charly started there.

Twenty minutes later, Charly had moved on to her mother's childhood bedroom.

Having played in Lavinia's house all her life, she'd been in the room more times than she could remember. Not surprisingly, her grandmother had left it like a time capsule. Its double bed was covered with a home-made quilt made by Lavinia. A few of Audrey's stuffed animals were still propped casually among the bed's mountain of throw pillows.

The posters hanging on the walls never failed to put a smile on Charly's face. Knowing that her mother was once into Alice in Chains, Metallica, and Nine Inch Nails blew her mind.

Charly made a note to roll them up. She'd have them framed and present them to Audrey on her next birthday.

Her mother's closet was a treasure trove of period clothing. But even back in the day, Audrey had a mature fashion style: slacks as opposed to acid-washed jeans; blouses, not tee shirts. There was none of the usual fashion faux pas from the teen era she'd lived through.

Actually, there were a few pieces that Charly coveted: wide-legged tan pants, a sleeveless black mock turtleneck sweater, and a raincoat with an empire waist. If any of these items were from Sienna's grandparents' store, they'd be worth a small fortune now. Although Audrey was shorter than Charly, both were slender, so maybe it would work out. She set these items aside in an empty box.

One fashion accessory that seemed a bit out of place was a pair of boots: pink Doc Martens illustrated with London icons. Her mother's other shoes were flat slippers, although there was a pair of Converse sneakers.

Because the boots were practically brand new, she put them in her take-home box as well.

The only things on the closet's upper shelf were old handbags and a cardboard box.

Charly grabbed the box and set it on the floor. One of the items inside was an Ashbury Academy yearbook from her mother's senior year.

The longest messages were scribbled along the borders of the pages showing black and white photos of her mother laughing and hugging her closest friends: Bliss, Davis, Tallulah, and Gemma—

And some guy named Jeremy.

Like the others, Jeremy's memories were relayed in a shorthand that only the writer and the recipient would understand. Whereas the other four messages were light and humorous, this Jeremy person's comments were filled with longing and regret.

My mother was a heartbreaker, Charly realized.

This unexpected revelation gave her pause. Even with visual proof in hand, the realization that her mother was once a teenager coveted by boys seemed to knock her world off-kilter, sending it spinning in the wrong direction.

The next thing she pulled from the cardboard container was a small lacquered burlwood box.

There wasn't much inside. The box's pull-out tray was divided into six square compartments. One square contained a bracelet covered in charms. A mood ring filled another. Tiny diamond ear studs and other trinkets were placed in the other chambers.

Charly pulled out the tray to see underneath it. There were a few torn music event tickets, most from the Fillmore. Some were for Maggie's concerts.

These are collector's items, Charly thought excitedly.

There was also a strip of miniature black-and-white photos: headshots of a young man, fresh-faced, with a cocky grin. She recognized him immediately: Egan, twenty years younger, maybe more.

A heart had been drawn around his face with a red Magic Marker.

Mom had a crush on Egan!

Charly blushed at the thought.

Is it difficult for her to see him now?

No, of course not, she reasoned. Mom's an adult. She's got kids.

And a husband.

She loves Dad…

But then she saw it: the last thing in the cardboard box:

Another book—

Extracurricular.

The title page was earmarked with a ticket to some event: Egan had been interviewed at UC Berkeley about his break-out debut novel.

And he'd signed the page:

Dear Audrey,
   You were the ideal fantasy.
   May our reality be just as wonderful.
   With all my heart,
   Love, Egan

My mother—was once Egan's fantasy?
And what had he hoped was their "reality"?

Emotions roiled through Charly. she thought back at the few times she'd seen her mother and Egan together. By her nature, Audrey was always reserved. But whenever Egan was around, Charly had noticed her mother's eyes brighten and her voice took on a charged lilt.

Then again, most women seemed to appreciate Egan's charm.

Charly looked down at the ticket. Its date put it just nine months before Chuck's and her birth.

She remembered how upset her mother was when, on the first day of school, the twins had teased her about their parents' wedding day. It took place less than nine months before their birth.

Stunned by the implication, Charly leaped up from the floor. Out of the corner of her eye, she caught sight of her reflection in the dresser mirror.

Oh my God—

Is Egan our father?

The book fell from her hands, hitting the hardwood floor with a loud thunk.

From Lavinia's old bedroom, she heard her mother exclaim, "Charly? Are you okay in there?"

"Fine! Everything is…just fine!" Charly shoved the burlwood box and the two books under the clothing in her take-home box. She then folded the box closed, wrote her name on a Stick-It note, and taped it to the box.

As quietly as she could, she tiptoed downstairs with it.

Her father's car keys lay on the foyer table. She placed the box in the far corner of his trunk.

She'd retrieve at home.

"WHAT'S THIS FOR AGAIN?" WARILY, CHUCK EYED THE SMALL PLASTIC TUBE Charly had handed him.

"Biology class. Extra credit. For my experiment, I need a sample from you." She nodded toward Noah. "No biggie. He's given me one as well."

Noah gave Chuck a thumbs up. "But only because she gave me ten bucks."

For Charly, the bribe was worth it. There was no way she could dare ask Daniel for a saliva sample. But since half of Noah's DNA was his, if in fact the twins and Noah had different fathers, they'd know immediately.

Chuck cocked a brow. "You're not going to clone me, are you?"

Charly snorted. "Trust me, one of you is more than enough."

Chuck laughed. "Alright, but let me grab my phone. If I'm going to spill my seed, I'll need to look at some porn. I'm not a bonobo, you know—"

"Why porn…?" When the reason came to her, she punched his arm, horrified. "Not sperm, you idiot!"

"Oh…" Chuck shrugged. "Okay, then at least let me drink a couple of glasses of water." He held up the tube. "Although, it's small enough that I might be able to pee without any—"

"*Ew…no!*" She raised her hand in frustration. "Look, just give me some *saliva!*"

"Oh!… Why didn't you just say so?" He spit it into the tube until his saliva reached the fill line.

As Charly took it from him, she shuddered. Not just because he was grossing her out, but because she hated herself for following up on her sad, sick hunch about her mother's secret.

Hopefully, she was wrong.

She wouldn't dare ask her mother. Not when a DNA test was easy enough to get.

In eight to ten weeks, I'll know for sure.

She wondered if getting a sample from Egan would be as bothersome to retrieve.

Somehow, she doubted it.

FRANKLY, IT WAS EASIER THAN CHARLY THOUGHT.

It helped that Egan was vain enough to keep a well-stocked toiletry bag in his bottom desk drawer. She'd learned about it a few months back. After his lunch shift, she'd noticed him carrying a toothbrush when strolling back into his classroom.

She'd teased him about it too. "Worried about gum disease?"

"That—and coffee breath," he'd admitted. She'd even joked that it was the same color as the one she had at home: pink.

"You're stuck with whatever colors they put in a four-pack," he insisted. "And using it here—doesn't that make me woke?"

She laughed so hard that he joined in.

Thankfully, his toiletry bag was still in his desk drawer. While he was out to lunch, Charly entered his classroom and swapped it out for a new identical one she'd taken from her bathroom closet.

She chided herself for her suspicions, but it was better to know for all their sakes.

At least, that's what she told herself.

CHAPTER 13

The months of January, February, and March were declared San Francisco's soggiest winter in a decade.

To Audrey's relief, it didn't help the sale of Lavinia's house.

"Don't realtors suggest that sellers frou-frou up a place before putting it on the market?" Daniel asked.

Audrey chuckled. "Exactly what do you mean by that?"

"You know…" Daniel struggled to find the right words. "They bring in nice furniture to fake the fact that someone is living there. And they make the place smell like chocolate chip cookies are baking in the oven."

Audrey shrugged. "I guess so. Maybe I'll suggest that to our realtor."

She was lying. In fact, the realtor had already recommended staging the house.

Audrey had told him not to bother. She dreaded the thought of selling Lavinia's house. In fact, she wanted to buy it herself.

But doing so would mean dipping into the children's college funds—something neither she nor Daniel could do, especially now that two university tuitions would soon be staring them in the face.

Both of the twins had applied to UC Berkeley—their first choice and parents' alma mater—and UCLA, their second.

Acceptances were due in late March, as was the case with the other UC campuses. Chuck had also applied to Davis, San Diego, and Santa Cruz.

Charly had also sent applications to Stanford, Boston University, Wellesley, and USC, but she'd refused to apply for early admission. In her mind, these were fallback positions should she not get accepted to Berkeley.

In any event, at the least, Daniel and Audrey would be shelling out

531

thirty thousand dollars per child per year unless scholarships could be wrangled from the schools.

So, even as a rental investment, hanging onto Lavinia's house was not an option.

Audrey sighed. "I'll call the realtor first thing in the morning."

"Okay, folks—listen up!" Egan scanned the faces of AA's Debate Team. "As you already know, tomorrow's debate is the last one before the state tournament. We'll be facing off against Saint Ignatius, which, like us, has a record of ten wins and no losses." He paced the floor. "We're in this fight because each of you has brought your personal best to every previous match. And"—Egan's pause warned the team to listen up; that what he had to say next was very important—"it's why, should we win our division today, I'll finally be making good on my promise of choosing our team captain—the person I feel could help us become state champions."

It has to be me. Please, God, let it be me, Charly prayed.

"But first things first. To take the division crown, we've got to win two out of tomorrow's three matches based on the questions you've researched, summarized, and drilled for all week."

Egan pointed to the whiteboard:

• *Should high schools drop football because of the potential for life-altering injuries?*

• *Is a college education necessary in this day and age?*

• *Should our political leaders be held to a higher ethical standard?*

"However, we're approaching this last match differently," Egan explained. "Each question will be the *sole domain* of one of our top three scorers. They will give pro, con, and rebuttal arguments for their questions. Their success is our success. But only one of them can lead us into the state tournament. Tomorrow will decide who that will be."

The students exchanged knowing glances. It was no secret that Chuck, Charly, and Fawn were the team's highest point scorers.

Egan scanned the room. When he found Chuck, he smiled. "Chuck, you'll do pro, con, and rebuttal on the first question," Egan declared.

Chuck's nod was accompanied by a shrug.

Since the SAT test, Chuck seemed more serious—stoic, perhaps.

I guess the test served its purpose, Egan reasoned. He's taking life more seriously.

As much as Egan had hoped for that, it also saddened him. Chuck's laugh was infectious. His sense of humor lifted the spirits of all around him. Egan never realized how much he appreciated it until now.

His gaze shifted to Fawn, who sat two seats to the right of the boy. "Fawn, you'll do the same on the second one."

She preened as she nodded, then glanced over anxiously at Chuck to gauge his response to her great luck.

The kid's yawn was hardly an acknowledgment.

I guess it's finally over between those lovebirds, Egan reasoned.

Finally, Egan turned to Charly. "The third question is all yours, kiddo." The bestowment came with a wink and a grin.

<hr>

Even before she found her mother's copy of *Extracurricular*, she'd already made up her mind to impress Egan so much that he'd have to make her captain.

If what she suspected about his real role in her life was true, it would mean more to her than ever.

She loved Daniel and knew he was proud of her and that he loved her too. And yet, she'd always felt the need to compete for his love.

Not that winning Egan's adoration would come any easier. She could see that already. If he suspected—or for that matter, if he already knew he was her father, he certainly didn't show it.

Charly had always scored high in Egan's Comp Lit class. But since her suspicions, she'd made a concerted effort to earn what his students jokingly called "Egan's A+++ Compliment of the Week."

They could jest, but Egan's acknowledgments were coveted nonetheless.

Fawn had worked just as hard for Egan's recognition, and bristled visibly whenever he complimented anyone else—

Especially Charly.

In Chuck's case, whereas he'd been enamored with Egan before receiving his exemplary SAT score, Chuck's attitude toward their teacher had changed. He no longer sought Egan's approval.

For that matter, he seemed to have distanced himself from Daniel too.

Even more shocking, he had totally dumped Fawn.

Chuck was now fully self-driven.

I guess that's a good thing, Charly reasoned.

For that very reason, she was glad that she hadn't revealed her suspicions about Audrey and Egan to Chuck. If the DNA test proved she was right, he'd be a victim to the same emotional turmoil that coursed through her.

Would her brother accept the test results, despite knowing it would crush Daniel?

Would he, like she, be upset with their mother keeping from them this life-changing secret?

Her guess was yes to both.

These days, Charly could barely stand looking at Audrey, let alone being around her mother. She was silent in the morning drives to school. And after school, she'd gotten adept at finagling excuses to stay away from home.

Thankfully, her loving friends indulged her. But by the concern in their voices, she knew they were worried about what she wasn't telling them.

She threw herself into the one thing she found joy in doing: working through every debate question, from every angle—not just the ones Egan had assigned her.

Charly was the undisputed star of Ashbury Academy's debate team.

Tomorrow she would prove it.

To Egan, especially.

She wondered how he'd respond to the knowledge that he was a father of two, and teenagers at that? If it turned out she was right about his relationship with their mother, she hoped that the time Egan had spent with the twins would make it easier for him to accept her love.

And hopefully, Chuck's too.

She had no doubt that Chuck's shock and awe at the revelation would mirror her own. He respected Egan. That could be the start of the bond between father and son.

Hopefully, one that would strengthen between them for the rest of their lives.

And yet, Charly worried how Daniel would take the news.

It would break his heart, she feared.

Could he ever forgive their mother for lying to him all these years?

For that matter, would Egan forgive Audrey for hiding the truth from him as well?

It would be difficult, Charly realized.

She knew this from experience. Her anxiety over the DNA test results grew with each passing week.

So did her antipathy toward her mother.

As anxious as Audrey was about Lavinia's house, she was even more concerned about Charly.

Her daughter was avoiding her, and Audrey didn't know why.

Ever since the night Charly came home drunk, she now found excuses to spend less time at home. Instead, she hid out in her friends' homes.

She never invites them here anymore, Audrey realized sadly.

She knew her daughter was competitive—especially with Chuck. Audrey wondered if his higher SAT score had shaken Charly's confidence to the point that she was now ashamed to face her family.

Was Charly finding solace in drink—or worse yet, drugs? Although pot wasn't allowed in school, it was ubiquitous with students everywhere.

Audrey prayed this wasn't the case. In the past, Charly had stayed away from it. She never saw the purpose of mind-altering substances—be they drunk, inhaled, or ingested.

If Charly was at Manya's house, Audrey avoided calling Nira to confirm it. A physician, Nira was rarely home before eight o'clock. She was also a strict parent and would wonder why Audrey was checking up on her daughter. The last thing Audrey needed was for Nira to forbid Manya from seeing Charly.

And besides, since Nira accepted the trustee board's offer to join it, the last thing Audrey wanted was anyone—even Daniel—to know she was concerned about Charly's behavior.

When Charly claimed to be at Zina or Sienna's homes, Audrey would wait an hour or two before calling the hosting mother. After small talk or gossip, she'd find an excuse to ask after the girls.

"They're fine," Gemma would insist. To prove it, she held out the phone in the girls' direction so that Audrey could hear their giggles or catch a snippet of their conversation.

Inevitably it was about their studies.

Bliss, too, always confirmed their whereabouts.

But today, after Audrey's seventh such call, Bliss bluntly asked: "Has something happened between you and Charly?"

Audrey didn't know how to answer that. Finally, she whispered, "Yes. But I don't know what."

"Oh—my dear, sweet friend!" The concern in Bliss' voice touched her deeply. "I'm sure it's nothing to worry about. I mean, let's face it. All girls go through a period of hating their moms. Last year, Sienna acted as if I was a leper." Bliss' chuckle was half-hearted at best. "Not to worry! It's just their way to prove that they're ready to…oh, I don't know. Maybe spread their wings without asking permission?"

"But… I never felt that way," Audrey admitted.

"Why would you?" Bliss exclaimed. "Lavinia never doubted you. And she never gave you any reason to doubt her either."

"Does Charly think I doubt her?" Audrey was confused. "Or does she doubt me? Bliss, what are you saying?"

"Audrey, you're asking the wrong person," Bliss explained. "Maybe it's a conversation you should have with Charly. The sooner the better too. Hey, the debate team match is tomorrow. Why don't you ask her if she'll join you for a mother-daughter dinner afterward?"

She's right, Audrey thought. Daniel would be flying home from New York late that evening. Noah would be sleeping over at a friend's place.

"I'm sure Chuck will be fine with us ditching him. He'll probably want to hang with Fawn anyway—particularly if her parents go out that night."

"You see?" Bliss exclaimed. "Fawn is a *perfect* example of a kid who hates her parents!"

Dismayed, Audrey insisted, "But...I'm nothing like Seamus or Gretchen McCoppin!"

"No! Of course, you're not!"

Bliss' attempt to backtrack hurt more than her honesty.

She's right. It's time for Charly and me to clear the air.

CHAPTER 14

*J*ust as the Newark gate attendant had informed him, Daniel discovered he'd scored the last empty seat in the first-class cabin of United's six o'clock San Francisco departure.

Another lucky twist of fate: Tallulah was in the seat across the aisle from him.

"Fancy meeting you here," she exclaimed as he bent down for a kiss.

"I don't mind changing seats," the man next to Tallulah offered. "Unless you two would prefer to join the Mile High Club."

Tallulah and Daniel roared with laughter at that.

Once they were airborne, he confessed, "I wish I'd known you were going to be in town. I hate eating dinner alone."

Tallulah chuckled. "Unfortunately, when I'm here, I'm wined and dined to death—and usually at midnight." She shrugged. "Such is the life of musicians and promoters. We keep vampire hours. It's aging me quickly." As proof, she pulled a compact from her satchel and scrutinized her face for telltale evidence.

"Don't kid yourself," Daniel insisted. "You could easily take ten years off your age, and no one would guess."

Tallulah's laugh filled the cabin. "Audrey has you well-trained." Her smile faded. "Speaking of my dear, sweet friend, how is she holding up, anyway?"

"I won't lie. Lavinia's death affected her deeply. Me and the children as well." Daniel hesitated. "I was sorry to hear Maggie took it hard too."

"Maggie always joked that she'd flame out first, what with all the drugs she'd ingested." Tallulah sighed. "I truly believe it never occurred to her that Lavinia might not always be there for her. Lavinia was her rock."

She attempted a smile. "I'm glad Audrey agreed to be on the search committee."

"Audrey wouldn't have it any other way. Lavinia's legacy is the school. She insists on safeguarding it." Daniel grimaced. "Unfortunately, Gretchen McCoppin is on it, too—and she's not making it easy for her. What with your role in chairing AA's anniversary gala too, I'm just glad you're also there on the board's behalf. Between the two of you, Gretchen can't do too much damage."

Tallulah nodded. "The gala is on a glide path now. Bliss is perfectly capable of wrapping up any loose ends. Replacing Lavinia with the right person is the priority now."

"I couldn't agree more." Daniel attempted a smile. "The only thing that's raised Audrey's spirits is Chuck's SAT score. Somehow he managed to pull off fifteen-twenty-two."

Tallulah frowned. "That's...interesting."

Daniel laughed, "I know. Hard to believe, isn't it?"

"No more than Quest pulling off fourteen-eleven. Jokingly, I asked him if he'd found some cheat sheet. He said no. That Egan had spent a long time drilling him on the basics. Still..." Tallulah shook her head. "Then he told me Jammerhead had signed him up for Miranda's concierge counseling program, which meant he could take as long as he wanted to answer questions. Quest said that when he went to her office to sign off on his application, he noticed she plumped it up with stuff he'd never done—like rowing crew and volunteering at some non-profit group he'd never heard of. When Quest questioned Miranda about it, she blew up at him. Told him that Jammerhead had paid her a pretty penny to quote-unquote assure that he got into a prestigious business music program." She frowned.

"How long ago was this?"

"Quest told me right as I was leaving for Manhattan."

"Have you asked Jammerhead about it?"

"He's on the road." Tallulah scowled. "Even hearing what little Quest knew, I quickly figured out it's not the sort of discussion one should have over the phone."

"You're right about that—especially if what Miranda has done involves bribery and fraud."

"Oh, my God!" Tallulah muttered. Perplexed, she slunk down in her seat. "The last thing we need is a scandal—especially one that could land Jammerhead in jail!"

"The school doesn't need this sort of headache either," Daniel pointed out. "Listen, Tallulah, give me a dollar."

Startled, she stammered, "What for?"

"Just do it," he ordered.

She reached into her satchel and pulled out a single bill.

Daniel pocketed it. "You've just retained me as your lawyer. That way, if Jammerhead has done anything illegal that he hadn't previously divulged to you, I've got your back."

"Thanks, Daniel." Stony eyed, she stared straight ahead. "So, what's our next move, counselor?"

"Don't say anything yet to anyone. I'll do a little background research on Ms. D'Arcy."

Tallulah nodded. "One thing we know: Miranda is an alumnus. And, supposedly, she built a business based on the success of her so-called college counseling skills."

"Both of which got her to sidestep any serious employment vetting—at least where Lavinia was concerned," Daniel replied. "Considering how competitive college is these days, it makes sense that she's playing with a loaded deck. I suspect she's bribing a few university staffers. Now, the big question is whether her clients know this is going on."

"Considering that they include Seamus, Jess, and Warner, my guess is yes."

"No wonder they pushed so hard to have her replace Lavinia," Daniel reasoned. "What better way to cover their tracks? For now, anyway."

"If what you suspect is right, Quest is going to be crushed when the shit hits the fan." Tallulah's voice trembled. "I guess Jammerhead is so desperate that Quest should be something more than just a musician. Why can't parents—my husband included—just let their kids live their lives?"

FAWN LOOKED AROUND ASHBURY ACADEMY'S AUDITORIUM. IT WAS A FULL house. Pride in this year's Debate Eight was sky-high.

One more reason she wanted to win the title of debate team captain.

But first, she'd have to impress Egan, which meant earning the best score in today's match.

Her plan was simple: memorize her arguments perfectly. Make eye contact with the judges. Speak with authority, but with brevity as well.

And most importantly, find some way to trip up Charly, who would also be doing all of the above.

Granted, even if her scheme worked, there was an outside chance that Egan would bestow it to Chuck.

That would undoubtedly present a conundrum.

Ever since they got back their SAT results, Chuck had been distant to her.

He no longer begged to spend time with her.

Worse yet, he found excuses to avoid her.

She was sure his bitch of a sister had something to do with that.

Miffed at Chuck's desertion, Fawn initiated the one failsafe ploy women had been using since Eve wrapped herself in live snakeskin: she flirted.

Hugo was the lucky guy, and didn't he just know it.

To her dismay, Chuck didn't seem to care.

Fawn's Hail Mary pass was delivered in a hand-written, scented note left in Chuck's locker:

I don't know why you hate me all of a sudden. At least have the courage to talk to me about it. My jailers will be out tonight. How about my place, tonight, after the match?
xoxoxoxox Fawn

She planned the best make-up session ever.

It would begin with a little move she'd perfected on her Cheerfully Yours website. She called it "Cherry Pie."

When she debuted it just last week, the clicks were astronomical, and new sign-ups went through the roof.

Best yet, the bid on the rainbow-hued spankies she'd worn during the erotic cheerleading routine brought in the highest bid in the site's history: an incredible ten thousand dollars.

Tucked into the spankies was a personalized note for the winner, someone who went by the nickname of BigBadDaddy:

Sweet dreams, BigBadDaddy!
XOXOXOX!
—Miss Cheer Fully

And should, for some unfathomable reason, Egan choose Chuck as captain, Fawn had no doubt that a double-dip of Cherry Pie would convince him to pass on the honor and suggest bestowing it on her instead.

This would peeve Charly to no end.

More importantly, it would shock Seamus into realizing she wasn't a bimbo after all.

Fawn loved the thought that becoming debate team captain would buoy his hopes about her chances for getting into Yale. She couldn't wait to say no to all the acceptances. That would teach Seamus a lesson for blowing her right to try for it on her own.

Until then, she'd have to play the good girl until her college acceptances rolled in. She had no doubt they would, and in droves. The package Miranda had created for Fawn, sent to the top ten universities touted on *US News & World Report*, had all the bells and whistles. Besides her sky-high SAT score, Miranda had doctored some of Fawn's previous grades.

She'd even faked Fawn's participation in some supposedly

international non-profit club called Best Face Forward. It was supposed to be like 4-H, but instead of pretending to be farmers, the members were supposed to do good deeds for the needy.

As if we're some sort of bleeding-heart losers, Fawn scoffed.

The catch was, there really wasn't such a club.

Fawn realized this when Miranda insisted she wear a tee shirt with the organization's logo and then marched Fawn out onto a nearby street corner to take a picture of her handing sandwiches to a couple of homeless guys.

But just as Miranda shot the picture, one of the men pinched Fawn's ass. Fawn slapped his face so hard that the dirty old codger lost a tooth.

When he howled for the cops, Miranda shut him up with a fifty-dollar bill.

"That's going on Seamus' bill," Miranda warned Fawn.

"Oh, yeah? Then I'll tell him about your so-called non-profit," the girl retorted.

"And I'll tell him about your whore-tart website," Miranda shot back.

Noting Fawn's blush, Miranda added: "And by the way, that lecher bait goes dark the moment you get home. Should any of the college recruiters find out about it, all of your parents' money for this little endeavor goes up in smoke!"

"Yeah, okay, sure," Fawn pouted. *Like hell, I will!*

The money was too good.

And besides, the more it made for her, the quicker she could leave Seamus and Gretchen in her rearview mirror.

First things first: make Seamus regret he'd ever doubted her.

So yes, tonight was important. She just had to make team captain.

Fawn watched as her parents made their entrance. She'd reserved seats for them next to Audrey Thorpe just because she knew they despised each other.

Served them all right.

THE JUDGES SELECTED FOR THE DEBATE MATCH—TWO WOMEN AND ONE MAN, all retired lawyers—were a solemn bunch.

As was the tradition, the debaters shook each judge's hand before taking their podiums.

Chuck's match was first. He considered himself lucky that he drew the con argument on the question as to whether football should be abolished from school sports.

It allowed him to expound eloquently on football's role in American culture: how it brought communities together and played an integral role in America's civil rights history.

"Football is as American as apple pie," he concluded.

He won a comfortable victory over his opponent.

Usually, when Chuck won at anything, his exuberance never seemed to fail him. This time, though, he nodded with a slim grimace as he left the podium.

He'd spent the last couple of months in a haze of doubt.

It had started when Fawn declared that Egan had nudged their SAT tests above the 1400-score sweet spot.

And that he'd done so at Miranda's behest. Apparently, it was something she did for all her concierge clients—for the right price.

He found it hard to believe Egan was on the take. At least, not from the way he'd worked so hard with Chuck to make sure he'd succeed on the test.

Miranda must be one great lay, Chuck thought. What other reason was there? Besides, he'd seen the way she simpered and preened whenever Egan was around.

Dad pushed hard for me to talk to Miranda. I should come right out and ask Dad if Fawn is right, Chuck thought.

But he quickly nixed that idea. He was afraid that his father would confirm his worse suspicions: that Daniel acted out of desperation because he'd been unsure of Chuck's ability to bring his A-game to the test.

The thought cut him to the quick.

Upon hearing Fawn's claim, Chuck's shock turned to anger. In time, it softened to sullen bitterness.

Had it not rained so hard all winter, Chuck would have come up with excuses for why he was no longer interested in the family's Saturday bike treks.

Lately, Chuck had been tempted to tell his mother his suspicions, but he couldn't stand the thought of upsetting her.

Not so soon after Lavinia's death.

Instead, he'd prove his father wrong.

It would start with winning the debate team captainship.

Too bad his father had missed seeing his son prove him wrong.

My turn, Fawn thought.

And she was ready to win her match. She'd felt she'd drawn a great question: whether college still was necessary in this day and age. She sauntered up to the judges' table with a beaming smile.

But as she shook the male judge's hand, she noticed he held it too firmly and for too long. She wondered why he was staring at her. She figured it out when he murmured, "Win one for Big Bad Daddy."

Oh....

Shit.

Suddenly, she couldn't breathe. It was as if her whole world was closing in on her. Her gaze went from her judge who gave her a broad wink, to her father—

Whose wink was even broader.

Shit, shit, shit!

Fawn drew the con argument.

She started out with a stutter, then willed herself to take control. But despite having memorized her argument and practicing it for an hour, she couldn't remember any of it.

There was nothing she could do but wing it.

She opened with some riff about lazy students who were only in school to party on their parents' dime. She then reeled into a speech about all the millionaires who, through sheer pluck and ingenuity, made their fortunes without a college degree. She tossed in survival of the fittest, charisma, karma, and good luck—none of which, she claimed, came out of a classroom.

Fawn knew she should be making eye contact with the judges, but if she dared to look at Big Bad Daddy, she knew she'd melt into a puddle of insecurity.

When the match came to an end, this decision counted against her.

Except with one judge, who gave her a perfect score.

After the match was decided, Fawn rushed out of the auditorium. She was too ashamed to face any of the men in her life: not Seamus.

Not Egan.

And certainly not Chuck.

The second she got home, she vowed, I'm deleting Big Bad Daddy's accounts.

As Charly had hoped, she drew the pro argument on her match question: whether political leaders should be held to a higher ethical standard.

Using the threads of wisdom sewn into the fabric of the U.S. Constitution, she began with a cautionary tale of executive power. Then, as if cross-stitching squares in a quilt, Charly presented historical examples of self-sacrifice during times of historical unrest.

The seamless pattern of selflessness, honor, and duty unfurled in her closing argument brought the audience to its feet.

On the heels of that, her competitor's argument unraveled like pantyhose.

Her score was the highest of both teams.

It won Ashbury Academy the district title.

THE AUDIENCE BROKE OUT IN PANDEMONIUM.

Charly was swallowed up in the team's group hug.

Finally, the others peeled away, leaving her with Chuck's arm around her shoulders.

Egan walked up to them. As he shook her hand, he murmured, "Congratulations, Captain…McKittridge."

She was struck by the way he grimaced and hesitated when saying her last name.

Does he know about us?

How she ached to ask him.

A moment later, Audrey was at their side. As she nodded to Egan, Charly watched his face closely for any sign of—

Of what? Sadness? Longing? Regret?

His benign grin betrayed nothing.

When Audrey put her arm around Charly's waist, the girl shrugged it off. Obviously dismayed at the rejection, Audrey's smile faltered. Still, she insisted, "We should celebrate. Just the two of us. Somewhere special! How about Gary Danko?"

"I'm too tired," Charly muttered stiffly. "Let's just go home."

Bemused, Egan declared, "You're kidding, right? You've wanted the captainship since I mentioned it! You've earned it fair and square. And Danko's? Are you really going to turn down that tasting menu? Take her up on the offer, Charly! You've earned it."

"But…I really don't want to." Charly turned to Chuck, but he was too caught up in his own thoughts to cipher her silent plea for help.

Noting her concern, Egan replied, "Don't worry about your brother. I'll buy him a burger. Besides, I need to pick his brain on our upcoming strategy for the state tournament."

Why does Egan want to eat with Chuck?

Why not me?

Chuck seemed just as surprised by the offer—and just as perplexed.

"That's very kind of you, Egan." The relief in Audrey's voice put a grin on Egan's face.

This was not lost on Charly.

Neither was the look on Egan's face: as if Charly had somehow disappointed him.

If only she could explain why.

CHAPTER 15

"Two burgers—and two Cloud Covers on tap."

Egan ignored the waitress' sly wink. She usually flirted with him, but now was not the time to flirt back.

Not with his son in tow.

When she walked off, Egan realized she may have not been coming onto him at all. "Jeez, I forgot…you're not twenty-one yet!"

"She doesn't know that. And besides, she likes you." By his tone, he didn't find that funny or for that matter, concerning.

"I guess it's not as if you haven't had a beer or two."

"You were a teenager once," Chuck countered. "What do you think?"

"I did," Egan admitted. "I usually snuck one out of my dad's six-packs. Nothing like the wild parties you AA kids throw."

Chuck snickered. "I don't throw them. I just attend them."

"College will be even more of that," Egan assured him.

"If I get there," Chuck muttered.

"You really are the full package, Chuck. You're personable. You're athletic. And you pulled your grades up. Your SAT was nothing to sneeze at." Egan tossed their menus aside. "For you, college is just the first step. You can do anything you set your mind on."

Chuck shrugged. "I may not go."

"Why would you say that?" Egan's eyes opened wide with surprise.

"Because I didn't earn it." The boy turned to stare at one of the big-screen monitors over the bar. A Warriors game was playing, muted.

Egan frowned. "What do you mean by that?"

"Fawn told me…she says you doctored our SAT scores so that we'd make at least fourteen-hundred." Chuck leaned across the table. He locked eyes with Egan. "Is that true?"

Egan never thought he'd have to face his son and answer that question.

At least, now I can answer truthfully.

"I swear to you, Chuck, on my life—*you earned your SAT score on your own.*"

Chuck's face was like an open book in which its pages, illustrated with the boy's emotions, were being flipped at breakneck speed. Doubt made way for wariness, which was replaced by comprehension, then relief, and finally jubilation. "I knew it! What she said—it was just too ridiculous!" His head shook, incredulous. "I mean like just because her dad doesn't believe in her, doesn't mean mine doesn't believe in me, right?"

"Your father...he will always believe in you. He will always be there for you." Egan spoke so softly that Chuck leaned in to hear him.

At that very moment, their waitress appeared with their meal on a tray. But when she placed their beers on the table, Egan waved them away. "We've changed our minds. We'll have water instead."

After she left, Chuck burst out laughing. "Dude...you're not mad because I accused you of doing something fishy, are you?"

"No, not in the least. To be honest, I wouldn't have had it any other way. I'd feel bad if you didn't trust me, and I didn't know why." Egan pointed to the burgers in front of them. "Let's dig in."

———

EVEN BEFORE THE SECOND DISH OF AUDREY AND CHARLY'S THREE-COURSE tasting menu came to their table, their conversation had gone off the rails.

For the life of her, Audrey couldn't understand why.

On the way over to the restaurant, Charly's answers to Audrey's questions about upcoming school events, her teammates, and their prep for the forthcoming tournament were clipped at best.

The girl said nothing at all during their short wait to be seated and instead busied herself by roaming through text messages.

By the time the first course was served, Audrey was upset enough to ask, "Charly, you seem so...so distant. Is it because you're missing Lavinia?"

———

THIS HAS NOTHING TO DO WITH LAVINIA.

This is all on you.

Guess again. Keep guessing. But trust me—

You'll never guess in a million years.

Unless you have a guilty conscience.

For over two months, Charly had made a concerted effort to avoid looking at Audrey. She was too afraid that her emotions would give her away.

But now that they were face to face across the restaurant table, everything—the elegant setting, even the diorama of San Francisco Bay playing out in the large picture window beside them to a cacophony of fog horns—receded into nothingness.

All she saw was her mother—pensive, hopeful, wary.

No—she is scared.

At that moment, Charly realized she'd never really seen her mother as an ordinary person. She'd always had her mother on a pedestal. Audrey Thorpe: a loving mother, adoring wife, perfect daughter, and loyal friend.

Audrey Thorpe, whom others counted on to pick up the slack; to come to the rescue.

To always do the right thing.

Audrey Thorpe, of whom so much was expected, but who never anticipated anything in return.

But that wasn't Audrey at all.

Once, Audrey Thorpe had been a seventeen-year-old girl who apparently had a crush on her cute, young, charismatic teacher. The two-inch-square photo of Egan marked with a heart was proof of that.

And once, Egan had been smitten with her too. The inscription in Audrey's copy of *Extracurricular* spoke volumes to that.

If they'd had a liaison, and if the result of it had been Charly and Chuck, and if for any reason Audrey didn't want to share that with him, surely the turmoil it had caused her had been tremendous.

And Egan's return to Ashbury Academy would be reason enough for each of the emotions now writ large on her mother's face.

If Charly were to ask Audrey all of this point-blank—right here, right now—would her mother answer her truthfully?

She hoped so, but now she wasn't sure.

After all, Audrey was just like everyone else: human.

Charly reached across the table. Taking her mother's hand, she murmured, "Yes, Mom. I miss Lavinia with all my heart. I wish she were here with us now."

Audrey nodded. Then, in unison, they turned and gazed out at the mist-kissed bay.

The DNA test results will arrive any week now, Charly reasoned. Until then, she would just have to pretend that everything was fine and dandy.

CHAPTER 16

"So, how do you feel about Netflix?" Davis' call to Egan came just as he was about to enter the school.

It wasn't the best time to take a call. The final first-class bell would ring at any moment, and at noon, the Debate Eight was driving down to Los Angeles for the state tournament, and there was still a lot of prep work Egan had to do before they departed.

To make matters worse, he'd just heard from Cornell. He had to bow out as the second chaperone because of a ruptured molar.

Egan would have to find a replacement quickly. He'd text the kids to put in calls for a parent volunteer.

At a loss for words, very cautiously, Egan declared, "Well, I was never a big *BoJack Horseman* fan, if that's what you're asking, Davis. But I enjoy *Living with Yourself.* I'm big on dark humor—"

Davis groaned. "I'm not asking you for a program critique. I'm trying to tell you that the network's suits flipped over my pitch to turn it into a limited series."

Jesus, he did it. Extracurricular *will be on TV...*

"Expect a call from Amy Sorenson. She's with ICA—International Creative Agency, one of the talent handlers I mentioned. I think you'll like her. If so, let me know, and I'll cc my option contract to both of you so that she can go over it with a fine-tooth comb. I'll release the option as soon as you sign on the dotted line."

"Great, then let 'er rip." Egan knew just how he'd use the funds: for Chuck and Charly.

Davis added, "Hey, listen. To up your fee, how do you feel about taking the first stab at the pilot script? I want to keep your voice in the show as much as possible, and I find that's usually the best way to do it."

"*Me?*... Sure, I guess."

"Great. I'll send a separate contract for that as well. No guarantees that everything in it will make it all the way to final draft or that I won't need to bring in a script doctor to massage it in places, but at least that will assure you a partial screenwriting credit. And as far as your commitment to the school, I know you'll be tied up through May, but don't worry. We have some breathing room. I'll just need a first draft by mid-August at the latest. I'll send you a care package with my notes on how I see the book breaking down into ten episodes. I'll also forward a few scripts from other series with similar arcs, and a link to the scriptwriting app you should use, so that you get the format down pat. If you could also watch the shows, you'll get a better idea of how they turned out in post-production."

"Many thanks, Davis. I'll be on the lookout for all of this."

AA's bell tower chimed the first-class warning.

Davis must have heard it too because he added, "I guess I should let you go. And hey, leave the bell tower scene in the script, okay? It wouldn't be AA—or *Extracurricular*—without it."

"Not to worry, it'll be in there."

Egan paused in front of the quad and stared up at the bell tower.

Thank you, Lavinia.

The first thing Egan did when he got to his office was write his resignation letter.

It said, simply:

> **Dear Miranda,**
> **Find someone else to abuse. I quit.**
> **—Egan**

He stuck it in his pocket as if it were a talisman.

Egan would turn it in as soon as he returned from the debate tournament.

"I just got a text from Chuck." Audrey's tone worried Daniel.

He'd just walked into his office when his cell rang. What could have happened in the half-hour since he left the house? "I'm sitting down. What did he do this time?"

"Thankfully, nothing. But...the twins need a favor. Debate Team is down one chaperone."

Daniel snickered. "Are you implying that I should fill in?"

"Frankly, yes. Every other parent has begged off."

"You too?"

"The search committee has two interviews scheduled this morning and two more for Saturday, so yes. Unless you'd rather swap Debate Tournament for finding Lavinia's replacement—"

"I guess the debate team is the lesser of two evils. Okay, yeah, text Chuck that I'm in."

He'd just hung up from her when his phone buzzed again. The caller ID showed it was one of the private detectives used by his firm: Francesca Upton.

"That was quick," Daniel declared.

"Your subject—this Miranda D'Arcy—is what we shamuses call a 'scorched earth personality,'" Francesca retorted.

"I take it that means I probably won't like what I hear." He sighed. "Okay, give me the highlights."

"The last school she worked at was Bobbitt-Hennings Prep in LA, in the position of a college counselor. When a parent reported that another had boasted she'd followed through on a guarantee to secure admission to a prestigious university, Miranda was not so politely asked to vacate the position."

"I would imagine that's just part of her sales pitch. Where's the beef in that?"

"Apparently, the student in question was a dullard who just so happened to ace his SATs and get onto the university's crew team despite having a deathly fear of water. As it turns out, to make the point, his loud-mouth parent felt compelled to name a few others who'd paid dearly for Miranda's bag of tricks. At that point, the school's trustee board figured she was too hot to handle and paid her a settlement to go away."

"Can you get me a list of the trustees' names?"

"I just texted it to you."

Daniel took a moment to scan it. "I've got an old classmate who's a partner at a law firm with one of these guys—Robert Edelson."

"Do you want me to follow up with your friend?"

"No, I'll do it. But see what you can find out about the loudmouth parent."

"On it," Francesca assured him.

Daniel's old acquaintance at Edelson's law firm, Terrence Owen, was out of town, litigating a case for an East Coast client. But Terry's assistant assured Daniel that she'd relay the message and its urgency the moment he called in.

Terry didn't call until just after eleven, Pacific Time.

When Daniel explained the purpose of the call, Terry didn't respond for so long that Daniel assumed they had been disconnected. Finally, he replied, "A few months ago, Rob asked to be bought out of the partnership. The other partner and I thought it was odd. He's still in his forties and healthy as an ox. His wife and kids are also in good health. Right before the buyout, a couple of FBI agents showed up, asking to see him."

"Interesting. Was it about a client?"

"Frankly, no one knows what it was about. He never said, and his assistant didn't sit in on it. I was curious enough to ask a buddy in the FBI's LA office. He told me he could say nothing about an ongoing investigation, but that the agents involved were from the San Francisco office."

Since Miranda is up here and she may be involved, that would make sense, Daniel reasoned.

"Thanks, Terry. You've been a big help."

"If you find out something interesting, don't hesitate to call back." There was no levity in Terry's request.

"I take it that Rob's buyout is still being negotiated?"

"Yes. And, frankly, if he's jumping ship for some reason that may later reflect on the firm, we'd like to close negotiations sooner than later."

"I hear you. I'll get back to you."

HAD CHUCK NOT BEEN SCHEDULED TO PITCH WHEN ASHBURY ACADEMY'S baseball team played Marin Catholic High School's some three years ago, Daniel would never have found himself in a bleacher seat next to Vance Melamed.

It was the last game of the season, and both men had arrived late. The overflow bleacher was a mix of families rooting for both teams.

As it turned out, Vance's son was the opposing pitcher.

Between shouts and cheers for their respective teams, the two men had struck up a conversation. Although Daniel's practice was corporate as opposed to criminal litigation, the fact that one of them was in law and the other in law enforcement gave them common ground.

When Daniel had mentioned he was on AA's trustee board, Vance cocked a brow. "Then, you know Darius Calder."

Daniel chuckled. "I would imagine you know him too."

"You guessed right."

"He's on the board because his wife is an alumnus, and his daughter is a student there."

At that point, an MC batter hit a double. Like others cheering on the team, Vance stood up and cheered.

But when he sat back down, he pulled a business card from his wallet and handed it to Daniel. "Just in case," he said.

Daniel had stuck the card where such random things were kept: the top righthand drawer of his desk.

He pulled it out now.

"So, how's your son's fastball these days?" That's how Vance assured Daniel he remembered him.

"Still going strong. But I'm happy he no longer has to rely on it for a college scholarship. He did more than okay on his SATs, and he seems to be pulling up his grades."

"That's...*nice.*" Vance paused before adding: "I guess AA's college counselor is doing her job. A real miracle worker."

Her job?

Miracle worker...

Daniel took the hint: Miranda was being investigated.

Vance chuckled. "So...is this a social call?"

Daniel didn't know how to answer that.

He's great, Audrey thought.

No—he's perfect.

If Lavinia were here, she'd think so too.

The Head of School candidate, Frank Michaelson, hailed from a prep school in a small Massachusetts town. He'd come with glowing letters from a decade's worth of the school's parents, faculty, and students. The school had won numerous scholastic and academic awards. Eighty percent of its students had gone on to college, sixty-eight percent of whom had been accepted to their first-choice schools.

Besides Audrey and Tallulah, Gretchen and Nira were also on the search committee, as was Odette.

Frank shook everyone's hand before walking out the door.

"He's ideal," Tallulah murmured.

"I was just thinking the same thing," Odette declared.

Gretchen shivered. "Hardly! He has no charisma! I can't see him as a leader for the students, let alone the teachers—"

"As the only teacher representative here, let me assure you I found him *scintillating,*" Odette huffed.

"That's because you're...well, you're *old school.*" Gretchen sniffed.

"*Merde,*" Odette muttered.

"I speak French, *mademoiselle*! I know what that means!"

"Well, in that case, you'll also know what I mean when I say '*Votre approche à cette tâche est des conneries—*"

Gretchen leaped up. "How dare you call me *'des conneries'*!"

Odette shrugged. "If the *chaussure* fits—"

"Ladies, please!" Audrey shouted. This was the fifth candidate in a very long day. Audrey rubbed her temples. "The reason we are using scorecards is for this very purpose: to quantifiably assess the candidates. Any further notes you have on your observations are to be added in the comment section. *Comprendre?*"

Both women glowered at the other.

Audrey groaned. Turning to Nira, she asked, "What did you think of him?"

Nira frowned. Her glance went from Gretchen to Odette then back again. "I…could see how he might appear milquetoast to some parents."

"In other words, you're siding with Gretchen," Tallulah muttered. "Why am I not surprised?"

Audrey was literally saved by the bell—in this case, her phone's ring tone.

It was Daniel.

"I have to take this. And considering this was the last interview of the day, we may as well adjourn until Saturday."

As the others filed out, she answered the call. "If only you'd called five minutes sooner, I could have avoided a French name-calling contest."

"Sorry. Hey, listen. I won't be able to chaperone the debate team."

"But—they're counting on you!" Audrey exclaimed.

"Something big just came up. If you care to go in my stead, I'll be glad to bach it this weekend with Noah."

"But…don't you want to be there for the twins?"

"Of course I do!" Daniel sounded impatient.

And tired.

And discouraged. "But something important just got put on my plate. It's…unavoidable."

Two nights out of town with Egan.

It would be torture for both of them, albeit for different reasons. Audrey hated the thought that he'd be mooning after her in front of the twins.

"Got it." She tried for nonchalance but knew she'd failed miserably.

Without a preface or notes, she texted him the info on Saturday's interviewees. He could figure out the rest on his own.

"You're working late." Daniel hadn't bothered to knock on Miranda's door.

Entitled prick.

But aren't they all?

Annoyed, Miranda glanced up at the wall clock. It was almost six o'clock.

It had been a hell of a long day—and far from over.

All the teachers do is complain, she thought. Admittedly, not as much as the damn parents. All they think about is one-upping their besties with whatever they can get out of me for their damn brats!

Frankly, the school was a daily shit show. She had been a fool to let Seamus talk her into even the interim Head of School position—and taking on two more concierge parents, since the knew the Feds would be tickled pink about it.

Instead of dealing with the ongoing headache of the AA universe, she should have been planning her getaway.

The crap was going to hit the fan any day now.

The moment the acceptances came in.

When they did, she needed to be as far away as possible.

Not that she could say that to Daniel.

She stifled a groan as she muttered, "So, what can I do for you, Mr. McKittridge?"

"You can leave. *Right now.* Before the roof caves in on Ashbury Academy."

What is he—a mind reader?

Miranda sputtered, "I beg your pardon?"

Daniel came right up to the desk. But he didn't sit down in either of the two chairs opposite it. He stood in front of her. "I know what you're doing, Miranda. It's the same game that got you dismissed from Bobbitt-Hennings."

Miranda sat back. She couldn't help it—she had to smile.

"Well, well, well! Someone in this school has done a little homework." She snickered. "Lavinia would have hated that. Not at all 'hands-on' learning."

"How many parents did you rope into your scheme?"

"Does it matter?"

"It will when the roof caves in on them—and their children."

Miranda smirked. "If you must know, I made dreams come true for nine AA students, including Hugo, Fawn, Buck—"

"Not surprising," Daniel muttered.

"As well as Manya, Quest, and Zina," Miranda added.

He winced at the names of his children's friends. "I'm sure they all made it worth your while."

She leaned forward. "It's the only reason I'm here."

"And Seamus' full-court press will assure you lots of victims for years to come. Let me guess—he'll be skimming off the top."

"Yes, that's the game plan. He's generously offered to manage AA's various endowments so that they reach their full potential."

"Not if I can help it. I'm turning you in, Miranda—to the FBI."

Her laughter filled the room. "No, you won't, Daniel."

"Try me." He took out his phone.

"You won't because you can't practice law behind bars. And visiting rights are very strict for the sort of crimes you'll be charged with committing."

She stifled a giggle when the color drained from his face. "What the hell do you mean by that?"

"The chair you sponsored—for Egan Gable? The funds went to pay for Chuck's concierge fee."

"*What?*... How could that be?"

Miranda shrugged. "A little financial sleight of hand. Your funds went into one bank account as opposed to another. And of course, there was a bit of paperwork to back it up—with your signature on it." She smiled. "Not to worry! Remember? Chuck passed with flying colors! Of course, it meant that Egan had to jigger the lad's SAT test to make him look as intelligent as he is handsome, athletic, and...erudite." Miranda laughed raucously. "All the more reason we should both forget this conversation—until I say otherwise. Shall we?"

"I'm a lawyer—an officer of the court! I can't turn a blind eye to all of this."

Noting his crestfallen face, she smirked, "Don't be ridiculous. We only see and hear what we want. Like that last compliment I just gave Chuck. For a parent who has always insisted on honesty, didn't you find it a bit over the top? I mean, let's just call your son what he really is: *a smart ass.*"

Angrily, he took two steps toward her.

Miranda cocked a brow. "And then there's Audrey's past with Egan."

Daniel stopped cold. "What are you talking about?"

"Trust me, they were much more than student and teacher. And let me tell you, that flame never went out, as you can see for yourself." She clicked onto her phone and held it out to him so that he could see what was on it:

A video of Egan and Audrey. They were alone in the school's reception area. She was leaning into him as he stroked her hair.

For once, Daniel's silence had nothing to do with his temperament, but his grief.

"I take it we have a deal?" Miranda asked.

He stalked out of the office without answering.

Her cackle followed him down the hall.

I HAVE TO KNOW IF IT'S TRUE, DANIEL REALIZED.

But first things first.

The mother of Noah's best friend was totally open to the idea of a sleep-over. "Why should I mind? My God, you and Audrey have covered for me more times than I can remember, so go for it. You lovebirds deserve an out of town getaway."

He had no answer for that. He couldn't even admit to himself that the only reason he'd be catching the next flight to LAX was to check up on his wife—

And the man who may have put his family in legal jeopardy.

His next call was to Vance Melamed. "I'm sorry to call you so late, but after our call earlier today, I needed confirmation before reporting something I feel falls in your jurisdiction."

Vance paused before asking, "What, exactly?"

"If you need proof that Miranda D'Arcy may be cheating to get her clients' children into certain colleges, I think I can verify it for you."

"Yes, anything you can bring forward will be useful, Daniel. Why don't we meet on Monday, say at noon, at my office?" He chuckled, then added, "You did the right thing."

<hr />

AFTER MELAMED HUNG UP, HE TURNED TO THE OTHERS IN HIS OFFICE: LIONEL, SallyAnne, and Riley. "I assume you were able to catch the audio on his conversation with Maleficent?"

SallyAnne smothered a grin. Lately, she'd noticed that Melamed had been calling Miranda by the nickname he'd once forbidden.

"Whenever she doesn't want us listening in, she leaves her phone in another room. I guess she didn't figure we'd tap Daniel's phone, which worked in his favor: it allowed him to get her to admit she shifted those funds in his name from the school's bank account to one of her offshore stashes," Lionel replied.

"We can now add embezzlement to Miranda's rap sheet," SallyAnne added.

"Now that we know Daniel is clean, should we cancel his surveillance?" Riley asked.

"Not yet," Melamed answered. "As angry as he is, he'll certainly confront Egan on what he knows about Miranda's activities. Who knows what he'll get Egan to confess to?"

"You mean, like the fact that Egan has never gotten over Daniel's wife?" Riley declared.

Hearing that, SallyAnne stared triumphantly at Lionel until he blushed.

"Yeah, that too," Melamed chuckled. "Ain't love grand?"

CHAPTER 17

*U*pon hearing from Chuck that Daniel had offered to chaperone the Debate Eight during the tournament, Egan had resolved himself to be civil and gracious to Audrey's husband, despite his suspicions about Miranda's payoff.

But at noon, it was Audrey who pulled up in the SUV that Daniel used for the family's bike trips: a Toyota Sequoia.

Egan's heart did a backflip.

"Daniel had an office emergency." Avoiding his gaze, she added, "I assume the sooner we load the kids into the cars, the sooner we'll get out of Bay Area traffic."

He nodded. Turning to the debaters, he exclaimed, "Okay, team, wagon ho! Choose your rides."

Since there were only three boys—Chuck, Quest, and Hugo—Fawn decided to ride with the boys in Egan's rented mini-van.

The other girls piled in with Audrey.

***

THE EVENT THAT WAS TO BE THE PINNACLE OF CHARLY'S SENIOR YEAR HAD JUST turned into a nightmare.

When Chuck had told Charly he'd reached out to their parents to substitute for Cornell, she'd bitten her tongue to keep from groaning aloud. With what she suspected, it was hard enough being around Audrey and Daniel. The last thing she needed was to have one of them smiling benignly at her as she walked onto the tournament stage.

Chuck later reported that Daniel had agreed to go. As anxious as that notion made her, she was fascinated at the prospect of watching him interact with Egan. Daniel had been gracious in underwriting Egan's chair. At the debate matches Daniel had attended, they were friendly enough with each other. This gave her hope that her assumption regarding her paternity would prove false. That Egan's inscription in Audrey's copy of *Extracurricular* was no more than a casual flirtation.

But now that Audrey was here instead, Charly almost fainted. She'd forced herself to dam up her fears about her mother's past until the DNA test results were in. But should Audrey or Egan show even an inkling of desire for the other, any respect she had for the lovelorn would release the torrent of revulsion barely contained in Charly's heart, washing away the promise she'd made to herself—to give her mother the benefit of the doubt.

Thank goodness the chatter of her friends shielded her desperate silence.

When they hit the halfway mark of the journey, both cars stopped for gas.

Egan suggested that the passengers change places. The girls were fine with that. Audrey figured they found it easier gossiping in Egan's presence as opposed to hers since he knew all the players in the perennial drama that was Ashbury Academy.

She was relieved when Chuck rode shotgun as opposed to crawling into the back seat with Fawn.

Obviously miffed at his choice, Fawn pulled Hugo into the far-backseat with her.

Quest groaned, "Can't you two wait until we get to the hotel?"

Audrey glanced over at Chuck in time to catch his scowl.

The tediously interminable trip just got even longer.

The caravan arrived at the Los Angeles hotel just after eight that evening.

Despite the two baskets of healthy snacks that Audrey had brought along for the ride—water bottles, apples, bananas, power bars, dried cranberries, and raisins—by then, everyone was famished.

"We'll check in first. Give yourselves a half-hour in your rooms to freshen up, and then we'll grab a bite to eat," Egan ordered.

He walked over to the front desk while the students and Audrey waited in the lobby. A few minutes later, he strolled over with a handful of keycards.

He tossed one to Quest. "This is for you, Hugo, and Chuck. The room has two queen beds and a fold-out couch. You can flip for who gets the couch. Like me, you guys are on the third floor."

He handed Manya another keycard. "Second floor, as is Ms. Thorpe's room. It has the same set-up as the boys' digs." He pointed to Zina and Sienna. "Have fun, roomies."

Fawn and Charly turned to each other, horrified.

"Ladies, I can think of nothing that would make me happier than knowing you're burying the hatchet someplace other than each other's skulls. For the team's sake, I hope the next two nights will result in a peace pact."

He handed Charly the keycard. "Also on the second floor."

Fawn frowned. "Only *one card* per room?"

"No, there are two," Egan replied. "But your floor chaperone—that would be Audrey for the girls, me for the boys—will be holding the second ones."

Incensed, Fawn snatched the key from Charly and stalked off to the elevator, suitcase in hand.

Hugo grabbed his bag and went off after her.

Egan handed Audrey her key and then two others. "Your room is in the middle of theirs. That way, if for any reason you hear anything suspicious, you can enter at your own risk."

"Just like old times," Audrey muttered. "Considering how much of tonight may end up being 'don't ask, don't tell,' maybe it's a good thing I came instead of Daniel."

Egan kept his mouth shut.

He couldn't agree more.

EVEN IF THEY HADN'T BEEN THE ONLY TWO PEOPLE IN THE ELEVATOR, FAWN would have slammed Hugo against the wall and ground her mouth in his as a clue of what he could expect should he deliver on her next request: "Hey, so, have you got any Valium in your goody bag?"

Hugo snickered. "Of course, among other products: pot, coke, Adderall, some E—you name it. With all these competitors freaking out over this tournament, there should be a lot of takers."

He unzipped his bag, pulled out a baggie, and plucked two pills from it.

Hugo handed them to Fawn. Scrutinizing it, she asked, "How potent is this stuff?"

"Five milligrams. It's a knock-you-on-your-ass dose." He eyed her curiously. "So, you into that stuff?"

Fawn shook her head. "You know me. I'm all about all-natural highs and lows." With a come-hither wink, she stuck her thumb in her mouth.

He showed his anticipation with a giggle.

If there was one thing Fawn hated, it was a guy whose laugh was higher than hers. But if he were willing to give her the pills, she'd plug her ears and follow through with a little quid pro quo.

"Nah. It's for a friend," Fawn explained. "She's with one of the other competing schools. Why don't you leave a couple of them with me now, while we're, um...*alone?*" She twisted his nipple as an incentive.

That's all it took—along with a promise to meet him after lights out in the private room he'd booked the moment he found out the hotel Egan had reserved for them. "It's on the fourth floor," he told her.

"Sure," she promised.

But only as long as it took for her to slip him one of the Valiums. She planned on crushing it into his drink so that he'd pass out.

Hugo Smallwood was a total dud in bed. He expected her to do all the work. And, ironically, living up to his last name, he gave her surprisingly little to work with. Not that it mattered. Better he was too zoned out to get it up than miss out on a good night's sleep before the tournament.

Yet another reason she missed Chuck terribly. When it came to sex, he always gave it his all.

Well, he wasn't coming back. She saw that now.

Her scheme to use Hugo Smallwood to make Chuck jealous backfired. Her ex was seemingly immune to her attempt to make him jealous. Instead, it now seemed he looked upon her with contempt.

Charly had won in splitting them up.

Payback would be sweet.

That's where the second Valium came in.

"MAYBE EGAN IS RIGHT. MAYBE WE SHOULD AT LEAST TRY TO GET ALONG—FOR the sake of the team." Fawn could tell her peace offering took Charly by surprise because the other girl quit brushing her hair mid-stroke.

The girls had staked out their sides of the room in silence. In a few minutes, they'd head downstairs with everyone else.

If Fawn was going to have her kumbaya with Charly, it was now or never.

"Being civil to each other would be better for morale, for sure." Charly's words were slow and wary. "Fawn, listen. I know we got off on the wrong foot this year for...for a lot of reasons."

"Only one reason, really," Fawn retorted. "Chuck."

Charly frowned. "Chuck and I love each other. And we respect each

other. And, admittedly, I couldn't really see you two together...long term..."
The second the words were out of her mouth, she regretted it.

From Fawn's wince, Charly realized the damage was already done.

"'Long term?' What do you mean by that?" But of course, Fawn knew.

"I didn't mean it the way it sounded."

Fawn shrugged. "Sure, you did. But, hey, if he was my brother and someone like me had him wrapped around her little finger, I'd feel exactly the same—insecure. Jealous." She put her hand on Charly's arm. "But now that I'm out of his life, maybe you can stop judging me. In a few months, we'll probably never see each other again."

"We may end up at the same college," Charly countered.

Fawn snickered. "Trust me—*we won't*. And in the long run, any memories we have about each other will seem like a bad dream." She shrugged. "So, at least for this weekend, let's put aside our differences. You know, take one for the team, as they say." She held out her hand.

She's right, Charly thought.

So, she shook it.

THROUGHOUT THE TEAM'S DINNER, CHUCK DID HIS BEST TO KEEP FOCUSED ON the group's strategy discussions as opposed to any chitchat.

Egan warned them that the participating teams wouldn't be given the debate questions beforehand. Once the questions were announced, the teams would have two hours to prepare their arguments.

He felt Egan had done the right thing by asking each teammate to assess the role they wanted at the tournament. Quest, Manya, Zina, and Hugo chose to focus on the research needed to make the arguments. Hugo's rationale was simple: "The last thing I need at this shindig is a high profile."

Fawn, Sienna, Chuck, and Charly were to rotate either the pro, con, or rebuttal arguments.

Occasionally, Chuck glanced over in Fawn's direction. It broke his heart to see her playing up to Hugo. He found it hard to believe that she was doing it to make him jealous.

I mean, come on already—the guy is the school's most infamous drug dealer! What's the future in that?

One thing that surprised Chuck: Charly and Fawn seemed to be getting along. Whenever Fawn interjected something into the group's conversation, Charly complimented her insights. Fawn reciprocated by deferring to some of Charly's suggestions. When both girls reached for the last garlic roll in the breadbasket, Charly insisted that Fawn eat it. Instead, Fawn split it and gave half to her roommate.

At that moment, Chuck felt there might be hope for their relationship—

Until she did something that curdled his stomach.

Halfway through the meal, he'd seen Fawn grab her purse and walk toward the restaurant's lavatory.

Chuck got up to follow her. He thought maybe they could have a word alone—

But then Fawn veered into the restaurant's bar. There, Fawn signaled the bartender for something. The man nodded, grabbed an empty glass, filled it with water, and handed it to her.

After she thanked him and he turned to serve another customer, she pulled something out of her pocketbook: a baggie. It contained some sort of powder, which she poured into the glass. She grabbed a swizzle stick, stirred the water, and then took the glass with her into the restaurant.

Chuck watched as Fawn moved the glass behind her so that it wouldn't be evident that she'd brought it with her. As the others laughed and talked, it was easy for her to place it on the table without being noticed.

With some sleight of hand, Fawn replaced Charly's water glass with the one from the bar while her head was turned.

Chuck was incensed.

What did she put in the water—a roofie?

Angered, Chuck was about to ask Fawn what the hell, but just then, Hugo leaned into Fawn for a kiss. Fawn glanced across the table at Chuck. Noting his scowl, she planted her lips on Hugo's mouth.

The kiss was long enough, and Chuck was angry enough to switch Fawn's water glass with the doctored one.

Chuck grimaced. Fawn was about to get a taste of her own medicine.

"Look, it's an Easter miracle! Fawn and Charly are getting along!" Egan murmured to Audrey. He nodded at the larger table behind her, where his students sat, eating and talking.

Her head whipped around. Seeing the proof, she let loose with a slow whistle. "Will miracles never cease—even on the Ides of March!"

Egan laughed. "By Jove, you're right! I've been so consumed with the tournament that I'd almost forgotten today's date." He tilted his wine glass at her. "Here's to a Shakespearean reference that few remember or care about."

Chuckling, Audrey moved her glass away. "I will not drink to that, and neither should you! The Sweet Swan of Avon is weeping in Heaven to hear one of his most ardent admirers turn on him that way!"

Egan laughed too—not at her statement but at the realization that Audrey was laughing and enjoying herself.

"Seriously, Egan, as inspiring a teacher as you are, you could be instructing at any university in the country." Her smile faded. "I wouldn't blame you if you left AA, what with the changes that are sure to happen now that Lavinia is gone."

"You sound as if you want to get rid of me." His tone was light enough, but he was dead serious about seeing how she responded.

"Not at all. I think of you as...a valued friend." She sounded as if she meant it.

"That means the world to me, Audrey. I would never do anything to lose your respect and trust."

She reached out and took his hand. "I realize that now. Thank you."

He was touched by the gesture.

He squeezed her hand tightly.

Yes, he thought, we can be friends.

But just beyond her head, something happening at the students' table caught his eye: Chuck was switching Fawn's glass with another.

He watched as the boy smirked at his former girlfriend and the new love of her life.

"Excuse me." Abruptly, Egan stood up. In a flash, he was next to the students' table.

CHARLY HAD SEEN IT ALL.

The ease with which Audrey and Egan bantered and laughed together.

The look of longing in Egan's eyes.

Audrey's gentle deflection of his adoration with a mere touch of acknowledgment and a gaze of appreciation.

She knew now that no matter what had happened between them, her mother had decided it had no place in her future.

It must be devastating to love someone who can't love you back, Charly realized.

Shamed at her own voyeurism, she shifted her eyes away.

It couldn't have been long—just a few seconds. Still, suddenly, Egan was shouting at Chuck.

Fawn was picking up her glass.

Egan snatched it away from her.

"What the heck?" she exclaimed.

Everyone at the table turned and stared as Egan pointed to Chuck. "You—with me—*outside!*"

Chuck's face lost all its color. "But...you don't understand!"

"You're going to explain it to me—now!" Egan held out the glass. "Unless you'd like to take a big swig of this."

Chuck's eyes grew large. "No!"

Egan growled, "Why not?"

"Because...I don't know what's in it."

"If that's the case, why did you change out Fawn's glass so that she'd drink from it instead?" Egan asked.

"I'd like to explain—in private," Chuck insisted.

Egan's stare shifted to Fawn. "Okay. We'll talk in my room." He turned to Audrey. "You should join us." To the others, he added, "Everyone, back to your rooms immediately."

Stunned, the group made their exodus in silence.

CHUCK SAW ME DO IT, FAWN THOUGHT. AND YET, HE WON'T SNITCH ON ME.

Knowing that shamed her.

She walked with the others back to their rooms, dazed by the knowledge that she'd just ruined Chuck's life.

CHAPTER 18

"What was in the water?" Egan leaned back on his bed as if to indicate they had all the time in the world to get the truth out of Chuck.

Audrey chose not to say a word. Instead, she took her place in the room's only chair.

That left Chuck standing.

And sweating. A sheen of dampness rose on his forehead.

He glanced at his mother. The look on her face—a mix of sadness and confusion—shamed him.

Finally, Chuck muttered, "I don't know what's in the glass." He raised his head to look Egan in the eye. "But whatever it was, I didn't put it there."

"I saw you myself, Chuck! You swapped her glass with the one you refused to drink from!" Furious, Egan rose from the bed. "Look, I know the break-up between you and Fawn hasn't been easy. And I see how she likes to tease you by flirting with Hugo. Still, I never expected you'd stoop so...*low!*" He shook his head.

"I'm telling you—I didn't do it!" Chuck retorted.

"But you knew something was in there. And you wanted her to drink it," Egan countered. "Am I right?"

Chuck couldn't deny that.

"If you didn't put it in there, then who did?" Egan asked.

Chuck stayed silent. But out of the corner of his eye, he watched as his mother bowed her head: in shame, he imagined.

"I'm sorry, but you're suspended from Debate Team," Egan murmured. "And when we get back to school, I'll take up the issue of your suspension with Miranda. If she agrees, it will affect your ability to graduate. I hope you realize that."

"Well, then it's a done deal."

Egan frowned. "What do you mean by that?"

Chuck shrugged. "I think you know what I mean."

———

THE SAT TEST.

He's going to mention it here—now, in front of Audrey.

Egan's glance shifted to his son's mother. Her anguish had drained all the color from her face.

Instead of responding, Egan muttered, "You may go to your room now."

Stunned, Chuck left the room.

Egan turned toward Audrey. "I'm sorry."

"Do you think he did it?" Audrey voiced the question with no fear, no malice.

"No, I don't. But I thought he'd be honest and tell me who did." Egan sat back down on the bed. "You know I'll have to follow through on the disciplinary action. If Fawn had been harmed—"

"I know," Audrey whispered.

Wearily, Egan closed his eyes.

He could feel Audrey drop onto the bed beside him. When he opened his eyes, she was staring at him. The concern in her eyes touched him deeply.

"Raising kids is hard, isn't it?" she murmured.

Egan felt a lump rising in his throat. Still, he was able to mumble, "Yeah. Go figure."

When he bowed his head, Audrey patted his hand. "Thank you for believing Chuck. And thank you for loving him enough to do the right thing."

The team was supposed to spend at least the next hour on drills. Between the drive, the anxiety over the tournament, and Audrey's sudden appearance, the day had already been too long.

All Egan wanted to do was get some sleep.

And mourn his son's mercurial fall from grace.

He dropped his head onto Audrey's shoulder.

She didn't move. Instead, she took his hand and squeezed it.

They sat there, just like that, for a moment before she asked, "What did he mean by that?"

"Who?" Egan murmured.

"Chuck. He said… Let's see…" she thought for a moment: "It's a done deal."

"Tell the truth, Fawn. Chuck didn't try to hurt you. Am I right?" Charly flopped down on Fawn's bed so that the girl would have to look her in the eye.

Fawn had been crying since they walked into the room. Charly should have felt sympathy. What Chuck tried to do was horrendous.

But that's just it. Charly wasn't sympathetic.

She was suspicious.

Fawn's sobs died away. She did her best to wipe her face with the palm of her hand, only to smear the mascara already running down her cheeks in damp black trails. "No. He was just trying to save…" Ashamed, she dropped her head. "The glass was meant for you. I'd doctored it with a Valium. It would have knocked you out through the morning, and—"

Charly was too astonished to speak.

At first, she wanted to laugh.

Then she wanted to slug Fawn.

She settled for asking, "Bitch! Like… *What were you thinking?*"

"That, finally, you'd be out of the running, and I'd outshine you!" Fawn fell back onto her pillows. "Do you know what it's like living in the shadow of someone who's so—so perfect? It's always been like that with you! You're the perfect student. The perfect friend. The perfect daughter. You were even the perfect granddaughter—"

"Lavinia never played favorites!" Charly retorted.

"That's the point! She didn't have to!" Fawn shook her head in exasperation. Suddenly, she was crying again. "And you were—*are*—the perfect sister too."

She was crying so hard that she heaved.

Charly couldn't help it. She felt sorry for her. As she put her arms around the girl, she muttered, "Jesus, Fawn…"

The crying went on for so long that Charly was worried Fawn would never stop. When the sobs finally subsided, Charly whispered, "What do you want to do now?"

Fawn shrugged. "It's not exactly up to me, is it?"

"Yes, it is." Charly leaned back on the headboard. "You just bitched to me about how you see me as 'perfect.' Well, here's your chance to be 'Charly.'" She sighed. "So, what would Charly do?"

Fawn sighed. "She–*you*—would tell Egan the truth and let the chips fall where they may."

Charly nodded. "Well, there you go. So now, what will *you* do?"

Fawn opened her mouth to speak—

But there was a knock on the door.

Charly got up to open it.

Daniel stood out front. "High, gorgeous." He gave her a kiss on the forehead.

Surprised, Charly stepped out, pulling the door behind her. "Wow, you came after all!" She looked around, perplexed, "Where's Noah?"

Daniel grimaced. "He's at a sleepover. Something came up that... It needs your mother's attention." He looked at the door. "Is she in there with you?"

Charly shook her head. "No, just Fawn. We're, um…getting ready to meet the others for rehearsal."

Daniel grinned, surprised. "Well, that's…nice."

Charly ignored it. "Mom is next door." She nodded to the door farther down the hall.

Daniel shook his head. "I knocked there first."

"Oh… Well then, she must still be with Egan. They—"

"What's his room number?"

"Let's see. It's next to Chuck's, which is over mine. So right over Mom's."

"Sounds about right," Daniel muttered.

He was at the elevator in a flash.

THE DOOR WAS OPEN—NOT ENTIRELY, JUST A CRACK.

Daniel nudged it open—not entirely at first, but enough to look in and see if anyone was there.

Yes, there they were. They sat side by side on the bed. Egan's head was bent over Audrey's. Their hands were clasped.

When he took a step closer, he noticed that their eyes were closed.

What. The. HELL?

Audrey murmured softly, "It's a done deal?"

What was a done deal? What were they planning?

Jesus—

Miranda was right.

It took all of three strides for him to reach the bed.

Egan opened his eyes at the wrong time—just as Daniel's right fist hit the left one.

Egan groaned as he fell back onto the bed.

Leaping up, Audrey screamed, "Daniel… *What are you doing?*"

As Daniel rubbed his fist, he muttered, "A better question is what are you doing—with him?"

"We were discussing our…son!" Audrey retorted angrily.

"Chuck? Why? What has he done now?"

SOMETHING IS VERY WRONG.

Charly had never seen her father so upset.

A thought struck her: *Does he know about Mother and Egan?*

Anxiously, she grabbed the keycard and exclaimed, "Fawn, look—I have to go up to Egan's."

Fawn stood up. "I'm going with you. I need to tell him the truth."

The elevator took a couple of minutes. By the time the girls got to Egan's, Daniel was already in the room—

And Egan was nursing a bruised face.

Audrey shook angrily.

Charly stared, horrified. Turning to her mother, she whispered, "Did you tell him?"

"I tried, but he didn't want to listen." She reached for Charly's hand. "I'm sorry you have to see your father this way."

My father…

Which one does she mean?

Charly was almost afraid to ask.

"Tell me what?" Daniel asked.

Oh…shit.

Before she could answer, Fawn exclaimed, "Mr. McKittridge, don't be angry at Egan! I was to blame."

Perplexed, Daniel declared, "What are you talking about?"

"The water glass—I did it, not Chuck. I was the one that put the Valium in there. It was meant for"—Fawn blushed—"for Charly. Chuck must have seen me do it, and he wanted to stop me."

"No, really, I wanted to teach you a lesson." Chuck's voice came from the front door. "It was stupid of me. I should have just dumped the water."

"You were protecting Charly," Fawn pointed out. "Egan shouldn't suspend you. He should suspend me."

"Don't tempt me." Egan warned her. He rose from the bed. "As much as you'd like to believe I was moved by your confession, I'm just being practical. Ashbury Academy deserves your best. *Lavinia deserves it*, God rest her soul. So, since no one got drugged, maimed, or killed, all your idiotic acts committed in the name of love, hate, or vengeance are absolved, and the confessional is now officially closed." Reaching for the ice bucket, Egan added, "Breakfast is at seven, at which time our tournament questions will have been emailed to me. If you are not in the hotel's restaurant by then, don't bother showing up to the tournament—*and you can find your own way home.*" He started for the door. "Now, if you'll all excuse me, I've got to grab some ice for this shiner. Unless you know first aid, don't feel the need to stick around."

He stormed down the hall.

A moment later, ice could be heard clanking into the bucket.

Chuck and Fawn skedaddled.

Warily, Charly looked at Audrey and Daniel. "Mom... Do you need me?"

"Thank you, honey, but no. Your father and I need to talk." Audrey's icy stare was aimed at Daniel.

My father.

Daniel.

Together, Charly and her parents walked to the elevator.

To Charly, the one-floor ride seemed the longest in her life.

"Why are you here?" Audrey's question to Daniel was simple enough.

Because Miranda is tearing down the school, one illegal act at a time.

Because the FBI will soon be arresting parents for helping her.

Because I don't trust you.

Daniel knew the answer he gave would be complicated. He took a deep breath, and started from the beginning:

He told Audrey about his conversation with Tallulah on the flight home from New York;

And how he got the firm's private investigator to check into Miranda D'Arcy and discovered that her previous employer had bought out her contract and sent her packing.

He mentioned his calls: first to his old acquaintance who was Rob Edelson's partner, who told him that the FBI had come looking for Rob, and then to his new acquaintance, Vance Melamed, who headed the FBI office.

"Vance didn't deny that his office was looking into Miranda—which is just as good as a confirmation," Daniel explained.

And, finally, Daniel told Audrey about his confrontation with Miranda, and how she told him she'd shifted his endowment donation to Egan into her concierge program's account to make him complicit in her scheme.

"That way, I'd keep my mouth shut," he explained. "But I told her I wouldn't. And I'm not. In fact, I've set up an appointment with Melamed for first thing on Monday."

Audrey took all of this in silently. When he was through, she replied, "Miranda had Egan drill the students involved. He was also their test proctor. Do you think he may be involved too?"

Daniel shrugged. "She didn't say. But that doesn't mean he isn't."

"You should ask him," Audrey insisted.

Daniel smirked. "Do you think he'd tell me the truth?"

"Of course! Why would he lie?"

"Because he may be involved." Daniel let that sink in.

"That's ludicrous! Why would Egan risk everything for—*for her?*"

"You mean, as opposed to you?"

She stared at him as if he were a stranger. "What are you asking, Daniel?"

"Audrey, tell me the truth: do you love him?"

HE ASKED.

And I will tell him the truth.

"Not now," she whispered. "But I did, once. A million years ago."

Numbed by Audrey's declaration, Daniel nodded slowly. "So, you and he...were lovers?"

Tell him.

"Just once," she confessed. "A long time ago."

Daniel dropped down onto the bed.

Audrey sat down beside him.

"How does it make you feel, seeing him now?"

She shrugged. "It was odd at first—like a ghost from your past who appears out of nowhere. You recognize his features, but you don't remember from exactly where. Then, when it dawns on you, you see that it's trying to communicate, but you no longer talk the same language."

"You said, at first. But not now."

He was seeking clarification. She knew that.

He deserves it.

Fervently, she declared, "Egan and I are just friends. He knows I love you."

Daniel took her hand. He opened it to kiss her palm.

Then he held it to his cheek.

Audrey didn't want it to stop there.

For that matter, neither did he.

There was no need to rush it. Gentle touches. Languorous kisses. Meandering strokes. Each subsequent touch piqued their mutual craving all the more.

In time, their rhythm picked up. Damp with desire, she called out his name.

Ripe with lust, he entered her.

In time, frenzied gasps gave way to slow soft sighs.

As they lay in each other's arms, spent, she whispered, "It was always us."

If only she'd known this back then.

CHAPTER 19

$\mathcal{A}$shbury Academy's debate team had already eaten breakfast by the time Audrey and Daniel went down to the hotel's restaurant the next morning.

While they finished their breakfast, Chuck texted his mother that the debate team had received its tournament argument and was working in one of the hotel's conference rooms and that she was to meet them there.

"Do you want to join me?" She asked Daniel.

He grimaced. "Yes. I need to apologize to Egan—if he'll let me."

"I can't imagine he'd hold it against you. Like us, he knows it was a misunderstanding." She laid down her napkin. "I'll walk in and ask. If he agrees, I'll hang with the kids while you two talk in the hall."

He nodded. "Okay, let's do this thing."

EGAN WAS SURPRISED TO SEE AUDREY. HE WAS SURE SHE'D HAVE APPEASED Daniel and gone home with him. If not, she'd show up when needed, but stay out of his way in any case.

He didn't blame her. For the sake of her marriage and her family's wellbeing, she wanted to protect their secret.

Even at his expense.

So be it.

Despite Audrey's denial to divulge his real role in their lives, he vowed he'd always find a way to be there for them.

To that end, that morning at the crack of dawn, he'd sent a formal termination letter to his literary agency. He also signed the contract proffered a few days ago by the talent agency Davis had recommended, ICA. His agent there, Amy Sorenson, was already crowing that Davis had accepted her price of half a million for the option.

"We asked for an executive producer credit along with creator and screenwriter," she informed him. "The network is excited about it. By the way, can you send me your other books? There may be fertile soil there too."

He was fertile, alright. Mossy, in fact.

"Amy, send it now, and I'll sign it. And I'll give you my bank account number too."

Half a million was enough to secure what he had in mind for Chuck and Charly.

He made the necessary call immediately.

Audrey would find out soon enough.

He wished he could tell Audrey about it now, but he knew it wasn't the right time, despite the wistful smile with which she greeted him as she beckoned him to the door.

He excused himself from the students, who were already busy dividing up the tasks for the four questions.

"Do you need something?" Polite, but cautious.

Audrey's smile wavered. She'd gotten the message. "Daniel would like to offer you an apology."

Egan shrugged. "Would he care to come in and do it? I can't leave the students alone."

"He'd like to talk to you outside. I can watch over them."

"They aren't toddlers. They're here to win their debates, and they need me to help them make some important strategy decisions."

"Yes, I know," she replied coolly. "As you remember, twenty-two years ago I was in their shoes. I won my debates. Perhaps I have something to offer."

Touché.

"If he's willing to apologize, I'm willing to accept his olive branch." Egan forced himself to grin as he walked out the door.

"I'm sorry I punched you." Daniel held out his hand to Egan.

Egan nodded grudgingly as he shook it. "I accept your apology."

Done. Now let's get on with our lives: yours, with the woman I love and the children I should have raised.

As Egan turned to head back inside, Daniel added, "Isn't there anything you'd like to ask me?"

Egan turned around. "Like what?"

"Aren't you even curious as to why I came down here?"

Egan shook his head. "I assume... I guess I thought you were here to watch the twins at the tournament."

"I wish that were the case." Daniel grimaced. "Miranda told me about your affair with Audrey."

"My...*what?*"

Daniel stared silently.

"Daniel, I swear—I am not having an affair with Audrey."

"I know," Daniel admitted. "Not because I believed Miranda. She's a conniver. I figured that out fast." His dismay showed itself with a tremor. "I hate to admit it: I jumped the first flight I could to come here because of what Audrey wouldn't tell me—until last night."

Audrey told him.

Last night.

He accepts the truth...?

"She told me that you and she...I know you were once lovers."

No. She hadn't told him about the twins, Egan realized.

The muscles in his face sagged under the weight of his disappointment.

"Two decades was a long time ago," Daniel continued. "The fact that you still care so much for her...I'm not surprised. Audrey is unforgettable. I'm glad you've accepted her friendship"—he put his hand on Egan's shoulder—"and mine too."

Egan nodded.

"One last thing, Egan. Regarding Miranda." Daniel looked him in the eye: "What do you know about her college cheating scheme?"

"Her...*what?*"

"I have it on good authority that she's being investigated for bribing influential college staffers, faking extracurriculars on admission applications, and fixing SAT tests."

He's testing me. He wants to see if I know he's involved.

Maybe I can make him sweat.

Egan smirked. "I wouldn't doubt it in the least. She'll do anything to prove she can live up to the reputation she's put out there."

Daniel frowned. "You've drilled the students in her concierge program and proctored their tests."

"Yep, I did."

"Has she given you any special instructions—you know, in that regard?"

"Are you asking me if she's bribed me to fix the tests—specifically, your son's?"

Daniel shrugged. "Yes, something like that."

"After last night, I know you'd like to believe the worst about me. But Daniel, I will tell you flat out." Egan looked him straight in the eye: "Chuck earned his grade fair and square."

Daniel nodded. In fact, he looked relieved. "Good to know."

Egan wanted to laugh. But if Daniel had paid Miranda to fix Chuck's test, sometime today he'd be screaming at her about being hoodwinked.

However, if Daniel wasn't bluffing and the Feds were onto her, Egan knew they'd be knocking on his door soon too.

And yet, Egan's respect for the man would be renewed.

But that still didn't stop Egan from wishing they could trade places.

CHAPTER 20

It was a true tribute to Ashbury Academy that its debate team placed sixth in the state competition, more so because—as Egan put it to Audrey—it was accomplished without anyone dying, ending up in the hospital, or going to jail.

The praise could be spread among everyone. The researchers (Quest and Hugo) kept their heads down and pulled together enough statistics, facts, and citations on each of the four topics. Convincing pros, cons, and rebuttals were drafted by Manya and Zina.

And although each portion of the arguments were delivered by Fawn, Sienna, Chuck, and Charly on a rotating basis, it was the twins who were the true stars, keeping their cool under pressure while delivering heartfelt oratories.

Although Audrey was disappointed that Daniel had to fly back immediately after the tournament for an emergency meeting on some major case, she noticed that Egan seemed relieved that her husband had made an early departure.

"I take it you worked through your misunderstanding?" she asked him during the team's celebratory dinner.

Egan shrugged. "He offered an apology. I accepted it. Case closed."

But she could tell he was worried about something. "Did he ask anything out of the ordinary?"

"You mean, about us?"

"Yes." Audrey admitted.

"He seemed to think he knew everything already—at least, as it pertains to us alone."

This was his way of saying: *He didn't mention the twins, nor did I.*

As her eyes misted over, she murmured, "Nothing stays a secret forever."

He frowned when she said that.

He wants us to come clean about the twins. I can't do that. Not yet.

Hopefully, never.

MIRANDA HAD DECIDED THAT SUNDAY WAS THE DAY SHE WAS TO CUT BAIT.

Just yesterday, she'd heard from two of the college coaches in her pocket that acceptances were due any day now. And besides, her conversation with Daniel made her uneasy. By revealing what she'd done to Chuck, she hoped she'd scared him into silence, but who knew for sure? Those by-the-book types were her worst nightmare.

Realizing that the Feds were surveilling her phone and home, and looking through her mail, in February she'd ordered a few burner phones on the school's account and had them delivered there, along with a couple of laptops and iPads, all of which she'd take with her to Ecuador. From what she could tell, it was the only place without a U.S. extradition treaty that wasn't located in a desert or frigid tundra, or run by some dictator.

Then, from one of the new burners, she ordered:

- New suitcases, which she also had delivered to the school.
- New clothes, knowing the Feds were watching her comings and goings for suspicious activities; and
- A private car to pick her up at the school promptly at five-thirty to take her to the private plane that would whisk her away to her new life as a well-heeled fugitive.

Unfortunately for her, Miranda had forgotten one thing: that the debate team was driving back to the school after the tournament, where their parents would be waiting to pick them up.

Gemma arrived first—around four-thirty—taking an empty parking space right in front of the large picture window in Miranda's office.

With no curtains, it was easy to see inside, so Miranda ducked down. *Damn it,* she thought. *I can't afford to be seen here today!*

She'd soon be on the Most Wanted List for having coerced seven of the debate team's families to join her scheme.

Including one she had set up unwittingly: Daniel McKittridge.

At that moment, Jess drove up too. He was there to pick up Hugo—yet another reason to hide. The last thing she needed was for him to look in the window and see her staring back at him. To bide his time while he waited for Hugo, he'd come in and suggest a quickie.

But one look around, and he'd realize what she was doing: going on the lam and leaving him and the others in the lurch.

She'd have to hide somewhere—and quick. If anyone saw her and then mentioned it to the Feds before the plane was wheels up, they'd be able to trace her whereabouts, or worse yet stop her from leaving the country.

Miranda knew the perfect place to hide: the clock tower. That way, she could watch as everyone drove off.

She crawled out of the office on her hands and knees. When she hit the lobby, she ran as fast as she could up the staircase.

THE TEAM PULLED UP IN FRONT OF ASHBURY ACADEMY JUST AFTER FIVE o'clock.

Everyone was tired and ready to go home. Egan was too, but as the others took off, he went inside the school instead. If what Daniel said was true, it was only a matter of time before the police would come for Miranda.

He pulled out his resignation letter and walked over to Miranda's office, where he would lay it on her desk.

THE DOOR WAS CLOSED. ODDLY, THOUGH, IT WAS UNLOCKED, SO HE WALKED IN.
Odder still, beside the couch were several suitcases.

Miranda is here at the school…

Jesus! I've got to leave before she comes back to her office.

Egan hurried to the desk. He was about to drop the envelope when he noticed that she'd left her purse and cell phone on the desk.

A passport lay on top of the purse.

He flipped it open.

The name on it read *PUCCI TEDESCHI*, but the photo was of Miranda.

She's fleeing, he realized.

He stuffed the resignation envelope in his pocket. He couldn't leave it now. Otherwise, she'd know he was there.

Just then, her cell phone lit up. Silently, a text message scrolled across the screen

> *Our apologies! Flight is delayed, as the equipment is still in transit from its last location. New departure time: eight o'clock P.M.*
> *—Galaxy Marquee Airline*

Egan hurried out the door.

BOOK THREE

CHUCK WAS UNPACKING IN HIS BEDROOM WHEN A PING INTERRUPTED THE music mix playing on his AirPods. Now that the Warriors had no shot in hell of making the NBA finals, the only alerts still active were for his college admissions.

He reached for his phone and saw

UC BERKELEY

Then another, and another, and another:

UCLA
UC SAN DIEGO
UC DAVIS

"Shit!" He cried. "*Shit! Shit!*" Even louder, he screamed, "Charly—*come here!*"

CHARLY WAS ALREADY IN THE HALLWAY—SCREAMING.

The rest of the family came out of their bedrooms.

"What the hell is going on?" Daniel exclaimed.

"Berkeley!" Charly and Chuck declared in unison. Then, to each other: "Have you read it yet?"

Both shook their heads, no.

Anxious, Audrey grabbed Daniel's wrist.

Charly did the same to Chuck. "Okay now, together on the count of three—Berkeley first, then UCLA."

Chuck nodded.

"*THREE!*" Noah shouted excitedly.

The twins clicked the links:

Jubilantly, Charly screamed, "Accepted! *Yes! Yes!*"

Chuck stood there, stunned. "Wait listed."

Charly's elation faded. "Oh…Well, look at UCLA."

Chuck grimaced but nodded. One eye closed as he hit the link:

He smiled. "Accepted."

"Hit the others," Charly insisted.

He nodded. Then, one by one: "Accepted…Accepted… Accepted…"

Audrey pulled them both close for a hug. "Congratulations, my scholars!"

Drawing Noah in with him, Daniel clasped his family in a bear hug.

"Ditto. And, by the way, Chuck: if you want to hold out for the final word from Berkeley, you don't have to accept any of the others immediately."

"I know," Chuck replied. "But…maybe it's time we split up the circus."

Charly frowned. "What do you mean by that?"

He put his arms around his sister's neck. "I love you with all my heart. But you cast a big shadow. I think it's time I quit hiding behind it."

Charly gulped back her tears. "So…UCLA?"

Chuck held up a fist. "Go, Bruins!"

CHARLY HAD BEEN SO BUSY UNPACKING HER SUITCASES THAT SHE HADN'T EVEN glanced at her desk.

But now, walking back into her room, the stark white envelope on the tidy surface of her desk stood out.

She walked over to see what it was.

Background Labs

It was from the DNA test center.

Had Noah left it there? Or perhaps Daniel?

The thought that it might have been the latter caused her to flinch.

With each step closer, Charly's heart picked up speed. Her hands trembled as she picked up the envelope. But she paused and took a breath before breaking the envelope's seal.

Charly and Chuck were Subject 1 and Subject 2, respectively.

Subject 3 was Noah.

The Paternity Subject was Egan.

If their Y DNA—paternal chromosomes— did not match Egan's, their CPI—Combined Paternity Index—would read zero.

Only Noah's showed zero.

Whereas the maternal half of Noah's DNA matched Chuck's and Charly's, his Paternity Index did not.

In fact, Chuck and Charly's analysis read:

Probability of Paternity: 99.9998%

STUNNED, CHARLY FELL TO THE FLOOR.

"Charly! Come on down! To celebrate, we're ordering pizza," Noah shouted.

She had to tell Chuck.

But not here.

Somewhere he wouldn't blow up. Break apart.

Cry.

But first, she had to compose herself.

Charly went to the stairwell and called down: "Can I go pick it up?"

After a moment of silence, Audrey called back: "Yes—and thanks."

Charly went back to her room for what she knew Chuck would demand: the evidence for her accusation.

Then she knocked on Chuck's door.

When he opened it, she shushed him. "You have to come with me —*now.*"

The look on her face spoke volumes: *Just do as I say.*

Nodding silently, he grabbed his coat and followed her downstairs.

CHAPTER 21

"*How* long have you suspected?" Chuck's question to Charly came after a few minutes of silence, followed by howling laughter in which he anticipated she'd join in when she felt the joke had gone on long enough.

Instead, she stared at the floor until he got the message that she wasn't kidding.

Charly was ready for his interrogation because she knew it would be the best way to counter his denial.

What worried her most was what form his anger would take.

They'd pulled the car over a few streets away from the house. Charly felt it was better than divulging the truth on some park bench. If things got ugly—if he shouted or cursed or cried—she didn't need any passersby to stare. Or worse, offer them sympathy.

Charly started at the beginning: how, as she cleaned out their mother's old room in Lavinia's house, she'd found Audrey's copy of *Extracurricular* and read the inscription Egan had written inside.

Then she pulled out the book and showed it to him so that he could read it as well.

Chuck was silent as his eyes scanned the page. Finally, he muttered, "He was flirting with her. Big deal! Guys do that all the time. Hell, *I do it...*"

The similarity stopped him cold.

"All guys flirt," he insisted.

"Dad doesn't," Charly countered. "Not even when strange women come on to him."

"He flirts with Mom," Chuck argued.

"No. *He shows her he loves her.* He's not afraid to hold her hand or to hug her or kiss her in public. That is not flirting."

"You're making too big of a deal about this," he protested.

Then Charly showed him the photo contact sheet of Egan from the year he taught their mother. Seeing the red heart drawn around Egan's face, Chuck blanched.

He shook his head, dismayed. He shrugged. "Girlhood crush. No biggie."

Finally, she opened their DNA results from the envelope. "Remember when I asked for your spit? It really wasn't for a science class experiment. It was for a paternity test."

Chuck guffawed. "But—for that, you'd need DNA from Egan and Dad too! How—"

"Egan brushes his teeth after lunch. I swapped out his toothbrush. Most importantly, Noah's sample shows that we have different fathers." She pulled out the information sheet provided with the test results. "Read this."

Chuck stared down at it.

When, finally, he spoke, she could barely make out his words: "Does Egan know?"

"I have no idea," Charly admitted. "Why don't we go ask him?"

EGAN FLINCHED AT THE SOUND OF THE DOORBELL.

He fully anticipated he was to be arrested. And yet, he hadn't expected it to take place so soon.

Or that they'd be so polite about it.

Egan assumed it would happen just like in the movies—that someone would bark, "FBI! Open up!..." a second before the door was shattered with a battering ram.

He peeked out the keyhole. Chuck and Charly were standing there.

My God—has something happened to Audrey?

He flung open the door. "Is everything okay?"

The twins traded glances.

Chuck coughed uneasily, "Egan, um… mind, if we talk?"

"Of course not." Egan moved to one side.

They walked in, looking around cautiously.

Egan could tell they were uncomfortable. Finally, he ventured, "Has something bad happened?"

Charly exclaimed, "No!" at the same time Chuck replied, "Yes!" Then they traded responses. Perplexed, they stared at each other.

Until Charly blurted it out: "You're our father."

Oh, hell, Egan thought.

<hr>

"Does your mother know?" Egan asked.

Chuck gawked. "What? *That you're our dad*? I would guess so! I mean… she's not stupid about *that* kind of stuff." A thought dawned on him. "Are you saying she was a slut?" At a loss for what to say next, he turned to Charly.

"No, of course not!" Egan exclaimed. "My God! She was—*is*—anything but that! What I mean to ask is, does your mom know that you're here?"

"No!" Charly replied. "We just now found out ourselves. And we thought that if you'd been kept in the dark too, you'd…well, that you'd want to know too."

As if proving the point, Charly turned off her cell phone, which had been buzzing persistently since they got there.

Audrey is trying to find them. But they're here. They're asking questions.

He'd dreamt of this moment. Damn it—why hadn't he prepared for it? *Here goes nothing.*

"I knew," Egan admitted. "But only since before Thanksgiving."

Charly's jaw dropped open. "And…you didn't tell us?" she sputtered.

"Your mother asked me not to," Egan pointed out. "She felt it was something that should happen at a later date."

"When?" Chuck retorted. "When she was dead—*or you?*"

"That's a good question," Egan admitted. "Once I found out, I was shocked, certainly. But I was also willing and open to taking on the responsibility of—I wanted to be your father."

"Then you should have, despite what she wanted." Charly's voice trembled with pain. "That's what Dad—I mean, Daniel would have done."

Egan looked sharply at her. "Would he? Do you really think that he would have gone against her wishes—which were based on knowing how much it would hurt the man who thinks you are his children? The man who raised you and loved you with all his heart? Whose every waking breath— *every action*—revolved around his wife and children?"

His words silenced them.

Charly whispered, "But doesn't it make you angry—that he took your place?"

"If you're asking me if she'd told me eighteen years ago that I was a father, would I have come running? Or if, instead, I'd have run away?" Egan shrugged. "Yeah, I'd like to think I would have manned up. I loved Audrey with all my heart. God help me, I still do! *I was just too full of myself to know how to show her.*" Suddenly, he was pacing the floor. "I thought that by writing it into a book and telling the world instead, she'd somehow get the point. But by the time we ran into each other again, she'd already fallen in love with Daniel." Egan winced. "But Audrey made the choice for me. He was the father she wanted for you."

"So, you met up with her again after they were dating?" Chuck pointed out.

"Yes," Egan admitted.

"God! That's so…*disgusting*," Chuck muttered.

Egan scowled. "I admit I'm not perfect!"

"I don't mean you," Chuck retorted. "I mean, our mom! *She wasn't loyal to our dad!*" He shook his head, dismayed. "The way he tells it, he loved her from the very moment he saw her; that he was head over heels in love with her."

Egan laughed wryly. "I know the feeling."

"And that, even when she quit seeing him, he knew he couldn't stop loving her; that he just needed to give her some space—"

"They had a breakup?" Egan interjected.

"Yes…for a few weeks, I guess. She was still at Berkeley, and he was already working for his firm here in the city. It was her senior year. Exams and all…" Chuck shrugged. "But then, one day, she showed up on his doorstep. He asked her to marry him, and she said yes."

Charly stared at him. "How do you know all of this?"

"Dad told me." Chuck shrugged. "It was after Fawn broke up with me the first time. He was trying to explain to me what true love means. That it's more than physical desire. It's when you realize that, no matter what, you never want to leave her side. *Ever.*" He glared at Egan. "Mom knew he'd be there for her, always. I guess she was right about you since it took you all this time to find out about us." Chuck tapped Charly's arm. "Let's go."

Egan blocked the door. "Don't pass judgment on me. You don't know all I've done—"

"What you *haven't* done speaks volumes—or don't you get that?" Angrily, Chuck shoved Egan aside.

Egan shoved back.

The tussle ended when Chuck slugged Egan, and he crumpled onto the floor.

Charly knelt beside Egan. "Chuck—*this is our father!*"

"No, he isn't." He nudged her. "Let's get out of here."

"We can't leave him like this!" she insisted.

"Hell, I can!" The door slammed on his way out.

THE LAST THING CHUCK WANTED TO DO WAS GO HOME. AUDREY WAS ALREADY worried. He knew because Charly's phone wasn't the only one she'd been calling for the past half hour.

And no way was he going to call back.

I have to tell Dad…

Daniel.

Chuck knew that if he were in Daniel's place, he'd want to know.

Once the shock had worn off, would Daniel still love them, or would he resent Audrey so much that it would turn his stomach to look at the twins?

For that alone, Chuck hated Audrey.

All his life, he'd put her on a pedestal. No more. Their mother had always insisted on honesty. But not telling the truth is just as bad as lying.

I need a drink, he thought.

Many of his friends lived there, in the Haight. He'd been at enough parties at their homes to know that the closest liquor store was a few blocks away. No need to drink and drive. Egan lived directly across from Buena Vista Park. He figured he could drink it there. Ruminate about the rest of his life.

The life that he now knew was a sham.

THE ONLY OTHER CUSTOMER IN THE LIQUOR STORE WAS CHECKING OUT THE tequila shelf. When Chuck walked past him, the man—bulked up, frowning—was still glaring at him as he turned the corner.

The store clerk barely glanced at Chuck's fake ID. Chuck had just thrown a twenty on the counter when a voice behind him said, "I'll take that—and anything else you have in your wallet."

Chuck felt something hard against his side.

He didn't turn around. He didn't have to. The frightened look on the clerk's face told him what he needed to know: there was a gun in the man's hand.

Chuck put his wallet on the counter.

"Open it, you moron—and pull out the rest!" To make his point, the man jabbed Chuck even harder.

Chuck nodded. Still, with his eyes on the clerk, he slowly reached for the wallet.

The clerk reached for something too.

Whatever it was, Chuck didn't know because he'd already blacked out from the bullet.

AN ICE PACK BROUGHT EGAN BACK AROUND. THROUGH THE ONE BLOODSHOT eye that didn't hurt when he opened it, Charly's face came into view.

She looked relieved. "How are you feeling?"

"Shitty. Your brother packs a meaner punch than Daniel."

She laughed weakly. "Let me help you up."

With her help, he stumbled to his feet. They stood there, staring at each other.

She broke the silence by asking, "Can you take me home? Chuck took the car."

"Sure. Let me grab my keys."

But when they got outside, Charly frowned. She pointed at Audrey's SUV. "Our car is right there! He must still be around—"

Egan couldn't hear her because of the sirens screeching past them: two police cars and an ambulance.

Instinctively, their eyes followed the vehicles down the block, where it stopped in front of the liquor store.

Fear creased Charly's brow. The next thing Egan knew, she was running toward the ruckus.

Egan didn't think. He just ran after her.

CHAPTER 22

*T*he call to Audrey came from Charly.

She could barely make out what her daughter was saying—something about Chuck and a robbery, and a bullet and all the blood—

And that Audrey needed to come to SF General as soon as possible.

To rouse herself from her stupor, Audrey washed her face in cold water. Then, as calmly as she could, she told Daniel and Noah to grab their coats and meet her at the front door; that she'd explain on the way to the hospital.

SALLYANNE'S MOTHER BELIEVED THE OLD WIVES' TALE—THAT THE WAY TO A man's heart was through his stomach. Since her mother was an old wife and SallyAnne wasn't a wife at all, she felt she had nothing to lose to try it: specifically, on Lionel.

Melamed insisted that the cases would hold up better in court if the charges went beyond intent. Until college acceptances went out and parents paid the requisite tuitions, arrests weren't going to be made. So, now, on a Sunday in which her case was in a holding pattern, SallyAnne baked. Tomorrow morning, she'd take her culinary handiwork into the office break room.

This time, SallyAnne chose to make a dozen lemon meringue pie-lets. She knew it was one of Lionel's favorites. She could tell because he always took two back to his desk.

When her cell phone buzzed, it took her by surprise. She'd been placing one of the tiny pie crusts in its fluted ceramic dish.

588

She glanced over. It was from Melamed:

Maleficent on the run.

Oh…hell!
A second text read:

Pick up EG

Egan…?
Ah, the moment of truth has come.

He's at SF GENERAL

What the…
SallyAnne turned off the oven, then covered the rolled-out dough with wax paper and put it in the refrigerator.

Unfortunately, she'd have to dump the pie filling and meringue mixture down the sink.

She untied her apron before going for her coat, badge, and gun.

It was silly, she knew, but SallyAnne took three minutes to put on some make-up and a dress. Even if Lionel didn't notice, she knew Egan would, for what that was worth.

———

"How did this happen?" Daniel asked.

He'd never seen Charly so scared. She was shivering and hollow-eyed, but the streaks from the tears she'd shed before they came there were still damp on her face.

Daniel's eyes shifted to Egan. "And what are you doing here?"

Egan opened his mouth to say something, then closed it. Instead, he looked at Audrey.

Daniel, too, faced his wife. "Is there something I should know?"

Audrey shook her head, confused.

Charly stammered, "Mom, Chuck and I… *We know.*"

Audrey's lips went white as if she'd received a blow to the back of the head that sent her into shock.

"Tell him, Mom," Charly implored. "It's why Chuck is in there right now!"

"Tell me what?" Daniel demanded. "What the hell is going on?"

"Excuse me, are you Chuck's parents?"

Everyone turned to stare at the doctor standing behind Daniel. Instinctively, Audrey, Daniel, and Egan exclaimed, "Yes!"

Daniel glowered at Egan.

"The wound is not life-threatening. Fortunately, it hit muscle, so no bones or vital organs were damaged. But Chuck has lost a good amount of blood. We need to raise his blood count," the doctor explained. "However, it will take us forty minutes to type his blood unless you're able to tell us now."

"He is …type O," Audrey replied. "Like me, if you need a donation."

"I'm O, too," Charly offered.

"Thanks, we'll let you know." The doctor took off.

Daniel stared at Audrey. "How could that be?"

Perplexed, she asked, "What do you mean? I'm his mother. Of course, I know his blood type!"

"No—I mean…my blood type is AB, so there's no way he's O… Or Charly…"

Daniel's stare pierced Audrey.

And yet, she couldn't look away.

Tell Daniel…about Egan.

"I…didn't know I was pregnant until after you'd proposed." She flinched, as if even whispering her long-held secret would send shock-waves through him.

She could see it had.

Daniel's head dropped to his chest.

When Audrey laid her hand on his arm, he shrugged it away.

Stricken with shame, Audrey shrank against the wall.

"Daniel," Egan muttered, "If it's any consolation—"

Daniel's punch told him it wasn't.

Egan slammed into the wall. As he staggered to his feet, he declared, "That's it! I'm getting a restraining order—"

"Mr. Gable?" The salutation came from a petite pretty brunette.

Pretty…

But vaguely familiar…

Perplexed, Egan replied, "Yes. Do I know you?"

When she held out her hand, it wasn't to shake his, but to show him her badge. "FBI. I'm Special Agent SallyAnne Jagger. We'd like to question you regarding an open case involving Miranda D'Arcy."

So, this is it.

In front of Charly.

In front of Audrey.

"WILL YOU COME WITH ME, SIR?" AGENT JAGGER NODDED DOWN THE HALL.

"I'm going with you," Daniel replied. The declaration slipped out before he could stop himself.

Egan stuttered, "*What? —You just slugged me!* You're full of yourself if you think I want you to represent me as my lawyer!"

Charly glowered at him. "Shut up, Egan! There's a reason my dad gets paid the big bucks."

As the color drained from Egan's face, it seemed to take his ego with him. "*Okay, okay!*" Wild-eyed, he turned to Daniel. "She's right. I... *I need your help, Daniel.*"

Daniel cocked his head. "No shit. But I'm not going for you. I'm going for my...*our kids.*"

"Jesus," SallyAnne murmured. "So...you know?"

Everyone stared back at her.

"Am I the only one in the world who didn't?" Daniel exclaimed. He threw up his hands. "You're right, asshole. Call someone else."

Charly seized his arm. She didn't say a word, but he knew she was begging him.

"Listen, Daniel," Egan muttered, "I know we've had—have—our differences. But...*Damn it, I trust you!* So, please—will you represent me?"

Smirking, Daniel shook his head.

You're one audacious son of a bitch.

Then his gaze caught Audrey's. She too was silent. And she was smiling.

She already knows how I'll answer him.

He should have hated her for that, too. But he couldn't.

Once again, she's putting the children first, he thought. Just like when she chose me over Egan.

He turned to SallyAnne. "I'd suggest you read him his rights. Then we'll cooperate."

CHAPTER 23

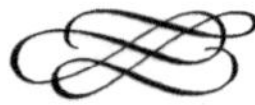

By the way Daniel shook hands with SallyAnne's boss, Division Director Melamed, the two seemed like old friends.

Egan didn't know if that worked in his favor or not. For all he knew, Daniel might allow the Department of Justice to lock him up and throw away the key.

Melamed must have shared the same thought. His eyes grew wide when he saw Egan right behind Daniel. "Wait... you're now representing him?"

"Yep." Daniel shrugged. "Keeping it in the family."

Melamed's laughter filled the room.

Egan didn't like that.

By Daniel's grimace, he didn't either.

Egan's gaze went to Lionel before moving to Riley, then to SallyAnne.

I swear I know her....

At that second, it came to him. "You're the pixie!"

She stared back. "I'm...who?"

"At the bar, that night!" That awful, wonderful, life-changing night. "You were there when I ran into Miranda and she offered me the position of proctor. I now recognize"—he took a good look below her skirt—"your legs, even if you're no longer blond and in mourning."

SallyAnne blushed.

Egan nodded at Lionel. "Teutonic Twit was there too, at the restaurant." He turned to Riley. "And aren't you the mime from Argentina who was at Lavinia's memorial service?"

Riley winced. "I think I said Bolivia."

Melamed slapped his head.

Daniel took a closer look at him, then groaned at missing the connection. "Okay, now that we're all re-acquainted, I'm sure Mr. Gable has information that will help your case." He turned to Egan. "Despite any deal we cut here, a jury will have to convict you, and a judge will sentence you." Daniel leaned in. "Egan, the fact that you're sitting here is proof that they already have the goods on you, which, as Ms. Jagger pointed out, includes bribes for whatever tests you doctored for"—Daniel turned to SallyAnne —"how many students?"

She cleared her throat. "Seven."

"You're wrong," Egan declared.

Noting Melamed's frown, Daniel prodded, "How? Why?"

"I own up to changing some of the tests. Specifically, those turned in from Buck Crawford, Hugo Smallwood, Fawn McCoppin, Quest Wishart-Jammerhead"—he grimaced as he added—"and Zina Sisley-Calder." Egan took a deep breath: "However, I didn't change Manya Patel's score. She achieved it on her own. As did Chuck McKittridge." He turned to Daniel. "I mentioned that down in Los Angeles."

"Yes, we heard it," Lionel replied.

Daniel smirked. "I take it then, I've been under surveillance as well?"

Melamed grinned. "I'm sure you wouldn't have wanted it any other way,"

Daniel shrugged. "You've got me there."

Lionel continued, "And we also videotaped the testing session and what you did afterward, Mr. Gable."

"Good," Egan declared. "Then you'll see I'm telling the truth."

Melamed motioned to Riley. "Cue it up—specifically his actions toward Manya and Chuck's tests."

To the agents' mutual surprise, Egan was right. Other than checking Manya's test, Egan didn't touch it.

He didn't even look at Chuck's.

Lionel shook his head, awed. "Egan, why did you accept Miranda's offer?"

Egan sighed. "Literally an hour before, I'd just found out that"—he glanced at Daniel—"I was the twins' father. To put it lightly, it was a shock. At the same time, I realized how important it was to me to know there were those who, if by their genes only, were my legacy to the world." He looked down. "So, I resolved to do what I could to leave them some sort of legacy too—a financial one, since I'd blown any opportunity for it to be emotional. But I'd just been wiped out. Between my mother's eldercare and the Blackwell settlement—"

SallyAnne snorted. "Yeah, well, you have to hand it to Miranda. She timed that perfectly."

Egan stared at her. "What does Miranda have to do with that?"

Riley shook his head, awed. "Seriously, Dude—you never figured out she's your old student, Mandy Blackwell?"

But then, seeing the shock on Egan's face, he choked back his chuckle.

FOR A MOMENT THERE, EGAN WAS SURE HE'D BLACKED OUT FROM HIS ANGER.

When he got ahold of his fury, it all made sense:

How, when she called on Lavinia's behalf, she'd mentioned being an alumnus;

And how she cooed about she and he "knowing each other in another life."

He remembered how she encouraged him to join the trustee board by claiming Lavinia would need his vote. She then had him nominate her for the board too.

All the while, she flirted with him, even as she was sleeping with Jess.

Even as she coerced parents into her program, behind Lavinia's back.

All the while she dangled carrots like the endowed chair while beating him with the cudgel of the defamation lawsuit.

She's played me every step of the way, he realized.

He nodded to Melamed: "Okay, let's make a deal."

Melamed grinned. "What do you have for us?"

Daniel nodded for Egan to continue.

Egan leaned back in his chair. "I'll bet you don't know where Miranda is now, this very minute."

"If you let us in on the secret, it'll certainly help your case."

"She's on the run—leaving now to catch a private plane out of the country."

"How do you know this?" Lionel asked.

"When I drove back with the debate team a few hours ago, she was at the school. I know this because I was going to turn in my resignation." Egan pulled the envelope from his back pocket so that they could see it. "I walked into her office. She wasn't there, but her luggage was, along with her phone and her passport. In fact, the airline—Galaxy Marquee—sent her a text about her flight being delayed until eight tonight. And by the way, the name on the passport was 'Pucci Tedeschi.'"

He spelled it out slowly as SallyAnne scribbled it down.

"You knew she was about to run. And yet, you stayed put," Melamed pointed out.

"You're right," Egan admitted. "Between what I'd done at Miranda's behest and what Daniel had asked me down in LA, it didn't take a genius to figure out you'd be knocking on my door next." He shrugged. "But I've been running all my life. The truth finally caught up to me. By that, I don't mean this, either. *I mean Chuck and Charly*. Had I run from the knowledge of them, I would have been the worst father ever."

Melamed nodded. "Thanks for the tip-off. Egan, is there anything else you'd like to tell us?"

"Yes. It's regarding the fees Miranda paid me for the students. Please note that the day I received the money, I donated it to the school's scholarship endowment fund."

Melamed grimaced. "Thirty-five thousand times seven…you mean, all two-hundred and forty-five thousand of it?"

Egan nodded. "Check with the receptionist, Clare. She can confirm it. However, Miranda claimed that the money Daniel donated for my endowed chair was Chuck's fee. I don't know how that could be, since Lavinia was good to her word in making sure I received the lion's share of the gift."

"She discussed that with me as well," Daniel added. "I told her I was onto her scam and asked her to resign."

"We heard it too," Melamed admitted. "Now that she's Interim Head of School, she has pulled funds in that amount from one of the school's accounts. We're trying to trace its destination now."

"The judge may be lenient in Egan's sentencing since he didn't actually profit from Miranda's bribe," Daniel pointed out. "It's already happened in a similar case."

"You've got us there," Melamed grumbled. "Considering your attempts to redeem your illegal activity, we'll ask for a lighter sentence. But everything is at the judge's discretion." He turned to Egan. "Maybe you'll luck out and the judge will turn out to be a fan. Gentleman, you're both free to go."

DANIEL RECEIVED A TEXT FROM AUDREY: CHUCK WAS OUT OF SURGERY, AND IN stable condition.

"So, what happens next?" Egan asked Daniel.

"I'm going back to the hospital," Daniel replied. "I assume you'd like to check in with Chuck as well."

"Yes, of course! I mean…I was asking about you and Audrey and…the kids."

"That's between Audrey and me," Daniel replied stiffly. "As far as the kids go, in a few months, they'll be adults. I guess we'll find out how they feel about both of us, now that they know the truth."

The men drove back to the hospital in silence.

As promised, Miranda's private jet was wheels up immediately after eight.

And wheels down after only fifteen minutes in the air.

"Technical difficulty," the pilot explained. "We're returning back to the airport for maintenance."

She stalked up to the cockpit. After giving him and his copilot an earful about their lousy service and lousy planes, she stomped back into the cabin and fumed silently.

When they landed, the pilot suggested that she "feel free to stretch her legs, since the issue may take a while."

Miranda huffed as she made her way down the airstair—

Where a welcoming committee waited to greet her:

Lionel and SallyAnne.

Angrily, she exclaimed, "How did you know where I'd be?"

"Egan," SallyAnne responded. "Welcome back."

By the time Egan and Daniel made it back to the hospital, Chuck was awake: weak, but lucid enough to see them.

Audrey, Charly, and Noah were already at his bedside. When the two men walked in together, Chuck murmured, "I'd like to talk to Egan and Dad alone."

Audrey wasn't surprised by his request. Since he'd regained consciousness, he'd made it a point to avoid looking at or talking to her, let alone answering her questions.

Silently, she left with Charly and Noah.

"I love you, Dad." Chuck's eyes met Daniel's straight on. "I'll never call you anything other than that. It's who you are and will always be to me: my father."

Daniel dropped into the chair beside Chuck. He reached out for the boy's open palm with one hand while he wiped away a tear with the other.

Egan tried not to stare at the tender scene before him, but he couldn't look away.

That could have been me, he thought sadly.

At some point, he realized Chuck had returned his gaze. Taken aback, he looked down at his feet.

"Egan, you will never take my father's place in my heart. But that doesn't mean my heart isn't big enough to open up to the place you hold in my life. To return your love. To appreciate your insights and your guidance. To know you have and will always have the best intentions for Charly and me." He attempted a weak smile. "I'm still a kid. I've fallen *in* love too many times. But when it comes to loving someone outright and with all my heart, there have only been four others: Mom, Dad, Charly, and Noah..." He stopped himself. "No, make that five. God, I loved Lavinia! I miss her now and every day. I hope I never feel differently!" Not willing to take his one good hand from Daniel's grasp, he shook his head so that his tears would break free from the lashes under his eyes. "If she were here now, she'd point out all the ways I'm your son. Don't think I haven't noticed it." He smiled. "I guess what I'm trying to say is that I want to love you too. And I know—no, *I hope*—that we'll have a great many years to prove it to each other many times over." He slid his hand out from under Daniel's and held it out to Egan.

Egan walked over to the bed and took it.

He kissed Chuck's forehead. "Thank you for that."

Then he walked out of the room.

———

"Eventually, Chuck will forgive you," Charly predicted.

Her suggestion, that Noah grab snacks for everyone from the cafeteria, gave her a few moments alone with her mother.

Audrey sighed. "I hope you're right."

"I know from experience. It's why I was so sullen these past few months—you know, after we cleaned out Lavinia's house."

Audrey frowned. "Why? What happened then?"

"I found your keepsake box at the top of your old bedroom closet. It had a small contact sheet of Egan. You'd drawn a heart around one of the photos—the same one that's in your senior yearbook."

"I did what?" Puzzled, Audrey tried to remember...

Mandy Blackwell.

Her guffaw startled Charly. "What's so funny?"

"I didn't draw the heart. Another girl did. She hated me. She even went so far as to steal a book from my desk that I'd used to research my debate topic. She'd used the photo strip as a bookmark." The memory brought a grimace to Audrey's lips. "It was Tallulah's idea that we raid her locker and take it back." She shrugged. "We also took her favorite boots."

Charly chuckled. "The Doc Martens in your closet?"

"Yes! *Oh, my God*! I'd forgotten I left them there!" Now Audrey was laughing too, which threw Charly into a giggling fit.

To keep from falling down, they held onto each other.

When their chortles subsided, Audrey gasped, "Goodness, I wonder what happened to *her*?"

"She must have been in your class, right?"

Audrey shook her head. "A class behind."

Charly smirked. "I wonder if she still goes by 'Mandy!' That's such a... I don't know, cutesy tweenish kind of name, don't you think? I mean—it's a nickname, right? For what?" She thought for a moment. "Amanda? Miranda?..."

Miranda.

MIRANDA D'ARCY.

The hair was different: blond and straight as opposed to red and curly.

She was no longer dumpy, but what had Bliss said? "Oh yeah: "She's had some work done on her face, and God knows where else..."

But the height was the same.

And that voice, too—when it wasn't drenched in syrupy sweetness.

And now this.

I need to tell Daniel as soon as possible.

She looked up to see Charly frowning at her. "Mom, what's going to happen to you and Dad?"

"He and I... Frankly, I don't know, honey. We need to talk." Audrey blinked away her tears. "He has every right to feel used. And I have no excuse for what I did, other than to say I didn't know I was pregnant until after I accepted his marriage proposal."

"Well, that counts for something."

Audrey pulled her daughter close for a hug. "We shall see."

CHAPTER 24

*R*ealizing that their parents needed time to talk alone, Charly suggested that she take Noah out for pizza.

Noah knew this too. Before driving off, he took one of his parents' hands in each of his. Squeezing tightly, he said softly, "I love you—both."

Audrey and Daniel drove home in silence. She assumed he was waiting for her to say something, but she didn't know where to begin.

After opening the front door, he let her walk through first. He followed her into the living room, to their favorite spot: the couch facing the fireplace. It was the first piece of furniture they'd purchased as a couple. The cushions had been replaced twice, but the fabric, originally a colorful brocade, was now fading.

Every now and then Audrey thought of replacing it. But it felt as if she'd also be tossing away eighteen years of memories they'd shared, and conversations they'd had, as they sat there, side by side.

Tonight, though, they sat on opposite ends.

It's just like our marriage, Audrey thought sadly. Worn thin by all the things I've never said.

Well, now is the time.

She put it simply to him: "Ask me."

He thought for a beat, then nodded. "Tell me everything. From the beginning."

So she did.

About how they met. And how they ended it.

And all the missed opportunities in between.

It wasn't easy: admitting what it was like to hold onto an ideal about love. Not the real thing, but the fantasy:

Egan.

"If I'd only known then what I know now. That we'd never have been a good fit."

"Why do you say that?" Daniel asked.

"Because he was used to it from everyone: the adoration; the flirtations." She grimaced. "I vowed I wouldn't be just one more AA schoolgirl with a crush on him."

"And because you weren't, he wanted you even more badly," Daniel pointed out.

"It didn't seem so at the time," she countered. "He made that quite clear, up to the very last time we saw each other."

"In what way?"

"He told me AA had been just a job to him. A way to pay the bills while he wrote on the side." She shrugged. "It must have been true because the one opportunity he had to kiss me—right after I'd graduated—he didn't."

"Is that why you went to see him after the book was written?"

"Yes," Audrey admitted. Tears misted her eyes. "How I wish you'd gone with me that night!"

"Do you think that would have made a difference?"

She guffawed. "Of course! Don't you?"

Thoughtfully, Daniel shook his head. "I think it would have prolonged the inevitable. You said it yourself: he was 'an ideal.'"

"And you were my reality," she insisted.

"As much as you'd allow me to be." He shrugged. "I tried hard, Audrey. Really, I did! To respect you. To honor your boundaries." He stood up. "But let's face it: they were there because of Egan."

Audrey frowned. "What do you mean by that?"

"When we met, you were in your last year of college. You were still a virgin because no one lived up to your ideal of him." He smiled wryly. "And, apparently, no one lived up to his ideal of you, either. But at least it made him money, got him some success."

"After he and I...after we made love, I felt ashamed."

"Why?"

"Because I'd waited too long for him! I wasted too much time! I needed to let others in. I should have let *you* in. I almost lost you!" She sighed. "And now, I may lose you again."

"For now, anyway." He smiled wistfully. "I'm moving out, Aud. I need some space."

Now the tears were flowing harder. She shook her head. "No, don't! This is on me." She stood up. "Please stay with the kids. They need you, now more than ever. In his own way, isn't that what Chuck told you?"

"What do you mean?"

"That, no matter what role Egan eventually takes in Chuck's life, you are and will always be his father? And that he needs you, now more than ever?"

Daniel cocked his head, surprised. "How did you know?"

"How could it be any other way?" Audrey smiled through her tears. "Daniel, I rocked their world. You can steady it again—if you stay at the house."

"Okay—but only if you insist." He took her hand. "Will you stay at Lavinia's?"

Laughing, she shook her head. "No. Believe it or not, we've already received an offer! It came while Chuck was in surgery." She shrugged. "Full asking price, sight unseen. Cash deal, so no escrow. Of course, I told the realtor we accepted. She suggested that I hand the keys to the new owner in person, tomorrow. That way—let me put it the way she did: 'The person who knows it best can walk them through all of its idiosyncrasies.'"

"The joys of San Francisco real estate. Even a fixer-upper sells itself." Daniel shook his head in disbelief.

They kissed.

Audrey could tell that, like her, he'd wanted to linger in the memory of it.

She was glad they'd been sitting on the couch.

AUDREY WAS WAITING ON THE FRONT PORCH OF LAVINIA'S OLD HOUSE WHEN Egan walked up.

Instinctively, she waved at him.

When he bounded up the steps, her puzzled stare was met with the grin that had once made her heart do cartwheels in her chest.

No more, but it still put a smile on her face.

"Out for a stroll?" she asked.

Egan looked down at his watch. "No. Quite frankly, I'm here to meet with..." He cocked a brow. "You."

She stammered, "But... Are you..."

"Yep." He leaped up the stairs and plopped down beside her. "So, do you want to give me the grand tour?"

AFTER CLEANING OUT THE HOUSE, AUDREY HAD DONE HER BEST TO STAY AWAY from it. The thought of losing it saddened her. Seeing it now, she realized the realtor had done a good job in staging it. It looked perfect: warm and homey, not at all ostentatious.

"I'm glad it's you who bought it, Egan," Audrey said. "You'll enjoy it here."

"Oh!… I won't live here—unless the trustees allow it."

"The trustees?" Audrey frowned. "But the school didn't get the house. It took the home's purchase money as a donation for Lavinia's scholarship fund."

"I didn't mean the school's trust. I meant the trust that purchased the house." He turned to face her. "I established it for Chuck and Charly."

Stunned, Audrey, murmured, "So, they now own Lavinia's house?"

"Yes." Egan smiled wistfully. "I've turned in my resignation to the school, Audrey. Davis sold *Extracurricular* to Netflix. The money was enough for me to buy the house for them."

"That is incredibly kind of you, Egan." Her voice trembled with her gratitude.

Tears welled in his eyes. "I can't think of a better way of showing my love. And, frankly, it's too little, too late." Egan shrugged. "Chuck made it clear that I will never take Daniel's place. I don't think he realizes I never presumed I could. But he's come to the same conclusion I have about my role in their lives. If their hearts are open enough to include me, I will always be there for them in any capacity they'll accept." He took her hand. "How is Daniel taking the news?"

"He is…distant. In fact, Daniel and I have decided to separate." She stared out at the backyard. "For a while, anyway."

"What does that mean?"

"It means he needs space to understand why I kept the truth of our children's paternity a secret from him all these years." Audrey turned to Egan. "He has a right to take all the time he needs."

"What I meant by my question is, what does it mean for me? For us?" His eyes were filled with hope.

"Nothing, Egan. I'm sorry. I know it's not the answer you wanted." She held out her hand to him.

He took it. "You'll always be the one who got away."

SEVEN MONTHS LATER

CHAPTER 25

$\mathcal{A}$udrey had just drifted off, lulled by the Pacific Ocean waves lapping against La Selva Beach's sugary crescent of sand, when she felt a light pat on her backside.

She groaned, her way of expressing her displeasure.

She'd been enjoying her dream. In it, she was pregnant again: with the twins, she knew, because of the number of feisty kicks that thrummed in her full belly like a drum.

In the dream as in real life, the sensation had awed her, filling her with incredible bliss.

Audrey refused to acknowledge the culprit with anything more than one cocked eye. "Go away."

Tallulah waved back. "You know, with all that cycling you do, I could bounce a quarter off that ass and I wouldn't have to lower my hand to catch it."

Audrey laughed. "I guess I should I take that as a compliment."

Tallulah snickered. "At our age, hell yeah, I would!" She plopped down on the lounge chair beside her friend. Gazing out toward the horizon, she declared, "God, I am *so glad* Maggie held onto this place—although she's come close to losing it on at least one occasion. Remember? The IRS almost snatched it for back taxes."

Audrey rolled over. "I'm glad she held onto it too."

"Me three," Gemma muttered as she tapped her iPad.

"Me four," Bliss shouted from the farthest lounge.

Bliss leaned over toward Gemma. "What are you reading?"

"Coverage on Seamus' trial. I still can't believe he pled not guilty! The jury is going to crucify that pompous ass."

604

Seamus' perp walk made the cover of the *San Francisco Chronicle*, and was picked up by newspapers all over the country. The laundry list of charges included mail fraud, wire fraud, federal programs bribery, and money laundering.

The charges for Jess Smallwood and Warner Crawford were almost identical.

Like Seamus, Jess had decided to take his chances and plead not guilty. Warner's guilty plea put him behind bars for eighteen months.

"If Seamus gets convicted, I hope he gets put away for a *looong* time," Tallulah muttered. "Between his plot to cut AA's scholarships to nothing, and to accept only parents who were willing to buy into Mandy's bribery scheme, can you imagine the devastation it would have caused the school?"

Months ago, when Audrey had revealed Miranda's former name to the others, the shock had been so great that no one spoke for what seemed like ages.

Tallulah had been the first to break their silence: with a litany of curses.

From that point on, they only referred to their nemesis as Mandy.

They wished they didn't have to think of her at all.

"Gretchen hasn't been the same since her prison stint," Bliss murmured.

"I would imagine not, after what happened to her there," Audrey shuttered. "Being tattooed by her cellmate! How awful!"

"At least they moved her into solitary after that," Gemma pointed out. "I'm just glad she was only sentenced for a month. With good behavior, she was out in three weeks."

Gretchen had been presiding over the Ashbury Academy fundraising committee when the Feds walked in the school auditorium, cuffing her in front of all her shocked acolytes.

In her case, the charges were negligible: merely mail fraud and bribery.

When Fawn's father and mother called her to bail them out, just out of spite she waited twenty-four hours.

"I'm glad Fawn forgave her after that," Audrey said.

Tallulah shrugged. "My guess is that there was nothing sentimental about it. Perhaps she thinks their mother-daughter dynamic will add more drama to her reality show."

It was no secret that on Fawn's eighteenth birthday, she'd been given control of a trust her father had set up in her name. The moment that happened, she thumbed her nose at all things Seamus and Gretchen and went her merry way.

CheerFullyYours was a goldmine. To make its success even greater, Fawn took a portion of her trust and plowed it into a large social media and publicity campaign.

In no time, a television network had offered her a reality show based on her exploits. As fast as its audience was growing, the entertainment industry pundits predicted it would mushroom to Kardashian proportions in no time.

"I can't believe how quickly the Feds moved in on the parents," Bliss added. "Right after acceptances!"

"According to Daniel, the FBI felt it best to do so then as opposed to allowing the students to start the school year. That way, the slots could go to others who deserved them," Tallulah replied.

"I guess the upside is that it saved the students caught up in their parents' shenanigans from having to be expelled for no action on their part," Audrey pointed out.

"The one silver lining: since the FBI confirmed that Egan never touched Manya's test and her score was legitimate, Stanford honored its offer to her," Bliss reported.

"It was the right thing to do," Tallulah replied. "How is Manya doing, anyway?"

"The other AA students who also got accepted are looking after her," Bliss assured her. "And if Sienna gets accepted for next year, they'll room together. Considering how much money Raffaele donated to the school, her chances are pretty good." She shook her head, dismayed. "Donations are legal bribery, but still acceptable—for now, anyway."

Gemma frowned. "Too bad Nira wasn't told that in time. It might have saved her from taking her own life. What was she doing with a gun, anyway?"

"Her ex had threatened her on numerous occasions," Audrey replied. "The thought of losing custody of Manya to that creep was just too much for her." Saddened, she shook her head. "The money she paid to Mandy was the smallest of all the fees—only ten thousand dollars! I don't think the judge would have sentenced her to more than a few weeks."

"Any conviction would have been reason enough for the state to revoke her medical license and to get her fired from her medical practice," Gemma pointed out.

Audrey patted Tallulah's hand. "I'm glad Jammerhead took Daniel's advice: pleaded guilty and showed remorse."

"Me too," Tallulah admitted. "Rumor has it the reason he was sentenced to only a month behind bars is because the judge is a closet 'Jammerhead Bobber.'" Tallulah rolled her eyes at the nickname for her partner's fans. "His trial wasn't the best publicity, but it certainly popped his album sales." She grimaced. "So has a video someone made while Jammerhead was being arrested. It's all over the internet."

"It happened at the recording session for his next album, didn't it?" Bliss asked.

Tallulah nodded. "We always hire a videographer—you know, so that we can use clips for promotional purposes and for posterity. But this clip wasn't from that camera. It was a bootleg from the security camera."

Audrey chuckled. "For once, Maggie was right. Didn't she predict he'd come out of it unscathed? I think her exact words were, 'Hell, look at the cred Johnny Cash got from his arrests, not to mention all those rappers.'"

"Her own stints behind bars—albeit overnighters for drunk-and-disorderly conduct—endeared her to ex-cons, so I guess she's right." Tallulah shrugged. "Jammerhead does seem humbled by the experience. And it gave him the time to write a couple of killer songs. In fact, he's now going to a therapist. He says he wants to work out some of his daddy issues before it ruins his relationship with Quest."

"How is Quest's tour going?" Bliss asked.

Tallulah smiled. "He loves playing back-up to Maggie. It makes sense, since he's been listening to her music since he was in the womb. He's even building a fan base. He did the right thing for himself." She turned to Gemma. "How is Zina?"

Gemma grimaced. "Still hating her father for taking away her chance to prove she could make it into a top-ranked university on her own. She refuses to visit his gravesite." She sighed. "Not that I blame her. But her boyfriend, Sven, has been true blue through this whole ordeal. He's convinced her to follow her dream. She agrees with him that she should take a year off to help me at my law center and then take the SAT again at a certified facility before applying next year. He also suggested that she embrace this whole horrid experience in her college admissions essays. After all, she was a victim of it—and the whole cockeyed admissions system, for that matter."

"At least one good thing came out of the whole experience," Gemma added. "Zina claims Egan instilled in her a fearlessness toward taking the damn test."

At the mention of his name, all eyes went to Audrey.

She blushed.

"How is Egan doing anyway?" Tallulah asked.

"Now that Chuck is at UCLA, he sees him often," Audrey replied. "He mentioned that Egan is adjusting to Los Angeles. Loving it, in fact. He's really taken to screenwriting. And having gone back to AA gave him ideas for a few more seasons of *Extracurricular*."

"I'll bet it has," Gemma muttered dryly.

Bliss guffawed. "Not a week goes by that *People* isn't running a photo of him and some starlet on his arm."

"He's the one person even prison couldn't humble," Tallulah declared.

Gemma snorted. "He wasn't there long enough! The judge sentenced him to 'time already served!' In his case, it was the one day he spent in jail before Daniel bailed him out. What were the judge's exact words?... Oh yes: 'I have not seen anyone who is less culpable.' It doesn't get much better than that."

"She felt that his having donated all his ill-gotten gains to the school offset the crime," Audrey pointed out.

"Bullshit," Tallulah replied. "I'll bet she sleeps with a copy of *Extracurricular* under her pillow."

"Charly mentioned that Egan is also going to therapy," Audrey offered. "In fact, Chuck offered to go with him."

Gemma winced. "Did Egan take him up on it?"

"Charly claims Egan is open to it. In the meantime, he's trying to understand why his obsession with me went on for so long."

"We are too," Tallulah teased.

"Frankly, that is the *perfect* place to start," Bliss exclaimed. "You know, in hindsight, finding out he was a father may have been the best thing that ever happened to Egan."

Audrey shrugged. "I'd like to think so."

It was her fault he hadn't learned sooner. Yet another reason to despise herself.

Gemma tapped Audrey on the arm. "Daniel says hi, by the way." She raised a brow.

Audrey blushed. "You ran into him?"

"Yes, in the courthouse. I'm glad you recommended that I let him represent me with the Feds. It gave me the distance I needed from all of Darius' tomfoolery. The only thing I can say about my dearly departed husband is that he was smart enough to pull Mandy's fee from one of the many bank accounts we didn't share, so they believed me when I said I knew nothing of their agreement. In fact, I've asked Daniel to help me untangle some of Darius' other messes."

"He's a great lawyer," Audrey replied.

"And according to Charly, a great father too," Gemma said. "He makes it a point to have dinner with her once a week, just the two of them."

Audrey nodded. "I take Noah on that night." Admittedly, spending quality time with the children separately had brought her closer to each of them.

Recently, even Chuck had responded to her conversational emails with more than a cursory one-sentence response.

And Charly had divulged that it was Chuck's idea that they offer her a temporary lease to Lavinia's house.

At first, Audrey had refused. She was afraid Daniel would think it was a condition Egan had stipulated in the twins' trust.

Only after Chuck called her and insisted had she given in. "Just pay the utilities, and it's a done deal," he told her.

"And the taxes. I insist."

"Sure, if it makes you happy."

Hesitantly, Audrey murmured, "Hearing your voice makes me happy."

"I miss yours too," Chuck admitted. "Especially since you're not using it to scold me about something."

"Was I really all that hard on you?"

"Yes, for good reason." He chuckled. "But at least now we know why. I guess I'm the one apple that didn't fall far from the Gable tree."

She couldn't argue with that.

Now that the sun was almost below the horizon, a chill had set in. Audrey grabbed the blanket beneath her lounge chair and wrapped it around herself.

"Okay, ladies," Tallulah exclaimed. "On our last day on the beach, please join me in a toast to our new tradition! Here's to our annual gal pal beach getaway!"

Reluctantly, Audrey raised her glass with the others. As much as she loved Lavinia's house, she hated the thought of leaving her friends and returning to it.

It was no longer the place she called home.

Family was home.

Things will never be the same, she realized.

She had only herself to blame.

OPERATION SIS-BOOM-BAH WAS DEEMED AN IMPORTANT ONE TO WIN BY THE Department of Justice; so much so that an additional prosecutor was assigned: Jeremy Blake, whose record of convictions was second to none.

Miranda recognized the name immediately.

Her old high school boyfriend's limp—her final and most lasting gift to him—confirmed her worst fears.

Miranda's groan was loud enough to worry her attorney, Gerald Breslin. He hissed, "What's wrong? Are you sick?"

"No," she muttered. "Just doomed."

Her prediction proved right.

Despite Breslin's argument that Miranda's cooperation had led to the arrests and convictions of those willing to partake in one of the largest college bribery cases in the country's history, Jeremy's argument—now honed far beyond his debate team skillset—proved much more convincing.

Miranda winced as Jeremy's voice boomed through the courtroom:

"Miranda D'Arcy preyed on the fears of parents who entrusted her with the future and wellbeing of their children. She created the web of deceit, and then entangled them in it. None of this would have happened if it weren't for her."

He walked toward the judge. "These are not victimless crimes. These are crimes that will resonate for years to come in the lives of those whose futures have been impacted by Miranda D'Arcy's actions."

Jeremy pointed to Miranda: "Isn't it time to impact her future as well?"

The judge agreed.

Despite Miranda's cooperation with the FBI, the judge felt the charges —obstruction of justice, money laundering, racketeering, bribery, and tax evasion—and her attempt to flee the country were worth a seven-year prison sentence.

This time, Miranda had no one to blame but herself.

"HERE'S TO A WIN FOR THE GOOD GUYS!" LIONEL TAPPED HIS WINE GOBLET TO SallyAnne's.

"I'll drink to that!" She giggled. "Or maybe I shouldn't. I'm already on my third glass." She looked around the bar as if she'd be scolded for the indiscretion.

"You earned it; wouldn't you say?"

"I guess so." SallyAnne held her head high. "Okay—hell, yeah, I earned it!"

Lionel raised a brow. "I love it when you talk dirty to me."

"Then maybe I should do it more often, *damn it*." Pretending shock, she put a hand over her mouth.

"I mean…in bed." There. He'd said it.

She shrugged. "That can be arranged."

For a moment, he quit breathing.

She stood up. Grabbing her purse, she added, "I'm through pussy-footing around. No more beating around the bush…" She stared at him. "Do those count as naughty?"

He laughed. "It's a marginal call, but sure. Works for me."

"Good, because I mean it. I want you, *Lionel Porter Polk the Seventh*." She sighed mightily. "My God—that's a mouthful!" Suddenly, she was giggling again. *"That's what she said!"*

Lionel was laughing too. And following her out the door.

THEY'D BOTH COME TO THE CONCLUSION THAT IT HAD BEEN WORTH THE WAIT.

Despite the difference in Lionel and SallyAnne's heights, anatomically speaking all the various pieces seemed to fit perfectly.

And in spite of their differences in temperament—or perhaps because of it—their lovemaking ran the full gamut of expression and exertion.

Afterward, they both agreed it had exceeded expectations.

As the excitement of the day and the exhilaration of the evening gave way to exhaustion, they fell asleep in each other's arms.

———

SALLYANNE WOKE TO FIND LIONEL WATCHING HER.

Embarrassed, she sat straight up. "I…I guess we shouldn't have—!"

"I'm sorry, but…*I didn't want it to ever stop*," Lionel muttered.

SallyAnne's heart dropped into the pit of her stomach. "You mean…working together?"

"No," he insisted. "This!" To make his point, he stroked her cheek.

Then he kissed her.

The kiss was so long—so deep—that she thought all time had stopped.

When their lips parted, she whispered, "Neither do I." She felt tears gathering in her eyes. "But…*we're partners.*"

"Not if I take the promotion Melamed offered me."

SallyAnne sat straight up. "A promotion?…But…he offered one to me too!"

Lionel frowned. "When?"

SallyAnne's brow furrowed as she thought about it. "A few weeks ago." She shrugged. "I'd be partnered with someone else, so I turned him down. I couldn't stand the thought of not being with you."

Lionel took that in. Finally, he asked, "For almost four years, we've spent nearly every day together. Can I convince you to trade that for a lifetime of evenings and weekends instead?"

And that's how he asked her to marry him.

———

WHEN IT WAS AUDREY'S WEEKEND WITH NOAH, SHE MADE THE TREK ON HER bike north to the McKittridge home before they took off through the Presidio and over the Golden Gate Bridge.

With her young son as her guide, Audrey was learning the bike trails that crisscrossed Mount Tam.

Sometimes Charly joined their outings. On those days, Audrey blessed Daniel for instilling in them his love for this communal experience.

All these years I've missed out on this, she marveled.

But no more. Now that her secret was out in the open, she could embrace a different kind of life with her children. Never again would she dodge their questions or couch her answers in evasive terms.

At last, honesty was front and center.

As she rode her bike up to her old house, she was surprised to see another bike outside.

Not Noah's, but a woman's.

Audrey's first instinct was to turn around.

Daniel has found someone else, she thought. Someone who feels comfortable enough to leave her bike by our front steps.

His front steps.

Daniel had moved on with his life. There was nothing she could do but accept it.

I can't disappoint Noah, she thought.

She jumped off her bike and walked it into the driveway.

As she headed toward the steps, the front door opened. Daniel stood there. He waved.

She forced her lips into a grin. "I'm here for my date."

He grimaced. "Noah slept over at a buddy's house."

"Oh..." Audrey looked around. "Then I should take off." She turned to leave.

"Will I do?" Daniel asked.

"Do...what?" Audrey shook her head uncertainly.

"Do, as your date." He walked down the steps and sat on the bottom one.

"But...don't you have company?" She pointed to the bike.

"That's for you." Daniel hesitated, then added, "Noah told me about some of the trails you've been taking. The frame on your bike will be shot in no time, so I thought you might like this one better..." His voice died away.

But his gaze was as steady as ever.

"You thought right." Audrey eased down beside him. "I'm heading out in a new direction. Would you like to come along?"

THE END